Fish Tails

Sheri S. Tepper

Fish Tails

A Novel

HARPER Voyager

An Imprint of HarperCollinsPublishers

Harper Voyager and design is a trademark of HCP LLC.

FISH TAILS. Copyright © 2014 by Sheri S. Tepper. All rights reserved. Printed in the United States of America. No part of this book may be used or reproduced in any manner whatsoever without written permission except in the case of brief quotations embodied in critical articles and reviews. For information address HarperCollins Publishers, 195 Broadway, New York, NY 10007.

HarperCollins books may be purchased for educational, business, or sales promotional use. For information please e-mail the Special Markets Department at SPsales@harpercollins.com.

A hardcover edition of this book was published in 2014 by Harper Voyager, an imprint of HarperCollins Publishers.

FIRST HARPER VOYAGER PAPERBACK EDITION PUBLISHED 2015.

Designed by Paula Russell Szafranski

Chapter-opener art based on *The Blood of Fish,* published in *Ver Sacrum* magazine, 1898 (engraving), Klimt, Gustav (1862–1918) / Private Collection / Bridgeman Images.

Library of Congress Cataloging-in-Publication Data has been applied for.

ISBN 978-0-06-230459-9

15 16 17 18 19   OV/RRD   10 9 8 7 6 5 4 3 2 1

With a huge thank you to LuAnn Breckinridge, whose daily assistance has made my "declining years" much easier

And, in memory of Frederik Pohl

Contents

Fish Tails

Prologue

THERE WERE ROADS DEEP IN THE WOODS LYING at the foot of the last great mountain range between the west coast and the lands of Artemisia. These would not have been called roads in most places; they did not even serve as roads very usefully; yet if one drove carefully, asked questions of the locals (also carefully, and not of just anyone), one could cover the distance with no more dangers and troubles than usual.

Abasio and Xulai were mindful of both the dangers and the troubles. They had been warned against the weather, against the solitary hunters and trappers, against the possibility of Ogres, even against the seemingly peaceful villagers that one might encounter here and there where a valley had opened up and submitted to agriculture: milk cows, sheep, and perhaps a few horses. And dogs, of course. Always dogs. And they were warned repeatedly about Lorpists.

Opinionated people were almost always a danger for someone, and Lorpists were men obsessed by a new opinion. New, at least, under that name. People had always been opinionated about "differences"—of skin color, of hairstyles, of language. Lorpists were a recently formed group who were opinionated about "wholeness." Their opinion was that mankind had been made as a whole creature. He, and she, were meant to have two arms and associated hands with five fingers each, two legs with associated feet and five toes each, two each of ears, eyes, nostrils, and, in men's case, testicles. Also, one navel, one mouth, one front and one rear aperture for excretion. The lexicon went on to specify where hair should grow and where not, and the completed description spelled out, according to Lorpists, how a "hyooman bean" should be constructed. Luckily the Lorpist inventory did not extend to internal organs or women.

Abasio and Xulai had been told that Lorpists were punitive toward people lacking any of the listed parts or having supernumerary ones. Since Abasio and Xulai's year-old twins, Gailai and Bailai, did not have immediately recognizable legs or feet, since they did have gills under their arms, since they could swim and sleep underwater, and, indeed, traveled in a tank of water that was kept inside their traveling wagon, their parents feared for them, and for themselves—not that Xulai and Abasio were unable to defend themselves. They were equipped with not one but two *ul xaolats,* extremely effective weapons that could easily wipe out an opposing army before it had a chance to act. And could do it without disturbing the sleep of those who carried them.

BUT . . . their "mission"—as it had been strongly suggested they call it—required peaceful acceptance, not threats or holocausts. They wanted to be greeted, not feared. They wanted to be accepted, not murdered. So far, the score was weighted a bit heavily toward their saying "Let's sneak off in the night before they all get out their weapons." Still, they had had some notable successes and felt, on the whole, their time was being well spent. From almost every village they had traveled through, a few people had set out to travel to Sea Duck 2, on the coast, where the "changing station" was.

Xulai, while pleased about their progress, was somewhat worried over the dreams that Abasio kept having. Each night, he told her, he visited a non-Earth planet occupied by humans—always the same planet and people, where he hovered in the air above a pool of sapphire liquid while a couple of these human females talked about either visiting or revisiting Earth. Abasio said the two women addressed each other as Jinian and Silkhands. The same dream also contained a couple of children and a statue of a woman named Mavin. Needless to say, Abasio didn't recognize any of them, certainly Xulai didn't know any of them, and the purpose or origin of the dreams was a complete mystery.

The best Abasio could say for them was that they were not violent or threatening—except, perhaps, to Abasio's sanity and rest. He seemed to sleep a good deal on the wagon seat to make up for the rest he didn't get on that other planet!

. . . which is what he was doing at the moment. Blue and Ragweed didn't care. Half the time Abasio didn't even hold the reins, just let them lie in his hands while the horses followed the particular "road" they were on, one they had been told would lead them to an occupied valley near the edge of the forest and thence, fairly quickly, over the high mountains to Artemisia via the Findem Pass. They had been furnished with an outrider, Kim, who rode some distance ahead of them on a horse named Socky. If Kim noticed trouble, he could ride back quickly and tell them to detour or wait or do whatever Kim thought sensible under the circumstances. So far they'd done a bit of hiding (once for several days) and some fast talking, but Abasio had never felt they were in mortal danger.

Just now Abasio was only slightly aware that Blue and Rags, their heads bobbing gently up and down, had entered a clearing among the trees. Off to the right, water from a clear pool leapt and skipped in a plunging stream toward the valley below, chuckling to itself as it went. Eyes now half open, reins still lax in his hands, he looked past the horses' heads to see they had entered a small clearing in which stood a shop with an exceptionally well-painted sign, glittering gold on black:

BERTRAM THE TAILOR

Quality Clothing for All: Fine Clothing for Those Who Have Time!

Abasio snorted. He was sure they would have time. He and Xulai had agreed. No matter what else they had to do, they simply could not go on without a few days' rest. And rest was needed by the horses, Blue and Ragweed, as well. As though reading his mind, the horses pulled the wagon into the shade of a large tree with a carpet of tall grass beneath it.

Blue remarked, "If you'd unhitch us, 'Basio, it'd be good to get a drink, and roll in the grass and eat a bit of it. That stuff where we were last night was the nastiest greenery I've tasted in some time."

"Didn't dare eat it," added Rags. "Mighta been poison."

Abasio got down from the wagon seat, stretched, went to the pool, and scooped up a cupped palm of water. He tasted it. "That's all right, at least." Yawning and stretching, he loosed the horses from the wagon. "Let's leave the harness on until we decide where we want to put the wagon. If the tailor is amenable, we may take a day or two for rest." Abasio had seen what Xulai had not. There was a smokestack in back of the shop, which, coupled with the stream that flowed from that direction into this pool, indicated the likelihood of a bathhouse.

Xulai murmured to him. "The fact that we've encountered a tailor is blessed fate. Or maybe Precious Wind has been casting favorable spells for me. The children have outgrown every garment we had for them!"

"Would Precious Wind suggest *tailored* clothes? For babies?"

"One gives thanks for what one is given, even the unexpected," she said piously. "Besides, we were given funds to pay for the unexpected."

Leaving Blue and Rags to test the quality of the grass, they each took a child and went up the steps to the porch of the shop. As they opened the door, a bell rang and a stout, cheerful-looking man came bustling from the back to stand behind the counter.

"Yes, ma'am. Sir. What may I do for you?" he burbled. "I note you're dressed for cold. Summer coming, you'll need something lighter, perhaps?"

"It's for the children," murmured Xulai, unwrapping Gailai and placing her on the counter. "I need new clothes for the children."

Bertram stared at her. Stared and then again. "Ma'am," he muttered, "it is not my custom to clothe . . . fish!"

Across the counter from him, Xulai drew herself to her full height and coupled a blazing stare with a suddenly icy tongue. "If you do not better school your tongue, sir, you may find yourself without any custom at all."

The stocky young man's sad, dark eyes widened in sudden panic, as though he had unexpectedly stepped off a cliff. He gulped. "I did not mean to offend." The walnut gleam of his skin hid his flush of embarrassment, but his shaking hands betrayed him as he ran them over his black, tightly curled hair.

"What *did* you mean to do? Didn't I hear you refer to my children as *fish*?" She turned from him, ebony hair swirling, dusty, no-colored traveling robe lashing around slender ankles—ankles, deplorably, that were as dusty as the hair, as the soiled robe. The wearisome roads, wet or dry, were dirty. Even her hands and face were covered with a gray film. She looked at her wrists in fury. She could plant grass in the creases of her skin. A little sweat and they'd grow! Or tears! Tears would do it. She turned her face away. The rain of tears was imminent.

"Children? Madam . . ." The tailor was beginning to sweat. He gripped the lapels of his impeccably fitted coat, one he had put on only when he had heard their wagon arrive outside his shop. The woman was furiously angry. He was not so frozen in embarrassment that he failed to appreciate her beauty, her perfect features, her hair . . . Well, it was luxuriant and—if washed—it would no doubt gleam with blue lights. Beneath the travel dirt her skin was an unblemished olive. Her manner, on the other hand, was . . . well, it might be aristocratic, possibly regal. But could she possibly be the mother of those . . . ? It simply wasn't believable!

The woman's companion stepped between tailor and fury. With obvious effort to overcome great weariness, he forced his lips into a smile. "Let us begin again."

The tailor turned toward him, helplessly starting to speak then stopping himself. He had not really noted the lined face, the drooping shoulders, the exhaustion in those eyes. If the man were left alone for five minutes he would be deeply asleep, and he moved as men do who have already been tried past endurance.

And yet . . . yet he managed a conciliatory smile as he laid his hand on the lady's shoulder, stroking it, calming it and her. He was as travel-stained as she, but he carried both the road dust and the weariness as if they were accustomed garments, fully aware of their condition, knowing that everything about them needed mending, laundering, or even better, replacing with something cleaner and more comfortable. He did not seem resentful of what their clothing accused them of. Negligence? Haste? The tailor thought not. Neither time nor effort had been spared, everything else had simply been . . . well, secondary. Yes, secondary to whatever else it was the man needed to do. Just now he needed to move his tired eyes first to lock on the tailor's, then to tug the tailor's eyes toward the lady as though to say, "Look, really look here, my friend. See?"

The traveler reached out and drew her closer with one hand while reaching the other to smooth the frown lines between her perfect brows. He stood back at arm's length and bowed toward her as he spoke over his shoulder. "May I introduce my wife, sir? This is Xulai, Princess Royal of Tingawa and daughter of the Duke of Wold. Wold, you probably know of? Tingawa is less well known to us on this side of the sundering sea. The stains of harsh travel do not betray her royal blood, but when she is extremely weary, her temper becomes fully—or shall I say perhaps *exceptionally* imperious." He swept an elegantly executed bow in her direction, his cloak making a practiced and beautiful swirl as it moved and fell.

The tailor was not so overawed that he failed to notice her fleeting smile, the elegance of that swirled cloak. Even under all that dust it was magnificent. Any tailor worthy of the title knew of Tingawa, and the only fabrics that could be spoken of in the same breath as those in that cloak could be from no other place. Tingawa. The west. Over the sea. The lining had to be Tingawan silk! And the drape of that wool. Heavens! What was it called? It was from some particular animals. Kazi . . . something. He had only read of it!

The traveler raked his dusty hair behind his ears, digging his thumbs into his neck with a grimace. The gray at his temples was not entirely due to dust. Holding the tailor's eyes, he spoke softly, with humor. "I, sir, on the other hand, am simply Abasio. Sometimes called Abasio the Dyer, sometimes Abasio the Traveler, also sometimes Abasio the Idiot, for marrying, or should one say 'espousing,' so far above myself."

He reached to take one of the babies from Xulai's arms, holding the child where the tailor could get a good look. "The future of our world, sir, depends upon these children of whom you spoke so hastily." He held up a finger, silencing the tailor's attempt at apology. "Spoke, may I say, thoughtlessly . . . But only in *words,* sir! Words are no matter, for Gailai and Bailai are too young to take offense, and my wife and I are sufficiently forgiving to ignore them."

The princess glared, taking note of the emphatic pledge without agreeing to it in the slightest. As the tailor attempted another confused apology, Abasio cut it off with a raised hand.

"Let it be forgotten! Our purpose is simple. We have come to find Bertram, the much-lauded Bertram; Bertram who makes clothing for people from as far away as the eastern prairies all the way to the western sea; Bertram, who for some unknown and no doubt imperative reason does his exemplary work on the hill above Gravysuck, in White Mountain Valley."

Abasio, in full cry, turned and thrust his arm swordlike toward the southwest, finger inexorably extended: "There, there is White Mountain, lunging upward, snow-clad as ever!" The arm dropped, the extended finger pointed down, to the south. "And there below us in the subsidiary valley lies the village of . . . yes, indeed, it IS Gravysuck." The pointed finger curved, joined its fellows to become a cupped hand, held pleadingly toward him, as though begging. The voice dropped almost to a whisper. "So here, here, indeed, on this hill, indubitably and without contradiction, we find that *you must be the paragon: Bertram!*"

Stunned by the drama, Bertram struggled unsuccessfully to find a suitable reply. "Yes, yes, but . . ."

Abasio patted him forgivingly on his shoulder. "Your mistake is understandable. And your patronymic, sir?"

" . . . Uh . . . patro . . ."

"Your father's name?"

"Also Bertram . . ."

"Then you are Bertram Bertramson . . . ?"

"No, sir, Bertram Stitchhand, sir, one of the Volumetarian Stitchhands." Had he not been incapable of doing so from birth, Bertram would have paled. He clapped his hand over his mouth instead. What had he done! What had he said! Why had he said it!

This time Abasio smiled from honest amusement, though he had no energy left to inquire into either the Stitchhands or the Volumetarians. His body was dirty, every crease of it was filled with the detritus that joins with sweat to form an intimate muck, an invasive slurry that itches and complains, drawing all attention only to itself. He was tired with the weariness that doubts the existence of sleep. Xulai, too, was tired, dirty, hungry, and petulant as a . . . dyspeptic pig! They desperately needed a few days' rest, *if this man would only cooperate by giving them an excuse to take such a rest before Xulai committed all three of them and the babies to enmity everlasting.*

Swallowing the exhausted sigh that was threatening to swallow him, Abasio said clearly, uttering each word separately, peering into Bertram's eyes to make sure the man understood him: "As I had begun to say, many of the children born during the next century or two will resemble these children you see here. They will live in the seas. The temperature of the seas is fairly constant, changing only gradually. However, our young ones are not yet full-time sea-children, and they are traveling across area where there has as yet been no significant inundation."

"I . . . ah . . ." gargled Bertram, his eyes fixed on the children in question. The two infants, about yearlings, he judged, were loosely wrapped in knitted shawls and were reclining in their mother's arms, regarding him, Bertram, with great interest. Down to their waists they were appropriately human-looking, their skin, where it showed beneath the knitted caps, was more or less the color of an aged ivory button. Not as light as their father's, though he was somewhat darkened by the sun. One little head of dark hair had reddish lights, the other blue. Their little faces were pretty, their eyes dark and very observant, and their smiles were delightful. Their nether appendages, however, whatever such limbs were called, were unquestionably fishy! But not scaled, no. The olive skin above the waist simply became darker—blue? Or green? More leathery, thicker, and it ended in feet that were . . . webbed. Quite webbed. Extravagantly webbed! The insignificant heels were companioned by very long, almost froggy toes!

Abasio's voice hardened. "So, since we must travel where as yet there are no seas, the children are sometimes cold. They require jackets! Coats! Something to keep them warm!"

The tailor mumbled something.

"Yes?" asked Abasio with a lethal smile.

"Why would aquatic creatures be here? You are so far from—"

Xulai interrupted, her voice like a well-honed knife. "They must be both, Bertram. If you'll let me explain. May I sit down?"

Her words were a question, her tone was not. The tailor's conscious mind finally received the information his subconscious had been trying to get through to him for some time. *"Forget your oath! Forget the books. Forget defending your life's primary purpose of being a Volumetarian. Shut your mouth and listen. Shut your mouth and smile and listen! Shut up and smile and listen sympathetically, as any decent tailor would!*

He scurried, fetching a chair while stretching his mouth into what he hoped was an understanding smile. She did sit down, with a weary sigh.

"We are in the age of the waters rising," she said slowly, carefully, hoping to sound merely didactic rather than lethally threatening. "About two centuries from now, all our world will be under the waters . . ."

She paused for emphasis, but did not begin again, for Bertram had stumbled back, not merely astonished as many were who heard this information for the first time, but shocked as though mortally wounded. His dark face was turning gray, all at once!

He gasped. "Surely . . . you must be joking, ma'am. I don't . . ." He put his hand to his head, suddenly dizzy. He gasped for breath.

Abasio stepped around the corner of the counter and helped the man sit down. He and Xulai realized almost at the same instant that evidently the flooding of the world meant something more to this man than it meant to most people.

Bertram was babbling. "Travelers have said . . . Coastal flooding, of course, yes, but . . . a few lowlands perhaps, but . . . surely not the world! *The books . . . the books . . . the books have to be kept dry! What can I do with the books?*" He went on babbling, almost wordlessly, his face gray, even his lips so ashen that they might as well have opened his veins and drained all his blood away.

While the tailor's breathing gradually slowed, Xulai shrugged off her heavy robe. Though she shared the dislike of dirt that was customary to cats and Tingawans, it would have to wait! Unlike a cat, she could not lick herself clean, but with the filthy robe removed, she could half convince herself that she looked acceptably human instead of appearing to be some monster made of muck. She reached out to touch his shoulder. Let him feel her hand. Let him know she was as human as he!

Softly, in her most unthreatening voice, she went on: "In order to survive in the changed world, our forms must change. There is enough time for this to happen; six or eight generations. When the earth is finally inundated, all of us who cannot exist underwater will have lived out our lives; so will our children and grandchildren; and in that same time new generations will have been born able to exist underwater, to swim, to dive, even perhaps to dance upon the waves.

"Abasio and I are . . . facilitators of that change. We—and some other couples like us—travel from place to place carrying with us the . . . the . . ."

"The process," Abasio interjected firmly. "The process by which people

can be changed. Once changed, *their children will be born like our children, able from birth to exist in the changed world."*

They glanced at each other. They tried not to talk about the first-generation change at all. Sea-eggs were needed to make the transformation, and Abasio still remembered his own transformation with embarrassment. He had behaved badly. Or, as Blue said, "Like a pig keeper just got himself knocked into the wallow." It was the first-generation changers, however, who subsequently gave birth to sea-babies like Gailai and Bailai, so no matter how embarrassing, the first transformation might be, it had to precede the second. They had learned to speak largely in generalities, to let people see the children, to explain that yes, they were their own children, and if others would like to bear children who would survive the world wide drowning, they could find out all about it in Wellsport on the west coast. The change center there was now called Sea Duck 2 by its inhabitants, for they had, each and every one of them, been "sea-ducked" and were able to breathe underwater. Sea Duck 1 was in Tingawa.

So far they had been unable to develop a satisfactory routine! Though they had been on this journey for almost a year now, their reception from place to place had been so varied they had been unable to settle on a routine. Words and phrases that were acceptable in one village turned out to be fighting words in the next place, even though they tried to avoid any fighting at all. If hostility seemed imminent, they had the means to leave, and they did leave: horses, wagon, and all. Essentially they had three duties: first to explain that the world was being drowned; second to let people know about the sea-children. Third: to survive!

Xulai, seriously worried about Bertram's seizure, had not left his side. He now had some color coming back into his cheeks, but he still looked woefully unwell, and Abasio suggested he go lie down for a while. Abasio escorted him back into his living quarters, settled him on his bed, and asked if he, Abasio, and his wife might pay him for the use of his bathhouse, if that chimney out in back did, indeed, indicate a bathhouse? Also, would Bertram allow him the horses to be unhitched to graze? Might they take advantage of his hospitality, perhaps, to stay for a day or two, just to rest?

Bertram could only nod repeatedly. Oh, yes, it would be so good to have company. And if they would stay, he could show them and explain about the books. He murmured distractedly, "Oh, Sir Abasio . . ."

"Just plain Abasio will do, Bertram."

"Well, if you see any people coming up from down the hill there . . . be careful. There's been a bunch of Lorpists down there . . . I didn't notice. Does your lovely wife have pierced ears? That would count against her 'wholeness,' you see. I suggest a scarf over the head and ears if she sees them coming . . ."

"Lorpists don't like . . . what? Any trifling with the human body?"

"That's it. Yes. And God help a man who loses a finger due to an accident. Lorpists feel it their duty to kill the rest of him so he doesn't walk about as an affront to the Creator."

Blue had stationed himself by the window of the tailor's shop, where he could hear the conversation. He relayed the word about the Lorpists to Ragweed.

"Wonder what one of 'em'd do if I kicked him in the you-know-wheres and he maybe lost a ball," murmured Ragweed.

"Now, Rags. Don't go kicking up trouble," said Blue.

When Bertram had somewhat recovered himself, he invited them to stay as long as they liked. They would, yes, said Xulai, if he promised to go to bed and stay there until he was breathing properly. If he had any customers, she would see to them.

Gratefully, Bertram said the horses could graze around the shop and into the little pasture that lay over that way. He was later amazed to find no horse droppings at all.

Xulai explored the place; Abasio fired up the water heater behind the shop and left it to gurgle warmly to itself. When it was hot enough, he and Xulai and the babies (though they didn't particularly like hot water) had a bath. Afterward, Xulai used their bathwater to wash all their blankets and she hung them over Bertram's side fence to dry. For some time, there had been no stream or pool to give them even a half-way convenient place to wash. The back of Bertram's house was built right up against the mountain for some reason—which they discovered later. Xulai invaded Bertram's kitchen, found the ingredients for a proper soup, took a bowl to his bedside, and fed it to him.

Meantime, Blue and Rags received a visitor. A very dirty small boy came sneaking out from under a bush and, seeing the wagon appeared empty, decided to explore it. The boy was blocked by a very large horse. The boy decided to go in over the wagon seat and found his way blocked by another horse.

"Blassit," said the boy. "I 'uz just goin' to look! Was'n gonna take nothing."

"What's your name?" asked Blue.

"You can't really talk, can you?" the boy asked. "Somebody's hidin' somewhere pretendin' to be your voice."

"Ragweed and I can talk. I was given the gift of speech by some very lofty creatures, angels maybe. Ragweed got her voice from a woman named Precious Wind, friend of Xulai's. It requires some trifling with the anatomy and it won't work on just everyone. What's your name?"

"I got a dog, maybe she could get him to talk."

"What's your name, boy? Either tell me or I'll kick you all the way down the hill."

"Willum," said the boy.

"WILLUM," came a call from down the hill. "WILLUM, you get yourself back down here and eat your supper."

"Quit upsetting your mother," said Blue. "Go on and get your supper. We can talk again later. Looks like we'll be here for a day or so.

The boy left them. "You don't usually talk to brats," said Ragweed.

"No. Have a strange feeling about this one, though."

The boy came back, some time later. "Horse."

"Yes, boy."

"There's Lorpists down there. They've heard about the fish babies. They're all set to do you some damage when you go down the hill. Where you going, anyhow?"

"Someplace over a pass, Findem Pass, then down into Artemisia."

"Well, 'f'you're going to the pass, you gotta come down through Gravysuck, where we are. Just remember, those men they got axes n' things."

"Why's your town called Gravysuck?"

" 'Cause . . . we used ta have this man . . . he was real nasty with women, even little girls. Y'know what I mean? He used to hurt 'em. So we had this other man visitin', and he told us the town needed a cata-pull-it, n' him and a buncha the men they built the cata-pull-it an' they put it out nexta Gravy Lake, and they call it that because it's kinda thick and brown like gravy. And it's gotta bottom in it you can't walk on, and if you fall in you can't get out, it kinda sucks you down. Then the man said we had ta tell everybody if they didn't behave, they'd get cata-pull-ited. And everybody got told. And the bad man didn't listen, so next time he grabbed some little girl, they were ready for him, and they cata-pullit-ed him right out inta the middle of Gravy Lake and it sucked him down, sploosh, like that. Three or four men got catta-pullit-ed since, oh, and one real rotten ol' lady use to poison people's wells. And since that, we haven't had any trouble."

"Very interesting," said Blue. "Well, boy, thank you for all the information. I guess we'll be leaving tomorrow or the next day. Do you think your folks and friends would like to see the sea-babies? If you think so, you ought to tell them to ask my people."

CHAPTER I

An Unexpected Lamentation

NEAR THE EASTERN EDGE OF THE GREAT STONIES, barely within the last jagged file of mountains before the long descent into the deserts and prairies beyond, there was reputed to be an astonishing landmark—*reputed,* for it was spoken of more often than it was remembered. Few sought it out. Fewer had seen it, and fewer yet had seen it in the season and hour of its glory. Those who lived near enough to consider the landmark a local thing—whether they had seen it or not—generally called it "the curly rock," and did not regard it as having any particular distinction beyond its odd shape. However named or referred to, it stood on a lofty prominence west of and equidistant from two jagged peaks that sheltered it from the rising sun three hundred and fifty days of the year. Only as Earth tipped the sun back and forth along the horizon during a few successive dawns in spring and again in fall did sun and season work in concert to create something almost miraculous.

In geologic terms, the Stonies—in their present form—were young. Some thousand years before, a great upheaval had shaken the continent, splitting off and drowning the western third of it and thrusting the western edge of what remained so far into the sky that air-breathing creatures who were along for the ride descended rapidly. Unlike its predecessor range, which had achieved a pleasantly rounded permanency, one that map makers felt secure in locating and labeling, this most recent cataclysm had awarded the Stonies a shifty and transitory reputation, as though any part of them might be subject to sudden erasure or change. Even the rivers moved about from season to season: like flea-bitten travelers, desperately and perpetually seeking cleaner and more comfortable beds.

There were not many roads through the mountains, and those there were often lasted no longer than a decade or so. Few penetrated all the way from east to west. A few—not the same few—penetrated from west to east. There was nothing mystical about this. Some roads one could scramble up but not down, where "down" would require putting a rope sling around the mules. All of which is to say that the mountains were dark, sneaky, and dangerous, and they made no exceptions for stubborn travelers who should have had better sense.

On a particular morning in a high, cupped valley, one such traveler stood weary and shivering. All the roots of things were asleep, darkness still lay in drifts; treetops trembled in the ice-chilled air that darkness had sucked down from the heights. The traveler and the child with her had walked a long way to get to this particular place at this very particular time. Lillis, usually called Grandma, had been here before, on several occasions. Her granddaughter, Needly, had not. Today was Needly's tenth birthday: she had been told this was to be an occasion, an announcement that had led her rather tentatively to anticipate something in the way of candy, perhaps, or a wrapped something, maybe even with a ribbon. Grandma was capable of such surprising details. In reality, the child's life had allowed few if any illusions, and she already had an adult awareness that planning and happening were quite different things. Cold and weariness, though extreme, were not yet accompanied by despair.

Grandma was equally weary, shifting from foot to foot at the edge of a fury directed entirely at herself! This journey had been a gamble, but she had foolishly allowed anticipation to trifle with details of her previous visits; allowed optimism to strengthen two sets of bones and muscles, one not yet adult, one no longer young. She knew perfectly well that lengthy waiting unrelieved by sleep or food or amusement could seem an eternity. During her life she had done a good bit of such standing about, enough to be familiar with that dagger point at which every successive moment attenuates into forever. Well, hope had outrun good sense. She had wanted so to show an enchanting thing to an eager, intelligent little girl whose childish strength her fatuous grandmother may badly have misjudged! She grieved for the child. The cold hand in hers was limp with weariness.

Both watchers, old and young, sighed in simultaneous exhaustion, looked down, rubbed their eyes, shifted their weight, sighed again, counted silently to one hundred—as the older one had taught the younger one to do in situations of a similar kind—and then, without particular hope, raised their eyes to the height above.

To glory! There it was! As though a heavy window curtain had been suddenly flipped aside, fiery light flooded over the fangs of the esker, darted between the two sheltering peaks, and blazed the landmark into radiance. Where had been only darkness was now a miracle: creation come upon the height, majestic and unbelievable! A thing, a living thing, red as ruby, huge as the most mighty monument, leaping up from the ledge that held it as though it had lain there through millennia and was now, impossibly, endlessly uncoiling itself upward into the sky!

Grandma squeezed a suddenly muscular and vibrant little shoulder, and whispered, "People, those few who've seen it, they give it different names. Mostly around here, people call it the Listener."

Needly was too busy marveling to reply. The enormous curlicue sprang from the ground angling toward the north, curving as it climbed, higher, higher yet, then circling back toward the south . . . no, perhaps slightly east of south, all that monstrous weight arched across the sky as though flung there, supported by nothing at all! It twisted, it spiraled, the narrow, questing tip of it finally pointing due east. In this light, it seemed to quiver! Needly thought it was most like the tendril of an enormous vine, one of those eager, trembling, impossibly slender fingers reaching out upon the wind, exploring the air for anything it can touch, and touching, grasp, and grasping, hold fast! What was it reaching for? Needly held her breath waiting for it to fall, knowing in the instant that of course it couldn't fall. Grandma had said other people had seen it before, long, long before, so it *had been there for a long time,* and falling was *not what it did.* But . . . but . . . it must have survived only by miracle!

Over the centuries, other travelers had thought the same. The area was not as remote as it seemed, particularly if one came from the east, but its approaches were hidden. If someone was crossing the mountains from the west and came from below, there was only one very short section of road from which it could be seen. In these mountains, winter came early and stayed late, so few travelers would have risked travel during the brief period of visibility in spring or fall. Fewer would have found a suitable campground within reasonable distance the previous night; fewer still would have left that campground in darkness, well before dawn, to have reached this one place on the road; only a fraction of *them* would have arrived there just at or before the moment of dawn; and of those, even fewer would have been looking eastward at just the right moment to see the sun burst through those gated mountains!

So, though the great rock formation—which is what most of those who had seen it supposed it to be—was indeed *visible* from other places and at other times of day, those who had actually *perceived* it numbered very few.

From the point of view of the thing itself, a few was barely tolerable.

Volcanologists had suggested that molten stone had been thrust into some deep, twisting cave and had solidified there to be heaved up during some great cataclysm. It had undoubtedly been smoothed by blown sand, washed by rain, polished by time. To Needly, how it had happened didn't matter. It was here now, majestic, marvelous . . . and alive. The child was quite sure of that. Stone, maybe. But unlike any other stone.

Grandma caught the child's thought as she often did (often hearing the thoughts more clearly than words) and was not surprised to find it mirroring her own. In this scarlet light, birthed bloody from the womb of morning, the reaching curl of it had the shape of vitality: the coil of a sinuous vine, the time-perfected veer of a wooded river; the arched line of a windblown tree, the flawlessly spiraling twist of a shell. All such transient living precisions were here frozen into an eternal reality. The substance was irrelevant.

Grandma remembered, decades ago, attracted as much by challenge as curiosity, she had come this far, camped overnight in this same cup of shadow, then when it was barely light—using rope, and metal spikes that she had pounded into cracks with a hammer, and, yes, no small measure of egotism—she had come from below, climbed the precipitous wall, and then crawled over the razor edge of rock onto the narrow ledge on which the pedestal rested. Once there, she had touched the Listener, touched it, stroked it, examined it closely enough to assure herself that the formation was in every sense solid and real.

Before deciding to make the journey, she had decided the thing had to be called "the Listener" for a reason, and she had desperately needed someone to listen. She had leaned against the glorious whatever-it-was, put her face against it, and pled for help: *"Someone help me. Someone please tell me what the hell is going on?"*

During and after this plaint, she had probably uttered the word "help" at least ten times. Then, all those years ago—as she turned to climb dangerously and laboriously back the way she had come—she had seen that her final, vertiginous effort to reach the Listener had been utterly unnecessary. There was a route visible only from this end, a short, simple way that led toward a well-traveled road and would have brought her to the monument with a fraction of the time and effort she had expended. On that occasion she had collapsed in tears and agonies of frustration that had absorbed a good deal of time and fury even though she used that easier route to return to the place she referred to and occasionally thought of as *home.*

She had intended to take Needly along that route as soon as it was light so the child could actually climb onto the pedestal and touch the Listener. That climax to the experience was now . . . not possible. The ledge at the foot of the Listener's pedestal was already occupied. She hadn't seen it at first. Half blinded by dawn, she'd been looking past it at that curling, crimson glory, but now her eyes had dropped onto the ledge that should have been empty. This morning it was occupied by an unreality.

Since neither she nor the child had seen it arrive, it must have been there during the darkness: a fantasy only slightly dwarfed by the Listener above it. It was obviously a mythical thing; anyone who could read knew that! No matter how the old woman blinked and wiped her eyes; incredible or not, there it was! As the sky-flung stone above it faded from fiery copper and blazing bronze, the creature below it on the ledge received the metallic sheen and, enlivened by it, moved its great wings, the long primaries unfolding upward, the arc of the feathers that followed repeating the arc of the overarching formation, successive quills rising on either side of the massive chest, two perfect vertical fans that framed the prone body, the regal head with its queenly crest, the burnished mane that seemed to shine with its own radiance; the great beak like a shield of bronze, all this living assembly shining while the morning held its breath until the escutcheon was complete.

There it was. Whole. Alive. And awake! A Griffin! A living Griffin!

Needly and Grandma were still hidden in the cup of shadow below. Before starting on this birthday journey, Grandma had shared certain memories: her own sensations on first seeing the Listener; her wonder and delight; her perception that Earth itself seemed to rejoice at this particular revelation. Now she felt something approaching fear. Not terror, not yet. But things with great beaks like that, they did eat things, and Grandma and Needly were very probably among the types of things they . . . ate. She and the child were still hidden. The trees were only a few steps away. If they did not delay, they could creep away. They should do that right now, while darkness hid them . . .

They did not.

Why? A subtlety. Though Grandma could not possibly have expected this additional marvel, its presence was a perfect and suitable completion of the occasion. One did not flee from perfection!

So, standing silent, her hand on the child's shoulder, she swallowed apprehension and assured herself it was good that she was not too old and the child with her was not too young to see and hear and feel. They stood while the quivering wings still cast reflected sequins of gold and glory across the valley, the fiery light faded slowly, and the Listener's brilliance slid into more muted shades. The darting lights seemed to evoke a tingling over the surface of her body and the child's, and she—they—heard an almost inaudible ringing, as of innumerable tiny crystal chimes.

Needly's eyes had not blinked since her first sight of the marvel. Her voice was only a dazed whisper, a sliver of sound emerging from a bubble of enchantment. *"Grandma. If you had a barley field made of glass, it'd sound like that."*

"Might. Yes."

"If the winds were gentle, if the stalks were made of music."

"Yes. Could be. If."

"And if the sound could go on and on and on, even when the wind stopped . . ."

"If all that, I suppose, yes." The old woman wondered—only briefly—if the sounds had been stroked into being by a particular wind or by the rays of this particular sunrise, or whether they had been uttered or created by the creature herself, and whether her own skin was reacting to sound or smell or something entirely extraordinary. That one . . . that winged one on the mountain had never been an ordinary anything. That one had not evolved, not accumulated, not adapted to become. That one had been created by someone, someone who had been striving for perfection.

Needly whispered, "It's turned green: the Listener."

"Yes. It does that."

Indeed, the stone had lost its fiery glow, drifted through orange and yellow into a transitory emerald green that had almost at once become muted, faded, as though lichen had crept over it. Now anyone looking casually toward it would have been unlikely to make out its outline against one or the other of the guardian peaks. On the ledge below it, however, still shining with bronze light, the wings of the other marvel folded abruptly, like the flick of twin fans. The great, thick bronze rope of her tail, tasseled in gold, lashed against the ledge of stone, and three great cymbal crashes broke the air into shards: *Gone, Gone, Gone.*

All other sounds ceased, and the echoes from those immense strokes had barely faded before the unreality opened her beak, the tongue within it quivering as the brazen throat uttered a sound of pain and sorrow and longing and timeless, universal grief: a cry that fled across the sky like a shadow only to return from the distant mountains, broken into a thousand echoes of mourning, again and again and again.

As the creature cried, rainbows dropped from her eyes, one by one.

"She's crying," mourned Needly, cupping her hands to catch her own tears.

Grandma squeezed her shoulder. She had once heard, or perhaps read, that Griffins wept crystal tears. The reason for the tears was evident as that marvelous beak dipped down between the front paws to greet another, smaller being creeping from the shelter of its mother's body. This tiny one was more gold than bronze—the larger creature's mirror but in miniature—and the watchers both knew that the mother was weeping over the child. Her child.

Then the smaller creature also lamented, and to her, also, the echoes responded, as though the world itself grieved and could not be comforted. The mother took her child between huge, padded front paws, enormous ivory-gold claws curving around it to enclose it safely, and launched herself from the ledge into the gulf of air above the watchers, her wings unfolding with a great crack of sound. They, mother and child, soared. They, grandmother and child, went to their knees under the buffet of downthrust air.

The winged ones spiraled upward until they were only a golden spark in the sunrise.

Silent time moved on, drawing no attention to itself. When it became certain the marvels would not return, Grandma showed the little girl the easy way to reach the Listener. See, she said, how the these hollows hid, how that little crevasse concealed, how this stone's shadows disguised the simple way to reach the Listener. They followed this hidden way quite easily and stepped together through a shadow on what appeared to be a solid wall to step out upon the ledge itself. Together they found a feather the baby Griffin had lost and several crystal tears the mother Griffin had shed, each enclosing rainbow lights. Together they leaned against the Listener to feel the far-off throbbing Grandma had felt before, as though there were a heart beating inside the stone. Their thoughts were varied and in no sensible order. Nonetheless, they amounted to a plea, which was what the Listener heard it as, yet again.

And so, strangely, as they turned to make their way back home—a place neither of them really thought of in that way—both of them felt comforted, almost as if they had heard a whisper, a murmur from some immense distance saying, "Coming . . . coming . . . I hear you . . ."

It was Grandma who had chosen the name "Needly" for the child. Even at birth she had been slim and silvery, white of skin and almost white of hair—the "almost" indicating no tint of gold but instead an almost metallic silver. She had wide eyes that went here and there, in and out, stitching the world together, making a shape of it at an age when most babies could not even focus their sight. This one was sharp, bright and perspicacious, as Grandma told herself. She was also an anomaly, for Needly was born to Grandma's daughter, Trudis, and Grandma had firmly intended that this disastrous daughter should *never* bear children!

Her intention had been thwarted at every turn. Trudis had borne seven, Needly being the last. Now, in hindsight, Grandma could not regret the other six—the two infant girls who had died, the four boy babes dropped into the world like gravel into a riverbed, losing themselves among unremarked heaps of other such gravel. Perhaps in some way they had opened the path for the seventh child, the wondrous child, Needly. Even Grandma—who often longed for marvelous and remedial things that had small chance of happening—even she had never dared hope for such a one as Needly.

The child was extraordinary, and in Hench Valley being extraordinary was a death sentence. Grandma had removed the baby from Trudis's erratic and often nonexistent care and went to considerable effort make the little one seem ordinary. Part of the effort consisted of naming the child without seeming to do so. The menfolk of Hench Valley used only ugly words for females, whether human or animal, and all females acquired their names by accretion of epithets. "Worthless" was a common valley name for a girl. "Ugly," "Slow," "Dirty" were others. Even if one had a treasured mare, the name would not hint at it. Glory-on-hooves would receive no better label than Mud. Grace-in-gallop would be nothing more lovely than Lump. Not that glory or grace had any place in Hench Valley. Except for Needly and Grandma and an occasional visiting cat or dog, all the valley's occupants actually were mud or lump, whether on four legs or two.

Grandma decided upon "Needly" at first sight of the child. The slender form, the steely pale hair and skin, those wide eyes, that pointed gaze made the name inevitable. Thereafter, Grandma had frequently sneered the word aloud, referring to the child thus, but without any apparent intention of naming her. In Needly's case, repetition succeeded where obvious intention would have failed. The label was not euphonious. It had no connotations of grace or fortune. It had the sneer of derogation necessary for females, and therefore it could be allowed where a loving or kindly word would have been jeered into nothing. Of course, when Grandma was alone with the little girl, the word was tenderness itself. The child understood this very well, though she was still too young to speak.

The power of names went unconsidered in Hench Valley. No one living there knew why the place was called Hench Valley. No one living there knew why the four settlements within it had the names they did: Tuckwhip; Gortles; Grief's Barn; Bag's Arm. Grandma thought, perhaps, that at that time, some centuries before, when love was still permitted, even expected, a father losing a woman in childbirth could possibly have named a child Grief, and that child might have built a barn. A son named Bagger or Bags could lose an arm in an accident and bury that part of him near the place he lived.

Male children were given names: Pig-belly, Suck-tooth, Fat-ass. These names were used only until the male in question caused a pregnancy. After that each added "Pa" to his name. Pig-belly-Pa. Suck-tooth-Pa. Fat-ass-Pa. Females lost their labels once they had children, each becoming a Ma, or, a generation later, a Grandma. Men never became Grandpas, however, since they were assumed to have had no part in producing the grandchild. So it was pretended, at least, though incest was not uncommon in Hench Valley. The only exception to these generalities was Grandma Lillis, who had first been identified as "Ma the healer," and was now called "Grandma healer," the word "healer" setting her into a separate category, making her valuable enough to leave alone at an age few other women reached, certainly not while still whole in body and mind.

Needly had been of no immediate value to her Ma or her putative Pa: Trudis had, in fact, put the child to the breast without even looking at her, and did not seem to notice when Grandma removed her from the household. If girls were valued at all by Pas, it was as a future source of profit. This child here, marveling at the Griffins in the dawn light, was still a year or so too young to prove profitable. Girls when just about beddable—those who lived that long—were very briefly profitable at eleven or twelve because they were in very short supply. Females had a high vanishment rate among Hench Valley folk. The reasons varied: girls were "Sold to somebody at Grief's Barn." Or "at Bag's Arm." Or "at Gortles." Girls "disappeared." Girls "up and died."

All this was part of the reason Grandma had intended Trudis to remain childless.

THE PROBLEM OF TRUDIS HAD begun with her birth in Tuckwhip, one of the small Hench Valley towns. Grandma was then known merely as Lillis. Lillis had moved into Tuckwhip with a stranger man and had built, from the ground up, a well-constructed house. No one moved *into* Hench Valley. No one had ever built a *decent house* there because no one there knew how. Somehow this man did. He was one whom the resident men had thought it unwise to either insult or attack, a man who made no attempt whatsoever to become acquainted, much less friendly with any of them. He was not a Pa, he would not use the title, his name was Joshua. Lillis had subsequently borne him twin girls—Sally and Serena (becoming a Ma in the process). When the little girls were around two, Joshua had gone away a month or so before Jeremy had arrived to father Jules the golden-haired. After Jeremy had come Jubal to father lilt-voiced Sarah, and then after Jubal, James, whose children were twins again—sturdy Jan and Jacky the dancer, who never toddled but went directly from a crawl to the extravagant grace of some creature born with winged feet.

Lillis thought she *should* feel it was promiscuity, this sequence, but she didn't. Each of them was different from the others, distinguishable, that is, but they were so much *alike!* It was a kind of faithfulness with the added spice of novelty! Each of them had returned every now and then to visit Lillis and his child or children. When each child, including the first ones, reached the age of four or five, his or her or their father arrived to take the child or children away. All Lillis's men had shared the way they behaved as well as their appearance. All of them were taciturn to other villagers, strong, capable, and—with Lillis—companionable, affectionate, and exceedingly intelligent. The one who had *actually* arranged such matters: a person? an agency? To herself, Lillis called them or it *the Planners*. It was clear that *the Planners* preferred that the person or agency found useful should live in a very unpleasant place among quite unpleasant people but *nonetheless* do it as happily as was possible *under those conditions*. Each time child or man went, Lillis had grieved: she had accepted grief as part of the bargain but she had not foreseen its weight.

When Lillis was twenty-five, Trudis was born: her last child; the child who confounded all assumptions. Her father had resembled those whom Lillis called "the J's," but he had been in some ways quite different. A little somber, perhaps. Not so musical. Unlike all the other of Lillis's children, Trudis had proven to be perfectly suited to Hench Valley and therefore—obviously—she was also an inappropriate candidate for leaving it. Inexplicably, despite her extremely select parentage, by the time she was two, Trudis was seen to fit the Hench Valley mold all too perfectly. It was as though the valley itself had engendered her. Trudis's father went away, returned saying he had sought advice and subsequently followed that advice. He told Lillis with regret and sorrow that Trudis had simply had not turned out to be . . . suitable, and when he left—reluctantly, as each of the others before him had been, though for a different reason—he left Trudis behind.

Lillis would not accept this. Her pride rebelled against it. Lillis was a stubborn woman. She believed, with all her mind, that the man had been as carefully selected as Lillis herself, and no child of *theirs* could be . . . what Trudis was!

In Hench Valley, the Rule was that each house was owned by the eldest woman in it. The owner could be a Grandma or a Ma or the oldest girl born to the preceding Ma: Lillis and Trudis occupied her house together. The rule also said that if there were any women of breeding age in the house, there should be a man in it, a Pa. In Lillis's case, however, once her last consort left, she had no man in the house. Only the fact that she was the Healer Ma kept possible invaders away. Though the reason was unspoken and very possibly indefinable by local standards, no one wanted her to be *owned* by anyone else. She was too useful to them all.

Someone had sent Lillis to the valley originally. *The Planners* and the people Lillis *thought* were responsible might not be the same person or people, which did not matter at the time. She had no real "relationship" with either. *The Planners* had governed her life until now—and she had agreed to it, for she had been told that the result would have "beneficial consequences for mankind." This promise came from a sufficiently exalted source in a sufficiently exalted place that Lillis believed it. Implicitly. The words were sufficiently lofty and lacking in detail to allow almost any interpretation, and "beneficial consequences" dropped into lockstep with Lillis's unbreakable habit of looking on the bright side. All went well and as planned, thus, until Lillis had her last child, Trudis.

Ah, Trudis! Those senders had looked deep, very deep, into Trudis within hours of her birth. Without dissent they considered Trudis to be both useless and hopeless. Worse (from their point of view) this judgment required that they look deeply into those of themselves who had arranged for the girl's parentage. Those individuals were evaluated also, and were judged as having been, at best, inept. Years of research had been backtracked. Hundreds of studies had been reviewed and re-re-reviewed. Fingers of various types had been pointed at faces of various species. Everyone agreed that it was an unfortunate mistake, and—given perfect hindsight—completely preventable occurrence. These particular foreseers, however, did not consider perfection to be impossible. Everything else in the plan was on target, however, and in the face of Lillis's furious determination they felt sufficiently distracted, and, moreover, sufficiently *guilty* to let her try to salvage Trudis.

Prognostication said that only tragedy would result if the girl's father stayed in Hench Valley for the length of time this salvage might take. He bid Lillis a loving farewell mixed with a feeling of loss. Lillis missed him, as she had each of them. People Lillis had grown up among were disinclined to use the word "love" as having too many possible definitions, but Lillis's "liking" would have met any of them. The ones who ruled Lillis's life (the ones who really did, not the ones who got blamed for it) rarely made mistakes; he, she, it, or they were usually very good at what he, she, it, or they did. He, she, it, or they gave her time and allowed her to try.

Lillis had set herself to the task with grim, unrelenting determination, a determination so rarely met with defeat that she assumed defeat was impossible. Only someone stubborn as she (as her last consort had mentioned, quite fondly) would have made the effort and, having made it, continued it. Each time a new strategy failed, she rethought the process: surely a change in method, surely inventing a new way, a new trick, a trap, a snare that would capture Trudis's . . . well . . . that was where the failure always snagged! Trudis's what? Imagination? Ambition? Better nature? Trudis had no imagination. Certainly no ambition that lasted longer than the five minutes needed for gratification. And better nature? Better than what?

Trudis grew quickly, a large girl who would be a large woman: tall and buxom and even attractive in a brutish, cowlike way. Years of patient teaching had taught her to string half a dozen words together in place of grunts and head shakings. This minor achievement had suggested there might be further progress, which was unfortunately misleading, for Trudis's mind remained as unformed as it had been on the day she had emerged bloody, brooding, and mute into the world. Trudis was still Trudis, as though carved from a rough block of greedy, lecherous stone. Trudis was not mendable.

As the years of Trudis's childhood spun by, a certain subsection of the Hench Valley Rule had very gradually forced its way to Lillis's attention. That subsection allowed that *if a house was without a grown male in it but had a breedable woman in it, then any breedable woman of that house could get up early on midsummer morning, cook a griddle cake, and carry it to the meadow, where she could offer it to whatever male she chose from those loitering there.*

The fact that the man might be half brother or even father to the woman bearing the griddle cake was not taken into consideration. Hench Valley did not keep track of such things. If the man who was approached took a bite of the cake and followed the woman to her home before sundown, then that man had henceforth the exclusive right to breed from any female in that house! This included the woman herself, her mother, even her grandmother, if the Ma had started bearing early enough. A woman of thirty-eight could have a daughter of twenty-five who had a twelve-year-old girl child and one Pa could enjoy them all. It wasn't even unusual—particularly inasmuch as few of the people kept track of their ages at all. This practice having been carried on for as long as anyone could remember, the Hench Valley population was very closely related to itself.

Lillis knew all about the Rule. It was not written down anywhere, but it was fully understood by everyone who lived there. Lillis was not going to let Trudis fall prey to the Rule. Trudis had to be taken from the valley before she reached puberty and fell prey to any of the Pas. Time went by, however, until the time came that Trudis would soon leave childhood behind her. Then, as though suddenly, time was running out.

Lillis knew that if she had been unable to change the child, she would be unable to change the woman. If the woman were made infertile and left here, she would end up being savaged for not bearing, as this would reflect on the Pa-ness of whatever male was consorting with her. However, since Lillis's presence in the valley was no longer at all useful to the powers that be (or powers, perhaps, that had been), there were places where Lillis and Trudis could live out their lives in less dangerous surroundings. Through her long, compliant service—and more important, by a certain admission of guilt among the powers that be, as they had been managing things and *one or more of them must have made a mistake*—they owed support for Lillis and for any other child she bore.

It was spring when Lillis made her decision. Though baby girls were generally ignored, if ever a beddable or nearly beddable female tried to leave the valley, the men hunted her down. Lillis decided to leave at Midsummer, both because it would be warm and because Midsummer was celebrated with three nights of bonfires and beer. Everyone in Hench Valley would be drunk and stumbling for at least three or four days, during which time no one would notice Trudis and Lillis had gone. If they left well after dark on Midsummer Eve, they would be able to get so far gone that the men of Hench Valley could not follow. Trudis could not be told they were leaving, however. Some other attractive reason for going into the forest would be invented for the occasion: maybe a neighboring village having a pig roast, or a crop of certain mushrooms showing up in a nearby valley. Trudis liked food . . . and drink, and she already liked sex.

The plan was made, the packs were ready and hidden. Shortly before Midsummer, lending a whiplash of panic to an already compelling motivation, Trudis experienced her first "womanlies." Lillis was so flustered by the event that when she explained to Trudis what was happening, Lillis actually used the word "womanlies," which was current in Hench Valley. If she had been thinking in her usual analytical manner, she would not have done so. Trudis heard "womanlies" and remembered it. *Woman* lies meant she was now a *woman,* and there was a rule about *women.*

Lillis didn't notice. She was busy with vital details of their disappearance, details assuring they would not be followed, not be caught. There were certain things of hers that had to be hidden or destroyed. Or, in the case of certain very rare and valuable herbs and roots, bottled or packaged so she could take them with her.

By the morning of Midsummer Eve, Lillis had everything ready; the packs were well hidden in the forest on the way they would go. She planned to leave as soon as it was well dark and the festivities were at their height. She had told Trudis they had been invited to a pig-roast feast at a neighboring village where Trudis had never been; a pig feast with cake and ale. Also, there was a certain herbal extract she would give Trudis just before they left, one that would make her biddable. Lillis allowed herself an extra hour's sleep that morning. As she was sitting over her tea mug in the all-purpose everything-including-the-kitchen room, however, someone fell through her kitchen door. The woman stumbled exhaustedly to her feet, babbling that she had run all the way from Gortels, a couple of miles north. Rotten, a woman of Gortles, was giving birth and seemingly dying of it. Rotten had begged—screamed—to her friend to fetch the Healer Ma.

"Did you call Ma Beans? She's good help with birthing!"

"Ma's dead, Lillis. Ma got 'erself kilt."

While listening to the details of Ma Beam's late-night fall from a cliff road, Lillis was gathering up her kit, and she walked quickly to Gortles, thinking to be back in plenty of time to leave that night.

During the subsequent day and night, as she battled for the woman's and the girl baby's lives—successfully in the one case, though not the other—her plans for Midsummer Eve were driven from her mind. Only when she started for home in the morning did she remember with exhausted horror what precisely it was that the Midsummer Day rule allowed. She prayed, actually prayed, that the second night of the festival would allow their departure as well as the first would have done.

Trudis, however, now that she was a woman, had actually, for the first time in her life, planned to do something. She got up early, baked griddle cakes (very badly, one side drippy, one side black), ate all but one of them with copious amounts of the honey that her mother allowed her only sparingly (it came from elsewhere, and it could not be readily replaced). She then took the saved griddle cake with her to the meadow hoping to find Gralf Garn, a man-sized boy she'd been looking at and sharing some fleshly amusements with for some time. Gralf Garn had taken a bite of cake, though he'd spit it out as he had followed her home, and after a lengthy interval in the one bed in the house, by early midmorning he was ensconced in Lillis's kitchen.

Lillis, weary past belief, came through her door at noon that day, saw Gralf Garn drinking beer in the kitchen while Trudis squirmed in drunken and lubricious pleasure on his lap. Lillis, silent more from exhaustion than prudence, thereupon received Gralf Garn's greeting: a few rude words, several of them the same word used as noun, adjective, verb, and expletive, and in that single moment of absolute weariness let all resistance go. The inevitable fell into place around her, splitting off determination and hope and mere stubborn will. Her long battle had ended in defeat.

Honorable defeat, she whispered to herself. At least that!

Lillis had known Gralf Garn from birth. He was the only child she had ever delivered who came from the womb with teeth that bit the hand that drew him forth. She knew him far better than Trudis ever would, and she was saddened thereby. Trudis was no longer a girl, and would undoubtedly soon be a Ma. It was no longer worth the battle it would take to get her away. She might save the girl from Hench Valley, but for what? Trudis would make a Hench Valley around her wherever she was.

She left the two of them drinking, and weary though she was, she recollected that she was still considered an attractive woman even after all her childbearing. Accordingly, she shoved a wedge beneath her door. In no other house in Tuckwhip would a wedge have held, but Lillis's house had been built by Joshua, not merely thrown together. She was already prepared to leave; she needed only to sleep a few hours first. Her few treasures and necessities were already packed, waiting for her in the woods. She would pick them up when she left that night. She further assured her safe departure by dosing Gralf's bottle when he left it briefly to go outside and relieve himself against the front wall of the house. All the men in Hench Valley did it, marking territory, like dogs. Well, he would have a good nap that would extend into a good night's sleep. A nice long sleep!

As a final drop of the bitterness Tuckwhip had held for her, she mused on the fact that Trudis and Gralf were undoubtedly well mated. As river stone to river stone, they were mated: each unyielding as stone, each mind shaped as river stone is shaped, worn, rounded, hard, unusable for any constructive purpose, shaped by long, aimless tumbling in careless waters so it would twist beneath your foot and break an ankle for you, only good for throwing, if one wished to hurt or kill. There were piles of such stones here and there throughout the villages. They were pointed out to women. Those were what would be flung at a woman "fer tawkin' back 'r not havin' supper ready." There was less stoning of women now than in the past. One did not destroy what one could not replace, though when drunk, the men sometimes forgot that. Men who lost their temper ended up with no woman at all, and most men in Hench Valley were already in that category.

At about midnight she left Hench Valley by the safe and easy ways she would not have been able to travel with Trudis, arriving very soon thereafter near the House of the Oracles. It was a short walk from there to her home. Though the Oracles saw her in transit, they took no particular notice, which would have surprised Lillis had she known. The persons/creatures/individuals, he, she, it, or they who had thus far actually directed her life, however, noted with deep concern that instead of looking at least fifteen years younger than her years—which she usually did—on this occasion she showed every year plus a few. She was desperately weary and slept for several days without moving.

Back in Tuckwhip, both Trudis and Gralf Garn discovered parts of the Rule that neither of them had considered. Morning came and Gralf Garn woke in a strange bed with Trudis sprawled beside him. There was no Lillis in the house. He searched the area around the house, the byre, the garden, even the privy. It being the Midsummer morning, no one was around to ask if anyone had seen Lillis going somewhere to do some healing. To say Gralf Garn was astonished was to say too much; the man was not capable of astonishment, for he had only two, perhaps three, emotions. There was the pleasant feeling of being drunk. There was the edgy feeling of being hungry or lustful. And there was often the heat of anger.

The worst of it was that when he followed Trudis home, he had not considered that Lillis wouldn't be there. So far as Gralf had planned—and he had actually *planned* to meet Trudis that morning—Lillis had been the most important part of the deal. Lillis was needed for several reasons. One of them was that she could cook. There were other important reasons also, one of which he had anticipated forcibly explaining to her, so he actually put down his bottle and decided to hunt her down! Everyone else was sleeping off a drunk, with another two nights of being drunk to look forward to. He had no luck at all in getting anyone to go with him to look for her.

Of his three emotions, anger seemed the most applicable. Trudis was surprised to find herself receiving both the blame for no tea water and the violent chastisement that accompanied it. She went to complain to her mother and was again surprised. Within a few days she had grown accustomed to the reality of constant surprise and constantly being hit for it. That was the way she would live in Hench Valley with Ma Healer gone. Trudis being Trudis, she soon decided being hit was easier than doing anything to prevent it.

Bein' hit required no effort at all. She soon didn't even bother to yell, and Gralf soon gave up hittin' as useless.

LILLIS HAD GROWN UP ON a small farmlike place with an oddly assorted pack of relations and quasi-relations. There was an uncle who spoke several languages, an aunt who had been a surgeon, two people Lillis had thought of as moms, one of whom had actually given birth to her, though Lillis was never certain which of them it was. Both of them knew about animals and farming. There was a man she called Poppa who might have been her father and who had certainly read every book ever written about the history of Earth. There were also several uncles and cousins who knew frighteningly exhaustive information about "ono-mies" or "ologies" from astro to zoo. All these people came and went; all of them had spent time with Lillis, who had learned to read at age three and had been kept well supplied with books ever since. It had not occurred to Lillis that she was being "managed" in any way, nor did it occur to those who helped in the matter that they were "managing" her. It was simply what people did with young ones.

The Oracles had arrived in the vicinity around the time Lillis was born. No one saw them arrive; they were simply there, occupying a series of well-explored and rather boring caves that had been, seem-ingly overnight, transformed into living quarters, storage rooms, and vaults. Though the adults in the "family" had always kept their distance from strangers, including these, Lillis had introduced herself to the Oracles during those few unchallenging months between learning to toddle and learning to read. She had been welcomed as a visitor and was welcome to use the multitude of education machines that stood in the front part of the Oracles' cave. They told her, when she asked who they were, that they were Oracles

She asked if they could answer questions, and was told, "All of them—if we want to." Since all representations made to her by adults had been accurate in the past, and since the Oracles looked (somewhat vaguely) like adult people, she believed this representation to be accurate also and therefore valued her association with the Oracles. She blamed her own ignorance when those answers were almost never particularly useful. She thought her lack of understanding was attributable to her age. In fact, the Oracles often told her she would understand it better when she was older.

And it was on her way to the House of the Oracles at age seventeen that she had met a man who said he was visiting the Oracles, who said he thought he'd stay for a while, who said his name was Joshua, that she was a really pretty girl, and would she have any idea what disease was bothering his chickens? Discussions concerning the diseases of fowl were followed by discussions about everything under the sun. They became acquainted, and better acquainted, and very well acquainted, and not long afterward he built a very solid house in nearby Hench Valley, invited her to share it, and fathered twin girls upon her.

While all this was going on, he also intimated he had not merely happened to meet her, but had been *sent* for that purpose. And, *she guessed,* it was the Oracles who had sent him and the Oracles who summoned him away, along with their child.

A year or so later, it was from the House of the Oracle, *she assumed,* that the other men came, four all together, counting Joshua. All these men shared certain attributes. She often thought they could have been brothers. One she remembered best for his beautiful voice, not that the others had not had nice voices. One had played the guitar wonderfully, like a master, not that the others couldn't play well. One could tell stories that kept you waiting eagerly for the next word; well, they all did, really. All of them were full of laughter and pleasure. Nothing about this was a surprise; Lillis had been told by her first consort why they would be coming and leaving, and from everything she had read and knew, it had seemed a worthy reason. Until the last one and the last child: Trudis.

Well, Trudis now had a Pa in the house, and Lillis did not intend to share either the house or her body with the Pa. Relinquishing the problem that was Trudis, Lillis returned home. Home was rather depleted, only three members of her earlier "family" were there, but others arrived. All of them were interesting and most of them were pleasant. There wasn't much news. This one had moved to Wellsport. That one had gone south down the Big River to see the ocean. A man named Joshua had built himself a house up the hill, and was getting to be quite an acceptable neighbor. Lillis eagerly went to meet him. *It was the same Joshua! Or Jeremy? Or Jubal? Strangely, she couldn't quite remember the little differences that had distinguished them before.* He was indeed very acceptable, and they subsequently shared many pleasurable activities from mushroom and herb hunting, to fishing, to exchanging views about the possible future of the world, to playing cards or "cubeys." This was a kind of spelling game involving ten dice with different sets of letters on the sides. One posited a question, then each player made an answer to that question by throwing the cubeys, then using the ten letters on top—or if one allowed oneself multiple throws, any multiple of ten—to spell an answer. The number of throws was determined in part by the complexity of the question asked.

At that point Lillis believed she had fulfilled every obligation she had incurred, every duty she had sworn. Now she could relax and delight in the simple pleasure of having a close and loving friend.

Though Lillis had never felt comfortable enough with the Oracles to penetrate very far into their "House," she had always had access to an area just inside the cave complex where various complicated machines were kept; some were food machines that could take any recipe and turn it into a meal. Some were information machines that answered virtually all questions; others would allow one to look at and listen to various places, if one knew the code locations of those places. Lillis learned the location numbers for the villages in Hench Valley, for a town over the mountain called Saltgosh, and for areas beyond that called Artemisia, as well as several other towns near roads where people traveled. One could see who was going where; one could hear what was being discussed. By using the device, she was able to find out what was happening in Tuckwhip or Grief's Barn or anywhere else in Hench Valley by listening to the women at the well. Whether by foresight or good fortune, each village obtained its cooking and drinking water from its own good well. Men did not go to the wells, and women could speak freely only there, so everything suppressed and buried came boiling out at the wells.

Lillis learned that Gralf had fathered, or "Pa'd" as the locals said, a baby on Trudis as quickly as any twelve-year-old female could manage it—though she was actually not far from thirteen when the baby was born, a girl. This baby lived until she started to crawl, her neighbor reported. She crawled into the creek and drowned. She was too young to have acquired a name. Not quite a year later, Trudis set the second daughter outside in her basket, got to drinking beer with Gralf, ended up in bed, and "fergot 'bout the baby," so Trudis said at the well. "Basket 'uz bloody. Wild dogs, prob'ly," said Trudis, dry-eyed, quoting Gralf. "Mebbe bobcat. Mebbe uh owl."

Many men made a strong town: that was the sum and total of truth. Nobody really wanted the bother of rearing girl babies and no one in Hench Valley planned for a future in which those females might be wanted. Gralf chastised Trudis after each female birth and again after each one died, though not as severely as for having had them in the first place.

After that came four boy babies, two sets of twins. None of them had suffered fates similar to the girl babies because Gralf kept an eye on them, though Trudis did not. Trudis didn't keep an eye on much—except perhaps Gralf himself. Time went on. After the second set of twins, Trudis did not conceive again. As the boys reached their sixth or seventh year, they joined the pack of boys who lived out in the wild. "Parenting" in Hench Valley consisted of a Pa pointing at a dirty, probably hungry, mostly nude boy and saying, "That-un's wunna mine." Lillis believed they recognized their sons by smell. She could not think of any other possible way. The boys took refuge where they could during the winters—often in the tunnels the Hench Valley men had dug into the buried city that lay beneath the valley, often earning their food by helping a Pa extend his "treasure tunnels" farther into the buried city. Eventually, if not killed in a fight, they went off "hunting women" and didn't return. If anyone had bothered to remember, it had been more than twenty years since any man from Hench Valley had gone off hunting a woman and had actually brought one back.

It seemed Trudis's childbearing was over. That fall, however, when Slap and Grudge, the second set of Trudis's boys, were six years old, a predator began killing livestock, including one of the half-dozen cows left in the valley. None of the cows were in milk, the men having inadvertently slaughtered their only bull calf for a barbecue, so amply supplied with beer that the recent death of the only other bull in the valley had been forgotten. When they sobered up enough to become infuriated—fury was always an acceptable substitute for thought in Hench Valley—the men went hunting for the killer, whatever it was.

The killer beast had left very catlike tracks, and the tracks led the Hench Valley men a great distance away, deep into distant woods, beyond twisted ridges. In their absence, a tall, strong, quiet sort of fellow made camp out in the woods at a point equidistant from the towns of Tuckwhip, Bag's Arm, Gortles, and Grief's Barn, and thereafter he became familiar to the women—and to Grandma, who watched his amatory adventures as though they had been a play on a stage. But then she had always thought of Tuckwhip as a stage and of herself more as bit-part player than as a resident. The women were quick to notice how clean he was, and how pleasant his manner. They noticed his very pale skin, his white hair, not from age but from birth. There was a sudden onset of bathing in hot springs among the village women, only two of whom—captured as children some thirty years before from among a group of travelers on the road—had ever before met a male who was either clean or pleasant. Several months went by. Shortly before the valley men returned, the stranger departed. There were three reminders he had actually been there: several women had become pregnant; some women so enjoyed being free of the itch that they kept up their habit of bathing and washing their clothes; and there was a young bull in the cowshed at Grief's Barn. The stranger had brought it, leading it on a leash, like a dog. No one had wondered at that, no one at all. One or two of the women thought fleetingly that the cows could be bred and would come into milk about the time the women would have their children, just in case cow's milk was needed.

Along with all this, Lillis learned that Trudis, the only woman of childbearing age left in Tuckwhip, was among the pregnant in Hench Valley. In the family home near the House of the Oracles, where Lillis now dwelt in a degree of comfort that almost repaid her years of frustration, Lillis recalled what she had heard of "Silverhairs," a race said to be preternaturally wise, able to read the future, able to set things in motion to achieve future ends, sometimes generations in advance—able, indeed, to do most if not all of the wonders the Oracles were reputed to achieve. If what was said of them was true, then Trudis's pregnancy might result in something other than the birth of another Hench Valley stone. Lillis talked with Joshua/Jeremy/Jubal/James about it, saying, "I think I'll consult the Oracles about it."

Joshua et al. grinned and said, "Now, Lill, why would you do that?"

"Well, it's important, maybe. And the Oracles are right here, pretty near here, anyhow. And with them available, wouldn't one be foolish not to consult them?"

"Well then, love, you go right ahead and consult. Just don't place much faith in what they have to say."

He was right. Why should she behave foolishly? Instead, why not simply find out? She decided to go back to Tuckwhip when the baby came. Selfishly, she preferred to return at the latest possible time: when Trudis was already in labor. If the baby turned out to be another stone, she would be able to tell at once and could leave without unpacking. When she reminded herself of Trudis's propensities, however, she utilized other bits and pieces of the Oracles' equipment to make a number of surreptitious visits during the pregnancy, enough of them to assure the child would be born without the handicap of a drunken mother. Unaccountably, though temporarily, Trudis lost her insatiable thirst.

NEEDLY WAS ONE OF THE six babies born in Hench Valley that summer, though no one except Grandma seemed to notice them. The babies seemed to slip through the mind like the shadow of trout in a brook: half gone before half glimpsed. Needly—from the moment Grandma finished washing and wrapping her—was tiny and pale, with hair as white as the moon, appearing to be almost silver in good light. Grandma visited every one of the babies: watched their eyes, their gaze, their quiet, and decided that none of them were stone. Not only were they not stone, they were very definitely something far superior. In the light of what knowledge she had about genetics, she found this . . . more than merely puzzling. It contradicted everything she knew about breeding. A metallurgical analogy would be to melt equal parts of gold and lead together and pour the mixture out as pure gold. It couldn't happen!

Or it could if an ovary could be induced to produce one golden egg out of ten thousand lead ones. Perhaps by chance. Or the impossibly favorable result of cosmic rays. Or if someone transplanted an already properly fertilized egg into the woman at the appropriate time.

Once she had decided it was remotely possible, Lillis gave up thinking about it.

It had been considered lucky to have "the Healer" provide a secret name for a baby, as she was one of the handful of residents who could read. So Lillis played cubeys to get baby names for the new mothers. The other two girls were named Clethra (discarding a Z, a Q, and an X) and Acrea (discarding two Us, two Ws and another R). Cubeys provided the boys with the names Brian and Galan and Victor. Like Needly, their hair was silvery, like spun metal. The people of Hench Valley glanced across Silverhair babies and, except for their mothers, forgot what they had seen. Needly had two half sisters and three half brothers, and every one of them survived: two in Gortles, two in Grief's Barn, one in Bag's Arm, Needly herself in Tuckwhip.

Lillis had left Hench Valley wearing Healer Ma's shoes. Healer Grandma Lillis returned to Tuckwhip wearing those same shoes. The only way she could guard this child was by living there or taking her away, and—yet again!—everything about the child spoke of a predestined life in which it would be unwise to interfere too greatly. Joshua thought it would be dangerous for the child and for Lillis if he came within reach of Gralf, and Grandma concurred, suggesting that Joshua take a short vacation, look up some old friends. She thought she wouldn't be staying long. Just long enough to find out what was going on, then maybe she'd leave and take the little one . . . *ones* with her.

She visited the other mothers just as a Healer Grandma would do, checking them out, seeing if they were healthy. Grandma Lillis decided that as soon as they were weaned she would take them away. All of them were alike: healthy, vigorous, and they cried seldom if ever. They looked at the world out of wide, knowing eyes.

And they disappeared. As they got to early weaning age, they disappeared, one at a time. Only Grandma Lillis realized this, and she nodded to herself: so these babies were intended for something specific, and someone had come for them! When they disappeared, the mothers of the babies behaved oddly for a few days, walking around, peering behind things, as though trying to find something that was lost without knowing what it was. Sometimes each would take a gold coin from a pocket and fondle it, wonderingly. The little ones had not been sold or killed; gold had been left behind to pay for what . . . ? The womb? The breast? Certainly no one had ever abused the infants, not by word or action. No one had abused the women who had borne the children either, which was most surprising! No one took the gold away from the mothers either, which was truly astonishing! The third boy was only a little under a year old when he, too, was gone. *All gone, except for Needly!*

Unfortunately, when the others had gone, so had the protective immunity that infancy had provided. Gralf had begun to notice the baby. Lillis, who was now a Grandma, managed to keep the infant out of his way while she waited for someone to come and collect the little girl. Her wait was a troubled one, as she half hoped someone would come soon, before the child fell to harm, half longed that no one would take her. Lillis had a great store of thwarted mother love saved up, and she had come to love Needly dearly. She had loved all her own but had given them up as she had *been told,* had *presumed,* had *accepted* that destiny required her to do so. This one, she rebelliously decided, would be taken over her dead body! She even threw a few tantrums with those . . . Oracles, asking them to find out what in . . . was going on?

The Oracles reacted to tantrums as they did to anything suggesting criticism. They disappeared. They were simply not there when one went looking for them. If eventually discovered and confronted, the Oracles were oracular, meaning allusive rather than definitive, indicative rather than directional, and always refusing to clarify until the matter in question culminated, at which time they invariably said, "Well, that's more or less what we meant." With Lillis occupied full-time down in Tuckwhip waiting for Needly to disappear, Joshua did disappear. Lillis had a crying fit over this, before deciding that she had deserted him, and in all honesty, she would have done the same if he had deserted her. When the second year passed, and the third, Lillis decided Needly's continued presence could mean only that she, Lillis, was considered to be an adequate custodian or keeper or guardian. This both pleased and annoyed her. Someone could have told her! It would have been polite! She could have told Joshua, and she could have taken the child to their home. If he had consented. Probably.

The child, though remaining as pallid as those strange growths sometimes seen in cellars, thrived and grew and no one . . . nothing ever informed Lillis, now Grandma, whether she really was the proper guardian or whether Needly had just been overlooked. Was Needly different in some way? Was she, Lillis, supposed to *do something* about Needly, or was *something else* supposed to happen? Fearing any attention paid to the child, Lillis did what all mothers in Hench Valley did for their daughters: she uglified the child so that nobody would look at her covetously. Even as she rubbed soot on the child's skin and made her hair look like a rat's nest with a carefully contrived horsehair wig, Lillis kept exploring, looking around herself for clues, going off into the woods and speaking into the silence of the trees, asking!

Once, only once, she went all the way to the Listener and asked it, not really expecting and not receiving any answer.

She wanted badly to take the child away but was fearful of upsetting some larger purpose. She had learned many things from her real family . . . the one she had supposedly been born into. *She had learned that there were larger purposes in the universe than those readily apprehended by human beings, and though it would be egocentric to believe one was, necessarily, part of any such predestined thing, if one truly thought one was involved, then it might be wisest to go along with it.*

Lillis did believe it: she thought she might be caught up in such a purpose. She was, nonetheless, annoyed. *If something was supposed to happen, someone or something ought to be kind enough to give her a set of directions!*

No one did. She struggled with her annoyance—sometimes outright rage—and kept the matter to herself as much as she could. Rage was wearying. It wore itself into tatters and the pieces eventually blew away. It was entirely possible she was already doing precisely what *they, whoever they were,* wanted her to do, and until something else was required, she would simply go on doing whatever it was she was doing. She had dealt with the Gralf-being-the-Pa-in-the-house problem early on by saying she had a disease, and if any man bothered her, his parts would fall off. Gralf believed her. Gralf told every other Pa, and they too believed. Also, Gralf was neither as young nor as insatiable as he had been at one time.

As Needly grew, Grandma taught her everything she could about healing, herbs, the nature of plants and how to distill them into useful, portable substances. She taught her about beasts and their treatment as well. She took the child, from the age of five, with her when babies were delivered and had her assist in the process, borrowing newborns now and then so that Needly could feel them. "See, that's the head. Feel it. Imagine it all slimy, but under the sliminess, that's the way it feels. That's the little arm, feel it, and the leg. See, if it's turned wrong in the womb, you might have to grab this and pull, so. Understand?"

Neely did understand. Her strong little arms and tiny hands proved extremely useful in several difficult births in the other towns in the valley! Lillis taught her how to clean wounds and treat them. She taught Needly to look carefully at the difference between what a person says and what that person actually does—putting this in context of "other places." In Hench Valley there were no differences between vile words and vile actions. And she went on waiting for a sign. The only thing about Needly she felt at all strange about was that when Needly was told something important, real, and meaningful, she always nodded, as though checking an item off a list of things she either already knew or had been expected to learn.

Lillis had been wearing healer shoes when she had left Hench Valley; Healer Grandma had returned to Hench Valley in that same pair of shoes. And though Needly was certainly odd enough to warrant stoning, for the Healer Grandma's sake, Needly had been let strictly alone.

As did any girl in Hench Valley, strange-looking or not, Needly grew up to live what the men called "a good life fer a wummin." Up early in the morning to fetch water from the well, and it not even an hour away, she had a nice stroll in the morning! The yoke across the shoulders was a burden, true, so the men said, females who grew up to the yoke grew strong under the burden! Besides, they weren't expected to carry full buckets until they were maybe six or even seven! And once the water was fetched, there was only the stock to be seen to—little of it though there was—and the byre to be shoveled and the house swept and the day's grain to be ground in the hand mill and the meals to cook and the garden weeded as the Great Fathers had intended. It was all good, healthful exercise for the strengthening, training of young females. Constant chastisement reinforced all three.

It was each girl's own Ma who broke the girl into hauling water and digging gardens, thus building up helpful calluses on shoulders, hands, feet. It was a girl's own Ma who uglified her by rubbing manure in her hair and mud and soot on her face, thus making her even fouler to see and worse to smell than the usual Hench Valley person. Girls were kept salable until puberty by making them as undesirable as possible. Repeated chastisement by a girl's Pa and her brothers kept her in line. Slap and Grudge tried chastising Needly only once. Grandma had heard their whispering and had been poised to intervene when the unexpected happened. Slap raised a stick. There was a loud noise. Still holding the stick he had intended to hit Needly with, Slap lay in a corner, black-and-blue in the face and upper body. Across the room from him, Grudge nursed a broken arm. Even after Slap and Grudge were healed, no one touched Needly. It was almost as though someone had dropped a veil of invisibility over her.

If and when girls were de-uglified to be sold or mated, most of them stayed alive for quite some time, just as Trudis had. Men didn't spend that kind of money on somebody who'd be around only a year or so, unless they were like Old Digger, and Old Digger bought really young ones, sometimes as young as eight or nine years old, and kept them only three or four years. Never past their womanlies, though. Once they started to get breasts, Digger was finished with them. They disappeared and he'd go back to digging salvage or gold out of the buried cities until he had enough to buy another one.

Gralf liked to annoy Grandma by talking of selling Needly to Old Digger. If he sold her to anyone else, he'd have to pay taxes when the king's tax-hogs came by Hench Valley, the far east edge of what the King of Ghastain considered his own lands, but nobody'd know he'd sold her because Digger didn't keep them long. There'd be no taxes on a girl who just disappeared. "There's no taxes owing on girls who just run off, and that's what I'll say she did, run off." Gralf considered himself clever, and he bragged drunkenly to Grandma about his plan to sell Needly and fool the tax-hogs.

"Who's going to fetch the water then?" Grandma asked the air in her casual murmur, speaking the garbled, half-swallowed tongue Hench Valley people spoke rather than the speech she had taught Needly to use when they were alone. "Needly goes, I'm gettin' too old to do much. Alla' yer boys but Slap and Grudge're gone. Y'think they'll decide to help? Y'think Trudis gonna stir 'rself allofa sudden? Wonder who'll feed the stock and hoe the garden?"

The mutter was mere misdirection. Grandma had spurred the first and second of Gralf's sons into departure with stories of cities and women and drink. Slap and Grudge would follow very soon. As for Grandma herself, she had no intention of being anywhere in Hench Valley once Needly was out of it, and the minute Gralf started talking about Digger, she knew it was time for Needly to go. *If some purpose was to have been served by Needly's being here, in this place, that purpose had had plenty of time to declare itself.* Grandma said this quite frequently and loudly! She was letting THEM, *the Planners*, know. Whoever THEY were.

Yes, Grandma decided. The purpose had either been *met* or *canceled*, and Grandma intended to be gone in the dark hours, taking the child with her. Dull-witted as he was, Gralf half suspected that's what would happen. Grandma had gone away before, she'd likely do it again. He could kill the old lady, of course, but that wouldn't get the water brought either. Besides, some said she was a witch, and killing old witch ladies was *jitchus, real jitchus.*

When he considered selling Needly, Gralf hadn't thought about who'd do the work. Trudis didn't turn her hand to anything. Couldn't cook worth spit. Couldn't fetch water without spilling most of it. Couldn't fork out hay without catching a pitchfork tine into the hide of the cow or milk goat she was supposed to be feeding! Hellfires, he had to put his own water in the kettle on the back of the stove at night to be sure he had tea water hot in the morning! Had to do it *his-own-self*! Well, he made damn sure there was only enough water for him. Trudis wants hot water, she c'n make her own fire, fill her own kettle! Far's he c'd figure there was only one thing Trudis did do fairly well, fairly often. He enjoyed it some, but—though he was incapable of expressing it in those terms—*surfeit had been sure death to appetite.*

Though Lillis well knew Gralf and the way his mind worked, he had one idea so ridiculous that she had never suspected it for a moment. On that long-ago Midsummer Day when Gralf came home with Lillis's daughter, one of his reasons, not the least one, had concerned Lillis herself more than it had her daughter. Lillis was known to be a midwife, a healer, she knew herbs; the people she helped probably paid her something for doing it. Certainly no Hench Valley man did anything for anyone without being paid. So, Gralf figured, since she was making all those pennies with the herbs and the healing and the midwife thing, those pennies could just as well add up in his pocket as in hers. A house always belonged to the eldest woman in it, which had never seemed right to Gralf, but that house was the man's to rule! If he ruled, then nothing said he couldn't take whatever pennies she got. Those theoretical pennies—in theoretically improbable aggregate—had figured large in Gralf's decision to accept the utterly inedible cake Trudis offered him before he followed her home.

Gralf had fully intended to get rid of Needly by selling her, but no boy with any pride would do girl's work, and if Needly was gone, Grandma likely wouldn't stay. So there'd be three men in the house and nobody to do for them but Trudis, and she wouldn't!

Unless! Unless he could buy a girl for Grudge or Slap, and that brought him back to Grandma Healer's pennies. Grandma, now she was back, would still be doing what she used to do, and he could probably lay hands on what people paid her, so he'd let her get into the habit of doin' it all again. Though Grandma could read what passed for thought in Gralf's mind as though it were printed on his forehead, the last thing she would have suspected to find there was money that she, Lillis, was supposed to have. Until, that is, one day when the pennies loomed so large in Gralf's mind that he told her he'd be taking what she was paid in future.

She could not keep the laughter inside her. So that's what the fool had been thinking of. "Well, Gralf," she said. "You're welcome to everything I get, but you'll have to come along with me each time to get it. The most I get from anybody is a mug of tea, and some days I almost drown in it! But I can't carry it home; you'll have to be right there to get any."

Grandma said Gralf never let Trudis have any money. Why would he think any other man would let a woman have money to pay for a healer? Gralf heard her say it. He went around hitting things for several frustrated days. He would have preferred to hit the old woman, but there was that *jitchus* thing! Kill an old woman who might be a witch, and it'd *jitchus*!

Needly herself remained blessedly ignorant of either Gralf or Grandma's thoughts. Thus far she was merely wary, as all Hench Valley females were when any of the men, including any supposed father, was involved.

Those were Grandma's words. Supposed father. When Needly had been about nine, she had considered those words. What, after all, Needly puzzled, did she know about Grandma? Only what Grandma had told her. Grandma's name had been Lillis; Lillis had birthed twin daughters, then four other children, then Trudis in this house. All but Trudis had been taken away while they were quite young.

Lillis had been told originally that they would all live well, elsewhere. Far elsewhere. Lillis had been told the several fathers of those children had been selected for Lillis by *people from elsewhere:* selected because children from those couplings would be born with certain attributes that fit long-planned purposes of *those people.* Lillis was told *those people* did not and never had lived in or near Tuckwhip, but *those people* had made sure each time that the right man would visit Lillis in her house and stay with her for long enough, however long that needed to be. *Those people* were not, Lillis reasoned, the same as those who lived in the House of the Oracles. *Both,* she assumed, might have contributed to her life and future, but the two groups were quite separate, though they *might* be aware of one another. She thought. Perhaps.

Whenever she told Needly things she thought Needly might at some time need to know, Grandma was careful to identify guesses and possibilities as just that. She never said definitely that she knew who was responsible for what. Needly, in fact, made no more sense of it than Grandma had.

More pertinently, she knew Grandma had purposefully learned herb lore and midwifery and healing because these would be useful skills in places like Hench Valley. Needly also realized that whoever had made the plans, whoever had sponsored the roll of the genetic dice, that individual had come up good for the three sons and three daughters who had departed as children.

"But they didn't stay with you, Grandma!" Needly had cried. "It makes me unhappy! I want someone to explain things. I really do!"

The woman had given her a long, measuring look, put the kettle on, made a pot of tea, and placed two cups on the table. She couldn't explain. She could tell the child only what she herself had wondered over.

"Needly, one of the men who lived in our family house for a time told me our world is very sick. He said lots of people know this, though there are even more people who deny it. I'm told that several groups of thoughtful people have looked into the future—using every tool they had, thinking machines, gatherings of the wise, reading of history— trying to come up with a way of straightening things out. They all agreed, finally, that mankind simply has not evolved far enough from the ape. Mankind still has parts of his brain that are *monkey-brain.* It isn't their fault, they don't choose to think like monkeys, it's the only way they can think. They need immediate gratification. They aren't able to look ahead, to consider the consequences of their own actions. It's like an inherited disease—no, more a condition. *Monkey-brain* condition."

She saw puzzlement in the child's face. "We don't have monkeys in this part of the world, Needly, but I've told you about them. Let's pretend, like we did when you were little. Let's pretend you're a monkey. Let's say you and your monkey husband somehow get blown by a storm onto a little island where there's nothing to eat except delicious fruit from one tree that bears fruit all the year around. Even the seeds of the fruit are delicious. Are you going to eat the fruit?"

Needly nodded. "'F I was hungry, I would. We all would."

"Yes. A monkey wouldn't look at the fact there's just that one tree. A monkey wouldn't think, 'Hey, wait, maybe we'd better plant some of these seeds.' A monkey would just eat the fruit as it gets ripe, year-around: him and his mate and their child. They chew and swallow the seeds and shit on the ground around the tree. And the next year there'd be another child. And the year after that another child. The children would mate and have other children. And the family would get bigger and bigger. And the fruit wouldn't quite fill them up, so they'd fight over it and some of them might be killed or hurt. And eventually there's so much poop around the tree that it burns the roots and the tree dies. That was the only tree, so the monkeys die as well. Monkeys don't know how to stop having babies. Monkeys don't know how to plant trees. Monkeys just know how to be monkeys: greedy, heedless monkeys. They have *monkey-brain*.

"Humans evolved from creatures very much like monkeys, and they brag about their children. Even here, notice? Look out there at that Pa, strutting on the road, pointing out this little one, that little one, 'That one's mine,' 'Those two're mine,' 'All these're mine!' The children are skinny little things that are always hungry; sometimes they have runny eyes and sores, but the men don't care. It isn't the *children* they're proud of. It's the *willy-wagging* they're doing. Those men are *willy-waggers*. 'Oh, look how my willy waggles to make little ones, looky at me!' And when the tree dies, they'll starve to death on whatever island they're on. They have *monkey-brain*.

"People are still evolving, you know. At first there wasn't much difference between the smartest ones and the stupidest ones. But gradually, over the millennia, the difference between the most intelligent ones and the least intelligent ones has grown wider and wider. Why do you suppose?"

Needly's mouth puckered, and the skin between her eyes. "Because . . . because, Grandma, when smart women have a choice about it, they'd rather have smart men as fathers for their children, wouldn't they? It's kind of . . ."

"Selective. Right. Women would rather. Men . . . not so much. They're usually thinking about breasts more than they are of brains. But, very gradually, over the centuries, the distance between the smartest and the dumbest has grown. It's not a huge difference, but it's a critical difference. It means some people have developed a part of their brain that others haven't. They aren't the majority, mind you. The people with *monkey-brain* are in the majority . . ."

"Why? Why are they?"

"What did I tell you about monkeys? They don't know how to plant trees, and they don't know how to—"

"Stop having babies."

"Right. Not every one, or each one, but in the aggregate, they have more than can be provided for. More than our island planet Earth can provide for. But because there are always more *monkey-brains* than there are the other kind, no one could do anything about it. The ones with the *monkey-brain* fished the seas empty. They polluted the oceans. They strutted their children. And whenever someone pointed out what they were doing, the people with *monkey-brain* said, 'There's plenty of empty space.' Or, 'Science will think of some new kind of crop,' or 'We'll farm the oceans.' Remember, *monkey-brains* aren't very smart. They don't realize that all the empty space is ice or desert or rock. They don't realize that there'd be no water to irrigate that new crop because they'd already used up the millions of years' worth of deep water in the underground aquifers. They didn't see that they'd already polluted the oceans with filth, and chemicals and deadly nuclear trash."

"Didn't anybody tell them?"

"Of course! But you can't tell a *monkey-brain willy-wagger* anything. It'd be like a dog howling at the moon. The moon doesn't care. And the *monkey-brain willy-waggers* . . . I need a shorter word for that!"

"'Mobwow,'" cried Needly. "Call them Mobwows, Grandma. It's

monkey-brain willy-wagger with an *oh-oh* in the middle. It'll work for women, too. *Monkey-brain* womb-wallowers."

Grandma started to harrumph, then laughed so hard she had to wipe her eyes. "Well, If anyone tries to tell a . . . Mobwow anything, the Mobwow says, 'Oh, that's a lie the *other side* puts out.' The *other side*, mind you, is anyone who disagrees with them, that includes anyone who says population should be limited, anyone who says anything except 'Wag your willy and use this world up.'

"Do you know that some religions used to say *not* having too many children was a sin! *Willy-wagging* without having babies was a sin. The myth instead of the reality. Oh, shame."

"Weren't they scared of what was going to happen when they ran out of room and food and clean water . . . ?"

"No. They either didn't believe it or they figured it wasn't going to happen in their lifetime, so they didn't care. Finally, back before the Big Kill, when the earth was actually dying, some very intelligent beings got together to try and find a solution. And they found there were actually two distinguishable races of humans. Not different colors or different languages or anything like that, but two distinguishable types. One kind had evolved a brain part that the other kind of people did not have. If you're born with that part, you don't have *monkey-brain*. My family calls it the 'if-then' part.

"Up until mankind, creatures didn't need an *if-then* part. That's the part that says, '*If* we add one more human being to our tribe, *then* we'll have to find a new cave.' Or maybe, '*If* this grain is growing clear here where I spilled that little bit, *then* maybe if I put a lot more in the ground near the cave, it will grow there, too.' Animals didn't need the *if-then* part because nature creates its own balance. IF there are too many rabbits, THEN the coyote population will increase to reduce the number of rabbits. Things will come into balance.

"But that doesn't work for the Mobwows. If there had been just the one race, the Mobwows, they'd have been wiped out, or at least there'd be many fewer of them. But nature was never allowed to balance *monkey-brain* people. The other race of people, the smarter ones, always found a way to survive, and the *monkey-brain* people always rode piggyback on top of the sensible ones. One can't tell them apart, just looking."

"Couldn't anybody teach the *monkey-brains*?"

"No, child. Whenever someone tried to teach them the 'if-then,' they smothered it with myths. One of their favorite myths was 'This earth doesn't matter. We won't really die. We'll just leave this world and be taken away to another world in heaven where everything is perfect and we'll live there forever.'"

Needly was thoughtful for a long moment. "I suppose if you believe that, you can be totally selfish, can't you. It wouldn't matter what you did to other people or your world. You could just go ahead and ruin your world."

"You can ruin. You can kill. You can pollute. You chop your way through the world, taking, burning, and destroying, without feeling any responsibility at all. None for your descendants, none for the earth. You can father twenty children, and if they starve to death, don't worry, they'll all live forever somewhere else. There's always enough well-to-do ones whose children are healthy and well fed to hold up as golden examples of Mobwowism. And every single one of those stories that they tell was started by a *monkey-brain* person who believed in *willy-wagging* as a way of life. You see, some of those people have only men to teach their religion—a religion is a collection of myths, different ones for different people. So if they have only men as religious teachers, they never get any other viewpoint at all."

"Religion?"

"One of my family members told me once there are over a thousand different sets of myths on this planet of ours, a thousand different ones with a religion following each set and people following each religion. Remember your litany. Some people are evidence-driven, some people are myth-driven. Mobwows are always myth-driven."

"You mean like herd smell? And hive noise? Recognition rites."

"That's partly what I mean, yes."

"You must have had a interesting family, Grandma."

"I suppose so. When I was very young I had a mother and a father and a grandmother. I had at least one sister and I think two brothers, full or half. It sounds disorganized, but you know, there were always good, caring people around me. The children in the family were always clean, well clad, well fed. I don't know who bought the food, or who had built the house, but there was always plenty of food and firewood, and the roof didn't leak, and I had warm blankets on my bed. No fleas. No hunger. Never any abuse, though I remember some very severe talkings-to, with me the one talked at. I don't remember grieving when any one of them went away for a while, but I do remember being glad when they came back. I don't remember feeling deprived or orphaned. The people were most always interesting and spent quite a bit of time with me; many of them brought books into the house that I read. Including some *monkey-brain* ones, as a warning."

"Is *monkey-brain* catching?"

"The groups that *teach* Mobwow try to infect as many people as possible. Some people are immune. My uncle Gren—he may have been a real full uncle, brother to my maybe mother—had a friend Holger who paid us a long visit when I was growing up. Holger called himself a 'half-assed philosopher.' I think that just meant he didn't have a license to philosophize. In times long past you had to have a license to call yourself anything fancy—some kind of document or letters after your name, maybe. I just remember Holger was the one who first told me about *monkey-brains* and about some people being immune to *monkey-brain* disease because they have bah-oh. I asked him what 'bah-oh' meant, and he said the word means 'thread.' I didn't understand that, so he took hold of my sleeve and he said, 'This is made of threads. What is it?' And I said, 'It's cloth, fabric.' And he said, 'Having bah-oh means knowing your threadness.' He wouldn't explain it. He told me to figure it out, so I'll tell you to do the same thing. Now there's a puzzle for you."

"Do you suppose maybe we could be part of something like a breeding program?" whispered Needly, who was fully aware of the mystery surrounding her own birth.

"Oh, I've always wondered that, wondered about it for both of us, Needly. I'm almost positive I was. That's the only explanation. You're not part of a plan I know anything about, but I'm sure you're part of something interesting and important. There's more to the world than Hench Valley. Things happen in places we don't know about. There may be many people working on the Mobwow problem and the solution might include you and your half sisters and brothers. I hope . . . I thought at one time that my children might be part of something like that, too, though I may have been lied to about that. Or I was just lying to myself, making myself feel better about things."

"Hench Valley doesn't seem to be the right sort of place for anything like that to happen . . . you know. It's such an awful place to—"

"Oh, Needly, I've asked myself that question! If Hench Valley is really being used for some kind of project like that, the only reason I can think of is *because* it's such an awful place. It would not surprise me to learn that Hench Valley is widely known as an awful place and has been carefully dropped into the vocabulary and consciousness of people everywhere."

Needly giggled, something she did not do often and never within the hearing of a Pa. "I can hear mothers telling their children, 'Wipe your shoes! Were you reared in Hench Valley?'"

"Exactly! It would be impossible for anyone from Hench Valley to have the brains to be involved in anything intellectual or demanding."

Needly murmured, "So . . . it would be like a . . . source disguise. So nobody knows what tree we've really been grown on. What seeds we carry . . ."

Lillis felt tears come into her eyes. "My children could do nothing useful here, child, no one can be useful here, but being *from here* might be a useful part of their story. If that's what the mysterious *they* are doing—which may only be a vain hope on my part—if they were, though, *people coming from a place like this would never be suspected of being part of anything sensible.*"

"What do you think it is?"

"Oh, Needly, when I'm wildly dreaming, I hope they're propagating a virus that will kill all the *monkey-brain* cells in people's heads. Gren and Holger said it was a brain pattern, a thought pattern. Wouldn't it be wonderful if it were just a neat little cluster of cells that could be targeted and killed without hurting people otherwise? Of course, it might be easier to disrupt a pattern." She stared wistfully into the distance, slowly shaking her head. "I can't pretend that's true, though. That's what we need, a pattern disrupter!"

"Maybe someone will invent one."

"Oh, we'll hope they do. And we'll hope they keep it secret. Because people with *monkey-brain* don't want their brains changed; they're happy with their do-whatever-you-want-to-and-then-live-forever myths. You and I can pretend it can be cured, we can dream about it being cured, we can imagine a world that doesn't have it, but we shouldn't talk about it to other people, because most of the world is in love with the disease."

ONE DAY, SOME MONTHS AFTER her birthday journey to see the Listener, Needly saw the sunrise creature again, the mother one, on a cliff top closer to the valley than the one near the Listener. She ran at once to tell Grandma the creature had returned. Gralf was gone and Trudis was curled up in bed with most of a gallon of recently brewed beer. Grandma decided the child's sighting the creature might be a hint as to what was intended. Perhaps they should, lacking any other directive, go to the bottom of the cliff where the Griffin roosted. The place was some distance away and had no village near it, but she took Needly with her, for the child was not safe left behind. She told herself she was looking for a certain root that she'd been unable to find any closer than a little canyon east and two steep ridges over. It would do as a reason for their journey, if she were asked.

She so convinced herself of that reason that two days later, when they actually came upon the plant she had supposedly sought, right there in front of them in the middle of the path they were on, she stopped utterly still in surprise—not at the seed head, ripe at the top of the stem, or the rosette of hand-shaped, furry leaves, like a cluster of tiny knitted mittens, that told her the root was there below, but at the other plant growing next to it. It was one she had been told of in whispered words, had seen its effects demonstrated, had copied a hand-drawn picture of, and had herself prepared from dried samples, but she had never seen it growing. She was also astonished at the things that lay atop the two growths, like shards broken from the sun. On the fuzzy mittens lay a Griffin tear, a multifaceted crystal tear as big as a pigeon egg, with sunrise colors all through it. On the other lay a bronze neck feather as long as her little finger, glowing as though from the forge.

"Is this a plant?" whispered Needly, staring at the second growth as she picked up the feather. "It looks like a rock, like a bunch of rocks."

As indeed it did: a paving cluster of small, smooth stones, each seeming pebble a straight-sided irregular polygon from being pushed tightly against its fellows. They could have been stones except that they had roots binding them to the soil. This plant, too, had a ripe seed head nodding above it. The feather lying upon it smelled of spice and sweetness and glory, but also of pain and loss. Needly held the crystal tear and the bronze feather while Grandma carefully planted both sets of ripe seeds along the path where the parent plants had grown, while she dug parts of the two roots with the little folding spade she had carried—the stone plant roots went very deep—wrapping each plant carefully, separately, so they would touch nothing else. There was enough coincidence and contrivance about the whole episode that she supposed she had been given the sign she'd been waiting for, and therefore, she would probably be able to determine what it all meant: the Griffins, the Listener, the two plants, the tear, the feather, all of them meant something, and maybe, oh, maybe she was part it. Even though she had Needly, the loneliness ate at her too much of the time.

Once they were home, Needly helped her find a nicer bit of wrapping to put around the crystal tear and the feather and tucked them away with the others, the ones they had found on her birthday morning. It was a good hiding place, where Trudis, Gralf, Slap, or Grudge could not find them. It had been during their search for a very good hiding place that Grandma and Needly had discovered Gralf's hoard. They had looked at it, counted it, and been amazed by it. It must have been accumulated over several generations. They left it as they had found it. Grandma had even dropped spiders on top of it to renew the webs they had disturbed. She had selected black widow spiders for the purpose, as the hoard was in the kind of place that particular spider preferred.

Grandma searched out two of the little bottles men sometimes brought her from their diggings in the buried city. She paid a dozen cookies per bottle. Keeping cookie ingredients took some doing, but she managed. If the bottle was of colored glass, she added another half-dozen cookies. Colored bottles were easier to tell apart.

So now she took two of the buried-city bottles, one blue, one green, and she boiled them for a long time. She waited until Gralf and Trudis were asleep that night before preparing the roots she'd found. She bottled the two syrups that resulted, being very careful not to let the stone medicine touch her skin and washing every trace of it from the utensils she had used, pouring the wash water in a certain place where nothing was growing. Needly watched the process, Grandma making sure she wasn't too sleepy to remember. These particular concoctions stayed potent for years, some said for centuries, so they would be ready if something of their kind were needed, which undoubtedly would happen. Why else, Grandma murmured, had she been led to them?

Later, she told Needly, "If you vanish, child, be sure to take my medicine bag with you. The new syrups are in there. Remember, the furry, hand-shaped leaves, that ones in the green bottle. That's the antidote for the stuff in the blue bottle, the stone medicine."

"What's the stone medicine for, again?"

"If . . . if it should happen someone is hurt bad, so bad you can do nothing to help, you can put a drop or two of that upon his tongue, or over his heart, and he will become as stone. And that stone will keep him as he is, alive, maybe forever, until someone comes who can fix him so you can give him the antidote and he can go on living. The little dark green bottle has the antidote. Not a lot because I found only that one plant and you saw I took only part of it."

"Not to be a *monkey-brain* and eat it all. You planted the seed."

"Exactly. So, you memorize the plant, and if you see it, you dig only some of it! And if it's in seed, you plant them and you remember where. The drawing of the plant is in the notebook, along with the way you make the antidote. They're unique, those two plants. I don't know of anything that looks anything like them. Keep your eyes open for them. They're rare, but the root dries well, so you can keep the dried roots and make the antidote later. If you vanish, be sure to take them with you."

"I'll remember," said Needly. "But I'm not planning on vanishing, Grandma!"

Grandma turned on her, taking her by the shoulder, shaking her firmly. *"Now you listen to me, Needly. Listen hard, remember well. If the time comes that life gives no choice you'd choose to put your hand on, not a one, don't you lie to yourself and say maybe it won't be so bad, or maybe you can bear it or survive it or anything of that sort . . ."*

Needly was both startled and puzzled. "Like what, Grandma?"

The old woman lowered her voice. *"Like Gralf telling you he's sold you to Old Man Digger, or, more likely, you overhear him tell someone else, Trudis, maybe. No girl has survived to reach womanhood once she was sold to Old Digger. And don't believe for a moment that Gralf would be ashamed to do that to a daughter, because Pas do it all the time in Hench Valley, and Gralf has no shame, none!"*

Needly was too smart to cry out or say anything stupid like "You don't mean?" or "That's just a story," because when Grandma said things in that particular tone of voice, she was telling the absolute truth. "Why would Digger kill them so fast, Grandma? Doesn't he want children?"

Grandma bit her lip, shook her head, finally nodded to herself. "No real reason not to tell you, child, 'cept it's so ugly. Long years ago Digger had a woman, and she bore him a child. She was a big woman, very big, but it was a huge boy baby, biggest newborn I ever saw. The baby grew fast. Boys here in the valley do grow up dreadfully fast—more like animals with short life-spans than humans with decades . . ." She stopped, suddenly thoughtful: *Hench Valley men have shorter life-spans than most men! Well. That's interesting. Now someone should look into that.* She shook her head and went on, "In any case, when the boy was twelve, he was nearly as big as Digger. When he was fifteen, he was bigger than Digger. The boy got mad at Digger, took a hayfork to him, nearly killed him before Digger found an ax near to hand.

"Digger swore he'd never let another child be born to a woman of his. So, whenever he buys a woman, Digger buys a little girl just maybe big enough to get some pleasure out of without any chance they'll get pregnant. Once they're old enough to be pregnant, they vanish. I suppose if one dug up the floor of Digger's barn, one would find what was left of them."

Needly swallowed and breathed hard a time or two. "Well then, you said Gralf knows that. Why would Gralf sell me to Digger?"

Grandma gave her a look. "Needly, you know very well why, but you want me to confirm it. Your senses tell you Gralf has no moral values whatsoever, your brain tells you he'll do anything for gold, but you can't quite believe your own intelligence. What have we just been talking about with the *Mobwows*? Making up nice stories instead of accepting uncomfortable reality? Living a myth-driven life?"

Needly flushed. It was true.

"Have you ever known Gralf to look past gold? Has he ever held on to anything that can be sold? You saw his hoard!"

Needly shook her head.

Grandma's voice softened. "His father was the same. Gralf had two brothers, they were the same, they had sons, and they are the same. They will give nothing for love or care! Nothing for comfort or beauty! But they will sell anything for gold. For hoarding! Not to spend, mind you. To have. Just to have. Like a dragon's hoard! All of them the same."

"They don't spend any?"

"You saw the hoard when we found it, Needly. It had cobwebs and dust on it. Nobody spends it. They trade things they find that a trader will buy. The main trader up there at the pass, he's called the Gold King. Always pays in gold. The men, they spend silver, but they hoard gold."

"Why do they have hoards?"

"Well, next time I meet a dragon, I'll be sure to ask her. Or him."

Needly grinned. Then she sighed. "I don't understand my Pa."

"Needly, you know full well he is not your Pa."

Since the child seemed accepting of this idea, Grandma went on: "All the menfolk went away for a hunt a number of years ago, and there was a stranger man around. I think he's your real . . . I don't want to say Pa. Any man who can willy-wag is called Pa around here, and every jackrabbit can breed, so the title's meaningless. One of my uncles told me of a place north of Wellsport where they raise fine horses. When time comes to breed the mares, they're bred to the finest stallion they have, because his get will be better than others. Better for the mare, too, so she can take pride!"

"Mares take pride? Grandma!"

"My uncle swore to me they do! And the man who came to live here the summer you were conceived, he was like that fine stallion. That man was a chosen sire, one you'd be proud to claim descent from. He was like the fathers of my children, maybe even more so. If you hadn't been born, I'd have stayed where I went when Gralf first came into this house, but you were different. So I came back to keep you safe."

"Why didn't you just take me with you, Grandma? Hmm?"

Grandma frowned at her boots, shook her head. "I don't know, and that troubles me. I grew up believing my life had a purpose. I was told so, several times, and though I don't know where the idea came from, I believed it. The things that have happened to me, the children I've borne, were purposeful. I thought the same about you, that you were here for a purpose. My raising you here might have been that purpose. Something just told me not to do anything drastic, to wait for it. Wait for something to happen. I don't know what. Just something."

Needly stared, all kinds of ideas clashing together, making strange, chaotic designs that spun into an instant's beauty and then lost themselves. "But what if nothing happens, Grandma?"

"Needly, there's always that chance. I've been disappointed before, one way and another. I know you have, too. But, don't forget, we've always kept your pack ready to go, everything in it you'd need. The best thing for you to do, child, is get up the mountain to Findem Pass, and down the far side. That's the limit of the country called Ghastain. Then you're in the land of the Artemisians. There's a woman there known as Wide Mountain Mother. She's the head person. She would know the way to the House of the Oracles, and one of her people could guide you there. The house where my family lives is quite near there. That house is mine now. There's a little map in my notebook, the one with the plants in it, and the House of the Oracles is one of the landmarks. Tell the people in Artemisia that Lillis Show-the-way wants you to go there. Don't giggle. That was my father's name. The Artemisians know that's my name and they'll show you where it is. Be sure to take the Griffin's tear and her feather with you along with the pouch with all the little bottles of things I make. I only tie them under my skirt when I'm going somewhere. If you take them, you tie them under your skirt. It's not comfortable and it'll keep them away from anybody but a child rapist. You have a weapon for that sort?"

"Yes, Grandma."

"Be sure you do. I taught you to read. I taught you the Great Litany. Do you remember the Statement of Study?"

Needly folded her hands. *"The existence of the universe is proof of the Creator. That which exists can be seen, measured, and studied, and it does not lie. As we know healers by their healing, craftsmen by their craft, singers by their song, so we know the Creator through its creation. The dedicated study of creation reveals the nature of the Creator."*

"And the Creator?"

"The Creator sends no prophets, requires no worship, heeds no prayers. Creation itself includes the evidence of everything that was, the presence of all that

is, and the possibility of everything that will be. Everything true is in it or will evolve in it. Creation simply is and cannot lie."

"And suppose a man brings forth a stone with words written upon it, or a scroll, or plate of engraved metal with writing upon it, claiming it bears the words of the Creator."

"At the moment of creation the Creator spoke, finally, absolutely, and infallibly through the totality of what was created. Having spoken the universe, which contains all that is, what need is there to speak again? Those seeking myths make them up out of their heads. Those seeking truth study Creation. The study may be arduous, but the universe remains there for any student and for all students. It does not reveal itself to some and withhold itself from others, it does not contradict itself in various languages, its changes and processes are part of itself, its laws are immutable. Those seeking comfortable myths and stories that children may learn without difficulty may go to the mythmakers and storytellers who are many upon the face of the earth and who dwell in houses of dreams."

"Suppose a man calls himself a prophet and claims he was inspired by the Creator?"

Needly sighed. "You paraphrased that one for me. 'Better wholly understand one grain of sand than follow any prophet.' The litany says, *'There is evidence for every truth, if there is no evidence, there is no truth, for the CREATOR is truth; CREATION does not lie or play tricks.'*"

"Exactly. Don't forget it. I remember one fool woman who told me the Creator put bones in ancient rocks just to fool us and make us think the universe was older than her book said it was. As though the Creator would LIE! Fool woman. She would rather worship a liar than pay attention to reality." She sighed, reached out, and stroked the child's hair. "Needly, you know, I first began to be . . . doubtful about the Oracles when I realized they don't live by the litany. The people I grew up among, the ones I called my family, they lived by the litany, certainly insofar as studying creation goes. They certainly never said a certain thing was true unless it came from a deep understanding of that thing and everything known about it. They didn't just quote some book or some scripture, they knew the proofs. They always told me that nothing exists without showing proofs of its existence, though sometimes one has to dig deep to find the proofs, deep into the edges of the universe or deep into the tiny of the atoms.

"Now, remember what I've told you. The book and the labels on the bottles are clear. Lucky for us, Hench Valley men think reading is a female thing. They have no patience with it. And it's a sorrowful thing to say, but I'm almost sure we're the only two females in the valley who do."

Needly hugged her and promised to remember. And there Needly's future rested. Until a later time.

CHAPTER 2

The Dreaming of
Abasio the Traveler

AT A SLIGHTLY LATER TIME, ONE RANGE WEST of the place called Hench Valley, Abasio Cermit, Abasio the Dyer, Abasio: First Father of the Sea-Children of the Future, Abasio who is much married to the Princess Xulai and who is the supposed owner of the horse Blue—a horse who knows very well he is not owned by anyone save himself—that particular Abasio is nodding on the wagon seat and is, yet again, in the midst of a recurrent dream that has been visiting both his night's sleep and his daytime dozes on the wagon seat.

Xulai murmured, "He's asleep again, Blue. And he's been making those troubled noises. I don't know what to do . . ."

"What you do," said Blue, "is make him tell you what he's dreaming about."

"He won't want to."

"He doesn't want to do a lot of things you make him do. Like come in out of the rain or eat green vegetables. Now me, I like green—"

Rags, Blue's partner in harness, interrupted. "She's not worried about what you like. Xulai, really, you do need to make him tell you.

Tell him it's in your . . . wedding vows. I've heard about them. You did have vows, didn't you?"

"I don't think he was paying attention."

"So much the better," the mare said, with the equine equivalent of a giggle.

"What?" demanded Abasio, suddenly wakening. "What?"

Xulai breathed in deeply, gripped the wagon seat with both hands, and squeezed it, noting with some dismay that all four ears were cocked to listen. "Where does the dream take place?" she asked, in as casual a voice as she could manage."

"Not on Earth," he murmured, still drowsy. "I know that much. The trees are all wrong."

"The trees?"

"The leaves are more blue and purple than green. And they group themselves differently. And I'll swear they talk to one another. When the wind blows, I get this feeling it's one grove speaking to another grove. And then there's the tower. I've never seen one like it here."

"That's interesting, Abasio. Can you describe it?" Before her, Rags's ears twitched in what Xulai believed to be the equivalent of a pat on the shoulder.

"It's white. Tall. It has arches all the way around the bottom except for one space where there's a spiral staircase going up to the balcony. Way up there. The balcony goes all the way around the walls of the tower, lighted by another set of arches, and, of course, the bell hangs there . . ." His voice trailed away.

The ears twitched. They were very expressive ears, saying, "Ask a question, stupid."

Xulai said, "The bell. Is it a . . . large bell?"

"Oh, yes. Large, silver. Beautiful tone. They strike it morning and evening with a long kind of rod with a leather-covered tip. Makes a soft sound, but it goes out of the tower like a flight of birds. I imagine they can hear it . . . all the way to the edges—"

"Edges?"

"Of Lom. The Edges of Lom. That's what the place is called. And I know that because the women in the tower are talking about it. Two of them. They're always the same women. The older one is named Silk-hands, the other is named Jinian. Then there are two children. Jinian's children. The boy—possibly seven or eight years old—is Crash, and the little girl, perhaps a year or so younger than Crash, is Crumpet."

"Very odd names!"

"Nicknames. Obviously. When the women get irritated they call the children something else, something long, probably with hyphens in it. I can never remember those names when I wake up. The children beg for a story, and their mother tells them a story about Lom. About how their people came to Lom."

Xulai's mouth fell open; her expression, if Abasio had been watching, was one of surprise, even shock. Silence fell, Xulai stared at the ears, which flapped encouragingly. "So, uh, we presume Lom is the name of the place where they are. Ah . . . where are you while this storytelling is going on?"

"I'm hanging in the air over the pool."

She made an abortive gesture. "You didn't mention a pool."

"Well, it's set into the floor of the tower, slightly raised, with a kind of seat all the way around it. Only the seat is too narrow and too low for humans to sit on. The two women are sitting on cushions next to the statue. The statue is of a woman, an angry woman? Or maybe one who's just been awakened or something. She doesn't look tranquil. The whole tower is very tranquil, but not the statue. And there are creatures coming in and out of the tower, people and other creatures. Some of them are little ones, furry ones. And they come over to the pool and scoop something out of the the edge of the pool and take it away . . ."

"Something?"

"They shine, like . . . jewels, only very thin. Oftentimes they put them in their mouths, so I think it may be some kind of . . . food or candy? I don't know. And I don't know what they're for. The dream doesn't say. But I think the women know, because they don't seem surprised at all."

"So you're hanging in the air, over the pool? You don't . . . worry about falling or anything?"

He shook his head. "I don't feel suspended and I'm not afraid of falling. I seem to be invisible to the women and to most of the creatures coming and going out . . . all of them very busy and purposeful."

"Invisible to most?"

"Once in a while one of them says hello to me. There's a Dervish who says hello. I think she is Jinian's mother; at least Jinian says, 'Good morning, Mother,' when she comes in. And there's what Crash calls 'a glactic ossifer.' His mother corrects him to say 'galactic officer.' A very strange-looking thing. It's standing in one of the arches, looking in. It nods at me, looks directly at me, smiles, seems to know me."

"Strange-looking how?"

"Nonearthly. Six legs, I think. Six arms. It really looks more like a shrub or short tree than it does a . . . person. Maybe it's a vegetable person." He laughed, a harsh, barking sound. "Do you think I'm going crazy?"

"Dreams can be crazy without the person who dreams them being at all crazy," she said firmly. "What's the story about, the one the women tell the children."

"It's evidently the history of 'How the Earthers Came to Lom.' About landing there, two ships of them, one in a valley, one on a mountain, how the people started settlements and also started behaving like . . . humans! That is, destroying the new world the way they did the old one, and how some being . . . a local god, maybe . . . gave them special talents that they used to play war games on one another. That kept the population fairly small. There was a . . . rebellion on the part of the local beings, the younger ones, against the humans, and during the conflict the tower was destroyed . . .

"You see, the important thing was that it was not just a tower, not just a building or landmark, it was an essential part of the . . . wholeness of the place. There were two towers, the *Daylight* Tower and the *Shadow* . . . or maybe *Twilight* Tower. There was a verse: '*Shadow Bell rings in the dark, Daylight Bell the dawn. In the towers hang the bells, now the tower's gone.*'" His voice drifted off. He sighed. "Mostly, it was very sad. The children seemed to accept it as history, but the women . . . the tragedy had actually happened during their lifetimes. When the talents were lost, it happened to them." He sighed again. "Anyhow, that's the dream . . . oh, except for the subject they were discussing." He laughed. "They were discussing an upcoming trip they're going to make with the 'glactic ossifer.' His name is Balytaniwassinot. His nickname is 'Fixit'—he's in that dream, and he's in some of the others, too. And they're coming here, to Earth."

He turned to give her a skeptical look. "Now, are you *satisfied*? I notice Rags and Blue have been very quiet. *Are all three of you satisfied?*"

"Yes," said Xulai, in a very relieved tone of voice. "It's all perfectly un-derstandable, dear heart! During the Big Kill, in an effort to allow the human race to continue, two ships carrying human settlers were sent to Lom. Lom isn't a planet, by the way, it's a geographic part of a planet, either a large island or a peninsula. The planet is called something else. You're merely making a dream out of historic fact, that's all."

He shook his head. "Oh, really? Now how did this historic fact, which you have just told me for the very first time, this fact that I never knew anything about, how did it get put into my head as a dream?"

"You probably heard about it as a child. It doesn't matter, Abasio. You're not going crazy."

"That's so very nice to know. The one called Silkhands says, in the dream, that the reason humans lost their talents is because they have no bow. Do you know what that means?"

"Not a clue," she said, smiling. "Do you think it's important?"

For some reason he did think it was important. Terribly, terribly important. Not important enough, however, to argue about with Xulai. Arguing with Xulai was . . . futile. One could tie her up and carry her over one shoulder (and on at least two occasions, under extreme provo-cation, one had done so), but one could not win an argument. He took a deep breath and tried to concentrate on the road, that is, the ruts ahead of him. They should be approaching a village called . . . Gravy-suck. Undoubtedly there was a good reason it was called Gravysuck. He awaited with great anticipation finding out what that good reason might be!

Not really. He was very, very weary of villages. Evidently he need not worry about it yet, for there was no sight or sound of it, only the ruts going on and on and on.

Xulai went back into the wagon to lie on the bed while she fed the babies. Blue and Rags kept discreetly silent. The road went on. He fell asleep puzzling yet again about the tower. What had it been about the tower . . . ? As if in answer to the question, the dream began again . . .

He was there, over the pool. The women and the children were there. Silkhands and Jinian. The children were hers, but Silkhands was telling the story . . .

"The people of Lom were called Eesties. The young ones rebelled against their ruler . . . their king? They wanted to destroy all the humans on Lom, and

finally a mob of them wrecked the Daylight Tower and broke the Daylight Bell that hangs above us. Before that there had been two towers, and there was a verse about it . . ."

"I know, I know," cried the little girl, Crumpet. " 'Shadow Bell rings in the dark, Daylight Bell the dawn. In the towers hang the bells, but now the tower's gone.' "

"That's right, Crumpet. Without the Daylight Bell to control them, the shadows were free to spread, covering everything and eating living creatures. The Eesties who joined the rebellion were glad, for they thought this would destroy all the humans in Lom . . ." Her voice faded and she stared sadly out through the arches.

"But, but," cried Crash. That was the boy, slightly older than the girl.

Their mother bit her lip, taking a deep breath. "But their leader didn't tell them the shadows would destroy them as well. Lom had depended on the towers and the bells to keep everything in balance. Without the towers and the bells, all the moving living things in the Lom part of this world began to kill themselves."

Silkhands said quickly, "So some animals and people had to go into Lom's memory and find the part where the tower was destroyed, and then dig out that part so it wasn't a memory anymore. And then the humans had to rebuild the tower and recast the bell. It took them a very long time because they no longer had the talents Lom had given them . . ."

"Like flying," said Crash sadly. "And going from one place to another one, zip, just like that. And shapeshifting, like Grandma. Like she was before she got froze, I mean."

Crumpet interrupted. "She didn't get froze. She got petrified!"

Silkhands went on: "Yes, all those talents were gone, so the tower had to be rebuilt just just with muscle and determination. But it was done, and now . . . Lom feels better . . ."

Jinian said, "And now, just as we told you both, Lom has been asked for help from the world our people came from, so your mother and I have temporarily been given back our talents and asked to go very far away to save some creatures there."

"Why can't those people on urth save their own selfs?" demanded Crash.

"Earth people have already found a way to save most of them, but there's some kind of problem . . . It's all mixed up with which ones have bow and which ones should be saved . . ."

"Do we got bow?" demanded Crash.

"Some of us do, Crash. But I guess a lot of Earth people don't, and creation has decided they've had their very last chance!"

"*Creation has decided? The whole universe, Jinian?*" *asked Silkhands, raising a skeptical eyebrow.*

"*Well, the galaxy, anyhow. There's a galactic officer involved. That must be fairly high up in importance.*"

"*What's a glactic ossifer?*" *Crash demanded.*

"*It's a . . .*" *She stopped, then leaned forward, whispering,* "*If you'll look to your left, Crash. No, your left, across the pool! See the person standing in the arch over there, looking this way . . . ?*"

Abasio looked where Crash was looking. There was indeed a . . . something standing there. It was not unfamiliar. It had shown up in several dreams. He might not have called it a person, for it had six . . . he counted again, twice. Yes. It had six legs, all the same length, and six arms of differing lengths. It had something that might be a face: it definitely included eyes—eyes that were looking straight at him, at Abasio. Now it lifted a hand . . . or whatever it was at the end of its arms and saluted him. HIM. Abasio. Looking straight at him. Smiling. Very definitely an . . . actually friendly smile. Abasio felt his face replying, smiling back.

Jinian went on, lowering her voice. "*That's the galactic officer. Its name is Balytaniwassinot, only it says we can call it Fixit. Fixit is a person responsible for . . . well, fixing things, like . . . oh, just . . . fixing things. I think that's what it said.*"

"*Oh,*" *said Crash offhandedly.* "*It's really funny-lookin'—*"

He was interrupted by a Dervish who came spinning in through one of the arches. Crash and Crumpet immediately stood up, very respectfully. The Dervish approached the pool, slowed down, stopped, its layers of fringes settling around it. "*Good morning, Silkhands. Good morning, daughter. Good morning, children.*"

"*Good morning, Grandma,*" *they said in unison, with excruciating politeness. Evidently, Abasio thought, Dervishes were held in considerable awe. She left them and came to the pool, scooping up one of the thin, glinting crystals that lay in the shallow edge of it.*

"*Morning, Abasio,*" *she said cheerfully, putting the crystal into her mouth and beginning to twirl once more. She spun her way out through the arch and away down the road, making a sonorous humming sound.*

The children did not sit down until she had gone, then Crash said, "*Silkhands, c'n I ast a question?*"

Silkhands reluctantly withdrew her eyes from the six-armed person. "*Crash, you always do ask questions.*"

"Who's that man hanging out there in the middle of the pool. The man Grandma called 'Basio. He keeps looking at me."

"What man?" asked the women in unison. "What man?"

"Me, for heaven's sake," shouts Abasio in his dream. "The Dervish can see me, the children can see me, even that weird . . . galactic officer [!] can see me! Why the hell can't you?"

And with that shout, Abasio's eyes opened.

He looked up, past the horses' heads, to see a shop with a sign declaring:

BERTRAM THE TAILOR

Quality Clothing for All: Fine Clothing for Those Who Have Time!

Abasio got down from the wagon. Yawning and stretching, he loosed the horses from the wagon. "We'll leave the harness on until we decide where the wagon can be parked. If the tailor is amenable, we may take a day or two for rest." Abasio had seen what Xulai had not. There was a smokestack in back of the shop that, coupled with the stream that flowed from that direction into this pool, indicated the possibility of a bathhouse.

Xulai murmured to him, "The fact that we've encountered a tailor is blessed fate. Or maybe Precious Wind has been casting spells for me. The children have outgrown every garment we had for them, including the ones we bought large so they could grow into them!"

"Would Precious Wind suggest tailored clothes? For babies?"

"One gives thanks for what one is given, even the unexpected," she answered piously. "Besides, we've been given funds for the unexpected. Father said he was sure it was the one thing we would encounter."

Leaving Blue and Rags to test the quality of the grass, they each took a child and went up the steps to the porch of the shop. As they opened the door, a bell rang and a stout, cheerful-looking man came bustling from the back to stand behind the counter.

"Yes, ma'am, sir. What may I do for you?" he burbled. "Summer coming, you'll need something lighter, perhaps. I note you're dressed for cold."

"We don't need clothing," said Xulai. "But the children do." She unwrapped Gailai, rubbed noses with the giggling baby, and placed her on the tailor's counter.

"Madam," he said. "It is really not my custom to dress fish!"

Across from him, Xulai drew herself to her full height and coupled a blazing stare with a suddenly icy tongue: "If you do not better school your tongue, sir, you may find yourself without any custom at all."

CHAPTER 3

Traveling Garments

THE STOCKY YOUNG MAN'S SAD, DARK EYES WIDENED in the sudden panic, as though he had unexpectedly stepped off a cliff. He gulped, "I did not mean to offend." The walnut gleam of his skin hid his flush of embarrassment, but his shaking hands betrayed him as he ran them over his black, tightly curled hair.

"What *did* you mean to do? Didn't I hear you refer to my children as *fish*?" She turned from him, ebony hair swirling, dusty, no-colored traveling robe lashing around slender ankles—ankles, deplorably, that were as dusty as the hair, as the soiled robe. The wearisome roads, wet or dry, were dirty. Even her hands and face were covered with a gray film. She looked at her wrists in fury. She could plant grass in the creases of her skin. A little sweat and they'd grow! Or tears. Tears would do it. She turned her face away. The rain of tears was imminent.

"Children? Madam . . ." The tailor was beginning to sweat. He gripped the lapels of his impeccably fitted coat, one he had put on only when he had heard their wagon arrive at his shop. The woman was furiously angry. He was not so frozen in embarrassment that he failed to appreciate her beauty, her perfect features, her hair . . . Well—it was luxuriant and—if washed—it would no doubt gleam with blue lights. Beneath the travel dirt her skin was an unblemished olive. Her manner, on the other hand, was . . . well, it might be aristocratic, possibly regal. But could she be the mother of those . . . ? It simply wasn't believable!

The woman's companion stepped between tailor and fury. With obvious effort to overcome great weariness, he forced his lips into a smile. "Let us begin again."

The tailor turned toward him helplessly, starting to speak and then stopping himself. He had not really noted the lined face, the drooping shoulders, the exhaustion in those eyes. If this man were left alone for five minutes, he would be deeply asleep, and he moved as men do who have already been tried past endurance.

And yet . . . yet, he managed a conciliatory smile as he laid his hand on the lady's shoulder, stroking it, calming it. He was as travel-stained as she, but he carried both the road dust and the weariness like an accustomed garment, fully aware of its condition, knowing that it needed mending, laundering, or even better, replacing with something more comfortable, yet not resentful of what it said of . . . negligence? No. Haste? The tailor thought not. Neither time nor effort had been spared, everything else had simply been . . . well, secondary . . . to whatever it was the man needed to do. Just now he needed to move his tired eyes first to the tailor's, to lock there, then to tug the tailor's eyes toward the lady as though to say, "Look, really look here, my friend. See."

The traveler reached out and drew her closer with one hand while reaching the other to smooth the frown lines between her perfect brows. He stood back at arm's length and bowed toward her as he spoke over his shoulder: "May I introduce my wife, sir!? This is Xulai, Princess Royal of Tingawa and daughter of the Duke of Wold. Wold, you probably know of? Tingawa, more remote, less known, is far, far west across the sundering sea. The stains of harsh travel do not betray her royal blood, but when she is extremely weary, her *temper* becomes fully—or shall we say perhaps—*exceptionally* imperious." He swept an elegantly executed bow in her direction, his cloak making a practiced and beautiful swirl as it moved and fell.

The tailor was not so overawed that he failed to notice her fleeting smile, the elegance of that swirled cloak. Even under all that dust it was magnificent. Any tailor worthy of the title knew of Tingawa, and the only fabrics that could be spoken of in the same breath as those in that cloak could be from no other place. Tingawa. The west. Over the sea! The lining had to be Tingawan silk! And the drape of that wool! Heavens! What was it called? It was from some particular animal: kazi something. He had only read of it!

The traveler raked his dusty hair behind his ears, digging his thumbs into his neck with a grimace. The gray at his temples was not entirely due to dust. Holding the tailor's eyes, he spoke softly, with humor. "I, sir, on the other hand, am simply Abasio. Sometimes called Abasio the Dyer, sometimes Abasio the Traveler, also sometimes Abasio the Idiot, for marrying, or should one say 'espousing,' so far above myself."

He reached out to take one of the babies from Xulai's arms, holding the child where the tailor could get a good look. "The future of our world, sir, depends upon these children of whom you spoke so hastily." He held up a finger, silencing the tailor's attempt at apology. "Spoke, may I say, thoughtlessly but only in *words*, sir! Mere *words* are of no matter, for Gailai and Bailai are too young to take offense and *my wife and I are sufficiently forgiving to ignore them.*"

The princess glared, taking note of the emphatic pledge without agreeing to it in the slightest. As the tailor attempted another confused apology, Abasio cut it off with a raised hand.

"Let it be forgotten! Our purpose is simple. We have come to find Bertram, the much-lauded Bertram, 'Bertram, who makes clothing for people from as far away as the eastern prairies to the western sea!' Bertram, who for some unknown and no doubt imperative reason does his exemplary work on the hill, above the village of Gravysuck, in White Mountain Valley!"

Abasio turned, thrusting his arm, swordlike, toward the southwest, finger inexorably extended: "There, there is White Mountain, lunging upward, snow-clad as ever!" The arm dropped, the extended finger pointed down, to the south. "And there below us in the subsidiary valley lies the village of . . . yes, indeed, it IS Gravysuck." The pointed finger curved, joined its fellows to become a cupped hand, held pleadingly toward him, as though begging. The voice dropped almost to a whisper. "So, here, here, indeed, on this hill indubitably and without contradiction, we find that *you must be the paragon: Bertram!*"

The tailor, stunned by the drama, struggled unsuccessfully to find a suitable reply. "Well, yes, but . . ."

"Your mistake is understandable. And your patronymic, sir?"

"Pa . . . patro . . . ?"

"Your father's name?"

"Also Bertram."

"Then you are Bertram Bertramson, right?"

"No, sir. Bertram Stitchhand, sir. Of the Volumetarian Stitchhands." The tailor would have paled, had he not been incapable of doing so from birth. That being impossible, he clapped his hand over his mouth in dismay. What had he said! Why had he said it!

This time Abasio smiled from honest amusement, though he had no energy left to inquire into either the Stitchhands or the Volumetarians. His body was dirty, every crease filled with the detritus that joins with sweat to form an intimate muck, an invasive slurry that itches and complains, drawing all attention only to itself. He was tired with the weariness that doubts the existence of sleep. Xulai, too, was tired, dirty, hungry, and petulant as a . . . dyspeptic pig! They desperately needed a few days' rest *if this man would only cooperate by giving them an excuse to take such a rest before Xulai committed all three of them and the babies to enmity everlasting!*

Swallowing the exhausted sigh that was threatening to swallow him, Abasio said clearly, uttering each word separately, peering into Bertram's eyes to make sure the man understood him: "As I had begun to say, many of the children born during the next century or two will resemble the children you see here. They will live in the seas. The temperature of the seas is fairly constant, changing only gradually. However, our young ones are not yet full-time sea-children, and they are traveling across areas where there has as yet been no significant inundation."

"I . . . ah . . ." gargled Bertram, his eyes fixed on the children in question. The two infants, not yet quite yearlings, he judged, were loosely wrapped in knitted shawls and were reclining in their mother's arms, regarding him with interest. Down to their waists they were appropriately human-looking; their skin, where it showed in the gaps, was more or less the color of an aged ivory button. Not as light as their father's, though he was somewhat darkened by the sun. Not the smooth olive of their mother's. Something in between. Their hair was dark. One little head reflected reddish lights, the other, bluish ones; their little faces were . . . very babyish. Pretty, even. However, their tails. Legs. Their nether appendages, whatever such limbs were called, were unquestionably fishy. Not scaled, no, the olive skin of their faces and upper bodies darkening smoothly below the waist, where tail joined other flesh, becoming dark and slippery, and ending in feet that were . . . webbed. Quite webbed. Extravagantly webbed! The insignificant heels were companioned by very long, almost froggy toes! The babies' lower halves were dark in color. Blue. Green. Or maybe black. As were their observant little eyes . . .

Abasio's voice hardened: "So! Since we must travel where as yet there are no seas, the children are sometimes cold. They require jackets! Coats! Something to keep them warm!"

The tailor mumbled something.

"Yes?" asked Abasio with a lethal smile.

"Why would aquatic creatures be here? You are so far from—"

Xulai interrupted, her voice like a well-honed knife. "They must be both. If you will allow me to explain?"

Her words were a question; her tone was not. The tailor's conscious mind finally received the information his subconscious had been trying to get through to him since the little bell above the door had jangled. *Forget your oath! Forget the books. Forget defending your life's primary purpose as a Volumetarian. Shut your mouth and listen. Shut up and smile and listen. Shut up and smile and listen* sympathetically, *as any decent tailor would!* He shut his mouth and nodded, pulling his mouth into what he hoped was an understanding smile though it felt like a gargoyle grin, a desperate disguise hiding his fervent desire to go back in time and lock the door before these people had arrived.

"We are in the age of the waters rising," Xulai said carefully, slowly, hoping to sound merely didactic rather than lethally threatening. "About two centuries from now, all our world will be under the waters . . ." She paused for emphasis, but did not begin again, for Bertram had stumbled back, not merely astonished as many were who heard this for the first time, but shocked as though mortally wounded! His dark face was turning gray! All at once!

He gasped, "You must be . . . surely you are joking, ma'am. I don't . . ." He put his hand to his head, suddenly dizzy, things becoming blurred . . .

Abasio stepped around the corner of the counter and helped the man to his chair, shaking his head at Xulai. A tailor dead of shock would do them no waistcoats! Xulai shuddered, comprehension striking her like a slosh of icy water. *Ordinarily, she would have realized that water meant more to this man than it did to other people. More than to the average villager. If animosity on the part of such villagers had not been so prevalent during their recent journey, she wouldn't have reacted with such . . . annoyance! She would have allowed for disbelief, yes: the initial response was almost always disbelief. But . . . but people had not been fearful. This kind of shock? The man had meant no real animosity, he simply couldn't believe what she had told him and it meant something dire to him! Something far worse than it meant to most people!*

Abasio was patting and murmuring, "Bertram. It will be some time yet before it happens. Breathe. That's it. Again. In and out. And again. Xulai tells you the truth. We did not mean to frighten you. You hadn't heard this before?"

Bertram swallowed, gulped, tried to speak, only gargled. He tried again. "Travelers have said . . . Coastal flooding, of course, yes . . . A few lowlands, perhaps. But . . . not the world. Surely not the world! *The books!*" His voice became shrill with hysteria: *"The books! By whatever Gods take into care, the books! What will I do with . . . ?"* He went on babbling, almost wordlessly, face still gray, even his lips so ashen that she might as well have opened his veins and drained him.

Abasio shared a baffled glance with Xulai. "It's not going to happen in your lifetime, my friend! Take another deep breath. Pretend for the moment that it's only a story you're hearing. A dream you're having. Let yourself relax into it." He patted Bertram's shoulder, whispering soothers, words meant to be used in couples: "now, now"; "there, there"; "tsk-tsk"; "come come" . . . Mentally he shuffled and redealt them. "Tsk! Come now! There, there, whatever you fear, it will not happen tomorrow! *Nor in your lifetime!* Now, relax . . ."

While the tailor's breathing gradually slowed, Xulai shrugged off her heavy robe. Ever since they'd left Woldsgard, months ago, their journey had led them upward, always higher, deeper into the forests and mountains. Often the so-called roads were only pairs of ruts virtually hidden in grasses—ruts filled with dust that became airborne beneath their wheels and settled upon them, enveloped them, encrusted them. In the shade of the forest at this altitude, the air was chill. Her inner clothing had not absorbed as much of the dust as the outer robe, and with it removed she could half convince herself she looked acceptably human. Though she shared the dislike of dirt customary to cats and Tingawans, it would have to wait. Unlike a cat, she could not lick herself clean. Sighing, she reached out to touch the poor fellow. Let him feel her hand. Let him know she was not a monster!

Softly, in her most unthreatening voice, she went on: "In order to survive in the changed world, our forms must change. There is plenty of time for this to happen. When the earth is finally inundated, all of us who cannot exist underwater will have lived out our lives, and so will our children, and our grandchildren, but during that time, many of our people will have been born to swim, to dive, to sing and dance and live happy lives—lives spent upon or under the waters. Abasio and I are . . . facilitators of that change. We travel from place to place, carrying with us the—"

"*Process,*" said Abasio, firmly. "We carry the process by which humanity is to be transformed." He had stepped back against the wall and now leaned on it, letting himself sag. He and Xulai were still struggling with vocabulary. Though they had been on this journey the better part of a year, their reception had been so varied that no single, effective pattern had emerged. Forty-something villages, so far. Forty isolated citadels to invade, forty armies of superstitious villagers to win over. How they explained their task successfully in one place might be badly misunderstood in another. The first generation of changers—as he and Xulai were—needed sea-eggs to make the transformation, and though they carried a sizable store of them well hidden in the wagon, they would not mention or distribute them until they reached the seacoast to the south. The first-generation change could be traumatic, as the two of them well remembered with a mixture of dismay and amusement. It could be done only in deep water, preferably seawater, and—to minimize trauma—among people who had already experienced the change. Abasio still remembered his transformation with embarrassment. He had behaved badly. Or, as Blue said, "*Like a pig keeper who got knocked into the wallow!*"

So, in these upland villages, he and Xulai didn't mention the first-generation change. The traditional prejudices of the mountain people ran too deep to risk it. They had learned to speak only in generalities, letting the people see the children, explaining that yes, they were their own children, and referring interested young couples or individuals to the Sea-Dwellers Center in Wellsport: Sea Duck 2, as it was called by its inhabitants, for they had, each and every one, been "sea-ducked" and were able to breathe underwater.

Abasio patted Bertram on his shoulder, relieved to see he looked less gray, less desperate. "Bertram, we're traveling about to explain the *process* by which parents can bear children who will survive the change. We tell people where they can go to find out more. We offer neither inducements nor threats. We're among the first such travelers, but as time goes by, there will be many more of us. Everyone now alive on Earth will have the chance to meet travelers like ourselves."

Xulai momentarily closed her eyes, fervently praying this would be true. Just now she could number the teams on her fingers and toes. Sea Duck 1 was in Tingawa, started shortly after the children's birth. Then she and Abasio had carried sea-eggs from Tingawa and returned to Wellsport to establish Sea Duck 2 while Precious Wind had traveled to the Golf Coast to set up Sea Duck 3. From Wellsport, two small ships were working their way south along an enormous length of coastline—Sowmari Cah—much of it mountainous—that ran almost to the southern pole. Across the western sea, there were almost a dozen teams fanning out to the west and north from Tingawa along the edges of Ahsiya that Abasio persisted in thinking of Ahsiya as "the backside of the world." He knew very well the world didn't have "sides," while at the same time knowing instinctively that he was on the front one.

Soon within the next two or three years, there would be a Sea Duck 4, 5, and 6—six couples were being trained—on the Brittns, offshore of Yurope. Yurope would come next, with sea-egg teams taking ships up the major rivers. Eventually, next century when the water rose higher, teams would go to Ahfreeka. Ahfreeka had been almost totally depopulated during the Big Kill, and the survivors had taken refuge in the midcontinent jungles. They would not approach the coasts and might not be reachable until the floodwaters inexorably moved the coasts to them.

But all that was "soon" and "elsewhere." Xulai and Abasio's work was "now" and "here." They would cross the Stonies to recruit young people from the area known as Artemisia who would be sent to Sea Duck 3.

Xulai's lifelong friend, Precious Wind, was there, traveling with other volunteers, and it was she who had told them the area had been named for the Golf People, a pre–Big Kill society led by elderly priests who performed the daily fertility rites. Wearing ritual garments and followed by acolytes who carried the sacred paraphernalia, the priests led processions across dedicated grasslands in pursuit of little white eggs, which, when found, were driven with sanctified spears or implements into previously bored holes in the ground—also sanctified and so marked with holy flags.

The symbolism was typical of most fertility rituals, requiring little explanation: ova being sought by the male organ and repeatedly pursued into the womb. The rite, as a whole, was well understood as begging divine encouragement of reproduction—much desired after the Big Kill, when population had dropped so disastrously.

Precious Wind—who was an inveterate accumulator of esoteric knowledge—was writing a detailed account of the ritual impedimenta. Egg, womb, and spear were obvious, but as yet no one had been able to explain why so many spears were employed in the ritual and why they had such odd shapes. Virtually all records of that time had been destroyed during the Big Kill, but small household idols of the priests in ritual dress and posture—one leg straight, one bent, spears held aloft, gaze directed prayerfully at the heavens—had been found during excavations.

All of which was neither here nor there. Xulai took a deep breath and returned to the reality of now. She pointed over her shoulder. "Bertram, we've come in a wagon. We parked it in the clearing, near your pond." She turned toward the window behind them.

As though upon cue, Redshanks obliged them: *"Kruk, kruk, kuraaawk. Kruk, kruk, kuraaawk."*

"That's our rooster," Abasio murmured. "Always nice to have a rooster along to wake one in the morning and encourage the chickens: fresh eggs for breakfast; a tasty something to look forward to after *wearying* hours on the road." Perhaps the man would hear the emphasis. Perhaps the man would take on the character of a tailor! At least temporarily!

On his part, Bertram was fully aware that both these people were charming and soothing him; it annoyed him that he felt both charmed and soothed. Volumetarians learned to be leery of charm, for it made one vulnerable. The burners of books sometimes hid behind charm.

His instinct was to continue dithering. Dithering had saved Volumetarians in past centuries when they had been confronted with burners and censors and who knows what else they called themselves? Inquisitors. Oh, yes, that, too. On the other hand, this man's clothes were far finer than those any book burner had ever worn. Bertram had not seen fabric like that in decades. Or style. The outer tunic, the way it was lined, that narrow band at the sleeve! Silk! How long since he had seen real silk! The woman's wide trousers and shirt, with an embroidered and beaded waistcoat—worn while *traveling*! It should be properly wrapped and carried in a silk case for some formal occasion! And their boots! The man's boots had been made by a very talented boot maker out of some leather he could not even recognize—as had hers. Yes. Hers were even better. Would inquisitors dress like this?

Xulai flounced impatiently. Both men heard the subliminal stamping of a not-altogether-imaginary foot: "Listen, Sir Tailor, *listen*! We're telling you that before long there will be many of us traveling about. Some of us will have children with us. We will go to places that are not yet inundated. Some of those places are damnably chilly as it is here, right now, and we can't keep the babies wrapped in shawls forever! They need JACKETS. They may even, heaven help us, need TROUSERS."

The young tailor drew a heavy breath and silently repeated a mantra that had to do with stitches in time saving one thing or another as he turned his eyes back to the f . . . the children in question. Actually, now that he was really looking at them, jackets wouldn't be a bad idea. Something in a warm fabric, with wide armholes for mobility, a style that nipped in a bit at the waist. They did have waists, obviously. Were they old enough to walk . . . he didn't mean that. Were they . . . "Ma'am, are they already swimming? I mean, can they?" He turned to take up a fold of paper and a pen.

"Certainly," Xulai replied, her annoyance subsiding. Questions were welcome. Questions meant involvement; involvement meant acceptance—eventually. "They were born able to swim, as most babies are. Prior to birth, all babies swim in the womb. We all evolved originally as sea creatures. Our children do not walk, as yet, though the anatomists tell us they will, though a bit clumsily because of the long feet, which will seem shorter as the bodies grow larger. When they go underwater the legs fit together and the skin overlaps—you can see the right-over-left fold—and there is also a very novel arrangement in the joints of hips and knees that allows . . ."

"Fluidity of motion," suggested Abasio wearily. They had not been doing this long enough to have it totally by rote, but they could let their mouths do parts of the work automatically, though only those parts including words they had previously analyzed for every possible invidious implication. If there was any way under heaven that some Stone Age villager could misinterpret what they said, they *would* misinterpret—and always to the detriment of their purpose!

"Fluidity of motion," agreed Xulai. Now that her spate of fury had worn itself out, she also sagged. A chair was close behind her and she sank into it, almost without volition. These last days had been hideous! They had fled from Churn-top, having been told by a sympathetic woman that some of the villager men intended to kill them during the night. They had already decided to detour around the next nearest two villages, for those two had been classified as dangerous from the beginning. The map had been made by the tax office in Ghastain. Since a troop of armed guards accompanied the king's tax-hogs—so named by the king himself, for their ability to *root out* assets carefully hidden by tax evaders—a place known by them to be dangerous was a place to be avoided.

The three dangerous villages had been separated by dense forest. There were streams, but none offered a comfortable place to camp nearby. When they were too tired to go on, they'd turned into the first available opening among the trees, erasing the hoof and wheel tracks behind them. They'd used *ul xaolat*, the thing master, to hide the wagon, and they had traded off, keeping watch all night while torch-bearing men in twos and threes went by on the so-called road, calling to one another in furious whispers.

Ul xaolat was a device that could, at command, dispose of the men by moving them far away or by killing them. Xulai preferred such measures be used only as a last resort. She and Abasio were the first to travel this route on this mission; there would be others later. Killing off half the inhabitants might prejudice later recruitment teams, so they stayed awake. Sleeplessness, however, added to general weariness, and Xulai could not remember ever having been this tired. Well, not within the last year, at least. Perhaps before that, that time she was hugely pregnant and being dragged up that dreadful cliff as bait for the Last Monster, half dead with fear and bitterly resigned to dying for her people but not at all . . . willing! She'd been frightened, yes, scared into paralysis, yes, but even then she couldn't remember being this tired!

And *even that* wasn't the real problem! She'd accepted it would be dangerous. She'd known that! The trip was long, but she could accept that! She'd expected that! The problem was that *she hadn't expected virtually everything else—all of it happening too quickly*!

The babies were growing faster than babies possibly could! The arrangements she and Abasio had planned for their care—smiling the while, telling each other how smart they were, baby-talking at the little ones and believing they were being extremely intelligent and prescient—those arrangements *might as well have been designed by a blind eeler for the care of snails*! The buckets that were expected to hold the children for the better part of a year had been outgrown months ago! A tinner in one of the towns they had passed through had put together three discarded stock tanks to make a shallow basin that took up half the floor of the wagon, but even it had become crowded! *Everything in the wagon was constantly damp!* Add the dust to the damp, and one was always filthy! The children accumulated toys. Tadpoles. Baby turtles. Efts. Each time they stopped near a river, Abasio had to take the old efts and tadpoles out of the tank, many of them newts and frogs by that time, creatures who considered Xulai's pillow an appropriate place to croak their territoriality. Xulai dreaded to think what the babies would bring home when they reached a real ocean. A baby shark, perhaps. A clutch of little octopi. Or would octopi come in sucks? "A suck of octopi." No. Clutch sounded better. It went better with eggs . . .

"I did suggest we leave them with the Sea King," said Abasio, leaning to embrace her, but doing it very gently. Heaving water buckets had left them both with shoulders that were sore to the touch. "He is, in one sense, their grandfather. But . . ." He lifted Bailai into his own arms, feeling the ache in the muscles of his back. *He wouldn't feel so weary if he could just sleep soundly. He had never had what people called nightmares, and the dreams he was having now couldn't really be called nightmares; they weren't frightening or horrible; some of them were even funny. There was one about a creature named Plethrob that was . . . silly! Now, that one had something to do with sex! No, everything that one did was with sex! Though how it was connected to anything else, God only knew. It was ridiculous, if anything. Purposeless! And if it was connected with what he and Xulai were doing, somehow, he couldn't figure out what! Except that the character, the six-armed character, was in that one as well.*

"The Sea King has too many children," Xulai complained, in solitary argument. She sounded petulant, even to herself, and she hated sounding petulant. A woman of her age, of her breeding, should be able to sound poised under any conditions, but damn it, she was just . . . She sighed and rubbed her aching forehead with her free hand. "The Sea King has so many baby octopods that he doesn't trouble himself if a few of his own get eaten. I don't think he's reliable. He'd leave them in his castle and go off to a seabed linguistic conference with the whales, forgetting all about the children. I think that's generally true of males in most oviparous races . . ." She scowled her disapproval of all such. "They're all parents in absentia!"

"Except for most birds," argued Abasio. "And some fish. And—"

Bertram interrupted the incipient argument by thrusting a sketch across his counter. "Something like this?"

Xulai looked at the pictured jacket and relaxed, rewarding Bertram with something halfway between pleasure and tears. "Oh, yes, Bertram. Yes! Perfect for Gailai. For Bailai, something a bit more masculine?"

The tailor peered at the children. "Which . . . ?" he started to ask, but stopped, his eyes going back to the child the man was holding. The one with hints of red in its hair had a more boyish face, he thought. He no doubt took after his father, who, though going gray, had shades of red in his dark hair: Bertram had an uncle on the lighter side of the family whose hair had changed like that. Instead of graying first, it became lighter, with red in it, then went to gray. This man's hair would have been much darker auburn when he was younger.

He said, "Certainly a bit more boyish, yes. Perhaps we can add some stitchery hinting at epaulets—stitchery only, not to increase the bulk or drying time—and larger buttons. Brass, I think . . . not! No. Not brass. I had forgotten the water. We need something that won't discolor. *Shell* would be perfect, wouldn't it! And bone would do well. I have a collection of buttons, some of them very old. They're here somewhere. I'll find them. If all else fails, I have steel hooks and eyes that needn't show at all. And, just for fun, how about a cap, just for wearing out of water.

Winter is coming. Caps with earflaps, yes? Little heads get cold, too. How many jackets, ma'am? And how soon do you need them? If you'll give me a little time, I can make them in several sizes. If they're growing rapidly, they'll soon outgrow anything that fits now. And don't forget shirts. Even though the jackets will be lined, they'll be more comfortable over shirts . . . Do they have nightgowns?"

"What a wonderful idea!" Xulai beamed at him, both pleased and relieved. "Oh, Bertram, that's such a very good idea! We'll take time! We really do have to rest, so we'll rest awhile . . . how long do you think, Abasio?" *A month or two would not be too long,* her eyes said. *Forever might just be a start!*

Abasio tried to concentrate on what she was saying. They had dozens of sea-eggs well hidden in the wagon, two dozen from each of three distinct genetic groups on the coast behind them—once a woman made the change, she usually produced one every ten days or so—and Xulai was adding her own sea-eggs as they traveled. They could not, however, distribute any of them until they were near seawater, preferably at Sea Duck 3. He sank back onto the wide windowsill, which seemed to have been cushioned for the purpose. He closed his eyes momentarily, while Bertram resumed his sketches.

Only for a moment . . .

Often as a child he had had dreams that troubled him. He very vaguely remembered his mother, his grandfather, shaking him awake and calming him down. During his Ganger years in Fantis, he'd had dreams, too. Dreams of horror and terror. Murder and mayhem. Those had jerked him awake, covered with sweat, staring around himself for . . . the threatener. The attacker. Those dreams were gone moments after he wakened. They did not last.

The dreams he'd been having on this journey were different. He remembered every detail of them, and the memory did not fade when he woke. *There was the tower one, with the two children: the place, the tower, was always the same. He was in it unmistakably. The graceful arches, the spiral staircase ascending to the balcony, where smaller arches echoed those below, and in the domed open center the bell was hung. The creature, being, person who struck it, morning and evening, used a long, almost wandlike striker. In those same dreams he remembered thinking the striker was* wrong, all wrong. The bell should ring of itself. *Would have rung of itself if this world had been left alone. If humans had left it alone. He had no idea where that thought came from!*

The pool was filled with a living fluid, bubbles and sparks continually swim-
ming within it, or rising to the surface to vanish in the air. Around the edge,
next to the rim, light glinted from the small, flat crystals the size of thumbnails,
slightly thicker than the leaf of a tree.

Sometimes creatures fished out a crystal and put it into their mouths. Some-
times the creatures took several crystals and made off with them, variously twirl-
ing, darting, flying out into the world. Some of the creatures were star-shaped.
Some were small, furry bipeds. Some were, he thought, animals and birds.

Abasio sighed.

Bertram heard the sigh and looked up from his sketch. Poor fellow.
He'd fallen asleep there on the windowsill. Oh, to have such a task
ahead of him, harder, perhaps, than Bertram's own task. The Great
Cause of the Volumetarians. The Preservation of Books. He said aloud,
but softly: "Tea. We need some hot tea."

He left them. Xulai and Abasio heard the slosh of water, the clink
of china from somewhere toward the back of the building, but they did
not stir. Both of them felt blessed merely to be sitting still, to be not
jouncing on the wagon seat, not hearing the wheels creak. It had been
a long, long way from Tingawa, where the children had been born:
first across the seas to Wellsport; a rather pleasant stay there, not too
tiring, no insuperable problems, one small excitement in an attack by
a Lorpian maniac who held Xulai to his chest with one arm and waved
his knife with the other. (Lorpians were shapists who believed anyone
who changed his physical body in any way was devil-ridden and should
be executed at once.) The shapist had been standing on the dock, his
back to the water. Below him, in the water, was a recent large, strong
initiate who was resting from his change. The initiate found the maniac
within easy reach for five out of his eight arms while the sixth removed
the knife and the other two remained anchored below the waterline.
The maniac, sadly enough, had not been able to breathe underwater,
though Xulai had found it easy enough.

Then when the Sea Duck station was set up and the first few couples
had been initiated, it was time to head eastward through the forests
to Woldsgard, stopping at villages on the way; from there south to the
lands above the Big Mud—with a stop in Elsmere to meet with an old
sweetheart of Xulai's father.

She had given them more recent maps, and from there they had come on eastward, through wooded hills and grassy valleys, and finally into the mountains themselves, following young Kim, their Tingawan outrider, into or through or around village after village, spending a day here, two there, sometimes backtracking because Kim came back to report—map notwithstanding—some road might go through, but this one did not.

They never stayed anywhere long enough to rest enough. They almost never had water deep enough to transform themselves—a transformation that had unexpectedly become a source of relaxation, recreation, peace. When too much time passed between transformations, they began to fret over it, suspecting they couldn't do it anymore. It made them feel they were pretending, no longer sure of what they were doing. Their lives were so . . . unlikely. Put into words, this journey was unlikely: almost a fantasy; a dangerous fantasy; a deadly one.

Add to all that: their attempted education of an often disbelieving populace.

People had to be convinced that the waters were rising. One had to get that over first, and it was often difficult, sometimes impossible, in these rugged mountains. Only after that could they speak of the transformation that could occur for their children and grandchildren. If they got that far, then Abasio and Xulai could paint a picture of a happy and productive life on and under the seas for their great-, great-, how-many-times-great-grandchildren: a lovely though largely speculative picture. When Xulai described floating hamlets constructed entirely of seaweed on which experimental populations were even now dwelling, it was all true, quite true. The structures were still experimental, and certainly the "populations" were first-generation changers, not yet many in numbers, but *they really were living in that way and many of them were relishing the challenge of inventing new ways of doing things. Or of doing without things or procedures they had previously considered necessary.* By this time there might even be additional second-generation children to serve as Bailai and Gailai were serving, as living proof!

Once in a while they had come to a place where the news of the inundation had preceded them. Another traveler from coastal regions had been there before them, or some native son or daughter had returned home from regions already flooded. Either of these happenings made the message more believable. They had had success enough that despite the episodes of weariness and hopelessness, they were quite honestly accomplishing what they had set out to do. They had sent a significant number of adventurous young people off to Sea Duck 2 in Wellsport, and a few would go later to Sea Duck 3; more than even the planners had hoped for. Xulai had chronicled it all. The name of each village, how many and who had gone or planned to go from it. Every now and then she leafed through her record book and counted them up, needing to convince herself their journey made sense, to assure them they were not wasting their time! Their youth, their love, their joy . . . That was another matter! Xulai grieved once in a while, stroking Abasio's head in her lap, seeing the gray hairs at his brow. He was too young to turn gray!

She resented that. Though she couldn't deny the importance of the task, she resented it. She resented it particularly among people who would not believe the waters were rising until they were standing in seawater up to their necks! If then! Often these people had no opinions, only convictions or hatreds forged of iron. "The world has always been as it is now. The world will never change." "This world was made for us, as we are, as it will continue to be." "As a matter of conscience" (or sometimes "As our deity commands," or "In accordance with our custom"), "we will kill anyone who suggests that the future will be different or that we should change in any way." More than one set of villagers had tried to do just that—unsuccessfully, of course. *Ul xaolat*, the device she carried, did not need to threaten. It became at need a spy, an alarm system, a defender. From a hundred whispered conversations among villagers, *ul xaolat* could detect those conspiring murder and identify not only the speakers but the sympathetic listeners, without error. Still, the feel of enmity was oppressive; the threats of enmity not easily forgotten.

Even in some villages where most inhabitants had been more curious than hostile, there had been individuals or small groups who felt the babies—along with their parents—should be destroyed because the world belonged to "their kind," and could not possibly include "otherness." Their world could contain only people who believed as they did and who shared their own color, cuisine, dress, habits, language, shape—and who were also, *provably,* one or the other of their two acceptable sexes. One particular village had insisted the babies Bailai and Gailai could not be considered girl or boy, never mind what Xulai said.

"Y'can't see they thingies t'tell, can ya? Any real baby, y'kin see they thingies 'f it's a boy, right?" When Xulai separated Bailai's legs to show that his quite normal little-boy thingy was hidden by the overlap in the skin, it made no difference. Thingies had to hang out in the open. That is, except for trousers. Or didies on babies. And why a trouser leg should be accept-able and a flap of skin not? Why, because that's the way it was!

In that place, aptly enough called Ramton, all the grown men gath-ered together in the evening and decided that since Xulai had "conner-dick-ed 'em" when she talked, killing her would show their own women that "connerdick-ing" men was not a good idea.

Xulai had quietly asked one woman what "connerdick-ing" amounted to.

"Oh, you do that, you cuttin' off they thingies, lady. When you talks back, you cuts off they thingies, so the menfolks say. Can't connerdick a man, 'cause anybody with a thingy, what he says goes. S'like a crown on a king, only he's born 'th it. Y'got a thingy, what you say is law! All a man hasta do here is take his thingy out an wave it, y'know yer in fer a real whopping."

"How did I argue with them?"

"You said you c'd tell if'n those fishy chil'ren was girl baby 'r boy baby. Men said y'couldn'. Not easy 'nuf."

"Which is easier, stepping your legs one step apart or taking off your trousers?"

"See, thass whuchur doin'! Yer connerdick-in'!" And the women fled, afraid they might have caught the connerdick-ing disease.

In Ramton, as was their habit, they had parked the wagon a little distance from the village. Early on, they had made a habit of putting the wagon where it could not be surrounded by villagers at any time, against a cliff or among several large trees. Add to that the fact that the new, improved version of *ul xaolat* could also make their camp fade into the background and surround it with what Precious Wind called a distraction field—one that made people turn right or left and wander off looking for something else. Though it was not as effective at night, when people relied more upon touch than upon sight, Xulai had felt that was protection enough, and one of the first things she had done on receiving the improved device was to tell it not to kill people. *Ul xaolat* accepted this. It also accepted her order to protect her and Abasio, their family, their horses, their wagon. Thus, when it isolated the whispered plotting among the men and older boys, *ul xaolat* accepted that they could not simply be slaughtered. They would have to be forestalled in some other way.

The conspirators, every male in the village over the age of ten, had come from the village intending to circle around the wagon, steal the horses, then kill the two monsters while their so-called parents watched, then kill the man slowly while the woman watched, and for a final thrill, amuse themselves with the woman and then kill her. That'd show her what came from connerdick-ing them. They had not had the fun of slaughtering a connerdicker for . . . a few years. Time to show the young'uns how to cut off breasts, n' ears, n' fingers without killin' 'em too quick. They knew the direction the wagon had gone. They went in that direction, circling, seeking here, there, searching for the wagon, at first whispering:

"Y' seen it yet?"

"Where's it?"

"M' torch went out!"

Then calling:

"Dam, butz dark, Jed."

"Where're ya, Balf?"

"Jed?"

And finally yelling at the tops of their lungs:

"Hal, k'n ya hear me? You, Balf?"

"Jed."

"Pong, m' torch burnt out! Where're you guys!"

Not one of them was aware that he was alone until the sun was well up. By that time the strangeness of the trees and the horizon, when any of it could be seen, suggested that each one was somewhere other than in the forest around Ramton. Where they were, in fact, was in a deep primeval forest that had no trails, roads, or villages in it at all. There was no smell of campfires, no human animals, only four-legged ones including large, hungry bears and several of the rare but ravenous big mountain cats. Each man or boy found himself as Xulai had required, totally uninjured.

Over the next several days, steering by the sun, Pong, one of the more sensible of the men, made almost thirty miles in a direction that would have, in another twenty or thirty, brought him into familiar country. There was plenty to eat in the forest; berries were ripe, mushrooms were plentiful; there were fish in the streams and snares could be rigged if a man had a knife, which he did. If he had been patient, he would have survived nicely, sleeping in trees, collecting food as he went, traveling only when he could tell what time of day it was and thereby which directions the shadows pointed. He was not patient enough to wait out three days of rain, however, and ended up returning almost to his point of origin, where the bears, who had finished off what was left of Jed a few days before, had just wakened to go looking for breakfast.

The *ul xaolat* had originally been designed more than a millennium ago, during the Big Kill, as an aide to those who traveled and who transported material from place to place and who did not want to fall prey to one of the monster killing machines. It obtained its power from receivers and broadcasters on Earth that received it from the sun cannons on the moon. Tingawa now guarded and maintained the receivers and broadcasters, devices so well constructed that they were still powering devices around the world, mostly ones of Tingawan manufacture. At the time of the Big Kill, *ul xaolats* had been designed to do almost anything that a traveler might need to do to survive in some degree of comfort. It could hunt game, cut firewood, light campfires, and clear campsites, and it could serve as a defensive weapon against predators—human and otherwise. Thus, even the original versions had been designed to detect hostile intent and provide defensive protection.

The new, improved *ul xaolat* had complied with Xulai's orders by moving the men without harming them in the least. New improvements had made it possible for the device to extrapolate the men's future behavior as well, and they adjudged the men's hostility to be of such determination and degree that it would persist indefinitely. The initial move, therefore, had to remove all threat existing at *present or future time.* The *ul xaolat* decided to set *future time* at eternity. The new improvements also allowed the device to extrapolate possible *user* reaction, and therefore to Xulai's request that the men be transported back once she and Abasio were far enough removed to be out of danger, *ul xaolat* merely replied "order understood." This was followed a day later by "Transported men fought, all were fatally injured. Shall separated parts of bodies be returned?" This was true; they had fought the bears, very briefly. It was also a test reply on the part of the device, as it wished to determine whether bodies or parts of bodies were to be further disposed of.

Xulai found the outcome completely believable. The men had been notably quarrelsome; they carried knives, and all of them, even boys as young as nine or ten—in addition to virtually all the woman—had knife scars. On consideration, it might be less disturbing if the men just disappeared rather than being returned in sections. She visualized separated parts as being ears, perhaps, or fingers. Maybe teeth. She replied, "In this case, no."

Meantime, *ul xaolat* entered into its data bank that men armed only with knives who fought large, healthy bears were almost invariably killed, and in such cases, body parts need not *routinely be retrieved*. The user had not, however, said this would be true in *every case*. In this case the device had supposed a "no-return" policy without knowing it to be true. The device found such uncertainties troubling. Itchy, as it understood that word. Incomplete. Being itchy or troubled used up power. Using power unprofitably was against the rules. This instruction had to be clarified.

Ul xaolat asked, accordingly, "When retrieving body parts for return to point of origin, is separate material at the cellular level to be included, i.e., blood, fingernails, and the like?"

Xulai shivered and answered promptly "No. Fluids and cellular level material need not be included unless specifically requested for laboratory use."

Not wasting power was an *ul xaolat* imperative. Bringing people back dead or in pieces was wasteful of power. Therefore, the device reasoned, it was up to the device to report in such a way that it would *not require bringing people or parts of them back at all* unless needed for forensics. *Ul xaolat* had the answer it needed. It immediately modified its internal procedure manual to implement the change. In future, in similar predatory situations, *ul xaolat* would submit "in-process" reports until sufficient time had passed for nature to take its course; a delay that centered on the oft-repeated question of whether bears poop in the woods. Poop would not constitute remains of the persons pooped; therefore when a body was entirely reduced to poop and bone fragments, no return would be necessary.

Moving this item from probable to certain gave the device a momentary surge of satisfaction. Since this journey was unique both in the way in which *ul xaolat* was being used and the fauna among which it moved, it was unlikely that anyone involved in refining the device or monitoring its activity would notice its autonomous acquisition of a sense of irony.

Ramton—and possibly Burned Hat—had been the worst towns they'd encountered. They'd heard all possible arguments and vilifications on this journey. As a result, they had learned not to talk about the *first stage* of the process. Any explanation of the first stage, which could be slightly traumatic, could be left to the people at Sea Duck, who could actually enact it before their eyes. Instead they simply referred to "the process." *"We are here to offer the process to those of you who are interested."* Those who were not merely uninterested but violently opposed turned their backs and muttered threats or attempted violence and were dealt with; those who didn't care one way or the other chatted about it for a few days before forgetting it; and those who were truly interested and young enough to be accepted packed up their necessary belongings and traveled westward, to Wellsport. One had to be of childbearing age, otherwise there was no point. Abasio and Xulai had been able to avoid preemptive defense except on the Ramton occasion and in the three-town cluster: Burned Hat, Saddlebag, and Rotch.

Burned Hat had been impossible. *"If the water comes the angels will come take us to a new world. We know this for a fact. No, we ain't interested and better get going before the men get worked up. They don't like folks comin' here tellin' us how we're s'posed to live."* Accordingly, they got going. This irritated the already-worked-up men, who knew shortcuts to Saddlebag and Rotch, and they had worked up the men of those villages into a fine fury before they figured Abasio and Xulai could get there.

Abasio and their outrider, Kim, however, had already decided on detouring via a long loop to the south that would avoid both the other towns. Men from Saddlebag and Rotch lay in ambush, intending to kill the travelers before they reached either place so that neither village could be contaminated by new ideas.

Abasio and Xulai never saw those lying in wait. When other villagers went looking for them later, the ambushers were gone, leaving no evidence of violence or, indeed, any evidence they had ever existed. Abasio and Xulai knew of the incident only when *ul xaolat* reported as one item in the day's activity log: "routine defensive maneuver completed." There was no mention of the village names. By that time *ul xaolat* had learned that reports were unlikely to be closely scrutinized when they were, first, given as general information, without any interesting details, and, second, were not provided until very late in the day, by which time Xulai was too tired to be picky.

In blessed ignorance, Xulai counted only Ramton and Burned Hat as total failures. The two villages avoided were not counted at all. She felt they had achieved an excellent acceptance rate, though she had tended to fret over some missed villages, regretting that they had not been able to take time to try to convince people. "If the men succeed in killing us, our mission fails," said Abasio, who had been schooled among gangers. "Living under the sea will require adaptability and intelligence. People without those qualities won't make it anyhow. Survival of the fittest is an absolute truth, and fitness implies being able to see reality. I think it's something called bough . . ." He stopped, momentarily confused. "No, that's in one of those dreams I keep having. I just mean some people don't ever see how things really are, and reality has let them perish. Who are we to second-guess reality?" There was something in *that* about bough, also, but he couldn't think what!

So now, in Bertram's shop, they second-guessed nothing but merely slept exhaustedly until Bertram returned with a tray. The jingle of china woke his visitors to be astonished by teapot, cups, saucers, even milk and white sugar—in little loaves! Like tiny building blocks! They had not seen sugar cubes since they left Tingawa! Abasio's eyebrows went up. Real sugar was virtually unknown on this continent.

Bertram flushed at their obvious surprise. "My family sends it to me. It is their business. It isn't from cane. We grew cane in the east, my family did, but the climate here is too cold for cane, so we grow sugar beets some way south of here. Cane or beet, the process is the same: crush the plant, collect the juice, boil the juice. The little sugar shapes are a conceit of ours. And all shapes of sugar are equally sweet in the tea, no?"

They sipped together. Xulai relaxed. It was a good tea, herbal, slightly floral, a touch of mint, and bergamot, with other ingredients she could not quite identify. It was not as satisfying as the teas in Tin-

gawa, where the tea shrubs of the ancient world were still being culti-
vated, but still it was flavorful and relaxing, with a pleasing scent. Tea
was one of the things that she would miss, though if her friend Precious
Wind had her way, the flavor would be transferred to one or several sea-
plants: cups would be carved from coral, and magnifying glasses would
be used to heat the water—if they couldn't figure out underwater stoves
or possibly ways to use subterranean hot spouts! Sea-plants tended to
be heavily mineralized, which interfered with flavor. Precious Wind was
much concerned with methods for distilling seawater so the tea would
not taste of salt. Xulai didn't worry over it: by the time tea no longer
existed, neither would Xulai.

She drank deeply and focused instead on the matter at hand, saying
gratefully to Bertram: "Make two jackets for each child, a little larger
than the size they are now: then two each, a size larger than that; and
two more a size larger yet. That's six for each, a dozen. Light shirts, also,
something *very* washable that will not need to be ironed. It simply can't
be done when we're traveling like this. I suppose that should keep them
clothed for at least a couple of years, perhaps longer, though I've been
wrong about every supposition I've made about them yet."

"Would you say they are growing about the same rate as ordinary
children?"

Xulai nodded. "I've been told they are, by committees of mothers
who've seen them."

"Can you weigh them, ma'am?"

Abasio said he could.

"Then if you will tell me their present weight, I have a chart that will
give me their probable sizes for the next couple of years."

"Wonderful." She sighed. "What payment do you accept, Bertam?"

"What have you to offer, ma'am?"

"Notes upon the bank of Ghastain. Letters of transfer from the Tingawan Reserve. Some barter goods, though they are small things only.
Or gold coin."

"Gold is always acceptable, ma'am. The smaller coin the better if
I am to use it." He lowered his voice and whispered, "Or I would take
books, ma'am."

"Books?" exclaimed Abasio.

"Shh," said the tailor. "I broke my vow when you came in, sir, madam. In my surprise, in my shock, I mentioned the books. I am not supposed to mention the books, ever. But . . . considering what you have told me . . . Ah. Nothing is as it should be! I am a Volumetarian, sir. Are you familiar with Volumetarianism?"

Abasio said wonderingly, "Volumetarianism, no. I'm not familiar with it."

"In the past, sir, books were burned." Bertram pinched his lips together and gave them a significant look. "Burned, sir. As a method of thought control. I presume, given your current . . . job? Task? Mission! I presume you are familiar with the history of thought control? With the ancient times of the religious or political imperatives? When only approved books could be read? Of the time of the Big Kill? Then, more recently, east of us, in Artemisia, the destroying of history by those in the Place of Power, in order to squelch ancient enmities!"

Abasio nodded. "I know what was done in Artemisia, yes. I was . . . I was there, at the end of that time. When the Place of Power was ended."

Xulai murmured, "Are you saying your title began even before that time? And survives even now?"

The tailor nodded. "It does, ma'am. Our title is millennia old. Of course, you will not spread it about? Ordinarily, I do not mention it, not to anyone. We have records of fifty generations of Volumetarians, same family. Not everyone is sympathetic with our goals. However, what you have told me is so . . . world-shaking in its implications that I must involve you, no? Back in the time of the Big Kill, when all books were being destroyed, our people hid volumes. We say they did it Volumetarily." He snickered, a mere moth-wing flutter of amusement. "Joke among ourselves, sir, ma'am. The Volumetarians sequestered them, protected them, and preserved them. My family has always been Volumetarian."

Xulai shared a glance with Abasio, eyebrows raised, indicating this was a thing they might discuss later. He nodded assent, and she went on. "I will pay you in gold, and we'll look about among our books to see if any of them can be spared."

Bertram busied himself with a tape measure around the children, and quite unexpectedly the girl child, who was slightly smaller than the other, reached out a baby hand and grasped his thumb. He stood, transfixed. The baby smiled. She was adorable! He smiled back. He sighed. "Ma'am . . ."

Xulai saw his confusion, this time with sympathy. "Yes, Bertram. What is it?"

"I do not wish to offend again. What name for these children of the subsequent race is considered polite?"

She looked startled. "We've always used their names, but they . . . Abasio, have we settled on anything like that?"

He nodded. "We've left it to the locals, and I haven't tried to enforce any uniformity. That place up where they played the drums, up the side of that red mountain, the people called them the Troutlings; Water-babes, I think in that place they farmed the pine-nut trees; Pollywogs, in one place, which we accepted, for the appellation was being used affectionately and we rather liked the sound of it. We usually call them sea-children when we speak of them."

"Sea-children will do," Xulai told Bertram, displaying more friendship than he had seen until that moment. "Collectively, they are sea-children. Individually, they have names, just as all of us do."

Gailai commented on this, her voice holding a querulous note. The tailor stepped back, jotting rapidly. There was a slight difference in measurements between the two, and he had them accurately for each. He was finished just in time, for the girl baby was obviously hungry. Xulai rose, took Bailai from Abasio, nodded pleasantly at the tailor, and headed for the wagon. Abasio took the chair she had vacated, seating himself comfortably, as though intending to stay awhile.

The tailor, from the table where he rummaged among fabric samples, looked up to say, "Sir, do you have to go to the town down there?"

"Not necessarily into the town, no, but the road through it is the road we need to follow to the places we need to go. We usually camp near a town, so we can buy provisions. Our outrider should have returned to us by now, as a matter of fact . . ."

Bertram frowned, nodded, then shook his head in troubled fashion. "Oh, gracious, sir. I think you may find, sir, that your outrider has been . . . detained. Some of the Suckians aren't very friendly. It's why I couldn't stay down among them when I came here. I set up business in town, but every time a customer wanted to visit, he had to fight his way past certain of the inhabitants."

Abasio was sympathetic. "Bertram—you don't mind my calling you Bertram?—it won't be the first time we find hostility. If a place is very unfriendly, when our outrider comes back to us we would ordinarily change our route if we can. Sometimes we can't, and that includes this stretch along here. This is the only road that takes us to Findem Pass, and we want to reach Artemisia, on the far side of the mountains. What do you mean, detained?"

"I merely thought it likely they'd captured him, sir. It's not likely they'll hurt him badly or kill him, but you probably will have to . . . pay ransom . . ."

Abasio tried to shake the weariness from his head. What was the man saying? "Kill . . . ? Who?"

"I'm afraid they've taken your . . . outrider . . . taken him prisoner, sir."

Outside, Xulai approached the wagon, where the horses, Blue and Ragweed, slouched in the traces. Blue's partner, a large pinto mare, mostly brown with white patches around the ears, rump, and legs, was seemingly asleep beside him. Xulai sat in the shade on the wagon step and let the children suckle.

Blue opened one eye. "The tailor man have a fit of startlement and stab himself with his needle?"

Xulai responded: "Not any more than usual. He's making jackets for the children, three sizes, so we don't have to do this again for a while."

Ragweed also opened an eye. "What fabric? Wool's best, if it's going to get wet." She shook herself. "Someone put a blanket on me once, kinnen, or maybe it was lotton, some name like that. Not Zilk, you can keep Zilk! Embroidered, that one was. Very fancy! Hadda silly woman in charge back then. She died. And not too soon for me. I might've kicked her to death had she not! That blanket was the coldest rag it could possibly be when it was wet! Give me wool every time."

"I didn't even think . . ." Xulai closed her eyes. The horses remained quiet, listening to her breathing. Asleep, she was. After a time the babies released her. A chill breeze struck her bared breasts. She shivered and wakened enough to take the children into their tank in the wagon. She watched as they curled into deeper sleep, the gills along their sides quivering. They would come up for air when the water became deoxygenated, as it would! The first few months of their lives she had hovered day and night, afraid they would stop breathing, unable to believe their bodies would do whatever the environment required. Even now she sometimes stood in wonder, simply watching them breathe. She adjusted her bodice and went out, intending to return to the shop, but stopped momentarily, looking at Abasio, who stood on the stoop of the shop, staring at nothing.

They had set out in good health, in good flesh, not fat but certainly in good condition, when the babies were three months old. The way was wearing on them both, no doubt, but she hated to see its effect on him. He had hollows in his cheeks that had not been there before, though that fact had done something dramatic with his cheekbones. The gray at his temples was pronounced now, not merely a sprinkle of snow but an ashen upsweep over his ears. Which was, however, remarkably attractive. When she had first seen him, his hair was full of auburn glints. Most of that was gone now. He was still strong, very strong, but he walked . . . wearily. Well, fiddle. So did she. And he wouldn't if he got some rest!

He looked up, saw her watching him, and smiled . . . the Abasio-smile that melted her. All love. All pleasure. When she grew angry at the fates or the people who had ruled her life since before birth, she soothed her anger with Abasio. *If it weren't for them, she wouldn't have known him, so she had to forgive them!* He lifted a handful of something and waved it at her: fabric samples.

"Wool," he said as he approached. "Bertram thinks it will be warmer. He says it holds moisture without getting chilly. Pick the colors out here in the daylight, and then tell him what you choose. He has enough material for six jackets in any combination of these." They conferred for a moment over the samples, several blues, two greens, several reds and browns.

She said, "Red and green for Gailai; brown and blue for Bailai; one of each in each color in each size, six for each of them. That way we'll know which belongs to who." She took the samples from him, went up on tiptoe to kiss his surprised lips, and moved toward the shop once more. He looked after her, touching his lips with a forefinger, smiling, and suddenly ten or twenty years younger. He ambled over to the horses and leaned upon Blue.

"No fair," said the horse. "You're not any more tired than I am!"

"I just need the comfort of a friendly shoulder," said Abasio. "The tailor says they're holding Kim a prisoner, down below here."

Blue murmured, "Then we should probably see about getting Kim loose." He shook his head thoughtfully, then whispered, "It's not that bad. We were in a worse place near Artemisia, when we were there last. D'you suppose it's all changed over the mountains, Abasio?"

Abasio had refused to consider this. He would have to consider it, and a number of other possible unpleasant things, before they approached the area. He knew there was a town named for him—for a certain image of him—north of the Artemisia line. Cat-land. Named for the heroic Abasio the Cat. He had been told that his picture was painted on its walls. He had heard that his former . . . acquaintance Sybbis was queen of the place. His one intimate encounter with her had been while Abasio himself had been drugged into virtual unconsciousness—at least his mind had been, though at least some body parts had seemingly remained alert enough to father her child. Or so she had claimed. While not being at all *responsible,* he might in fact have been *responsive.* Or so might a number of others, including his onetime friend CummyNup. Sexual morality was unknown among the gangers except as affected by ownership. Women were often owned by particular ones of them, and no other ganger should trespass on what another ganger owned. The boy would be how old now? About four or five years?

Any association with Sybbis's child could mean trouble. He would need to look as different from his former ganger self as possible when they reached Artemisia, the end of this leg of their journey. He shook his head, feeling the uncustomary fall of hair around his ears and shoulders. He had been younger then, and his hair had been cropped—long hair was a disadvantage in a fight!—so now he had let it grow and was letting himself age, as though there were any *let* about it! Soon he would have to cut it or braid it. He muttered, "Sybbis is there. Y'think she'd know me, Blue?"

"You're older," said Blue. "And you're grayer. You should go with that, become a bit grayer yet. Quit shaving your face. By the time we're down the mountain, you'll have enough for a mustache and a neat little beard."

"Xulai says kissing a man with a mustache is like trying to suck berries from a thornbush."

"Don't grow one, then. Your hair's enough longer you can braid it and put stuff in the braids. Feathers and ribbons. That's Etershore doings, and it'd add ten years or so to the age you seem to be."

"Sybbis knew me as one of her father's gangers. We were all known by our scars and our tattoos, and during our one encounter, she identified me by mine. They removed both scars and the remnants of the tattoos in Tingawa, so that won't help her. She's never seen the wagon, but her consort, CummyNup, was told all about it by one of the locals, so she might suspect something even though it's been repainted."

He did not want his history in the area to complicate matters for him and Xulai. When he left Artemisia, years ago, he hadn't known the waters were rising. No one in Artemisia had known. The only places aware of it were coastal areas and river basins, and not all of them had considered it to be a worldwide thing. The three great beings in the Place of Power had had a specific task— self-determined or imposed by something even more powerful. That had been to get rid of the cities and the walkers and to make sure no one brought back any of the ancient weapons stored up near the moon. Abasio shook his head. He hadn't thought about any of this in ages! Now it was all flooding back: "The place. The terrible battle. The angels . . ." He did not realize he was speaking aloud.

"Angels!" whinnied Ragweed. "That's who's going to save that Burned Hat place! Didn't they tell us, '*Oh, the ocean isn't coming, no, but it wouldn't matter if it did because before anything happens to us, the skies will open and all the angels will come down to carry us away. Our prophet told us so!*'" Ragweed yawned, rotated her head upon her neck, and said in her normal voice, "Made me wish the angels had carried them away before we got there."

Abasio shook his head: the people of Burned Hat would not have been talking about the angels Abasio had met! Those beings had not been malign, but they had been divinely pragmatic. Few humans could manage that kind of pragmatism. *They had done what they came to do. They had left him with one certainty: there were other intelligences in the universe besides humans and earthly animals.*

He had to keep reminding himself of that. *The terrible walkers were gone; the shuttle with his beloved Olly was . . .* His mind shut down and he thrust that thought away. *All that was past. The future was with him and*

Xulai and the babies and, he hoped, the people of Artemisia, who were very good
people whose customs and pattern of life deserved to survive!

He patted Rags's shoulder. "Xulai tells me not to fret over things.
She says just to thank whatever Gods may be, there are several generations of recruitment left before total coverage, and every generation
enormously increases sea-egg production."

"That 'we' of people doing recruitment better not include me. Another trip like this, and I'm finished," said Blue. "I am not a colt, Abasio."

"It's that water tank," said Ragweed, fixing Abasio with a very penetrating stare. "It's too heavy, Abasio. If there's no way to get another
team between here and any more mountains, you'll have to figure
something else out for keeping the children's tails wet. I'm no more a
filly than Blue is a colt. Willing we are, but it's impossible."

Abasio knew she was right. He had thought there might be need
for a four-horse hitch; he had even obtained the extra set of harness in
Woldsgard and stored it in a compartment under the wagon, thinking
surely they could add a team somewhere on the way. Finding a team
that anyone was willing to part with had thus far been impossible. They
had actually been nearer horse country in Wellsport than they were
now! They should have sent someone north to Valesgard to buy another
team from the Free Knights who bred Prince Orez's horses, but everyone had been in a fever to get started. They wanted to get moving, to get
on with the job of saving the human race. Moving around would have
been easier without the babies, but people would have been less likely to
believe! It made recruitment so much easier if people could actually see
what the second generation looked like. Most people thought they were
cute. Of course, babies of many creatures were cute but became less so
when full-grown—unfortunately. Perhaps an end to babyhood would
relieve Xulai and him of the current task!

The door to the tailor's shop closed with a snap and Xulai trudged
toward him. He reached out to help her onto the seat. "The town is
just down the hill," she said. "Shouldn't we see to getting Kim free of
them?"

"I was just waiting for you." He chirruped to Blue; the horses shifted,
tugging the wagon slowly over the small crest. The moment the village
came into view, the horses stopped, halted by a sudden clamor! A ca-
cophony! Pots and pans, banging and clattering, people pouring out

of the buildings onto the roadway, where they formed into a consolidated mob. Some had staves, a few brandished rusty-looking swords, there were even a couple of torches . . . *Torches?* Abasio and Xulai shared a look of consternation. Below them, their outrider, Kimbo-niro, tied hand and foot and somewhat bruised, was being held between two large men. Bertram had been right!

"Whoa," breathed Blue.

"Yes," agreed Abasio. "Certainly, whoa. I think wagon and horses go no farther than this."

Xulai was already climbing down from the wagon seat. "I'll go down on foot," she said.

From inside the wagon came an enormous splash. Wailing followed.

Abasio smiled. "We can't risk you. Blue, Rags, take the wagon back where it was and Xulai will unhitch you both. Bertram won't mind our stopping over by the pool, he says the grass over there is good grazing. When Bertram told me he has a bathhouse out back of his shop, I could no longer think of any reason for camping any closer to that mob. I'll just walk down and collect Kim." Xulai's hand came from her pocket, offering him *ul xaolat.*

He took it, put it in his own pocket, raised his other hand in salute, and ambled down the hill alone. The small mob before him shifted one way and another, muttering. He stopped a good twenty paces from them. He took his time, looking from face to face, not smiling, and taking on a stance he had copied from Xulai's father and grandfather. It was one of absolute mastery in posture, gesture, or word. It had taken a good deal of practice before a mirror, but he was now capable of lifting one nostril. He could do only the right one, but doing so conveyed disdain. He conveyed it now. "Do I understand that you will not allow us to go through your town on the road?"

There was a hasty flurry around Kimbo, and he was pushed forward so violently that he fell. Abasio went forward, picked him up, noted the bruised face, pressed the *ul xaolat* to the ropes that bound him, and stood the young man on his feet. There was an exclamation from the crowd as the ropes vanished, knots and all.

"Where's Socky, Kim?"

"Buncha horse thieves!"

"They say anything?"

"Said they'd heard we was turning people into monsters. They don't want you anywhere near."

Abasio murmured, "Go on up the hill to the wagon. Have Xulai tend to your face, and I'll be along in a minute."

Kim staggered up the hill. Abasio looked at the muttering crowd with his loftiest expression. "We did *not* plan to stop in *your* town; it is *not* on our list. We *do not visit* towns that *are not on our list.* We will simply go through on the road. If you are not thieves, you will bring me Kim's horse. If you are thieves, the King of Ghastain has agreed to send fifty or a hundred armed men to deal with any problems we may have."

More muttering. One red-faced challenger pushed himself forward. "You don' wanna stop here!"

Abasio nodded firmly. *"You are absolutely correct. We do not want to stop here!"* Each word was firmly bitten off with an unmistakable sneer on the "here."

This agreement seemed to puzzle the speaker. "Where ya goin?"

"To the Findem Pass, over the hills. I came from the plains beyond. We're going back there to visit my people for a while."

"Not stoppin' here?" The spokesman sounded put out.

Abasio said with utter boredom, "We were given a list of worthy villages to visit, and *this place is definitely not on that list.*"

More muttering. "Cata-pull-it!" "Whatzee sayin'?" A spokesman stood forth. "Whatchu call wor-thee?"

"We have a list of towns given us by the King of Ghastain and the High Lord of Tingawa: towns that are known to be well managed and useful, whose people are worthy of surviving. This place is called something like what? Grabslack? Graystink? So the tailor told me, and there is no such town on our list."

"Cata-pull-it, all! Why i'nt it?"

Abasio yawned at some length, shaking his head before looking down his nose at the crowd once more. "How should *I* know? I don't *know* and I don't *care.* I didn't make the list. We received it from the High Lord of Tingawa, I doubt you've heard of him, but you've heard of the King of Ghastain—he's the one who sends the tax-hogs around to get your taxes every five years or so. They decided which places were worthy."

"Where'zat *Tinky-wah?*"

"Across the western sea."

More muttering. More explosive "cata-pull-its." Evidently a local expletive.

"We heerd you got monsters."

Abasio yawned. "We have no monsters. We have Kim and Kim's horse, two wagon horses and a wagon. We have my wife and our two babies, who are sea-children but most certainly not monsters. The tailor thinks they are charming. If you are not thieves, you will bring me Kim's horse so we can plot a way around Greepslunk and leave you in peace. If you attempt to keep Kim's horse, it will be very bad for you."

More muttering, from which a childish voice soared: *"But I wanna see the monsers!"*

Abasio sighed and began to turn. "You are a town of thieves. Very well, we will simply go around you. The men sent by the King of Ghastain will arrive before winter. They'll take twelve of your men hostage. Meantime, one of you will disappear each day until we get the horse back, so you can start choosing which ones you're willing to get rid of. I will remark that we do have weapons, so please do not attempt to treat us as you treated our guide."

A male voice shouted from the crowd. "Yer guide was askin' us to give ya place to camp. Yer guide said you was stayin' here."

Abasio snarled: "Our guide said . . . *nothing . . . of . . . the . . . kind!* He probably asked *if we could have your permission to camp.* We camp only in places where we are welcome. All you had to do was say no. Instead, you have made it clear you are thieves and slavers. All roads belong to the king! Since you are blocking the king's road, the king's soldiers will come to remove you and your village, as you are an impediment to honest travel. The king will slaughter your livestock to feed his soldiers and use you as laborers to build roads up on the highlands. Once your village has been removed, there will be no reason for anyone not to use the king's road. I bid you good afternoon." And he strode away up the hill.

He heard the shocked mutters behind him. "Ree-moved?" "Who'n hell started this grabbin' people?" "Ree-moved?" "Dradblum you, Lorp!" "Where's 's 'orse?"

He got about a third of the way before feet pounded after him. He turned.

"Mister, mister. C'n I see the monsers?" He was skinny, brown, dirty, tousle-headed, big-eyed, and about ten years old. Maybe a little older than that, around the eyes.

Abasio shrugged and continued walking, paying no attention to the voice from the crowd. "Willum, you, Willum, you git yerself back 'ere."

Abasio trudged. Willum kept up, showing no sign of having heard himself summoned. "Mister, what's yer name?"

"Abasio." The boy had evidently inherited his much-mended trousers from an older, shorter, wider brother or cousin. The faded cloth was gathered around his waist and failed to reach his ankles by a handbreadth.

"Mr. Baso, what's sea-children?"

"My children. One boy. One girl. They can swim like fish. They can live in the water. When the waters cover the earth, they will be able to live in that water."

"How soon's that gonna happen?" The boy's eyes were luminous with wonder, deeply brown as a peat pool, fringed with lashes Xulai herself would envy.

"In about two hundred years."

"Oh." Trudge, trudge, bare feet scuffing more dirt onto his feet and legs. "Thassa long time. How come you got sea-chil'ren now?"

"Because it takes twenty years for a sea-child to grow up and have children of its own. And it takes a long time to find all the people on Earth who are worthy of having sea-children. And if we wait until the last minute, it will be too late. By starting well in advance, by the time the waters rise over the whole world, we'll all have children that can live in them. All but places like this, of course. Your people wouldn't want to. They don't care if their children all drown, and if they don't care, we certainly don't care."

Trudge, trudge. The eyes had gone even wider, the mouth suddenly set in wounded disgruntlement. "*But I'm their chil'ren!* One of 'em! *I don' wanna drown!*"

"Yes. Well, when you get a bit older, you can travel to one of the towns on my list and maybe they'll let you become one of the sea-people." *Which would take care of the dirt.* Perhaps the child attracted it, as metal attracts a magnet. He came to himself with shocking awareness: the child was no dirtier than he himself was! Bertram had offered his own bathhouse, behind the shop. Oh, yes! With a stove to heat water! That was something to be done today! Before sundown!

When they reached the wagon, Abasio introduced Willum, who went in to meet Bailai and Gailai. He knelt beside the tank, saying, "Wow. Wow. Wow. Wadda they eat?" Surprisingly, for the babies often reacted adversely to strangers, each of them had grabbed one of the boy's hands and tested it to decide if it was edible.

"Their mother is still nursing them," said Abasio. "You've seen mothers nurse their babies?"

"Thought so," said Willum. "They suck fingers like the baby goats do. D'ya haffa climb inna water ta feedum?" Willum asked Xulai.

"No," said Xulai crisply. "They can stay out of the water for a while. They just can't stay forever, because the skin on their tails dries out and cracks . . ."

Abasio left the boy to amuse the babies, went back outside, and stood looking down on the crowd. It had not dispersed. While Willum was probably an excellent ambassador, it was probably best that he return home before some new cause of hostility occurred. "Willum," he called. "Come on. Go back down to your mom. Tell the people they're welcome to come visit, no more than six at a time. Okay?"

The boy backed out of the wagon, face alight, and raced down the hill, waving his arms and yelling. "Hey, Ma, Ma, *they're babies, not monsers!* Ma!"

"I told them they weren't on our approved list," said Abasio. "I said we have an approved list prepared by the King of Ghastain and the High Lord of Tingawa, and they're not on it. I told them the king would see that their village is removed, they will be taken into slavery, and I think we will find they have changed their minds."

"Then you'd better get another team," said Blue in his seldom-used, ponderously put-upon voice. "I don't think we can manage cross-country. Not that the roads are that much better."

"Excuse me," said a mild voice.

They turned to see Bertram standing on his shop stoop. "I'm afraid I overheard some of that. Is it . . . are the horses talking? Ah. Interesting. I have always thought horses and dogs had the intelligence to talk. Not only they, of course. Also goats and pigs, I'm sure. Has someone recently given them the right vocal apparatus?"

"Yes," said Xulai, surprised. "Someone has indeed. My people in Tingawa invented the process. Prior to the Sea King's War, some experimentation was done on this side of the ocean as well. In parts of the lands west of the mountains, there are probably still a good many talking animals. Abasio's horse no doubt descended from that group."

Abasio did not comment, though he thought Blue had not descended from any such group. The three great ones that had destroyed the Place of Power had given Blue a voice in order that the horse could keep Abasio from dying of loneliness. Or maybe . . . *Olly* had asked them to. Which had been very nice of them, in a way. Blue had been annoying him—though companionably—ever since.

Xulai went on: "Dogs and horses are now being adapted to underwater living as well. Sea dogs, sea horses."

The tailor beamed. "Remarkable! Quite. However, my intention was to say that I understand the problem the horses are having with the wagon. Water is remarkably heavy, isn't it! Perhaps I can help by making the children some wet suits."

Abasio and Xulai stared at each other. "Wet suits?" said Abasio. "I don't understand."

"You were mentioning a tank? Wool holds water very well. If I make some trousers out of lambskin—with the layer of soft wool on the inside and something to prevent evaporation on the outside—they should be able to travel without a tank. And then, for nightwear, a similar garment closed at the bottom, like a sack? Fastened around the waist? It should take far less water than a tank. I should imagine a quart or so would keep them nicely damp all night while leaving their bed dry. Which, I presume, you prefer."

Kim, who was nursing his bruised face at the side of the road, said, "Try it, 'Basio! We're not gonna find another team anywhere close, and Blue's right. They can't haul the wagon up the pass with all that water in it."

While Xulai quieted the children, Kim and Abasio accompanied the tailor into his shop. "That's a good idea you had," said Abasio to the tailor. "How did you come up with it?"

"A very old book. I was reading it just the other night. It spoke of wet suits. Something that divers wore. If I read it correctly, it was to prevent their being chilled in deep water. There were pictures of people wearing them. The outsides looked very much like the surface of your children's . . . tails, legs, they must serve both functions, no? There were no detailed illustrations showing the construction of such devices, so I don't know what they were made of." He fetched the book from the back of the place and showed them the picture. The surface of the suits did look like the children's tails: shiny, slick, dark.

"Old book?" whispered Abasio.

Bertram looked about, as though afraid to be overheard, and whispered, "Can I trust your discretion, sir?"

Abasio smiled, feeling how wry the smile actually was. "A great many people seem to have done so, Bertram. If it's a secret . . ."

"The books are in a cave behind the shop. They've been there for more than a thousand years. Many volumes go back to the before time. You'll have to wait until tonight to take a look. I never go into the cave until all the Gravysuckers are asleep. The books have been preserved, but I wouldn't trust the townspeople to leave them alone. Many of them are like squirrels. What they can't eat, they chew holes in! Or in this case, they'd use them to start fires. Or as toilet paper, though the Suckians seem to have found a dried leaf that works better. Flexible, soft, absorptive. They're thinking of making it a market crop, sold in bundles of one hundred."

Abasio whispered. "Tonight or a later night would be fine. I've committed us to staying here near you, Bertram! I've upset the people below by threatening them with the King of Ghastain. I hope you don't mind our camping here awhile and letting the horses rest while Gravysuck considers its position.

"The pond is just a few yards from the wagon. The children will likely spend hours playing there. About half of what they're eating is solid food, now, but Xulai really needs to wean them. Nursing them is wearying for her on top of everything else, and she needs some time to relax. We're all filthy; we need to clean up. When that's done, then you and I can spend some time in your cave." He turned and raised his voice. "Kimbo-niro can heal from his bruises a bit."

"I'm all right!" blurted Kim. He had come all the way from Tingawa to serve Xulai and he was determined to do his job well. He did not want to be sidelined because of injuries.

Abasio shook his head. "I didn't say you weren't all right, Kim, but taking a little time off to heal is always sensible. It saves trouble later on. Go get some of Xulai's special heal-all tea and take a nap."

As Kim moved away, Bertram actually smiled. It was an exceedingly sweet smile, with some longing in it, and it came to Abasio suddenly that the tailor was probably an extremely lonely man. He asked, "About grazing for the horses?"

The tailor said, "The area just through the trees, beyond the pond, excellent grass. And I mentioned the boiler out back. The water is piped down from a stream uphill where it's perfectly clear. Tailors have to be clean, otherwise everything we stitch would be filthy by the time it is completed. There's a tub, and a kind of shower-bath arrangement there. If you build the fire under the boiler—it holds enough water for two tubsful—and get it started now, it should be quite hot within the hour. Several families in Gravysuck have similar arrangements. Not all. Some prefer being filthy to chopping wood for the stove."

Abasio thanked him, remarking, "You said you had to move up here onto the hill because customers had to fight their way to you down in the town. Was that the real reason?"

Bertram ducked his head in chagrin. "Partly. People would come looking for me, meet somebody in town who'd snarl at them, utter a few 'cata-pull-its,' and direct the poor souls the wrong way—"

"Cata-pull-it? A local swearword, right?"

"More or less. Definitely a localism. The way I understand it, they used to have a man in the town who was . . . well, not normal, shall I say, about women and little girls. He tried to make off with some female children, and another man in town, a visitor, told the inhabitants they should have a catapult. He built them one. They showed the rapist the catapult, put him in it, and catapulted him out into the middle of Gravysuck Pond. It does—suck, I mean. Once in, you cannot get out."

"Don't you get lonely up here?"

"I do. But the books are here, and I moved here mostly so they wouldn't find the collection up here in the cave. You see, for the last several centuries, it had been cared for by a local family of Volumetarians. Not tailors, needless to say! They had a farm a bit east of the village down there. All they had to do was keep an eye on the place, keep local people away from it. A few stories about ghosts and evil spirits, an occasional manifestation of weird lights and howling, that took care of keeping them away. Well, whenever the Volumetarian in charge died, the duty would be passed on to the next family member. Eventually the local family died out, word got passed to me, and in accordance with our usual vows, I came. I had a house built for me down in the village; one adequate also for the shop."

He sighed. "However, I was a stranger to Gravysuck and did not resemble them in the way they all seem to resemble one another. You'll note the lean muscularity, the strong cheekbones, the almost uniform straw color of the hair and the pale eyes. Long breeding within a restricted population, I should think. Strangers are anathema in Gravysuck. After putting up with them for a time—a time and a half, actually!—I hired a couple of carpenters who were traveling through. Volumetarians who relocate are always supplied with adequate funds. While we dare not move the book repositories, each of us can certainly arrange to put ourselves in an appropriate relationship to the one we guard! Pursuant to that, the carpenters and I took my house down, board by board, and rebuilt it up here, backed right up against the mountain. My cellar door opens up into the cave, so I can go back and forth unobserved. If Gravysuck ever found the books, someone would very probably yell, 'Monster books,' and they'd burn them all."

"And yet you mentioned them immediately to us?"

Bertram's mouth dropped open. "I did. I really did. At the moment it seemed to be the right thing to do. I've never, never done that before. I haven't figured out why it happened this time!" He was quite pale, obviously upset over the lapse.

"In this case, it was the right thing to do, and something probably told you that. Are you here alone? You have no family?"

"I was only twenty-four when I came. My brothers were both grown, off on their own, adventuring. Mother and my older sister, Linian, came here with me, but Liny first married a man in Flitterbean—that's the family she and mother taught to make sugar after waiting two years for a supply of beet seed to reach them—and some little time after her husband died, she married a man from Saltgosh, next town south, on the east fork up in the mountains. Mother stayed in Flitterbean with Liny's son—they'd taken him into the sugar business—but Mother passed on, five years now. I travel down south or up the hill—isn't it interesting that 'south' is *down* directionally but can be *up* altitudinally—to see my nephew and his family or my sister Liny in Saltgosh when I get a chance. That's about it."

"What did the villagers have against you?"

"I'm an outsider, I don't look like them, I'm not a farmer, and I'm a very good tailor who actually entices strangers to seek me out, isn't that terrible? Why, I had people from Saltgosh and Flitterbean and south beyond the turnoff to Saltgosh about twelve miles from the town of Asparagoose, and—"

"Asparagoose?" said Abasio. "Asparagoose?"

"Have you never seen a goose with green, sort-of-ferny feathers? Well, they had one hatch, so they named the town after it."

"Did *you* see it?"

"I did. Looked like an asparagoose to me. It grew up and laid twelve eggs, hatched six regular geese and six asparageese. There were ganders and geese both in the hatch, and they've had flocks of asparageese ever since. I say green, but the goose color is really more toward the celadon. It shouldn't be surprising—the color, I mean. Many waterfowl are brightly colored. At any rate, at my suggestion, a few of the village women have taken to making couturier cloaks: asparagoose down on velvet! Special order only, and they're selling quite well."

"Who in heaven's name around here would have the money to buy—"

"Oh, not around here. No. To the traders that come through. We're on a main trade route for wagoners. Sugar, salt, wool, dried fruits, hand-carved toys . . ."

"And did you say Flitterbean?"

"There was once an oddity called jumping beans. I found them mentioned in my books, back there." He nodded furtively toward the back of the shop. "Actually, of course, it was the movement of newly hatched worms inside the shell of the bean that made them hop. It was very much the same kind of thing down in Flitterbean. They always raised crops of red beans—with the usual green pods—and apparently one year the pods grew wings and flew away, right off the vine. What actually happened was that a new kind of insect with a long green body and long green wings laid eggs inside the pods. The little ones matured and crawled out; the long green bodies looked like bean pods that took wings and flew away. The locals thought it was the beans that flew, so they named the town after the event. Prior to that time, the village was called Thwonkville after the Thwonk family there."

"Didn't the Thwonk family object to the change?" asked Kim.

"As I understand it—and of course the tale may have been embroidered—by that time, there were none of the Thwonks left to object. The townspeople had been killing them off for about twenty years. Killing Thwonks was, as I understand it, a collaborative though covert project undertaken as a civic responsibility. It took a long time because there were a lot of Thwonks, and whenever one of them was disposed of, the event had to look accidental. As the family shrank, I understand that some of the Thwonks seemed to feel a certain disquiet and moved away. The last pair remaining, Urgle and Orgle Thwonk, twins, were caught in a propitious avalanche just a week before the beans flew off. Extremely unpleasant people, the Thwonks."

Bertram was dead serious, but Abasio had to struggle with his face.

"What's all the business about monsters?" Kim asked. "They were bound and determined we were bringing in monsters."

"Oh." Bertram shook his head. "That dates back a couple of decades, at least. There was a woman named Villy who lived here in Gravysuck. She fell in love with a traveler—a man who moved about peripatetically, rather as you seem to be doing, sir," he said, giving Abasio a long, analytical look. "She married the man—his name was, I believe, Gurge, or perhaps Garge—and went off with him. She was gone for quite some time—he was killed, she returned pregnant. She gave birth to something that didn't look human at all, and it died. Villy told people they'd been living in a place the locals called 'the burn,' where the animals were all wrong. The town claimed she'd brought back something bad with her, which proved prophetic. She died of it, too, about a year later. Nobody else has ever suffered as a consequence, but that has been the town's excuse for screaming 'monsters' ever since. That and the Lorpists. I'm sure you've been warned about Lorpists."

"I think I've been near a place known as the burn," said Abasio sadly. "Full of deadly radiation. If this all happened six or eight years ago, it's not there anymore. Someone . . . something cleaned it up."

"Now, that sounds like a story."

"No reason you shouldn't know, and I can make it a short story. North of Artemisia was the area called Manland, because there were still cities in it, including the one nearest my home: Fantis. It was a final survival, I guess, the only place where there were still . . . *are still* enclaves with a high level of technology, subterranean communities around the cities: the so-called Edges. The city itself was divided into gang territories, even though the gangs were dwindling. The death rate was very high. The Edges remain, but the city is gone now.

"Some days' journey south of Fantis was the so-called Place of Power. Some of the partly or mostly human creatures in the Place of Power were conspiring to start the Big Kill all over again. They were stopped by three very powerful beings who had been overseeing things there for several generations at least. In the end, they stopped the conspiracy from happening. There was a Kill, but it was mostly the killers who died." He fell silent, musing.

"And you know this because . . . ?"

"Because I was there. I saw the place destroyed."

"Were the powerful ones good beings?" asked Bertram in a wondering voice.

Abasio frowned. He tried to keep his voice level as he said, "Bertram, that's a question! The old, powerful beings I'm talking about didn't hesitate to act, and bad people died for what seemed good reasons. Good people died for what we hoped were even better ones. Terrible destruction happened. And in the middle of dire happenings on all sides, I could not say whether it was for good or ill. I could only wait and see what it all led to. My . . . my dearest friend helped them, and she died doing it. I hope desperately that it was for good. So far it seems to have been."

"Where was this Manland?" asked Bertram in a very gentle voice.

"East of here, well north of Artemisia."

"Then Liny and Mother and I came may have come along the southern edge of it on my way here. We were told to avoid the cities, and we did so. Our people were originally a forest people, part of the Black and White Tribes from the east."

"But you had heard of Artemisia?"

"Some good way south of here, and east. Let's see, settled originally, someone told me, by an association of LIFFs: Librarians, Injuns, Friends, and Feminists."

"Librarians? Really? I didn't know that about the original settlers, but I should have guessed at it. There were places called 'burns' still scattered around, but people there know enough to stay away from them. The walkers were beings that created burns every time they stood still. I'm surprised nobody told Villy's man."

"Oh, Gurge or Garge had been told, but he thought they were using the threat to hide treasure. He was that kind of man. Never believed anything, always supposed that the other man had some ulterior motive for his warning. Gurge could talk the leg off a lamb without the creature knowing it was gone. You could follow Gurge's trail by the three-legged sheep left limping around behind him, not one of them with any idea what had happened. Unfortunately, he usually talked himself into the same kind of situations. Poor Gurge never gave himself a chance, according to Ma, and of course he passed his death on to Villy."

Abasio nodded to himself. "So, since then, anyone coming into Gravysuck is supposed to be bringing monsters or changing people into them, that right?"

"If they're strangers, that's more or less it." Bertram placed a friendly hand on Abasio's, and Abasio surprised himself by gripping it strongly. Yes. They would be friends. He had not had a true male friend with only two legs for a very long time.

"Now, getting back to business," said Bertram. "I can make you some trousers for the babies, wool linings and canvas outside, I can treat the canvas with beeswax. Make it pretty well waterproof. Then you can dump all that water and have less weight in the wagon, and—"

"Abasio!" Xulai spoke from the door she had opened just a crack, her voice suspiciously sweet. "We have visitors."

Abasio put on his meeting-questionable-strangers smile and went outside. There, shifting nervously from foot to foot, were three men and three women, with Willum behind them, dancing up and down in joyous expectancy. He cried, "They come to see the sea-babies, Basio. My ma and pa, Aunty Enna and Unka Gum, Lorp and Aunty Liz."

Abasio went to the wagon and brought out two sleepy babies. The three couples stood at a distance. One baby woke up and put a thumb in its mouth.

"Oooh," said Ma. "It's a *tweety baby*." She turned to Xulai. "May I feel its hair?"

"His hair," said Xulai. "That's Bailai: a boy. The other is Gailai: a girl."

"Ooh," twittered Liz, "how can you? I mean they don't have . . . there's no . . . How do you know which is which?"

"They actually have two legs," said Abasio. "The legs fit together closely when they're swimming. They'll learn to walk before long, and it will be more obvious. Also, Bailai seems to have a little red in his hair, as I did when I was younger. And when Gailai is older . . ."

"The girl will have . . . ?" Aunty made a curving gesture toward her chest.

"We believe so, yes," said Xulai. "Except for the arrangement of the legs and the gills along their sides, everything else is completely human." She did not mention the extensive rearrangement of internal organs discovered by the doctor in Tingawa. "Since these babies are the first ones, we're not completely sure how early they will mature. They're doing what completely human babies do at the same ages, so we're guessing about age fifteen or so." She put on her own "let's be friendly" smile. "I was about to put on some tea. Would you like a cup?"

Abasio left Xulai serving tea and cookies to Ma, Aunty, and Liz— their stock of cookies was running very low. As Bernard later informed him, a sibling of a parent was a named person, as were Aunty Liz and Unka Gum. Liz and Gum were siblings of Pa or Ma, Gum's wife was Aunty, or Aunty Enna, but Lorp had not been accorded the "uncle" because, so Abasio gathered, the others, including Aunty Liz, did not consider him family. What was immediately more important was that Ma was cuddling Gailai and Aunty was rocking Bailai, and Liz was passing cookies. Both the babies had gone back to sleep. Pa, Gum, and Lorp stood apart, Lorp muttering and waving his hands about.

Willum had worked his way around to Abasio and now tapped him on the arm, whispering, "Uncle Lorp thinks they're monsers. He said so. That's why my ma made him come along. He just told Pa they'd die, like that other one did that got borned before."

"I heard about that, but I don't think that's going to happen," Abasio said. "The babies are almost a year old; they're very healthy, they're almost weaned, and they're growing fast. When we get to the ocean, down below Artemisia, they'll probably start eating seafood, that is, fish and seaweed, things right out of the ocean."

"Give 'em back the damn horse," shouted Pa suddenly, yelling it into Lorp's face. "You are all the time getting us into trouble, Lorp. You and your prophecies and your shapist sillyness! Tryin' t'kill that traveling lady just because she had earrings on! Now this nonsense! None a' us care 'f yer a Lorpian or a crawdad! We're going to give them back their horse, and you're going to be shut about it, and if I hear any more about it out of your mouth, it'll be the last thing you say!"

"Wow," whispered Willum. "Pa don't let go very often, but when he does, look out!"

Pa stood at the top of the hill, waving his arm. In a moment someone came out of the town, leading Kim's horse.

"Meet him halfway," said Abasio to Kim, and Kim started down the hill. When they met, the reins were handed over, and Kim brought white-footed, mostly black Socky to rejoin Blue and Rags. The ladies from Gravysuck had finished the obligatory cup and were preparing to leave. Xulai waved them farewell, with smiles, but Ma looked around, searching. "Where's Willum?"

Everyone looked. No Willum. "Did he go back to the town?" Abasio asked.

"Must've," said Ma. "That boy's gone more than he's anywhere. He'll show up for supper. Seldom if ever he misses supper."

THAT NIGHT, WITH KIM, THE babies, and the horses asleep, Xulai and Abasio met with Bertram in his cavern, entered from the shop basement through a narrow slot in the mountain. Air moved freely through the space, making the candle in the lantern flicker. The first space they came to was empty and uninteresting, a cave, merely a vacancy in the stone, but a narrow and twisting crevasse led them to a second, very different cavern. It was huge, high, echoing, and filled with transparent cases of books. One of the cases had been unsealed, the others were misted inside with gray vapor. Bertram confessed to having opened the one.

"That case held the inventory, and also it had the book about the wet suit," he said, pointing. "When I opened the case, the gas inside came out. I wouldn't have opened it except that I had more gas canisters, so I knew I could refill it when I put the books back. Strictly speaking, I shouldn't have opened the case even so. But, since I knew I could reseal it, I decided I could at least take a look at the case that had the inventory in it."

"Are there more of these places?"

"Book repositories? Oh, yes, wherever there are Volumetarians."

"They're books about the oceans," said Xulai, who had been looking more closely at the books in the open case. "They're scientific books, full of graphs and charts and mathematics. Gracious. I wonder if my people know about all this."

"Would they understand them?" asked Bertram eagerly. "I've wanted someone to come who could understand them. Or someone who would take them to someone who would understand them."

"Oh, yes. That's exactly what my people in Tingawa do," said Xulai. "Bertram, keep your secret just a few months more while I arrange for people to come. They have arranged for all the information to be kept in a form that will still be accessible when the waters have risen. Would all the Volumetarians want their books to be copied?"

"Copied? You mean, written down?"

"It's easier than that," said Abasio. "They have machines with eyes. The eyes look at each page and store all the information that's on it. It goes as fast as the machine can turn the pages."

Bertram's face lit up and he heaved an enormous sigh. "How wonderful. I've thought of it over and over. If I can be sure there are people coming, I'll seal up the little slot we came in through—make it look like a natural fall, you know. Then, when the people get here, they can go in and copy them all. I'll give them the list of my kindred and friends, each of them will give others, and so on until all of them are reached. None of us have the complete list. There were times when that just wasn't wise. But when that's done, all of us Volumetarians can quit living like hermits!"

"There's someone you're interested in?" asked Xulai.

He blushed. "There is a girl in Asparagoose . . ." He sighed. "We're sworn not to reveal to anyone outside the fold, as it were, that we are Volumetarians."

Abasio asked, "Do you have any idea what the rest of the books are about?"

"There are sections on everything. Astronomy through zoology. Everything."

They slipped back the way they had come. "Would you like our help in sealing it up?" Abasio asked. "The fact that you seemed friendly with us may stir up some talk; it could lead to troublemakers hanging about."

Bertram lifted his lantern, pointing to the pile of stone next to the crevasse entry. "The ones on top are the ones that go on the bottom," he said. "I thought it'd make it quicker, putting them back. It shouldn't take us any time at all."

While Xulai held the lantern, they stacked the stones, mostly a matter of tumbling the large stones down and tossing the small bottom ones on the top. Repiling was obviously easier than unpiling had been. When they were finished, the pile looked like several others around the walls of the cavern. As they were about to leave, Xulai stopped. "Footprints," she said. In the lantern light, their footprints led straight to the pile of stone.

"I'll get a broom," said Bertram, leaving them momentarily.

"Strange," said Abasio to Xulai. "Bertram, I mean. So . . . unlike the other inhabitants of Gravysuck. It's almost as though he belongs somewhere else."

"Place I was before, it wasn't that different from here," said Bertram, returning. "But a long time ago, I opened one of the cases there and started reading the books in it. I read almost every book in it, and it was a big, big case. Fiction, the books were called. Stories. It's like I'd lived the lives of hundreds of other people, you know. I believe it would be hard to be just a Gravysucker or a Saltgoshian or a Burned-Hatter once you've done that."

Abasio, thinking of the wonders of the library helmet that he had hidden in the wagon, knew exactly what he meant, and so did Xulai. Olly had given him her helmet before she left. She had been given it by one of Artemisia's librarians. They had received the helmets originally, so they said, from helpful creatures who had come from some other place or time or universe. In any event, Abasio had taken his helmet all the way to Tingawa, where the babies were born. There a scientist named Savanker Kyn Dool had found not only that the Tingawan labs could duplicate it, but also that new, empty helmets made exactly like the sample one were able to access the same information source as the original helmets. In addition, they were waterproof. When humanity was at last consigned only to the sea, their books could go with them. Savanker Kyn Dool was the same man who had given them the key to making humans and other creatures "seaworthy."

Bertram was very busy for the next several days. Willum came and went and came again, often bringing others with him, children and adults, to watch the babies swimming in the nearby pond among the trees, to play with them under Xulai's watchful eyes. Willum was uniformly gentle and playful with the babies—he said they were pretty much like baby goats and sheep, except for being wet—and they soon adored him. Lorp (who, it turned out, had taken his name from the Lorpist sect) was still trying to convince the village that Abasio and Xulai and their children were "monsers," but he made very little headway against the babies' chortles, grins, and happy splashes.

Xulai, using the Tingawan far-talker that had been installed in their wagon, spent most of one night reaching her friend Precious Wind, who was traveling toward them and was now somewhere southeast of Artemisia. Precious Wind had far more practice in using the device—which, like most devices, ancient or modern, had its quirks—and she in turn reached the appropriate people in Tingawa and reported back that they were sending a mission from the University to record all the books in Bertram's hoard and getting his list of Volumetarians so they could record everything that existed in print. On hearing this, Bertram burst into tears and hugged both Abasio and Xulai repeatedly, confessing brokenly that he could not forgive himself for having been rude to the lovely children. Xulai patted him into a semblance of poise and forgave him yet again.

Later Xulai told Abasio, "I told Precious Wind about the Lorpians. They haven't shown up in her area, not yet at least. She has several groups well started along the coast down there, and she feels they can continue the work without her. Most of the people down there can actually see the water rising; they're not skeptical. So she's decided to head back in our direction to be with us in case we meet up with a Lorpian threat. She'll meet us in Artemisia, and according to the map, it's just two valleys and a pass away!"

Abasio nodded, glad of it. Xulai had been lonely for female companionship. She had actually borne the bulk of the "fatedness" they shared. It was she who had borne the children, she who nursed them, she who did most of the caring for them. Having Precious Wind with her once more would give her some help and make him feel far less guilty. Not guilty of anything in particular, just for existing in a kind of not-particularly-helpful male matrix of some kind. Being the one responsible for constant alertness to danger and constant readiness to meet it did not qualify as "doing something." This journey had for both of them been an isolated, anxious, sometimes angry time—angry not at each other, but infuriated by certain villagers. Or sometimes reduced to hidden laughter.

A schoolmaster had explained to them: "Y'see, when there gets t'be 'nuff a' that water, see, it'll all run t'the bottom, see, and the earth 'll just float on it, see, with the north half outta the water an' we're not worried 'cause we're on the north half!"

When Xulai had asked which way was the bottom, it was carefully explained that all the maps showed which way was up and which way was down. The south was down because it was heavier and water always ran downhill. The village schoolmaster had been delighted to explain the matter to them and delighted to calm any fears their visit might have occasioned. He was quite, quite sure they were far enough north to be above the waterline.

That village had not been dangerous. Other villages were dangerous, but Xulai and Abasio had been warned. They'd known. The constant abrasion of implacable ignorance and focused animosity had not yet rubbed through their defenses, but the everlasting watchfulness had been extremely wearying. That night, soothed by the fact that Precious Wind would soon be with them, Abasio totally relaxed into sleep. He dreamed once again of the not-Lom place. It was the Plethrob dream. He paid attention. Maybe this time he could make sense of some of it . . .

And in the morning, Abasio awoke suddenly with the whole dream firmly in mind. It stayed with him for at least ten seconds. Then he realized what had awakened him was Bailai, loudly shouting his first word: "Il-lum. ILLUM. ILLUM."

Beside him, wrenched from sleep, Xulai burst into tears.

"There, there, dear," said Abasio to Xulai, holding her closely while she wept. "Come, come, sweetheart. I know you expected them to say 'Mama' or 'Papa,' or 'Dada' or whatever, but since we don't address one another by those names, it was illogical for us to expect that the babies would read our minds. We do address Willum as 'Willum' frequently, and Willum is far more ubiquitous than we! He's in constant motion. He's noisy. He brings people who bring treats and toys. He is unfailingly amusing. We, on the other hand, are merely part of the environment."

"I was looking forward to their saying 'Mama.'" She wept.

"Now, now, dear heart. I don't call you 'Mama,' Willum doesn't call you 'Mama.' They will say something like 'Oolai,' because that's what they've heard. Oolai and Baso probably. You'll grow sick of hearing it soon enough." He believed what he said, then during the rest of the day tried to remember how he knew that.

The next day Gailai's first word was "Oolai," and by evening Xulai knew that Abasio had been right. Gailai said it: within hours, Bailai said it, then shouted it, and very soon they were both shouting it at every opportunity.

"Lug them over to the pond, will you, Willum?" said Abasio, his ears ringing.

"Drown them," muttered Xulai.

"Don't think they drown," said Willum thoughtfully. "Y'want me to try?"

"She was joking, Willum!"

"Oh, fiddle, 'Basio. I know that," said Willum, with the scorn of which only a very bright child is capable. Abasio, as a matter of fact, recognized the tone as one he himself had sometimes used. As a child.

"It's time to wean them," Xulai announced. "They're teething. They bite! Remind me what the people in Tingawa said I was to feed them. We've only given them fruit and vegetables . . ."

Abasio recalled the instructions: "Anything we eat, a tiny bit at a time, mashed up. Not too much of any new thing, at first, and easy on the seasonings."

Some days passed. The children grew fond of eggs. And crackers. And leaves and moss and insects. Willum carried a damp handkerchief about with him for wiping out mouths. The people of Gravysuck grew familiar with the concept that the waters were indeed rising. Several young people announced their intention of traveling to Wellsport, to see about taking part in the future. Xulai began to look less weary and laugh more often. Kim rode off to find reputed horse breeders, here and there, but could not locate another team of horses.

They had become too well accepted to suit at least one villager. Arising from bed and leaving the wagon one morning, Abasio almost tripped over a body stretched out on the ground, near where the horses were grazing. Lorp. Lorp with a knife in his hand and a horseshoe-shaped depression in his skull. He was quite cold.

"Tried to cripple me," said Blue. "Came around midnight, but had to do a little bragging about it first. Leanin' up against me, tellin' me what he intended to do. Man got kind of startled when I told him I didn't like the idea. Mighta managed to cut me if he hadn't had to call me names first. 'Cordin' to him, only HYUman shapes're allowed to talk."

"He had to call you a monster, I suppose," said Abasio mildly.

He pointed the body out to Willum, calling his attention to the knife. Willum said matter-of-factly, "Ayeh. That's his knife." He went to summon the family.

No one wept, not even Liz. "Notcher fault," Liz told Abasio. "Not t'horse's fault neither. He'uz allus a mean'un, Lorp. Allus was. Glad I din't have to killum m'ownself. I was 'bout ready t'killum! Musta bin crazy t'marry that'un."

After an appropriate silence, Abasio said to Willum, "Bertram finished the jackets and pajamas and shirts for the little ones yesterday. The children wore the pajamas last night, slept well, and they didn't show any sign of drying out." He turned to Kim, who'd been waiting for his instructions. "Kim, your horse is well rested. You can ride on toward Saltgosh early tomorrow morning. We will follow you an hour or two later. Saltgosh is the last town before we go over Findem Pass and down into Artemisia—the last one on the road, at any rate. Bertram goes down to Flitterbean and Asparagoose fairly regularly, he has promised to serve as our recruiter there, and that leaves us free to take the northern route and stop in the village of Odd Duck. Leave sign if you see anything we should look out for, and we'll see you each evening, as usual. Ask Bertram if he has anything to send his sister Liny, and if he does, either put it in the wagon or carry it with you. She lives in Saltgosh."

He turned back toward Willum. "Tell the folks in Gravysuck we're moving on tomorrow, Willum. It'll take me most of today to get rid of the water tank and plug up the drain holes in the bottom of the wagon. In this dry air, the floor should dry out in a few days. The map says the stream runs along the road all the way to the Findem Pass. Would anyone know if that's true on the north road?"

"Oh, it's true," said Willum. "Gum goes to Saltgosh ever' year, and he says the river from there runs down both ways. Like it splits there, or something. And, I heard from one a' the wagon men there's a little creek starts up pretty quick on the other side a' the pass, too."

Abasio nodded. "The map says there's a little lake about a half day's travel down on the downhill side, so we can actually get by without even filling our drinking-water tank as we travel uphill."

Willum gave him a long, searching look, and loped down toward town.

"I'm almost out of cookies," said Xulai. "We've used up all the ones we brought along, and I can't bake cookies over a campfire."

Bertram had been listening. "When you get to Saltgosh, you'll be seeing my sister Liny. She and a dozen or so of her women friends do all kinds of catering things for Saltgosh, and they'll be glad to bake hundreds and hundreds of cookies. You seem to use a lot of them . . ."

"Tea and cookies. That's the way we do it in every village. Even if people don't want to hear about the inundation, they'll come along for the tea and cookies."

"Ah. I see." He gave her a saddened look, turned it toward Abasio, and asked plaintively, "I shall miss your being here. It has been . . . a friendly time. Do you, perchance, have any idea when the mission from Tingawa might arrive?"

"It's already fall," Abasio mused. "We'll reach them as soon as possible, and if the ships have a good wind, they'll get into Wellsport about thirty days after that."

Xulai nodded. She thought the earliest they could be here would be late winter or spring. The people from Tingawa might travel faster, but their speed might depend on the weight of their equipment. *But if they* use ul xaolat *to jump them here once they're across the sea* . . . "Bertram, it could be as soon as a month or two, depending upon how they come."

He sighed. "Now that I know it's not for my whole life, it's silly that a few months can seem so long."

"It'll be sooner than you'd expect," said Abasio. "When they get here, ask them to use their far-talker—the device we told you about—to reach Xulai. We're very interested in what happens."

"Abasio . . . ?" Bertram seemed to be fumbling for words.

Abasio gave him a sympathetic look. "What is it, Bertram? Something we can do?"

"If I . . . if the books are all taken care of and I don't have to keep the Volumetarian Oath anymore, and if my friend in Asparagoose—her name is Mirykel, pronounced like the *miracle* she is, but not spelled that way—if she says yes . . . I mean, if she does, and well . . . where should we travel to, to get the best chance at sea-eggs?"

Abasio grinned widely. He had already spent considerable time regretting being separated from Bertram. If one ignored fathers-in-law and grandfathers-in-law—which one sometimes had to do to save one's sanity—he had not had a close male friend since he left certain gang members in the city, years ago—and even they had not been . . . well, not fellow thinkers. Or thinkers of any description. If Bertram traveled to Wellsport, chances were good Abasio would see him there.

"Go to Wellsport!" he cried. "I'll give you a letter to the distribution people there and Xulai and I will give you two sea-eggs. Put them in a safe place. Do not use them until you're at the Sea Duck. They are not like a bird's egg, they're solid, they seemingly keep for years. The people at Sea Duck should know where we are, and we're sure to see you there at some time. You and . . ."

"Mirykel."

"You and Mirykel should go as soon as you can. Is she . . . younger than you? Good! The whole purpose, of course, is to give sea-eggs to those who can have children. And be sure you visit Mirykel frequently, because I'm counting on you to get some of the young people from her village ready to travel to one of the Sea Ducks. It may be that from there, the nearest would be the one south of Artemisia. Sea Duck Three. You've heard everything we have to say, you can do the telling for us."

Bertram's eyes lighted up. "Oh, yes, I mean to do it, Abasio. And Mirykel will help. She's a wonderful woman. None of this Lorpian stuff about her."

"Lorpian?"

"You didn't catch that? They never called him 'Uncle,' they called him 'Lorp' because he was a Lorpian, a follower of Akra Vechun Lorp. He's the Great High Shapist!"

Abasio shook his head, not getting it.

Bertram said patiently: "A man named Akra Lorp—he actually calls himself 'the Great Lorp'—started a Shapist sect. He uses as his authority one of the old books in which it is said that God made man in the image of God. Some of us call him Aggravation Lorp. Whatever we call him, he says anything a man does to change his shape, that's heretical. That's where Lorp got all that Shapist stuff he was preaching."

"Change his shape?"

"Well, you know . . . for instance, girls. They acquire bosoms. Though I've never understood it, no tailor is unaware of the fact that there seemed to be great dissatisfaction attending this acquisition. Either the bosoms are not thought large enough, or they're too large, or they . . . droop. Accordingly, women create—sometimes doing it themselves and sometimes it has been known for a tailor to do it—fancy underwear to hold themselves up or make them more . . . protrusive. This is not such a great matter in these villages where anatomy is taken for granted, but in the more sizable towns, well, you know: the greater the population, the greater the number of silly people. According to the Great Lorp, bosom stitchery is heretical. Or if a man loses a leg, that's a sign God's cast him out; and if somebody makes him a peg leg, well, that's heretical. Or if a man puts on a wide belt to pull his belly in."

"So the Great Lorp's God has breasts?"

Bertram flushed the glossy red-brown of well-oiled mahogany. "Well if God made both sexes, I assume that meant he had all the requisite patterns in stock. It never made any sense to me, Abasio. But that's where all that monster stuff is coming from. Just so you'll be informed."

While Bertram was available, Abasio asked if he would look over the map and give his opinion as to the northern route.

"Odd Duck. Oh, yes, we came through there on the way here. Nice little place, rather isolated, though not that far from Saltgosh, a one-day, maybe one-and-a-half-day trip, I should think. Of course, it was around eight years ago, but I don't suppose it has changed much. It's named for a peculiar long-beaked water bird that visits the chain of ponds down that valley and supposedly has never been seen anywhere else. They fly south in winter, but usually not this early, so do take the opportunity to see them."

Xulai had used the time they were near Gravysuck, which had orchards, gardens and fields, flocks of chickens, and various animals, to replenish their supplies of dried and preserved meat, legumes, grains, and fruits, dried or preserved, as well as a food new to her: various dry shapes made from flour, water, and eggs that, she was assured, "kep' practical f'rever." Willum's mother had showed her how to boil the shapes until they were rather soft, then put them in a sauce made mostly from a local vine fruit, a large, rather soft red one called, for some unremembered reason, Tom's toes, which could be used either fresh or dried. There were great racks of them baking in the sun down in Gravysuck—and Xulai bought a goodly supply of the dried ones. Sausages could be added to the sauce, so she purchased sausage as well, along with a very hard cheese that lasted well and could be grated into other foods. Since they were assured of clean water at least as far as Findem Pass, they could keep the wagon weight down on the uphill trail.

To pass the time and keep her muscles working, Xulai always gathered field herbs, nuts, fruits, and roots along their way as they traveled. Some they could use themselves, some were for chickens, some few for Blue and Rags, who enjoyed certain fleshy roots but hadn't the ability to dig them up.

Traveling in coops on the roof of the wagon—coops that were moved under the wagon at night—the chickens would yield a few eggs most days. Redshanks had a coop of his own to which he retreated at sunset, as the hens did to theirs, and all the coops had secure doors that Abasio was careful to close and latch to keep them safe at night. The owls of the region were huge, feather-horned creatures that could lift a chicken or a rooster with no trouble at all, and whatever scratching about the poultry did in the pen sometimes set up for them during the day, they always returned to their coops under the wagon at dusk as though well aware of the risk.

In very cold weather the area under the wagon could be warmed at night by enclosing it within a wagon skirt. The smokestack ran across the bottom of the wagon before ascending at the back corner of it. With a slow fire in the little ceramic stove inside the wagon, and the wagon skirt hung on little hooks screwed into the floor, the area beneath the wagon stayed much warmer than the outside air. Now that the drain holes in the wagon floor had been closed, the area under the wagon would be dry once more, so Abasio moved the wagon skirts to a place he could reach easily. Likely nights on the heights of the pass above Artemisia would be considerably cooler.

They set out before cockcrow, leaving the chicken coops to be uncovered later, when it was warmer. The village was still. They went through it quietly, even the rooster lulled by the familiar motion of the wagon.

Xulai murmured, "I thought Willum might stay up all night so he could say good-bye."

Abasio smiled. "He may have tried to do just that, and fallen soundly asleep around midnight."

Beyond the village, scattered farms would take the place of the huddled houses; the little tavern with its oasthouse out back; the tiny general store, resupplied at intervals by traveling merchants and local farms who raised special crops; the mill with its creaking wheel; the tiny open-fronted chapel or shrine dedicated to a goddess presumably of vegetation and sheep, for her body was made up entirely of the former (pumpkin belly, melon breasts, sheaves of grain for arms and legs) and she was clad in wool. Willum had identified one little building as the school where all children were taught by Ma Garney. Everyone learned to read and write. Some families even had books, for in addition to the big wagons that came by two or three times a year to stock the little village stores, peddlers also came through every now and then. Bertram had standing orders from suppliers in the east, and they included a few books as well as paper and ink to sell. Willum's school had a dictionary, half a dozen books (which Willum knew by heart), and a few maps of the surrounding countryside. It had a book of poetry, too, and Ma Garney taught them how to make verses and songs.

Most of the buildings were of stone, some roofs shingled with cedar splits, some thatched with reeds or straw. Any wagon that went into the forest for wood or nuts or wild mushrooms to dry picked up a few angled stones on the way home; stones suitable for building formed a considerable hillock at the edge of the village, there for the use of anyone who needed to repair a chimney or a wall. Some barns and sheds were laid up in earth brick that was replastered with mud each summer, and these had wide eaves to drain the water well away from the walls, walls in many cases invisible behind huge stacks of wood cut for winter fires.

Sheep and goats were grazing in stubbled grain fields that had been harvested of oats, wheat, corn, and barley, their dung fertilizing the ground for next year's crop. The orchards had been stripped of pears and apples; the fruit preserved or dried or stored away in lofts. Plums and cherries had ripened earlier, and they, too, had been dried or preserved. In sunny places on the south sides of barns and houses, dried Tom's-toes vines rattled in their conical trellises among the drying melon vines, all to be raked up and added to this year's compost pile along with the barn cleanings. This year's pile was one of five, next to last year's pile and piles for two, three, and four years ago. The well-rotted four-year-old pile would be dug into the gardens next spring. In places where the soil was light and sandy, the trenches from which potatoes had been dug awaited spring replanting. Along the stream there were several small rice paddies, now drained for the winter. Rice, said Willum's mother, was finicky stuff—all that sprouting in advance and handwork to plant it, but it was traditional for one local family who, legend had it, had been "different" when they settled in Gravysuck. That had been generations ago, and though they now looked just like everyone else, they still grew rice and traded some of the grain for things they did not grow.

By the time roosters began crowing from distant farmyards, they had left the village and the close-in farms behind and had passed an evil-smelling gray swamp with a strange, angular construction on its far side, the whole surrounded by stiff, rattling reeds that carried faded, lilylike blooms. Redshanks, traveling in his covered cage, saw fit to answer the dawn challenges of the distant cocks with a muffled response. As Abasio climbed onto the wagon seat to uncover his cage, he saw tears on Xulai's cheeks.

"Oh, love. What?" he asked.

"It's just so peaceful and perfect and fruitful and . . . well kept. And it's all going to be gone."

"I know." He reached for her hand and held it tightly in his own.

"There's pastures beneath the sea," sang Rags. "Planted for you and for me. If we all behave, then beyond the grave, there's pastures beneath the sea."

"Good merciful heavens, Mare, what are you on about," said Blue. "You sound like that humanish choir in Gravysuck!"

"They were singing it down in Gravysuck. I wandered down to listen."

"Really, Ragweed?" cried Xulai. "Who got them started on that?"

The horse said thoughtfully, "Willum, I think. He and his ma make up songs. He plays a whistle kind of thing, too, with holes down the sides, and another thing like a . . . what is that thing with strings, Xulai? You play on something like it."

"An ondang?"

"I think Willum calls his a bango; he bangs on it some," said Blue, taking up the song: "There's pleasures beneath the sea, provided for you and for me. If we behave well we will not go to hell, we'll have pleasures beneath the sea."

"A boy of many talents." Abasio grinned. "Is the local religion one that speaks a good deal about hell?"

"Oh, horse apples," said Ragweed. "That's just some Lorpian idea. People don't really believe in it. They figure stuff like that was made up by some cult or other that wanted to control how people acted. You can get rich if you control enough people, they say."

By midmorning they had left the last scattered farms behind them. Only a distant croft here and there, a cluster of sheep on the hillside, a skein of smoke from a charcoal burner's fire, told them people were settled on the land. By noon they were in a forest, mixed evergreens and hardwoods, freckled with sunlight and a-flicker-twitter with the cries of birds and the peripatetic scurry of small creatures. The stream ran along beside them, larger than it had been near Gravysuck, for it had been joined by several streamlets on the way. The horses suggested a rest and drink, to which Abasio readily agreed: "Next opening where we can get at the water."

It came up soon, a long swale cutting through the forest from higher land on the left down to a winding and widening meadow on the right where the stream ran into a sizable pool fringed with reeds and tall flowering plants before leaving it to meander across a small meadow. The road split ahead of them, an old signpost at the parting directing them east to Saltgosh and Findem Pass; south by west to Asparagoose and Flitterbean.

"Break time," said Xulai. The babies had been angels all morning, sitting quietly, watching the world go by, comfortable in their traveling suits. By now the suits would need washing out, and the pasture near the pond would be a good place to do it. Blue and Ragweed trundled the wagon down to the pond. Humans and babies got off. Babies got stripped on the grass and their traveling suits turned inside out to be rinsed out by buckets of water. Then the babies themselves were rinsed by buckets of water before being pitched into the pool, where, with shrieks of joy, they plunged about seeing what they could find.

"Please, not another turtle," said Abasio.

"I just thought," said Xulai, "are there any poisonous water snakes?"

"Historically there were," he said. "I haven't heard of any existing now."

"Then the one Bailai is waving around probably isn't poisonous?"

Abasio turned quickly, dropped his clothes in a flurry, and plunged into the water. Two of his arms grabbed the thick, black reptile, two others grabbed his son, another two his daughter, and with the last two he pulled himself onto the grass. Xulai took the children from the waving tentacles.

"Ut's only a water snake," gargled Willum. "Won't hurt nobody."

He was standing beside Xulai, his eyes like moons, watching Abasio's tentacles pull him slitheringly onto the bank of the pond. He looked up at Xulai. "What'd he do?"

"He changed into an octopus," said Xulai matter-of-factly. "Before one can have a sea-child, one has to change into what Abasio is. The next generation are born with fish tails, like the children. But the first generation comes as a . . . shock."

"Firs' generation. You n' him! You mean you can do like him? Like he did?"

"I can, yes."

"Oh, wow. Could I do that?"

"If we decided to give you a sea-egg, yes."

"I *want* one!"

Abasio slithered toward his hastily flung clothing as he said, "Willum, what in hell are you doing here?"

"I'm off to see the world," said the boy, totally unabashed.

"How did you . . . ?"

"I hid up on top under the canvas, atween the chicken coops. I crawled up in there this mornin', after you fed 'em."

Xulai stared at the wagon top. She and Abasio always tied a canvas over the coops each night, as protection against predators, rain, and wind, though the sides were left partly uncovered for ventilation. Hens did not like being either stifled or wet. There was plenty of room up there for one skinny boy. "We'll have to take him back," said Xulai. "Really, Willum! Your mother will be so worried."

"I awready tol 'er I 'uz goin'. She's the one said hide atween the chicken coops. She's the one said best get it out of my system while I'm young. She told me what kinda people t'look out for. She says most people take pity on young'uns. When I get older, in a year or so, they won't be so nice to me."

Xulai stared at Abasio, who stared back. After a time Xulai mouthed the word "bay-bee ten-der," and waited while Abasio considered it. When he nodded, Xulai breathed deeply and said, "You'll have to work to earn your way."

"I figgered so," the boy said contentedly. "Older those fish tails get, the more trouble they'll be. I knew you'd need help." He turned curious eyes on Abasio, head tilted at the writhing eight-legged form for a long, long moment. "Y'gonna eat that snake or let it go?"

CHAPTER 4

Saltgosh Music

THE WORLD WAS EMPTY OF PEOPLE AND PEOPLE'S doings on the northern road. The widely scattered farms had vanished entirely. Valley led into valley, the river to the right of the road dwindling as they climbed. Tributary brooklets wriggled down from the left into the road ruts, gargling beneath the wheels before slipping away on the downhill side. Each evening they camped by running water and fell asleep to sedative night sounds: *slup-plip* of ripples; intermittent *ri-i-i-p* of grass torn by grazing horses; drowsy rustles from the chicken coops under the wagon; the fluting *hoo-whoo-hoos* of hunting owls as counterpoint to the erratic, echoic piping of bats. If it had not been for Willum, the days would have been even quieter: the plop of hooves into dry dust, the sigh of a breeze through tall, dried grasses, crisply sequential beats from invisible wings. Ducks, Abasio thought. Ducks or crows; both had distinguishable wing sounds, sharp and purposeful and far more rhythmic than the other wings they occasionally heard. What else could they be but wings? Out of utter silence, a *whooosh*, then a long, long silence, and then again *whooosh* . . . from somewhere. Of course, Willum transformed every tranquil moment into one of imminent peril.

As Willum yodeled it: "Too much nothing!" with the *ing, ing, ing, ing* coming back from all sides like the resonance of a huge bell.

"Hush, Willum," snarled Xulai.

Which he did, for perhaps four or five wheel revolutions. When Willum could be silenced, if only briefly, they could hear other things, particularly an anonymous cooing that seemingly arose from the depths of the black and featureless forests farther away. The cooing didn't come *from* anywhere. Abasio remembered pigeons from his youth. They had inhabited the barn as though by right and had made similar sounds. Softly insinuating. Sugary sweet. The barn sounds had not, as these sounds did, raised the hairs on the back of his neck or set his eyes searching for a defensible position. Thinking to dispel childhood terrors, he mentioned it to Xulai. She thrust herself into the circle of his arms, whispering that the sounds frightened her. She hated what she called their "ubiety." She didn't mean ubiquity. Not that they *were from everywhere*. She meant they *could be from anywhere*!

Then, a moment later, with a shaky laugh, she admitted that she might be generating some of the effect herself. In rebellion against the stupefying silence, she had been counting how many echoes each sound evoked. Bailai's shriek of hunger on last waking, she said, had bounced back at her clearly at least six separate times. And, of course, there was Willum's constant racket. The boy generated noise merely by existing. If he wasn't using a stout stick to whack stones off the road, each whack accompanied by a shout, he was making a yodeling search for a new echo—or a new footstep. Shivering deliciously, he claimed he heard footsteps from behind them, or maybe across the valley, or up one of those side hills. "Crunch, crunch, crunch," he yelled. "Something big!"

Neither Abasio nor Xulai had heard anything, but then they had been on the wagon seat, where the rattle-crack of the wheels snapping across fallen twigs would cover other sounds—even a few of Willum's. Asking for, even *insisting on* quiet from Willum had thus far done no good at all.

On what the maps declared would be their last day's journey to Saltgosh, Willum raised his usual noise level by yodeling an unfamiliar song:

"Fahma Donal hadda fahm, see, I seed, I sow ah. Onna fahm he hadda cow, see, I seed, I sow ah. Feeda cow with corn I grow, feed it so the cow will know, moo-moo here and moo-moo there, moo-moo moo-

moo ever'where, see, I seed, I sow ah . . ." as it went on from the cow to the goat and sheep, pig and horse, chickens and geese.

"What does it mean?" asked Xulai, having been unable to decipher either the words or the sense of it.

"It's the bargain song," said Willum. "Din't you ever hear it? Ages old, Ma says. About the bargain the farmer makes with his stock. He grows food and feeds them, they give him eggs or milk or meat in return. He tells 'm, 'See, I seed, I sow all.' Only when ya sing it, it gets kinda what she said, you know, when ya run the words together an make 'em sorta soft?"

"Slurred?"

"Thassit. Gets kinda slurred when ya sing it. Grandma—that's my ma's ma—she says ever child ever was learnt that song, even when they weren't farm people. It wuzz . . ."

"Traditional."

"Like that, yeah."

"Who was Farmer Donal?"

Willum shrugged. "Justa name, she says. Could be Fahma Brewer or Fahma Miller, whatever farmer was aroun' back then. She says ya go back far enough, wuzza time afore there was even cities an' near ever'body was farm folks."

And that gave Xulai something to ponder over: this current age of Earth was not, as she had supposed, new and strange. It was *old* . . . and strange.

The road was double or triple the length the map indicated. Every straight line on the map was actually a lethargic snake, slowly squirming along the outthrust elbows of the mountain. The map also indicated the village of Odd Duck was a fairly sizable place, but they had almost passed through it before they knew they were there. A short length of fence on their right alerted them, five or six erect posts with most of the connecting rails in place: both rails and posts of that silver-gray, grooved and striated appearance that spoke of long drying. It had been kept standing by a gnarled grapevine, still waving tattered guidons of dried leaf as Willum strained at it, jerking it away before Xulai could stop him. Only then she and Abasio saw what he had seen: the white rib cage, the arm bones thrust through the rails, the neck bones still supporting the front two-thirds of a skull.

Willum, farm-raised, accustomed to butchery, was seemingly unaffected as he cried loudly, "Somethin's bit the back of its head off! Izzit a man or a woman?"

Xulai, unwilling to set an example of weakness, swallowed hard and promised herself a crying fit, later, after she looked at the pelvis. She and Willum searched. There was no pelvis, or any legs. She explained to Willum why that particular bone was needed for sexual differentiation, pleased to note that her voice stayed reasonably level when screaming would have been more appropriate. She had been well prepared for rejection and hostility on this journey, but not for . . . whatever this was.

Abasio unhitched Blue and Rags so they could have a look around. Horses, along with dogs, cats, indeed, almost any animal, could often see—or sense—things humans did not, and Blue often offered helpful insights. Now that they knew where they were, they could interpret the fragments of rafter and beam on the dust piles spaced out along the river, the scattered falls of roughly squared chimney stones. The village was now occupied by beavers who had created an extensive waterway along the river, one with several smaller ponds and at least two lodges. Across the river a dozen cows lay chewing their cud at the edge of the forest while an equal number of horses grazed nearby.

Blue had in mind recruiting an additional two-horse hitch, but his mere approach sent all the animals galloping wildly into the cover of the trees. He returned, shaking his head.

"Wanna know why it's called Odd Duck?" he asked. "That pond over there's got a bunch a the oddest ducks I ever saw. Red feathers, beaks like on—what you call those tall ones with long, long necks, Xulai? Ones that eat fish?"

"Herons?"

"Like them. One was out there swimmin' around like a duck, stabbin' down till it got a fish speared on its beak, then it paddled to the edge, waddled out, shook the fish off on the ground. Rest of 'em gathered around, all'v'em pinchin' off bits an' throwin' their heads back to swallow! Odd ducks. Ha."

Willum returned to exploration, scuffling through the fallen houses, calling out his findings. "There's more bones, they got tooth marks, Abasio." He came toward them carrying a human thighbone. "Look here. That's the mark of a dog tooth, that's what Ma calls 'em even though she says no acshul dog'd want the ones we got. And see here, how it slid off the bone, and there's the back teeth."

The marks were clear, a canine tooth that had bitten down, then slipped off the far side of the bone, each tooth imprinted on the bone by a jaw wider than the thigh had been long.

"See the shape a' that jaw," Willum went on. "See, that's not pointy like a bear or a wolf. That curves more like yours and mine, Abasio. See that. But it's big. Lot's bigger'n you." He laid the bone down and went off to see what else he could find, in a few minutes summoning them both to examine a pile of huge dried turds that he was poking at with a long stick, raking out the inclusions: small skulls. "How old'd you say those are, Xulai?" he asked in a suddenly quiet and grieving voice. "Just babies, an't they?"

"About the age of the twins," she said, swallowing horror. "A year or two old."

Willum dropped the stick and was off again, wiping at his cheeks with the backs of his hands. Abasio murmured, "What do you think?"

"I think what you think. I think after Bertram came this way, something else came this way: Giant. Or Troll. Or Ogre. Or something not necessarily human-shaped, but big."

"The giants I met before . . ." He cleared his throat. "They didn't eat people."

"The ones you met before were actors in the whole archetypal village thing. Precious Wind has a saying. *Hunger finds its own meat.*" She stared at the cattle, slowly emerging from among the trees. "Why not the cattle, though?"

"Probably the cattle stayed closer to the trees and could run faster. And did." He purposely did not add, "And do." Instead he cleared his throat, adding, "Cattle and horses can lose themselves pretty well once they get into the forest. They, too, were once wild creatures." He picked up the thighbone and the little skulls, wrapped them, and put them in one of the hidden compartments under the wagon. At some point, he might have to convince someone that he hadn't been seeing things.

Abasio beckoned to Willum and took a last look around while he slowly rejoined them, still searching every corner and pile. They moved leisurely, reminding one another of things that should have warned them: there had been no roads leading away to farms or neighbors; no one had spoken of the village in Gravysuck—except Bertram, but he had been in Gravysuck for fifteen years. Perhaps this destruction had been old news. Or perhaps no one in Gravysuck had known of it.

"No Fahma Donal here," said Willum with finality. "Was once, but he's gone." He paled, head coming up, listening. The cooing again. Rebounding. From every direction. Some of them very close. They all heard it. If a pigeon made that sound, it was a pigeon the size of a very large cow. *Cow elephant,* Abasio thought to himself, remembering books he had seen in Tingawa. Tingawa claimed there were still elephants alive on the mainland west of the islands.

Not far from the ruined village the road made a brief climb, then went down into another, narrower valley that led more nearly eastward. The tumbled stone at the bottoms of the walls on either side had left extravagantly toothy ridges above what appeared and disappeared above the trees, gradually coming closer and closer to one another. Willum once again amused himself shouting and listening to the echoes that volleyed back and forth until Abasio, whose prior nine warnings had been ignored, told him to be silent or be gagged. Xulai remarked sleepily that they seemed to be inside the jaws of some long-snouted monster.

Willum took the remark as possible truth and managed to talk himself, loudly, into a pleasurable panic that would have become even louder had they not emerged from the trees to confront a problem more immediate than being eaten by mountains. Kim stood awaiting them in the middle of the road; Socky grazed on the verge. Not far behind Kim, both river and road disappeared into a gaping hole. Abasio, Willum at his heels, left the wagon to stand as Kim was standing, staring at what confronted them. Xulai, who could see quite well from the wagon seat, did not join them. She was mentally, angrily, reviewing the map they had used in planning this route. *The map had not shown any sign of . . . this barrier.*

The two sidewalls that had been angling toward each other met here, in this pocket of stone. At some much earlier time, someone had made a hole in the pocket. Both road and river emerged from the hole, a notch barely wide enough for the wild riot of water on the right, even less adequate for the road on the left. Abasio peered at the narrow, canted shelf the road occupied, his back rigid with . . . probably terminal annoyance. Xulai heaved a deep breath.

Though the spray obscured all but the nearest bit of the tunnel, Abasio surmised from the way the light fell from above it that the passage rose—not very steeply—then turned abruptly to the left toward another source of light. At that point, presumably, the tunnel had reached the other side of the wall. The tunnel was lit by light falling through jagged gaps from above, enough of it reflected back and forth to have encouraged the growth of a glistening green slickness on every surface.

Kim said, "There's rings set into the wall over the road, Abasio. Metal rings, and they look like they'd hold . . ."

Willum was already peering into the hole. Abasio said, "Willum, I wager you are most surefooted of us. Stay tight against the rock on your left and *do not run*. Find out for us how far this . . . burrow goes—wait!" He turned slowly, peering into the west, his finger to his lips . . .

Xulai whispered, "Abasio?"

He stilled her with a gesture. Then she heard what he had probably heard: a very loud sound quite a way off. Abasio didn't move. They waited: another sound. And another. And another: footsteps.

"It's coming this way," said Abasio, turning. Willum was already gone.

"Wagons have been through here," murmured Blue, his voice shaking. "There are places where the wall is scarred. I think it looks worse than it is. The road's washed to rock, Abasio, no mud . . ."

Willum's treble voice came back to them, the echoes in the notch making him sound like an army. "It's no way a'tall, Abasio. Jus' one long sorta curve, and that's it."

Abasio stuck his head into the notch, calling, "Stay there." He reached up to the hooks high on the left side of the wagon and lifted off two coils of rope, a thin one over his right shoulder, a long, heavy one over his left. He called, "Xulai, you and Kim get the babies through first! Follow me!" He beckoned and she came toward him, one child on each arm. Kim took one from her.

The horses followed, getting as close to the entrance as they could get. Abasio placed the coil of heavy rope against the wall and tied the end of it to a heavy iron ring that formed part of the wagon frame at the right rear corner. "Blue, everything's covered with green slime, and it's slick. Wait here until I get them through . . ."

The huge footsteps were louder.

Abasio felt his way along the left wall. A shallow declivity in the rock wall began a few paces inside the notch, the hollow hidden from the entrance by an almost smooth pillar of stone. A metal ring had been drilled into the wall near the pillar, and there were others along the wall, about shoulder high. He tied the thin line to the first ring and threaded the other end through the other rings he found as he followed Willum. He was trying to do it quickly while counting arm spans of rope, but the footing was as treacherous as Abasio had feared: the road did slope rather steeply upward as well as canting toward the water. Luckily enough light was reflected off the wet surfaces above to let them see where they put their feet.

"It's not a tunnel," Xulai shouted from close behind him, barely audible above the roar of the water. Abasio glanced back. Both she and Kim had one hand on the rope. He nodded. No, it wasn't a tunnel. He thought it likely someone had attempted a tunnel, but at some point while making the initial bore, the wall above it had shattered and dropped huge, sharp-edged chunks into the flow. The metal rings set about head high into the tunnel wall had been there long enough that they were almost totally obscured by the same slick growth that covered the road.

Willum had been right: the wall they penetrated was not a thick one; the notch led south at the point of entry, but it soon angled to the left and emerged pointed southeast. From this point on, the road was level. Abasio tied off the rope handhold and beckoned Xulai past him, and Kim. And Socky, who had very sensibly decided not to wait.

He ran back toward the wagon, one hand on the rope he had strung. Blue and Rags were already inside; both horses were trembling. Abasio heard the crashing sound of approaching footsteps even over the roar of the water. The rocks in the stream sent enough water splashing upward that every stone above them poured like a pitcher. It was like standing under a waterfall. Water streamed down the back of his neck under his collar, onto his bare back, and down, leaving the bottoms of his trouser legs in tributary streams. He dropped two loops of the thick rope around the smooth, pillarlike stone he'd picked, took a position in the declivity behind it that was hidden, he prayed, from the entrance. He pulled the rope tight, calling, "Go, Blue. Take it slow." The wagon was not a full length beyond the pillar before the wheels began to slide toward the water. Abasio braced himself and pulled, keeping the rope tight. The road was barely the width of the wagon, giving him just enough angle to keep the wheels from sliding off. He counted arm lengths of rope as he played them out, mentally counting down from the total he had strung getting to the angle where the road flattened and was not wet! If they could only get past that angle . . .

The crashing of enormous, running feet was loud enough to be heard over the water by the time the front of the wagon reached the angle. At that point, the road flattened instead of canting to the right. Abasio held fast until the wagon end was almost past the angle, then let the rope fall and scrambled along the wall, one hand on the rope through the rings, reaching the wagon just as it angled away. He called Blue to a halt and reached for the knot on the wagon. Having the wagon immobilized by a rope entangled among the rocks would not be a good thing. The knot was wet, impossible. He cursed himself. Wrong type of knot! He knew better! Stupid! He drew his knife and sawed through the rope, held on to the cut end of it, and shouted to Blue, "Go! Go!" as he jumped for the ladder on the left rear corner of the wagon. The few seconds taken up in reaching and passing the angle seemed to last an eternity. Everything was slow. If he'd used the right knot, it would have untied. Maybe. He'd never tried it with wet rope. If he'd had an ax he could have cut the rope more quickly . . . well, next time he'd have an ax. Next time?

The rope in his hand tugged. He dropped it as he would have a snake, watching it. It didn't move, so it hadn't been grabbed, it was just . . . stuck somewhere. He looked over his shoulder; something was blocking the light from the tunnel behind him, but the wagon was well past the angle. There was a sound from behind them, a shout magnified by the tunnel walls as a great howling. The horses shook; Abasio clung to the ladder and called to them, as much to himself as to them, "It can't get in here. Take it easy. Don't panic." The opening was close ahead of them, the walls were smoother, the waters less violently constricted, the road almost completely flat and dry. Some quiet part of Abasio's mind noted that a tunnel had been started from this end and decently cut in a workmanlike manner that continued as far as the turn before being disastrously interrupted.

The horses emerged into sunlight. Abasio had already decided the thin rope would stay where it was, threaded through the iron rings. It made a good handhold, at least, and it would take too long to loosen. Not to mention bringing him within reaching distance of whatever . . . However, several turns of the heavier rope he had tied to the wagon lay at the bottom of the pillarlike stone near the entrance where he had dropped it; the rest of it lay along the wall all the way to the corner and a little past. With the light blocked at the other end, it was unlikely any . . . thing would see it moving. The near end of it was probably far enough on this side of the angle to be invisible from the entrance. Probably . . .

He dropped from the ladder and went back. As he approached the bend, however, he stopped. The tunnel seemed much darker. If he pulled the rope from here, he couldn't be seen, and with so little light, a moving rope couldn't be. Had they seen the wagon and the horses, or merely heard Willum's noise? He stepped back and located two rocks in the river's edge with a narrow slot between them. If he could get down behind them, he would be able to see the entrance at the expense of getting soaked. His feet squelched inside his boots, and he fought down a ridiculous urge to laugh. He could not possibly get any wetter than he already was.

Dropping into a crawl, he went over the edge of the road and down among the rocks that made up the riverbank, cold water now running up his back and sloshing over his shoulders while an endless torrent dropped on his head. It *was* possible to get wetter. He raised his head to look through the slot, staying motionless. The interrupted and jagged hole that served as tunnel entry now contained two faces. No, the entry was now *almost filled* with two faces and parts of shoulders. One of the bodies that came along with the faces must be lying along the road; the other had to be kneeling on the far side of the river, bending forward, the top of its head next to the cheek of its companion. Yes, what he saw beyond the chin of the one to the left was not a pile of rocks. It was a hand. A thumb, really. Just one thumb.

These were not giants as he remembered them from the war at the Place of Power. Those had been big, yes: fifteen to twenty feet tall, their proportions had been in keeping, stocky, thick-legged. They had been very wide, very strong. These were vastly bigger. He solemnly resolved not to pull on the rope if it gave any resistance. A tug-of-war would not be appropriate. The one to Abasio's right had thrust his right hand into the river, feeling its way up the stream. The water, already half blocked by the huge lower arm, became even deeper. The hand at the end of the arm came out of the water, a hand the size of the side of their wagon, and smacked down in irritation, which drove a fountain of icy water upward—into the hugely gaping nostrils of the wide, flat nose. The nose wrinkled.

Abasio wriggled back around the angle, grabbed the end of his rope, and ran. The sneeze caught him halfway along the angle and propelled him out onto the road. He was still holding the end of the rope. Evidently it hadn't caught on anything. Or . . . perhaps the sneeze had made the thing in there . . . drop it. Or . . . it really didn't matter which. No. It really *didn't*.

He got to his feet and plodded out into the sunlight, shivering only partly from the cold. Water was draining from every part of him. He simply stood, incapable of any further action, the rope trailing from his hand. Kim took it from him and began to coil its sodden length onto its usual hook. Abasio was staring, counting: three horses. Blue, Rags, Socky. Correct as to number and name. Four people, including him. One female, one male, one noisy brat, and him. Right. Babies? Must be in the wagon. Otherwise Xulai would be screaming, and she wasn't. Yet. Everyone was here and safe. Maybe safe. Willum and Xulai were staring at him from terrified faces, unspeaking. The horses were visibly trembling—even phlegmatic Blue . . .

Everyone was carefully not asking the question he didn't have an answer to. Can those things at the other end of that notch get in here?

"Good grass," remarked Blue in voice that sounded almost normal. "That'll be nice for a change. *Animals seem to be enjoying it.*"

Momentarily derailed from either fright or fury, Abasio looked past them. Blue was right, as usual: the fields were dotted with grazing animals, sheep, goats, cows, horses; every one of them could hear that howling, but none of them were in a panic, none of them were running. Abasio simply stared at them, his mind frantically scanning for something, anything that would put the enormous faces out of his mind.

What came, ridiculously, was himself, in his dream, hanging above the quiet pool in that dreamworld while the little boy, Crash, asked: "What's bao? Do we got it?"

Why would his subconscious come up with that? Perhaps *bow:*

weapon. Well, yes, but it was also a gesture of respect or subservience, a tied ribbon, half a dog bark. Perhaps it was *bough:* a branch of a tree. Was that helpful? At one time people had carried green boughs as indications that they came in peace. Not helpful. What did the little boy mean? Why was it important? Could it be a magic spell to quell monsters? Silently Abasio answered Crash's question: "What is it? I dunno if we have it. Do we need it? No, to all of the above and *get out of my head!*"

Blue said calmly, "Forest grass doesn't have much flavor, doesn't get enough sun."

Slowly the tower dream evaporated, the giant faces dissolved into mist, and their surroundings penetrated reality. The wagon had emerged into a green, sunlit valley carpeted by rich grasslands, a valley limited on the south by forested mountains and in the near west by a tumulose of low, furzy hills. Abasio turned to look at the wall behind him again. The near side was a sheer vertical wall running from east to west, as far as he could see: a true wall, perpendicular to the valley floor they stood upon, towering above the trees as it disappeared into the west. The only scenario he could think of was that it had been one thick stratum of hard stone, originally laid down horizontally, as a thick sheet of lava, and then improbably thrust up in a vertical wall during that most recent upheaval . . . a thousand years ago, more or less. It could have had softer layers on either side that had since eroded away. Abasio stared at wall, wall at Abasio. He could not estimate the actual thickness. Panic had thickened it, increasing fear; fear thinned it, lessening good sense. Did it matter? It was high enough, thick enough, and strong enough to keep those things out. Otherwise, *as Blue kept trying to tell him,* all these placidly grazing animals would be in complete panic.

If the tunnel had been completed as started from this end, if it had been made neatly, smoothly cut all the way through, then the things on the other side could have crawled through long since. One at a time, of course. If the workmen had done a good job, the giants would be in here right now eating his family. However, the notch was anything but neat or smooth. The opening extended all the way to the top of the wall, projected in splintered fangs of rock that interlocked viciously with others from the far side. Preventing the giants from getting through. And obviously they couldn't climb the wall. And if one of them tried to crawl through, its body would block the water. Probably neither one of them liked water up its nose.

Xulai, Kim, and Willum were waiting for Abasio to acknowledge being alive. They weren't going to do/say/think/decide anything until he did. When he finally blinked owlishly at them, they were evidently . . . reassured, though Abasio was . . . not.

"When I got here and saw that," Kim said, choking on the words as he waved at the notch, "I thought you might need help with the wagon, so I waited. Didn't expect . . . the other thing."

Willum could hold himself no longer. He shouted, "Wuz it giants, 'Basio?"

Willum's question was answered by a shout/cry/yell, something-or-other kind of furious sound issuing from the tunnel. As Abasio had feared, the cry was one of hunger along with the anger/frustration. He did not trust himself to speak. He merely held up two fingers. When his breathing slowed, he said, "Willum, if you don't keep your mouth shut, they'll probably follow the sound here. I'm going to give you to them. They can eat you first!"

Turning to Xulai, he murmured, "The livestock in those fields wouldn't be there if those creatures hunted in here. They evidently can't get through there."

Xulai, forcing herself to stop shaking, had spread her cloak along one side of the wagon and fastened it there to dry. Now she took Abasio's to the other side while Abasio sat on the wagon step to strip off his outer clothes and boots. Barefoot, cursing, he stepped into the wagon, dried himself, put on dry underclothes and trousers, and came out to take towels and brushes to the horses. They were still shivering, only partly from being soaked with very cold water, a state that was not improved by Abasio's continuous, fluent, polysyllabic damnation of map makers who'd had the stupidity, malfeasance, and egregious unprofessionalism not to bother indicating either this barrier or the fact that there were giants on the prowl. There was a taxable city beyond this point, he muttered. The map had been provided by the tax-hogs. *They had to have been here! They had to have seen this road!* Were tax collectors predation-proof? There was no excuse for it! He choked, gargled, stopped to clear his throat and breathe. Breathing felt . . . pleasant. He bit his tongue and went on breathing.

Certainly this valley gave no evidence of predation. The trees were alive with birdsong. River and road wound peacefully down toward them from the east, the road swerving back and forth in languid S's as it paralleled the north side of the river's meanders.

Abasio held out his hands. They were still trembling. Willum was pouring questions from an uncountable store, but for the moment he was not yelling them. Of course, he hadn't seen giants. Abasio wished he hadn't seen them either. He was not allowed to forget, for Xulai asked, "What did they look like?"

"All I could see were faces."

"And?"

Abasio shook himself like a dog. "I need a dry shirt."

Xulai busied herself finding a dry shirt, socks, and shoes for Abasio; she had already put dry blankets around the babies. Though it was clear to everyone who had been around the children for any length of time that they did not feel cold as Xulai and Abasio did, she was unable to convince herself the babies were not in frequent and perpetual need of dry blankets. Xulai would put blankets on fish, so Willum said. Abasio thought Willum was probably right. She would; and without asking them first, either.

He stopped at the wagon step to pick up his boots and turn them over to drain. He had only the one pair. He did have two pairs of shoes, however. Which he had told Xulai he didn't need to bring. Which she had insisted he bring. He wondered, briefly, where he might find a boot maker. Considering . . . everything, he really needed a spare pair.

"Now tell us what you saw," said Xulai, handing him a dry shirt.

He breathed some more. It took a while before his throat would open. "I saw two faces, part of one shoulder, one hand and lower arm. I should say each eye was about the size of my hand. The one . . . the one that was lying in the road had his mouth slightly open. The teeth were a lot wider than . . . those marks on the bone Willum found: eyebrows, hair, dark. Skin and hair dirty or dark or both. No clothes, of course. That is, I didn't see any. The ones I used to know wore clothes. I think. I don't remember their being naa . . ." He choked, unable to force the word out.

"Abasio. Shhh. Breathe."

"*I am* breathing. *They were breathing.* They had very wide noses. Possibly they hunt by smell. Couldn't see the ears, but I'm quite sure they had located us by sound."

"Oh, wow," said Willum.

Xulai handed him dry socks and gave him time to get them on.

He said, his voice grating, "If we'd fiddled around just a few moments more outside that notch, they'd have had us, horses and all. And the babies. And the sea-eggs."

"But they're not in here! They can't get in here," cried Willum.

"I hope that's true, yes. *And if you, Willum, hadn't spent the last hours on the way here making as much racket as you possibly could, they might not have found us in the first place.*"

"You mean I brought 'em," said Willum, eyes wide. "I didn't mean ta—"

"Willum, you never mean ta. I'm not angry at you *yet*. However, it is not necessary for you to make all possible noise at every possible occasion. When there are evil things out in the world, smart animals are quiet. You do not hear mice making echoes in the kitchen when the cat is there." He heard his own voice, loud and trembling with . . . what? Just plain fear was what.

Willum actually seemed to be listening. Abasio turned away and took a deep breath to calm himself. From behind him Willum crowed at the top of his lungs, "It's a room, Abasio!"

Abasio turned, glaring. Willum went on loudly, "Did'ja notice we're in a room! Doesn't have a roof, but it's a room. Like for giants, Abasio. The ones you saw. You think they'll keep tryin' to come in here?"

Abasio grabbed him and shook him, hard. "Well, now they can hear you yelling again, so my bet is they'll sure try, won't they? They're hungry, Willum. And *you are food*. Maybe if I let them have you, they'll leave the rest of us alone. At least they won't be able to find us so easily!"

"Y'mean they're still out there?" Willum paled. "I thought we got away!" He looked puzzled. "Ya mean—I shouldn't yell, huh?"

Xulai shook her head at Abasio, took Willum by the shoulder, and escorted him into the wagon, where Abasio heard her voice raised. Willum had a very thick skin. It might be necessary to get through his hide with something like a bullwhip. It might be necessary to cut through that skin with a chisel first, then use the bullwhip! Though, come to think of it, Xulai's voice could flay one almost like a whip when sufficiently aroused. She did sound aroused. *Go to it, Xulai!* He sat down on a convenient stump and tried not to think of anything. Not giants. Not Willum. Not Willum's skin . . . ears . . . hearing . . . he didn't listen.

Or, he thought to himself in a moment of revelation as he recalled the time they had spent in and near Gravysuck, the conversations he had overheard, *it was possible that Willum had never learned to listen because very little if anything had ever been said to him or within his hearing that required listening to.*

Xulai came to the wagon door and handed Abasio his shoes. Kim was standing next to Socky, both of them shivering. She cried, "Kim, you're freezing! Come in and get yourself changed. I put a towel and dry clothes out for you." Kim and Socky carried only what would be needed during the day; everything else traveled with the wagon.

Abasio put on his shoes and forced himself to examine the surroundings. The great upheaval that had created the northern wall behind them had created the eastern wall as well. They were now enclosed on north and east by cliffs of ruddy stone. That northeast corner of the space did have, as Willum had suggested, the vertical walls and enclosed feeling of a room—if one could accept sky as a ceiling. The south side of the valley was all mountains, rising rather steeply and thickly forested. They were not enclosed on the west. The wall went on west, the mountains went on a little south of west, the area gradually widening the farther one looked. The enclosed space was triangular, the tip of the triangle chopped off by the eastern wall, which was not complete. It had a gap at its southern end where the road and the river came through. Through that gap they would come to Findem Pass.

Xulai came out of the wagon carrying cups and a pitcher. She was followed by Willum, a Willum who was neither shouting nor running anywhere, who did, indeed, seem rather thoughtful as he moved away down the road. Abasio gave her a questioning look.

She handed a cup of hot tea to Abasio. When Willum was out of earshot, she cleared her throat, with only limited success. She still sounded choked as she murmured, "Two things, Abasio. When I heard them coming, the . . . the giants, I reached for a weapon, that is, for *ul xaolat.* I started to ask it to . . . to kill those things. Then I remembered Precious Wind insisting that before I did anything irrevocable, I ask the device for possible . . . side effects. So I did, and it said don't drop those bodies out there or everyone within several days' travel would die along with them. It didn't say why."

"Will it tell you why?"

"Probably. When I stop shaking enough to sit down and read it. Second thing: Willum. He's a liability, Abasio. He's a risk to our . . . duty, our quest. We may have to send him back. I've pointed out as forcibly as possible that we cannot possibly take a mere farm boy with us. I told him that farm boys don't have to think, because they just do the same things year after year, and so long as they get the chores done the way they've always been done, nobody cares if they spend the rest of their time yelling and pounding on things. I explained that traveling through strange territory is not like that, and his mother should have thought of that before she told him to go with us, unless maybe she just wanted to get rid of him and his noise. Traveling is always dangerous in one way or another, and if Willum cannot change from a farm boy into a traveling boy VERY quickly, when we get to Saltgosh we'll make arrangements to send him back to Gravysuck."

Abasio nodded. "Well, when he came out he looked . . . dare I say 'thoughtful'?"

"It's barely possible I got through to him. Maybe we can think of some other image he could work toward, you know, the adventurer or swashbuckler. Problem is, there are no images in these farm communities that would be helpful to us. I've been trying to think of stories he might know that have intrepid heroes he might want to emulate, and I can't come up with one. I don't know. Something has to get through to him, nothing seems to faze him, and he just doesn't listen! Ever!"

"Not unless it's something he's curious about," muttered Abasio. "Then he listens. Xulai, I had one of my rare fits of revelation a moment or so ago. Do you remember anyone in Gravysuck saying anything that *you* thought was important enough to listen to? I'm not including Bertram, obviously, but I'm wondering if Willum doesn't listen because nobody in that village listens. They make noises at one another, like chickens clucking, a generalized flock noise to assure the flock everybody's there, but I never heard anyone saying anything worth remembering. Lorp was the only thing they argued about, and those weren't real arguments, they were just 'shut up about Lorp' retorts."

Xulai's eyebrows went up. "Chicken talk!" She turned, staring into nothing, considering. "Like hive noise, with bees. Just a comforting cackle that lets you know you're among known people. You might be right! Bertram was different, of course, but then he reads books. Willum may just let words flow through."

Kim came out in dry clothing and took a towel to Socky. Once they were dry and had had a chance to catch their breaths, there was no reason for further delay. When Socky had warmed up and been furnished with a dry saddle blanket, Kim mounted and headed up the valley at an easy canter. He would get to the town and make whatever arrangements were necessary long before the wagon got there. The actual distance wasn't great, but the road still followed the river, back and forth, over and over, loop after loop, multiplying the distance. Now dry and relatively calm, Blue and Rags ambled. Abasio left them to determine their own pace. It was a longer distance than people needed to be hauled; he and Xulai followed Willum, straight across the pastures. Those that were fenced had gates; if the babies yelled, Blue would let them know.

As the tumult of white water faded into silence behind them, they turned to look back. A grove of huge dark trees stood along the base of the wall, their drooping branches shadowing and hiding the entrance to the notch, while the road to the west stood open and clear. The river forked into north and south branches some distance east of the notch, not naturally, but because of a V-shaped diversion wall built of stones and set into the riverbed. As the river forked, so did the road, the north-half road veering away to accompany its half of the river through the notch while the south road crossed the north fork by a stout timber bridge and followed the south-half river westward.

"Abasio, have you ever seen such a tree?" Xulai cried, pointing at the notch. "Look at it."

Abasio had been looking at it, or rather looking past it, to see if there were huge hands clawing over the top of the wall. The enormous tree stood just west of the notch, one side of the trunk quite near the vertical wall, a trunk so thick that it would take more than ten large men to make a hand-to-hand circle around it. The other side of the trunk reached almost halfway to the south branch of the river.

"Hundreds of years old, I imagine. I wonder if there are more of them." He thought the diversion must have been built centuries ago.

Neither wall nor notch was recent, yet neither wall nor notch was on the map!

Willum had removed his shoes and hung them around his neck by the laces in order to better investigate something in the river. When they caught up to him he said, "One time some explorer came to this place, and he asked some fellow, 'What's all that white stuff?' So they gave him some to taste, and he shouted out, 'It's salt. Gosh!' That's how it got named!"

"Is that true, Willum?"

"Gum says it is," the boy replied, suddenly serious. "'Bout those giants back there, I got to thinkin' about them. How did they make them?"

"Will you listen if I tell you?"

"Yeah, I wanna know, 'Basio."

Which was, Abasio thought, the key. Willum listened only if Willum wanted to know. There was a key there somewhere. He'd have to think about it!

"All right. Now, it's a long story, so pay attention. First, you have to think of time, because a lot of this happened a thousand years ago. Can you get your brain around a thousand years?"

"Ma Garney teaches 'rithmatic. I c'n add it and divide it and stuff."

"One generation is about twenty-five years. That's about what it takes for a person to grow up and have children. Sometimes less, sometimes more, but that's kind of an average. About four generations every hundred years, so a thousand years is forty generations. It's a long time. Gravysuck wasn't there. Saltgosh wasn't there. These mountains we're in, they pushed up about that time. You with me?"

"Oh, wow. Thassa a long time."

"Right. Now, back even before that, some hundreds of years before that, the world was packed with people: cities, roads, things called railroads, people everywhere. It got so full of people that they were always fighting over space, or over food or over fuel or power. So some people got the idea it would be nice to get rid of everyone in the world who wasn't just like them. People built killer machines. The killer machines could read people's minds, and the machines would kill everyone whose mind was different from the people who made them. Can you guess what happened next?"

" 'F it was me, I'd build me my own machine to kill those people that made the first ones," Willum said belligerently. "Ma allus says people oughta think what they want."

"They did build their own machines. By the time it was over, there may have been dozens of different sets of machines killing people for what they believed, or killing other killing machines for killing the wrong people. That's what finally stopped it. The machines started killing one another. BUT by that time, ninety percent—you know about percents?"

"Nuh-uh."

"Nine people out of every ten were dead. How many people in Gravysuck?"

"Sixty-two if y'count the farms."

"There would have been six people left in Gravysuck. That's ten percent."

"An one of 'em was about seven weeks pregnant, right? 'Cause there ought to be about two-tenths part of another one."

Abasio and Xulai shared an astonished glance. Well! *Sparks of light in the impenetrable darkness.*

Abasio went on: "So the machines killed each other, and almost all the machines were destroyed. Last year, Xulai and I were there when the very last one was destroyed. It had gone on killing for a thousand years. Now, that whole time the machines were killing people is called the Big Kill."

"Whassat got to do with those giants?"

"Well, during the Big Kill, what would you have done?"

"Gone n' hid, I 'spose."

"That's exactly what some of the very smartest people did. They left the cities, they went outside the cities into the country, and they dug in. They made refuges for themselves underground. The machines couldn't read minds that were underground, and these very smart people made their places very strong. Because they were at the edges of the cities, that's what the places were called: Edges. They were full of people with very good brains who invented all kinds of things . . ." *That they shouldn't have,* he said silently. "When I was a boy I lived near the ruined city of Fantis. Within a one- or two-day journey north, east, or south of the ruined city, there were about a hundred of those Edges . . ."

"The people stayed in there, Willum," Xulai offered. "Generation after generation. They were safe there, and they stayed there, and they got awfully bored. So they did what people do; they had hobbies, something to amuse themselves. The Edgers decided to create villages copied from fairy tales; have you heard of them?"

"You mean little kids' stories. Like 'Sweet Dreamer and the Seven Dinkies'? An' 'Princess Ladder-Hair'? An' 'Three Skinny Piggies an' the Big Coyote'? Ma Garney tol' us all a' them. She used to have a book a' stories like that, but it wore out."

Xulai nodded at him. "Stories like that, yes. The Edgers created places like those stories, and they put people and creatures in them to act the parts. Some of them were real people. Some of them were machines, dressed up to look like people. And some were living things that they created in their laboratories and then put in the villages. Abasio lived near such a village. His mother had . . . an injured mind, and they put her in the village to play a part—"

Abasio interrupted, not wanting to revisit old tragedies. "If the story had a giant in it, then the Edgers created a giant. There was one near the village Xulai's talking about. He was a perfectly nice giant, a little over twice my height, didn't eat people. He was all human, but very, very large. Because we know the Edgers could do that, we're pretty sure the Edgers made those giants that're trying to get in here.

"I lived just over those mountains." He pointed eastward, toward the final range. "Chief Purple, the chief of the gang I joined in Fantis, had people digging into the city, the buried city, finding things, and he sold a lot of those things to the Edgers. When he had something they wanted, he would send some of his gang members to deliver it— sometimes I did the delivering, so I got to know some of the Edgers. He ended up finding something valuable enough that he used it to buy his way into an Edge. After that, he lived in the Edge, just using the gang members to protect him when he went back and forth.

"So, this one Edger that I talked with quite a bit was all excited about using the genetic patterns of some animals in the creatures they made. He told me about various kinds they'd obtained from who knows where! One was called a hyena. It had this wild, laughing cry. Trolls cry like that. Some fool had decided to make both male and female Trolls, and the Edger told me there'd been breeding between giants and the female Trolls. That's where the first Ogres came from. He thought it was hilariously funny."

"Part giant human and part Troll," Xulai breathed. "I hadn't realized that . . ."

Until that moment, Abasio hadn't really thought about it, had, indeed, refused to think about it. He felt his skin turn cold, and he shivered though the sun was warm upon him. He shook his head, forcing the images in there to go elsewhere. The creatures on the other side of that wall were like those prehistoric beasts he had read of in Tingawa: menacing, indomitable, and always voraciously hungry . . .

He tried to get them out of his head by concentrating on where they were. Xulai put an end to distraction by passing him the *ul xaolat* she had been fiddling with and pointing to the text screen. He read the line of rolling text and snarled. "Plague?"

"*Ul xaolat* said don't kill the giants. That's its explanation. It says biting insects will lay their eggs in those huge bodies. The eggs will hatch into larvae that eat the bodies. The giants have some kind of growth hormone in them that will transfer into the larvae, and the next generation of the biting insects will have no limit on their growth, they'll grow so big they can kill people before laying eggs in them. We'll have substituted thousands of huge insects for each giant."

"So we can't . . . we can't kill them?"

"Not unless we can bury or burn the remains, so bugs can't get at them. So far, the giants have eaten all the dead ones, so it hasn't happened."

"Couldn't *ul xaolat* dispose of . . . ?"

"Of course it could, with enough power, Abasio. It would draw an immense amount of power. There's no way to do it slowly that would stop the plague."

Cursing the Edgers did not soothe Abasio's anger. It would take half a forest's worth of wood to burn one of those huge bodies. If they couldn't kill the creatures, what in the devil could they do with them!

(*"She's right about the power,"* ul xaolat *fumed. It had been watching the fluctuation, hoping to find a time when use was low. There was none. Usage was virtually level around the clock. Others had had the same thought, tried the same thing, moved their delayable usage to the lower-use times and evened everything out.*)

Their road led upward, toward the eastern wall of the canyon, a wall that extended from the north wall without a break, ending in a clean, vertical cut across from a rocky precipice on the south. Through this cut the road and the river climbed on eastward toward Findem Pass. At the north edge of this gap, next to the road, the cliff wall ended in a towering square pillar so regular in shape that it seemed built rather than natural. Below and some distance north of this tower, glued to the vertical eastern wall of red stone as though placed there by a flock of enormous cliff swallows, hung a . . . well, what was it? It appeared to be a glittering collection of refractive gems, mirrors, and crystals, all sparkling and generating rainbows of scintillating light across the valley's walls, like a diamond necklace for a giantess, or a display of spun and crystallized sugar in a confectioner's window.

Xulai and Abasio shared the thought with a glance. "Candy . . ." she murmured, licking her lips. He nodded, managing a weak grimace. In the citadel of Tingawa complicated sweets had been the confectioners' pride. Sugary elegances had marked the climax of many of the celebratory meals that had honored Xulai's marriage, Abasio's "adoption" as an honorary Tingawan (princesses were traditionally not allowed to marry outsiders and this "adoption" was a delayed bow to tradition), and the birth of "her" children. She was, after all, a princess of the realm. Abasio, when in Tingawa, often felt like an appurtenance. Now, of course, all that elaboration seemed remote as a dream. A man whose duty it was to assist in saving the human race should not be dreaming of candy! In the company of giants, no less!

He shook his head in mock dismay at himself, lifting and staring at his hand. Well, at least *that* part of him had stopped shaking. He couldn't say as much for his insides, which still quaked, stopped, then quaked again, as though something in there kept waking up and screaming. The wagon might have reached that corner one second later . . . He could have tripped and fallen . . . If that hand had grabbed the wagon, it could have pulled it back, horses included . . . It had been so close, so terribly, terribly close. His mind was on other things, but his body went on remembering, time after time convulsing with sickening internal spasms.

He forced himself to concentrate, instead, on what lay below the spun-sugar town, at the foot of the cliff. As they came nearer, the area of meaningless clutter gradually resolved itself into purposeful order. The patches of darkness were mine-shaft openings: white-coated machinery stood against the pale wooden sides of storage barns or warehouses; men clustered at this task or another, variously dressed and equipped and moving among saw pits, crushers, and grinders. Wagons were pulled by horses clad in what looked like raincoats and masks; they moved here and there to be loaded and unloaded, all of the activity surrounded by the pale powdery substance that was being shoveled, ground, cut and piled, bagged, stacked, stored.

"What do they do with all of it?" Xulai murmured.

Abasio replied, "According to Bertram, it's the only salt mine left within hundreds of miles in all directions. They do blocks for livestock, granular for kitchens. Some of the salt goes over the pass to the east, some is bartered for provender from local villages. Some will be sent as far west as Ghastain. Areas west of there, the people get their salt from seawater evaporation ponds along the coast. There are a lot of them just south of Wellsport."

Socky and Kim were mere blotches, far up the valley, both of them, man and horse, trying to run away from their terror. If people could only do that. Poor Kim. Though the boy had been longing for adventure and thrilled to be picked for the job, Abasio would not be surprised if he chose to do something . . . less adventurous in the future.

As they drew nearer, they could see the town was set on a narrow horizontal ledge that crossed the face of the cliff. The white cubes topped with domes were houses, many of them multistoried, some edged and faceted like gems, often diagonally slashed by exterior stairways, here and there penetrated by doors and windows that stood open or were covered with brightly painted shutters. Since the ledge itself was virtually invisible from below, the entire conglomeration did appear to have been cemented in place. Not by swallows, however. No bird could have achieved the purity of color: the silver that whitened into snow, then shaded to ivory before glinting toward silver again, constantly shifting shape and hue as the ledge was shadowed or disclosed by an early evening flock of woolly clouds, grazing southward across the glowering sun.

They passed an area of mire, almost against the north wall. It was grown high with reeds and grasses and emitted a more-than-merely-swampy stench that gradually dissipated behind them. Only a mile of road remained, now swerving only slightly through pastures dotted with small groves where cows lay, placidly chewing. As the road came back toward them, Xulai met the wagon and climbed onto the seat while Abasio walked beside Blue. They were now close enough to see that the buildings of the lofty town were divided by narrow alleys that penetrated from the lip of the ledge back toward—and possibly into—the sheer wall of stone behind. As they neared, moving dots of anonymous color became bright shirts, capes, skirts, and head scarves worn by people who watched their approach from behind a sturdy rope railing supported by fantastically carved pillars of salt.

Willum joined the wagon and walked beside Abasio. He said, "See those carved things, up there? The ones t' hold the rail up? Gum told me 'bout them. They carve all kinds a' things for fun, the people do. See that one at the end. Thassa unicorn, that is. Next one, thassa horse with wings. Looky, Xulai! Thassa mermaid, like Gailai!" And, indeed, one of the salt balusters, though a good deal more bosomy than Gailai was likely to be, had the requisite tail.

"And that's the town," said Abasio unnecessarily.

"It's got no road to it!" exclaimed Willum, crowing at the discovery. The only visible access was the narrow stairway path, also well railed and netted, that zigzagged up the face of the cliff to a single gate. The tall and burly gatekeeper had just opened it to allow two figures to descend, immediately identifiable as Kim and Gum. They came down far more quickly than seemed advisable to the watchers.

"Salt! Gosh!" said Willum again. "They built the whole town outta it! Gum tol' me, but I didn' know it'd look like that."

"Willum, did you know Gum would be here?" asked Xulai, staring at the back of the boy's neck . . . which turned slightly red.

His face was as flushed when he turned to answer her. "Well, he hadda bring t'wagon anyhow. Bringin' stuff t' barter for salt, for Gravysuck this winter. We gotta have salt before the animals get slaughtered, y'know, to salt the meat n' the cabbage n' make pickles an' stuff."

"And?"

Willum flushed. "And Ma said in case you didn' want me by the time we got here, Gum could bring me on home."

Ah, she thought. So Willum's mother had not been as casual about his departure as she and Abasio had supposed. "And?" she asked. "Did she tell you anything else?"

"Ma said somethin' . . . I forgot until I saw Gum's wagon." He made a face, digging one horny toe into the dirt.

"And of course you can't possibly remember what she said." Abasio sighed.

Willum turned red. "Suthin' about no runnin' off or teachin' the babies bad words, I think. An' helpin'. I'm pretty sure she said helpin'."

Xulai and Abasio shared a frustrated glance. "Did she also tell you that you were to *listen to us* and obey us?" asked Abasio.

Willum turned almost purple, seemingly unable to answer. He cast a sidelong glance at Xulai. "Tell him," she ordered. "Tell Abasio what you told me!"

"Yeah, but . . . I didn't take it . . . for serious. I mean, Ma always says stuff, but she never does—"

Xulai said sternly, "Willum's mother makes the girls mind her, but she never made Willum mind her because he is a boy. And what did I tell you about that?"

"You tol' me sometimes women give up on that 'cause they b'lieve men're too stupid to listen."

"And?"

"And lately I been provin' she 'uz right."

Abasio said, "I imagine when you're there on the farm, maybe it doesn't make a lot of difference. If you get yourself killed, that's just you. But when you risk getting both of us and the babies killed, along with Kim and the horses, then we just can't have somebody like you along. It's too dangerous for us. You might try this, Willum. Imagine you're home, back in Gravysuck. And imagine there's a couple of those giants in the forest up the mountain. And they're hungry. They'll eat you or your ma or anybody else. Try to figure out whether you'd make noise or not."

"Ma never did nothin' to me . . ."

"Answer the question." He saw the boy's blank look. *He hadn't listened to the question.* "We won't do anything to you either, Willum. We'll just send you home. Not worth our time trying to teach you if you're not willing to learn."

Xulai said, "*We're serious, Willum.* If all you are is a noisy young one who does not listen, you'll definitely go home, if not now with Gum, then later by whatever route is handy. Do you know that I mean that for sure? I'm not going to let you risk our lives by playing games."

Abasio remarked, "I think maybe your ma knew that Xulai wouldn't let you get away with being ornery. Your ma probably figures if you're with us, we'll treat you as family."

Willum shook his head. "Ma thinks more a' Xulai than that, Abasio. Ma says you got to earn bein' fam'bly. Lorp was married in, but he never earned bein' fam'bly."

His words reminded Abasio of something he'd been wondering about. In most places, if a local was kicked to death by a horse belonging to an outsider, there would be some fuss about it, but there's been none over Lorp's death. "I didn't think to ask about it before, Willum, but did they have any kind of funeral for your uncle Lorp?"

"He wun't really a uncle, an' nah. Wasn't no funeral. They jus' cata-pull-it'd him into Gravysuck."

"They *whatted him*?" cried Xulai. "Into Gravysuck? The town?"

"Didn' you know about Gravysuck? Y' know that swamp south a' town? The one with the corpse flowers growin' all around it?"

"Corpse . . . ? Those things that looked like lilies?" Abasio asked. They had passed it when they left, and he had regretted not having had time to explore it. "I never did get over to take a look at it."

Willum looked at him, shivering. "Well, thassa good thing you din't go anywheres near it. Dad says more'n a few people and kids got themselves drowned in there. Didn't nobody tell you about that? See, the town is really named Gravysuck Swamp Town, but people leave the 'Swamp Town' part off. Gravysuck is the name a' the swamp. It's all brown and kind of like gravy, only it smells bad—Pa says it oughta be called Poop-suck—and if anythin' falls into it, the swamp goes *suuuck,* an' whatever got in there goes down and it never comes up again. That's where we put Lorp."

Abasio shared a glance of incomprehension with Xulai.

Noting this, Willum continued: "See, there's a cata-pull-it over on the far side, like a big spoon, and it's got a pivot in the middle, see? Like a little kid's teeter-totter. Well, not e'zackly, because one end's a lot longer than the other one. Anyhow. There's a kinda basket at each end. The basket at the short end—that's the *cata* part—is kept fulla rocks.

When they need t'use it, a whole buncha men go down to the long end, the *pull-it* part, and they use a whole buncha pulleys to pull the long end down. Usin' those pulleys, that's the *pull-it* part, an' that pulls the *cata* part up into the air. It takes a whole buncha men t'*pull-it*, 'cause the stones are heavy. When they get the stones alla way up, they tie the *pull-it* end down. They use a short piece a' real strong rope that's left over from something. The *pull-it* end's gotta basket on it, too.

"Then somebody—whoever feels like doin' it, maybe more'n one—makes a speech about how this par-tick-u-lar person is a *cata-stroll-free* and he's been strollin' free at it long enough and now should be *cata-pull-ited*! If somebody wants t'make an argyment, that's awright to do. Maybe his ma or pa begs for 'im, but if he's a real *cata-stroll-free*, likely they've given up on him anyhow. When the argyments're done, they takes a vote."

"A vote?" Xulai asked, almost in a whisper.

"Yeah. Whether they *cata-pull-it* the person or don't *cata-pull-it* the person. An' if they vote yes, the drummer does a *dum, dum, dum* on the drum. Loud, so ever'body c'n hear it an' anybody wants ta watch, they know it's time. When ever'body's there, they march the *cata-stroll-free* aroun', lettin' everbody see he's the right one, y'know, givin' everbody a las' chans' ta say if he's the wrong one 'r not. Then they tie up the *cata-stroll-free's* legs an put'm in the basket, and then they cut the tie-down rope with a hatchet and *wheeeeowee*, the *cata* end with all the rocks falls down WHAM, and the *pull-it* end whips up real fast and *cata-pull-its* who's in the basket right out into the middle a' Gravysuck. 'At's where Lorp landed, anyhow."

"Catapult," said Xulai. "Your people do that with everyone who dies, too?"

Willum shook his head at such willful misunderstanding. "Din't you hear me say, Xulai? I aweady said just *cata-stroll-frees*. People free ta stroll aroun' bein' no good for nothing-at-all!"

"Like what?" asked Abasio.

"One stroll-free, he use ta foller t'women. N' if they got somewheres with nobody around, he'd grab at 'em and try to drag 'em off, n' you know whut he'd do. N' little girls, too. All the time. N' if anybody ast him why, he'd jus' giggle, like some little kid, giggle and point at hisself, his parts. 'Basio, you know what I mean! An' one little girl he mos' kilt."

"Sex-mad, mentally defective lunatic," murmured Xulai.

"He was a *cata-stroll-free*. Free ta be rotten! That's the kinda folks the man who built it said t'use it on. The man who made the cata-pull-it, he lived in Gravysuck in my grandma's time. He wan't from around here, but he stayed here for a long time. Ma, she sez he was sweet on Granma, you know? Anyhow, he got to know the folks, and he said we had a need for a *cata-pull-it*. He even picked out the first two or three *cata-stroll-frees* folks used it on. My gram knew two of 'em. All they did was steal from folks and beat on people—even little kids an' women—and stay drunk. She says the town people should be *everlastingly grateful* to the man who built the *cata-pull-it*." It was obvious that Willum had learned and enjoyed rehearsing those specific words. "Anyhow, when they did Lorp, there was no argyment about it. Whole buncha people made speeches about him bein' good riddance and sayin' thank-yous to the horse that kilt him. 'Sides, he 'uz dead anyhow when he got *cata-pull-ited*."

Abasio and Xulai shared a glance, Xulai frowning as she considered the ethical considerations. Perhaps the inventor had been a Volumetarian? A wandering Tingawan? Someone who shared Abasio's horrific sense of humor?

Willum went on thoughtfully: "We don't *cata-pull-it* fambly or good folks. We bury them up on a hill where flowers bloom in the springtime. It's nice up there. People go talk to the buried ones, too. They bring lunch, y'know, and fix a plate for the people that's gone. The spirits, they eat the spirit of the food, Ma says. We only *cata-pull-it* people like Lorp. Even Lorp's ma said he cert'ny was irritatin'. 'F a person din' have ten toes and ten fingers and two eyes and ever'thin' else all correct, then that person was 'sposed to be kilt—right then, no argyment. Girl's mama made a hole in little girl's ear to put a gold ring in, she was 'sposed to be kilt."

Xulai asked very softly, "Do the town people always wait until the catastrophes die, Willum? Before they catapult them?"

Willum shook his head firmly. "Not alla time, no. 'Member, I said they march 'em aroun', the ones that're live? March 'em aroun' with the drum goin' *dum, dum, dum, dum* an' ever'body makin' sure that's the real cata-stroll-free. Folks don' wanna make a mistake 'bout that! An if it's a real one, nobody's gonna wait till he dies nachrul. Kids arn 'sposed to watch, though."

"So?"

"So? Us kids sneak inna woods an' watch from where folks can't see us. But I never saw'm do a live one, so I dunno. Lorp was the oniliest one in a long time got *cata-pull-ited.* Now, mostly, if some man—or some really awful woman—hears people say they're 'checkin' out the cata-pull-it to be sure it's workin',' they figure maybe it's them and they oughta leave town on their own."

Xulai smiled evilly. "Willum, now that we know what you do with *cata-stroll-frees,* we're warning you: just make sure you don't turn out to be one for us."

Willum gave Abasio a pale and frantic glance. Abasio contented himself with a serious-faced nod toward Xulai, indicating his complete agreement with her sentiment.

By this time, Kim and Gum had made their way through the mine workings, where they had been joined by half a dozen of the Saltgoshian men, who turned and straggled by ones and twos across the road and reassembled beside the fence of a large stretch of pasture between the road and the south wall of the valley, where the wagon would pass it very shortly. Xulai put the babies inside and took her place on the wagon seat. Abasio and Willum continued on foot beside the horses.

As they neared the Saltgosh group, one of the Goshians came to meet them, offering a hand to Abasio.

"Name's Melkin, sir. Supervisor this season. You'd be Abasio? My pleasure, sir. And you, young'un. You'd be Willum? Nephew to Gum there, right? He told us you'd be coming. Ma'am, nice to see you well. Your children also well, ma'am? Good. Good. All of us very interested in hearing about them. Now, as you can see, the path up to the town doesn't allow for wagons, so this pasture here's the place for visitors." He waved toward the enclosed area. "We'd offer the use of the visitors' dormitory, over behind the mine office, but Gum says you've got the wagon fitted comfortable and we keep a watch on this area, so nobody'll bother you here. This side here's for people to camp; the west side, through the gate, that's for the horses. Take your water from the east side, there where it's clean. Horses can water in that little side pool off at the west end, and there's a nice, tight shed for them if it comes to rain.

"Privy over there next to the trees away from the stream. We ask that users put several buckets of water down it before you leave. One bucket per day per user is about right. It's leached in a contained area, ma'am, no danger of reaching the water. You can rely on its cleanliness. There's no fee for graze. We expect visitors to leave the place as clean as they found it; there's a place for rubbish yonder," and he pointed to a bin at the upper near corner. "Burn what will burn clean; what won't or didn't burn clean is rubbish. Manure pile there against the wall."

"Do you hear the man, Blue? Rags?"

"Certainly," said Blue. "Thank you for pointing it out, sir."

Melkin's jaw dropped. "The horse . . . he . . . talks?"

"Yes," said Abasio. "He does. So does his partner."

Melkin swallowed, breathed deeply, and continued. "There's places for cook fires already laid up; there's the wood bin there, next to the fence; take what you need, either go up in the woods and find enough deadwood to replace it or pay the children to collect as much as you've used. The children always appreciate it. Rule is, little ones six years old and older have to earn what they spend, and traders generally have something the little ones covet. Children do a lot of chores for travelers, but there's very few travelers this late in the season.

"Now, even though you prefer your wagon, ma'am, you're welcome to use the warm-water showers available behind the works, separate one for the womenfolk. Place there to do laundry, too. Can't work salt without a way to wash it off! No fee for use of the place, ma'am, just leave it clean as you find it."

"I hope everyone is polite enough to do that in return for your generosity," said Xulai.

"Well, let's just say we never forget the ones who don't, ma'am. Next trip they make, they find showers and laundry and all locked up tight and a very high fee to unlock 'em."

Abasio and Xulai murmured their thanks and their assurances for this well-rehearsed recital. Abasio asked what amount the children would expect for wood gathering and was shown the marks on the wood bin that measured usage, and what amount of coin of what types was considered appropriate per mark to be deposited in the slotted box by the fence. The men bowed to Abasio, again to Xulai, neither scornfully nor subserviently. Melkin turned toward Blue, then shook his head, deciding not to bow to the horse. Blue spoiled the whole thing by whinnying at him ingratiatingly, extending one front leg and bowing to him.

Melkin gulped, fought with his face for a moment, then returned the bow. Abasio, swallowing laughter, returned Melkin's bow, to precisely the same level with precisely the same expression, and spoke his own thanks simply, without flourishes. Melkin waved a hand and left them, saying, "Gum'll bring you up to the town. Tavern's open yonder."

Abasio followed him until they were out of earshot and detained him with a touch on his arm. "We came through the notch down there," he said, pointing.

Melkin frowned. "So the watch told me. We get . . . very little traffic that way."

"We just escaped, barely. I'd like to know . . ."

Melkin whispered, "The watch thought there'd been a problem, the way you came through! Please don't talk about it in the town. Only takes one or two to get everyone hysterical. I'll make an opportunity to talk with you about it, but we don't want the whole town stirred up. If that's all right with you? I can say this, just so you can reassure the lady and the boy—oh, and the animals . . . what's considered polite with speaking horses, by the way? I had no idea! Anyhow, you're safe here, and when you go on east of here all the way to the pass, you'll be safe from that particular problem. The giants can't get in here."

Abasio nodded, smiled, letting everyone see he wasn't fearful or unhappy. No, not if it was something they preferred to keep quiet. "You asked about the horses. Blue and Rags are partners of ours. We treat them as we would ourselves, we chat with them, we make sure they're well fed, well informed, and well cared for. As for people like yourself, who know they can speak but are not familiar with them, they still appreciate being acknowledged. I follow their lead. You may have noticed that animals treat people differently. They sense things about people that other people may not. So, around certain people, the horses do not speak because they do not trust them. If the horses don't, I follow their lead."

Melkin mused, finally allowing himself to smile. "Well, at least I've passed the horse test."

As Abasio waved Melkin good-bye, he grabbed Willum, grasped him firmly by both shoulders, and said very briefly that Willum was not to mention the giants.

"Not to get the womenfolks stirred up," said Willum.

"That may very well be true. But, Willum—look at me! No, do not look at six other things you want to find out about, look at me! Remember what Xulai told you about not needing farm boys. She meant it, I mean it. Keep your mouth shut about it."

Willum swallowed. "I thought he maybe meant just the womenfolk . . ."

Abasio crouched to the boy's level, one hand on each side of his head. "I don't want to hear what you *think*! Maybe in Gravysuck you know enough to think; here you don't. *Your eyes are off everywhere, you still aren't concentrating on listening.*" He shook the boy hard. "The man said please don't talk about it in the town." *Shake.* "That means you do not open your mouth and say one word about it in the town." *Shake.* "Not to men. Not to children. Not to the horses. Not to anyone." *Hard shake.* "You don't even stand out under the stars and talk to yourself about it! You don't know enough about anyplace but Gravysuck to do any thinking! I want you to listen. Are you?" *Shake.* "Now hear me. You will not say the word 'giant.' You will not mention it to anyone. If someone asks you if you saw a giant, you are to look stupid and say, 'What, what giant?' If some group of people mention that there are giants out there somewhere, you are to keep your own mouth shut. You are not to ask any questions." *Shake.* "You are not to say the word! You are not to hint the word! You are not to pretend to know something that you can't talk about to make yourself seem important!" *Very hard shake.* "And if you do any of those things, or make anyone think you have done any of those things, or tell someone and make them promise not to tell, I *will* be told about it, and, Willum, you will go back home with Gum, no joke, no second chance! Do you understand me?"

Willum had a very strange look on his face.

"What?"

"I 'uz just thinkin' you musta been as bad as me, 'Basio. You sure covered ever'thing I mighta thought of."

Abasio, rejecting laughter, adopted ferocity. "Then I'm going to add something else. You are also not to do anything that I didn't mention that you may think of later!"

He returned to help Kim unharness the horses while Gum rambled on about the evening's menu at the Tavern—which was down near the mine workings, so taking the babies along would not be a problem.

"Shouldn't think there'd be enough traffic to support a tavern," called Abasio from the wagon, where he was rummaging for a clean shirt.

"Oh, Tavern's for the mine folks, 'Basio. They need a little 'muse-men', too, y'know. Tavern serves stuff a little fancy, y'know, things the town families likely wudden cook for their selfs. Got 'em two furriner cooks, they do, him n' her. Tasty's what they do. I allus looks forward to eatin' at the Tavern. Men n' women here work four days, two days' rest. Rest days, folks all drink a little, sing a lot! Children's playgroun' jus' outside. Young'uns can't do much runnin' up inna town. Space is kinda tight up there, but up there's mos'ly jus' for livin' safe an' outta the way of people causin' trouble. The town's guarded and safe, y'know."

Guarded and safe, Abasio repeated to himself silently. At least two giants just outside that slot down the valley, giants quite possibly tall enough, if they got in here, to reach those houses up on the wall, but the people considered themselves guarded and safe. He looked forward to his chat with Melkin. Yes, he certainly did.

"Is the town really built of salt blocks?" Xulai asked. "Doesn't it dissolve in rain or snow?"

"All salt!" Gum said. "Whole thing! They paint it with stuff makes it waterproof. Tops've all gotta dome on, like a beehive, painted like the rest. Rain runs right off. Insides're painted, too, so it don't rub off on yer clothes 'r yer skin. Gotta be careful about that, salt's awful irritatin' when it gets rubbed in."

Xulai suggested they put off visiting the town until morning, and they accepted Gum's suggestion to have their supper in the Tavern where rest day and evening meals were provided quite inexpensively to those traveling and also provided to the Saltgoshians—along with their housing—as part of their pay from the mine. Men going on duty in the morning advised the Tavern if they and their families wanted supper in the evening or, on going off duty on day four, what meals they would like on the two following rest days. There, after a meal as tasty as Gum had promised, Gum loaded his pipe with some unfamiliar but fragrant combination of leaves and told them about the town perched above them on the ledge while the babies slept curled into their blankets on the settle beside them.

"I was thinking how dreadful winters must be," said Xulai. "That narrow little path, slippery with ice . . ."

"Ah, no, lady," said Gum, half mumbling around the stem of his pipe. "Saltgosh folks don' live up in Summer Town in wintertime. Like you jus' said, way too much snow n' ice. It gets deep, taller'n me."

When cold came, he told them, the Saltgoshians moved from their cave-swallow houses on the high ledge down into "Snow Town," an old section of the salt mines that had been fitted up for subterranean living with ventilation pipes, tight doors, stoves, and chimneys. Down there, the inhabitants went through the cold season "snug as bears in a cave," said Gum. Especially since among the more important barter items he and others brought were many sacks of the grains needed by the Tavern for the brewing of ale. There was a large cave below, big enough for the young ones to play ball games, and school went on all winter for the young ones, too, and he described the system of water pipes and sewers.

"Waste pipes all run down t'that marsh place, long the wall. Stinks consid'rable, but don' seem to bother the critters none," said Gum.

"We noticed the smell on the way here," remarked Abasio. "Did I understand right when you mentioned kennels?"

"Sled dogs, 'Basio. Come snow, t'dogs pulls sleds. Y'go rescue some-body treed by a bear in winter, y'need sled dogs."

The city on the ledge, he said, was occupied only from thaw until threat of first snow, for even early snows at this altitude soon covered the town completely, sticking tight to the wall behind it. At the end of the wall, near the river, where the stone tower went up—and it was, he said; a natural formation with a natural vertical fault into which stairs had been built—"Way up, on top, 'ere's a warm li'l room 'at's a watch-tower!" It had a closed little stove that burned special fuel with almost no smoke. It had glass windows that looked in every direction, windows set deep so that they reflected no light. People entering the valley would not even know they were observed. Abasio's wagon, said Gum, had been watched from the moment it entered the valley.

Xulai murmured sleepily, "So, nobody could take over the town in winter?"

Abasio said, "I think what Gum is saying is that after the move be-lowground, the dwellings are deeply buried in snow and there's literally nothing there to take over. It must take a lot of effort to move every-thing, Gum."

"Oh, it do, 'Basio, it do. Movin' takes three, four days, spring an' fall.

Hoist goes up n' down, up n' down, dawn to night, an' ever'thin' gets moved—down 'r up, it gets moved, ever'body doin' it, even the little 'uns! Then 'ey has a party. I was atta Springtime Move-up party wunst!"

"Salt!" exclaimed Xulai, shaking her head. "What do they paint on it to keep it from melting or rubbing off?"

"Dunno." He shrugged, obviously not caring what it was so long as it worked. "Ever' early summer a wagon fulla it comes over t'pass. Kinda like paint, only no color. Both places, up n' down, gets painted outside n' inside, ever' year. Tavern, too. It's built outta salt."

"The Edges are still there," Abasio reminded her. "Over the pass, near where the cities were. They've always made things for trade, and they need salt, too, just like everyone else."

"How do you get into this Snow Town?" Xulai asked.

Gum's eyebrows rose in astonishment. "Oh, missus! Outside folks don't know! An' the chil'ren don't know. Even some person got saved from bears or t' like, even one a' them, they'd blindfol' afore they'd take him down and afore he come up agin. Jus' like they do little ones, too baby yet to keep their moufs shut."

Xulai still wasn't satisfied. "It sounds sensible enough, and I can understand their going underground, but what danger are they always watching for?"

Gum had to think about this. His furzy eyebrows drew together as he brooded for a long moment before saying slowly, "I 'ud say—nothin' in par-ticaler lately! But one time? Oh, my, yes! Old Oaster tol' me, he did. Right. Long time ago. He tol' me in t' Tavern. Women stealing."

"Women were stealing from Saltgosh?" Abasio said disbelievingly, trying not to laugh.

"No, no, 'Basio. It 'uz Saltgosh women bein' stole. Or wudda been, if those raider men'd got any. Not in my life, boy. In my pa's time. When he wuz a lad. That'd be seventy years ago."

At this evidence of real danger, Xulai cried, "Who was stealing women?"

"It wuz some little towns off inna woods, kinda strange people, had this notion stealin' women wuz . . ." Gum made a two-handed gesture of puzzlement. "It wern' so much t' gettin' of some women. *It was more the kind of women they got!* Raiders said a only way 'ey cud get a *good* fee-male wuz stealin' one."

Xulai pursued the question. "And they're still watching for them to come back?"

"Oh, *cata-pull-it,* NO, lady! I SAID! Non'uv'm come t'Saltgosh *fer seventy years*! See, back 'en, the Goshians here got ridda big bunch uv'm, n' they never come back."

Though Xulai felt an actual physical pain at letting go of any possible danger that she might intervene to prevent, she did get the point. As Gum said, Goshians weren't geese, but there was this one little thing that bothered her. "If the villagers don't steal women anymore, why do the Goshians still keep the watch during wintertime?"

At this, Gum's speech slowed into his *important mode:* the pipe withdrawn from his mouth, each syllable separately enunciated and containing all the consonants habitually ignored. "No, no, lady, they keeps the watch *all* times. Daytime. Nighttime. All year round! Maybe those women-stealin' crazies don't come no more, but it don't matter! Now, y'see, keepin' watch is *tra-di-shun*! When a boy outgrows singin' t'high notes, gets his man-voice, t'sing, y'know, then he gets ee-ni-shee-ated to the Watch. Takes a oath an' all." Gum's voice deepened, he intoned: "*'Will not rest, will not sleep, faithfully my watch I'll keep.'* Then his daddy gives him a red hat with a badge on, gives him a drink a' beer. Ever'body in t' Watch cheers, an' they have a feast! Makes a boy proud t'do his part: watchin'! That room up there, it's so high up, they saw you afore you even came the wet way inta the valley."

"*Ah!*" said Xulai, with satisfaction. "Rite of passage," content to let it be so, now that she had properly categorized the matter. *"Male solidarity system."*

Abasio, however, though he did not react outwardly, felt his body tense. If they had seen over that wall, then they had seen into the valley beyond. He smiled and nodded at Gum, resolving yet again to meet, very soon, with Melkin.

Next day they carried the babies up the path and walked through the village as they routinely did, showing the babies, explaining, letting the villagers follow them back to the pond in the meadow to see the babies at play. The Goshians had displayed the usual fascination, asked the usual questions—though with none of the hostility shown in many other places. Then, at lunchtime, they had gone into the Tavern, and it was there that they learned what occupied the Saltgoshians during their free time, for Gum announced to all assembled that these folks from Tingawa had never heard local music.

There was immediate enthusiasm. People went up the path to fetch people who were in the town. People came hastily down again. Chairs were arranged. All the instruments were kept in the Tavern back room, as the Tavern was the only place large enough to hold everyone who wanted to take part. Accordingly, though the music was mostly vocal, the back room was plundered of its astonishing variety of drums, gongs, bells, and chimes so that Saltgosh might offer its visitors an impromptu concert. Virtually everyone except the young children and some of the very old wore a red hat with a badge and had a vocal or instrumental part. The director was an elderly man, possibly retired from work in the mines or relegated to less physical work, but he had acquired extensive musical knowledge from somewhere, for he held the music in both mind and heart as he directed his musicians.

It seemed almost everyone in Saltgosh was part of the music. The singers covered the entire range of the human voice from a basso so deep that it made Xulai's bones rumble, to one clear, elegantly crystal soprano that lilted and leapt, utterly unstrained. That singer was part of a cluster of soprano, contralto, and tenor voices that rang out like bells from a group of five dark-haired young people who stood together and looked much alike. Too close in age to be siblings; Xulai thought they were probably cousins.

Xulai had not heard such complex harmonies or memorable melodies since she'd left Tingawa. The words of the songs praising trees, wind, birdsong, and other natural things were simple, but their effect was not. Xulai heard the music with her whole body. "Deep mine" songs were dense, in men's voices only, giving Abasio shivers about lost men who walked galleries far under the earth. Xulai's favorite was one they called the "rain song," which started with a patter of rain on a tom-tom, the sound of rain on a roof, built into a thunder of barrel drums, a lightning strike of gongs and cymbals, all the while the voices building in a rush of air, a torrent of wind, the storm rushing this way and that, on and on, finally fading into the patter of rain, once more, slowing, slowing, ending with a serious-faced five-year-old girl child's solo on a treble drum the size of an apple: a delicate, two-fingered *tap-tap-ping, tappity . . . ping . . . ping . . . ping . . .* and silence except for a distant mutter of barrel-drum thunder, fading . . .

After the concert, they went to congratulate the director, Burn Atterbury, who flushed with pleasure to hear the singers praised. Xulai asked about the youngsters she had particularly noticed, and his smiling mouth turned down sadly for a moment, then smiled again.

"Ah, they are happy here, I think, for all their tragedy so early in their lives. They were just babies, not two years old yet, when they came here to our Home. They're orphans, the children of three brothers, Pembly was the name. The youngest brother fathered the two girls and one of the boys, Brian. The older brothers each fathered one of the other two boys, and they had older children as well, but the older children were with the adults when the tragedy happened."

"A tragedy?"

"It was some kind of family celebration, grandparents' birthday or anniversary, something of the kind. The five littlest ones were left at home together with a couple hired to look after them, rather than subject them to a rather arduous journey, and all the rest of the three families went to the celebration. They were staying together in the little town there in the mountains where the grandparents lived, and there was an avalanche! That was a terrible year for snow. They had a string of them that year, and not one since!"

"How did they end up here?" Xulai asked, in wonder. "Someone related to them?"

"No. It was a very unexpected thing. Turned out the family had been very fond of music, and their business had taken them back and forth traveling through here many a time, so they had had occasion to hear Saltgosh music many times, even going out of their way sometimes just to hear it. We do sings for people, you know, when we have a bunch of 'em here. Don't remember the Pemblys, myself, but we have visitors coming through from snowmelt to snowfall every year, and no way we'd remember 'em all. Anyhow, the Pembly brothers had left wills if anything ever happened that left family members needing care due to age or health, if our Home would take them in and let them share in our music, the Home was to receive the family estates. They were very well-to-do, the Pemblys, so it was quite a fortune, altogether."

"Your Home?" asked Xulai. "I don't understand . . ."

"No reason you should, ma'am, we don't make a big thing out of it. I'm sure you know that many jobs can be dangerous, and mining—even salt mining—is no different. Sometimes there's accidents and people may get crippled up, or maybe some young ones are orphaned. Folks get elderly and can't quite manage on their own, maybe it gets to be too much for them even to go up and down stairs to the Summer Town. They're our people, and they don't want to be sent away somewhere among strangers, none of them. So, it was over a hundred years ago the miners' 'sociation—that's who owns and runs the mines, ma'am, and all of us here, we're members of it—we built a Home back up in the woods, real pretty south-facing clearing with a pond in it up there, little garden for folks as like to putter planting things, not far away, and o' course, people that planned it put a nice warm underhome below it for winter. The 'sociation sees to it there's good people hired to do the cooking and cleaning and caregiving. Tavern here does the food buying and storage for them.

"Well, that's where the young Pemblys grew up. We already had a dozen grown-ups and seven or eight orphaned little ones up there, and figured with the Pemblys added on, we'd maybe need another good schoolteacher and music teacher. We've got our own school here at the mine. Have to! Can't let the children grow up ignorant. The Home's connected by a tunnel so the little ones from there can go to school with the little ones from here. We got us some edubots, too, and I got involved, oh my, yes! *I got involved right off, because way before those Pembly babies could talk more'n a few words, they could sing!*"

"Sing? Words to songs?" Xulai marveled.

"I'm saying *before they could say the words, they could sing the music!* They could sing. In harmony! Hear a tune one time, and the five of 'em could sing it in harmony and make it sound like they'd rehearsed it for a year! We bought a lot of instruments, too, and later on they learned instruments as well. Some of the old folks are pretty good musicians, too, and sometimes the Home gives the rest of us a concert. Last time, all the music they played and sang was composed by one or another of the Pemblys. Truth to tell, ma'am, I think their folks had more than just an inkling about how talented those little ones were goin' to be, somehow, because with all of the elder Pemblys lost at one time like that, well, those families left quite a sizable amount to our Home just because they'd been real impressed by our music."

Xulai murmured, "Well, one doesn't ordinarily think about marvelous music and salt mines at the same time, so I can see why you said it was unexpected."

Mr. Atterbury frowned. "Oh, if you lived here you'd think of 'em at the same time, ma'am. Sometimes we hire an outsider, or I should say, sometimes we don't have a young one coming along to take a certain job that needs filling, so we have to bring someone who's qualified in from outside. No matter how qualified somebody might be, he or she wouldn't stand a chance of gettin' the job if they can't make music. Why, we'd all go crazy back here alone in these winter mountains if we didn't have our music."

As they were helping put away the instruments in the back room, Xulai and Abasio noticed several stacks and baskets of little carved animals, people and creatures, most of them quite funny. According to Gum, the children in Saltgosh were born with music in their throats and carving knives in their hands and the carved toys were part of the "what all" that was done down below, in winter. The small wooden creatures had cleverly jointed arms and legs, or wings and fins, or—later, after Willum had informed the entire village about "first-generation changers" (Abasio had not thought to silence him on that matter), multiple tentacles, each tentacle with a dozen or more joints that writhed with an amusing jerkiness. If the Sea King were to see them, thought Xulai, he would be most offended.

Abasio immediately bought a quantity of toys to take with them, letting it be known at the same time that he would buy all the sea-children toys modeled on Bailai and Gailai that the carvers could come up with in the next few days. All that afternoon, carvers came to peer intently at the babies, who, now that they wore Bertram's jackets, were unmistakably male or female. Abasio and Xulai had agreed that mer-toys would be excellent selling tools. "Who could be afraid of a creature that looked exactly like a doll one had played with as a child?" asked Abasio. "Maybe one with a jacket and hat that a child could put on and take off?"

Xulai's eyes lit up! Dolls! That was the word she'd missed! Yes! *Soft dolls!* The kind of thing one put into cradles with infants! She had had such toys, and Abasio remembered having a fuzzy bear with a red, red tongue. Others recalled piglets, raccoons, yarn-haired little-boy and little-girl dolls. No doubt there were women in Saltgosh who would enjoy making extra money by sewing dolls, soft, stuffed sea-person dolls, sea-baby dolls, for the cribs of ordinary babies, so they could get used to the shape and the idea. Yes. They subsequently spoke with Bertram's sister Liny, offering her a sizable sum in advance to pay whatever women might enjoy making the dolls.

"You can send batches of them on to Bertram with this letter from us asking him to send on to Woldsgard and Wellsport. He may also want to sell some of them to people who come to his shop."

Liny gave him a searchingly mercantile look. "But your real wish is not so much that they be sold for profit as that they be sent far and wide, eh?"

"Oh, profit was not the point at all," said Xulai. "No, our needs are supplied by the people who planned and worked on the sea-children project. Selling the dolls simply gets the wherewithal to buy materials to make more of them! Spreading the image, getting the shape to seem natural to people was what we wanted to do."

Liny nodded. "Well then, I think we can do that on our own, take our own modest profit, and thank you for the suggestion. The women of Saltgosh have always sold handicrafts of the needle, the loom, the carving knife, or the oven. A nearby sun-pocket farm raises ginger root for us, and our hard ginger wafers are in great demand by the wagoners—they keep very well. Though it's not apparent this late in the season, this route through Saltgosh is well traveled, it's the only wagon road that fords the Big River and goes on to the coast. Wagoners who come here take our orders for things we need and bring them on their next trip and buy our crafts here to sell elsewhere.

"I'm sure they'll buy soft sea-children dolls for their toddlers. Soft dolls would travel well; they don't have to be packed carefully as the wooden toys do. All we would need you to do is send us the initial supply of fabric and stuffing together with instructions for ordering more. I can't think of anything local that will do."

She went on murmuring to herself: "It's too late in the year for a wagon train. A pack train . . . cloth, if there's one returning empty. Sheep's wool . . . perfect, but . . . may prove too expensive. There are shepherds . . . driving the stock through soon . . . on their way to winter quarters . . . yarn for the hair . . . yellows, white, reds, browns, black—and suitable fabrics in various flesh colors . . . Well, we'll suppose so . . . the legs . . . those may have to be dyed."

Gum had stayed longer than he had planned, and he would go as he had come, by the western route that would take him through Flitterbean. Wagoners came that way, Gum remarked, to avoid the wild-water notch, not the giants, for the giants were a fairly recent addition to the landscape. Or, he admitted, maybe they had only recently reached a size that made them truly troublesome.

"It's not a natural cut, through that wall," Abasio commented.

Gum shook his head. "Nah. Story is, long ages ago, two men thought they wuz important. Important-Joe an' Important-Jeff, mebbe. Dunno what they wuz important for. So Joe had a place here in the valley and all down to the west, the way the road goes. Jeff had a place t' other side a' t' wall. Jeff needed water, so he had a fella start a tunnel through for him t'get some from t' river. So Joe sez he had no right, to get the hell out, so Jeff got hisself some stuff from over the pass, and he blew him a hole. Alla top rocks fell in, an' he took t' whole river."

"Then what happened?"

"Story is 'ey had a battle. Kilt each other. Saltgosh was just a little place then. When it grew some, Saltgosh fixed the river so it went both ways 'cause by that time there 'uz beavers and fish and all kina birds both places, an 'ere was villages growed up along that north fork and all. Goshians say they haven't seen folks from that way recent. Nobody uses that way much now, 'cep Gold King."

Abasio was almost afraid to ask. "Gold King?"

"He's a fella got a wagon comes over t' pass two, three times a year. Men up there, in those little places, where t' old cities wuz. Those men're diggers. Moles, some call 'm. They find stuff, oh, joolry, stuff made out a' silver. N' they goes up 'ere to the pass n' they trade what they dug up for stuff the men want: some trades fer gold, or fer drink, mos'ly. Gold King's got a wagon purty much like yourn. 'Cep it's gold, a'course."

"Made of gold?"

"C'mon, 'Basio. I ain't total stupid, y'know. How many horses it 'ud take to haul a wagon made a' gold? Nah. Got his wagon painted gold is all. An' he's usual got six or eight horses hitched to it, at least, and anywhere from six to a dozen riders with all kinds a' weapons. T'keep the Gold King from gettin' robbed, y'know."

Abasio did know. It had to be the Edges, again. "Where does he go from here, Gum? What's west of here?"

"Goes all the way t'the sea, I 'spose. The road goes all that way."

The Gold King bought things from the diggers in the ruins, sold these things to the Edgers, and then . . . what? Took what he got from the Edgers to trade near Wellsport? Wellsport was the only place Tingawa sent ships. That Abasio knew of. Oh, he would like to know what the result of all that trading back and forth was!

Returning to the subject of the cut through which the river poured, and the farms along the way they had come, Abasio sought out Melkin and suggested it might be time to talk about what they had found beyond the notch. About fifty of them assembled in the men's hall at the works, and Abasio told them of Odd Duck, displaying the chewed bone and the little skulls, following this with a description of the difficulty they'd had getting through the notch.

"Everything back to Gravysuck is empty. The villages shown on our map don't exist anymore. We found houses, fallen in, all empty. But we get here, and no one seems fearful."

The men looked at one another. It was Melkin who said, "Caltrops. Do you know what I mean?"

Abasio did not. Melkin nodded, and a basket was fetched from a storeroom. One of the items in it was set before him: a metal shape of four spikes, so arranged that no matter how it fell, one spike would always point up. The points were very sharp.

"I was told smaller ones of these were used long, long ago when men fought on horseback," said Melkin. "If one of these got into a horse's foot, it would cripple him, and when the horse fell, the man might also be injured. At least he would have to fight on foot. We trade salt for these, many thousands of them. We go over there." He nodded to the north, vaguely in giant direction. "One quiet man with a few very quiet packhorses or mules and a few men to keep watch. Giants're so big, they leave clear trails behind them, trees knocked down, everything squashed. We find their trails wherever they come close to our borders. We go a few miles down their paths and come back, putting these behind us. These spikes are big enough the livestock can see them and smell them. Livestock tends to stay off Giant trails anyhow. Giants, well, their eyes and noses are way up there, they don't see 'em or smell 'em.

"Nobody human has come that way in . . . two years, maybe more, but we never put any on the roads people used, just in case. We didn't figure on crippling horses or people. We've already got signs made and men ready to go west and put up warnings. Giants don't read. Don't speak any language we know of, either. Make noises, sort of like cows." He looked at others for confirmation, and they nodded at him. He repeated. "Mostly like cows. Mooing and bellowing."

"Anybody coming that way will come through Gravysuck," said Abasio. "Or through Flitterbean or Asparagoose. Be sure your people let them know, because it's around there where the road forks. These spiky things don't look like they'd do much damage to the giants I saw."

"Not designed to, Abasio. The spikes are just long enough to go through the thick skin on the bottoms of their feet. But before we place them, we dip all four points into something else. The something else is a kind of disease, a kind of rot that goes on working to cripple them, even if the giant pulls this out of his foot. Or hers."

Abasio shuddered. "Hers! You mean there are now giantesses?"

"There are. And giant babies. And whatever fool created them made them even larger than the giants we had more or less learned to live with. The giants coming this near us is recent. Couple of years ago was the first time, I guess, and very rarely then. We figured the only place that'd create such things would be the Edges. So how come they're here, all the way over the mountains from where the Edges are?

"We're just now putting plans in place, letting people know. First riders went out about a month ago. Place the boy comes from? They should've heard by now. Some of the villages, the ones that are well up on the sides of the mountains, are safe enough so long as they stay high. The big things can't breathe up there, they like the valleys. The men were due to go over there three days from now to spread caltrops. We were surprised to see the two coming after you. That area near the wall's been safe."

"I'm afraid they heard the boy with us making a lot of noise."

"We hope he's learned how stupid that is."

"If he hasn't, he's hopeless. You said the stuff goes on working to cripple them. What happens to the cripples?"

"Their feet rot, they can't walk, their families kill 'em and eat 'em," said Melkin. "The mothers coo over the babies, but once they can walk, they're meat and on their own. We think the more of the giants there are, the fewer of their children survive. They don't seem to have much . . . much brain. Not much thought. Instinct, some, and that's about all."

Abasio could not speak for a moment. He only whispered at last, "If they eat their own kind, they definitely have Ogre in them?"

One of the other men, a tall red-haired one called, as might be supposed, Red, laughed harshly. "They have every damned thing in them that was ever thought of, Abasio. Ogre! Troll! Ghoul! A year ago, sir, I'd have sooner killed you than looked at you, bringing those babies, coming to suggest that we meddle with ourselves the way those creatures have been meddled with. Well, I've seen the babies and I've heard about the waters, and both have convinced me this particular meddling thing was well intended and lots of sacrifice made for it to be accomplished. Can't have been easy for you or your good wife, but I believe what I can see: a person can swim like a fish and still be a human being. I can look at your pretty little ones, listen to them laugh and have them grab my finger like my own do, and call out for Mama or Dada or Willum, and I don't really mind if my grandchildren look like that. Hope I live long enough to see it, maybe swim alongside 'em. Maybe I can believe that, all right, but those doubly damned giants are another thing altogether, and if I had the doing of it, every Edge that was involved in making them . . . I'd drop a gas bomb down it and kill every creature there, just to stop everything they're doing!"

The others were nodding in agreement.

"Any idea which place made them and why that size?" Abasio asked.

"All we know is Edgers," said someone. "They may be customers, but I hate 'em. Who else is so shut off from the world it doesn't matter what they do? Had a contest, probably. Who could do the biggest ones."

"It's more likely the giants have just gone on growing ever since they were made," said Gister, a quiet, elderly man who spoke little but was always listened to. "I don't believe they're new, I think whoever created them just forgot to include the stopping point. Like the tree down there, next to the tunnel. Just goes on growing. If I could only find a male one, I'd be a happy man." Seeing the question in Abasio's face, he shook his head and added, "All the trees are female trees, so we're not getting any seeds. No way to grow new ones. I'd give anything for some pollen from a male tree. Anyhow, I think those giants have just gone on growing like the trees . . ."

On hearing this, Abasio took a deep breath. It had occurred to him, too, and he agreed that it was most likely. Perhaps even the gentle giants he had known near the archetypal village had gone on growing. He said gravely, "No matter what size they are, they're going to drown, too, you know. And, gentlemen, I know the Edgers are your customers, but it would be a very good idea not to mention anything about the sea-children to them or to anyone else moving through. If any of the people from the Edges actually come here, don't say a word about it. If they bring children, be sure your children don't talk of it. If someone asks, laugh and tell them it's a fairy story the children like to play at. Just as well let the Edgers be in the dark about it. Otherwise they'll be trying to take us over and keeping everyone else out."

"Well, their drowning couldn't be soon enough," snarled Red. "And everybody here'll keep shut about you and the little ones. We're used to talking careful around the Edgers."

Melkin announced, "That's why we've got some other weapons coming, Abasio. We've been drilling into the wall, behind the town. We've bought cannons to go in there. That's just in case; we won't even get them for a couple of years. So far, the caltrops have worked well enough. There's still cattle and horses over there for them to eat, but there's fewer of them than there were, say, ten years ago. We hate bringing big weapons in, but there's no way we can just get along if they come into this valley."

"Instead of cannon in here, I'd try to hit them with something like your caltrop poison. I'd try very hard not to drop one of them dead in this valley."

"Why's that?" Red wondered, a little belligerently.

Abasio took a deep breath. He did not want to mention *ul xaolat*. Still . . . "Figure out how many tons of meat one of those critters weighs, and then figure out what you're going to do with that much meat rotting in your valley, where you can smell it," said Abasio. "Or how you'll work the salt or keep traders coming even supposing the dead giant isn't lying across the road. And that's not mentioning other giants smelling it and coming in to eat it."

It was quite apparent they had not considered that. Abasio, who had lived for a time in Fantis, where bodies were left for the rats, was familiar both with the smell and the animals who ate corpses. "We've also received word that if the bodies are not disposed of promptly, say, by being eaten or burned, certain kinds of flies will lay eggs in the rotting body. The larvae will eat the body, the body has a growth hormone in it that will change the larvae, and they'll hatch into giant biting insects. We got this information from Tingawa, and information from there is usually accurate. Tingawa is trying to find a poison that would not only kill the giants but also the flies and the fly eggs, but right now it's only the fact the bodies are being eaten by other giants that's keeping you free of giant, biting flies. When you get down to the last few, be ready to dispose of the bodies. If they aren't eaten, you must either bury or burn them."

Abasio left them talking about what fuel they could order that would burn hot enough to get rid of the bodies. Just outside, he encountered Gister. "What was that you said about a male tree?"

"There's about a dozen of those trees anywhere within reachable distance from here. Nobody's ever seen one anywhere else. They're all female, that is, they don't produce pollen, so they don't produce . . . whatever it is, cones with seeds, probably . . ."

"My wife says they grow near Tingawa. If you'd like, I'll try to get some pollen for you. Would it be too late for this year?"

Gister grinned at him. "If you could do that! Oh, yes. This year or next or whenever, so long as I'm still living. Even if the waters come, like you say, I've got a hunch there'll be a mountaintop of two could stand having trees on it. And I'd see the seeds were kept, too, ready to plant when the time came. Or take to some other world, maybe. I can dream that!"

Abasio promised. Later he gave Gum a sample caltrop, a jug of the poison, and a letter to Willum's mom, explaining about the giants and suggesting that they be prepared if the Giants came into their area. The village had a blacksmith. He could make the spikes, and they could buy the stuff that went on them from Saltgosh, or trade for it. Gum shook his head over the information. When he left for home the next morning, by the southern route, Willum sat atop Abasio's wagon watching the Gravysuck hitch on its way back home, disappearing and reappearing as the road rounded the plump shoulders of the mounded hills.

Xulai, while tucking the wet-suited babies into a basket for their nap inside the wagon, remarked, "Don't forget we have to stow the cookies." Liny and a dozen other women had made them in the huge Tavern kitchen between the regular breakfasts, lunches, and suppers for the residents. Those made by the Saltgosh women were plainer-looking than the ones from Tingawa, but even Xulai admitted they tasted just as good. It had taken several tries before they had come up with a way of packing and stacking them that would keep them whole as the wagon bumped its way up toward the pass. Certain drills the miners used came in long fiber cylinders, perfect for packing stacks of cookies that could be slotted into the hollow ceiling of the wagon.

Abasio took their map from the wagon and spread it on the shelf that folded down from the wagon's side. "Since we know the map isn't accurate, I'm not going to trust it entirely, but since it shows no peopled place between here and the plains on the eastern side, and since the people here in Saltgosh agree with that, we won't plan on stopping anywhere. Liny says the kitchens here are well provided from their Home farms and the wagons that bring barter, so if we need anything in the way of food to last us until Artemisia, now is the time to buy what we need."

"Gum mentioned people from around here who raided for women . . ." said Xulai.

"If you're thinking of a place for us to recruit, there's nowhere. Remember, those people came seventy years ago. If they still exist, which I doubt, they're too deep in the woods to get the wagon in, and considering what Gum said about the people from there, they are not candidates for the sea change." He laid his hand on Xulai's shoulder. "The next likely place to do any recruitment is going to be inside Artemisia itself. You'll like the people there."

"How come you know so much about the place?" Willum asked.

Xulai answered. "Abasio was born east of the mountains. A lot of the ancient scientists and technicians lived in the same area . . ."

Willum's face twisted oddly, half curiosity, half annoyance. "I hear you and 'Basio alla time sayin' *sine*-tist, *sine*-tist, sine-*tist,* but nobody tells me what one *is!*"

Abasio grinned at Xulai. "Not keeping up with your educational responsibilities, madam?"

She took Willum by the arm, handed him a bucket, took another one herself, and started for the pool, saying as she went, "Well, Willum, a scientist is a person who studies things. One might study animals, another might study birds, or stones or stars . . ." Her voice went on, discoursing on scientific method, Willum interrupting at intervals, and as they returned, she was saying, "One person may say 'tall' where another says 'short,' or 'thick' where another says 'thin,' but two is always two, four is always four. It is the scientist's job to prove how something works by recording and measuring, and they can't say it's so until they can prove it."

Willum stared at her. "How would one o' them prove something like . . . like a rainbow?"

Xulai threw a glance to Abasio that said, "He may be a brat, but he isn't stupid." Abasio had already figured that out. He leaned back and drowsed, the sun on his face, while Xulai set Willum to chopping cabbage during her explanation of raindrops and prisms and the scientific method, concluding " . . . and even though one man quotes his holy book as to what's true and another man quotes his traditions as to what's true, a scientist will not say anything is true until he's proved it."

Willum looked puzzled. "But how come the holy book didn't know what was true? I mean, if it was holy and all that?"

Abasio opened his eyes and joined the conversation. "Willum, there's a holy book some folks have that tells about God making the first man and then taking one of that man's ribs to make the first woman out of. Everybody in the world was supposed to be descended from that man and that woman. So a lot of the people who believed in that book said the book explained why men have one less rib than women do."

Willum drew himself up, hands flying to the area in question. "Do I have a fewer rib?"

Xulai murmured, adding chopped apple to the salad, "No, Willum. You've got the same number we all have, same on both sides, men and women."

After a moment of frowning concentration, the boy's face lighted up. "So you mean *they never counted?*"

Abasio was delighted. There was intelligence hidden behind that stubborn, unthinking behavior. "You're right! They never counted. That's why Xulai and I have to be so very careful about people's religion when we're traveling. If your religion tells you to believe you have one less rib, you're not allowed to count them."

"My ma, she'd say that's just plain silly."

"Well," drawled Abasio. "In my experience, often people with very little brain find life easier if they turn the brain off entirely. Thinking is work, and for some people, that's like harnessing a pair of field mice to pull a hay wagon. It's lots easier to shut your mouth, ignore reality, and believe what people tell you to believe."

Xulai, moved by Abasio's challenge, was considering what her duty was as temporary mother to Willum. She had assumed that duty would include telling a child whatever that child wanted or needed to know, promptly and fully. Including the embarrassing details, if any! Abasio had waited with some anticipation for the unveiling of the embarrassing details, but Willum, being farm-reared, knew about sex already, including things about the sexual behavior of animals that Xulai would have preferred to remain ignorant of, much to Blue and Rags's amusement.

Each of them had a plate of lunch, Willum walking back and forth with his, and she became slightly apprehensive about what else the boy might have on his mind. Since he usually approached food as though it had to be disposed of before it grew legs and got away, she expected an immediate resumption of discussion. Today, however, she noted the boy's furrowed forehead, the brows drawn together over his nose in puzzlement, the slowed movement of hands to mouth. She shared a glance with Abasio, who shrugged slightly. The boy was bothered about something.

In a moment Willum looked up and said, "Well, tell you what, Xulai! I think that rib business is just . . . like I said, silly. Now, God took that rib, right? And so my uncle, he had a accident, and he lost his thumb. N' after that, he had a little boy and the boy had both thumbs, so losing some part of you doesn't mean your children are gonna be missing that part."

Abasio laughed out loud. "You're perfectly right."

"Even back then there were enough examples that people should have known it," admitted Xulai. "But people thought since God made man in the first place, any changes made by God would turn out to be hereditary. Of course, that was mostly before the Big Kill . . ."

Willum shook his head in stubborn, red-faced confusion: *"Ma n' Pa*

*never tol' me about any Big Kill! You and 'Basio say there's not many people any-
more. Nobody tol' me there wasn't many people anymore. Nobody in Gravysuck
ever tol' me that!"*

Abasio frowned as he pulled the boy closer to him. "Hey, Willum,
settle down. We told you, these things happened way in the past! Forty
generations. Remember? That's what we said. Nobody talks much
about things that happened that long ago. Most people talk about what
they've done, sometimes about something their parents did, and even
more seldom anything their grandparents did or saw. The Big Kill happened long before Gravysuck was even there. I imagine your family
didn't get started in Gravysuck until hundreds of years after those
things happened."

A long silence while Willum actually snuggled against him. Abasio
caught Xulai's eye, and she nodded. She had noticed. Too many new
ideas! And actually being disciplined! The boy was feeling lost. And
maybe homesick. And perhaps scared. He'd never before thought it was
necessary to listen or be obedient. Now he probably found the thought
frightening. Maybe? *Could one hope so?*

"Was there really truly lots more people then, 'Basio?"

"You can answer that for yourself, Willum. I know you've heard
about all those buried cities!" He paused for a nod of agreement.
"Well, if there were big cities, they had to have been filled with people.
Where did they go? What did you think I meant when I talked about
the Big Kill?"

Willum frowned, chewing his lip in annoyance. "I didn't conneck it
up, I guess. If they was killin' hunnerts a' people, I guess there had to
be hunnerts of 'em to kill, but I didn't conneck it up." He turned toward
Abasio. "'Basio. What was your story about why we don't have all those
people? Where you lived, what did they say about it?"

Abasio half smiled. "Well, I lived in farm country along the east side
of these mountains. Just over the pass, where we're going. We didn't
know about the Big Kill because almost all the killers had been destroyed by the time my grandparents were born. But the ruins of the
city, Fantis, were there. Lots of people had seen the ruins. Even though
the city was mostly buried, anyone could see how huge it'd been once
upon a time. You could see buildings that had had ten floors in them,
even twenty! So, all those people had to have gone somewhere, and

nobody remembered the Big Kill because that had happened too long ago, right?"

"I 'spose. Right."

"Everyone along the mountains knew there were spaceships at the Place of Power. No one knew much about them, but it wasn't a secret. People knew power got sent down from the moon to the Place of Power and there were ships that went up there to maintain the machines. Nobody thought much about it. People at the Place of Power didn't mix with other people, so they didn't know much about one another.

"So what I think might have happened is some men were drinking beer somewhere near Fantis, that's the big buried city where I was. Maybe they were digging into it for treasure. And one of the men maybe said something like, *'This place was really BIG. I wonder where all the people went that used to live here?'* And one of the other men maybe said, *'Oh, they prob'ly flew to the stars in those ships they got down at the Place of Power.'* And the first man says, *'Sure, that's prob'ly what happened.'* And then they drank some more beer, and when they went home they talked about it, and their families talked about it, and pretty soon everyone along the mountains there decided that everyone had flown to the stars in spaceships they had down at the Place of Power!

"And then later, maybe one night some boy about your age asked his mom, *'Mom, why didn't our family go to the stars on the starships?'* And Mom didn't know, but she didn't want to say she didn't know . . ."

Willum blurted, "And she didn't want him thinkin' like they hadn't been asked neither. Moms can get real mad if somebody has a do and they don't get 'vited."

"Right. Nobody wants to be left out, so maybe she said something like"—he screwed up his face and gave it his best falsetto—"*'Oh, my family said if those other people want to leave this good earth that's been our home, well, let them. We're going to be faithful to our home and stay right here.'* And the boy repeated that, and someone else told someone else, and before long, everyone said it. *'When I was a boy, all the people in the cities went to the stars, but we chose to stay right here!'* And, of course, there had been millions of people in the cities."

"Is that a lot? Millions?" Willum asked Xulai.

"It was way too many people in one place, yes."

Abasio was rubbing his head, casting his mind back to that teenage boy who had left the farm for the city. "Where I grew up, on the farm, twenty or thirty grown people and their children was a village. So when we spoke of a million people, it seemed an enormous number."

"So it *is* a 'normous number," said Willum. "Isn' it?"

"Yes," said Xulai. "But it's only a tiny bit of how many there really were."

Willum frowned. "If people knew how many there really was, how come they thought they all went to the stars, then?" He frowned, then shouted, "Wait! I know, I know. It's what you said about not counting! But it seems like they would . . . I don't unnerstan' that!"

Abasio gave him half a real hug, which Willum—obviously not thinking—returned. "Willum, how do your folks measure farmland?'

"Pa says it's achers, like a backache. 'Cause whether you plow it or seed it or whatever, it makes you ache all over when you're done."

"Now, your pa might have told you your farm is a hundred acres, or four hundred, or whatever . . ."

"Four hunnert twenty."

"Four hundred twenty. But have you ever measured it?"

Willum started to get up, then decided he was comfortable where he was, resting against Abasio's chest, with Abasio's arms around him. He frowned and shook his head. "No. Nobody does that. Dad just takes us out and shows the land starts from the big white rock by the road, the one with his great-great-grandpa's name cut into it, then you walk straight by the shortest way to the creek, left along the creek all the way to where it runs into the big gully, left again, back along the gully to the big red rock shaped like a cow, and then straight across to the black standing stone by the road, and from there down the road to the white rock again. Like that. Dad must've showed all us kids twenty times 'zackly like that."

"Yes," Abasio agreed. "And you believed that was the way to do it, right? We tend to accept things people tell us, especially family and good friends. So when some of our folks told us everyone else went to the stars but we were left behind or our families chose not to go, we believed that. We thought everyone else going off to the stars was perfectly believable. Just so long as nobody counted up—"

Xulai interrupted him, crying out, "But, Abasio! Remember, there were two ships that did go to the stars from there!"

"I know, you told me. It bothers me a little. You know Olly, she went in that last ship, and she did it to keep those crazy people from getting to the solar cannons on the moon. And when she left, she gave me her helmet, and she said to me, 'Man never went to the stars.' But you say two ships did go . . ."

Xulai nodded. "Yes, that's exactly what she said. She did NOT say, 'Men never went to the stars.' Or even 'Men and women never went to the stars.' She said *'man,'* as in *mankind, the race of man*! The people of Earth, all of mankind, all the missing human population of the planet did not go to the stars. I only know of those two ships that went to Lom, about two thousand people, and that didn't diminish Earth's population one bit. There were probably more than two thousand babies born on Earth the same day the ships went." She fetched her own pillow and came to sit in front of Abasio.

"So it really was the Big Kill that took the population down to almost nothing," he said, shaking his head.

Xulai concluded, "It's all in the library helmet, Abasio. You can find it there."

Abasio said softly, "But Olly is in the library helmet. So wouldn't she have known? And it was she who told me."

Xulai never talked to him about Olly. Olly was one of those almost sacred memories that many people have, the ones that must not be intruded upon. Like her own deeply secret memories of her mother. She had been afraid to say too much to Abasio! But *someone* had obviously said *too little*. She put her hand on his free shoulder, shaking it gently.

"Abasio, Olly gave you her helmet when she left. Before she gave it to you, she asked the helmet to grant her residence. It's the same technology that was used to send the two ships all that way, a thousand-year flight. It records the mind and puts the body in stasis. With the helmet, it only records the mind: it read her, right down to the least little memory she had, and gave her residence within the helmet. *The Olly in the helmet* knows only what that Olly knew at that time or what the helmet Olly has chosen to learn since."

He murmured, "I thought all the information inside the library was shared among the people in there!"

He sounded so dismayed, so hurt. Willum stirred. Xulai said very softly, "Abasio, dear heart! If that were so, then they'd all be alike, wouldn't

they? They wouldn't be human people, they'd be helmet people, no difference among them, no individuals. That's not how it works."

"Then how the hell does it work!" It came out as an accusation. He
didn't mean that . . .

She kept her voice low, quiet, unemotional. "A person taking residence in a library helmet can say where they want to live. The person
might say, 'I want a sunny room, looking out on a lake that changes with
the weather.' Or, 'I want a little house beside a stream.' If the person
wants it to be very real, the person can ask to live in the helmet as it
would on Earth, sleep, wake up, get hungry, eat and poop just as they
would if they were alive. Or the person can experience hunger and the
taste and repletion of food perfectly well without experiencing diges-
tion. People can define what kind of existence they want . . .

"However, one thing is the same for everyone: whatever the person's
place is, house or palace or tent, it has some kind of an entry or door on
it. When you put on the helmet and ask for Olly, the helmet knocks on
her door or rings her bell or shouts into her tent and tells her Abasio is
there to asking for her. Then *it's up to her* whether she talks to you or not.
If she talks to you, she can remember anything you tell her. She learns
things the same way she would if she were still with us: either *she asks
questions and gets answers, or people tell her things.*"

"The library helmet could tell her!"

"*Only if she asks it to tell her!* It's up to her! It isn't the helmet's job to
educate her or inform her. It's the helmet's job to keep her as a whole
person, as she is or becomes. People who visit her can tell her things,
but the telling is just like in real life. *If she isn't interested in what they say,
she will probably forget it.* Or she can ask the helmet to file it for her and
bring it up if she needs it or wants it. Just the way you would yourself,
writing yourself a note and putting it away."

"So I could have gone in there, been with her . . . Olly never asked
me to do that . . ."

"Abasio, that's *not what she wanted.* She didn't want a helmet Abasio.
She wanted *to share your continuing life out here, where you are.* She wanted
to be visited by the Abasio who is living in the world, an Abasio who is
experiencing new things to share with her."

"Because she knew she would not have any more . . . experiences."
He felt his own tears and turned his head away.

"That's not true. She *can* have them, through you and others who enter the library from the outside world and knock on her door and say you have things to tell her. Or she can experience anything she asks to experience. I hope you have told her about your life, about our mission, *about your children*. I am positively sure that what she most wanted to know was whether her sacrifice had been worth it. Knowing about your children will convince her of that! She wanted to share your life. That is what made her sacrifice worthwhile. Don't deny it to her."

She stood up and went to refill her glass, her eyes wavering between Abasio's still, white face and Willum's sleeping one. She had assumed he knew! Wrong assumption. He had *not wanted* to know about it. He had preferred to think of her as if she were living in some other country. Living there, aging, changing in accord with what was happening to her, as though this outside world still affected her. And, of course, if she asked the helmet to do that, it would do that. If the helmet person grew weary of being, the helmet would let the person age and die. And if one did, then someone who asked for that person would be taken to the grave.

Willum sighed, yawned, half opened blurry eyes, and took advantage of the momentary silence. "Tell about the two ships that went to the stars, Xulai."

"Yes," said Abasio, as from a great distance. "Tell us a little about them."

Her mind was wandering, scattered, like a flock of sheep! She mentally circled the flock, making shooing motions, forcing her voice to be as soothing as possible: "Well, they already had the core of a station on the moon, because they'd been beaming sun power down to Earth for several generations. The shuttles took the pioneers up there a hundred or so at a time to be processed and stored in the ships. Processing meant the minds were recorded and filed, the bodies were preserved for later revivification.

"Three ships were planned. Things got so bad on Earth that they decided not to wait for the third ship to be finished. They decided to send the two that were ready. That meant there was one whole shipload of passengers up there on the moon that might not get to go at all, and there was some last-minute shuffling around as to who would be put into the two ships that went. That's why we don't know for sure who went, unless they were mentioned in messages after they got there."

Willum asked, "So they did get there?"

Xulai looked up, surprised. "Oh, yes, we know the ships got there. The ships left in our year 2140. In Earth year 3110, after roughly a thousand Earth years, both ships reached what we called the Q System and landed on the fourth planet from its sun. The planet already had intelligent life on it, and both ships sent messages saying they'd landed."

"A thousand years?" Abasio mused. "Forty generations of people here on Earth. Why doesn't anyone outside your little circle know about this?"

She shook her head at him. "Oh, for heaven's sake, Abasio! As you told Willum, it happened over a thousand years ago! Everyone who had any interest in it knew! By that time, we were beginning to hear about the waters rising, and Tingawa switched its attention to long-term survival here on Earth—that was also about the time of the Visitation!"

"Visitation?"

"Yes. In Tingawa. Shortly after or concurrent with people on Earth learning about the waters rising, they received a visitor. In referring to the episode, the people in Tingawa always referred to it as 'the Visitation' because the visitor was so mysterious, wearing long robes and a veil, speaking in a strange voice. He—our people assumed it was a he—told them he had just completed a translation of some pre–Big Kill documents on genetic research, and he had thought it best to bring them to Tingawa."

"Odd, but scarcely memorable for later ages," Abasio remarked.

She looked past him with a peculiar smile. "Well, dear one, I'm of the later ages, and I choose to remember it because those documents are why I was born, and my mother, and possibly you, and certainly our babies. What the Wazeer Nawt gave to Tingawan scientists formed the basis of the sea-children research. We wouldn't be here except for them."

He turned to her in amazement. "You're joking? You're not joking! Who or what was this Wazeer Nawt?"

"That's almost a rhyme. I wish we had an answer to who or what! Our people evidently asked the strange visitor what his name was, and he told them they could call him *the* Wazeer Nawt. Our people believed 'wazeer' was a title, like doctor or professor or reverend."

"Did he say where the documents came from?"

"Salvage. He was quite mysterious about it. He said they'd been salvaged from a buried university. What were we talking about before I mentioned the the Visitation?" She leaned into the wagon and retrieved a light blanket.

"The ships. You were saying you did hear from the ships."

"Well, one of the ships landed down in a valley, all the women on it left it, and the men who were left there started what they called a 'university.' That was kind of strange. It blew itself up later, some fault in its systems. The other ship sent its settlers out; they joined the women who had left the other ship, and within fifty years, there were a dozen villages and many farms. The place was called Lom, as you know. You've dreamed about it."

"Did they know about the waters rising?"

She spread the blanket over the sleeping boy. "We didn't know the whole world was going to be drowned. We didn't know about that until much later, but yes, Lom was told about it."

Leaving Willum asleep by the wagon, the two of them took a stroll along the road, taking time to admire the late-blooming flowers peering up through the drying grasses. As they returned, they passed a gooseherd with his flock of geese just leaving one of the little river ponds downhill from the Saltgosh poultry houses. Abruptly, responding to some stimulus Xulai neither saw nor heard, the flock changed its character as simultaneously each slowly walking, gabbling goose suddenly extended its wings and ran to get under cover. Being domestic geese, too large to fly, they moved instead in a kind of foot-pumping, wing-scooping pace that propelled them rapidly in a series of neck-stretched, half-sailing broad jumps. In a moment all were hidden among a grove that clustered against the cliff wall. Here and there a muffled honk marked a hiding place. Xulai saw one bright yellow beak stretched vertically alongside a young, white-trunked tree, bill pointed straight up, beady eyes searching the sky.

Xulai looked up. High! Higher! Wings at the very summit of the sky. The thing was far, very far up there, flying east toward a mountain that loomed enormously on the serrated horizon. After a time, wings slipped *behind* the mountain, almost at its peak. The wings . . . too large! Far too large! Nothing that flew could be large enough to be seen at that distance! Not flying *behind* that peak and still be seen from here!

Abasio's voice was sepulchral. "Speak of the devil—or near as: Griffin! That's the only thing it could be. The one I knew lived on the eastern slope of the mountains where we're going." Though the one he knew had not been anywhere near that size! Could it have grown? Surely it had been fully grown when he had been carried back to the Gaddir House, cushioned in its mane.

Something stirred in Xulai like a live thing in a burrow, an occupant of a closed box, something moving that did not often move. She felt it with all of her. As she had felt when she met Abasio. As she had felt at various other times when warnings had been sent or traps had been laid in her path. She did not want to speak of the feeling, but could not do otherwise. Something portentous, busy portending!

"Is it possible," she asked ruefully, "that the thing up there is looking for us?"

"Or," he said, taking her hand tightly in his own. "Or possibly not *us*. Possibly . . . just me."

At that moment he realized the probable actual size of the thing. The apprehension he felt was a shudder of possibility, like the subliminal detection of a far-off avalanche, barely heard but inevitably headed in their direction. A creature that size . . . so much larger than the one he had seen, talked to, been carried about by when he was last in Artemisia. So? What might that mean?

"Sexual dimorphism," murmured Xulai. "Do you suppose?"

Abasio scowled at the sky. They would be leaving Saltgosh in the morning; they would be moving toward that distant peak. He did not want to suppose any such thing.

CHAPTER 5

A Departure, and a Departure

IN THE HIGH VALLEY NEAR FINDEM PASS, THE time came that Needly had to leave Tuckwhip. She was moved by two happenings: a tragedy and a meanness, either of which would have been reason enough by itself.

The meanness came first. She heard Gralf, the House-Pa, tell his cronies he'd taken an advance payment from Old Digger, who would be wanting Needly right soon, since she was the only female in the village who was "purdy near beddin' age."

The following morning, when Pa crowed about it to Grandma, she lost her patience and told Pa what she thought of men who sold their children. Pa had no patience to lose, and one of those nice throwing stones was near at hand. It struck Grandma's forehead. One stone was all that was needed. That was the tragedy, or so Needly saw it. Gralf, seeing what he'd done, ran off. He'd killed the healer. The only one in the valley. It was *jitchus*! Some might not take that too kindly. Needly, seeing what he'd done, ran for Grandma's medicine bag. The little blue bottle was there: a drop of what was inside it was placed on Grandma's tongue while Grandma still breathed. This done, Needly relaxed in tears. She did not grieve. She thought there was no reason for grief. Not yet. Perhaps not ever.

There were no obsequies. The people of the village were superstitious about dead people left unburied, so Grandma was buried
deeply, though evidently not deep enough, for the grave was opened
to its bottom that night and Grandma's body was gone in the morning. This fact served only to intensify Gralf's fears. Too late he had
remembered *jitchus.*

Needly had gathered from various things Grandma had said that
Grandma's people would come for her body. That Grandma had *people,*
Needly had never doubted, nor had she doubted those people would
be her own, if and when they chose to reveal themselves to her, or if she
ever found them, which she now intended to do.

Without any prompting, Needly had decided the men in the village should believe that killing a woman would bring retribution. They
knew *jitchus.* Therefore let *jitchus* be manifest. Early on the day prior to
her departure, she mentioned to Slap that Grandma had come out of
her grave, looking for Pa because the goddess of the valley was tired of
the men killing women or girls, killing them or hurting them.

Needly's announcement was known village-wide by nightfall. It gave
Pa only an hour of apprehension between supper and sleep and a few
moments' serious discomfort the following morning. That night Trudis
and Gralf and the boys had slept very deeply, helped by one of Grandma's little bottles: this one a clear, tasteless liquid. One had to be sure
of the justice of the matter before using Grandma's potions, but for the
most part, they were not unmerciful. Just before Needly left the place,
at about midnight, she put a few drops from the yellow bottle in the
kettle on the back of the stove, the one Pa would use in the morning for
his tea. Pa always poured any extra water out, to prevent Trudis finding
any hot water when she woke. Pa was mean that way, as he was mean in
all ways, but this meanness was useful, for it meant no one else would
drink what was in the kettle. Needly bore Trudis and the boys no fatal
ill will. Trudis was her Ma. Slap and Grudge were at least her half brothers. Pa-who-was-not-her-father, however, was no kin to her at all and had
murdered her grandma. His fate was fitting.

"With this preparation, Grandma wishes you farewell, Pa," she said,
making the same hieratic gesture she had seen her grandmother make
on similar occasions. The gestures had a meaning. They were a kind
of summons. Grandma had indicated that these gestures, when used,

were *seen* to be used. If Needly used them, she would be seen to be using them, though how and by whom Grandma did not say. Nonetheless, the girl made them gracefully, completely, as instructed. "With this ceremony, with this elixir, Grandma and I say good-bye to you, Gralf. Fare far and unwell."

Her provisions had been ready packed and accumulating in hiding since she had turned eight. They had been regularly updated as she had grown. She was eleven now, or thereabout. Her small pack contained a fire starter, a good knife and a spare, leggings and boots, warm knitted sweaters, and a hooded raincoat that unfolded into a cover for her bedding. All the clothes were familiar, tested, broken in during private walks in the mountains. The pack was rolled inside a blanket, with another waterproof cover outside it and a strap to hold it across her back. Among the other equipment was a metal stake with a hook that would hold a tiny pot over a fire and a water bottle Grandma had found somewhere, made out of some flexible stuff that would not break. Could have been an animal's bladder, Needly thought. Something like that. One end of it wrapped around a short piece of hollow bone that was bound there with waxed thread, a hook to put on a belt loop, and a kind of cork thing that screwed in. It was to be used to hold water, whenever she left the vicinity of a stream.

In the pocket of her jacket she had a comb and a spare. Grandma and Needly had kept a secret from Gralf. They had only pretended at Needly's uglification. She had always washed and combed her real hair and braided it tight to her head, covering it with a wig made out of horse combings from the one horse in the valley with a white mane and tail. The dirt had been real, but it had never been allowed to grind in or accumulate. There had been frequent baths in the little hot spring in the hollow over the ridge; long midnight soaks while Grandma told her old stories and drilled her on survival matters. Since that first time, Slap or Grudge had not used Needly as their target. Since reasoning from cause to effect was beyond them, Grandma had finally told them Needly was protected by a forest spirit who cut off boy's parts if they abused girls. After that, they had left her alone. Along with gold, those "parts" were a male's most important possession.

By the midnight following Grandma's burial, Needly was clean, clad, equipped, and well away from the valley, gone by a different route than the men ever took. It was unlikely they would even hunt for her for some time, perhaps not until Old Digger decided he wanted her. It would take several days for Needly to get to the pass, but she did not hurry. Better to go slow and careful than quick and careless. Grandma had "foreseen" something useful for Needly would await her at the pass. Once at the pass, she could decide where to go from there so long as it took her east and eventually to the area near the House of the Oracles.

Behind her in Tuckwhip, morning came. Gralf rose, made his tea, and drank it. He felt very sleepy afterward and went back to bed. Trudis finally decided to wake him in the early afternoon, but his body was cold by then. Cold and starting to stiffen. Trudis went down the road to tell the other Mas. They said *the men'd wanna bury him afore dark.* The men were afraid of ghosts, so they did bury him. One of the men who had no woman announced to the others his intention of moving into Trudis's house. Two others saw fit to fight him over it. He killed one of them and sent the other fleeing into the woods, then waited for a couple of days after the burying, as tradition required, before moving in with Trudis, announcing he'd take Gralf's place. Trudis poured herself another glass of beer. She subsequently noticed no difference. Gulped food the same. Snorted and farted the same. Smelled the same. Rutted the same. Only that one fellow had been any different. The one that probably fathered Needly.

Needly. She yawned and rolled to face away from the new man, wondering if he'd get her pregnant and become a Pa, wondering why Gralf had gone and died, wondering where Needly had got to. Girl hadn't washed the kitchen stuff from yesterday. Girl oughta be here, takin' care of things. She hadn't been around for . . . a while.

CHAPTER 6

Encounters on the Road

AT FIRST LIGHT, ABASIO DROVE THE WAGON PAST the watchtower of Salt-gosh and up toward Findem Pass. They were well provisioned. If all went well, they would be on the plains below the mountains before serious cold struck. Willum knew all about what would be done in case of cold, but he much preferred not having to sleep in the cold-weather fold-down bunk above the big bed in the wagon. He preferred to sleep next to Blue and the chickens and come and go as he pleased.

On the journey, the horses needed no guidance. There was only one road and only one way to go up it, so up it they went, the walkers variously trailing behind, rushing ahead, or plodding alongside. The babies were perched on the wagon seat, carefully strapped in, regarding each turn in the road with solemn interest. They met no one at all for the first two days. It was, Abasio thought, as though they were the only living two-legged mammals alive, though four-legged ones were plentiful: deer, elk, wolves. He had more or less expected wolves. Precious Wind had adopted a pack of them during their former travels and she would guarantee that they survived the waters' rising. How water wolves would differ from water dogs, he had not asked. He did not see coyotes; they were usually creatures of lower altitudes.

The scenery was so uniformly grand as to become unremarkable except for one view they came upon in early morning as they made a turn on the way up and saw it against the sky.

"What in heaven's name is that?" cried Xulai.

Blue and Rags brought the wagon to a halt, looking up as Xulai was doing. She had actually walked forward, as though to get closer, though the thing was far and unattainable from where they were. They were looking across a straight-walled crevasse, over an intersecting ridge, up another vertical wall. At the top of the wall stood a sizable grove of blackened trees, an isolated grove occupying the only soil pocket for some distance in any direction. Nothing was left now but the charred trunks and the larger branches. Through this black veil they could see the curved, soaring lines of a remarkable stone formation.

"I see it," said Abasio. "Actually, I've heard of it. It's called something odd. Oh, yes: the Listener." He leaned back into the open window of the wagon, feeling dizzy. "I don't remember anyone saying it could be seen from the road here."

"It's huge."

"It is that," he mumbled, fighting nausea as images cascaded through his mind. *The tower. The women. A forest, a group of creatures dancing . . . a huge red egg . . . a building that squirmed and changed its shape . . . Then the tower, the pool. Then, suddenly, the throne room, Plethrob. . .*

Xulai stared at the thing. The light around it was a halo, a sphere, contracting, narrowing, becoming a single beam that reached from the formation toward them, arrowing toward them, past her, ending at Abasio. He was outlined with a scarlet glow, as though on fire . . .

She cried out, "Abasio? Love, what is it?" As she moved toward him, it vanished.

He slumped, breathing heavily. Casting a glance at the formation, Xulai said, "Blue, Rags, get us out of the line of sight of that thing, will you? Quickly."

The horses moved quickly; the formation vanished as quickly as it had appeared, visible only from that one angle, and it would have been invisible, even from there, if the grove of trees had not been burned. Xulai gritted her teeth. It was almost as though someone . . . something had burned them just so something could get a look at Abasio. She climbed onto the seat beside Abasio and turned his face toward her: he was pale, his nostrils flared. She could see the pulse in his neck, hard, fast. Suddenly he took a deep breath and straightened up. "Whoosh."

"Hold it, Blue, Rags. Let me get him something to drink."

He gulped at the water she gave him, his breathing slowed. His eyes darted, here, there, coming to rest on her face. He muttered, "Those burned trees. Looked like a lightning strike, didn't it. Just burned that one isolated bunch. Thank goodness it was isolated. Otherwise, there'd have been a forest fire."

"We goin'?" asked Blue.

Xulai answered. "Yes, Blue. Let's get a little distance between us and that whatever. Abasio, what do you know about the thing, the thing we just saw?"

"Ah. Not much, actually." He took several deep breaths, another gulp of water. His head didn't hurt, but it felt odd. As though it had been rummaged through. There were . . . adjacencies in there he didn't remember. Whatever did it wasn't required to be gentle. He fumbled for words. "I've never heard you could see it from here. Well, normally one couldn't, of course. It's supposed to be a vivid red at dawn. That's really all I know about it."

"It's very strange," murmured Xulai. She kept glancing at the skyline as they went on, though a turn in the road had put it behind an intervening ridge. According to a sign by the side of the road, Findem Pass was a day's travel farther on. They paused briefly in a clearing beside the road to put together a late, cold lunch. Willum, who seemed to have several extra pairs of eyes—to go with his multiple mouths and lungs—called their attention to the height still above them where a dozen horsemen were briefly silhouetted against a high rock wall. The men were perhaps an hour or so away, and Abasio noted with some apprehension that they had no pack animals with them and . . . the last horse in line seemed to have a rider who was bound. It was too far to tell for sure, but the horse looked *very much* like Socky. The bound man was probably Kim.

Poor Kim. He'd had nothing but trouble on this trip, and Abasio said as much to Xulai. Unfortunate young man. A Tingawan chosen for the task, but just possibly not as well fitted for it as someone else might have been. Xulai thought Precious Wind would not have been caught so. Nor would her former companion, the Great Bear of Zol. Poor Bear. Honorably dead. But still, dead.

The wagon had been sheltered behind trees when they saw the men; it was unlikely that either it or they had been seen. The wagon was quickly pulled into the next shielding grove. The trees were too thick to get it very far among them, so they removed their stores and anything that looked useful into the nearest hiding place they could find, a small cave not far away, invisible among trees and fallen stones. Everything went, including the chicken coops, which were covered to eliminate any clucking or crowing to betray them. All of Xulai and Willum's clothing was hidden, as well as the babies and all their accoutrements. The sea-eggs, which, along with themselves, were the most precious things they carried, were already well hidden in the walls of the wagon, cushioned against any accident. When they had finished, the wagon carried nothing much but a sparse diet and clothing for a single traveler. The last thing removed was the harness.

"Why, dang nab it?" said Willum to Xulai. "We was just about all the way up!"

"We don't know that group coming down," Xulai told him. "Men traveling in groups without pack animals and this far from a town have to live off the country—and we're part of the country. They could be slavers or thieves. Abasio and I would rather not have wounded people or animals while we're trying to get the babies to safety, so we're going to give them no fight and no reason to steal. Also, Abasio thinks they may have captured Kim. Understand?"

"Abasio says you got something could stop them!"

"Yes, but only by killing all of those men while they're in a close group, and probably some of their horses." Although, she thought, the new devices might well be able to discriminate. No time to experiment, however . . .

(*Of course I can discriminate, you silly woman! thought* ul xaolat. *I know Kim, I can release Kim, kill all the others—without gore—quiet the horses, and then recite in a solemn voice, in any chosen language, your choice of requiems, with appropriate musical setting. Given an extra few moments, I can manage an interment. With flowers. You don't have to push a button. You have only to say so!*)

Xulai went on. "Their horses are not at fault and killing them would upset our horses—and us—to see them needlessly murdered. So we are putting all our tempting things away, including you and me, Willum, and the babies."

"My ma'd tell you, nobody'd steal me," said Willum.

"They probably wouldn't steal you if they knew you, no," agreed Xulai, quite seriously, "But if they are gangers, as Abasio thinks they may be, they may make a specialty of beating brattish boys into doing what they're told, and in any case, they don't know you, so the question doesn't arise."

(I could have moved all that stuff in a tenth the time, thought ul xaolat. There's a better cave, too, and it's no farther away. And I don't suppose they'll tell me to put their possessions back either. Honestly! I could stow them so much more efficiently! Hasn't anyone read the new directions?)

About an hour later, the mounted men reached the clearing. They made up a column of twelve, riding in pairs except for one rope-bound man, tied to the horse being led behind the group. The two men at the head of the column dismounted and walked toward Abasio, where he sat beside a lonely fire, eating a very small pot of boiled grain. The wagon was parked inside a grove of trees. There was no sign of the horses.

The fatter of the two called, "Well, traveler, you're out here all alone." His eyes flicked toward the wagon and away.

"Ayup," replied Abasio, chewing, his eyes on the tethered man. Kim. And Kim's horse.

"Where's your horses?"

"Wun'a'um los' a shoe. T'other went to keep 'im comp'ny." Abasio let his eyes drift along the mounted column. When he saw the bound man was looking at him, he winked with the offside eye, the one the others would not see. The bound man nodded, very slightly. He looked only slightly battered. Far less so than he had outside Gravysuck. Probably they had been laying for him, jumped him.

"Went, where?" Fatter had eyes like two weasels peering out of holes in his face.

"Blacksmith," said Abasio, pointing down-road. "Couple days that-away."

"You had somebody who could drive them down, huh?" Leaner breathed through his mouth, loudly. His eyes were vacant, but that was a lie. Someone nasty was home in there! Now, who did that remind Abasio of? Another life, another story.

Abasio chewed, swallowed, wiped his mouth. "Nope. Nobody t'drive 'em. Went by their own selfs. They know where a blacksmith is. Otta know. Gone through here alla their lives. Up n' down the mountain. Up n' down, up n' down. They knows the way."

The two looked at each other, then at the wagon. The leaner one demanded, "Whatchu got in there?"

"Dye pot," said Abasio. "Raw stuff for dyein'. Not much dye lef'. Used mos' of it up."

"Dyer, huh?" said the fatter one. "That's intresting. Mind if I have a look?"

" 'T's a mess," said Abasio, "but suit yerself."

The two men inspected the wagon, which *was* a mess, a carefully created mess—complete with dye pots and slight smelliness. There was a small supply of grain, small enough that if it was stolen, they'd have plenty left. They had left no interesting food in sight or easily discoverable. There was nothing that looked worth stealing. The other ten men sat on their horses on the road, variously squirming and muttering. Two of them took out pipes and filled them. Fatter and Leaner returned from the wagon, one looking annoyed, the other vacant. Fatter said, "Where's yer harness?"

"Horses took it," said Abasio. "It b'longs to them. Whenever they d'cide to go off, they take the harness with 'em. See, they're just hired horses. I pay 'em a fee at the end of the trip. They use the money to buy oats, pay the blacksmith, and like that."

"Yer not carrying any fodder," said Leaner.

"Han't needed any," Abasio replied, scraping the bottom of the iron pot with his spoon to make an irritating, screeching sound. "Got good forage, so far. Should last till we get down to the prairie on the far side."

Fatter shook his head. "Never heard such a thing. How can horses own their own harness?"

"Man who owned 'em lef' it to 'em in his will. Set 'em free and lef' it to 'em. Do that alla time in Artemisia, so I hear. You musta come through there to get up on the mountain."

Fatter and Leaner went back to their own horses, muttering and growling to a couple of the other men, meantime glancing over their shoulder at Abasio, who was doing nothing but staring after them while holding a deadly weapon in one hand and planning his first stroke if he was forced to use it. *If Fatter and Leaner approach, fall to ground, take their heads off, aiming up to miss the horses. Then skip the last rider and make one slice above horse-head level back along the file.* Abasio had borrowed Xulai's *ul xaolat.* In an instant, it could move him to another little glade some way down the mountain.

However, whenever possible, both Xulai and Abasio preferred to avoid violence. Flicking off to some other location, however, would leave the wagon and its precious cargo of sea-eggs unprotected. If the mounted men gave him no choice, he would kill them, though it seemed less likely when he heard one of them say, "Y'can b'leeve mos' anythin' 'bout Artemisia. Crazy people."

(If they attack, thought ul xaolat, *I shall take what he is thinking as an order. Heads off, horses to be preserved uninjured, release Kim. He didn't say cauterize the necks, but I will. And dispose of the corpses by burial. I think over where the burned trees were. And I'll transplant a new grove from the big ones down at the bottom. I can do that even without corpses. It'll give me something to do tonight. It's neater.)*

Eventually, Fatter and Leaner remounted their horses and clattered off down the road, not bothering to wave. Abasio went out onto the road and watched them go. When the bound man on the last horse looked back, Abasio made a signal, an upright right hand making a circle toward the sun. It meant something like, "Within a day we'll see to it." Meanwhile he was carefully noting which stretches of the downhill road could be seen from this particular place.

There were three places, all within a day's travel, the first one only an hour or so away by horse—and by road. Without a wagon one could go downhill through the trees instead of by road, in less than an hour. He remembered the first possibility as a good place to camp, near the river—which at that point was merely a streamlet trickling through a rocky crease. The men probably had no plan requiring speed. Robbery, rapine, and murder needed no advance timetable. Plans were made after one had assessed a target. He wondered, briefly, if they knew how well Saltgosh was protected, deciding they not only did not know about Saltgosh but also did not know how to ride. If they were all like the two he'd seen dismounted, every one of them rode ugly and walked sore. He thanked something or someone he had not had to kill them. A dozen corpses to dispose of. He and Xulai couldn't simply have left them on the road. Possibly with a few dead horses!

Willum and Xulai appeared out of the woods, bearing chicken

coops and babies. Blue also appeared to tell them that Rags had gone down, slightly uphill and inside the forest, to be sure all the riders would indeed camp some distance away. Abasio mentioned that Kim was a prisoner of the men who had just passed.

"Why didn't they grab you?" Xulai asked.

"No horse for me to ride," Abasio replied. "I'd have slowed them down. And no harness for the wagon, so they couldn't take that. My guess is, they plan to pick me up on the way back. By that time, they figure on having extra horses."

"You want me to get Kim loose," asked Blue. "Tonight? While they're camped? I can follow them down now."

"Both you and Rags go. If the horses could be silently cut loose, maybe they'd wander off in the night and make it difficult for the men to go anywhere tomorrow. Or they might follow you. That'd be fine. But you . . . you might have to cut Kim loose. I'll have to—"

"Me, me, me," cried Willum. "I'm sneaky, 'Basio. Real sneaky."

Abasio gave him a long, thoughtful look. "Can you handle a knife without cutting yourself?"

"Oh, fer, 'Basio! You know me better'n that!"

Without further comment, Willum was furnished with a sheathed knife, which he fastened to his belt, his face tense with concentration. He scrambled onto Blue's back and the horse turned to go down through the forest, silent as a deer.

Abasio turned to find that Xulai was glaring at him. He said mildly, "When I was nine years old, four nasty men came by our farm. They took over our barn, where they had a little girl all tied up. She was a bit younger than I was. They were holding her for ransom, some folks in town who were well-to-do, I guess. They shut my father and me in the cellar. Snow could be heavy on the farm, partway up in the mountains as we were, so many of us farmers had tunnels connecting barns and chicken houses and such. I got out of the cellar into the chicken house, and then cross-country to the three farms nearest ours, got six men to come back with me. Three of them were good bowmen, the others had axes. The men in the barn had only knives; at least that's all I saw. While the men helped my father keep the place surrounded, I got into the barn and got the little girl loose, and got her and me down in the tunnel they didn't know was there.

"I tell you this to explain why a man is never too young to learn how to gag some female who is intent upon screaming when silence is absolutely required." He removed his scarf and moved purposefully in Xulai's direction.

"All right! I won't yell! I grant you are probably more aware of Willum's propensities than I am."

"Both his propensities and his talents. You need to examine his pack one of these days. He thieved half Saltgosh of this and that and no one saw a thing. He's a petty pilferer. I'll bet he's been sneaking into places since he was three." He saw the shock on her face. "Never mind! He and I have jointly recompensed or returned property to those who were stolen from. He owes me several dirty, unpleasant, onerous tasks for having supplied him with the wherewithal to repay and having taught him how to apologize. He deeply resented having to apologize. It made him feel ashamed, thank heaven! I was afraid nothing would! His ma evidently never taught him the thou-shalts and shalt-nots."

"Thou-shalts?"

"Some ancient rule most folks seemed to know when I was a boy. Thou shalt not steal was one of 'em. Not kill people was one. Not tell lies was one."

"What happened to the little girl in the barn?"

"After we killed the four men?"

"Presumably after, yes. Since you were a bit young to commit rape."

"Which would not have been at all tempting to me. If you had ever seen or heard her, you would have known that. Particularly heard her. Doing so would make one covet deafness. Don't worry about Willum. Even if he were caught, no one knows he's connected to us. They wouldn't hold him long."

Xulai did not look greatly comforted, but then she worried over Willum's morality more than Abasio did. Morality proceeded from conviction, and at some point she hoped Abasio would take the trouble to convince him. Ability to trick and dissemble, however, was inborn, and Willum had an immeasurable supply of that!

Abasio stalked out to the road. He would prefer that the men stop at the place he had picked out for them. He took off his boots and climbed a convenient tree.

From below him, Xulai asked, "And you are doing what?"

"Seeing where they stop, dear heart. So I'll know when we can expect Kim and his horse back. Also Willum and our horses. Also, perhaps, all the horses they were riding. I'm wondering about that group, hoping Kim has listened to them and can tell us something when he gets back. They acted almost as though they were looking for something in particular."

"You think the Griffin sent them . . . ?"

He shook his head. Griffin did not need and would not use such scruffy agents. Compared to that gang of offal eaters, Griffin was a model of purity.

Xulai prepared their supper, something a bit more satisfying than boiled grain, putting a goodly share at the edge of the fire to await Willum and Kim's return. When she took Abasio his bowlful, he remarked, "They stopped at that clearing we noticed on the way up, the one with the little tributary creek running through it. They've built a fire." He came down from his perch. "We can't expect anything until well after dark. Let's get everything repacked and ready to move. We'll want to get out of their observation range before light."

(*That's it*, thought ul xaolat. *Hurry, rush, scramble around, drive yourselves crazier. Why not just say, "Put the stuff back in the wagon"? I am being totally wasted on this trip. Maybe they make a model for very young children two or three years of age that would be more suitable for this . . . group.*)

BLUE AND RAGS ARRIVED IN the vicinity of the troop's camp well before it was dark. Willum slipped from Blue's back and slithered to the largest tree between him and the encampment—though he considered it not much of a camp. Everyone sort of suiting himself, finding his own bed space, nobody collecting wood to keep the fire going, nobody preparing anything hot to eat. And each one of them seemed to have a bottle of something besides water, which could be good news so far as Willum was concerned. Particularly if they all got sleepy-drunk fast.

Kim was tied to the tree Willum was behind, his hands tied in front of him.

"Kim," whispered Willum. "Don't talk."

"Crmm," coughed Kim.

Willum looked up. Kim had a gag on his mouth. "If I cut the gag off, they'll see. I don't want to cut you loose till they're asleep. Can you sit down?"

Kim sagged, worked the ropes downward inch by inch as Willum silently shaved off chunks of tree bark to let the rope go by. Kim finally managed to sit. He was tied once around his chest, once around his belly. "Put'cher legs up," whispered Willum. "Hafta cut the bottom ropes, but they won't see with your legs up. Hafta leave the top rope for a while."

The bottom rope—with a knot that had been pulled so tight it could not be untied—had been wrapped several times around Kim's body. Willum cut it next to the knot and pulled it slowly away, inch by inch, providing a nice length for someone to do something else with. He set himself to watch.

Each man carried his own provisions, just as each man had his own bottle, and they were settled separately, each eating and drinking from his own supply.

"Y'gonna feed 'im?" one asked.

"Na," said the fatter man. "Later, mebbe, when we get some provisions down in Saltgosh. Don't have any extra now."

"Y'wanna keep the fire goin'?"

"Nah," the leaner man replied. "S'not cold yet. We'll get some sleep, make a fire for tea in t'mornin'."

"We gonna do Saltgosh in the mornin'?"

"Whenever we get there. Queen Sybbis says Saltgosh's got a whole winner's wort' a per-versions. Got salt wagons and horses, too, an' prob'ly money. We're gonna load their wagons with their per-versions and drive them over the pass."

"Y'know how t'do that? Like harness n' all?"

"It's justa buncha straps. Shouldn't be hard."

A horse, hearing this, snickered. Willum gave Blue a look, which was returned innocently.

"Think there's enough of us?" yawned another of the men.

"Nobody there that fights, is there? Sybbis says it's justa mine. Men diggin' out salt. No gangers. Might be some women. If there's women, kids, we might take some."

One of the other men asked, "Whatchu gonna do with him?" —pushing his chin out in Kim's direction.

"Sell 'im when we get back."

"Don't think so," murmured Willum into Kim's ear.

It grew dark. The clearing resounded with whurfles, snores, grunts.

Kim was released. The moon rose, giving Kim and Willum enough light to release all the horses from the picket line after Blue had spoken to them about the need for quiet movement away through the trees, quiet movement upward off the road inside the trees, leaving no tracks while following Blue and Rags to a far better future than these idiots were offering. All the horses agreed.

Kim mounted his horse—the men had left the horses saddled—and followed the herd as it moved. Willum was on Blue's back, holding on tightly. The herd ghosted upward along the hill, mostly in among the trees, the shorter way that Rags and Blue had come, well spread out and leaving, as Willum had requested, no easily visible hoofprints. Willum could have tracked them, he knew, but those idiots asleep back in the clearing probably couldn't.

Willum announced his return well before midnight. " 'Basio, I got all the horses an' the saddles. Kim's back."

Xulai had heard them, and had also felt the soft noses of some other beasts smelling her where she lay beside the wagon. A brief conference ensued while Kim and Willum were given food and while both they and the horses drank.

"They didn't even unsaddle the horses, Abasio!" snarled Kim. "They're stupid. They don't know anything. Didn't even let the horses have a drink! No campcraft, nothing! Those saddles have been on those horses for days! They prob'ly got sores, even!"

"Well, their ignorance was luck for us," muttered Abasio. "Let's see if we can stow the saddles inside the wagon for a while. They may have to carry them daytimes, but we'll give the horses' backs a rest. I have stuff for saddle sores if you see any."

The extra harness was removed from its traveling rack under the wagon, Blue, Rags, and two volunteer horses—Blue said there were four in the group that were harness, not saddle horses. The Catlanders hadn't known the difference when they got them. Kim mounted up once more and headed uphill, followed by ten horses. In the pale moonlight, the wagon trailed behind them, moving a good deal more rapidly behind four horses than it had traveled with two. The second team made a difference.

"What did those men think they were doing?" Xulai asked Willum.

Willum said, "Two of the men were talkin', an' one said Queen

Sybbis says there's a whole season's worth of supplies put away in Salt-gosh, and they're supposed to steal winter 'perversions.' What're per-versions? And maybe they'll steal some women and children. An' when the others was asleep, it was just those two guys, Skinny and Fats, awake, and they said Saltgosh prob'ly had money."

In the moonlight, Xulai stared at Willum. "They were talking about provisions, Willum. That'd be food for winter, mostly, I imagine. Abasio, you have my *ul xaolat*, don't you? I created a destination place in Salt-gosh. It's not that far away in real distance, though the road winds so much that it seems much farther. I can be there in two minutes, warn them, let them lay whatever trap they like. Just because that crew lost its horses doesn't mean they still won't attempt to rob the place."

"What place in Saltgosh?" he asked.

She flushed. *There had been that lovely little mountain pool above the pasture, surrounded by pines, with the softest mosses . . . Abasio had been in a loving mood. The children had been asleep. And Willum had been, for a wonder, somewhere else! Never mind. It would be a good place to flick to, with very little chance of being seen.*

Abasio, reading the flush correctly, changed the subject. "Well, you'll have to wait until we reach a camping spot you can enter into *ul xaolat* so you'll know what place to come back to. There's plenty of time. They won't move until morning and they won't move fast even then." He turned toward Willum. "Did you or Blue hear anything else about who or why?"

"Seems," the horse said over his shoulder, "our information is correct about there being two countries now, down where we're headed. Artemisia is one of the two, Catland lies to the north of it. We know what philosophy Artemisia follows. Catland follows another one. That dozen are employed by Catland." He gave Abasio a significant look. Abasio shuddered.

"Catland?" said Xulai. "They worship cats?"

Blue made a whurfling noise, suspiciously like a whinnied giggle. "Not cats, no. Not just any old cat. Abasio the Cat. Who is evidently the sainted father of the current boy-child leader and the sainted spouse of the leader's mother, or regent, perhaps. Queen Sybbis, ha."

"The one you told me about?" whispered Xulai. "The ganger's daughter-in-law?"

Blue flipped his tail in amusement. "Better if her sainted spouse didn't suddenly turn up alive."

Abasio corrected him. "Blue, I was never Sybbis's spouse, and I'd rather not be a sainted anything! The single encounter I had with Sybbis took place when I had been drugged. The only way she could recognize me was by my scars and tattoos. Sybbis never saw the wagon, and it wouldn't matter. It looks entirely different now. None of the gangers ever saw Willum or Xulai. My scars were removed when I was in Tingawa. I'm older and grayer. I can dye my hair to be grayer yet. And starting now, I'll grow a mustache and beard."

"But they're talking about your son, Abasio," Xulai whispered. "Don't you want to . . ."

He put a hand on her shoulder and shook her, not entirely gently. "Bailai is my son. Gailai is my daughter. Willum is . . ." He had been going to say "my son." "Willum is—at least temporarily—my foster son. I was only ganger on my father's side. Sybbis is completely ganger both on her mother and father's side. If CummyNup is her boy's father, which is most likely, he's ganger head to heels. Knowing what I know of Sybbis, I'm quite sure she would prefer me to be dead. If she thought I was alive, she might take steps to assure I didn't last long."

"But, for heaven's sake, ganger isn't a race! It's not like skin color, or blue eyes! It's not something one inherits—"

"That's not quite true, Xulai. Personality is largely genetic. The ganger personality is a pack personality. If you don't have a pack personality, you don't last! Before the Big Kill some countries were tribal, pack civilizations all with the same language or background or religion, and with a dominating leader—an alpha male, one who is willing to do anything inside or outside the pack to maintain dominance: kill, rape, torture, murder. No one outside the pack matters. Anyone else can be killed without remorse. Sybbis has this 'pack attitude' and so does this bunch who are intending to rob Saltgosh. I, on the other hand, do not have it.

"We talked about my using another name when we get down on the plain. We'd better start practicing while we have some little time to get used to it. You and Willum need to practice hitching the wagon to four horses. We're all the ones who own the wagon, having bought it from a stranger man somewhere far west of here."

"You said we were gonna call you 'Vahso,'" said Willum.

Xulai murmured, "Yes. It sounds enough like your own name that if we forget, we can claim we said 'Vahso,'" said Xulai. "You're Vahso Gormley. I am Shooey Gormley. Willum is, of course, Willum Gormley. Will we reach the pass tonight?"

"Easily. If there's a good place to stop where we won't be seen, I'd like to see what those men will do in the morning. I don't see any sign of them, back there."

Blue said, "They let the fire go out. Didn't even cover it. They're not forest people or country people. Have they built themselves some new city?"

Abasio muttered, "I doubt it. Something more like a camp. Gangers aren't talented in any useful way. They create nothing, build nothing, grow nothing, harvest nothing but 'riches,' which usually means other people's belongings and lives. Nothing gangers do is useful."

Sooner than they had thought possible, they reached a switchback, high upon the mountain, where they found Kim resting the horses. He told them they were within half an hour or less of the summit but could rest where they were, unobserved, in order to see where the raiders would go in the morning. He pointed them into a glade opening from the end of the switchback and extending some little distance along a cleft in the mountains, rock on both sides, a few stunted trees, a little rock pool full of rainwater. They pulled the wagon in, unharnessed the four horses, and made all the horses more comfortable with a ration of oats and hay. Blue moved among the new horses, asserting supremacy and assuring good treatment. Xulai stared about herself as she entered landmarks into her device. She would return after visiting Saltgosh.

"Abasio, wasn't that ridge down there where the burned trees were?"

Abasio went to look. "I don't see the Listener."

"I don't either, and I don't see the burned trees. Shouldn't we see them from here?"

(*No, idiot,* thought ul xaolat. *You shouldn't. I've replaced them. The Listener wanted them replaced. I also found the remains of the campfire that started the blaze. And the bones which were all that were left after the body burned. And the horse that was wandering around down in the valley behind it from which I removed the halter and saddle. To summarize: one traveler, one horse, one campsite, one large bottle of spirituous liquid resulting in one drunken camper, one runaway campfire, one very large blaze resulting in one cremated camper, one grove of burned trees: sole survivor, one horse. I have entered the facts into the daily report. And by the way, if anyone's interested, that Listener thing is talking to itself. It says requests for aid have been received, help is on the way.)*

"If it starts to get late and I'm not back, you go ahead," Xulai said finally. "I may stay long enough to help the Saltgosh people, and I can catch up by taking short visual trips."

"No!" Abasio said, his voice rising. "Xulai, do not pin us down here with what you *may* or *may not* do. Don't make us fret and worry and maybe endanger ourselves or the children because we're worried about you."

She gave him a look of annoyance. He took her by the shoulders. "Dear heart, have you forgotten that our children won't wait quietly to be fed while you spend hours back down the road? And have you forgotten that Saltgosh has been right where it is for some hundreds of years? If you feel they're incapable of surviving without your assistance, then go, but come right back! If the people of Saltgosh have asked for your help, you can flick back to help them from our next place on the road. We will still be within range."

"It's more sensible," offered Blue in his minatory voice. "Really, Xulai."

"Of course," Xulai agreed, flushing ruefully. "It's awful of me, but I keep forgetting they're not weaned yet. I keep forgetting I'm a mother!" Her eyes began to fill.

"You have a history of behaving like a heroine," he said, hugging her and swallowing the grin she would have resented. "It's not a history one drops in a few months of parenthood. I have the same problem. I find myself irresistibly moved toward intrepidity and heroism! It is all I can do to remember I have other responsibilities!"

She gave him a frankly disagreeable look and flicked away, leaving Willum with his mouth open.

" 'Basio? What's 'in-trep-edy'?"

"Foolish behavior, like small boys teasing giants. It often results in death."

It was about an hour later, as they were just settling into their beds, when she returned, slightly shamefaced. "I don't need to go back. Gum was perfectly right. The Saltgosh people have had it happen before.

They'd already seen the group, already diagnosed the situation, but were waiting for them to get a little closer before ringing their big bell. Evidently, even though we didn't see any towns close to Saltgosh, there are clusters of woodsmen, hunters and trappers, back in the hills. When the bell rings, people from all over the valley come to help, and all non-combatants go underground—including the people in that Home they told us of. I told them how many men there were and what they were after. I told them we'd taken their horses and suggested they put their own horses where they can't be destroyed or run off if any of the raiders get that close. They'd started moving them before I left, the entrances are in the woods, not easily found. Everyone was quite excited about having someone to fight . . ."

She stopped, head cocked. They all heard it, far away but clearly tolling. *Bong* . . . Long wait. *Bong* . . . Long wait. *Bong* . . . Soft echoes bounced among the hills, *ong, ong, onng, onnng.*

"I think we'll sleep quietly the rest of the night," said Blue. "That is, if nobody minds."

Nobody minded.

IN THE FOREST SOME DISTANCE from Tuckwhip, Needly found the going slower than she had thought. There was a certain sense of urgency about her, as though some spirit were at her shoulder, tapping it, saying, "Hurry, girl. Get a move on." Still, Grandma had always cautioned against undue haste. It killed people, she had said. Always look before you step, so she had looked and was still looking when she heard the whurfle away to her left in the woods.

There was no doubt in her mind that it was a bear. After a few minutes' careful travel, she had no doubt it had smelled her trail, footsteps, or just her aroma in the air. She was being followed. Well. She'd been told what to do. Now if she could only do it.

She had to assume it was a grown bear, not a cub. A cub wouldn't hurt her, but it probably wouldn't be without a mother, and the mother would. Therefore, find a skinny tree. One with a diameter too small for a large bear to get its claws into. One standing fairly well alone. Which she did. She took a length of light line from her pack and tied one end to her pack. Another length made a loop to go around the tree. She put her knife between her teeth, remembering that the sharp edge went to the outside, fitted Grandma's foot claws over her shoes, and started up the tree. There were enough little stubs of broken branches here and there to give her feet good purchase. Her legs were getting very tired before she came to suitable branches. Three of them, a pair at one height, one slightly below, the three together forming a basis for her pack, which had straps on either side that could be tied around the side branches. She pulled it up beside her, settled it into place, and tied it there, then sat on it, back against the trunk, more or less at her ease. As per Grandma's instructions, soft things were all at one side of the pack, the top side.

The bear emerged into the clearing below her, approached the tree, smelled it, backed up, and looked up at her. Needly received the very strange impression that it smiled. The bear meandered around the little clearing, sniffing, finding some red berries that seemed to be enjoyable, for it sat down among them and ate them slowly, one at a time. It had finished the berries just before the music began.

Needly took a deep breath of disbelief. Music? She had never heard music. She'd heard Grandma speak of music, certainly, and she had heard Grandma sing, though only when they were far from Tuckwhip, where no one would hear. She had a beautiful voice, though she said that her range—explaining this meant low to high notes—had decreased as she had grown older. Grandma said singing, beauty, imagination, art . . . those things were threatening to people in Hench Valley, so she did not speak of them or do anything that might make herself seem unusual. This was the first time Needly had heard music that was obviously being made by some not-voice thing. Oh, there was the music she had felt, that time she saw the Griffin. She wasn't counting that. That had been . . . a kind of miracle.

The bear rose to its feet, brushed itself off with finicky, very human motions of its front legs, and began to dance. Left arm across chest, right arm extended to the right, nose pointed left, right foot raised, tapped, tapped, right arm swung across chest as the left arm extended to the left, nose pointed right, left foot raised, tapped, tapped. Turn left, turn right, both arms up, both arms down . . . the music went on. The bear went on dancing. The music went on playing. After some little time, both stopped.

The bear bowed in the direction from which the music had seemed to emanate. He or she then came to the foot of the tree Needly was sitting in and clumped down against the trunk. It yawned several times before putting its nose straight up and looking into her face, which was peering down.

"Needly," said the bear. "Are you going to sleep up there?"

Needly thought it over, finally nodding that she was.

"I'll scratch the trunk to wake you early in the morning," said the bear. "The people you're supposed to meet will be only about an hour from here." It yawned again. "By the way, you should take that knife out of your mouth. Otherwise, you might cut your own head off."

WILLUM WOKE EARLIER THAN THE others and went exploring down into the woods. He returned while breakfast was still hot and helped Kim and Abasio partly fill the water barrel, just in case there would be no water until they'd moved some way down from the pass. A little wind came up the mountain toward them, bearing the clear sound of the distant bell once again, *Ba-bong . . . Ba-bong . . .* Double rings, this time. Xulai said, "That means enough men have arrived! They need no more. They have dozens of deadfalls all around the works, and they've been out in the night, uncovering them—that is, they're taking off the safety covers that prevent Saltgoshians falling in by mistake."

"And, I suppose," said Abasio, "that also prevented our falling in when we were there." He strode about, examining their surroundings and noting certain features he had not noticed the previous night: a small track led from the main road through their campground and farther down a shallow fold of mountain to the north; old wagon ruts along it indicated that one of the little villages shown on the map might lie at the end of the tracks. He didn't want to leave their cover until the men down the hill could no longer see them, so he came from among the trees to lie behind a conveniently cleft stone and watch the road below them. After a time, the men emerged from the woods, strode or limped about, searching for tracks and evidently finding none. There was a good deal of arm waving by men who were obviously yelling at one another. Eventually they started down the road, bearing packs as men do who are unaccustomed to carrying anything. They would be very, very lame at the end of the day, walking like that.

Very shortly the men limped around a shoulder of the mountain.

They had taken no great time in searching for the horses or for their prisoner. They might have heard the bell, but they didn't know what it meant. Or they knew but thought they were numerous enough to disregard it. Or they were idiots who had no idea what they were doing, which was what Abasio considered most likely. Sybbis had probably ruled in Catland for a number of years without learning anything much about the countryside. No one had ever spoken of her of as a curious or intelligent woman. As head of the women in Purple House, she had enjoyed food, drink, and fancy clothing. And, maybe, sex. She would know that gang leaders sent men out to find out particular things, and were not surprised if some of them didn't make it back. Not returning was almost as frequent as getting back relatively whole. If Sybbis's men did not come back, she was very unlikely to send anyone looking for them, though she might send others elsewhere, on the same errand of robbery and mayhem.

Only the one short stretch of road was visible from where they were now, and the valley into which the men had moved slanted away from the peak above. Before the retreating walkers came to the next place where they could see this stretch, the wagon would be over the pass and out of their sight.

Kim left immediately with ten horses, wanting to be enough in advance of the wagon to let the dust settle before the wagon followed. Not long after noon, they had crossed the pass and come a goodly way down the far side, where they spotted a skein of smoke rising among a clutter of great boulders. Blue whinnied, was answered. Kim had chosen the end of a short length of road that led from a north-heading switchback, a spot that lay almost immediately east of the mountain peak behind them. He had built his fire among a grove of smallish trees, and came toward them, saying, "There's no water or forage here, but a bit farther down it gets grassy and there's water. The horses can have a small drink from the barrel, and we'll get to good water by evening."

They gave the horses a ration of oats and water and settled to their own midday meal. Willum was here, there, and everywhere, looking aimless. Abasio pointed out Kim's shelter among the stones, but Willum said he'd found a place he liked a bit along the mountainside, he'd take his blankets and sit there.

They fed themselves, Willum taking generous helpings off into the woods, though usually he ate with them. They rested only briefly, then went on their way downward, Kim riding ahead to scout their next stopping place. Well before sundown, they found him on a wide, wooded ledge that protruded from the side of the mountain. There was grass among the trees and water trickling from the crest—once again above them to the west. They had covered miles going north and south but had seemed to make only slight progress down the east side of the mountain.

Water had accumulated in a stony declivity from which the horses could drink. They followed their usual routines, put water to boil, cut bread to toast over the fire. The babies had wakened earlier, had been fed, had played and been dandled, and were having a nap on the bed inside the wagon. Abasio went out onto the road to see the downward way for himself. This area of the mountainside was extremely steep, and the upper stretch of road had been deeply incised into it, like stairsteps, short lengths of road running back and forth, many of them with trails leading off into the forests from the switchbacks. Game trails, perhaps. Or those used by hunters from the villages he had noticed on the map. Hench Valley was somewhere to the north of them, behind the peak, but it could no doubt be found at the end of some trail or other leading around the north side of the mountain.

Each section of road, as well as the wide ledge they were camped upon, had a vertical rock wall rising on the inside, and another such plunging down on the outside. These vertical walls were broken here and there along their length by great, faceted pylons, individual stones too huge to have been moved or broken by road builders, left standing along the roadway like sentinel guardians of some ancient, stony people. He lifted his eyes to the sky to see what weather portended, swallowing an oath before it left his throat.

What portended was wings! Huge ones that were circling the peak above him! He looked toward the cover of the trees. Too late. The creature tilted on her wings, swerving to face him from high to the north, then stooped, like a monstrous hawk. Dropping, wings folded, diving, upon him . . .

Eyes like glowing opal fires, light reflecting from a brazen beak, spread wide around a cavernous throat, huge feathered wings spreading out, out, out, covering half the sky. The flight feathers copper, gleaming as from a forge, the throat feathers bronze, darkening toward the huge brazen beak. He knew this one! From the corner of his eye, he saw Xulai fumbling frantically for a weapon and screamed at her. "NO! Xulai. NO!"

Her mouth dropped open; her hands fell to her side. The Griffin's wings widened, scooped air. She stood erect in flight, dropping less swiftly: curved, sword-length back talons extended downward to grip one of the great boulders of the cliff edge a few arm's lengths away from them. The great beak turned toward Xulai, opened, spoke: "I have no immediate intention of damaging you or yours, woman. Do not make the mistake of attempting to use your weapon."

It returned its gaze to Abasio. "Do you remember me, man? From the battle at the Place of Power?"

"I do," he said, fighting to keep his voice calm and level. Despite the creature's reasonable words, her eyes, focused upon him, blazed with anger. They burned like the coals of an unquenchable fire. He swallowed deeply. "I remember you kindly. You were of great help to us all."

It spoke again. "Your woman was owed a kindness. It was done for her. Not necessarily for you or anyone here. It seems our battle was all to no purpose."

He was honestly astonished. "Why? It achieved a good end."

"For you, perhaps!"

She turned her burning gaze on Xulai, on Willum, who stood frozen at the edge of the trees. Still with that anger, that . . . hostility. Perhaps hostility toward *what he was* rather than *who he was*. Perhaps.

The great head tilted, the eyes moved over him, totally intent. "It seems the world is to be covered in water."

Abasio swallowed again and nodded. "The people here are only now learning of it, though across the ocean to the west the Tingawans have known for some time that it would happen. They thought it would have stopped long before now. They don't know where it's coming from. It is continuing, but it is estimated it will take centuries to cover everything."

"We, those like me, are, in certain respects, rather like cats. We are not fond of water." The content of the words did not convey hostility; their tone conveyed nothing else.

"As I said, it will be several hundred years. A lifetime . . ."

The Griffin turned her head and rattled her beak, preening and rearranging the long strands of feather, almost like hair, around her face and on the upper neck. The sound was that of a smithy, though softer, almost melodious. Music played on gongs and cymbals. The beak was serrated along the edges, like a comb, an instrument for grooming as well as tearing flesh. She finished with the edge of one wing and turned to face him, the light glinting from the edge of the beak as from a sword. He knew the effect was calculated. Willed. The beak was lethal. She wanted to be sure he knew it, sure Xulai knew it.

She rumbled: "I am now nine hundred and some-odd years old, man-person. I look forward to a thousand more, at least, so a century, give or take, is hardly a lifetime. My child, whom your friend saved—is it true your friend gave her life to save the people of that land?"

Abasio nodded, summoning courage. "All lives, including yours."

"She was heroic, that one. My child was newly hatched, tiny, naked, helpless, when the child who became your woman found my hatchling at the foot of the cliff, put my child in her hat." There was a rumbling sound that Abasio interpreted, after a moment, as a chuckle. " . . . A hatchling she was! She carried my child back to my nest. Almost I attacked her. Luckily, I did not." The voice hardened, all humor gone. "Now my child is feathered and furred, she is some years older, but she will live perhaps two thousand or so. As will I. Given opportunity."

Abasio struggled. "We didn't cause the inundation. We can't stop the inundation. It's beyond any powers we might ever have had . . ."

"Oh, we are not fools, Abasio the Dyer. Abasio the Traveler. We are not fools! I have seen Tingawa! I made it a point to fly there, a long journey. I have perched on towers in the darkness and listened to talk of how people such as mine were made. I have learned how your seachildren were made! I have crouched beside your wagon when you were not watching for me. Even very large creatures may fly silently and low, in the tops of the trees. I have watched your children at play."

Something changed in the Griffin's face. That huge, metallic beak could not change, no, but the soft tissues at its sides were capable of expression, and he saw a moment's humor there as she said again, "At play."

"You are amused, great one?" he asked, unable to keep his voice steady. She was not threatening him, but there was a terrible implacability in her voice.

"It would take a great tragedy indeed for man to give up his shape,

Abasio. Humans have always been very proud of their shape. I was told they are so proud they believe their God is shaped as they are! So proud that they think all other shapes—shapes, colors, languages, all—inferior to their own! Even in creatures that are superior to them. Vastly . . . superior. So I see you change your shape and I am surprised. We live long and it takes a great deal to surprise one of us. I am surprised at your changed children. Children who will live in the waters. You have done this for your people. I have consulted with others. We have somewhat of a claim upon you. All we ask—no! All we *demand* is that you do the same for ours."

"Lady, mother animal?" said a small voice.

Abasio and Xulai spun around. Willum was coming toward them from among the trees; he was holding the hand of a little girl, perhaps a bit older than himself but small, small, pale as a ghost, hair white as frost braided into a complex helmet. She was approaching the Griffin, carrying something . . .

"Lady Animal, mother animal, is your baby here? I think your baby lost this." And she held out a feather.

The huge beak gaped in actual astonishment, then cried, a sweet sound that had scarcely died before another Griffin dropped before them . . . a tiny one! Well, not tiny, no. Half the size of Blue. It would make more than one Abasio. It rubbed its head against its mother's beak and spoke sounds, not words they knew.

Abasio was looking at the big one. He saw the tears gather. Like diamonds. He heard the whisper. "Once before a Griffin child, a hat-hatchling! Once before a human child, Traveler. Girl children, both. The human child found my little one and brought it home. My people are few. *You* created us, *you men.* You gave us brains to think with, feel with. Even language, though we have since adapted it as our own." Her voice hardened, like iron. "*We are not mere beasts.* We have only a few hatchlings during our lives. They are very precious to us."

"The other girl was Olly," he said in a half-strangled voice. "It was she who went with the ship, it was she who made sure death would not rain down from the moon, who made sure that the ship would never return."

"Oh, sir," cried the white-haired child. "Oh, sir, is it true that the baby will drown? No, no, you must save her, sir. And her mama and her mama's people. She is too young to be without a mama, without people! Even older children . . . like me, we . . . we need our people."

The young Griffin pranced toward the child, head cocked. It chirped, "Is that my feather?"

"I think so," said the child. "Grandma found it and gave it to me. Along with some other things. And then she died because Pa threw a stone at her. And he was going to sell me to Old Man Digger, who kills all his women because . . . because . . . I don't really understand why because." Tears dripped from her own eyes.

Xulai ran to gather the child into her arms. "What's your name, little one?"

"They call me Needly."

"Neelie?"

"Needly. Like a needle. Because I have sharp eyes, I think."

The Griffin was as surprised as the others, and as curious. "Do you have another name?" she asked.

"I have a record name, for the tax keeper to write down. My Pa's family is called Stormstone, and he's called Gralf. My Ma's family is Trailfinder, and her name is Trudis. My name for the record man would be Stormstone Trailfinder's Needly. Mostly I'm just Needly. And Grandma was just Grandma—she says her name is Grandma Find-the-way, but that may be a joke. And Pa wasn't really my father anyhow. My real father was a Silverhair."

As the child's voice faded, Xulai tucked that word "Silverhair" into the corner of her mind and asked, "Where do you live?"

Needly glanced at Willum, who flushed and dug his toe into the ground.

"Willum," Xulai murmured. "You know something about this?"

Willum drew a toe through the soil and studied the groove it had made. "Well, um, where we stopped before, there wuzza little trail, so I kinda . . . you know, follerd it. An', she had a little camp out inna trees, cryin' acuz . . . they wuz gonna sell her to this old man who kills all the girls and women he gets, and she had to hide from a bear last night, an' turned out the bear was a guide, and it brought her there, but she was scared—"

"Was not!" said Needly.

Willum risked a quick look at her. "—or maybe she was jus' real tired, and I said that wuzn' right, and she should come away with us."

"And where was that?"

"Where we stopped t'other night an' you went back to Saltgosh. Where we watched those men find out they lost their horses. I hid her on top a' the wagon, longside a' me."

Abasio reflected on the stop. They had commented on the wagon track leading from the road down over the hill. They had commented that there might be a community there, or perhaps only a farm. He glanced at Xulai, who was rubbing her forehead while staring at Abasio. His lips quirked and he shrugged.

She interpreted his shrug correctly. "How old are you, Needly?"

Needly did not look up from her labors. She had taken a comb from her pocket and was busy grooming the mane of the little Griffin, who had begun to purr. "Eleven or about, I think. Grandma kept track. But she died before she could tell me. Last time she told me, I was ten. That's when I first saw the Lady Animal . . ."

Abasio thought that she and Willum seemed to be of an age. The girl was clean, no dirtiness that could not be accounted for by the dust of travel. Her hair was neatly braided. He cast a glance at the Griffin, who seemed to be watching the child in fascination. Well, good. He swallowed and asked the child, "Will someone be looking for you?"

"Old Man Digger, maybe," she said, looking up a bit fearfully. "Though maybe he won't come this way. Hench Valley people don't go over the mountain hardly ever, because they don't know what's on this side. But there's ways to come round north side the peak, to here. He could come here."

The child looked very young and thin. Xulai asked, "What are you able to do, Needly?"

The child turned, tucked her comb away, and came to stand beside Xulai, to take her hand and lay it upon her own narrow shoulder. "That there that feels like bone, that's my skin," she said matter-of-factly. "Grandma said I grew a good patch on both sides, and that's good. That's from carrying the water every day. Two big buckets. From the well."

"How far?" murmured Xulai, astonished at what she felt. A callus like wood. Thick and hard.

Needly shrugged. "As far as from here to that turn in the road down there," pointing to a switchback half a mile or so down the road.

"Isn't there any water closer than that?"

"There's water everywhere," she said. "Little streams, all kinds of water. But that water isn't well water."

"Wouldn't the stream do as well? For washing in? Or scrubbing clothes. Or whatever," the Griffin asked, her voice low and soft.

"Oh, no, Lady Animal. No, water used in a house has to be covenanted water. From the well. The well has the only covenanted water. Going to get it makes the women covenanted, you see? We wouldn't be covenanted if we didn't haul the water."

Abasio, frowning, started to say something, but Xulai held up one hand. "Will you be able to use regular stream water on this journey, if you come with us?"

"Oh, yes, lady, gentleman! The Kindlies told me the covenant thing was made up by the Founder. The Kindlies told me all about him, the man who settled Hench Valley ages ago, him and his five wives—four, really. He thought he was a god, populating a separate place. Each wife had her own place, and he put them far enough apart they couldn't talk with one another and plot with one another. The older ones had one child right after another. One of them was only twelve years old, though, and she died in childbirth before her house was even finished. The Founder had named her place Child Wife, and there's nothing left of it, but the other four places are still there. Tuckwhip and Gortles and Grief's Barn and Bag's Arm. All the men in the valley are descended from the Founder and his four wives, but they don't keep girls alive much now.

"Grandma says all covenanting does for a girl is make sure she dies young. She planned for me to vanish. She even told me the timing of it: I should do it when danger was soon coming. They were suddenly going to give me to Old Man Digger, and that was surely danger coming. And, Grandma said, when someone sympathetic came by— that was Willum . . . or maybe the bear. And when there's a way to hide me until I got away—that's the wagon. She told me if danger came, I shouldn't bother with either sympathy or hiding, I should just git, she said. Just git! Fast!"

"Is that what you did?"

"Pretty much. They weren't going to give me to Old Man Digger for a little while, but Grandma said don't wait, so I didn't."

"No doubt," said Abasio grimly, looking up at the Griffin, who had followed all this with considerable interest. "Does your child want her feather back, Great One?"

The little Griffin raised her wing. "It goes here," she said, indicating a place beneath her wing with the tip of her beak, a tiny opening, like a pore. Needly went close, slipped the quill into place. It made a tiny, woodlike click. The small Griffin commented, "A new one would grow, but it would take a long time, Mama says." Needly stood stroking the Griffin child, a child several times her own size, but Needly treated her as she would an infant. Xulai realized that she really was: if a creature lived two thousand years, then its infancy and childhood would last at least two or three hundred years.

The great beak above the Griffin child stroked down, the baby snuggled to her mother's breast. The Great One's head came back, the expression hardened once more. "Listen, both of you. Man-person, woman-person; you, children, also!"

They froze in place, even Willum motionless, caught by that voice like a fish on a spear.

"Your people made us. You gave us pain, you gave us joy, we are not machines! You gave us language, or you lent us your own, we are not machines! You are responsible for us! You must help us—at least those of us who ask for it, for we have sworn that if you do not help us, your children will not survive either. We are not many, but we have friends who feel as we do, created as we were created. Some live in the air, but *many created as we were created now live in the seas.* Dogs are being made who can live in the sea. Horses, too. Cows and goats and sheep. And those who are not being changed are being . . . moved. Moved away, to other worlds that are not being drowned!"

"Moved?" cried Needly. "Moved where?"

"We don't know where, but we know it is being done. There are enough of them to make us sure what you have done for them can be done for us! Oh, be sure, you men, be sure none of your little ones will survive unless ours do as well," the Griffin whispered. "You see?"

A single crystal tear dropped on the little one's plumage, slid off the feather, and clinked glassily as it circled before coming to rest on the rock beneath.

Xulai, tears in her own eyes, murmured, "Yes, we see. I don't know what we can do, Great One, but we will try. We truly will!"

The Griffin reared onto her hind legs, picked up the little one in her front paws, the claws curving around beneath it like a cradle. Her great wings beat downward, stirring a hurricane of dust and pine needles and gravel as the great body lifted, lurched upward, and dropped into the canyon below, where her wings caught the air and soared upward. "Think deeply on that," it cried, not loudly, but loudly enough that they heard it clearly. "How you must do for ours what you have done for your own!"

"Think on that?" whispered Xulai to Abasio, who had come close behind her and put his arms about her. "By all the soul lanterns of all the Tingawan generations under the depths of the sea, Abasio! It took my people—our people—a thousand years to do it for humans. We don't have another thousand; so how do we think *upon that?*"

ANOTHER HALF DAY SHUTTLED THEM north to south and south to north, repeatedly, switchback after switchback. At noon they found themselves not a great deal lower but considerably farther north of the peak, a small clearing among towering pines. Abasio and Xulai sat beside the fire late into the dusk. While Needly slept in the wagon—wearied out, as Xulai thought, by too much labor, too little food, too much apprehension, not enough security—Willum took it upon himself to badger them about the Griffin, blaming them for not having invited the creatures for dinner so he could have asked it for a ride.

Finally Abasio, aggravated past endurance, snarled at him. "I thought you were a smart boy, Willum! You're doing it again, just as you did back there before Saltgosh. You're not listening. You didn't listen about the giants, now you're not listening to what the Griffin said! She is not pleased with humans, and much though you sometimes give me reason to doubt it, you are human! She might well choose to drop you from halfway up the sky just to prove she meant what she said! If you don't shut up I may emulate that event by kicking you off the side of the road!"

At that, Willum gave up. He rolled himself in his blankets, and finally stopped mumbling to himself and began to breathe like a sleeper. Xulai had begun her own analysis of the situation earlier in the day, listing both in writing and aloud what the people of Tingawa could and could not do, as she had understood the genetics of the changes made in Xulai's mother. Something similar would have to be done for the Griffins, and she explained this aloud, to herself and to Abasio, who tried to be attentive. He was losing the battle to drowsiness. However, when she repeated for the tenth time, "It was done genetically! We didn't have the before-time machines that could put together the genetic units in sequence, one after the other. We didn't have them! That meant it took generation after generation of breeding to isolate each characteristic, and it took a thousand years! But I think they have built a sequencer recently. Precious Wind said something of the kind. Of course, by itself, that's meaningless. Even if we started tomorrow, how could we manage enough generations of Griffins to change their . . . their shape? Their function?"

"If there is no time," he murmured from a half dream, "I rather imagine it would need to be done all at once."

She repeated the words. "All at once! How could it possibly be done all at once?"

THAT NIGHT, FOR A CHANGE Abasio did not dream of Lom. Instead, he dreamed of his first watery meeting with the Sea King. The great Kraken had tricked him into going swimming by lending him a fisherman's mask; they had swum among the coral, seeing the wonders of the sea, including the coral palace that had been built for the king that was full of his children. All those wonders, and by the time they had come up onto the beach once more, the mask had been long forgotten, and Abasio had acquired eight tentacles without realizing it. He had crawled out onto the sand, however, looking down to see a great writhing, sucker-laden serpent instead of an arm, and had gone into panic and shock. The realization of what he had become had taken days—months—to become accustomed to, even longer to accept.

But tonight, in his dream he was talking to the Sea King, repeating an earlier comment: "It had to happen all at once! All at once!"

The Sea King replied in Xulai's voice, "Hush, dear. All at once, we know, but go back to sleep."

WHEN ABASIO WOKE, KIM HAD taken the extra horses and ridden away down the road, giving the dust time to settle before the rest of the group came along behind him. Xulai was muttering to herself beside the fire.

He interrupted her. "When the people in the before time made the Griffins, what genetics went into them, do you think?"

Xulai, who was concentrating on timing the hen's eggs she was boiling by counting to two hundred, ignored him.

"You'd need something catlike for the body. A lion maybe. Her beak is very eagle. Though, actually, the Sea King has one much like it."

Xulai said, "If Precious Wind were here, she could probably tell us what would work."

"And we're meeting her, where?"

"She's moving toward us now. If we haven't arrived in Artemisia when she gets there, she'll come on west until we do meet."

"So, what do we tell the Griffin?"

Xulai gave bowls of porridge to Willum and Needly, each topped with a soft-boiled egg, scooped from the shell. She carried the other bowls to the grassy bank where Abasio was sitting and sat down beside him. Around a mouthful of breakfast, she said, "The first thing we need to do is find out where the Griffins were created. The Griffin may know, and that will give us a place to start. The only thing we can tell her immediately is to keep in touch with us until we meet Precious Wind. Her far-talker will reach the people in Tingawa." She mused for a few moments, seeming puzzled. "Did the Edgers make all the fantastic creatures? Why don't we know specifically where? And by whom? Doesn't that seem strange to you?"

Abasio shook his head at her, considering the question. "Considering everything else we don't know, love, it's not terribly strange. The men in Saltgosh have heard the Edgers brag about making many kinds of strange things. I know they did. Just last night, as I was getting drowsy, I remembered one time, while I was still living in Fantis, old Chief Purple was going through one of his half-drunk speeches about his friends the Edgers, telling us they had taken over an old place east of the city. A factory, he said. A place where large things had been manufactured long before. The person who told me . . . he said the place, the building or whatever it was . . . he said it was huge. They had made ships there . . ."

"Ships? That sounds unlikely! So far from the ocean?"

"Airships, Xulai. Flying ships. They were called something else, I've forgotten what. I thought it was 'planes,' but that's a kind of woodworking tool! The place was mostly underground, so it was well preserved, a lot of the machinery was still there. That place was large enough to have made Griffins, and even giants."

"One of the Edges? Or perhaps more than one Edge? Cooperatively?"

"Old Chief Purple used to make visits back to the gang house to visit 'his concs'—I guess that was short for 'concubines,' his women. He would get drunk and brag about the things his friends in the Edge could do. The wonders they were creating in this new place they had found, so much bigger than the Edges themselves . . . And it hadn't been just one Edge but several who had been working in the place. Several of them!" He shook his head, "The word 'cooperation' doesn't fit with the word 'Edger,' does it?"

"Not from what I've been told, no. But if the place was huge and they wanted it badly enough, I suppose two or three of them could have cooperated." She sighed, "There's one thing we can do almost immediately. We can ask my grandfather in Tingawa to find out if they have information about the Griffin's design. Who did it, where, when. That may give us some information the Griffin will accept as evidence that we're working on it, at least."

Willum had been listening. "Oh, wow, then I'll bet she'd give me a ride," he said. He caught Abasio's admonitory eyes on him and said hastily, "Never mind, 'Basio. I won't talk about it."

He turned away, mumbling to himself, "But I'll bet she'd give me a ride 'f I asked her."

Xulai looked up from her bowl, her eyes ranging along the downward road. She put down her bowl and said in a tone that held their attention. "Needly, don't stand up. Stay low behind the bushes. Take your bowl and cup and get into the wagon quickly. Willum, Abasio, stand up and walk over toward the drop-off, wave your arms, babble about something to draw the attention of that group of angry men coming down the road. As soon as Needly's in the wagon, Abasio, lock it, hide the key, then come back here."

Willum, surprisingly, did not argue, though his eyes darted toward the road. He went over to the drop-off, pretending not to see the men coming around the switchback. Abasio joined him, waving at the prospect below while noting from the corner of his eyes that the girl child had disappeared behind the wagon. He went around the wagon, leaned in, saying, "Needly, hide under the bed, take our babies under there with you, and try to keep them quiet." Blue and Rags were behind the wagon. He spoke briefly to them as he locked the door behind him, and put the key in his pocket. When he returned to the fire, he stood tall and very apparently "noticed" the group of men who were approaching. Just behind the men, part of a vertical column of stone moved very slightly. He shivered. That was all he needed; threat from both sides. Unless, maybe, just now, one of them wasn't threatening *him*!

There were ten men in the group, two out in front carrying shaped clubs, perhaps ax handles, three behind them with knives in their hand, then a clot of five more, two carrying bows, complete with nocked arrows, the other three carrying axes, sun glinting from the edges of the blades. Xulai, he noted from the corner of his eye, was now standing by the wagon and had reached deep into the pocket where she carried *ul xaolat:* she could move away in an instant or she could remove all ten of the advancing men more quickly than the gang of them would believe possible. Before the men could come two steps nearer, Xulai could put her hand on the wagon and go away, taking wagon and child—children—with her. Abasio took a deep breath.

"Hiya!" called one of the foremost marchers. "You dere."

Abasio raised his hand in a gesture of acknowledgment. "Yes. Something I can do for you?"

"We hadda girl runoff," cried the first man. "You seen her?" He brandished his club threateningly.

"Only female here is my wife," Abasio said, indicating Xulai with a nod in her direction.

"That'un," cried one of the others, pointing at Willum. "That'un's 'bout the right size!"

"Except that he's not a girl," objected Abasio. "Willum's been with us for a long time, and he's a boy."

"Gotta be sure," growled the first one. "Gotta be sure."

"Willum," called Abasio. "Come over here and pee for these men, will you?"

"Sure, 'Basio," said Willum. He came to stand near the drop-off, unlaced his trousers, and let fly. "Needed to do that anyhow." He settled himself, relaced his trousers, and followed Abasio's whispered instruction to seat himself next to Xulai.

The club wielder snarled, "How 'bout in the wagon?"

"I always lock it when we're outside," said Abasio. "There's nothing in there but our supplies."

"We'll have to see," growled a gray-haired, bearlike man with an ax. "Havta look. Havta find 'er."

Another one cried, "Oh, Digger, they don' got her. F'r grief's sake!"

"I bought 'er! I want 'er! Got to be sure! Havta look." Digger was huge; his hair was tangled and filthy, like his beard. His eyes were an odd, pale color, like sour milk; they did not look, they burrowed, cut, lanced, dissected. His eyes, thought Abasio, were knives made of pain and ashes.

"Ja' mind, mister?" asked another.

"Yes," said Abasio. "I do mind. Just as you would mind if we came to your house and demanded that you let us scuffle through it."

"Mor'v us'n you!" snarled Digger. "Mor'v us. Try n' stop us, get yersef killed."

Something very large had lighted on the road soundlessly, behind the men. There were now only five men standing, the five rearmost having been put quietly out of action.

"I only count five of you," said Abasio. "And two of us, not counting Willum. That's about even."

The group of three turned, looked back, and howled as though they shared one set of lungs. The two foremost also turned. The Griffin lifted one limp body in her right front claws, turned her head to the right, and opened her beak to its widest, upward, dropped the body, and swallowed with an audible gulp. Four other bodies waited under her other feet, the two under her left front foot squirming frantically to get free.

"I'm not really fond of human meat," said the Griffin in a conversational tone as she extricated one of the two squirmers and held him aloft: Digger. "But I am rather hungry this morning and you are interfering with my messengers. They carry a message to others of their kind. I will not have them interfered with!"

"She's only eaten one of you," said Abasio, struggling to get the words out. His mouth and throat were dry. "She may just take Mr. Digger and let the rest of you go if you go quickly. Either that, or she'll be happy to dispose of all of you."

There was a furious nodding of heads, a sideways scuttle toward the road behind the Griffin, who was lifting her feet, one at a time, slowly allowing the other victims to escape. Abasio pointed at the one she was holding and drew his hand across his throat. She flipped him, as a farmwife wrings the head from a chicken, throwing both head and body in one furious motion over the outside edge of the road.

Abasio counted eight men disappearing up the road in frantic haste. Though he had resolved to say nothing, the words "How'd you do that eating bit?" came blurting out.

"Sleight of beak," murmured the Griffin. "Spread my wing, turned my head up, dropped him behind my wing. He probably gave me lice or fleas as it was."

"Is it true, what you said? You don't eat human meat."

The great amber eyes fastened upon him, half closed, considering. "If we have to kill one of you, we try to use the talons—the back feet have talons—or only the claws on the front feet. The claws are retractable. Talons are not. We find it interesting that our makers could not quite decide which it was to be. Either is preferable to the beak, for if we used the beak, the foul taste would be inevitable and persistent. Humans taste like something rotten." The Griffin wiped her beak swiftly along the top of one wing, as though to eradicate a remembered flavor. "I'm told that babies are not as foul-tasting, but a being that would eat babies would eat corpses." She paused, staring into the distance, adding, "And *has* eaten them, no doubt." She shuddered, an apparently unconscious movement.

"You mean the Giants?" Abasio blurted thoughtlessly.

The Griffin glared at him for a long moment before speaking. "Giants? You've never met a Ghoul? The offspring of certain Ogre-Troll relationships? You must hope you never find out, Abasio the Cat!" The shudder went through her again. "To be clear, I like the meat of sheep and cattle. Deer are flavorful, as are elk or those huge shaggy beasts that have returned to the plains around Artemisia. I have killed and eaten all of those, yes. And I have killed men, too, but I have always avoided getting any part of them near my mouth." She paused, asked, "What did you mean, Giants?"

"I mean very big ones, over the mountain from Saltgosh."

Willum and Needly emerged from behind the wagon. Willum, actually speaking quietly, said, "We went out the window and we climbed a tree back there so we could watch."

Needly said, "They went back up the road a little ways where there's a place the rock's broken, and they climbed up to the next road, then they headed for the cut, around the mountain at the last place the road turned. Grandma didn't think they'd be able to track me! That was Old Man Digger who came after me."

Fearlessly, Willum close behind her, she approached the Griffin, holding out her hands. "Did you throw him down on the road below, Lady Animal?"

"That would have made a mess," said the Griffin with a fastidious shudder. "The road below you tends toward the south; the man's parts went into a crevasse north of it for the carrion eaters to enjoy: skunks, crows, magpies, no doubt, coyotes and bugs as well."

"You said she'd eat me," Willum cried to the girl, outraged. "She doesn't even eat people."

He had come too close to the Griffin and found himself suddenly pinned to the ground with one great forefoot, claws on either side of his head, driven into the ground, only now terrified as he stared up into the huge amber globes of her eyes.

"You don't *listen* well, boy!" growled the Griffin in a voice like rattling metal. "If you had *looked* and *listened* you would realize that I can kill you without eating you! Either talons or claws would go through you without difficulty, and I could wash them in the nearest stream. If you annoy me enough, be quite sure I could and would do that. I have given these people a task, and if you interfere with their getting it done, if you delay them, it will annoy me! I might even forget myself and bite your head off out of irritation, for when intelligent beings are sufficiently irritated, we all do things we would not ordinarily do." She dropped her voice almost to a whisper. "You would be wise to help your friends, for if they do not do as I have asked—they and their kind—you will die along with them."

She took her foot from the white-faced boy, saying to Abasio, "I will follow your trail southward. You will always be within my sight or the sight of my people." The great wings came down and she was gone, up and over the mountain, dropping behind the peak as into an abyss.

For a long, long moment no one said anything. As was typical, Willum restored himself to impudence before the rest had managed to shake off paralysis.

"See," he said to Needly, puffing his chest somewhat. "See. She wuddn' really hurt me, wuddn' hurt you neither, Needly."

Needly stared at him, shaking her head in solemn negation. "Oh, Willum, you're being silly! Lady Animal is right. You don't listen. You're always looking at her wings. You're always thinking about riding around in the air. You didn't watch her eyes when she talked. She keeps her voice nice, almost quiet, but if you were a threat to that little one, she'd kill you quicker than you could say 'scratch.'" And she turned to Abasio. "And whatever she wants you to do. Oh, Mr. 'Basio, I do hope you can do it. I don't know how many like her there are, but I suppose even one or two could do an awful lot of damage and she's probably got different kinds of friends, things that see in the dark and under the water or under the ground . . . If she knows her children can't live on, she won't care if anything else in the world lives on at all. I think she'll make sure nothing does."

Abasio, unlike Willum, had watched the Griffin's eyes and knew very clearly the intention they held; the creature had not exaggerated. The child was right: the Griffin meant deadly finality. Complete eradication. And there was that other thing . . .

"Back, over the pass, there was that Listener thing," he said, reluctantly. "Do you know about that?"

"Oh, yes," she said. "I came that way. Something had burned the trees. They were still hot. Griffins don't do that, do they?"

Abasio said, "I thought maybe lightning. But there hasn't been a storm."

"From down in the valley the way is long and twisty," Needly said. "Sometimes . . . people coming up the road from the east don't have time to take the long way, so there's a quicker way to get there. It's very well hidden, but Grandma showed me. I heard the Listener humming. All kinds of talk was going and coming. The air was busy. I imagine it won't take very long for the trees to grow back, not very long at all." She had been witness to replacement trees, magically soaring up from the valley below, great balls of earth around their roots, those root balls plunging into holes prepared for them from which the charred remnants had been removed.

"They were a century or more old," argued Xulai, "great tall things."

"Some people can move . . . great tall things," the child said. "I imagine."

"So you think some assistance might be coming?" asked Abasio.

"To help? Oh, yes. I should think so. Grandma and I asked for help quite a while ago. And you all just did, when the Griffin told you her terms. We're close enough here, the Listener would have heard that. Oh, yes. I imagine there'll be someone to help." She gave a funny, quirky smile, then said in a completely different voice, "Whether we like it or not."

Somehow Abasio was not surprised. He had expected for some time there would be some other, even more troublesome involvement. Even though he and Xulai had for the last several years done everything expected of them and a good deal more, it had all been . . . fairly easy. Tiresome, yes; possibly dangerous—had they not been carrying *ul xaolat*—but not repugnant. Not vile or mind-numbingly boring, merely wearisome, heavy, an unending tension during which the analytic part of him waited in dread for the counterstroke, the obliteration that seemed inevitable, coming from someone, somewhere. It was as though he had been warned without being able to remember by whom or when or how. Maybe he'd dreamed it. He couldn't remember dreaming that particular dream, had there been one, but then the dreams were full of half-remembered details. He hadn't been surprised at Needly's remarks about the Listener. He wouldn't even be surprised if they turned out to be true.

He was, however, repeatedly surprised at her perception. Where had she learned to look that clearly behind and within? Even now, as she came over to him, put her hand on his arm, looked up at him as though reading his mind—no. *She was reading what he had been looking for in his own mind and could not find there.*

"*What is it?*" he asked in a desperate whisper. "*Where is it?*"

"You have it." She returned his whisper with that same little smile. "Stop worrying about it, Abasio. You have it, your family has it. You don't have to worry about it or worry for them. It's all right."

Abasio breathed deeply and tried to believe that. He tried to believe he already had whatever he had been feeling he needed, even though he had no idea what that thing was. A weapon? A . . . dictionary? A translator? A quiet period of a few months during which he would not have to worry about anything?

He met Xulai's eyes. If he told her right now that it didn't matter what was happening, not so long as Needly knew what it was and where and how . . . would that effectively excuse them from having to play the game anymore? Because this journey, this life they led, it was like that game they had played in Tingawa. One player gave another player an imaginary gift without telling him what it was. The recipient had so many questions to find out what he was supposedly given. "Does it have legs?" "Is it furry?" "Is it galactic?" "Does it have more than four dimensions?"

Or, would it be enough simply to stop . . . worrying. To believe, as Needly said, that everything was all right. Whatever he needed, he had it. How did he know? Needly told him so.

Needly: named for the needle's eye, because she saw things very sharply.

CHAPTER 7

In the Company of Griffins

THE FEELING THEY WERE BEING WATCHED MADE THE descent an anxious one. Going down was less laborious than climbing had been, but without a concurrent sense of accomplishment. Nothing distinguished one switchback from another. Some sections of road led along sheer, cliff-like drops where even the tops of the nearest trees below did not reach to their height. At either end of each stretch, darkly forested slopes ran unbroken down to the east. Only far down, where the road debouched onto either prairie or desert (as rainfall would have determined by the time they reached it), did the forested wilderness give way to vague, no-colored plains, broken by the scars of scattered arroyos that winked fugitive gleams from deep inside themselves: little pools there; tiny streams; seasonal gatherings of blessed moisture, habitats for the fanged and scaled, the rarely seen, the scarcely known.

From time to time, almost unconsciously, Abasio and Xulai looked up, eyes keyed to wings even as minds prayed there were no wings. So far there had been none, but Needly was not alone in feeling eyes, and the feeling led to whispered suppositions among the four of them, five if one included Blue. Rags seldom spoke while hitched, as she felt it inappropriate for a speaking creature to be harnessed, though Needly had pointed out to her that heavy clothing and backpacks were just as much a burden.

Suppose, Needly wondered to herself, *suppose the Griffins have friends among other creatures, many other creatures . . .*

Suppose other things are watching us and will report to her . . .

Certainly the Griffin was not depending on human spies. This late in the season the threat of storm limited traffic on the road. Once they passed a man loading a donkey with the scattered deadwood that accumulated at the uphill edge of the road. Though the donkey saluted them loudly and persistently, his bulky owner did not acknowledge their presence. He faced into the mountain, head down, still as stone when they spoke to him. Xulai wondered if he was dumb or disdainful. His attitude fit nicely with Abasio's description of the northern mountain men's rejection of company. As did his smell. This gave Xulai something to amuse herself with: Can a human creature be said to be dis-odorly? Wasn't there something she had read concerning dis-odorly conduct?

Trails led away at many of the switchbacks, south or north. In order to siphon off some of Willum's overabundant energy, Abasio asked Blue to pick a placid horse familiar with brats and give Willum temporary ownership: a mount of his own! Freed from the boring trudge, Willum was off, exploring up and down, returning at a gallop to say a nearby trail split into networks of smaller tracks—by the look of them, seldom used. *"But,"* he cried enthusiastically, swollen with self-importance. *"But 'f I could just go just a little farther down!"*

Abasio threatened repossession of the horse; Xulai announced that she would send him home with the next traveler headed in that direction; Needly deflated him with elaborate descriptions of the bears she (might have) barely escaped during her own forest journey; and Blue made it clear that given a choice between bear getting horse or bear getting rider, most horses immediately disposed of their riders—and in Willum's case, without a qualm. Among all of them—though only by returning to the subject at intervals—they managed to shadow Willum's ebullience with a faint tint of caution.

Xulai usually sat beside Abasio on the wagon seat. When the day warmed sufficiently, she opened the shutters behind the seat so the babies could be passed through when they were hungry, though they were no longer nursing with any frequency. Needly and Willum had taken over the task of feeding them spoonfuls of mashed apple, mashed potato, mashed peas. "Mashed ever' darn thing," Willum griped as he pushed hard-boiled egg through a sieve with the side of a wooden spoon.

"Gently, Willum," Xulai admonished. "That's the only sieve I have, and you're pushing it all out of shape!"

Each night Xulai and Abasio shared the bed in the wagon, the babies curled up in their baskets beneath it, top halves dry, bottom halves wet. If the weather was good, Kim put his own bedding near the horses; if it threatened rain, he shared Willum's space beneath the wagon—already shared with Needly, who also preferred it to the small bunk bed that could fold down above the big bed in the wagon. Though Willum had brought nothing with him to sleep in, after several early-morning encounters with him in his natural and extremely shivery state, Xulai had adapted an old shirt of Abasio's, shortening the sleeves and eliminating the buttons. Though Willum considered this totally unnecessary, he admitted he was warmer at night in the shirt, along with the pair of soft, drawstringed undertrousers Xulai had made from half an old sheet. Also, Abasio had told him the people of Artemisia allowed nakedness only up until the time children were toilet-trained, so if Willum were observed running around naked it would be assumed he still pottied in his pants: shameful at his age.

Xulai's notebook, kept for the benefit of the Tingawan chroniclers and historians, benefited from the discussion of cultural differences: in Gravysuck, children were regarded as asexual until puberty and went naked whenever weather and surroundings allowed. Xulai approved of the custom, for she had noticed there was little or none of the preadolescent sneaking, peeking, and nastiness in Gravysuck that she had noticed in other places. Needly, however, had grown in a society in which uglification and shapeless clothes were necessary for females almost from birth. Another of Abasio's old shirts and the other half of the sheet were sacrificed promptly to meet Needly's need, and Needly was left wondering why Grandma had not included at least one of Needly's nightgowns in the getting-away pack.

"But, when you travel afoot, you sleep in your clothes, don't you?" asked Xulai.

"Yes. Of course you do. If something comes at you, you don't have time to get dressed. You grab your pack and run, or hide, or climb a tree—if you're not already up one."

"Well then, that's why. Your travel pack was just to get you where you were going. Once you're there, the other things you might need would be available. Besides, you knew exactly what was in your getaway pack, didn't you? You didn't think of it either."

Needly agreed that was probably the case but was still left with a small, aching doubt she had never had before. Grandma had always thought *of everything.*

Each morning Kim and the extra horses set out an hour or so ahead of them. Abasio occupied the wagon seat out of habit, though he did not pretend to drive the team. His only duty was to apply the wagon brake when it was necessary. Usually it wasn't, for he had designed the wagon to be brakable by the team itself. The wagon body had two short, widely spaced shafts in front. Between these shafts stretched a stout leather strap, securely fastened at each corner so its wide, flat surface was perpendicular to the road. Blue and Rags could simply back their rear ends against it to slow or stop the wagon as needed. Blue and Rags preferred to be the rear hitch, as they were the ones most familiar with the stop-strap, and also because they enjoyed hearing what the humans had to say to each other; this despite the fact that most of the conversation was dull.

"Not horse-ful," complained Rags.

"Y'could hardly expect that!" Blue replied.

"You n' him were alone together all that time in the north forests. I shoulda thought he'd have absorbed some horse sense by now."

"He has. He just doesn't always talk like it."

Each night they caught up with Kim to share food and campfire, preferring sites open to the east so they could watch the widely separated skeins of smoke that rose above the shadowed slopes below: faceless gray specters with glowing feet; ghostly, blood-tinged arms reaching upward into oblivion. Each wavering spirit marked the location of someone alone in all that darkness, and no obvious track or trail led toward any of them. If there were such trails—Abasio explained with a direct stare at Willum—they were hidden from above by trees and on the ground by endless convolutions as well as by deadfalls or other traps. Abasio took some time to describe the traps he had seen in the north—including vivid details of the partly or wholly consumed bodies found therein.

"Only bones," he confirmed to doubting Willum. "Ask Blue. He was there."

One evening Willum pointed out an unusual gathering of smokes that had risen almost to the level of the road they were on: a dozen or so of them, near enough to one another that they were being braided by an eddying wind.

"That many forest camps close together is unusual," Abasio agreed. "The trader up north told me sometimes kinfolk would share a good home place, one close to water and well protected, because three or four together would be better able to defend against raiders who might to steal their furs. Even then, he said, no matter how they depended on one another, they would never share trapping territory."

The braided pillar, much larger than the usual smoke ghost, danced on into the night, its top flushed with rose by sunset rays still slanting through high valleys behind them. For a long, breathless moment several smaller spirits undulated in attendance until light vanished all at once, leaving only far-separated sparks of campfire glow to populate the dark.

Xulai shivered. "I wouldn't want to be lost in there."

Abasio nodded agreement. Seeing these fires reminded him of his long trek through the north country on his way to find Xulai. He'd almost forgotten that journey, so much had happened since. It had been long and tiresome and dangerous, but it had taken him to Woldsgard: where the child Xulai had been; where he had needed to go. And all the way there he had wondered why he was going! No prize had been offered at the end of the road; no glory or riches would be forthcoming. Just . . . go, go there. Get there as soon as you can.

"But at least there *were* roads," Xulai commented.

He half smiled, ruefully. "They were given that title thereabouts. The trader told me if night was coming on, it was better to keep going, to get some distance between my wagon and the nearest camp, for the horse and wagon might prove irresistible if trappers thought they could take it without too much trouble. Blue and I got very, very good at hiding the wagon and ourselves."

This interested Willum to the extent that he, Needly, and Blue spent most of one evening discussing techniques of hiding oneself and one's belongings in the midst of a forest.

Abasio fell asleep promptly on lying down. Later in the night, he dreamed.

In this dream he knows who he is: he is Abasio Cermit, Abasio the Dyer, Abasio the Traveler, who is married to the Princess Xulai, Abasio the father of the Children of the Future and the supposed owner of the horse Blue, a speaking horse who knows very well he is not owned by anyone save himself. The dream Abasio knows also that this particular Abasio is dozing on the wagon seat and is dreaming yet again of a throne room in some very distant place . . .

The one enthroned—is that one Plethrob? Or is Plethrob something or someone else? Of course, if this is a new dream, Abasio wouldn't know who it is. It could be anyone. The dream feels familiar, however, and those blood drinkers on the perches—Abasio has seen those before; something like birds, but birds didn't have long, tubular tongues that unroll endlessly, from the perch all the way to the floor—so the thing on the throne is probably Plethrob.

Abasio looks down at . . . itself. It is wearing a sort of vertical brassiere with three—no, five lumps protruding. If it were female there would be . . . six? Or four? Some even number, surely. The wall opposite him or her or it is mirrored. He, it moves slightly, watching for movement in the mirror. Ah, there. An apparently bipedal, two-armed, erect creature wearing a circlet on its head to hold back a full head of slowly squirming tendrils? Tentacles? A short, open-fronted jacket and whatever garment it is down the front to cover the bumps. Not breasts. Not testes or anything similar. No. This body is not a he or a she. It is the body of an IT. An IT in the service of Plethrob, surely, who is now . . . thinking, his broad brow furrowed, the two nostrils under the right eye slightly elevated in . . . annoyance? Perhaps. Or simple irritation.

Plethrob speaks: "So this world decided to intervene, is that it, Jeples?" The words are not in Abasio's language, but he understands them nonetheless.

"Yes, great corpuscle of heaven." The glabinour replying is an old one with gray integument, wrinkled earflaps, vlagators veined in blue, age spots all over them. Which means, thank heavens, there will be no dominance rituals or . . . any of that. Uninvolved people could get accidentally dead during dominance rituals.

"This is a world name of Lom?" Plethrob inquires.

"It has upon it a place named Lom, indeed, O golden lymph node!"

The very masculine presence narrows his several eyes: "Jeples!"

"Yes, O marvelous bone-marrow, master of miracles."

"*Make a note.*"

Jeples takes a deep breath and makes a note. It is r'datitch (B flat, says Abasio's mind in the dream). Very slightly off. Abasio knows this without knowing how he knows it or caring very much. He seems to be alone in this disregard, however, for everyone else in the throne room is suddenly . . . stiffer. The old person tries again, and this time the note emerges purely. Everyone breathes carefully, silently, enormously relieved. Abasio finds himself thinking that deheadings are so damned messy, especially early in the morning, and it, Feblia, hates mess. (So that's who Abasio is! Abasio is an IT, probably named Feblia!) It—Feblia—will speak to the old thing's carapace polisher and tell him to serve old Jeples a bulb of herb tea with ziblac nectar first thing in the morning. Ziblac removes that accumulation in the throat, a precaution made necessary when a Ruling One has a tendency to poke, poke, test, test, call for a note here, a note there, purely to annoy, purely to irritate, to give an excuse for slaughter so he can watch the blood drinkers slurp!

Jeples is a nice old glabinour, but not of sufficiently high rank to have a personal sustainer. It would be terrible to witness an execution for being out of tune when a little personal care would carry it through. Another season or so and it would be retired from court to spend its aged years in safety.

Besides, when a great HE becomes annoyed first thing in the morning, it usually doesn't stop with one deheading. It can go on and on until the moppers are in hysterics and all the blood drinkers are falling off their perches from inadvisable repletion. Not that Feblia is concerned for itself. Early-morning annoyances are virtually always same-sex-directed and glabinours are arbitrarily considered to be male. That old rivalry thing. Every few octads someone proves morning dominance reclusions are a complete myth, that they are not caused by anything physiological or psychological, that no glands are spewing anything at all!

Oh, yes, it had been conclusively *proven that morning dominance reclusions resulted from a* specific *irritation: a night's sleep not being as restful as usual; the night cook not as well prepared as he-she-it-or-they should have been; the shes of the previous evening not as skilled as they should have been. HOWEVER, in this particular case, one had to ask, "How could they be skilled? Look at that creature on the throne! Look at its amtrog! How can anyone NOT look at its amtrog? Has anyone even IMAGINED an amtrog of that size? Immensely swollen, out of all proportion to purpose! How could any she or any* consortium *of SHES and ancillary ITS do* anything *with that monstrosity except regard it with fear and revulsion?"*

Oh, Feblia had seen the devices developed by the Erotory Society for pleasing monsters like this. Disgusting! Terrible fleshy pink naliwags, made out of glafwood and that slithery Vantec stuff, twenty times, one hundred times normal size, requiring eight to ten erotory specialists to manipulate them. Manipulate . . . that meant with the hands! What word did one use for hands, arms, legs, filquabs, shoulders, and thrugs? One must, quite literally, throw oneself into the work! All that trouble and pain simply because a He (Plethrob) had decided to become more He (!) than anyone else.

In south Gobanjur, where Feblia was reared among its egg siblings, any male who showed any sign whatsoever of developing that bigger-bigger-bigger ambition was mercifully and quietly done away with. It was the only sensible thing to do. But here in the north? They enthroned them, what else? The net effect was rizziwanks of infant males running about shouting, "Ooky me, ooky me. I gotta bigger amtrog'n you do!" And then, when the children got old enough to see a real monster, they suffered terminal frustration and either died or relieved the pressure with indiscriminate slaughter.

And lately there'd been entirely too much of that! When would members of the Jiptwik—the almost-royal-families—realize they could not help their kinfolk and snafluggers by nominating them to positions at court for which they were not well trained or equipped! Inevitably such a one would draw attention to him, her, it, or them selves by improper costume, inadequate abasement, or failure to hrack soon enough. At which point the dominant HE—who would inevitably be all too full of HIMself—would execute the creature for inability to shlub or some other such foolishness. Such heedless nominations were inexplicable— unless, of course, the Jiptwik had wanted to get rid of the nominee all along. It could happen. It had happened, as Feblia knew, when the Snafluggers (one of the Jiptwik clans) had wanted to rid themselves of Feblia's own brood brother, Plikkub. Of course, Plikkub had always been an idiot.

Nobody, absolutely nobody is unable to shlub! One learns shlubbing in infant school! Seventeen damned cycles of it. One could shlub in one's sleep! In over thirty languages. One could shlub while laspinking, and one's partners would not even notice!

Ah! The great HE is speaking.

"This Lom-world was asked for help, yes?"

"It truly was, Eyelash of Heaven. Urth-world asked Lom-world for help."

"Because this Urth-world was being destroyed?"

"Magnificent Muscle, it was indeed being destroyed by a plague of mankinds."

"Mankinds? Am I aware of mankinds?"

"Why would the Glorious Skinflake take any notice of such inconsiderable trifles?"

"Most Magnificent Self would not. So how did Lom assist this Urth?"

"It offered to drown the destroyers, O heavenly hair follicle."

"Ah. How?"

"How, most Marvelous Cuticle?"

Feblia felt a drop of sweat forming. Oh, no.

The great HE actually swelled. "Are you blamfozzled, Jeples? One means where did they get liquid? Space is abundant. Burning hydrogen is abundant. Metals are abundant. Light fills the very void. But liquid is not a condition universally available."

"Ah, forgive my stupidity, Magnificent Nosehair. Hydroxic liquid is found in abundance on the-very-large-world-Squamutch, most Marvelous Mandible. You will remember that the-very-large-world-Squamutch had asked the planetary scrutators for more dry space on which to grow crops, those crops Your Magnificence has been kind enough to endorse. By taking one world's overabundance and placing it upon this other world—"

"Which is named what again?"

"No, sir."

"No, sir, what?"

"It is not named Whatagain, sir. It is named Urth."

"Now that is a most demeaning untruth, Jeples. My Glorious and Utterly Unique Self has used its third retractable manipulator to access the catalog of acceptable worlds. Our own world of Barfram is there. Others are there. But my Astonishingly Masculine Self has found no planet with the name of Urth."

Jeples bowed. Abasio/Feblia is amazed to see that its legs went down like a fold-up ruler, five sets of knees bending in opposite directions, thus allowing Jeples to stop with his nose touching the floor. Jeples bounced up a few moglors in order to speak: "Your Magnificence is as ever utterly correct. Urth is never included in the catalog of acceptable worlds. As one said, it is infected with mankinds. It should have been fumigated aeons ago and IGGI ETC, the Inter-Galactic Group Investigating Eradication of Toxic Creatures, is currently study-ing the problem. But all sensible creatures know how long such a study is likely to take, and meantime Urth is infected with hordes of mankinds who could at any time explode further into the great void to settle on other worlds as they have already transgressed upon Lom.

"*Therefore, Miraculous One, Lom has prayed for succor from Squamutch, a conorbited world of vast size but only a tiny bit of land area, all dedicated to the farming of Fligbine. Through an utterly dependable, long-life wormhole discovered by completely qualified and respectable Galactian Locators, liquid substance from Squamutch is being poured into the planet Urth. The wormhole being used has no inappropriate deviations and only one egress, which is buried deeply under the ocean on the planet Urth itself—a location called the Mariana Trench. The wormhole has no lesser contiguities; it is direct and uncomplicated; and through it, one-fifth of all liquid on Squamutch will be redirected into Urth. Urth—a much smaller planet than Squamutch—will be completely covered in ocean. Mankinds—as air-breathing, land-dwelling creatures—are being eradicated as IGGI ETC has ordered." Jeples bounced slightly and began to hrack its way up.*

"*And as a happy side effect, Your Magnificence, Squamutch will end up with three times as much dry land on which to grow Fligbine, the Fligbine Your Utterly Flawless and Superb Magnificence so much enjoys in the evenings, or before the wake-up meal, or after the afternoon nappy.*"

Or any time at all, thought Feblia, when His Magnificent Muchness had nothing else to keep him amused.

"*I am pleased," said the Great One, almost smiling. The room hummed with pleasure and relief. The Great One had almost smiled! And before breakfast! The blood drinkers hummed.*

Feblia reflected on the truth that Fligbine is delicious when eaten or sipped as a tea. When inserted into one's lateral anstrackle—an anatomical feature of both males and neuters, but not of shes or frigles—it produces a long-lasting euphoria. It is also addictive. At the current time, this Great He Plethrob was, all by himself, *utilizing half the annual crop produced on Squamutch in each Barframian year. In addition to His Enormous Maleness, the rest of Himself was actually getting fat! Which everyone is pretending to admire, for the Great One is soooo much less bloodthirsty when he is on Fligbine!* Lots and lots of Fligbine!

"*Fligbine," murmured Feblia as it moved back through the surrounding draperies and into the hallway, bumping into someone as it closed the curtains behind it.*

"*Oh, pardon me," Feblia murmured, making the correct gesture of appropriate avoidance.*

"*Not at all," the creature it had bumped replied. "I was waiting here for you. You are Abasio, aren't you?*"

"Feblia," he/it said. "Feblia. I don't want to cause any—"

"Of course not. And it was nice of you to think kindly on old Jeples. He hasn't been the same since his snardat died. Little Pootsie."

"Oh, no! Not the pretty little one with the purple ears. Really?" Abasio/Feblia found him/itself remembering a tiny creature, fluffy, with long . . . no, was that the right . . . ?

"You probably never received the dream transmission at full resolution," said the bumped creature. "Pootsie was a snardat. Furry? Rolled around like a ball? A beloved pet."

The bumped creature had six legs, Feblia/Abasio noticed, and six arms, and a determinedly cheerful face. The six-legged creature smiled. It had a very pleasant smile. Abasio/Feblia remembered that smile. It had seen that smile before . . .

The creature spoke: "I have just injected myself into this dream transmission to introduce myself. My name is Balytaniwassinot. Bally Tanny Wahsi Not. Among my people it's a fairly short name, but others sometimes have trouble with it. Earthers do, I've noticed." The creature put two of its arms on Abasio/Feblia's shoulders and stared deeply, hypnotically into his, its, Feblia's eyes.

"Please try to keep this in mind, Abasio. I have inadvisably involved myself in the mankind problem! It's against the regulations! I admit that. However, I have an overwhelming aversion to what was going to happen if we let matters take their course. Humans are a galactic nuisance; one can accept that, one has to accept that, the evidence is overwhelming. They are also, however, a very creative and innovative people. One has only to look at this new thing, this aquatiforming of their race. Well, in the last analysis, it all comes down to bao or no bao. If we can fix that lack . . . well, I think of it rather like a blood transfusion. One that carries certain antibodies. You're not following? That's all right. You will remember! You'll add two and two to get four and four plus four to get barflic and a half, like humans always do. Nonetheless . . .

"I wanted you to know that you and your sweet wife have my congratulations. You're managing very well. I've been observing the sea-people process for some little time—time jumping is such a help!—a century here, a century there. Forbidden, of course, so one has to fix the logs to cover. I've become an expert at that. (Dream transmissions, being my own invention, are not monitored or recorded in anyone's logs, so this is just between us two. You may not recall the details, but I intend that you shall retain the feeling of reassurance.)

"At any rate, it's all coming to a—what does one say—to a climax? To a crisis? I've heard your plea to the Listener, as well as those of others, and since *the, ah,* the nitty-gritty—*the phrase is archaic but descriptive—looms ever more closely on our horizon, keep in mind that I will be there to assist. If things appear particularly upsetting, don't despair. That final tending to details is often the worst part, but they will be tended to. I just wanted you to know."*

The dream had wandered off into never-never land. Abasio felt the outlines of things wavering. "Very kind of you, Mr. Bahlee . . . ah . . ."

"Oh, do call me by my nickname. Fixit. So much easier. And it's what I do. *Sometimes in accordance with policy . . . sometimes, as in this case, not entirely. Policy is all very well, but it never makes room for the exceptional, does it? I do hate to see any race of creatures totally expunged, and that would have been the alternative. And everything comes down to a question of bao in the end. It was nice to see you. And it was interesting to learn about the Fligbine . . ."*

"Fligbine," said Abasio to himself as he wakened. "Good old Fligbine."

ABASIO HAD AWAKENED BECAUSE KIM had put his head into the wagon to report that one of the horses had a foot problem.

Abasio reviewed the dream, quite clearly. He lifted his shirt to be sure his belly was not . . . unbellylike, wondered briefly how someone injected themselves into someone else's dream life, decided it had merely been part of the whole dream, none of which made much sense. Or . . . hadn't Xulai said something about the amount of water exceeding the size of the presumed source? Or had that been something Precious Wind had said?

He shook the dream from his mind, got up, dressed, and went off to do something about the horse's foot, leaving Xulai and the children to their breakfast.

Xulai had spent a troubled night worrying over things Needly had said—and had not said—and asked suddenly, "Needly, your Pa wasn't with that group of men that came to get you, was he?"

"Pa wasn't one of them, no." Needly didn't think Xulai needed to know Pa was deader than week-old bear kill. She hadn't mentioned the little pouch of remedies tied under her skirt, day and night, and she didn't intend to. Grandma had been very clear about the morality of using certain substances: *"Passive watchers are as guilty as doers!"* Needly felt Xulai's morality would be somewhat . . . less stringent, more . . . merciful than Grandma's, and she did not want to be confused by a second opinion from someone she considered, for the most part, admirable.

Xulai did want another opinion, or at least a clarification, since—though she believed Needly was telling the truth—she was unable to accept that any father would sell his child in that way. Unfortunately, she adopted a somewhat chiding tone: "Surely you don't think your own father would have agreed with those other men?"

Needly gritted her teeth. There it was. Xulai was admirable, just not always . . . realistic. She understood that Xulai avoided unpleasantness. Farm people accepted that some creatures had to die if others were going to live, but Xulai, from what Needly had been able to learn, had not been reared in the barn, the paddock, or the kitchen. Xulai inevitably wanted to fix things so there would be no pain for anyone or anything, and on occasion the tendency became exasperating, as even Abasio had remarked.

Needly took a deep breath before saying calmly, "No, Xulai, YOU believe that my father, any father, would not do such a thing. YOU are limited by YOUR experience. I, on the other hand, know very well that he would, and I heard him brag about the deal. That is MY experience. Yes, my father agreed with them, ma'am. He's the one who sold me to Digger. All the men from Tuckwhip believe the same."

Xulai made her "Oh my, something should be done about this" face. "So there are no . . . pleasant people in Tuckwhip?"

"Lady, the only folks you could find at all pleasant were Ma and Pa Siffic, a pair of religious folks who lived down at the ford, half a day's walk away. They are Kindlies, followers of the Kindly Teacher. Kindlies come around every now and then, trying to convince those who live in Hench Valley. They tried with the Pas, but it was like trying to convert rocks."

"Convert them to what?"

"To bein' less like rocks," Needly snarled.

Xulai ignored the snarl and considered the conversion of rocks. "Hard, you mean?"

Pressed past endurance, Needly cried, "HARD, AND DENSE, AND INERT!," each cleanly enunciated word spit into the silence like an arrow. Her voice sounded both womanly and angry. Hearing herself, she shivered and covered her mouth with a trembling hand. "I'm sorry, Xulai. Sorry. That was Grandma."

Willum had been refilling his bowl from the porridge pot and had stopped, spoon half lowered. Xulai's mouth had dropped open and her head had turned to give Needly a surprised glance. She shook her head. *"That was Grandma?"*

Needly rubbed her forehead, troubled. "When Grandma and I talked, we . . . talked the way her people did. Do." She looked up, fixing Xulai with her eyes, the words coming with individual, icy clarity: "Our conversations varied considerably from the style of communication common among the village men: among them, or from them to women. Women are allowed very few words in Tuckwhip. As one grows up, one learns to use only the . . . accepted ones."

"Such as?" breathed Xulai.

Needly's reply was in a whining woman's voice: *"Yes, Pa." "I'm getting it, Pa." "It'll take just a minute, Pa." "The water's boiling now, Pa."* Her lips curved into a knife-edged smile. "Conciliatory words and phrases of that ilk, if said quickly enough and in a properly groveling and subservient tone, could sometimes forestall a beating which could end as a killing and did so with some frequency." This voice was a woman's voice, stern and unrelenting.

Willum, who had been busy emptying his refilled bowl, was staring at her as though she had grown horns.

Xulai paled in dismay, remembering what Precious Wind had once advised her. *Read your informant, Xulai. Do not demand painful words when the answer is there in the face.* She had hurt the child by pushing her like that. She took a deep breath. "Since you and your grandmother spoke together in that way, please feel free to do so with us whenever you want to." She frowned, mostly at herself. "Abasio and I would enjoy it. Willum might even learn something if you did."

"I may be able to teach him some vocabulary," said Needly, with a sigh. Willum had come to stand beside her, and she dug an elbow into his ribs in time to stop his immediate disclaimer. "He's boyish, which is a handicap, but at least he's not stone."

Willum, now much offended, put his empty bowl down and went off to join Abasio and Kim.

Needly took a deep shuddering breath, catching Xulai's eyes with her own and holding them. She did not want to have this woman as anything but a friend! "Xulai, lady, *I do not lie to you.* I can tell what you are thinking, even now. You believe that children exaggerate, that no doubt I am provoked by old injustice to intensify the preposterous in what I tell you. Some children may indeed do that, *but I do not.* It's hard for you to believe Hench Valley. It was hard even for my grandma to believe Hench Valley and she had spent decades there. She told me there is a reason that Hench Valley exists and is allowed to remain in existence when everything about it calls for extermination. I can, however, explain one part of your puzzle. You are thinking the man I called Pa was my genetic sire. *Had he been, he would still have acted in the same way, but it may make your belief easier to know he was not.* He was called Pa because that is what all women in Tuckwhip call any man once he has got some woman with child. Other males call such a man by his name or a nickname, but *all women and children call him Pa.*"

Xulai, frozen in place, was suddenly enlightened. "You mean . . . as a servant might say 'sir' or 'ma'am' in other places?"

Needly thought about it, gave the idea a twisted smile of recognition. "More *slave* than servant, but yes, *precisely like that.* 'Pa' is a title of ownership. Command. Territoriality!"

"And fathering a child gives him that title?"

"No. No man in Hench Valley is a father in the sense you use the word. Impregnating a woman—or assuming that he has done so—gives him the title. Having assumed so, they may take credit for the child, if it's a boy. The credit, mind you. Not the responsibility. Hench Valley men frequently 'walk their dogs' in the woods for the purpose of becoming a Pa. However, Gralf was not *my* father in any sense of that word."

"You're sure of that?" This time the words were not disbelieving.

Needly relaxed. Xulai was now interested, not . . . doing that digging, that pursuing, that determined uncovering that she had been doing before. "Oh, yes. Grandma told me how I was conceived, I and my half siblings. All the Tuckwhip men went off hunting lions one summer— there'd been cows killed by such a beast—and a stranger man came into the valley, like a new rooster into a henhouse, as Grandma said. *'A kindly speaking, gently holding, sweetly wooing man. A man as unlike Hench Valley men as it is possible to be.'* There were six of us born the following spring. The rest of us were taken from the valley as babies."

Abasio had returned earlier in this conversation and had seated himself by the fire. Neither he nor Xulai had failed to notice that Gralf had been spoken of in the past tense. They shared a glance. Xulai asked, "You said, six of *us* were born?"

"Children that were pale like me and with hair like mine. Silver-hairs, they called us." It was one of the politer things the children had been called. "Whitecaps," was another, which was the local name for a particularly angelic-looking but poisonous mushroom that Grandma called "the angel of death." Grandma preferred to use another substance, because it was painless. The angel killed surely, but it took a long, excruciating time to do it. Needly had some of both in the little bag under her skirts.

"How did the other children leave?"

"Grandma told me each of them disappeared at the time they were weaned, but no one ever saw the children being taken."

"Perhaps they were killed by predators," said Abasio.

Needly smiled a knife-edged smile. "No, Abasio. No wolf or bear or great mountain cat has ever been known to leave a gold coin to pay for his dinner. No one saw how it happened, but each women received such a coin. Grandma told me the mothers sorrowed but were glad the babies had been taken somewhere safe. They loved them, you see. As Grandma loved me—though Trudis did not."

"Ah." Xulai frowned, looked to Abasio for help, received none. The more she learned, the less she understood! "But *you* weren't taken?"

"No, because when I was born, Grandma came. Or, I should say, returned."

Xulai turned this over in her mind, trying to find some way into its real meaning, which was there, somewhere, though hidden. Purposely hidden from her, Xulai? Or simply hidden as a matter of habit? "Your mother, Needly, forgive me, but was, that is, *is* she an intelligent person?"

Needly stared into the sky, her brow creased. Oh, Grandma had wondered that herself, so many times. "Grandma told me that my Ma, Trudis, could have been a reasonably intelligent woman if she had had the aptitude and the inclination to be so. Gran was being sarcastic, of course. Grandma's other children had been intelligent, which is why they had been taken away while they were still children. That had been planned for even before they were born." She saw Xulai's lips half open, saw her eyes concentrated, her face muscles tight. *Oh, Xulai was desperate to know all about it.* Well, so was she, Needly, for all the good that did her.

She took a deep breath. "Xulai, I know you're curious about that; so am I; but I don't know why it was planned. I can only assume it was because Tuckwhip was the right place for the breeding or birthing, but not for the rearing."

Xulai stared through her, formidably alert, eyes glittering.

Well, thought Needly, *so that means something to her.* "Trudis was Grandma's last child, and Grandma had intended to take Trudis away well before Trudis was old enough to get involved with any of the boys or men."

"Before anything disastrous happened?"

Needly nodded gratefully. "While she was still a child, yes. There's some mystery in the matter of Grandma's children. She told me many things, but I'm sure there were many things she didn't tell me. She was the only healer, herbalist, midwife in the valley. I believe she would have taken me away long ago except that she was the only one who could help the women when they were sick or giving birth. They were helpless without her."

She stopped, tears gathering. Abasio, concerned about her feverish look, had filled a mug with water and now handed it to her. She thanked him with her eyes and drank the mug dry before returning it to him and gathering herself to tell the story of Grandma's return to her home on Midsummer's Day.

" . . . and when Grandma came back from Gortles on Midsummer morning, Gralf was sitting in the kitchen with Trudis on his lap, drinking beer. He had already taken his dog out hunting . . ."

Abasio, seeing Xulai's bewildered expression, said, "Is that the phrase they use for a man having sex with a woman, Needly?"

She nodded. "The connotation is not so much *having* as hunting down. The men tell stories about their dogs going hunting: finding prey. You can imagine." Her voice faded, she stood, staring at nothing. "I always speak of her as Grandma. I don't know that she was necessarily a grandma to anyone else back then, except to me. She told me stories about her other children later. She had six before Trudis. Boys and girls. When she died, if, indeed, she has died, which I doubt. Though she did not look at all old, she may have been . . ." Her voice trailed into silence that was for a time unbroken.

After a respectful quiet, Xulai broke it. "So your mother, that is, Trudis, had her first child when she was twelve?"

"Almost thirteen, I remember Grandma saying."

"When I asked about her intelligence, I was thinking of her as a grown woman . . ."

Needly shook herself, "She was a grown woman in body. Grandma told me that whenever a population is threatened with extinction, one of the signs is early puberty. It's as though each body gets a signal telling it to breed in a hurry because it won't have a chance later on. Perhaps the earth knows something awful is going to happen. However, Trudis never changed from what she was that Midsummer's Day. Gralf and Trudis, sex and beer. Grandma said nine-tenths of the valley's barley went to make beer. With Gralf there in the house, that's mostly what both of them did. Got very drunk and took the dog hunting. Grandma knew there was nothing she could do about it, so she left."

"This was long, long before you were born."

"Oh, yes. Trudis had many children before she had me. Six of them. I would have had two older half sisters, the first two Ma had, except she let one of them drown and coyotes get the other. She would probably have let me die, too, but Grandma came back in time to see I was taken care of."

"Just a moment!" Xulai cried, abruptly reverting to her imperious manner. "Why didn't she come back to protect the two girls your mother had earlier?"

Needly felt her body stiffen. The voice was like . . . Pa's voice. Sometimes.

Abasio rose, stretched, came to put his hand gently upon Needly's shoulder. "Xulai, we're not conducting an *inquisition* here, are we? Are you accusing Needly of something?"

Xulai's mouth dropped open; she bit her lip. "Oh my, I did, didn't I? I'm so sorry, Needly. I didn't mean to sound inquisitorial! When I get interested in something, Precious Wind says sometimes I go after it like a terrier after a rat!"

"Terrier? Precious Wind?"

Abasio answered. "Precious Wind is Xulai's oldest and best woman friend. One who has a soothing effect upon her. A terrier is an extremely energetic, rat-killing dog that can drive people crazy digging at things." He gave Xulai a studied and admonitory look. "*If it cannot find a real rat, it will mindlessly and protractedly seek to uncover a hypothetical one.* However, neither terrier nor friend is pertinent to this discussion. And it is merely a *discussion,* isn't it, Xulai? Hmm? *Of course it is,* and Xulai wonders—merely *wonders*—why your grandmother did not protect Trudis's first two daughters."

"She said there was no point in saving any child parented by Trudis and Gralf," she answered flatly. Seeing Xulai's body go into a spontaneous shiver, as though she were shaking off fleas, Needly laughed, an uncomfortably strained sound. "I know, Xulai. I know it sounds dreadful to you. *But given that heritage, no Hench-born child could be changed! Whatever Grandma was doing, she had to do it in the valley, and it was because Gralf was* not *my father that Grandma came back when I was born.*"

Xulai, very pale, stared at the toes of her shoes. "I understand genetics, to a degree. I don't understand what contribution may be made by geography, but presumably your grandmother did understand it. In any case, it's not fair for me to harangue you about it."

"I think you should well understand what it meant, being a Silverhair," said Needly very softly. "For Willum says you yourself were born for a purpose. Were you not?"

After a long, silent moment, Xulai nodded, sharing a glance with Abasio. Needly was surprised to see a note of despondency in it. "I was, yes. When I finally learned of it, I felt . . . I don't know exactly what I felt. Anger, certainly. It seemed intrusive. Later, I accepted it, though reluctantly. Recently, mostly I've been able to be glad of it."

Needly nodded agreement. "Grandma often said being born for a purpose makes life very difficult, as one constantly has to measure oneself against an unknown scale: any success may be a failure, every failure a success! Unless one knows what the purpose is—and she did not—one never knows whether one measures up! You know the purpose of your life! You can feel gratification! Even if you did not, it may be superior to being born, as many are, for no purpose whatsoever except that some man's dog was barking. Even if his children are starving or parasite-ridden through drinking foul water, their existence, however brief, testifies to the supremacy of his dog." She sighed, wiping at her eyes. "Grandma came to Hench Valley when there was something useful for her to do there—useful in her terms, Xulai! Not necessarily yours or mine. Living there was a trial for anyone, especially I suppose for anyone who had ever known a more . . . pleasant kind of life. So, whenever there came a time when Grandma could do nothing useful, she went away. She came back when I was born, believing it would be useful for me to live."

"Knew so, I should think," said Xulai, regarding Needly with frank amazement. It would be easier to believe this conversation if she shut her eyes. If Xulai did not look at Needly, if she heard only that calm, factual, lucid voice, she would believe her fully adult. It was the sight of that childlike face, that delicate body, those thin little arms—muscular though they were—that made the conversation seem unreal. "And why were you left behind when the other little ones like you were taken?"

"Grandma told me that when children are planned for a purpose— that is, by some sensible human agency—then parents or caretakers are usually appointed for each child well before the child is born. Some-times, perhaps often, these are people other than the birth mother and father. The other children like me were evidently intended to be reared by parents outside Hench Valley, for once the children were weaned, they were taken away to be reared somewhere else. Grandma had evidently been chosen to be my parent. Since she was well accepted as a healer, she could raise me there. I don't know why she couldn't take me elsewhere. It would have been so much easier, almost anywhere else, but she either chose to do it there or it was chosen for her."

She paused, as though judging what she would say next, and took a deep breath. "I've wondered why, so often. Since meeting you, I've thought perhaps I had to be raised there so I would know and accept—as you are finding it so hard to do—what some cultures can be like and what they can do to people. At some point in my life, that knowledge may be necessary. I am assuming that when someone is planned—as both you and I were planned, Xulai—the planners have the ability to see far, far ahead."

Xulai flushed. The point was very well made. It wasn't the geography that was important. The importance was the familiarity with the hideous culture that went with it, with a respected—or at least much needed— grandmother as the barrier between the culture and the child.

Needly went on: "I was taught to read. We had books, kept secret, but we had them. Grandma was a good teacher. She was sure she could keep me safe until . . . until it was time for me to go somewhere else. I don't think she planned on Gralf killing her, but from the time I was about six she told me repeatedly that if she was killed, it was time for me to go."

"And she was sure you'd survive," Abasio said.

Needly actually grinned. "I have a feeling there were people . . . creatures watching out for me when I left Tuckwhip. If I'd gotten into really bad trouble, I think they'd have rescued me."

"Bears sound bad enough trouble to me!" said Willum.

"Would you believe me, Willum, if I told you the bear followed me to the tree I climbed. It sat down and ate some berries. Off in the trees, something played some very strange music while the bear danced very nicely, showing me that he wasn't simply a wild bear. Then the bear told me I should get to the pass, because someone there would be waiting for me. And you were."

"You met my bear!" cried Abasio. "Or one like him. My bear liked music, I saw him dance, and you say he talked?"

"Either he talked or I had a very vivid dream," murmured Needly in a voice that was amused but frighteningly weary. "At the time I didn't doubt for a moment that he talked. Later . . . well, come morning, I wasn't sure."

"It's just one more case of planned genetics," said Abasio, making a face as he turned toward Xulai. "Are the geneticists in Tingawa still using people all over the world for breeding stock, Xulai?"

"If they are, I know nothing about it," she replied. "Just because I'm part of what they regard as one of their more successful efforts doesn't mean they tell me what else they're doing. Besides, isn't it equally likely the culprits are some of your former acquaintances from the Edges?" She turned back to Needly. "Let me get all my curiosity attended to in one fell swoop and quit bothering you about it. You've been very patient with me, Needly! I need to know about your being sold, and that whole Digger business? What was all that?" She took the kettle from the fire, poured some of its contents into the dishpan, and began to clean their breakfast bowls.

Willum sheathed his knife, found a dish towel, and took each bowl and cup from Xulai as it was cleaned. Needly settled herself next to Abasio in the place Willum had warmed for her.

"That has to do with the Hench Valley myth. Would you know it?" Seeing their blank faces, she went on. "Grandma said some people believe what their senses tell them, and some people prefer to believe myths. Stories, you know?"

Willum cried, "Xulai and Abasio were talking to me about that! Not very long ago either. They said the stories are different, everywhere you go . . ."

Needly nodded. "Grandma told me a lot of different ones, from other ages and other places on earth. The Hench Valley myth is a purely local one, but it's been told for quite a few generations. Grandma said it lacked 'the conventional embroideries' that are common to most mythology, but then, Hench Valley wasn't much for decoration of anything at all."

"Wot did she jus' say?" demanded Willum in a loud, sulky voice. He had begun by considering himself Needly's protector, and was becoming mightily annoyed by feeling he might be relegated to some other and inferior role.

Xulai replied, "She said that the Hench Valley story is very simple-minded."

Needly went over to get Willum's bowl, taking his spoon hand between her own. "Willum, you told me some things your ma said, like, *'Leave a cock his bluster or he'll forget how to crow.'* And that meant men had to brag some in order to feel right about themselves, right? Well, in our village the men say, *'Many men make a strong village, strong villages make a strong valley.'*" She took the bowl and spoon to Xulai, dipped a cloth in the dishwater, and returned it to Willum for his face. He scowled at her and she tapped her foot at him until he used it. "You forgot your ears," she said. "They're disgusting."

Abasio commented, "There was probably some truth to there being strength in numbers."

Willum had made a dab at his ears, a bare sufficiency. Needly took the cloth, pounced at one neglected ear, then the other before taking it back to soap it, scrub it out, and fold it.

"The Hench Valley myth started out as 'many men make a strong valley.' Of course. Women weren't in the saying, so they weren't very important and nothing about them was very important. One way to keep men *many* was to keep women *few*. That's more or less how it started."

"But it went on," said Abasio, frowning.

"To keep women few, no one bothered to protect and rear girl babies, and except for bedding them when one felt like it, women were kept to themselves and trained to work hard and be silent. Training them to do that involved hitting them. The conventional embroidery to the myth became 'For men to be strong, women must be chastised.'"

Xulai's face was stony. "I have read of such places in the ancient histories."

Needly went on: "One embroidery begets another, and eventually you end up with Hench Valley, where the fewer women the better, which means you have no extra ones, and if some man needs one, there's weak stupid towns where he can steal one. This culture was so pervasive that when a woman bore a girl child, oftentimes, knowing what kind of life she would lead, the mother chose to smother her in the basket."

Her voice broke and she looked down. The tears dropped into the dust at her feet instead of running down her cheeks. She wiped her eyes on her sleeve. "You can imagine the result? Boy babies survived, girl babies didn't, the female population dwindled to almost nothing. This didn't disconcert the men, however, because they continue to rely on stealing women when necessary."

"What's 'dis-con-sert'?" demanded Willum.

"It means it didn't upset them," said Xulai.

"She coulda said that," mumbled Willum angrily.

"Or you coulda *listened* and learned a new word, Willum," said Abasio threateningly. "Which is what a smart boy would do." He turned back to Needly. "I think you're telling us, Needly, that the Hench Valley myth depends upon women who are also mythical."

Needly's lips twisted into a wry smile. "Grandma told me *as a fact* that there are no women anywhere within reach of Tuckwhip available to be stolen. Ages ago, she said, they successfully raided a few wagon trains, until the wagon trains added armed men. Once they set out to raid the salt-mine place. Most of them were killed or badly wounded during that attack, and the few who came back brought no women." She stared off into the distance, her brow furrowed in thought. "Grandma told me it's something logical people struggle with constantly when they try to use facts to educate other people. She told me every human is like a horse-back rider: he either rides a fact-horse or he rides a myth-horse. AND, to people who ride *myth-horses, fact-horses* don't exist. Fact-horses are just stories *made up by the other side.*"

"*Whut other side?*" Willum demanded.

Needly shook her head. "Grandma said back in history people in power made lists of books other people were not allowed to read, because *they had information in them written by the other side.* Did you know that?"

Xulai nodded, pinch-lipped. "I was taught about it, yes. Hierarchies—religious or political—held on to power by forcing people to believe as they did. I remember reading that in some very stupid areas—there was one, Precious Wind tells me, just south of Artemisia in the Golf Coast—they refused to teach science in the schools because it contradicted ancient holy books." She wiped her forehead, which felt very hot and angry. "It is easier to control people if you control what they think or learn. Religions have always held power by controlling people."

Abasio put his arms around her and squeezed quite tightly. "Your cogs and wheels are coming loose," he murmured.

"I get very angry," Xulai mumbled, muffled by his chest. "Humans are capable of such dreadful stupidities!"

"How many men and how many women in your village?" Abasio asked Needly, without releasing Xulai. "Do you know?"

Needly laughed, this time a sad trickle of descending sound. "Those men who came hunting me, there was one from each of the ten houses in Tuckwhip."

Xulai struggled away from Abasio. "So your Pa . . . I mean, Gralf was with them!"

Needly shook her head. "No. The youngest one, the one the Griffin dropped on his head? That was my brother . . . half brother, Grudge. A season ago in those ten houses. Besides Trudis, there were four women past bearing, and three girls: Needly, Flinch, and Slow: eight females in all, and Flinch and Slow are . . . Grandma used the word 'retarded.' When Grandma was killed and I ran away, that left six. Trudis won't have any other children, she's had none since me, and I think Grandma did something to be sure she won't. I was the oldest girl, the one Digger wanted."

"So there are no fertile women left, and two little girls who might bear children in seven or eight years. If Digger hadn't taken them and killed them first. And that's it. How many males?"

Needly shook her head. "It's hard to say exactly how many. The ones who don't have houses come and go. Sometimes they go live in the woods or in another village; sometimes they're counted and sometimes not, but there are at least fifteen grown men and as many or more in the bunch of little boys living closer to Tuckwhip than anywhere else."

"What about the other villages?" Abasio asked.

"The other villages may still have a fertile woman or two, but their number is . . . similarly disproportionate." She lowered her head, tears still falling into her lap.

"Needly, don't . . ." Xulai left Abasio to put her arms around the child. "I'm so sorry. I've upset you . . ."

Needly gasped, her throat full. "It's just, Xulai, I do miss her so much . . . Talking with you the way Grandma and I used to was almost like having her back, but then you went . . . strange. You sounded like a *Pa*! Horrible and dangerous. Missing her makes me want to cry. Things were just awful in Tuckwhip, but, oh, sometimes we had such . . . such joy together."

Xulai hugged the girl close. "I apologize for sounding like a . . . an inquisitor. Abasio is right. I dig like a terrier even when I shouldn't. You speak in whatever way you are more comfortable, love. Abasio and I enjoy literate speech, though we try to speak as those around us do!"

Needly wiped her eyes on her sleeve. "There's one more thing about Tuckwhip so you'll understand the whole thing." Her face said what her mouth did not: she meant these to be the last words about Hench Valley, for she was desperately weary of it. "When the men and boys decide they need to steal women, the villages get together and build a huge bonfire. The men and the boys take their bows and axes, they make a barrel of extra-strong beer and drink it, they whoop and dance around the fire. When they're tired of doing that, if they're not too drunk, they go off to *steal a woman* just like the myth tells them to."

"Did it happen while you were there?" Xulai asked.

Needly nodded, gesturing openhanded, as though discarding something. "I remember the fire and the dancing, but I think I was only five the last time it happened."

Abasio said, "Let me guess. No one came back."

"No," said Needly with a crooked smile. "Grandma made a list of all the males who went, and she and I watched for more than a year. She made it a game, asking the women when she went to tend them, had they seen this one or that one. None of them came back."

Xulai said, "We know Saltgosh made itself raider-proof, and it's the closest. So, given the village life as you describe it, the young men who are supposedly hunting woman actually just get out of sight of the village, wash off the paint, and keep going."

"That's what Grandma told me. She said the woman-stealing myth was a kind of safety valve for the village. Every ten or fifteen years, if there got to be too many postpubertal males to feed, they'd go through what she called the 'woman-stealing rite,' but once they were away from the villages, they'd pick up whatever pack they'd hid somewhere and wander off in any direction that looked interesting. She knew that because whenever it happened, the women left behind in Tuckwhip always looked for the men's clothes—nobody has much more than one spare shirt or so, not in Tuckwhip—so the women would want to find any that might go to waste. They never found any at all."

"Which meant they'd hidden their clothes and packs in the woods somewhere?"

"Yes. The fire and the dance and all was just . . . kind of a lie they all told each other."

Abasio mused, "I think the behavior is fairly common. People have certain acceptable rites or observances. *At this new moon we eat apples. At midwinter, we build bonfires at the old sun's death and pray for the new baby sun to be born.* People grow up: they learn the words; they memorize the story; it gets to be habit. They don't believe that the observance is really necessary, but they go through the motions. Where I grew up, we enjoyed the festivals mostly for the food! There was almost always special food!"

"It's not just Hench Valley, then," said Needly, with a sigh. "Grandma said if we peeled away all the stories, the real reason the men went and didn't come back was there was nothing to stay for and nothing to return to. What is there in the valley? A few sheep. Not enough anymore for spinning much thread, weaving much cloth. Grandma used the loom a few times; sometimes the women gave her thread as payment for her help, and I have one shirt made from homespun. Cloth was something the men traded for up at the pass. There were a few small fields of wheat; some oats; some barley. A few vegetables in the house gardens, but the women do that. There are a few fruit trees, but no good apple trees anymore. The people who knew how to graft the good apple trees died long and long ago . . ." She stared into nothing. "Grandma had one little tree, off in the woods. She'd grafted it herself, long ago, off an old one in the village that she knew wouldn't last much longer. It had tiny, bright red apples; four would fit in my hand. They were so sweet, they tasted of heaven . . ."

Xulai put some honey in a cup of tea and offered it to Needly. "Have some sweetness here, too. So the men really don't do anything but drink?"

Needly took the cup gratefully. "Oh, they're not totally idle. They can raise barley and make beer, but they need to buy the barrels to put it in and to buy other kinds of drink. To make money they spend all their winters digging in the buried city that extends under the whole valley. They dig for parts of machines, for glass, for a metal that runs like water—live-silver, they call it. Gralf had a hoard of gold—we found it one time, an amazing amount of it. They hoard it. Grandma said many of the men had hoards. Old Digger did. They may use a little of it to trade for cloth and things they need, like knives and scythes. Some of the things they find, they keep. Things they can use."

"Or things women can use?"

"Only if it's something the women use for the men. Like cooking. The men don't cook because that's women's work, but a man might buy a pan or bring one he's dug out, because he knows it takes a pan to cook what he likes to eat. The men without women mostly end up chewing parched grain or eating half-burned bits of whatever they can kill. A man won't buy cloth for women, but he'll buy it for himself. Maybe he'll ask her how much he needs for a shirt. She'll tell him twice as much as it really takes. She makes the shirt and hides all the leftover and scraps. She cuts up the big pieces and sews them back together so they'll look like scraps. She makes her clothes, the children's clothes, out of that. And she hides what she manages to spin and weave and uses it for herself or her children."

"I should think the men would see . . ."

Needly shook her head impatiently. "Xulai, you *have to look at something to see it*! A man wants hot tea in the morning. That's what he looks for. If it's there, good; if not, he hits the woman. He never watches her making it. He never watches her do anything. What she does is unimportant." She stood at the edge of the road, looking out over the far prairies, wiping at her cheeks with the back of her hands.

Xulai sat next to Abasio, who whispered to her. "I think you probably sound a good deal like the child's grandmother, love. It's part of what's troubling her. She talks to you as she would have talked to her grandmother, and when you get imperious, it's as though Granny slapped her face."

"Oh, Abasio! I don't mean to."

"I know, but when you become the Princess Xulai, none of your adoring courtiers are quite sure what you mean to be."

"Well, no more inquisition. If you see me doing it, scratch your nose. Or shake me. Or something." She stood up and went to empty the dishpan at the side of the clearing where they'd camped, stopping to put her arms around Needly, which she had not done until now, and giving her a close hug. She was a child. Willum's age. A child. No matter she spoke like a professor and acted like a judge, she was a child!

Willum, seeing this, went to Needly's side and gave her a slice of apple, neatly peeled and only very slightly grubby. "I think it'd be more comf'tuble to jus' sort of not think about those old myth things."

Needly gave him her best excuse for a smile and went to help Xulai clean the campsite and stow things ready for departure. Let them get on their way and think about something absolutely . . . different. External, like . . . ah, Lom! Lying on their straw mattresses under the wagon, they talked about all sorts of things, and last night Willum had told her about that distant world where the two Earth ships had gone all that long time ago. Did they have myths in that world? They spoke of how wonderful it would be to have a clean, new world without any of the old myths in it.

Once they were under way, they all tried to throw off the morning's preoccupation, but their early-morning thoughts had set the mood for the day. Willum was wondering if there might have been myths back in Gravysuck that he had not known were myths. Needly had been thrown back into grieving for Grandma. Xulai was seriously considering using *ul xaolat* to jump to Hench Valley and obliterate it. Except . . . Needly's grandma had told Needly the place was . . . necessary. Abasio was reviewing the dreams he'd been having, dreams, often repeated, and varying from the pertinent to the ridiculous, each with its own internal inconsistencies. When he had been Feblia, Feblia had known what shlubbing was. Feblia, the character, had known! And Abasio had known that Feblia had known. BUT he, Abasio, *did not know.* How could he be aware of knowing something in a dream that he knew nothing about when he was awake? And the creature he had bumped into, Fixit. He . . . or she or it . . . made no sense. Too many things made no sense. He wanted not to think at all, simply to let the time pass until supper, until the warmth of the fire, the aroma and taste of food, the bedtime comfort of Xulai's arms. Or—if she was still feeling snappishly regal—he would simply regard her simmering warmth as a hearth fire to sleep beside—not too closely.

Xulai said, "We should be seeing Kim soon, shouldn't we?" she asked. "It's getting dark."

Abasio started out of his self-absorption. "No, not really. The plain below is still sunlit. The sun's directly behind the peak, and we're in the shadow of the mountain. We'll see him soon."

Xulai murmured, "I've been wondering how we could get the babies safely around the Catlanders, if we have to."

"I think the Lady Animal would help you," offered Needly. "If she thought it would help us help her . . ."

"No!" Abasio growled. "I don't know what weapons those gangers have, Needly! The Griffin isn't immortal. When she came down on us yesterday, Xulai could easily have killed the great creature. Some of those same weapons could have ended up in ganger hands. It's not likely, but it is possible! I don't want to put the great creature at risk: not she, not her child, not their kindred. I know . . . I know how she feels." He, too, had felt the loss of marvelous creatures. Marvelous people. He felt that one more such loss might . . . break him in two. There had been too many losses.

"Abasio is right," Xulai agreed, having given him an analytical glance. "When the Griffin appeared, I was startled into action without any thought at all. Evil things happen when people are badly surprised. Let's not borrow trouble. We hoped to come out of the mountains into

Artemisia, and we still may do that that. Just because that group over the mountain was made up of gangers doesn't mean we'll find them at the end of this road. Maybe Abasio, as 'Vahso,' should leave us somewhere and reconnoiter down below. I don't want Kim encountering gangers while he's driving horses that may have been stolen."

Blue threw up his head, jingling the harness he wore. "They weren't stolen. That fat ganger, back there when we got Kim loose, he said they'd bought those horses before they started up the mountain."

"Bought?" asked Xulai. "Not thieved? That surprises me!"

Blue nodded. "The men talked and talked. They said that Sybbis doesn't want any trouble from the Artemisians, so she gave her men money to buy horses so nobody'll claim they're stolen. That is, not *originally stolen.* I 'spose we stole 'em, though." He whinnied laughter.

"Considering how they intended to use the horses, my conscience is clear," Abasio snarled.

Needly, hearing him, was pleased. Evidently her grandma's definition of morality was shared by other people, some of them, at least. *"So long as unnecessary pain is avoided, don't worry what happens to the guilty. Just be* dead sure *they're guilty before they're* surely dead*!"*

The sun sank behind the hills. Abasio yawned, blinked, came around a slight curve, and saw Kim's encampment at the end of the stretch they were on. Good. They were weary and needed rest. He looked again. Kim was not alone. "Whoa, Blue," he said. "Xulai, I'm going to get off and check a wheel, take a look down the road. Do you see any threat?" He jumped from the wagon seat, stretched, bent, twisted to get the kinks out, then knelt beside the left front wheel.

"Don't think so, Abasio," she said. "Kim has met up with a pair of travelers. They have two saddle horses, one packhorse. All the men are drinking tea by the fire."

"Remember? From now on my name is Vahso," he reminded her. "Needly? Willum? You listening?"

"We got it, Vahso," said Willum. "Who are we 'sposed to be?"

Xulai murmured, "Willum, Needly, Vahso is your uncle Vahso and I'm your aunt Shooey. Your mother . . . What's your ma's name, Willum?"

"Bess."

"Bess sent you two children with us on this trip so you could see something of the world. Uncle Vahso is her brother."

"Needly and me, we'll both call her Ma." He and Needly put their heads together and agreed upon what they would say about Da and Ma and what was going on back home. "You and me, Needly, we live on a farm between Gravysuck and Saltgosh, and ever'body there says you're a throwback to some gran-cestor back a ways 'cause you're so white. To-night, I can tell you what crops we farm and what animals we have so's you can tell people 'f they ask."

"And everything else is simple truth," said Abasio, making an ostentatious examination of a front wagon wheel. "We are traveling to tell everyone the waters are rising. I have acquaintances in Artemisia because I'm a traveler and I've been there before. The only name we have to avoid is my real one, and it's simpler if people think we're a family group." He stretched again and climbed back onto the wagon seat. "All right? Wife Shooey, nephew Willum, niece Needly, let's go meet whoever it is camping with Kim."

"Who's Kim supposed to be?" whispered Needly. "Is he related to us?"

"Oh, yes," said Abasio. "Since they're both Tingawan, he'll have said he's a cousin of Shooey's. Remember to call him Cousin Kim. He'll expect you to." He had intended to spend a few days practicing this slight deception before they reached the bottom of the road, and he prayed attempting it now, without adequate rehearsal, would not prove a disaster. He climbed onto the wagon seat and picked up the reins, saying softly, "Hup, Blue, my faithful, nonspeaking equine, let's get on down the road."

"Yes, O profoundly wonderful master," muttered Blue, leaning into the harness. Needly, reassured by the talk on the way down the road, giggled. Xulai looked up in astonished delight. It was the first time she had heard the child laugh.

The men sharing Kim's fire seemed harmless, which immediately put Abasio on guard. They were too smiley. Too welcoming. Too "My-oh-my, let me help you step down, ma'am, and what's this lovely lady doing out here in the wilderness"-y. Xulai greeted them without smiling.

"Good evening, gentlemen. Kim, is the water hot?"

"Yes, cousin! I knew you'd want to wash the dust off first thing."

Abasio indicated a place. Blue and Rags, silent, maneuvered the wagon into the place, the door on the side away from the fire. Abasio and Willum removed the harness. Xulai took a bowl of warm water behind the wagon and washed the dust from all her available surfaces. Abasio had told her the Artemisians had real baths, baths near hot springs that one could submerge in, and she was looking forward to hot water in volume. She had not had an all-over warm bath since leaving Saltgosh, in the women's bathhouse. Before that, she'd had several dips in Bertram's pool, after dark, and had taken advantage of his hot shower. While she was at it, she cleaned the babies' bottoms and used the last of the water to wash out their wool-lined trousers. They were, at the moment, contentedly full, scarcely waking as she unclothed and reclothed them in the shelter the wagon provided.

Kim knocked on the wagon corner and whispered, "Ma'am?"

"Yes, Kim?"

"There's a pool a little way off. It's getting a little late to use now, but I thought maybe you'd like to know about it in the morning. It'll be chilly, but—"

"Kim, you are a very thoughtful man. Do the men with you have their own stores?"

"Yes'm. They've had their supper. I waited to eat with you all." His voice dropped to a whisper. "Didn't want to be . . . in their debt at all."

She nodded, understanding, dried her face and arms, and went into the wagon to gather foodstuffs, returning to the fire with a stew already assembled, needing only to be heated. "Gentlemen," she said again.

Abasio spoke: "My wife. My dear, the dark-haired young man is Clume," he advised her, nodding in Clume's direction. "The other is Walkin. Traveling to see the world, they tell me." Clume's hair was dark, as was his skin, a rich tan, all in all a good-looking young man, in his late twenties perhaps. Strong, from the looks of him, though not as bulky as Walkin, whose muscles bulged alarmingly whenever he extended an arm.

"Ah," she said, maneuvering the grill across the fire and setting the pot firmly upon it. "What have you seen of it so far?"

Clume set himself to be charming, and Xulai responded nicely to his charm, smiling, nodding. They had seen the ruins of the city to the north, he said. Fantis. Almost covered with tiny trees of various kinds that were still being planted by the Sisters of the Trees. There were many birds. They had gone north of there, even, into the deep forests, but had hesitated to continue where there were no roads.

Abasio nodded. "I've been up there. Got lost one time for the better part of a season before I found my way out. Got down into a valley somehow and could not find a way out of it again."

"You couldn't backtrack yourself?" asked Walkin.

"Got in there in the midst of a blizzard," Abasio explained. "Then the weather turned warm, everything was slipping and sliding, avalanches here and there, water dripping. By the time it dried out enough to travel, the landscape had changed to the extent that I had no idea where I was. Could have come out easy if I'd left the wagon, but I didn't want to do that."

"Family wasn't with you then?"

"Oh, no. That was years ago. When I was still a young man seeing the world, just as you are. How far east have you traveled?"

Well, it seemed Clume and Walkin had started from the south. Now they were going over the mountain and west to the sea. "We've been on our way up two days," they said. "We stopped at a village a day or so away from the climb: Artemisian village. You know the people there?"

Abasio swallowed a huge sigh of relief. Wonderful! It meant they would come out of the mountains into Artemisian territory! He need not leave the group and go inspecting the countryside. "I do know the people of Artemisia, yes; very good people."

Xulai saw his relief and grinned at him. "You'll have roads, such as they are, most all the way," she told the visitors, tasting the stew and deciding it was hot enough. The meat was left over from a roasted leg of venison, the last of the fresh meat they'd bartered for in Saltgosh. From here on, they would have only salted and smoked meat, but it was only two more days down!

Abasio took over the conversation, telling them how the road went from here over the mountain. A baby cried from inside the wagon. Xulai excused herself and went to tend to the twins. She would avoid their being seen, if possible. It was too late in the evening for explanations.

Needly and Willum, meanwhile, ate their supper nicely, without argument, being polite to Uncle Vahso, Aunty Shooey, and Cousin Kim, as though they had never behaved in any other way.

The men rose, said they would go a bit farther up road before dark, thanked Kim for sharing his fire. They rode away. Sometime later, Xulai and Abasio heard their horses on the road above them, the clop of hooves and the inevitable slide and splat of gravel that always seemed to rattle down whenever there was traffic on the next switchback up.

The nights were cool, though not actually cold as yet. They covered the chicken coops and put the "winter skirts" around the bottom of the wagon, canvas barriers to keep out the cold so that Needly and Willum could sleep warmly there. Abasio had put a line along the bottom of the wagon so the children could hang their daytime clothing over it, to air.

Before going to bed, Abasio and Kim spent some time with the horses, talking to them, finding out from Blue if any needed a hoof cleaned out or a bur removed. Later, from their bed in the wagon, Abasio and Xulai could hear the children talking, sometimes a word or two, sometimes, if it were very quiet, whole paragraphs. Tonight, Needly was telling Willum something her grandma had told her, and the two adults lay mesmerized, listening . . .

" . . . and see, a purpose of the Creator is the universe—we always say 'A purpose,' not 'THE purpose,' because we can see only this one but must allow that there may be others. And a purpose of the universe is life—there are bits of the chemicals that make up living things floating around all through the universe. People studied meteors, and they analyzed what they carried, and there's life stuff in them. And a purpose of life is intelligence . . . Thing you have to remember is that because something has a purpose doesn't mean more of it is necessarily good! Even though a purpose of the universe is life, having ten stupid children doesn't fulfill the life purpose, which is making intelligence. You have to follow the litany clear to its end. A purpose of intelligence is language. And a purpose of language is communication. A purpose of communication is knowledge, of knowledge is discovery, and of discovery is the universe, and of the universe is the Creator. It's a circle. We learn the will of the Creator by observing creation."

"So you'd just kill off . . . like the birds or fish that can't talk?"

"No, no, no. They're part of the universe. Part of creation. Speech evolved on Earth—and probably in millions of other places—but that doesn't mean every creature on earth has to speak. Grandma said each step in the litany is kind of like a . . . a mountain. You pile up a lot of life, and at the top of the mound you get intelligence, but that intelligence rests on the whole mountain, and all of it is important. It's part of creation. You don't kill off any part of creation; you can eat one fish but not all the fish there are! Then you pile up a lot of intelligence, and at the peak you get language. Maybe in some worlds they talk in smells or in whistles. And there may be a whole mountain of words stacked up before you talk back and forth to some other planet—that's communication."

"An' a mountain of back-and-forth before you learn somethin' new."

"Exactly, Willum! And you pile up the knowledge to discover new things, and you pile the discoveries to understand the universe. Then you're working toward understanding the Creator, see? Not that we do. Not that we monkey-brains do understand, not yet, but it's important to try!"

Xulai breathed deeply. Abasio reached over and put his arm across her. Both of them listened, fascinated as Needly explained Mobwows: *monkey-brains* and willy-waggers, which Willum accepted with comments about some of those he knew of back in Gravysuck. The two adults were yawning and smiling at the wagon roof above them when Needly moved on to something else.

"World spirits are supposed to help. As a planet becomes life-ful, it develops a spirit, a world spirit who helps keep the balance, tells creatures when they're too many or dangerously few. Grandma said most olden-time people understood this, or at least perceived it, because they always had a name for the Earth spirit. Some called her Gaia, or Persephone; others called her other things. Some just said Mother Nature."

"That spirit, she'd be lonesome," murmured Willum. "All by herself . . ."

"You'd think so, because all the worlds are far, far apart in the great wheel of the galaxy," said Needly. "So far apart that it would take thousands of years to go from one to the other the way normal creatures would have to go. But Grandma said world spirits can talk together across that space. They can kind of fold up the space that's in between, fold it up and make little holes from fold to fold so they can talk to each other. She called it wormholes. She says they can travel through those wormholes, too, but mostly they don't. The way Grandma used to talk, I think she thought the Silverhairs might be like . . . servants to those world spirits."

"Why'd they need servants?" murmured Willum between yawns. " 'F they c'n do all that foldin' an' stuff, why'd they need any servants?"

"Maybe to take messages?"

"Y'awready said they could talk to each other . . ."

Needly sighed deeply. "Maybe not take messages. Maybe do something important. I guess a world spirit wouldn't leave its own world and go across the galaxy if they could just as well send some Silverhairs to do whatever . . ."

"Like what?" asked Willum.

"Like to save this person or let that one go, like tell this one to go to another place. Like Abasio says he was told to go to another place, and that's where he met Xulai."

The sound of a long, unmuffled yawn. Then, very sleepily, "So, if you're one o' them, you don't acshully have hair. You've got like antennys on your head." Another yawn. "Antennys to pick up those signals they send."

"Where'd you hear about antennas."

A long pause, then, barely heard: "Xulai said bugs have 'em."

"I guess. Maybe. That might make sense. Willum. Willum?"

There was no answer. There was a child's sigh, a rustle of cloth, then silence.

Abasio slept the sleep of an exhausted man. He half wakened once, thinking he had heard the frantic whinnying scream of a panicky horse at some distance, but all was utterly silent except for two owls, talking over a considerable distance. Hoo. Hoo? Who? Who? Who indeed?

WHEN MORNING CAME, XULAI WAS first up to prepare breakfast so that Kim could get on his way with the horse. He was as eager to get started as they all were. Abasio rose, went into the woods with the latrine shovel, and returned to lean it near the wagon door.

Xulai called to him. "Wake the children, will you? Willum's usually first up!"

Abasio pulled the curtain aside from the wheels and leaned down. "They're up," he called. "They're not here."

She turned from the fire, suddenly alert. When the children were awake, they were inevitably audible and, usually, visible. Kim rose and came to stand beside her. "No, they're not up, Abasio. I would have seen them."

Xulai bent over to stare under the wagon. The bedding was disturbed. Their clothes were still hanging on the hooks. She knew at once they were not merely *up*. They were gone! There were footprints near the wagon, large ones that had not been made by Abasio or Kim. There was the sign of a very small struggle at the place the canvas skirts reached the ground. There was no sign of Willum or of Needly.

When they pulled the children's bedding out, a note came with it, a piece of heavy paper, somewhat wrinkled, as though it had been clutched in someone's hand.

Our children are at risk. It is only fair that your children should also be at risk. I would have taken your own had they been older and other than they are. These are not born to you, but they are dear to you, nonetheless. They are hostages being held against your word that you will do for ours what you have done for yours.

There was no signature. The writing itself was . . . clear but clumsy, written by someone who did not write a lot. Its provenance was made clear by the tiny bronze feather, half the length of Xulai's smallest finger, threaded through two slits in the paper—which wasn't really paper. It was the skin of something: maybe a lamb; maybe something else. Xulai sat quite still upon the wagon step, white-faced, while Kim and Abasio trailed the footprints back into the forest a bit, then up the hillside toward the road above, where they joined the hoofprints of two horses, hoofprints that wandered into the forest, headed south. And shortly after that, disappeared entirely!

And there had been that frantic whinny in the night!

"Lifted," Abasio whispered to Xulai when he returned, ashen-faced. "Two horses, two riders, two children lifted, carried through the air: gently no doubt. The Griffin may have made several trips. They were set down somewhere else . . . I think I heard one of the horses last night. It screamed as it was hauled into the air, no doubt. I should have, should have . . ." He should have nothing! It had been too late even then.

"Another Griffin may have helped her," said Xulai hopelessly. "She spoke of others, Abasio. She may not have planned this alone."

He went on, doggedly. "Whether the children are with the men or with her, we don't know. Where they may be, we don't know."

"Where *she* may be, we will know," grated Xulai. "She will be following us!"

AT THAT MOMENT THE GRIFFIN was not following anyone. She was poised on a ledge above a canyon, her back to the cave behind her, from which two voices continued to speak as they had been speaking querulously for far too long a time. Her command to her two prisoners that they lie down and go to sleep had not been obeyed.

" . . . and just shows you don't know much about humans if you think we can sleep on that rock! You better figure some way to soften it, then, 'cause if we try to sleep on that, you might just as well kill us and get it over with. Without some kind of mattress we're already so sore we can hardly move," said a small female voice.

Another, slightly louder, continued another plaint. " . . . and what in all that's holy do you expect us to eat—raw rabbit?"

"There's firewood there," the Griffin muttered, turning to stare at the lump of fur Needly was confronting.

"There's nothing to start a fire with," Willum replied, with scornful indignation. "An' I didn't notice you breathin' fire. Griffins don't do that anyhow. Dragons do. You got a pet one hid somewheres? There's no pot to cook anything in even if we had a dragon. There's no knife to skin a rabbit, supposing there is any rabbit flesh on that particular carcass, though it looks to be mostly bones."

Needly remarked, "If those two sneaks and villains had brought my pack, I'd have what I need, but they didn't bring anything at all useful." This was not quite true. The sack containing the Griffin's tear and all the little bottles was still tied around her waist, under the loose shirt Xulai had given her to sleep in. Following Grandma's precept, sleeping or waking, she kept it always with her.

"I've got a little knife in my nightshirt pocket," said the sullen voice from the back of the cave. "But I can't start a fire with it 'less I have tinder and a piece a flint, which I don't! 'Less maybe the lady has flint claws? That'd help. What I want to know is where do we go when we need to go. I'm not goin' to hang my bottom out over that edge and let the wind blow me off! An' Needly can't piss off the side neither."

She, the Griffin, had never considered pissing. She and her like did it catlike, first digging a hole. Obviously, the stony ledge would not be suitable.

" . . . and besides, if you give us nothing but meat," Needly continued, "we'll get sick. Humans have to have roughage. Grandma insisted on it!"

"Roughage?" the wholly carnivorous Griffin muttered. "And that is . . . ?"

"Whole grain! Fibrous fruits and vegetables! Oats and rice and wheat and corn stuff. And grain has to be cooked. That's what. And what are we supposed to drink? That water back in that cave stinks . . ."

"It's pure rainwater," insisted the Griffin.

"It may have started out as pure rainwater before it got a whole lot of something dead in it," snarled Needly. "You go take a sniff of it! I'd say it's pretty good rotted-bat soup by now."

The Griffin went to the edge of the precipice and dropped into the canyon below, snapping her wings open at the last moment. She often slept on ledges! She scorned such things as mattresses! So did her little one! She found herself wondering, however, whether having an exceptionally thick coat of fur on belly and sides might not serve the same purpose as a mattress. The children did not have a thick coat of fur. They did not even have adequate clothing. She had not considered that when they were sleeping, they would be largely unclothed, that they might wear only thin little garments, without shoes. Whenever had Griffins had to consider clothing? Her little one had kept the children warm last night. Both the children cuddled with the little one, but neither of them would come near her, the little one's mother, even though she had not hurt them. Except that she had not thought to tell the men to bring their clothing or bedding. She had had enough trouble getting the men to write the message correctly!

She circled, climbed, landed once more on the ledge, in time to hear Needly saying, "You know, I don't think your mama figured out this hostage business in advance!" The little Griffin had come out of the cave and Needly was sitting on one of her front legs combing her mane. When the big one landed, Needly turned toward her, stared upward into her right eye, and said in a pathetic little voice, "You really should have figured it out in advance, Lady Animal." She turned her face back into the baby's mane and began to weep, heartbreakingly.

Willum came out of the cave with tears in his own eyes. He put his arm around Needly, and the Griffin child snuggled up to them both, giving her mother a very angry and puzzled look that said, "Why are you being so mean to my friends?"

"Ax," muttered the Griffin to herself. "Knife. Clothing. Mattresses.

Blankets. Pot. Food supplies." Her eyes raked the surroundings, looking for any diggable surface. None. Only rock. "New location where they can dig holes. Something to dig with! "

Her angry soliloquy was interrupted by a sound from the sky: a scream, as of tortured metal, rent into shards. A shout as of a monstrous ripping of the very firmament, shrill and deep at once, a sound that cut into ears, pierced brains. It hurt. The children cowered as the sound neared from behind the peak above them.

The big Griffin's head snapped back, and she hissed, her voice full of barely suppressed panic. "Into the cave, quickly! Quickly, or he'll kill you!"

The little Griffin was already up, butting Needly with her head. Willum stood, peering up.

"Now," the Griffin hissed, in a voice that allowed no dissent, bowling Willum through the cave entrance with one vastly outstretched and very muscular wing.

The children had been virtually launched into the cave. The little Griffin righted herself, opened her own wings, and pushed them farther back, hissing with alarm. There was a place, there, where the roof went straight back only a few feet from the floor, making a long, low, horizontal niche mostly hidden behind a litter of fallen stones. They squirmed into it, scratched by the floor of it, bruised by the walls of it. Once inside, they were hidden, the little Griffin in the middle where the roof was a bit higher, a child pressed tightly against her on either side, their heads invisible behind the stones in front.

"Who's up there?" whispered Willum.

"It's the male Griffin. He is named Despos," whispered the little one in return. "Little things stay hid when Despos comes."

"Why?" whispered Needly.

"He kills things. He wants to kill all mankinds now, before the waters come. Mama and the other Griffin mamas say no. Mankinds can help us live, but Despos says no, vengeance now, no waiting. He is very angry."

"He'd kill us if he saw us?"

"He kills everything," said the little one. "He was made very angry, you see. He did not get that way. The ones who made him, they made him terrible to begin with. So he would kill, without thinking, without considering . . ."

"If you have lots of female Griffins, I should think they could conquer him," said Willum.

"Oh, no, no," cried the little one. "To conquer Despos they would have to kill him. There is no conquering unless it is to kill Despos, and if he is killed, then we would be no more!" She began crying, crystal tears, falling onto the stone like shards of tinkling glass.

Needly stared. "Child, tell me about the people who made the Griffins. Did they make many female Griffins?"

"They made several, not many. One time I have seen ten in one place. Mama said that was more than half."

"How many male Griffins did they make?"

"They made several, but Despos has killed all the others. Despos is . . . never thinking of tomorrow. For Despos, everything is now."

As she whispered, the cave went dark as something moved before the entry. They could detect the glitter of dark, almost black scales edged in bronze. Scales the width of a human head, as long as a forearm. They could note the expanse of a shoulder that blocked out the sun. Limbs as thick through as great trees! Needly shivered and put her hand over Willum's mouth, all in one motion, for he had been about to make an unconsidered sound out of sheer surprise.

"Shhh," she whispered. "It's bigger than the female one."

It was bigger . . . and louder; and more violent; and more vehement. The muscular arm that blocked half the cave entrance reached out. They saw it grasp something, heard the sound of an avalanche, saw the claw come back holding an enormous boulder. A moment later came heard a thunderous crash from the forest below. Voices roared. His deep, so deep it was like listening to thunder talk. Hers softer, higher, submissive. Too submissive.

Came a questioning roar, verbal but unintelligible. "Not here," replied the female. Another roar. "Far from here," came the answer.

Needly threw her arms around the little one's neck, put her face against that much larger face, her cheek against the smooth beak, her hands stroking behind the ear, as one might a cat, along the jaw, as any self-respecting cat would demand one to do. She whispered, "What does he want?"

"If any of the females have eggs, he wants to break them because they might be males. If they have young, he wants to see them to be sure they are not males. Mama says they are far from here, Mama says they have no eggs, no young ones."

"She's trying to delay him?"

"So there haven't been any baby-boy Griffins?"

The little one wept crystal tears. "There have been, yes. Despos kills them. It takes a long, long time for the egg to hatch. After it hatches and when it gets a lot bigger, the mother has to build a nest for the little one, because she can't hunt if she's carrying the baby. She plucks her neck feathers to keep the nest warm. But Despos, he follows the females to the nest. Sometimes he kills female babies by mistake. And we cannot kill Despos, for if he dies, Mama says, so do we all."

All sound had ceased upon the ledge. Then an enormous blast of air laden with dust and rock chips buffeted them. The huge wings outside had flapped, down! Again and again, and the black bulk before the cave opening lifted with a tumult like a hurricane. The sound lessened, lessened, and was gone. The she Griffin had lured him away, somehow. The children crawled from the horizontal slit. Needly took her comb from the shirt pocket, and began to comb the little one's mane, snarled and tangled from being caught on the rough stone. The individual filaments emerged from the flesh as quills, feathered at the sides, gradually lengthened into thick hairs, still with tiny feathery protrusions to either side, and at last thinned into real, silky hair that was very like human hair.

"First thing," said Needly. "First very important thing: we need to know your name."

"I don't think we have names," whispered the little one. "Mother calls me 'little one,' or 'wing child,' or things like that."

"Well, we need names to call you by. So you know who we mean when we speak and do not think we are impolite. You must have a name. And your mother must have a name. Grandma and I, we saw both of you first at sunrise, you know. I saw your mother unfold her wings against the mountainside with the sunlight all around her. We will call your mother Sun-wings. And as we stood there, the wind brought your voice. So, we will call you Dawn-song."

"Her ma should be a queen," said Willum. "Queen Sun-wings. And she should be Princess Dawn-song. Like Xulai is really a princess, you know."

"And Despos is the king of them all, I suppose," said Needly, frowning. Then silently, only to herself: *We should be very sure to do something about that! No wonder the Griffin mother is so frightened. She is threatened on all sides! Even by her own kind!*

"Poor thing is probably just worn out," muttered Willum, as though he had read her mind, which, he would have been somewhat surprised to know, they had both been doing to each other since the morning they had met.

Needly knew it already. She had chosen not to tell him, as he might be embarrassed at her knowing some of the thoughts he had had. Needly had been astonished how anticipatory they had been. No. Not anticipatory. Presumptuous! What boy of eleven or so goes about thinking what names would be best for his grandchildren?

KIM, ALONE AT THE HEAD of his herd, was surprised to receive a visitation. His surprise came mainly from the fact that the horses did not stampede when the creature landed on the road before them. The Griffin said something to them, however, something slow and sinuous to the ear, which made the horses lower their heads and fix their eyes upon their hooves, as though contemplating grass. The only one who still moved, and he only slightly, was Blue, who had joined the herd this morning so he could get to know the other horses. He swiveled his eyes, focusing on the great female where she crouched on a spur of stone above them.

"Your name is Kim?" she said.

Kim nodded, that being all he was capable of.

"The child, Needly, tells me I did not think things through well enough," said the Griffin. "I neglected to take clothing and mattresses for them—the cave is of stone—and blankets, and what she calls a latrine spade, and food, and a fire lighter, and roughage. I understand this means grain or something similar. I will hunt meat for them, so you need not provide that, or firewood. I will find a place with firewood. If you will tell the others to assemble the things they feel the children will need, packed in a bundle, well tied, so I can carry it. They can leave it on the road behind them; I will pick it up and convey it. It would be well if I could provide some comfort for them before tonight. I do not wish to harm the children unless it becomes necessary . . . to show that we mean what we say."

Kim did not look up to see her fly, he merely stayed absolutely still, right where he was, not moving a muscle until Blue raised his head and peered into the sky, now empty, saying, "Kim, she's gone."

The herd was already nervous. They had been disturbed all during the morning by distant sounds of conflict, screaming, tearing, metallic clanging and ringing sounds mixed with organic bellowing and screams of pain and anger. It was as though some titanic argument was taking place among minor gods, somewhere in the atmosphere, invisible but clearly audible. The sounds had come from a distance but were still loud enough to stop every living thing where it was, as it was, perched, crouched, grazing! During that time everything alive was petrified. Before noon, the noise had stopped as abruptly as it had started. Then, not very long later, the Griffin had arrived.

Blue had heard something in the Griffin's voice that reminded him of the morning tumult. Her voice, multiplied, deepened. Perhaps . . . no, probably a male? Something had been bothering Abasio lately. A male Griffin might be very bothersome indeed! Blue came to himself and followed the herd the very short distance to the next switchback, where they waited until the wagon arrived, as it did very shortly. Kim was barely able to speak; he had been frightened into a state of sustained terror. Blue butted Abasio away from the others and spoke more to the point. He and Abasio had been through things like this before. He hoped this would not end as that other time had ended, with one of their group gone. Or even two of them. Willum was what Abasio called a brat (*which,* thought Blue, *Abasio ought to recognize, having been one himself, even when much older than Willum*). The little girl, though. Oh, she was something. Blue very much wanted to hear what they made of her, down in Artemisia. What his speaking friends, Coyote and Bear, might make of her . . .

While Blue ruminated, a flurry of packing went on: three straw-stuffed mattresses, two small, one larger—the children's and a spare—Xulai had a very strong mental vision that included the little Griffin. Young things tended to group, even those from varying species, for company if nothing else. They would need blankets and foodstuffs and clothing and various small tools: knives, a small bucket, a pot, a spit, and a grill for cooking, a pan for water; rags for cleaning bodies, soap; two water bottles—filled. They would need a fire-starter and a supply of tinder; a roll of strong twine. Needly would need her pack, and they would pack another one for Willum, including combs, brushes. They would include the little hatchet for firewood and one of the thick-bristled brushes used for currying horses—probably that would feel good to a Griffin child: large combs, same idea. The whole made up into a single bundle, wrapped in canvas, roped with loops on top that the Griffin could seize in her claws.

"She will want to move the children as we move," Xulai snarled under her breath. "We must make a package that will be easy for her to carry."

"And one easy for the children to repack," growled Abasio. "I'm using knots I've already taught Willum to use." He felt strongly that the children were in no immediate danger. All morning he had been having one of those premonitory notions that sometimes came to him, out of nothing much. The current notion was that this particular incident could prove to be, in the long run, a good—or at least workable—thing. Building on the basis of such notions had never harmed him in the past. Some had alerted him to coming danger, others had warned him not to react violently if it merely seemed so. It was much the same kind of feeling that had carried him all the way from Artemisia to Woldsgard.

Xulai, however, was not at the moment of a mind to hear any such notions. She was too busy excoriating herself for not having protected the children better. He asked, "Why the third mattress?"

"To show her we care for her child better than she cares for ours! Besides, I have the idea the three young ones will become friends."

When the package was ready, Xulai stood on the road, looking at all of it, the rocks at the side, the view east from it down the canyon below them, forests, glades, the road running east. She would come back here to make sure the bundle had been picked up. She took *ul xaolat* from her pocket, spoke into it, and held it above her head while she pushed a button to record the destination before restoring it to her pocket. Neither she nor *ul xaolat* would forget this place.

The large package was left behind on the road as the horses and the wagon went on their way down. The trees on these lower slopes were higher, thicker. The wagon was only one road below when the Griffin came, but they had gone a long way north and did not actually see her behind them as she picked up the bundle. A little later, however, Abasio caught sight of her flying south and slightly eastward, the bundle dangling from her front feet. Well, the mountain range bent eastward as they traveled. Xulai was right. The children would be kept within watching distance of Abasio and Xulai and whatever it was they might do to save the Griffins.

Sun-wings—Queen Sun-wings, according to Willum—had moved them to a new cave immediately after the male had departed. The new place was at the top of a low rise, well hidden behind tall, old-growth trees. It was a location the Griffins, mother and daughter, had to approach by landing well downhill and walking upward among those trees, though Sun-wings had dropped the canvas-wrapped bundle closer to the cave itself. The refuge was shadowed by the overhang of the cliff above it and trees grew tight around it, leaving no landing place near the opening large enough for Despos to come at them. At the bottom of the slope a tiny stream wended its way south. It was a place, so the Griffin child, Dawn-song, told the children, that Despos did not know about and would probably be unable to find. It was the place to which Sun-wings had brought Dawn-song years ago, after Abasio's friend Olly had rescued Dawn-song near the archetypal village.

Customarily, Griffins slept on the peaks and flew in the chasms. Typically, their nests were inaccessible to any unwinged creature, for the protection of the young. With Despos now flying in the chasms, constantly on the hunt for rivals, even those who might exist inside an eggshell, there was no such thing as inaccessible. He found the young too easily. According to Dawn-song, her mama had been talking to the other females. They were trying to decide what to do to protect their eggs, to protect the little ones like Dawn-song. Building nests in caves was one thing they considered.

The cave where they were now was unfamiliar territory for the human children, and not totally familiar to little Dawn-song. Still, by nightfall, the three of them had dragged the contents of the bundle into the cave and had made themselves comfortable. The baby Griffin had been combed and petted and given her own mattress, where she was fed bits and pieces of roast rabbit after being offered a share of the boiled grain that Needly had seasoned nicely with the herbs and salt

Xulai had sent. Dawn-song tasted politely, but refused the offer. Griffins were carnivores, the children agreed. They were definitely pure carnivores, which should make the matter of turning them into sea creatures easier.

Willum and Needly discussed this, loudly but calmly, as though the process had already been accomplished. They had decided to speak of saving Griffins frequently and lengthily. This would put Sun-wings— and her sisters, if they happened to overhear at some point—in the right frame of mind. In all such conversations, the saving should be spoken of as inevitable! There were lots of things for carnivores to eat in the seas. Omnivores could manage well, but pure herbivores might have a problem. After making sure that Sun-wings could hear them, Willum and Needly discussed this at length and in exhaustive detail with Dawn-song, who asked a great many questions. Sun-wings overheard it all.

By the time night came, Willum and Needly had set up their camp in the cave. The smoke from their fire, they told Sun-wings, would seem no different from the smoke from many fires they had seen as they came down the mountain. They had fetched water, found a latrine ground close by, and Willum had dug a trench, heaping the earth neatly along the backside to be shoveled in as needed. Using the little hatchet, he had cut forked sticks to hold a stout crossbar as a seat and another as a back. They had washed themselves in the spring, changed their clothes, and, at Needly's insistence, washed the ones they had worn when they were "dragged onto sweaty horses" and "bumped up against muddy places" and "made generally filthy." All of which Needly said loudly and with obvious disapproval: "I wouldn't have let anyone treat Dawn-song that way!"

Sun-wings heard it all with a good deal of chagrin.

Now Dawn-song was lying on her very own mattress, purring, and the two children had lain down upon theirs, one close at each side, all of them blanketed for warmth. All three were curled in earnest, whispered confabulation, making plans to save themselves, their captor, and all her fellow Griffins—except for Despos—and, perhaps, the world. They had even agreed upon the rules for discussion: Willum could not introduce any factor that was not achievable, including aerial bombardment by men (including Willum himself) mounted on Griffins. Needly had foreseen the difficulties presented by endless one-to-one argument and had made sure Dawn-song had a vote from the beginning. Xulai, Needly knew, had foreseen their becoming close friends. The third mattress had been as good as a letter of instruction!

LATE IN THE AFTERNOON, ABASIO turned from the now-only-slightly-sloping road—it had for some hours tended slightly east of south—to the one below that led toward the eastern horizon: a flat horizon on a flat plain. There were still canyon walls on either side of the road, now only dwindling arms of the mountain that fingered the desert farther and farther from the road itself. The stream that had followed them the last bit of the way down had turned gently upon itself after trying a few north-ish or south-ish bends and deciding that running east along the road would do satisfactorily. Xulai, watching the stream burble happily along, knew they were still descending. Both sides of the stream were wooded. Among the various pines and spruces, the deciduous trees carried a few dried and no longer golden leaves that whispered together in any vagrant breeze. Still, they kept to the road for another hour or so, until they were able to see the ends of the canyon walls swallowed by the flatlands beyond. Then they moved away from the road to make their noon stop in a last outpost of the trees, a grove of towering evergreens and white-trunked shivering gold birches, very near a pleasant pool. The whole was surrounded by grass, still green and succulent.

"I think you can relax," said Abasio, rubbing his thumbs into Xulai's neck muscles, which seemed to have frozen into two solid knots of rope. "The fact that the Griffin picked up the supplies we sent, the fact that she asked for them in the first place, indicates that she has no wish to hurt the children. They are hostages, and hostages are usually very well cared for."

"Abasio, intellectually, I'm sure you're right." She drew away from him and settled her gown as she rotated her head. The neck pain was from tension, of course . . . only tension. "Emotionally, however, I want to scream. I can't do that or I'll upset the babies. Sun-wings won't want to hurt the children, but she knows nothing about children. Ignorance can hurt."

"You want to scream because your baby tenders are missing."

She gave him a look that might have charred him to his boot soles had he not been fireproofed some time ago. "I want to scream because I'm concerned about the children and I'm not sure they're all right!"

He put his hands on her shoulders and shook her. "Then you're just feeling, not thinking. The Griffin didn't come up with that list by herself. It had contributions from both Willum and Needly. They are, therefore, in sufficiently good shape to think reasonably and sensibly. Needly is considering the whole event calmly. I believe that child was born of some very strange heritage that makes her mental age something like two hundred years, give or take a quarter century. And how long has Willum been asking whether the Griffin would take him for a ride? He has no doubt had that ride, and I cannot imagine his being anything but invigorated by it."

"Those men who took them, I don't trust them!"

"Nor do I. Obviously. It's extremely unlikely, however, that those men are anywhere near where the children are now. If the men had been readily available, the Griffin could have sent them to round up the materials Willum and Needly needed, but she came herself. Also, the children are no doubt being kept in some very remote area. Ferrying men and horses would have required multiple trips, and I can't see the Griffin wanting to continue providing for them. That indicates she has paid off her lackeys and sent them away. I'm intrigued by the fact she must have paid them something. What was that, do you suppose?"

"Someone held hostage, perhaps. And we don't know where the children are . . ."

"They didn't ask for firewood, so they're in the forest, where they can find their own. The Griffin will have picked a secure campsite. They're not on a pinnacle; they're where a latrine shovel can be used. I'm glad we had a spare. They asked for a bucket, so I'm sure they're near water."

"You're dreadfully serene," she snapped.

"If I thought either of us could do any good by yelling and screaming and rushing about in circles, we could do that. I'm willing to do so if you'd like. We can do it together, hand in hand. Shall we go clockwise or counterclockwise to begin with?"

She hit him, or tried.

He caught her hand between his own. "Xulai, love, I trust Willum's sense of self-preservation and Needly's education at her grandmother's knee. As Gum once remarked in several other contexts, they are not geese! If they were, they'd be far less trouble. I'm much more worried about something else."

"That 'something else' being?"

"I'm worried about the Griffin, our Griffin. She's female. She has a child. She's the one I met before, the one Olly met. They no doubt move about. Olly met her in a forest, I think. Olly saved her baby when the baby was a hatchling. That would have been when Olly herself was a child. When Olly left on that ship, she was . . . in her early twenties. That was over three years ago. So the baby is at least twenty-some-odd years old. When will she reach maturity?"

"The rule for most animals is that one-sixth of the life-span is spent in growing to maturity."

"So, the mother said she might live two thousand years. Maturity, then. would arrive somewhere around three hundred years of age." Abasio scratched his nose, thinking.

"I wonder what the incubation time is."

"Geese can live fifteen years. Hatching time is, I think, thirty days or so. They are goslings for some time after that, however."

Xulai stared at him. "With that measurement, hatching would take over ten years."

"It sounds . . . unlikely. Some animals have precocious development. They gain adult attributes very rapidly, but they grow to full size only very gradually. I think that's probably what's going on here."

"So you suppose they could nest near . . . volcanoes? Someplace that stays warm?" Xulai frowned. "But the hatchling you described was in a nest, up a tree, wasn't it? Something like that?"

"It was actually up a cliff. There's nothing to prevent the baby being moved, after it comes out of the egg. Well, that's something we have to figure out. The thing I am supposedly making clear, to myself if not to you, is this: the Griffin is female and had a child, and that fact implies the existence of a male Griffin . . . but I've never seen one, or not up close, though I think I may have seen one at a great distance while we were back near Saltgosh. It was the biggest thing I have ever seen flying; far bigger than . . . our Griffin. And it was black, or blackish—metallic, rather. And if so, it makes me fearful."

"Perhaps parthenogenesis," murmured Xulai.

"Possible, but I think that's unlikely. The original designers would probably have had enough trouble using bisexual genetic mode—eagle, lion, who knows what else?—without trying for a less usual one. Instinct tells me the male of this species could be quite different from the females, not physiologically but psychologically. He may have a very different agenda. And I'm more than a little worried that we may encounter him, or them, at some point." He felt that they had already almost encountered him. He had not liked the sound of the battle they had heard.

"We have weapons that could handle that situation." She turned, confused by Abasio's expression. He looked troubled. Far more troubled than he had when discussing the children. "What is it?"

He shook his head at her; she was not seeing the problem! "Yes, we have weapons; weapons that kill. I've seen, females, several times. I've possibly seen a male, and I know there has to be one if there are young! Perhaps only one was ever created, or perhaps there is only one left? In which case, our weapons would kill not only him but the race of Griffins forever, including the descendants of that female-child Griffin that Needly is so careful of."

It was not something Xulai had considered. It was something that kept her awake late into the night.

WHILE QUEEN SUN-WINGS WAS AWAY, picking up their supplies, Needly had amused the Griffin child by telling her a story, one that she and Willum had spent some time concocting on their way to and from the latrine ground or the stream. It was a story that Grandma had supposedly told Needly, about an island of ice in the north, across the eastern ocean. There was a tribe of Griffins there, said Needly, one created long since who had lived there always. The tribe included three very large, fierce males whose names were Devastation, Disruption, and Destruction: the Dreadful brothers for short.

That night, snuggled into their straw-filled mattresses, well wrapped in blankets, she and Willum pretended to be sleeping. They were actually listening as Dawn-song told the story of the three male Griffins to her mother. The next morning, Sun-wings questioned Needly at length about the story: when had it been told, who had told it, how did Needly's grandmother know? Needly was properly unsure about the details. It was only something her grandma had told her, and yes, Grandma was a very intelligent woman, but she was very old. Needly couldn't say whether it was true or not. Needly privately thought that in an infinite number of galaxies there must be one planet that had such an island, properly inhabited.

The next night another Griffin, female, arrived, announcing herself from the woods so as not to take them by surprise. Needly and Willum listened again as Sun-wings told the story to her friend on the cliff above their cave. They spoke people language, local language, which Needly found faintly surprising. Somehow she had thought they would have a tongue of their own. But then, they were human-created! On this continent! Humans from here! Of course, if they spoke, they would be hatched into a world speaking that language, the language of their creators.

Dawn-song lay between them, also listening. "She's my mama's favorite friend," she told Needly. "She needs a name, too."

The three of them considered what name would be proper. The new one had remarkable plumage, a shining flow of the partially feathered mane that went well down into the fur of her belly: golden, gleaming, almost metallic in its reflection of light. Together the three of them decided this one would be "Golden-throat."

Golden-throat departed. The exhausted children slept, scarcely moving until morning, when Sun-wings summoned Needly and Willum out of the cave.

"I am told you create names for each of us."

"When we refer to you, we prefer to distinguish among you," said Needly. "It is polite to do so. You would, I think, prefer us to be polite."

"There is nothing evil in that. Name us, then, and tell us what the name is when you have done so. We recognize one another by the voice, the style of flight, the outline against the light, the very direction from which we come. Names will be something interestingly new to the more thoughtful ones among us."

"The more thoughtful, Sun-wings?"

"The more thoughtful, yes. The more curious. South of here, far south of here, there were some Griffins hatched who . . . are driven by . . . what is it that drives Despos?" She paused. "What is the word you use when you want something someone else has? Or want something like it?"

"Envy. If I wanted your beautiful mane and wings, I would be 'envious.' I might even dislike you because you had something I did not have. That dislike would be 'hostility.' Those Griffins are *hostile*. They feel *hostility*."

"Hostility. Yes. It is like that, yes. I do not think it is envy, no." The Griffin's beak tightened, the flesh around it gathered in harsh lines. Her eyes were slitted in concentration. "They do not want something of mine. It is only that they dislike . . . everything that is not theirs. With me, with my friend, you are more safe. Among the . . . *hostile*, not so safe, I think. There are three of them. They are full of violence and they do not . . . think about things."

"We have named your friend Golden-throat. We noticed how pleasant her voice was. Such voices are described as 'golden' in our shared language, and also the . . . fur of her throat is golden, so we can recognize her." Was it fur? It was really something between fur and feathers, or down. Needly shifted, a little uncomfortably. Willum was watching her from close inside the cave. She drew in a breath before asking, "Did I hear you telling your friend about the story my grandmother told me? The story about the three Griffins on that island?"

Sun-wings shifted in discomfort. "Despos intends to go there and kill them. Before he goes, he demands to see each of us females; he demands that we take him to each nest, to be sure we have no eggs, no male young. It would not matter, male or female in the egg. He would break the eggs, he would kill the young females trying to mate with them. He half kills us!"

"Then you must let him look."

"We can't," she cried. "We can't. He will kill them . . ."

Needly laid her hand on the creature's foot, the only part of her within easy reach. The bones shifted under her hand, the short, very short fur of the foot moved under her fingers as though the hairs were individually mobile. Needly forced her hand to stroke, advising herself to speak very softly. *Stroke, stroke.*

"Sun-wings, he will not see eggs or children if you bring them all here. Willum and Dawn-song and I can keep the eggs warm for a time. We can care for the children for a time. If you made a big kill, Sun-wings, if you did, and brought it close to our camp here, we could feed the little ones. I have seen you tear the meat in little pieces, Willum and

I can cut the meat up like that. We can make a fire to keep the eggs warm. Despos does not know this place. Bring the young here! Then let him see only females without young. Let him see only empty nests!"

She looked up into two orbs like bronze suns, staring down at her, two huge eyes that seemed to bore into her, suck at her, draw her strength from her own body into themselves. She stood back, straightened her back, and stared back, eye to eye. From somewhere, strength poured into her, like liquid metal down her backbone: only warm, not hot, a comforting warmth. She did not question its source. Its presence was enough.

Sun-wings stepped back. "We will try. It is the only thing left to try."

The great creature had to go some distance down through the trees before she came to the place she could best fly from. Dawn-song had told Needly that the Griffins chose high places for their aeries because of the drop; it was so much easier to drop into flight than to pound one's wings against unwilling air until one lifted. She, Dawn-song, could fly a little, but not for long. Her wings were not even fully grown. Wings were rudimentary in a hatchling. Only gradually did they lengthen and strengthen. Once they were fully grown, Griffin wings would hold the Griffin aloft for days while she soared on the air currents moving above the canyons. But, to get into the air initially, they preferred a good drop.

Needly watched until she was out of sight, then she went back into the caves, into Willum's arms that were waiting for her, hugging her tight. He whispered, "It's all right. It's all right. It's gonna work, Needly. It will, you'll see, it will."

They watched Sun-wings flying north, circling, finally turning west, toward the peaks. Once they were alone, they began on the duties they had already assigned themselves: collecting as large a pile of firewood as possible; filling all their pots and pans and water bottles at the spring. Needly sorted through her kit, repacked it neatly, put it where it could be grabbed up in a moment if needed. She went down into the forest, hid, took the little pouch from beneath her skirts, and checked it over, being sure everything was tightly corked, the corks tightly bound to the tiny bottles as she took an inventory. One bottle for sleep: three drops for a person; probably a small spoonful for something as big as a grown Griffin. One bottle held peaceful death: one drop for any creature of any size, even a very large size. One bottle held medicine for healing wounds: just a little diluted with water, then the water wiped onto the wound to moisten it. One bottle for questioning: one drop—then, as soon as the person's eyes went funny, ask the questions. The person would answer. One bottle held a long, terrible dying: one drop, only one. Grandma said she had seen it used only once, in order to elicit information that saved many lives.

Grandma had not said whether the healing mixtures she made would work on a Griffin. Well, along with parts of lions and eagles and who knew what to make Griffins, men used the patterns of parts of men's brains to create speaking creatures. Chances were Griffin brains worked very much like men's brains did! Altogether, there were ten tiny bottles, each with its own purpose. She put them into the pouch, closed it, knotted the bottom tie around her leg, fastened the top one to the belt she wore next to her skin day and night, shook down her skirts, and returned to the cave.

Some time later, crashing noises from the forest below heralded Sun-wings' approach, dragging behind her the gutted carcass of a young buffalo. Willum and Needly were summoned to learn which parts were most suitable for feeding children, human and otherwise. "Without the inward parts, it will stay good longer," she said, to which Willum nodded, then, noting the thickness of the hide, he asked Sun-wings to draw her beak here, and here, and there, creating flaps of hide that could be folded back to give him access to the meat below.

Still later, Golden-throat arrived with a child somewhat larger than Dawn-song. The child walked through the trees beside her mother. Only moments later, another Griffin, one they immediately titled "Silver-shanks," arrived. She also had a child, a bit smaller than Dawn-song. The mother carried it like a mother cat carries a kitten. As dusk approached, the children were cutting meat from the carcass when they saw another, a fourth Griffin, arriving, a bundle dangling from her feet. She landed down the slope somewhere, and they heard her hurrying up toward them, past them, and into the cave, sparing them the briefest possible glance. The children picked up their burdens and followed, naming the one they had just seen "Bell-sound," for they had heard her calling like a great bronze gong from the sky.

Bell-sound's burden—carried in the hide of some recently killed animal—contained three eggs: her own very large one and two others, smaller but distinguishable by size.

"We have to leave you here alone," Sun-wings told them, speaking directly to Needly, her wings twitching with the strain they could hear in her voice. "Some of them got Despos to fly off west so the others would have time to get their eggs and young here. Now, of course, he will demand to see our nests, to see us, to determine that there are no young, no eggs. Ordinarily, Griffins do not change their nests. Ordinarily, we build one and one only, deep and soft with plucked feathers to keep the baby warm. Now . . . well, now he will see empty nests. Now, hear me carefully, Willum, Needly."

She fixed them with her huge eyes, and even Willum, oblivious as he sometimes was, saw the pain and tension there. "I have pulled the buffalo carcass as near as I can to the cave door. Willum has had me pull the skin and cut it in several places so you can get at the meat. Cut what you will need from it for two or three days and bring that part into the cave. Do it as soon as we leave. There is a large piece of . . . human house-skin there. I took it from a man-place. Use it to cover the body outside, so it cannot be seen from the air. You do not want a gathering of crows or vultures drawing attention to this place. The eggs were carried here in a hide; I will carry that hide away. After that, do not leave the cave. Listen to me! If you go out, some small things may watch you, from the trees, from the ground, from the air! They are little, harmless things. You think, 'Oh, they can't hurt us.' You are right. But those little harmless things can be seen! And Despos can see them! And Despos can think, 'Aha, what is that little bird looking at?' "

"So he would come to see what the bird was looking at," said Willum.

The huge head nodded. "He would come to see, and you and Needly and my child and the other children, the eggs, all would be gone within . . . moments. If he roared into this cavern, your ears would burst. If he reached into it, you would die on his claws. If you need to pee or poop—that is your word, yes?—do it in that earth-floor corner of the cave. Our children will need to do the same, they can use that place as well. Despos has spies, some who fly, some who walk under the trees, and some who burrow under the ground. None of them are near this place. Not yet. It should be only a day before he goes! One day. Do not go out in daytime until we come to tell you he has gone." And with that, she herself was gone, walking off under the trees toward the precipice at the bottom of the rise, from which she could drop easily into flight.

Willum and Needly stared at the three eggs. Bell-sound's egg, the largest one, could have held a three-year-old human child, if it were curled up. One of the two smaller ones could have held a one-year-old; the smallest was half that size. Needly remembered Abasio's story of the woman, Olly, who had saved a hatchling as a child. So that huge egg must be mostly other stuff and quite a small baby.

Needly asked, "How long does the mother have to sit on the nest?"

"Sit on a nest?" questioned Golden-throat's child. "Why would a mama do that?"

"To keep her egg warm. So it will hatch?"

"But it is always warm. It is in her pocket. The baby does not stay in the nest until after it has hatched; then, if the weather is warm, it can stay for short times! If the mamas have an egg in the pocket, if they hear Despos coming, they fly away and hide so the egg doesn't get broken. If Despos attacks them, he kicks the mama, hurts her, breaks the egg, he even breaks the mamas. He is very . . ." The little one shook her head.

Needly knew the word. Grandma had very early taught her the word. "Abusive." It was the word for Gralf, the word for most of the men in Hench Valley. Someone had created an abusive male. Like the three hostile females. Surely not intentionally? She set that thought aside in order to find out something more important. She asked, "You have a *pocket*?"

The little one reared onto her hind legs, reaching down with her beak and running it across just below her front legs, a slit that ran from just below one armpit to the other. "Feel inside," she said, then giggled as Needly reached out to feel the warm softness within. "It tickles. It's always warm there. When a mother lays an egg, it's small. You know those birds that fly in long lines?"

"You mean a goose?"

"Gooses! They lay eggs in nests, near water, I have seen them. Griffin eggs are the size of maybe two or three of their eggs. The shell is soft. And the mama right away puts it in her pocket. The egg goes on growing there. The baby inside it goes on growing. It takes a long time, but Mama says it's no trouble. The egg takes food from inside the pocket, too. The skin kind of sticks to the shell and lets the food go through and it goes on like that for as many years as we have claws on our front feet!"

"Counting the little one that sticks out behind?"

"Yes. That is how many?"

"Ten. So it takes ten years to hatch."

"Yes. Or a little more. But finally the baby breaks the egg from inside. That big one over there, it's about ready to break. The mama pulls the pieces of the shell and the insides of the egg out of her pocket, because most of the egg is other stuff that makes food and air for us to breathe. We're not very big when we hatch out, just big enough to climb in and out, and we don't have any feathers or fur. So we stay in the pocket most of the time after we hatch, to stay warm until we grow our fur. When we first come out, the mamas give us meat, more and more as our fur grows on us."

"Did your mother tell you to tell us all that?"

"Yes. My mama and Dawn-song's mama. And they said you would give me a name. I think that's nice, having a name. We never did that."

Willum and Needly shared a glance, both of them feeling the weight of these lives settle heavily on them. What was it Willum had said? *Name something, you're responsible for it.* Needly adopted an oracular posture and intoned: "I name you 'Amber-ears.'" The word echoed in the cavern . . . *eers, eers, eers.*

Willum repeated the phrase and the name, matching the tone of voice. The little one frolicked around them, repeating the name. "Ammereers. Ammereers. Amber-ears." They stared as the ears rose and spread above her head like the wings of a bird, shining, long and tufted. "Amber-ears," she caroled delightedly. "Amber-ears."

Willum asked the air: "Is there anything else we're supposed to know?"

"I need a name," said the other little one. "Does my mama have a name?"

Needly answered. "Yes. Your mother is Silver-shanks, and you are 'Snow-foot.'"

"Snow-foot," the little one said, examining her feet. They were white. She ran out her claws, as a cat does when it stretches. They were silvery white, metallic. "Snow-foot."

Dawn-song had joined them. "We have to take care of three eggs.

Mama said this big egg is almost ready to hatch. That's usually when a mama finishes the nest she's been building somewhere safe and warm. From then on, the mamas can sometimes leave it for a little while, while they hunt. Sometimes big animals fight back, and the baby in the pocket might get kicked or gored, so they leave the baby for a little while they find food."

Willum frowned as he asked, "Dawn-song, do you and Amber-ears have big enough pockets for the two little eggs to fit in?"

Needly turned toward him. His face was a little flushed, as though he were embarrassed. He went on doggedly. "The eggs aren't very big at all. Would it be it be all right for you to . . . tend the eggs in your pockets?"

The two little ones stared at each other, turning the idea over and over. At last Dawn-song said tentatively, "Willum, Mama told me a long-ago story, about a Griffin who had sister babies, and the older one took care of the egg."

"Is it unusual for a Griffin to have both a half-grown girl child and an egg?" asked Needly.

Amber-ears cried, "Oh, yes! Yes! What she said about the long-ago! Yes, it made me remember! In the long-ago, before Despos got so big and before he killed the other fathers, Mama said there were more eggs then, more young, no one was breaking them, killing them! There were big . . . sister babies, yes. And big—what is a he-sister?"

"He-sister? You mean a brother?" Willum asked

"Bro-therz. Brothers, yes. Brother children. Brothers even helping mothers bring food for children, brother ones protecting the little ones!"

Needly turned to stare at Willum, several layers of thought going on at once. How sensible of him to have thought of that! And how helpful! With a two-thousand-year life-span, a three-hundred-year childhood, and babies needing to be fed fresh meat . . . mothers would need all the help they could get!

Willum nodded, his mouth set. "Well then, that's all three of the babies named and two of the eggs provided for." He took Needly's hand, an icy little hand. The air coming through the cave entrance was cold. Her lips were almost blue, and he drew her toward the fire in the back corner of the cave. "What about the biggest egg, Needly?"

She collapsed near the fire. "We'll just have to bring it over here and keep the fire going." As Willum went back to get the egg, rolling it across the cavern floor toward her, she held out her hands to the flame as she asked, "Dawn-song, how are we to nourish the eggs properly? Our skins won't provide food. Nor yours, probably."

"Mama said it will only be for a little while, Needly. The mamas have all flown back to their nests. When they get there, they will try to find prey nearby that they can kill and take back to their nests. When Despos comes looking to see their pockets and their nests are empty, there will be meat there, and he will eat it. When he eats, he is sleepier, not so likely to hurt things. When he has seen all the nests, he will fly north, east, where the island is said to be."

Willum said, "That's what's 'sposed to happen. Yeah."

Dawn-song said, "While that happens, we will keep the two smaller eggs warm in our pockets, and the biggest one can go here, near the fire. We can keep all of them moist on the outside by wiping them with water. Sometimes, if mamas have to go far away, hunting when the egg is very big, she will leave it behind and the egg dries out. That keeps the inside of it safe until she gets back. It doesn't let any moisture out that way. But then, when she comes back, she has to moisten it and get it soft again so it can go back in the pocket. Usually, a mama licks it all over. As soon as Despos goes away, the mamas will come back and get their eggs or their children. It won't be long."

Despos going away seemed to be the final word on the matter. With one quick glance Willum and Needly shared hope that Despos would indeed go before he killed anything else. Following the instructions Sun-wings had given them, Willum went to cover the carcass left outside. The house-skin she had mentioned was there: Sun-wings had robbed someone of a tent, ropes and pegs dangling from it. He examined it for bloodstains, finding none. At least it had not been taken forcibly while occupied. And it would serve the purpose Sun-wings had intended for it. He tugged the tent across the buffalo carcass and laid some branches atop the pile. From above, it should look only like a pile of debris at the foot of the cliff that loomed above them. The cave entry was shadowed by an overhang. It was not a bad place to be—under the circumstances!

They had already brought in water and a sizable supply of firewood; the fire had been placed in the most sheltered corner, and the smoke was leaking into a little recess and away through a fissure at its top. It was almost like a fireplace, Needly thought as she pulled the mattresses where they could gather near the warmth. Everything above them was forested. The smoke would indeed appear to come from a hunter's camp, like all those they had seen from the top of the pass.

They laid the three mattresses in a triangle, one corner of the triangle quite near the low and shadowed recess where the fire burned. The big egg went at that corner, taking up the end of one small mattress. When they had wiped the egg with warm water, they covered it with a blanket, and Willum pointed out the other end of that mattress and announced that it was his place. The larger mattress came next, Needly on the end next to Willum and Dawnsong at the other. The other small mattress held Snow-foot and Amber-ears. Willum stood, considering the arrangement, and asked Needly, "Y'think it'll work?"

From her place next to Dawn-song she murmured, "From what I've heard them say, Willum, all the Griffins in the world are here, on this side of the world, this continent and the one to the south: Grandma called them Normery Cah and Sowmery Cah. The Griffins were designed to live among mountains, and they've stayed in this range for hundreds of years—it goes way up into the northlands—or the one to the south that lies all along the western sea. They need companionship, just as we do, but remaining together has made them easy prey for Despos. He's too big. He's too powerful. He's too . . . Grandma used a word . . . 'paranoid.' It's a kind of insanity! It means he's always afraid something, everything is trying to kill him, so he kills everything before it has a chance.

"When they're sure he's really gone, the egg mothers will come back here for their eggs; Sun-wings, Golden-throat, and Silver-shanks will come for their little ones and they will go south and then turn westward to fly island by island to Tingawa. That's the way Xulai said they had to go so they won't need to fly too far in each step. It's hard to fly a long way carrying the little ones."

Willum murmured, "It'd be good to send a message to Xulai; she put paper and a pen in the things she sent. She has ways to talk to the people in Tingawa and she c'd let'm know the Griffins are comin'. And we might be able to help. We might be able to cut up that tent out there and make a harness so they could carry the little ones easier." He yawned gapingly. "I tell you one thing, Needly. Whoever made those

Griffins didn't know much about keepin' a healthy flock or herd. Even my grandpa—and Grandma allus said he was no wizard—but even he knew you have to breed out some. Y'can't have only one he-critter for a flock. One at a time's all right, otherwise they fight, but you got to switch between 'em. She says that's why men get the wanderlust, so they'll go breed out some, and it's why some families fade away to nothin'. Royal people in olden times, like. They got all family-proud and they died off from inbreedin'. You gotta watch it, Needly. You do."

He nodded to himself in confirmation, then, with a determined expression, strode across the cave and just outside, to the carcass. After an arduous session of slicing around bone and sinew accompanied by half-swallowed curses, he returned with a large, bloody chunk off which he and Needly carefully cut small shreds and fed them raw to the three Griffin babies until the young ones said enough. Then they salted and roasted bits for themselves, talking about salt and did Griffins eat salt? And where did they find it? Saltgosh, they decided. At night, when no one was watching.

This matter talked out, the young ones began to think of possible names for the three not yet hatched. Both Willum and Needly were indignant that the babies already hatched had not been named before! "Like they were just things," whispered Needly. "Like they didn't matter!" They and the little ones agreed, however, that babies not yet hatched could not be named as yet. It could be done far better after the Namer knew at the very least whether they were male or female.

"Male or female?" whispered Willum, recognizing the possibility for the first time. "Oh, Needly, what if . . . ?"

"Shh" She put her hand across his mouth. "Don't even think about it. And not a word, Not until . . . you know. Later."

They could go without sleep no longer. Willum took off his boots and lay with his head and shoulders near Needly's, his own stockinged feet beneath the blanket that covered the largest egg. The warm air flowing past it was keeping it warm. It moved, and he could feel each tremor with his toes. Blanketed, Dawn-song lay aslant on the larger mattress, leaving a triangular space next to her belly where Needly lay, her back against the little Griffin's pocket. From there she could whisper to Willum and feel the touch of his hand as well as feeling the egg inside Dawn-song's pocket as it shifted and stirred. Little Snow-foot and Amber-ears were cuddled together like kittens, Amber-ears' pocket against Snow-foot's warm belly, both well covered.

Three baby Griffins, three Griffin eggs, all of them warm, and those that needed feeding had been fed. Thank heaven Xulai had been liberal with the blankets. *One way or another,* as Grandma used to say. *Whatever needs doing, we will do! One way or another!*

CHAPTER 8

Unnatural Beasts

THE GRIFFIN NEEDLY AND WILLUM IDENTIFIED AS SILVER-SHANKS returned at dawn. Though Xulai had told Needly that she thought no reptile genes had been included in the Griffin heritage, everything about this particular Griffin evoked the image and idea of serpents. Only moments before she landed outside the cave, they heard her screaming from the height and Needly thought of snakes. She reminded herself that snakes were voiceless, that they certainly did not scream. Nonetheless, her involuntary mental picture at the cave entrance moments later was that she confronted the fanged strike of a snake.

She and Willum came hand in hand no farther into the cave entrance than needed for Silver-shanks to see them as she went on shrieking: "Despos went to the nests . . . lusting for killing . . . for blood . . . for tearing and rending . . . Despos wanted something to kill . . . no eggs made him more angry . . . there were no young . . .

"No one was near enough except your . . . *friend*." The word became a foulness, spit from the beast's mouth with particular emphasis. "He would kill her. Aha." The laugh was exultant. "Aha, *she* was not quick enough!"

"What happened?" Needly asked from a dry, trembling mouth, feeling the blood drain from her face.

"He hit her. Oh, he hit her with his talons. She went down, down. I went to see. She is still alive." Silver-shanks preened, her crest rising, her claws extending as she gloated. "Not for long, perhaps."

Needly felt Willum's hand clench in anger. She squeezed it with all her strength, saying silently, *Be still, Willum. Be still*. Needly felt as he did; she wanted to hit at the creature, call an avalanche down on her. Anything to stop that voice. She swallowed the impulse, contained it, concentrated all her anger, all her hatred into a point of fire, as Grandma had taught her to do. "Where is she?"

"There!" The Griffin shrugged toward the southeast. "She cannot fly. She cannot walk. Despos, he did not kill her. Enough she was down. He found rising air, he circled in it upward and upward, until he was the size of a bird! I am here to get my child now. The others are coming."

"Won't you help us get to Sun-wings?" Needly asked calmly, calmly. "Can't you take us to her?"

"I am not going that way," Silver-shanks snarled.

"It wouldn't take long to take us, and her child."

"I have my child to carry. I will not try to carry two mankinds or a Griffin cub."

Needly swallowed deeply. "Did you bring Sun-wings any food?"

"She's not a hatchling!" Silver-shanks sneered. "Let her look to herself!"

The words slipped out before Needly could stop them. "So you do not really care for one another. And yet you let her help you with Despos? Does that not seem to require that you help her?"

"What is this *help*? This *require*! Griffins feed selves. Griffins feed hatchlings! If Griffin cannot kill, Griffin dies." Though her great beak did not have the expression lips would have given her, the tissue around it and between the eyes was capable of movement. Silver-shanks emitted scorn, dislike . . . actual hostility. Needly remembered Sunwings' words all at once: "hostility," "envy." This was one of the other kind she had spoken of.

Needly's body was momentarily paralyzed, but her mind was rushing wildly: Sun-wings understood "help." Silver-shanks did not. Sun-wings spoke fluently; Silver-shanks seemed to resent speaking at all, or, perhaps, resented speaking to humans. Which one of them was typical of Griffins, or was there such a thing as "typical"? As with humans, one would have to evaluate Griffins as individuals. Humans were both good and evil. Humans had created both good and evil things. But generally each separate kind of creature had been one or the other, not both! Now it seemed that Griffins were likely to be as variable as . . . as human beings? As variable as Gralf from Grandma!

Adding to her immediate dismay was the struggle inside her own body. It had always belonged to her, done what it was required to do, been what it was expected to be. Now . . . now it had become a container for strange new feelings, unfamiliar new intentions!

She took a deep breath and did what Grandma would have told her to do, if she had been here. Analyze. How did it feel? If it had color, what color would it be? What part of her felt it the most?

It felt as though there were something new inside her, an actual physical thing that started inside the top of her skull and reached, stretched—yes, it had a defi-nite feeling of effort, that stretching—reached all the way down to the bottoms of her feet. It was taut as a bowstring! Something light that hummed and was hot! A red-hot something vibrating inside her! Even in Tuckwhip she had been this angry only a few times: When Grandma was killed. When Gralf announced that he had sold her. Everything went up in flames . . . as though the world were on fire!

She shut her eyes, breathed deeply, spoke to herself in Grandma's voice: "Derail it, now!" Her mouth began the recital of meaningless syllables, *amaba, bamaba, camaba, damaba, eamaba, famaba, gamaba* . . . Grandma had called them "derailing words." Of course, Grandma had then had to explain what rails had been, and used for what, and how "being on rails" could describe a mental state, and why "derailing" was sometimes a bad thing and sometimes an extremely good idea because rails went only where they went. One could not choose a route, and if one did not want to go where these particular rails were going, one needed to derail. *Hamaba, iamaba, jamaba,* the red fading, *kamaba, lamaba* . . . cooling the fiery orange-red to softer scarlet, then to rose, to pink, a quiet, gently intimate pink. Thus one could move one's concentration away from fury into a more . . . controllable state.

Controllable state! Oh, she'd had years of experience in that! Quiet! Control your steps, your mouth, and your eyes. Do not stare in disbelief, do not look in anger, do not trip over the foot this HE puts in your way, do not stumble and spill the milk. Do not anger Pa! Do not anger Slap or Grudge!

There was the source! Silver-shanks was Gralf, and all the Pas in Hench Valley. She too would harm anyone who confronted her, contradicted her. She too would maim, wound, and kill. And it wouldn't help to argue; that would only make her angrier! Needly turned to Willum and whispered rapidly. He nodded and went back into the cave. They had a secret to protect, and they had already decided how to do it.

Needly breathed deeply and faced the scowling Griffin once more, saying quietly, sturdily: "We will go by ourselves to provide food for her and care for her. I will not leave Dawn-song here alone. We will go together to find her mother. Please, tell us now how to get there."

"Find her for yourself!" The creature half crouched, crest up, claws out, threateningly ready for a kill.

Needly froze in place, moving not at all in the face of that deadly glare as she said calmly, "Did you say Golden-throat is coming to get her daughter? And the other mothers, they are coming for their eggs? I think I hear them returning now."

Silver-shanks' eyes darted side to side, edging closer, head weaving as she snarled. "Oh, in time they will . . ." Abruptly her head went back, her eyes focusing upward. She snarled again, with what sounded like frustration. "I hear them." Whatever she had intended to do, she would not do it in the presence of the others.

Needly risked a quick glance over her shoulder. Willum had managed to hide the eggs, the little ones, and the secret they were keeping. He sat by the fire, seemingly alone. Needly turned back to see Golden-throat landing only a short distance away. She signaled Willum by raising her hand.

Golden-throat came quickly, thrusting Silver-shanks aside without saying anything or indicating even that the other one had been seen, and making space for herself at the cave mouth. Now little Amber-ears was close behind Needly, where Golden-throat could see her clearly. The Griffin child was dancing from hind feet to front feet, capering delightedly as she cried to her mother. "Mama, we have names!" she chortled. "My name is Amber-ears! Mama's name is Golden-throat. Oh, wonderful, wonderful names!"

Needly drew back and bowed, her arm extending, gesturing for Golden-throat to come inside, hoping desperately that the Griffin would come in alone . . . Beyond her, Needly saw wings, a head, two . . . a third! Three other Griffins were already approaching.

Golden-throat's eyes flicked to one side, widening slightly as she took in Silver-shanks' crouch, her glare, her claws extended like curved swords. Deliberately, Golden-throat shouldered her way past and entered the cave. Past her gigantic shoulder, Needly saw Silver-shanks' head turn toward the three that had just arrived. Abruptly, her crest fell flat, her claws retracted.

So. The snake did not threaten when she was opposed or outnumbered. One or more of the new arrivals might not be an ally of hers. Which ones were her allies? Which were likely to be Sun-wings' allies . . . friends? Silver-shanks had used the word "friend" as though it were a curse. Did they even have friends?

The newly arrived ones pressed close to the cave entrance, immediately caught up in the babble about names, names, wonderful names. The heat from their bodies warmed Needly like a campfire as she slipped deeper into the cave, into the shadows, becoming less visible, less central. Small creatures, like Needly and Willum, were so very vulnerable to those talons, those claws, those beaks. With Golden-throat inside, none of the others would be able to enter the cave, and Needly relaxed momentarily against the wall, swallowing hard. Her mouth was dry, as though she'd walked miles without water. Past Golden-throat's rump she could see Willum, still quiet by the fire, but his hand was under his shirt, and she knew his knife was in it. Pray he kept still. It would be using a needle to fight a . . . one of those huge extinct things . . . an elephant!

Golden-throat, with surprisingly gentle care to avoid crushing Willum, turned her huge body to face the entrance. She preened herself, crest raised, crying out to the others that she herself was now Golden-throat, for she had been given a name by the Namers. Oh, yes, the Namers. *The Givers of Names!* How fortunate that the Namers had been here, just at this time! Just when they all *needed names to identify themselves in Tingawa!*

Needly felt the tension inside her relax a little. *Oh, clever creature, Golden-throat! She had seen the hostility, judged it for what it was, and given the hostile creature a reason not to kill her or Willum. Like Sun-wings, she knew their hope for survival depended upon Abasio and Xulai and on keeping their* hostages safe! So their hostages were no longer merely human nothings, they were Namers! They had been given status among the Griffins! Maybe. At least they had a temporary standoff there in the cave entrance: Golden-throat in the center, Needly at one side of her, Willum at the other. She could read his face where he stood, just across those huge paws from her. Now, if he would just . . .

One of the new arrivals, who had an almost scarlet rump and tail, thrust her head forward and ordered in a trumpetlike voice—it was a command, not a request—that these Namers come forth to tell them the names of all the mothers, all the children, all those that were as yet egg-children, not yet hatched!

Willum's face showed what he thought of this. Needly could see that he was inclined to be truculent about the whole matter, but Golden-throat said something to him very quietly and he stopped scowling and waited, more than slightly subdued.

"We will need to prepare if there is to be a . . . an OFFICIAL naming ceremony," Needly cried, giving the idea all the weight she could. "Go a little farther away while we prepare!"

Golden-throat cried, "Yes, move away while the Namers prepare to name us and our children!" Somehow she managed to lend a very special resonance to the word "Namers." The word seemed to hang in the air, humming, long after it was spoken.

Needly went to stoop over, putting her mouth to Willum's ear. "Willum, whatever else we do, you and me, we need to be necessary to these . . ." She risked a glance at Golden-throat. "These very large and dangerous creatures who are not likely to be patient with the oneriness of children!"

Golden-throat blinked slowly. Needly could swear she smiled. How could she smile? Nonetheless, the flexible tissues at the corner of Golden-throat's beak quivered, as though she was considering laughter. She did not laugh. She merely said very softly, without moving her clenched beak, "Listen to her, young one! She understands what's going on."

As Needly glanced into Golden-throat's eyes, her heart leapt at the complicity she saw there. Well then. Perhaps Willum had not been as wrong about the Griffins as she had thought! Perhaps they were capable of . . . empathy. With the support of even one Griffin, perhaps she could exact a price from the others—if they were sincere about wanting names. She murmured, "Sun-wings is injured. I have to get that one out there—we call her Silver-shanks—to tell us where she is."

Golden-throat nodded very slightly. "You have not yet told her the name you have given her? Good." She turned and went to the cave entrance, effectively blocking it.

The children mumbled together, and Willum went to get their stew pot while Needly dug through her pack to see what she could use. The little ones came out of hiding and watched closely when she found a long, wide sash in her pack, heavy red silk lined in white. Unnecessary baggage, but she had brought it because it had been Grandma's and it smelled of her still. She tied it around her head, knotted on her forehead, tucked the ends back so they hung down in front of her ears, down across her chest. She made a stripe across each of her cheeks with soot, another down the bridge of her nose. She whispered quick instructions to Willum, then put a handful of fireplace soot into a bowl with a little water and picked out the straightest, thinnest stick she could find from the woodpile to use as a wand. Willum grabbed it from her and trimmed it with his knife to make it neater, more . . . official-looking.

Finally, taking a deep breath, Needly tapped Golden-throat on her huge shoulder. The Griffin backed farther into the cave, leaving a space for Needly to stand in the entrance between Golden-throat's huge paws. Willum had settled himself on the other side of the right paw, crouched over the upturned kettle and holding the handle of a wooden spoon with a strip of rag tightly wrapped around the spoon end. Needly wanted a *bong bong*, not a *whang whang*.

Four huge Griffins were lined up outside, facing her, tongues lolling very slightly from their huge beaks. Needly blinked at the sight, but kept moving. They looked very carnivorous. Thank whoever had designed them that she, as a human, tasted bad, though she had only Sun-wings' word for that! Thinking about it didn't help her situation. She stepped from between Golden-throat's paws and strode to one end of the cleared space outside the cave door, her stage. She began to chant, the same nonsense syllables she had used to calm herself before. Back and forth, striding, striding, while waving her rod at the sun. She paused at one side, bowed, then waved at the trees with more chanting.

Back at the center, she made hieratic gestures and let her eyes roll up until only the whites showed.

Behind her in the cave door, Willum, his face also painted with soot, bonged rhythmically on the stew pot with the padded wooden spoon. She had explained: "You want to sound mysterious and marvelous." Occasionally Willum accompanied the bong with a shrill whistle and a high treble, quickly chanted string of syllables. *"Fahma Donah hadda fahma ee-ai-ee-ai-ohwaaah. Onna fahma wassa cowah ee-ai-ee-ai-owaaah. Cowah mu-mu, awies mu-mu. Ee-ai-ee-ai-owaaaah."* Needly fought down hysterical laughter. Oh, Willum!

They had already settled on a name for the Griffin who had brought the eggs, she who had called from the sky with a sound like the ringing of a great bell. Needly dipped her fingers in the soot bowl and marched toward that one, at the extreme right, laying her hand upon the bridge of that huge nose beak, between the nostrils, slowly marking it, chanting, finally crying in a high, shrill voice: "A-*hai*, a-*hai*, a-*hai*. The Namer names! *You are named Bell-sound!*"

She turned her back on her audience, bent, bowed to Sun-wings while she caught her breath. Then she repeated the entire ritual, trying to do it precisely as she had done it before. More waving, more bongs, another sooty marking: "A-*hai*, a-*hai*, a-*hai*, the Namer names. *You are named Copper-beak*," gesture, *bong.* Then it was the turn of the red-rumped one who had demanded a name. "A-*hai*, a-*hai* . . . the Namer says *you are named Flame-tail.*" Finally, Needly faced into the cave, marked her huge guardian, made a wide gesture with both arms, and cried, *"You are named Golden-throat, and your child is named Amber-ears."*

"My child," shrieked Silver-shanks. "A name for me and for my child!"

"I will give you a name and a name for that child," cried Needly, "when you have told me how to find the one we call Sun-wings."

The screamed reply could have been heard halfway across the sea! "You will tell me now a name for my child, or I will tear off your arms . . ."

Amazingly, the other three turned on her, their beaks wide, a hissing roar bellowing from three throats. From inside the cave, Golden-throat screamed, "You will not hurt the Namer! Tell the Namer! Tell the Namer what she wants to know! She is the name giver; tell her or we will kill you and take your child!"

Silver-shanks was taken completely by surprise. She had been backed almost into the trees, snarling and snapping the whole way, and was able to launch herself into the sky only by a frenzied flapping of her great wings. Needly watched every flap, noting that the process was indeed as Sun-wings had described it. Taking off from level ground could be done, but it wasn't easy.

The three Griffins outside watched Silver-shanks circling above them. To fill the silence, Needly extemporized a few rules to simplify Namers' lives, marching back and forth as she chanted them in her Namer's voice, Grandma's voice, only louder and more like . . . singing: *"By the laws of Earth and sky, Namers may not name children still in the egg. Namers may not name children still in the pocket. A name must reflect the Griffin as a pool of water reflects the reality, so names cannot be given until the child appears as a Griffin, furred and feathered! Mothers may use baby names for their little ones, but the real name can be given by Namers only when they are fledged! The Namers have saved your eggs, have saved your young. The Namers have cared for your eggs, your young. Now you must depart and go in great haste to Tingawa!"*

She had to stop for breath, leaning over, panting, filling the pause with a mumble that might have meant anything, or nothing. Then, erect once more, she proclaimed: "When you are in Tingawa, when the young ones hatch from their eggs, when their fur is grown in, when the feathers on their wings and neck are grown, take them to the ruler of Tingawa and say this: *'I come from Princess Xulai, chief of all naming. I come from Needly and Willum, the Namers. They have told me you will give us names.'"*

She spoke to Golden-throat. "You will say this to the ruler of Tingawa: 'Xulai, your granddaughter, says to her grandfather, 'Emperor, I beg of you names for the Griffin young and for generations of Griffins not yet named. And Xulai's children, the Namers, have sworn mankind will do all within its power to give the Griffins lives in the sea.'"

She turned away, fighting to stay on her feet. The huge beasts emanated a kind of . . . aura. It wasn't hostility. It wasn't a smell or taste, not wholly, even though she could taste a sourness that reminded her of sickrooms. There was a hint of nausea in it, a vertiginous lurch that made it hard for her to keep her balance. What was it? Those huge, dripping beaks? Those lolling tongues?

Not the most calming atmosphere for someone assuming the role of seeress!

said a well-remembered voice in her mind. She came to herself, amazed to find herself leaning against Golden-throat's side, half under one huge wing. Warm. Steady.

"Good," whispered the Griffin. "It will do. Hold on."

Hold on? She wanted to crawl in a corner with Willum so they could tell each other fairy tales! Tales of heroes who always won their battles! Of heroines who were always brave and whose monsters were always manageable!

Only moments later, Silver-shanks dropped outside the cave like an eagle onto prey, raising a cloud of dust as she thrust her kin aside, screeching: "The little stream where you get water. Follow it down to the place where another stream comes in from that way." One huge wing pointed southwest. "Follow that stream, up. It goes into a canyon with a waterfall. Go past the falls, on up to a place where there is a rock bridge across the stream. At the top end of the bridge, farther up over the hill in a little clearing, Sun-wings is there! Now, name me and my child!"

Needly took up her rod, gestured a command: Willum began his bonging; it took all her determination to approach the creature and mark it—hard to think of it as *her*—and she did not name it until she was well away from that beak. *"If you have told us true, your child is named Snow-foot. You are named Silver-shanks. If you have not told us true, your names will vanish, no one will remember them."*

She turned away from the four of them, wondering if Silver-shanks would now lie in wait for her. Perhaps she would just go away.

Golden-throat was speaking to her, whispering actually, her head turned so the others could not hear. "Namer, are you aware that the largest egg—"

"I know," Needly whispered. "I don't want some of them to know. Golden-throat, have you noticed that three of them have scales?"

"Scales?"

"Like Despos has. Instead of feather or fur, on his belly. They don't have many, but there are some . . ."

"Those are scales?"

"Like a serpent, a snake, yes. I get a weird feeling about those three."

Golden-throat murmured, "Yes. You are wise to do so."

"Get Bell-sound to stay here, but get the others gone! Can you . . ."

"Does little . . . Snow-foot know?"

"None of the little ones know. They were asleep. I didn't let them see what had happened."

"Bring the other two eggs to me, but stay behind me!" Golden-throat picked up Snow-foot as a cat does a kitten, by the scruff of her neck, interposing herself between the children and the cave door. There she put the little one down, saying, "Here is your child, Silver-shanks. You can take her down through the forest, there's a cliff there. You must begin your journey now to Tingawa! Go west! Island to island. Go swiftly, before Despos returns."

There was a breathless quiet that stretched into an eternity before it was broken at last by the loud snap of wings opened to catch the air! Golden-throat breathed deeply and turned toward Needly, who laid the two eggs on the ground before her. Golden-throat rolled them out through the entrance, saying, "Flame-tail, this one is yours, the other is yours, Copper-beak." She said their names slowly, giving them weight and importance. "Get them into your pockets and follow Silver-shanks. Go south along the shore, then go west by the way we decided, island to island. Now go quickly, to Tingawa!"

Peeking through the crack between Golden-throat's huge shoulder and the cave entrance, Needly saw the eggs being tucked into very large pockets. She noted particularly that the eggs did not make a bulge. There was room there in the mother Griffin's flesh, a kind of pocket protected by ribs so the eggs and the young ones would not easily be hurt. If Despos had broken eggs in the pockets, he had no doubt badly injured the mothers, too. She listened to the sound of receding voices followed by the sharp sound of wings catching air, like a pair of gigantic hands clapping.

Only Bell-sound was left outside, her eyes fixed on Golden-throat, who moved from the entrance, saying, "Bell-sound, you have a child hatched. It is safe and well cared for. The children have fed it."

Bell-sound cried out, a joyous sound very like a peal of bells. Willum brought the hatchling out, wrapped in the shirt they had put around it when it hatched during the night. A tiny pecking sound had wakened him, he had wakened Needly, and they had watched, fascinated, as a little hole appeared, a beak sharp as a pin poking through as tiny bits of the shell fell away. The being inside was so very tiny, naked, ugly. Pale, tender skin stretched over grass-thin bones. The wings seemed mere scraps of skin. When it had emerged, the little creature had been covered with something milky and sticky, and the shell had been full of stuff. "Gunk," said Willum. Gunk it was, obviously organic, rather smelly, and they had caught almost all of it in their cooking pan. Willum had buried it in the far back corner of the privy ground. Silently, not waking the other Griffins, Needly had warmed water and cleaned the baby just outside the entrance to the cave. Willum had fetched some of the raw meat from outside the cave entry and had cut it very fine. They had fed the child as it eagerly gulped meat until its tiny head fell to one side as though its thin little neck had snapped. For a moment they feared that had actually happened, but the baby had made a gurgling, contented sound. It had simply fallen asleep.

They had made a pile of bedding where the egg had been and covered it with the blanket so the Griffin children would not know the egg had hatched. In an attempt to hide any remaining odor, Needly took a brand from the fire and carried it around the cave, letting the smoke make a stink of its own. She had no idea how sensitive Griffin noses—or equivalent—might be, but there was nothing more they could do but wash the pan and put it over the fire with bits of the meat and herbs from their food stores to make an aroma of its own. The wrapped hatchling went inside her shirt, next to her skin The full cloak that Xulai had included in their stores had covered the bulge it made. In the hours since hatching, the baby had developed a fine downy coat, and they had fed it surreptitiously several times, keeping the cloak well around Needly as they did so. When Silver-shanks had appeared, Willum had taken the baby inside his shirt, his own cloak hiding its shape.

Now Bell-sound and Golden-throat stared down at it. Needly stroked it, petted it.

"It's a boy child," she said. "Bell-sound, this is a boy child." She had had time to study Dawn-song's anatomy in the last few days, and she had compared it to this newly hatched one. It was indeed a male. Her voice deepened: *"His name is Carillon."* The unintentional words had been uttered in Grandma's voice, as though the old woman were standing next to her.

Golden-throat said wonderingly, "A male child, and we have time to get to Tingawa before Despos returns. We have time, but none to spare. We must leave now." She turned to Needly. "We must go west, and you must go south to Sun-wings. We cannot risk this little male to go with you . . . Carillon, did you say? You have broken your own rule to name him so soon."

"The name means a chime of bells," said Needly. "He will have a voice like that, a beautiful voice. There is no rule for this child, this child is beyond rules. He is not of Despos."

Bell-sound whispered, "We are ashamed not to go with you, but . . ."

Needly felt the tears on her cheeks as she said, "Of course you can't risk it. I know what this baby means. It means if Despos is killed, he isn't the last male. And this one will not be like Despos! I know how important that makes him! And, I know you'll be safer if you go together. But don't go yet! You will be over the ocean, stopping only at islands that may be bare. You will need to carry food for the baby."

She staggered back, feeling a sudden weakness. The two Griffins were murmuring together; Golden-throat whispered to Willum, and he nodded. He started to cut meat into thin strips; Golden-throat took the meat from him and clicked her beak along it like a machine ticking as the cleanly cut shreds fell on top of the piece of canvas Willum had cut from the tent. He made a bundle of it, with a long slit in the top that would admit Bell-sound's beak and a strong loop on top for Bell-sound's claws. "We didn't send any with the other babies . . ." he said, sorrowing.

Golden-throat said, "They are old enough to go several days without food. Now, you young ones, it will take all the day to find Sun-wings at the place *that one* described."

Needly noted the tone of voice in which "that one" had been said. Silver-shanks was not a popular Griffin—at least, not with Golden-throat and Bell-sound.

Golden-throat went on: "Take what you will need with you; Sun-wings' child is big enough to carry some things. You will need to stay there, I think. If Despos hurt her badly, perhaps she will not live very long. If she does not, her child . . ."

"We will take care of her child," said Needly, whose brief respite had restored her determination, if not all her strength. "But before you go, there is one thing I must be sure of. Does each of you know who fathered you?"

The two Griffins stared at her, heads cocked, as though surprised.

Bell-sound said, "Despos was hatched or made far south of here, in great tall mountains along the western ocean. He is father of the ones you have named Flame-tail and Copper-beak and Silver-shanks. He is not father of Silver-shanks' child—Snow-foot, you named her. He is not father to this child! I sorrow—is that the proper word? Feel . . . sad? Yes. I feel sorrow to know that Despos is probably father to the eggs you tended." She glanced questioningly at Golden-throat.

The golden Griffin nodded. "I believe that is so and I, too, sorrow. Any eggs still unbroken by Despos are younger than Bell-sound's hatchling. Would they be of Despos? Was that the time he killed the last of the other males?" The two Griffins nodded to each other, considering it, thinking it over. When considering things, Needly noted, they made a deep purring sound, like huge cats. Grandma and Needly had had a cat. It was very old. Grandma had had it since it was a kitten. Its name had been Plush. He had died when Needly was seven years old. How strange. She had not thought of silky, black Plush in a very long time. That deep purring had brought him back . . .

The purring ended. Golden-throat said, "We believe the two eggs you tended are of Despos, and their mothers are of Despos. The mothers of Flame-tail and the other two may still be in that place to the south, or Despos may have killed them. At that time there were other males there and here, where we are, and those males were our fathers and fathers of our children. They stopped growing, as we do. Despos never did stop growing."

Needly held up her hand. "Is he still growing, Golden Throat?" She was thinking of the giants Willum had told her of. The Griffin nodded, a very human nod, and Needly turned back to the other griffins. "Sunwings, Bell-sound, and you, Golden-throat, have nothing of Despos in you. Dawn-song, Snow-foot, Amber-ears, and little Carillon, they are not of Despos. The eggs Copper-beak and Flame-tail have, those are from Despos, and so I believe with Despos as both father and grandfather, *the young ones will be as he is.* If those eggs were . . . accidentally broken, it would not be a bad thing."

"But even they will bring their children to a Namer in Tingawa, will they not?" said Bell-sound. "And you have a way to communicate with that place, to let them know who should be . . . helped and who perhaps should be . . . stopped."

Golden-throat murmured, "All of us, no matter where we were, we were first created by mankind. We were fathered and mothered by them."

Needly cried, "I know that, but please don't tell the other three that you have a male baby, Bell-sound. They have no way of knowing, do they, unless you tell them? Not for a while?"

"No," she said, the word humming like a chord stroked from muted chimes. "They will not know it has hatched. Babies do not leave the pocket at all until they begin to get enough fur to keep them warm. Then they may be left in a properly prepared nest for short times while the mother hunts, but they still spend most time in the pocket. It is safer. Why do you ask this?"

"Because even if you were all created by man, I think there are two different races of you. Mankind created many things: some were evil, some were good. Some were not intended to be evil but turned out that way anyhow. Among the Griffins, some are like Sun-wings and you two, and some are like Despos and his daughters, full of anger and killing. We believe any that were fathered by Despos are going to be like Despos. Do you use the word 'evil'?"

"What Despos does is evil," said Golden-throat. "Killing without thinking. Doing everything without thinking."

Needly nodded. "We think he has serpent in his making. Serpents don't think. They just react." She sighed deeply. "If you know the word 'evil,' you must know the word 'good.' If you would care to do a good thing, merely because it is a good thing, stay near Silver-shanks and Snow-foot. Snow-foot is . . . she is like Dawn-song. She is good, but her mother is not, so look out for Snow-foot. If ever she needs someone to take care of her, take her to the emperor in Tingawa, or if you are near, bring her to us. The emperor is grandfather to Xulai, he will help."

Two huge heads turned, two great pairs of eyes staring at each other. "Good?" murmured Bell-sound to the other. "And who shall say what is good?"

"I shall," said Needly, and Willum's head swiveled as he turned to stare at her, for her voice had reverberated like an enormous gong that sends reverberations away to the farthest mountain. "I am the Namer. I shall name what is good, and what is bad."

"And how shall we know?" Golden-throat demanded in a knife-edged whisper.

Needly murmured, as from some other place far away: *"You will see, you will hear, you will know. Pain is part of the fabric of creation, given by the Creator as a warning, to tell us when something outside ourselves is dangerous, to tell us if something inside ourselves needs care. Sometimes we must cause pain for a good purpose, to set a bone or sew up a wound. But one who causes pain intentionally for no good purpose is evil. To feel pleasure at someone else's pain is an even greater evil! Look into the eyes of any creature to see how they react to pain in others. We know Despos is evil because he rejoices in the pain of his victims. We know Silver-shanks is evil, for she rejoiced that Sun-wings was hurt, that she may die. Flame-tail and Copper-beak are the same, as their children may be as well."*

Now the great eyes were staring at her. The Griffins' bodies were trembling, a barely detectable shiver. Needly faced them, unconscious of her own being, merely there, a conduit for something . . . someone else. She looked down, whispering, "Grandma?"

Willum did not like the tension that was building or the expression on Needly's face as though she were holding an explosion within her. He broke it deliberately. "You remember, both of you mothers, it's real important you get to Tingawa. If you and your babies want to go on livin', you got to get there!"

The Griffins sagged. "Yes," said Needly, coming back to herself with a start. "If this baby has a chance at life, it will be in Tingawa. He will grow to be a male for you. He will not be like Despos. You should all go quickly, before Despos learns he has been tricked."

"Despos will come to Tingawa," said Golden-throat. "He will come there."

Needly nodded. "He may, yes. But the people of Tingawa have the power to kill him. And now that you have a young male, the Tingawans may allow themselves to use that power. I hope . . . Xulai's grandfather will use that power. It seems very important to me."

Golden-throat's voice was low, musing, as though she were finding her way among new concepts, new definitions. "If Despos has not killed more of us, there should be at least sixteen of us females. Bell-sound and I know them all. I think . . ." She looked into Bell-sound's face and the other Griffin nodded. "We think only those three who were here are, as you say, serpent. Only six of us, those you have seen, nested here. Ten of us nest other places, far to the south. We will pass their places as we go south to the islands. We will tell them all, we will warn them all."

Golden-throat moved away into the trees, Amber-ears beside her. As little Amber-ears reached the trees she turned, reared upon her hind legs, and waved both front paws.

Bell-sound took longer, licking the tiny, naked creature all over. The children watched as she tucked him away. Needly caught a glimpse of the inside surface of the pocket, oozing a pale liquid. "How long will it stay there?" she asked.

"Some tens of years," murmured Bell-sound. "Or more. It varies. I had two others. Then I had them not, for Despos killed them." The pocket closed smoothly, seamlessly around the child. The great creature leaned forward and touched both Needly and Willum on their foreheads with the very tip of her tongue, like a caress. "I give you my thanks. Sun-wings says that is the . . . appropriate thing to say. We have heard you, Needly. Golden-throat and I speak of you. We believe you were sent to us, maybe both of you sent to us, to be Namer and messenger. We believe you have done well. Because of what you have done, we can now believe your people will also try to do well for us. We . . . what is the word . . . ?"

"Trust," said Needly.

"Yes, trust. Do for us what you can." She turned away and walked toward the trees. They watched until she disappeared among them. Evidently Golden-throat had waited for her companion. The two wing snaps came only moments apart, as did the two voices as they flew away. One small one—"Amber-eeears"—and then from afar, Bell-sound's resonant, rejoicing utterance: "Belelelelel-souououound."

Willum took a deep breath and said in his most practical, getting-on-with-things voice, "Even if Golden-throat hadn't told us, I'da picked Silver-shanks, Copper-beak, and Flame-tail as kin t'that Despos. We'd need a really big cata-pull-it for one a' him."

Needly whispered, "But little Snow-foot was as delightful as Dawn-song."

" 'Spose she'll grow up like that?"

"I'm almost sure she will, but no one will know until after she's grown, three hundred years to maturity. Our great-, great-, great- . . . oh, twelve-times-great-grandchildren might know!"

"Ours? You n' me?"

"If we each have some, Willum. I didn't mean necessarily yours and mine together."

"Oh," grumped Willum as he turned away to confront their pile of supplies. "I wunt'a minded if you'd meant yours and mine together, you know."

"I know, Willum." Needly allowed herself only a hint of smile. "And I wouldn't have minded either. But it isn't . . . fitting to discuss it at our age or this stage of our journey. We have to focus ourselves on what's needed."

"What's 'focus' mean?"

"It means to look hard, to really concentrate on seeing something. Grandma showed me with a kind of glass she had. It pulls the light all together in one place so you can see very clearly. Dewdrops do it, too, she said."

"Like Xulai told me, about the dewdrops making rainbows."

"Well yes. Part of the same thing."

Willum heaved a huge sigh. He felt very tired. They had slept very little the night before. "We could tell the good ones from the bad ones just how they talked, couldn't we? That's a good thing, that we can tell. It'd be bad if'n you didn't know!" Then, without waiting for an answer, "We gotta go!" He cast a look aloft. The sun was midway to noon. "We got to get down the hill to Sun-wings."

Needly gave him a quick hug and a smile. "Remind me to wash my face when we get to the stream. If I look like you, we look like we been in a forest fire. And we need to fill our water bottles there, too."

They had already sorted aside the things that Needly was sure they could manage without. They couldn't carry everything. They couldn't carry half! Not the mattresses. One pot or pan would have to do, to wash and to heat water and to cook in. Two mugs, two spoons, two bowls. Small sacks of grain. A couple of onions. Some of the meat from the carcass outside, a little for them and a lot for Dawn-song. Tiny sacks of herbs for flavor. Willum took the ax and a small coil of rope, mumbling about unraveling rope to make rabbit snares. Dawn-song carried the blankets, all of them, piled across her back, with a rope tied loosely to hold them on. All three of them noted that the pile of things left behind was a great deal larger than the ones they could carry.

"We'll manage," said Needly.

"'Course we will," echoed Willum.

"Go find Mama," urged Dawn-song, for the fiftieth time. "Now. Enough talking."

"Enough talking, Dawn-song. Yes. We go." Still, Needly stood outside the cave, memorizing it. Xulai had the thing that could go anywhere, if you just knew exactly what it looked like. Maybe she would come back here with Xulai and get their things, hers and Willum's.

DEEP IN THE NIGHT, BLUE was aroused from sleep by a slow, tickly furriness around his rear legs. He shivered uncontrollably, not yet awake enough to decide whether to kick with one or both lethal back feet . . .

"Not eating you, Blue Horse," snorted a voice as furry as the touch.

Not-quite-memory swamped him. There were no words in it, just . . . feelings. From before, when he was . . . only horse . . . not . . . . not whatever-it-was he was now. Kicking, stamping on, fleeing away from feelings. When his body reacted in this uncontrolled way—which he considered unsuitable for any speechified equine—he had to surmise that he, or horses in general, might have an instinctive response to *that particular type of snort*, that piggish—*no, boarish* snort, which had a lot of teeth or tusks behind it: an omnivorish, "I'll eat anything alive or dead" sort of snort.

AND, he told himself sternly, all this cogitation was unwarranted given the urgency of the situation. He calmed himself. The words he wanted were *"That's Bear."*

"Bear?" He managed to get the word out. "Bear, is that you?"

"No. It's my cousin, twice removed," grumbled Bear. "Of course it's me. We heard you were coming. Griffin told us. I thought you'd know it was me."

"Ah," murmured Blue, grasping at the word. "Griffin told you. Well. I wish she'd told me you were coming as well. You . . . startled me." A tremor in the furry creature's vicinity told him Bear was laughing. So! The assault on Blue's feet had been quite intentional. Blue considered revenge. "Now, that'd be the big roan-mare Griffin, would it? Very haughty and kind of . . . um." What was it Xulai had said? "Disturbed?"

The furriness touched him again, and Blue, quite ready for it, executed a nicely targeted, nonlethal but quite definitely bruising kick, followed by a whinnied "Oh, sorry, did I hurt you?"

Bear had made an explosively oof-ish sound. Feeling in the skin of Blue's legs that the horse might do it again, Bear moved away, telling himself silently: *Think herbivore! When talking to herbivores, omnivore must think herbivore!* He heaved a huge breath and moved away from the feet, slowly circling around where Blue could see him, or at least his shape could be made out—including the location of his teeth, which, hoping to reassure his friend, he mistakenly displayed by smiling, widely.

Now Blue's front legs were doing that peculiar kind of spasm thing.

Mistake! Bear sighed and backed off a bit farther, letting his lips close gently over his remarkably handsome teeth—so he had been told, repeatedly, by a sow bear with whom he had a pleasant association more or less annually during what humans called "the breeding season." *Bears did not think of it in that way. In fact, when that time came, bears did not think . . . much at all. There was probably a word for it. Humans seemed to have a word for everything. He and Abasio had talked a lot about words, the different kinds of words. Names, doings, hows. Hows were important. Not just whats and doings but the hows of whats and doings. Whenever he thought about language it made him wonder if his cubs could talk. He would very much like to know! If he approached the mother, who was not languaged, how could he ask? Any approach to cubs would be a battle to the death with the mother. He could only wait. Wait and try talking to young bears. If they talked back . . . Oh, he really hoped some of them would talk back—though how would they have learned?*

And Blue was still dancing nervously.

Bear sighed tiredly, saying, "Well, Blue, if I had a family and my cubs were going to be drowned, I'd be disturbed about it! The she Griffin seemed quite sensible to me."

"That drowning bit is what's got the Griffins all worried," Blue agreed, concentrating on clear enunciation. *See there, he even remembered the word. Ee-nun-cee-ai-shun. Good word. If he concentrated on that, he'd quit shaking! Though maybe Bear had the idea by now that it was not a good idea to nibble a sleeping horse's feet! If he had really kicked, the way Rags had let go at that Lorper . . . well, Bear might possibly have survived, but he'd be very seriously injured! Then Blue would have that on his conscience. A conscience seemed to develop once a creature had the word for it. He couldn't remember having had one before . . . though perhaps he had had one without knowing it.*

Bear went on: "What I meant was, if what the Griffin says is right, seems Bears should be worried, too. And Coyotes. Maybe all us critters in general. Horses, too!"

Blue's skin had almost stopped twitching. He did a purposeful shudder to settle it further. "Well, actually, we probably don't need to worry that much, Bear. Abasio and Xulai went to Tingawa not long ago, and they took me with them. The people there are working on saving Earth animals, the few that're left. They were working with sea horses and sea dogs when I was there. Wolves, too. All the animals who are natural to this world, you know, bears included. Those Tingawan people, some of them really sorrowed over the fact that so many Earth animals aren't . . . aren't still living."

Bear muttered. "Extinct! That's the word. They've gone extinct or almost. Lions, you know. And hippowhats, and some big kind that ate with their noses . . . critters like that. But the Griffins aren't extinct. Not yet they aren't."

Blue shuddered, remembering Griffin's huge amber eyes. "No, Griffins aren't, but they're a different kind of creature. Mankind didn't make you or me, or coyotes: we're of nature. Needly says direct from the Creator. We evolved! From what do they call it? *Lower* life-forms! *Ha*. But the Griffins and the other unnatural critters, mankind made them up in legends, and then mankind decided to make them real, so the Griffins think mankind should be responsible."

"I know. That's what Coyote says."

"Where is Coyote?"

"Over at the pool getting a drink of water. Takes him forever! Lap, lap, lap, lap! I keep telling him, just suck it in!" Bear scratched his neck with a hind leg, reflectively. "Sometimes I think he does that lap, lap, lap just to annoy me. You think this waters-rising business is true?"

"All the sane people I know are convinced of it. It's supposed to come from ice in some huge cavern way inside the earth that nobody ever knew was there. From what Xulai says, they still don't know why they didn't see it thousands of years ago on their echo machines and whatnot. They thought for a while it was left over from when the earth collected itself out of a whole skyful of space trash, but there's not room enough down there for that much water, and it just keeps coming. That's what Abasio said. He says it's coming through some kind of hole in space from a whole different world called Squamutch. He says he dreamed it. When did Griffin tell you about it?"

"Short while ago. We were nearby when she fell. She's been hurt bad, Blue. She can't fly, her wing's all . . . ripped . . . She's got a lot of pain, but she told us where Abasio and Xulai probably were and she said you'd probably help her. Coyote and I, we hunted for her, brought her food enough to last her awhile. Broke necks, didn't let the prey bleed, kept it bloody as we could, 'cause we had no way to get water to her . . ."

"She made off with Willum and Needly," said Blue stiffly. "I'm not sure any of us want to help her."

"Blue Horse! Didn't know you were a jackass! That's what she's mainly worried about: her little one and yours, too. She was takin' care of them, good care, from all I could tell. Who's gonna protect the little ones if she's down in a canyon and can't get out. Them little folks all alone up there in the hills! Nice juicy little ones, no doubt, with bears around who don't talk and aren't inclined to be as reasonable as I am either. And she also says—what was it? I was 'sposed to be sure to tell Abasio. Ah—some Griffins do not have any sense of community, whatever that means!"

"Well then, why'n't you bring the children back. You were comin' this way!"

"Because we'd've had to *find* them first, if they weren't off trying to find *her.* Coulda wasted days doin' that. And then we'd had ta come all the way here, and they'd mighta been too scared to come with us, and by that time Sun-wings woulda been dead, and anyhow, Sun-wings said to *get you first,* that's why. We been on the way here all that night and one full day and last night with just little . . . naps."

Blue took only a moment to think it over before wandering over to the wagon, sticking his head through the wagon window, and making a soft, lip-fluttering *braaapp* noise directly over Abasio's head.

"What?" Abasio lurched upright and stared at Blue's head, inches from his own. "What? Blue, what are you . . ."

"Bear's here." Blue spoke softly, not to waken Xulai or the babies.

"What? Who?"

"Abasio, wake up. Bear is here. THE Bear. The talking Bear. From the Place of Power, remember?" Blue felt sharp teeth nibbling at one fetlock, very delicately tickling. He muttered, "Also, his idiot friend,

Coyote," and stamped down, hard, pleased to hear a yip and an explosive four-footed scramble as the idiot friend got away from his feet. What was it with these fangy creatures and other creature's feet!

Abasio got out of the bed by climbing through the window.

"You'll freeze," said Coyote. "Where's your fur?"

"On the other side of the bed. I don't want to wake Xulai. Come away from that window! Now, what's going on?"

They moved away from the wagon and held a muttered conference, interrupted by Abasio's recurrent explosions. "She what? . . . Left where?"

After several more exchanges, Coyote departed, Abasio went back into the wagon, through the door to get his clothes, then he wakened Kim, who was rolled into his blankets under the wagon. The two of them talked for a few moments before Abasio returned to Blue.

Abasio said, "I'll send the wagon, with Xulai and the babies, on with Kim. According to Bear, it's a straight run from here into Artemisia, less than a day on the road. I've given Kim instructions as to who he's to look for down there. Xulai knows already. You and Rags and I will go find . . . what did you say Coyote called her?"

"Sun-wings. Willum and Needly named her."

"And she accepted that name? Remarkable! I suppose there's no reason why a speaking, thinking creature should prefer to go around without a spoken name. They probably have recognition patterns like birds and animals do, but it's not the same thing." He scratched his head and yawned uncontrollably. "Bear says there's no road that would take us anywhere near where the Griffin is, so we'll have to go afoot and a-horse. If Bear and Coyote came straight here, which they claim they did, and if they counted the ridges correctly, we should be able to find her. Coyote has gone back up the hill to locate a few creatures in the area that need to know we're coming. He said he'd be back shortly; he and Bear will guide us to the Griffin."

"What creatures in the area?" asked Blue in a wary voice.

"I don't know who. Others of their kind, presumably, who can be asked to keep a friendly eye on us." He looked up. Blue was regarding him with troubled eyes. "Blue, I'll have some kind of weapon, so don't worry. If we meet with danger, we'll have a way to get out of it. Before we leave, will you tell the rescued stranger horses we expect them to behave themselves and not give Kim any trouble."

Blue wandered off to the picket line where the other horses were. Though only he and Rags were speaking horses, he had found he could communicate ideas to the other horses fairly well. It helped that they considered Kim, Abasio, and Xulai far preferable to their former owners, who enjoyed whipping and spurring and jerking on reins for no reason. This came to Blue through some kind of unspoken horse-to-horse communication. Herd-com, something like the hive-com bees do. When he told Rags what was going on, she joined him and they returned to Abasio together.

"The big Griffin is hurt? Who did that?" she asked Abasio.

"The male Griffin we've been worried about, Rags. There really is one. Bear says he's black with sort of bronze edges to the scales on his belly."

"I never noticed scales on the one we saw."

"It could be a sex-linked characteristic, I suppose. Or it could be a different genetic line. Bear says the male has scales beginning on the throat, between the front legs and continuing down the belly. He's huge and extremely violent, and surprisingly, he actually has a name— has had, since he was hatched. He's called Despos! Bear quotes the Griffin—ah, Sun-wings—as saying Despos was created when most of the other Griffins were, both the females and other males. All but him reached a maturity when they stopped growing, but Despos did not. He never has. Now he's of a size and temperament . . ."

"Knew a stallion like that once," said Rags. "Big old bastard! No lineage to brag about, no form, no grace, but oh, my mama-mare-on-grass, he was big! Huge! They had to get rid a' him. He killed mares, one right after the other. Had no sense, none. Battered 'em!"

"Why'n't you an' Xulai just kill this big one?" asked Bear, from behind them. "I know those Tingawans have weapons that'll do it. I heard about 'em."

"He's the only male left," said Abasio without turning around. "He's killed all the others. The females don't live forever. Without young, the Griffins become legend."

"What they was to begin with," muttered Bear.

"Well, according to *your* legend," said Xulai from behind them, "you should be living in a little house in the woods with your wife and one child, sleeping each in his own bed at night, sitting each in chairs at a table in the mornings eating breakfast porridge out of bowls, and receiving gratuitous visits from an unconscionably perky human child with terrible clothes sense and no appreciation of territorial boundaries!"

Bear stared at her, the tip of his quivering pink tongue protruding slightly. "Where'd you hear that?"

"It's a well-known human-ish legend. According to Willum, all children know it just as they know that Farmer Donnal has different kinds of animals and Lunnon Tressel's fallen down. I'm surprised you haven't learned it so you can tell it to your cubs. If you have cubs, though I understand boar bears refuse to take any responsibility for their children. That may be legend, too. For all I know, bears never were natural. Maybe all of you were man-made!"

"Well, WE know different," snarled Bear. *From now on, he would make a point of talking to young bears! Even the she ones!*

Xulai put her hand on Abasio's shoulder. "What's all this noise about your going off without me?"

He took the hand in his own. "Bear brings us word that our Griffin, the mother Griffin, has been badly hurt by the big male. She's down and can't fly—her wing's ripped, according to them. She can't walk either. She left Willum, Needly, and the little Griffin holed up some distance from there, and they're all alone with no one to protect them."

"That doesn't answer my question!"

He shook his head at her. "Xulai, let's not waste time arguing, or even discussing. Neither of us will accept leaving Willum and Needly up there on their own! And we can't risk our sea-babies' lives by taking them up there! Equally, we can't take the very grave risk to our babies if we leave them with Kim while both of us go find the children. Even though they're almost weaned, what would happen to the babies if Kim were accosted by an accusation of Lorpers?"

Her eyes filled. "I suppose you're going."

"What would *you* have me do?"

"Oh, go, go, Abasio, of course you have to go. What else!"

"That's rather what I thought," he said, putting his arms around her.

She pushed him away and wiped her face, muttering, "I shouldn't even question your going. It's not that big a problem! I used the talker last evening, and Precious Wind told me they'd already entered Artemisia. She'll be here day after tomorrow!" She looked up. Above the peaks, a crescent moon mocked them with a pale, disembodied grin. "No, it's almost moonset. She'll be here tomorrow."

His face lighted up. "Then you and Kim won't be alone more than a few hours! Knowing Precious Wind, she'll be here as quickly as she can. Don't move from here! We'll keep this place here as our meeting place. When we've found the children and done what we can among the Griffins, we'll return here. If you all leave here before we get back, ask Precious Wind to leave a few people here to meet us, or carry messages or whatever."

"If the big Griffin can't move, what will you do?"

He stared into darkness. "I don't know, Xulai. I truly don't know. I'm hoping maybe she isn't that badly hurt, that we can hunt for her and get water to her while she heals."

"That may be overly optimistic."

"Well, you know me. Always look on the shiny side." He tried to smile, without great success.

"Ha."

He drew himself up and attempted to look capable: half the battle, looking capable. "I do know one thing for sure. If I could move her, Artemisia would be the best place I could pick for the care and feeding of a large, wounded mythical beast. And her child. And if she can't be moved, then Artemisia is the most likely place to find healers who will go to her and help cure her. When I know what the situation is, I can have someone—Bear or Coyote maybe—come here and guide any willing helpers back where the Griffin is, hopefully a healer of some kind . . ."

"You would really need several people left here, then. To carry messages and so forth."

"Any help would be welcome." He tried a confident grin, unsuccessfully.

She said, "You haven't noticed but I am helping. I began this conversation with help in mind. You've forgotten *ul xaolat*, haven't you?"

He stared into the darkness, momentarily gone elsewhere, mouthing *uhl SHAH-oo-laht*. Then—of course, *ul xaolat*! *The thing master:* the hunter-protector device they had used during their travel to Saltgosh; that Xulai had used when she jumped to Saltgosh to warn them about the marauders. He'd become so accustomed to using it as either personal jumper or defensive weapon, he'd forgotten it could also move *big* things! He had forgotten all about that particular attribute! *It could move big things!*

"Do you think it could move a full-sized Griffin?" he asked, wonderingly.

She made a face. "I have been told if the holder of *ul xaolat* puts his hand on something, anything, the device will move that thing. It could probably move a mountain, given sufficient power. Moving a Griffin should be no problem. Distance is the problem, the thing only jumps about a day's foot journey at a time, and since several people now have the devices, they're all calling on the same power source. Depending on available power, the device may not always be able to make even that distance—especially with a heavy load! To be safe, I would say half a day's foot travel maximum with a Griffin. If it's a two-day journey, it will take four or five jumps to bring you back, and you will need to select and record locations on your way there."

"One each evening and each noon? Through the forest?"

She considered former journeys and forced marches that had been off-road, through woods. "Yes, noon and evening. The device should be able to jump you a half day's journey each time with no problem."

He frowned. One had to picture a destination clearly in order for the device to move one to that place. One destination could be easy, but a whole line of them . . . "I don't know if I can remember . . ."

"I know, I can't either! That's always been the problem with the thing!" She laughed. "It's easy enough to go from the gates of a city to a temple on the hill, and from there to the ship at the shore. But on a desert? Going from one clump of cactus to a very slightly different clump of cactus half a day's journey away? I could never do it more than one jump. I couldn't even do it twice. Even Precious Wind told me she had trouble with more than two.

"So, around the time I was in Tingawa having the babies and you were there being bewildered by fatherhood, the Tingawan technicians were modifying the *xaolats*."

"I wasn't exactly bewildered . . ."

"You looked bewildered at the time. For days and days. I told Father we couldn't possibly travel until you stopped looking that way. I was afraid you'd fall overboard in your bemusement."

He rubbed his stubbled face, wearily fighting laughter. His grandfather had had a saying about wives: *Any man who's been married more than once gets into heaven automatically, 'cause he's already fully accustomed to hell.* He was not going to explain that to Xulai! He put his arms around her instead, trying rather vainly to focus his own thoughts. "Xulai, are you now, amid intermittent and lengthy circumlocutions, telling me that your 'thing master' has been modified so that remembering destinations is not necessary?"

"Yes, it has been so modified." She relaxed against him. "Now it takes hardly any brain at all."

"Oh, good! Imagine what Willum would do with an *ul xaolat*!"

She shuddered and stepped away. "We haven't used it on this trip except to provide passive protection for us and the wagon and horses, and I honestly hadn't thought about using it as a mover. I didn't even use it as a weapon when those . . . giants came after us."

"For good reason."

Xulai went on: "Well, yes. But, I didn't think about *ul xaolat*'s other functions until those men captured Kim, and that reminded me I could jump to Saltgosh. However! I do have one of the modified ones that will take an imprint of the selected locations on the way, and when you want to return, *ul xaolat* will automatically jump from location to location in reverse."

"Is it very complicated?" At the moment he did not believe he could manage anything more complicated than . . . his razor. If that. Maybe.

"They made it as simple as they could. I'll show you how. And, if you're going to take the *thing master,* you'll also have a weapon."

Abasio shook his head. "No, Xulai, you'll need to keep that!"

"*I don't plan on killing anything this morning!* Precious Wind will be here very soon, and she has at least one *ul xaolat* with her, complete with the same offensive capabilities this one has. I can move the wagon and the horses and all our clutter farther back into the woods before you leave. We'll wait for Precious Wind to arrive before we come out of hiding. She says she's coming with a good group of people from Artemisia!"

He could think of no argument to that. Certainly he couldn't move Sun-wings by himself. What would it take to move a beast that size? Not counting the wings. He'd need a wagon with at least six sets of wheels; the wagon would weigh more than the load, and it would take at least four teams to haul it! And a decent road! No such wagon, no such teams, no such road. No way of getting any.

He put his arms around Xulai and held her very close. When young, he had longed for adventure and travel. He had since learned that adventure and travel usually meant leaving loved ones, and leaving them was often a dangerous thing to do. He hated being separated from Xulai, from the babies! Olly's departure had taught him that separations can be forever. The thought left him shaking. When he did think of Olly, the memory made him feel . . . like some goblet of very thin glass that reverberated to particular sounds and was likely to shatter from its own empathetic echo.

As with Xulai! When Xulai fretted, he fretted. When she feared, he feared for her. He had absurd notions of somehow keeping their vibrations from touching one another, because if she were in danger, he might be immobilized by his own fear for her. And it didn't stop there: Willum and Needly had somehow been grafted into his protective . . . area. He hadn't even realized it until now.

He could actually understand those lone men of the north. It was more comfortable to be alone, with no one at risk but himself. None of that terrible fear of separation . . . Yet, no matter what Xulai was up to at any given time, he preferred to be where she was. Even if what she was doing at the time was fuming at him. Fuming was as natural to Xulai as it was to a volcano. One simply learned to ignore the scent of sulfur and the heat. Unless, of course, the heat was . . . ah!

Here she was, her face nestled into his neck, her lips moving. She held him closely for a long, silent moment, feeling the thud of his heart, the breath moving in his lungs. At one time she had tried to disdain her feelings for Abasio, whatever they were, because she was annoyed that he and she had been meant for each other, meant in the sense of livestock, bred for the purpose. Sometimes, like now, she had to admit those who had done it had done it wonderfully well.

When she could forget her annoyance at being fiddled with, she could take a good deal of pleasure in life—or in those *infrequent bits of it not totally taken up with the task that took virtually every instant of their time and effort.* Enjoyment in those infrequent bits was a rare and marvelous thing. She kissed his neck again. Such a kiss would ordinarily be a prelude to lovemaking and they had no time for that!

She pushed him away with a final touch of their lips and said in a not-quite-calm voice: "I'll make up a packet of things to take with you. If the creature is wounded, you'll need some things to stop bleeding, to ease pain, to sew wounds closed if they're not too deep."

Such things might be helpful in treating Sun-wings, though the word "wounded" was not specific enough to describe the extent of injuries. How could one splint the leg of something that size? When Xulai had put a packet together from among their supplies, she took *ul xaolat* from the secure cubby where she kept it and went over its workings with Abasio.

"In the pack I made up for you, there's a complete set of directions for using the *thing master*. If you need some of the *things* it's the master of—the hunter, the defender, the collector, and so forth—the directions are there: pages of them. You should need only the ax master on this trip. You need it to make clearings—"

"To make clearings?"

"Clearings, Abasio. We've done this before. On your way back you don't want to land on top of a bunch of pine trees, or with your body half inside one of them! As you go you need to make . . . landing sites, clearings, every half-day journey, big enough for all of you and Sun-wings. They are the places you will hop to on your return journey, one right after the other.

"This is the new, improved *ul xaolat*. It will simply do what you tell it to. Tell it you're going to start a series and give the series a name. We'll call it 'Finding Sun-wings.'" The device made a beep, and a mechanical little voice said, "Recorded."

Xulai said, "That name is your code word for this particular journey. The first thing you do is clear a landing site and tell the device to record the site as Site One in Finding Sun-wings. When you stop each noon and evening, make another space and record it as Site Two, Site Three, and so on until you get there. If you forget the number, ask the device. When the first site is the right size, tell the device to make each succeeding site that same size. It has to be big enough for the whole assemblage: you, the children, the baby Griffin, the mother Griffin, and all the creatures you're traveling with.

"When you return, you have some choices. One of you could probably do the whole trip in one jump. Moving all of you at once, you'll need to make shorter jumps. You're limited by available power. So, to bring everyone back, you say, 'Finding Sun-wings, *series* return.' It'll jump you back in short hops, through the series, but you'll need to push the red button or say 'continue' at each site. It will not run the whole series."

"Why not?"

"If someone was waiting at Site Four to tell you Site Three was an ambush, you would not like to land in the middle of it. If you heard, for example, that someone was waiting to ambush you at Site Three, you could skip over that site."

"If there was enough power."

"You can always reduce the load: only half of you make the jump from Site Four to Site Two; then you jump back and bring the other half. If you wanted to make notes about each site, you do that by merely asking the device to record what you're saying about it. Then some time in the future, when you might be traveling alone, you could go to any one of them by number."

"By saying, 'Finding Sun-wings Site Three,' for instance."

"Exactly. Or ask the device to remind you what you said about each site. Now listen carefully. Bear says Sun-wings is more or less in the middle of a clearing. When you get there, record the site immediately as 'Finding Sun-wings, end.' That way, if you see a dangerous situation or need to back off and regroup, or if someone was left behind, you could go back.

"Also, if you push the button and you don't move immediately, it's because the device can't find sufficient power. Don't move around once you've pushed the button. Tell everyone with you so they're prepared to stay quiet and in touch. Whoever is touching you is being touched by other people, and so on. It should take only a minute or so—though I admit that's a wild guess, since I've never tried to move a Griffin. If you simply sit there and sit there and don't move, after a while you can say 'cancel this move.' Then try again in a few minutes. It's better than someone moving impatiently and getting left behind."

While Xulai moved the wagon and other things and creatures, he went through the routine several times. He wrote it down and put the paper in his pocket. He packed one change of clothing in case what he was wearing got soaked or ruined. Blankets, too. In case the children didn't have any. Bear could carry a pack without even noticing it. While Xulai watched, he directed the device to call up one of its "things" to make a sizable clearing, slightly up the hill and well hidden from the road. He thought of his previous use of the thing as having happened decades ago. Actually, it had only been a couple of years, and it came back to him as soon as the shimmering "thing" appeared under the trees.

One had only to tell the various devices what to do, which he did. "Make a clearing here large enough to hold a big Griffin, one little Griffin, two horses, a bear, a coyote, and three or four people."

He heard Xulai scream, but it was too late. A tree came down so close to her face that she was almost brushed by one of the smaller branches. He had said "here" instead of "there, around that rock" as he had intended to do. The device had not only cut the trees, it had removed them to the edges and arranged them as a border around the empty space, the fallen logs neatly trimmed of side branches.

Xulai said, in a very chilly voice, "Next time please specify something in the middle of the space, Abasio. Tell it to make a clearing around the rock. It's programmed not to hurt any sentient creature, but it can certainly give this one a heart attack!"

"I forgot that part." He was snarling at himself. This whole thing would have been easier if they hadn't wakened him in the middle of the night . . .

They were soon assembled. Xulai stepped well away from them while Abasio recorded the location they were starting from. They had already said good-bye, and Xulai watched wordlessly as Abasio and the horses walked off into the darkness, following their guides through the woods in a direction that Bear had described as "a little bit that-way from that-way." He had waved his his front paws to illustrate a little south of west.

She comforted herself with the idea that Bear and Coyote had traveled for the equivalent of two travel days to get here; that they should find Sun-wings by tomorrow evening; that they should find the children shortly after that; that they would return quickly by the same route and would not end up any farther from Artemisia than they were now. When they were out of hearing distance, however, she went into the wagon, where she let herself cry quietly without disturbing her sea-children at all. Since they had stopped needing to be fed during the night, they slept all night, every night, like perfect angels. No. More like hibernating bears! Hibernating . . . dolphins? Right now she found herself resenting it, regardless of how silly it was. They could at least wake up and distract her a little!

Finally, knowing sleep was impossible, she made tea for herself and Kim. He had spent enough time with Xulai that he did not attempt to comfort her. Precious Wind herself had sat down with him over a glass of wine to tell him about young mothers. Precious Wind had never been a mother, and Kim had had the temerity to wonder what made her the expert. Her advice had been simple and useful, however, and he had followed it.

Precious Wind had said young mothers are frequently under a lot of stress, usually because they are tired. In traditional surroundings, with older women to cluck and cuddle, the mother did not get so tired, but sometimes such helpers were lacking. Therefore, young mothers should be helped in whatever way possible, but not lectured or argued with.

Kim had no intention of arguing, and throughout the trip he had remained fully alert to provide help whenever he saw a chance. He was grateful this morning (though the sun had not yet risen) to find that nothing was required except to build up the fire and sit silently beside it with a mug of tea, sip, sip, sip, sigh, murmuring assents or negations as seemed required by the monologue Xulai was uttering, and refilling their mugs occasionally. Sip, sigh, refill, nod in agreement, sip again, until the sun rose.

As soon as it was light enough to see what they were doing, and after checking any visible portion of the road up the mountain to be sure they were unobserved, they made the wagon even less visible. The wagon itself was a tree-bark brown. With the shutters closed over the window, it faded into the background of trees. A sapling or two draped over the top hid it from the sky. Ever since their visits from the Griffin, they had been very conscious of being visible from the sky.

The final step was to obliterate the wagon tracks and picket the horses even farther from the road. They were somewhat handicapped by not having Blue and Rags available to help. The horses they had "rescued" were willing, but they had to be led instead of told. Finally they scattered the ashes from their fire and covered their own and the horses' tracks before setting themselves to "keeping busy," in order, as Xulai announced, to avoid useless fretting. Kim had such complete faith in Abasio that he hadn't been fretting, but keeping busy was always a good idea.

All three of the human adults on this journey had become experts at busy-ness. There were always small things that hadn't been done because there had been no time. Mending a pair of Abasio's trousers where he had snagged them on a thorny tree was not done because they smelled like him or felt like him, of course not, merely because they needed doing, as did fixing new spokes into the broken wagon wheel that they had replaced with a spare, and replacing the iron tires and greasing the axles. Since they would not build up the fire, as they did not want to be located by the smoke, they ate cold bread and cheese from the stores, followed by chewy slices of dried apple. Bailai and Gailai had applesauce and eggs that had been boiled well before dawn, before the fire was drowned.

Everything was done in bits and pieces, between sessions of tending babies, but none of it served to make them any less alert than they already were. Whenever they went out on the road to look eastward, however, they found it empty; its only traffic the mad darting of ubiquitous long-eared hares who seemingly had no homes and were always on their way somewhere else. One found their babies under sagebrush, as long as one's finger, fully furred and open-eyed, silent and virtually invisible, where Mama had left them to await her return. Xulai always wondered if the hare had an *ul xaolat* in her brain, one that could tell one particular sagebrush from every other possible sagebrush, one's own hare-baby from any other possible hare-baby.

Xulai hoped she and Kim and the children were themselves invisible, though they could not achieve silence. All day the trees resounded to "Dada? Willum? Eedy? Mama . . ." Yet again, Xulai remembered with regret those not-long-gone days when they could not speak at all. Of course, even then they could scream.

She and Kim had agreed that if they spotted someone inimical approaching, the babies would go into their baskets, into the wagon, under the bed, with all available bedding draped over the bed to muffle their noise. With Xulai close beside, of course, to keep them company. Xulai prayed it would not be necessary. She also had some drops to put in their mouths that would put them to sleep, but Precious Wind had said they were for emergencies only, not something that should be routinely used.

"You got any beer?" asked Kim when she mentioned this to him.

"Why?" asked Xulai.

" 'Cause if you really want them quiet, you can give them some beer. Willum said that's what they do with teething babies in Gravysuck. It makes them sleepy."

"Does it work?"

"He says it doesn't hurt them any, so long as you don't do it every time they start yelling 'cause then they get used to it and it doesn't work anymore."

Xulai spent the next while wondering what among their stores might have a similar effect, deciding that one of the jugs of cider had possibly turned into something else, as sometimes happened. If not yet turned, it was on the verge of it. It didn't matter, however. When she offered it, the babies preferred to spew it widely and then laugh like . . . like ravens making fun of the world!

Ravens. Xulai felt an overwhelming sadness. When the world was underwater, what would ravens do? Magpies? Eagles? Butterflies? She caught herself weeping and told herself it was over the inexorable fate of butterflies.

CHAPTER 9

Finding Sun-wings

NEAR THE BOTTOM OF THE HILL BELOW THEIR cave, Willum, Needly, and Dawn-song had turned downstream. Tree growth near the water was thick, so they paralleled the flow at some little distance, where they did not have to push through undergrowth. The forest was mixed, conifers and broad-leaved trees, these now bare. The ground was carpeted with leaves. They had filled their water bottles but drank from the stream, Dawn-song lapping water like a cat. "Y'don't drink from t'bottle when y'r near water," said Willum, as though quoting regulations. " 'Less you refill it right then. Then, when y'need it, y'll have y'r bottle full."

"Yes, Willum," said Needly, who had never thought of that particular rule but believed it was probably sensible, for all that. She had come to believe that Willum had a very good brain that had not been used for very much. She had come to believe, also, that this was not out of laziness, but simply because there had been very little in Gravysuck requiring much thought. All duties and problems had been ritualized in Gravysuck. Everything was done as it had always been done. Why think? It had all been decided long ago.

Even accidents and disasters had their rules and systems. If there were a flood, someone would recite Great-Grandfather Omnuk's solution to the flood of his time. Each disaster had its legendary cure.

Chickens were plucked with the size of the feathers in mind, the little, downy ones into this sack being kept for coverlets and pillows. Goose feathers, the same, though more rarely. Goose quills for pens. Of course, one did not want to kill a good goose, one that laid plenty of eggs and hatched them well, but poultry had to be limited to those that could be fed in the wintertime. Chickens liked meat, too: grasshoppers, crickets, all kinds of little creatures, including tiny snakes and lizards. *Little snakes and lizards, fillin' chickens' gizzards.* A child's rhyme. True, for all that.

Pigs, cows, sheep, and goats had their own systems. Someone in or near each village or among several villages had to keep a bull; someone a stallion; someone else a ram or two; someone a couple of billygoats. The same for boar pigs. Each of these male animals had one or two young ones picked to succeed him. As individual male animals aged, someone or some ones, in conference, selected a few males from the spring crop as possible successors, to be the bulls, stallions, boars, bucks, and rams of the future. A family could winter only the animals it could feed, so the keeping of the male breeders was divided up: this family kept the boars, that family the bull, that family the billygoats (because they lived somewhat away from the others where the smell was less noticeable). Those who housed and fed the breeders were paid a breeding fee to cover the cost of the food and care of an animal they all needed but that gave no food in return.

Willum knew all these things in all their slight variations depending upon weather and temperature and availability of labor. And he knew the shape of the land. And he knew how to mark a trail so they would not get lost in the going. Yes. He had a good brain. Though he crowed considerably, he was not *entirely* cockerel. So thinking, Needly smiled wearily to herself as they trailed easterly down the little stream.

At noon they had come to the place where the other stream came in from the south. Then they had to climb upstream, though it wasn't a steep slope. From a high point, looking south, Willum was dismayed to see canyon beyond canyon, vertical walls, hideous depths, one beyond the other, as far as he could see. He prayed they would not have to go that far! By midafternoon, they had reached the canyon, and Dawnsong was growing very tired. Despite a generous dose of genes from big cats, Griffins were not walkers, or trotters, and certainly not gallopers—

not for very long or very far. Needly suggested they stop for a while. She removed the blankets to let Dawn-song drink deeply from the stream and take slices of bloody meat from Needly's hand, to roll in the grass, wings held tight to her little body. Willum, whose energy seemed inexhaustible, went to the top of the nearest ridge and looked around.

He came galloping back. "That stone bridge is just up ahead, not far, but the middle's broken out of it. We can be there before long."

"We're going to let Dawn-song have a little nap," said Needly. "Just a few minutes. She's not a packhorse, and she's not used to walking very far either."

Willum subsided. He sorted his pack and repacked it. He took off his shoes, shook the pebbles out of them, took off his socks, turned them inside out, put them back on, and then the shoes, which he carefully relaced to make the laces the same length at both ends. He went into the woods and came back with a walking staff cut from a sapling and neatly rounded at one end. At which point Needly woke the Griffin child and they began again.

Willum had been right. The stone bridge was not far up the canyon. The walls at that point looked too vertical to scale easily, but there was an easier place just beside them, so they climbed out on the left side, the side where they should find Sun-wings. Here they were on rock, uneven, sharp, difficult to cross. Dawn-song struggled, Needly walking beside her, helping her place her feet. She made a mental note to create some slippers for the little Griffin. When they came opposite the stone bridge, Needly shook her head. They would have wasted time if they had come this far on the other side of the canyon, counting on the "bridge" to get across to the eastern side. It was only half a bridge, or two-quarters of one, one-quarter at each end. The central half had fallen, perhaps not long before, but long enough that the ends had weathered. More of Silver-shanks's malice? Probably. And it was malice. Bred in the egg.

They went on, paralleling the canyon as its edge continued almost to the ridgeline before them, keeping watch off to the left for the place Silver-shanks had described. Nothing. They went all the way to the ridgeline, and once there, stopped, horrified. In a clearing below them, Sun-wings lay, wounded, prone, legs splayed, her head lying limply on the ground.

Without any warning at all, Dawn-song took off, half running, half fluttering, calling, "Mama, Mama, Mama, we're here," as she plunged down the slope. It was clear of most tall growth. The few shrubs she encountered were brushed aside.

Needly had followed, more slowly. She, too, was very tired. She saw Sun-wings raise her head, look dazedly around her. There was blood on her wings. She saw her child, and then . . . her face changed. Her beak gaped wide.

"No, no, no, it's a trap," she cried. "No, child. Go back, it's a trap."

As it was, for all three of them.

IN THE GROVE WEST OF Artemisia, as Xulai was preparing their evening meal, she missed Kim and went looking for him. He was out on the road, standing very tall and peering into the east. "People on horseback coming," he called at last. "Enough to raise some dust. What do you want me to do?"

She walked out to the road, looked at the considerable dust cloud to the east. "Saddle the fastest horse and stay near it, out of sight. When the people get here, if all is well, I'll call you by name and you can join us. If I don't call you or call the wrong name, stay out of sight and watch what happens. If it seems needed and you're sure you're not seen, circle south, then back to the road and go on toward Artemisia for help. Precious Wind is on that road; the only question is how far. Take all the horses you can manage if you can do it easily. Otherwise, leave them."

She, meantime, stayed by the fire, tending her stew of lentils, onions, and smoked sausage. She would drown the fire in a moment, as soon as the stew was warm. She batted at her ear, aware of a gnatlike buzzing, realizing after a moment that it was the buzzing of the far-talker. She went back among the trees to the wagon and reached inside the door, where the device lived.

"Xulai," it said. "It's me, Precious Wind. Last landmark I saw was a hill named the Devil's Ah, at the end of the canyon. Where are you?"

At which Xulai screamed a welcome, suggested several mutually contradictory courses of action, grabbed up the babies, and ran back to the road, standing there as a distant dust cloud came slowly closer, resolving itself eventually into several wagonloads of people and five or six dozen riders. Two horses cantered forward, and their female riders dismounted at her side—Precious Wind and a woman she did not know.

"Arakny," said Precious Wind, introducing the dignified, slightly graying woman dressed in one of the fringed leather dresses the woman of Artemisia wore on ceremonial occasions. "Arakny, this woman with tears running down her face is my dear friend Xulai. The man over there coming out of the woods is Kim, a countryman of mine who has obviously recognized we are friends. Though where Abasio is, I do not know."

"I shouldn't greet you like this," sobbed Xulai. "Arakny, Abasio has told me about you. I apologize for being so . . . emotional, but I'm so glad that reinforcements have arrived! It has been a difficult trip, Precious Wind, and just now I'm terribly worried about the children."

"What's wrong with the babies?" cried Precious Wind, coming forward to look at them more closely.

"The babies are fine, of course. I mean the other children . . ."

"Xulai, give me that child! Bailai, is it? What a nice jacket you have, Bailai! You remember Aunty Presh, don't you! And you're getting so big!" To Xulai, "You say the wagon is in cover of the woods? And the horses? *Never mind,* tell me later. Let me get our people settled; there are enough of us to be quite safe making a fire near the pond there. We'll put on the kettles, and while we're doing that, perhaps you can tell us about these *other* children . . . ?"

All of which was more or less the order of things that were told, partly with Kim's help: Willum, who was off to see the world; Needly, whose father had sold her to a man who kills children; a Griffin named Sun-wings, who has a child named Dawn-song; both of whom were off in the forest, separated because Sun-wings had been wounded. And, add to that, a male Griffin, almost a dragon, huge, that they didn't know the location of, though he should be headed northeast as far as northeast went, if what Sun-wings had told Coyote was true! It all poured out, in and out of order.

Eventually Arakny said, "So Abasio has gone off with Bear and Coyote to help the wounded Griffin who is somewhere up there," and she waved in the general direction of the entire western part of the continent. "And your two foster children are up there, also, heaven knows where, with another Griffin, a child Griffin. And the large male Griffin is far gone in blood lust? And one of the children is a strangely silver-haired child who seems remarkably adult for her age. Is that about it?"

Xulai could only nod. That was about it.

"You see why I felt we should hurry!" said Precious Wind to Arakny.

"You knew about all this?" said Arakny reprovingly. "I'm not sure we even brought enough supplies."

"No, Arakny, I didn't *know about it*. I suppose I *knew of it*. Knew, that is, that something was wrong! I've known Xulai since she was born. One gets feelings about close friends and family. And then too, she and Abasio have a history of collecting these *situations* without at all meaning to . . ."

The dignified woman nodded. "Well then, I'm glad we hurried." She turned to Xulai, smiling. "She has driven us like a slave master, getting the group together to come meet you. She was sure you needed help."

"Oh, yes we do," Xulai admitted. "Should we go back to Artemisia, do you think?"

Precious Wind shook her head. "Before we think of returning anywhere, I think everyone needs food and sleep and consideration of what's going on." She turned to her companion. "Arakny, your folk are standing about over there waiting for your orders. Would you approve of our setting up camp here with Xulai? We're not going to go off on any rescue missions until tomorrow, and perhaps not then. If Abasio is as competent as when I last saw him, he may well solve this dilemma. He has this Bear and Coyote with him? And your *ul xaolat*? Bear and Coyote, I am very, very eager to meet. Arakny, didn't I understand that Wide Mountain Mother met one of them, long ago?"

"Indeed," said Arakny, her lips twisting to keep from grinning. Meeting a speaking bear had been one of the few occasions when Wide Mountain Mother's imposing poise had been severely tested.

"You haven't brought your wolves?" asked Xulai, apropos of absolutely nothing.

Precious Wind shook her head. "No. One of the men's lodges has more or less adopted them in Artemisia. Quite happily. They all go hunting together."

Within a short time, a camp had been established; the horses were brought back to graze nearer the far end of the pond; and Precious

Wind's group of men and women had surrounded their area with small campfires, as though they were building a fortification. Kettles were hung over fires. Xulai walked into the camp to introduce the babies, only to have them seized from her immediately and passed around like a favorite dessert, everyone, male or female, wanting a taste. After an initial hesitation, Gailai and Bailai decided they had gone to aunt-and-uncle heaven and spent the next couple of hours being cuddled, dandled, and fed bits of mashed this and mashed that before each was given a nice, greasy chicken-leg bone to gum happily as they moved from lap to lap.

When Xulai mentioned that they needed their "trousers" washed out, a group of women accompanied her to see how this procedure was accomplished, with a good many "Isn't that well done" remarks about the sleep garments Bertram had designed. Xulai, restored to equanimity by companionship, noted the interest gladly. Precious Wind regarded the Artemisians as *preferred stock* and had hoped these people might provide a good many first-generation sea-dwellers!

When the babies finally slept, Xulai was introduced to other people whom Abasio had mentioned, and when she told them of Bertram's books, Arakny's eyes lit up.

"That's another reason we hurried. The weather should hold long enough for half a dozen of us and one wagon to get over the pass and down the far side as far as Gravysuck. The people in Tingawa decided it made more sense for someone to go over there from Artemisia than to send people all the way from Tingawa. We have a small, portable machine that Tingawa sent to us. All we need to do is put our little conveyer belt together, have someone stack books at one end and take them off at the other. Of course, if there are as many books as you say, it will take us well into winter, at least. Once we have everything in the library, we'll duplicate it a few times here, then Precious Wind says it needs to go to Tingawa to be duplicated there!" She beamed with excited pleasure. "We haven't had any new books in a generation or more!" Her face calmed, and she shook her head a few times, smiling at nothing.

Then she frowned, looked perplexed, turned to Xulai, and said, quite suddenly, "Xulai, did I simply not understand the core of this Griffin story, or have you not told us? You have not mentioned why the Sun-wings creature took the children in the first place."

And, of course, that was the core of the whole matter, which Kim spoke of, and Xulai spoke of, and the babies, wakened by all the noise, also spoke of when they heard Willum and Needly's names: "Illum, Illum, Illum. Eedy, Eedy, Eedy."

"So your children are actually second-generation sea-children," murmured Arakny, spoon poised, waiting for Gailai to either swallow or spit out the bit of potato she had been given. "Do you intimate that the first-generation changers are not so attractive?"

"I think it would depend on your point of view," said Xulai a little stiffly. "Having eight sinuous, sucker-laden, leaden-gray arms enables one to do remarkable things, really."

"What would the Griffins change into?"

"I have no idea, nor do they. Whatever race of creatures did this first, that race needed an interim generation as a logical transition step. That race, humans, had to be able to recruit others. We could not travel overland if we had a purely aquatic shape nor could we demonstrate the change if we had a purely terrestrial one. We need both. The sea-children should never need to travel on land, so they don't need the interim generation. I'm reasonably sure all that was planned in advance. Abasio and I were not given a choice." She paused. Whatever she said next, Precious Wind would remember forever . . . She breathed deeply and went on: " . . . but whatever it might have been, we would have chosen to live through it together. Having that choice was the important thing!

"The Griffins do not want their race to die out, any more than we do. They believe they too need to be offered a sea life and we understand why that longing among Griffins is even more urgent than ours! You and Precious Wind and I will be gone long before the waters have completely risen, we will not be personally faced with drowning or watching our children drown, but when the waters have covered everything, Sun-wings and her child will probably both still be alive! They were designed to live, they have said, two thousand years or more! And not only Griffins want a sea-form. As they left, I heard Coyote and Bear asking Abasio if Tingawa was doing anything for bears, anything for coyotes to make them seaworthy."

Xulai rubbed her face tiredly, feeling the grime on her skin. It had been too long since Saltgosh's bathhouse. She no doubt smelled of travel and dust and sweat and horse. She stood up, shook herself. "It all makes me feel tired and inadequate. I think of the thousand years the Tingawans and the Sea King spent on creating my mother, Precious Wind. All those generations of breeding and testing and breeding, generation after generation, each human generation being only fifteen or sixteen years to sexual maturity. The Griffins take three centuries or more! There isn't time for enough generations to be born to do it the way it was done for us!"

"And they have threatened you?" Arakny commented.

"Yes. Sun-wings says if we don't provide for them, too, they'll call on their sea-living friends to kill every sea-child we have! Has the Sea King ever said anything to my grandfather about man-created sea monsters?"

"Kraken is the only sea-monster name I know."

Xulai shook her head. "Kraken is the Sea King himself. Our children are, in a sense, his children. His genetics are included in us, first generation, at least, and I can't believe he would destroy us or them."

"It's not a question that we can solve, certainly," said Arakny. "We will stay encamped here for a time, at least until Abasio returns. If some emergency arises that Wide Mountain Mother needs to know of, I'm sure Precious Wind can use her device to go back and inform her. She already knows about the sea-children and is eager to see them."

"We have that whole bunch of extra horses, too," offered Kim.

And that, of course, involved the telling of still another story.

RATHER THAN RIDE, ABASIO CHOSE to walk with Bear and Coyote. The trees were close together and the branches were low. It would be all too easy to be swept onto the ground if Blue or Rags misjudged the distance between their backs and the branches. When they came to stretches of ground that were open to the sky, he climbed onto Blue's back and let the horse carry him until they entered forest again. The sun rose and they went on until noon, then stopped for food and a brief nap. Coyote woke them at midafternoon. They went on, holding to their direction, stopping now and then to have a conversation with some other creature, usually invisible in the foliage or up a tree. A tribe of squirrels accompanied them for a long distance, turning them over to an owl as dusk approached. They followed her until it got too dark to see, then stopped and made a quick camp, eating quickly and lying down to sleep almost immediately afterward. Bear, Coyote, and the horses had decided to alternate a watch throughout the night.

" 'Basio not gonna watch?" Coyote commented.

"Let 'im alone," said Bear. "He's worryin' himself sick about these children they had with 'em. Prob'ly han't slept good for some time."

Blue said softly, "Took you two days to get down where he was. Take us at least that to get back. You think the big one's alive?"

"We did half a day last night. We did almost a full today today. I think she's still alive. I think the woods'd know if she died."

"Critters, you mean."

"An' trees. They know quite a bit."

"Trees do?"

"Sure. They just think real slow. Takes them a year to think one thought. Like bears do when it's winter and they're asleep. One thought's about all you can think, all winter."

"What do trees think about?" asked Coyote.

"Everything," murmured Bear. "Rivers, ponds, squirrels, birds, saplings, sun, wind. Everything there is. You ever notice how the whole world sometimes seems to . . . have one huge thought? As though every bird and every animal is all at once part of one huge word? Ever notice that?"

Coyote started to say no, but as he thought about it, there had been times. Certain times. There on the prairie, when he had been much younger, when the whole world had almost said something to him. If it took trees a year to think one thought, what did it take the world to come up with a word? And who would listen to it if the world spoke? Could be that mankind was too short-lived to even hear the world's remarks. He sighed. Well, he had the last watch. When on watch, he preferred to move around, so he spent the last few hours of darkness listening to the world, guessing at all the things trees thought about . . . supposedly!

IN THE CAMP OF THE Artemisians, Xulai, sleeping in the wagon, was awakened by someone putting a hand on her shoulder. "Wha . . ."

"Xulai, shhh. It's Precious Wind. Arakny had four sentinels posted a good way down the road east. A couple of them just rode in. There's a troop of armed men, horsemen, and wagons coming slowly down the road, torchbearers out front. They came from the direction of Catland, and from what one of the sentinels managed to overhear, their queen is with them. Arakny thinks Tingawans—you and Kim and I—ought to stay well out of sight. Kim's just outside. What do you think we should do about your horses?"

"Have Kim help you put them in with yours. Drive the herd out of sight and put some good bowmen to guard it. From what Abasio has said about gangers, they would be likely to steal the entire herd, so they're better out of sight. This wagon's well hidden, I think." She struggled to think what Abasio might have done. "Abasio didn't want to be seen by any gangers, but they wouldn't recognize me or the wagon. How many are in the group coming?"

"The sentinel didn't count them, but he says it's a good-sized group. Could be as many as we are; could be more. All Arakny's people are armed and awake. She's got bowmen out in the darkness where they can't be seen but can see firelit targets."

"Well, I'll get up and be ready to go into the woods with the babies. I need one helper for me—that would be you—and one for Kim. If things don't go well, if they find the wagon, it'll be empty except for the sea-eggs . . . There aren't too many to carry, Precious Wind . . ."

"Xulai, that's not necessary. I have *ul xaolat.* You and Kim and I, and the babies, can all get into this wagon, and we can move it and us in an instant. It's far more sensible to do that than to go off into the woods."

Xulai blinked, shook her head. Of course; she wasn't thinking clearly! "How far off is the troop? And where will you move us to?"

"We have some time. They are still some miles off. We can move to the place we were going anyhow, to Artemisia, the plaza next to Wide Mountain Mother's place. I took particular care to put a series of sites in memory before we left there and on the way here."

"Will you fetch Arakny? We need to tell her what we're doing."

Arakny listened. Arakny should put the horses with those of her own troop to avoid their being stolen . . . The three Tingawans would use a Tingawan device to move the wagon, with its cargo of sea-eggs to the plaza in Artemisia . . .

"A moment," Arakny said, puzzled. "If you can move the wagon and yourselves, why not simply move it somewhere close by from which you can keep watch? Up the mountain road you just traveled, perhaps.

Then, when the troop moves on, come back here. This large a group approaching at night may well be something you will need to know about immediately!"

"One must have a destination already in the device, or have a clear mental picture of the destination," said Xulai. "I don't have a clear destination . . . wait. Of course I do. The place where we left the package to be picked up by Sun-wings! If she didn't pick it up, I wanted to be able to return and get it! From there I could see the road down here, the whole straight stretch of it as it leaves the canyon. I need to be sure we could see this exact place . . ."

"And do you have a clear memory of the place you are now?"

"No. And it's too dark . . ." she murmured.

"No it isn't," said Precious Wind. "Remember, the devices have been improved. Darkness is no impediment to the new ones." She turned to Xulai. "How do we decide whether to come back here? If the troop moves on, toward us, where we are up on the mountain, or if they go back as they came . . . either way, we need to know if it's safe to return."

Xulai said, "We also want to be able to see what's happening, so I think we should test the location. I don't know that Arakny's campsite is really visible from there. If it isn't clearly visible, we'll have to think of something else. This time's just a test, Arakny!"

"May I watch you go?"

"Stand away, over in the trees."

The wagon door was open. There was no sound, no sense of movement. They were in total darkness, somewhere else. Kim made a gagging sound. Precious Wind said, "Lantern?"

Xulai called, "There's a little one by the bed. I should have lit it first."

Precious Wind brought the tiny wick-in-oil lamp that burned as a night-light over the bed. Xulai used it to light a larger one that was stored under the wagon seat. By its light they could see the road outside the open door. They got out and circled the wagon to look down. Far below, to their right, the campfires glimmered through the night. Farther out, slightly to the left, blocked occasionally by the ridge that ran out into the plain, they saw other, much smaller lights, torches, numerous torches, at a greater distance. Those approaching had turned at the fork in the road, the forested mound called the Devil's Ah behind them, backlit by moonlight.

They climbed back into the wagon and were, quite suddenly, back in the grove again. Across from them, Arakny held on to a tree, her mouth wide open.

Leaving the wagon, Xulai called, "It worked, and we're ready, Arakny."

"It was startling," she breathed. "I didn't believe it until it happened. What powers it?"

Precious Wind said, "Energy collectors up on the moon. They collect sun power and beam it to the few satellite receiving stations still circling the earth, as well as to a few stations on Earth itself. These devices receive that power. In Tingawa we had access to the power grid at the time of the Big Kill and we've gone on using it very carefully ever since. The power is a tiny fraction of what it once was, so the number of devices powered by it is limited."

"Could the power be increased?"

"If we could get back up to the moon, yes. The machines need only to be cleaned and repaired—all the parts and equipment are there. But there's no ship to take us there, we have no spacesuits—they'd have to be manufactured—and we have no recorded destination that would let us use *ul xaolat,* even if we were sure we had enough power to jump that far. I think it's been considered, but the power needed would be very great. Breaking the gravitational barrier, mostly. Besides which, we're not at all sure we *should* go. The lust for power was the downfall of previous ages. It might be so again. And what would some maniacal idiot do with it? With the waters rising, someone would probably try to boil all the water away, killing every living thing on Earth in the process."

There was a long, thoughtful silence before Arakny asked, "Will you go when they get slightly closer?"

Xulai said, "I don't want to go at all unless we have to. Kim will go with you and hide himself just inside the trees. Will you make some kind of signal, Arakny?"

"If I think there's danger, I'll pull my head scarf off."

"If you see her take her head scarf off, Kim, you get back here. We'll leave the door open, and the minute you're inside, we go up on the road where we just were a minute ago. This time we'll have a lighted lantern with us. Now, find a place where you can see her without being seen."

Arakny and Kim went off into the night, leaving Precious Wind and Xulai to put things away. The chicken coops were tied to the roof. There were a few scattered things in the grass that gleamed at them in the lantern light. A cup, a spoon. They went inside and waited.

NEEDLY AND WILLUM WERE BARELY over the top of the hill when something huge rose from a pile of leaves and branches and grabbed Needly by one arm, hoisting her off her feet. She caught only a glimpse, at first, enough to make her suppose it was a man, a very large man. She drew a deep breath and added to her "man" supposition a certainty that the very large man smelled a great deal like . . . a cow barn that had not been cleaned for . . . some time. No, no. It was far, far worse than that. Holding her at arm's length, the man-creature nodded at Willum, then in the direction of the glade below, all the time muttering:

"Git down 'ere. Gwan, git. Move it. Y're gonna hep me. Yessir. Needed hep, I did, and ol For'ster, he sent hep. He did, he did. Thot there'd be sumpin' come fer this'n. Yep. Did. Here t'is. Hep."

Needly had quickly taken stock. Dawn-song had fluttered down the slope toward the place where her bloodied mother lay, obviously unable to move. She and Willum were being herded or hauled in the same direction by a bearded, man-shaped being with a long knife in the hand that was not dangling her by one arm. He had a large ax at his belt. Willum was trying frantically to decide on his own next move when the huge man kicked the boy's feet out from under him and dropped Needly more or less on top of him. They were near a clutter of bundles, a circle of stones, the ashes of a fire, the creature's encampment. *His stomping ground,* Willum said to himself, seeing the huge boot prints radiating from the area. Oh, yes. Very, very big stomping feet. And a terrible smell. Oh, dearie, dearie me, as Willum's ma would have said, what a stink that is!

Dawn-song hadn't stopped running until she had reached her mother's side. The two of them, mother and daughter, only a few steps away, remained silent, watchful, though Sun-wings' eyes were only half open. Needly had caught Sun-wings' look, had watched as the eye focused on her. Needly nodded, once toward the man, then toward the Griffins, as though to say, "I see the situation. Be patient." Sun-wings lowered her eyelids, left them almost closed.

Willum had looked about to explode, but Needly had preempted him. She took a deep breath, to her immediate regret, pinched her nostrils closed, breathed through her mouth, and then declaimed: "Now, *Willum*, we must be *helpful* to this nice person. You heard him. He asked for help and *Old Forester* has sent us to help him. You understand that, *you heard Old Forester tell us to come here and help him just as I did.*"

Willum had been only momentarily mutinous, realizing very quickly that she was intending . . . something, and though he didn't know what, it was probably more sensible than nothing, which is what he'd come up with. "Well, of course, Needly. That's what we're here for, in't it?"

The creature stood slightly above them on the slope, hands on hips, greedy eyes on Sun-wings. Needly sat down on the grass. "May we know your name, sir, so we know who we are helping?"

"Yung For'ster, tha's me. Hunters. Us For'sters. Got more . . . meetup'nus t'others, so we do huntin'. Fer the ressa th' Ahgars. Pa 'uz Ol' For'ster. That's why I'm Yung For'ster. I 'uz younger'n 'im."

"That's very logical," said Willum, attentively borrowing one of Xulai's favorite words. He glanced at Needly. "Isn't it, Needly?"

"Very logical," she assented, straight-faced, still regarding the Yung whatever. He was definitely the source of the almost stifling smell. "You say you need help?"

"Yeh. Ahgars get mos' a' meat. Hides goes to hunters, n' we getta sellum, buy . . . good stuff." He licked his lips at the thought of the good stuff. "Gotta skinum firs. Never done one'th wings. Skun all kinds a' them, but never done one'th wings. Donno how, y'know, whur t'cut'm."

Needly was terribly afraid she did know. Oh my. Was this then, one of the forest men Abasio had talked about: the hermit hunters, trappers, the ones who stayed aloof and alone. She could see why. Abasio hadn't mentioned the stink! Let that go for the moment. This one was a hunter; hunters got to keep and sell the hides while "Ahgars" got the meat. This one wanted to skin the Griffin and sell the skin to buy good stuff, but he didn't know how to skin something with wings. He was staring at her. Waiting for her to . . .

She said quickly, "I understand. Yes. That would be different. You are a trapper, sir? Or only a hunter? Or both, perhaps?" She flashed a glance at Willum, who nodded at her.

"I be that. All 'at. Got traps, yeh. Got some 'at way, some yon." He gestured widely, taking in the entire countryside. "Hunter, thas me. Hunter

fer Ahgar feed grounds. Killsa meat an' put it out fer the Ahgars. Didn'
shoot this'n, tho. This'n jus' fell in. Wham! Looka that hide. Jus' looka
that. For'ster me'll git gold fer it, they'll gimme. True gold. More'n a
whole messa trappin'. 'F I can figger out to get a'skin offa it. It's them
wings . . ."

"You'll receive a lot more gold for the Griffin's hide than for a lot of
small hides, yes, I know. And you're right. The wings make skinning it a
very difficult process. It takes a lot of time. It's a good thing my helper
and I happened along. We're part of a very special group of experts who
know how to do this. It will take time, though, so you have to be patient.
Do you mind if I go over and take a look at it?"

"Stay way fr'm th' front part. Tha' mouth thing. Tha's sharp, that is."
He looked ruefully at his lower left arm, which had a large wound, just
scabbing over. "Real sharp."

Needly stood up and walked over toward Sun-wings, keeping her
eyes fastened on the enormous orbs that were returning her look. Her
back was to the . . . For'ster, and she raised one hand and put a finger
before her lips. Dawn-song was already huddled against her mother's
side.

Needly stood a small distance away and whispered, "Don't speak,
Sun-wings. Don't let the man know you can speak."

"I did not say anything," whispered Sun-wings, without moving her
beak. Needly had never been this close to her, close enough to see the
soft tissue behind the edge of the beak. Lips. Well, almost lips. Even
they had not moved, but their existence explained Griffins being able
to pronounce human language.

"Are you in pain?"

"Yes." The word was only a breath.

"I'm going to see if I can send . . . For'ster to go kill some meat. I will
give you meat and water, and I may put something on the meat or in
the water for your pain. If you taste a bitterness, don't worry. Just eat or
drink it anyhow. Will you do that?"

"Yes."

There were a few clumps of the Griffin's hair on the ground where
Needly stood, probably torn out when Sun-wings had attempted to
crawl. Needly crouched to pick them up. "I also have some herbs that
prevent infection. Do you know what I mean?"

"Healing." The word was only breathed, laboriously, as though her lungs could not get enough air.

"That's right. I'll definitely put that in water. Whatever I give you, eat or drink it all, even it if tastes bad. Only when I give it to you, all right? Can you show me where you're hurt?"

Sun-wings lifted her left wing, slowly, painfully, and only slightly. It was torn, the tear beginning near the wing joint and running along the bone to the outer edge. The feathers at the top edges of the wound were soaked with blood. Sun-wings whispered, "Other-side hind leg. Not 'roken, just hurt."

She was choosing words that did not require lip—or beak—movement, and Needly was amazed that she could keep her wits, wounded as she was. If it was only the wing, then perhaps . . .

"Lookie out dere," cried the man behind her. "She c'n git ya 'itha wing."

Needly turned and came back to the man. "My helper and I will need to make a small fire. We will need water. Where is the closest place? I will need to feed the creature."

"Feed'er? By boghost, not gonna. Feed a critter'm gonna skin? Not gonna!"

"You can't skin her for at least three or four days," said Needly. "It can't be done. Her hair is already starting to come loose." She held out her hand, the long neck strands dragging from it. "If you skin her now, the hair will all fall out, and the hide will rot, too, and you won't get any good stuff for it. She needs to be fed and watered and made comfortable so her fur is all shiny and thick. Otherwise the hide is worthless. The same is true of the little one. A Griffin can only be skinned when it is in perfect condition."

He did not look properly impressed. She put her hands on her hips, using pretended temper to hide her trembling. She shouted furiously, "Time after time Old Forester sends me to help people and I find they have already ruined the hide! They've gained the enmity of the whole Griffin race for nothing, trying to skin a wounded one."

"Amitty o' griff'n wha'?"

"When you try to skin a wounded Griffin, she makes a noise that is heard by all Griffins everywhere in the world. Then they all come and find you and kill you. It's only when Griffins are in perfect condition that they agree to be skinned."

"Thasso?"

Needly drew herself up, adopted a posture suitable to "expert being annoyed by silly questions." "How many Griffin hides have you seen? How many hunters or trappers have brought in Griffin hides?"

He shook his huge head, confused. "N'body. Not seen one."

"That's because everyone who has ever skinned a Griffin did it because they found the Griffin wounded, they tried it, and every Griffin from miles around came and killed them! You've never hunted one. You've never trapped one. The only way you could get one would be to find a wounded one. But you don't know how to skin her. Skinning her won't do any good unless you wait for a few days while we get her into proper condition. Then you ask her, politely, because you were so nice to her, will she let you skin her, and she will nod her head. That's how they were made, Griffins. That's the way they live and die. Isn't that right, Willum?"

"Exactly right. As my teacher told me in skinning school."

"Furrier college, Willum," Needly said in a fussy, schoolmarmish tone. "Griffin hides are classified as furs. Except the males, of course. Those are classified as merely hides, because of the scales. Suitable for making boots! I do wish you'd use the right words for things. I'll never be able to send you out on jobs alone unless you use the proper terminology! People will think you're not professional!"

"Sorry, ma'am," he said, ducking his head to hide his mouth, which, despite the situation, had turned relentlessly upward at its ends. "I really will try to do better."

"I do hope so. You, Yung For'ster, you have an excellent hide. It would do well for gloves, I think. Who have you left your hide to? Family? Friends?"

He looked confused, slightly upset. "'m only part Ahgar. Don' get peel s'ahfen!"

"They peel the Ahgars . . . do they?"

"Peel'm fer the stuff. Yep."

She lost the sense of that, but ignored it. "Very well. I didn't know. Now, sir." She approached him. "We need meat and quite a lot of it, a deer, perhaps, a mountain sheep or an elk?"

"Y'mean now?"

"The later we start, the more hair she will lose and the longer it will take."

The huge face wrinkled in unaccustomed thought. "Howkum you knows, huh?"

"Does your father know all this?"

"Did, I 'spose."

"Didn't you ask him for help?"

A nod. "Sorta said Pa'd know how. Not loud."

"And he sent me."

"He's dead, mos' pars rottin' inna groun'. "

"Mos' parts?" The words slipped out before she thought. She bit her lip.

"Pars 'ey din' want. Sum pars 'ey kep fer a nex' one."

She set aside for the moment the parts they didn't want, some parts kept for the next one, making a mental note to remember it. That and the Ahgars. "You asked your pa for help. His spirit, from the ground where his . . . parts are, his spirit heard you. His spirit is not dead. He sent us from the spirit world. We work there. We work here, too."

If expression meant anything in such a creature, this one was confused. Which was more or less what Needly intended. Cursing, slavering, mumbling, the creature got to his feet, wandered to a tree where he had a hung a quiver full of arrows and a bow taller than most men. He put the one over his shoulder, took the other in his hand, and wandered off into the trees.

"Oh, boy," said Willum. "He's sure . . ."

She silenced him with a gesture and went to speak into his ear. "He's smart enough to have heard us coming. He's smart enough to know we can't move Sun-wings, and he knows she can't move. He's smart enough to know we came here with the little one. He's smart enough to know he can track us, anywhere we might try to go, right? So smart or not, he's taking a gamble that we're real."

Willum spat. "And we know he's real because the smell is real."

"Oh, Willum, doesn't he stink! I've never smelled anything that awful: like rotten and swampy and dead and . . . all at once! It does make you spit." She did so. The stink seemed to thicken her saliva, making it syrupy, dreadful. "He'll be back with meat. Let me have the pan and our water bottle."

Willum put down his pack and dug it out. While he was occupied with this, Needly turned away from him and fetched the little pouch tied beneath her skirts. She selected three of the little bottles and removed them, returning the pouch to its usual hiding place. Looking carefully at each bottle as she did so, she put one in her skirt pocket, one in her jacket pocket, and one she thrust into the top of her sock. When Willum handed over pan and bottle, she poured the pan half full, took the two bottles from her pockets, added about one-quarter of the contents of one, and a spoonful of the other to the water and carried it to Sun-wings, holding it while the Griffin drank it all, beakful by beakful, lifting her beak to allow swallowing each time. Needly thought her throat must have been dry as dust. She had had no water.

"Not so bitter," Sun-wings said very softly. "You will feed us?"

"We will feed you, Sun-wings, and Dawn-song. Are you still thirsty? I'll bring you more water now."

Willum was suddenly beside her, holding out the pan, full of water.

As the Griffin drank slowly, Needly murmured, "If you feel me on your back or fiddling with your left wing, don't throw me off. I may be able to do some good there, too. You're going to sleep now. I've given you something to let you sleep and something for the pain. The pain will lessen, it may even go away. I don't know how much to use for something . . . someone your size, so you must tell me if it doesn't work. Somehow, we will get you healed and down off this mountain, though I don't know how."

"Despos?"

"He's gone, as we planned, to kill the male Griffins who live in the far, icy north. His search will take him a very long time. I am told the land up there looks alike, everywhere, all snow and ice. He'll have trouble even remembering where he has looked."

"And the others?"

"They're going south. The children have been picked up, the eggs have been returned. We had a conflict with three of them, but your friend Golden-throat and her friends helped us. And I have wonderful news. The Griffin we named Bell-sound because of her voice—"

"I know which one."

"Her egg hatched. It is a male baby, Sun-wings, and not from Despos. She is taking the baby to Tingawa."

The huge eyes opened wide, actually glowed. "Oh, that is wonderful, that is good!" She struggled to speak. "But that is good only if the others don't know, if they don't tell Despos when he returns. Is help coming?"

"You hid us well, Sun-wings. Golden-throat will tell those in Tingawa that we need help."

"You gave her a good name. She would have been helpful." She blinked drowsily. "Did you name her child?"

"We named her Amber-ears. They have all been told about Tingawa, and how to get there? The one we call Silver-shanks was not very helpful."

"White feathers down to her feet, that one?"

"Yes."

"A few of us are like that. Not many . . ."

"The ones Despos fathered. Only those."

The medication was working. The huge eyes were falling closed.

"Sleep," murmured Needly, bending toward Dawn-song. "You too, little one, Dawn-song, sleep. Nothing is going to happen to you. Not while Willum and I are watching." She turned wearily and went to the place where the giant had had his fire. Willum had already shaved tinder and laid a small fire for them. He had his fire starter in his hand. The sun was very low in the west, it was already chilly; the two of them wrapped themselves in blankets and sat beside the blaze.

"I got the water behind that rock left of you," murmured Willum. "A tiny little spring comes down there. There's plenty for us and for Sun-wings."

"Good. She's had enough for now, but she needs liquids, so we must bring her water as soon as she wakes. Are you as tired as I am, Willum?"

"I'm tireder. I been doin' all the thinkin'."

"Willum, you're shameless."

"Yeah, that's what Ma says. You n' her got a lot in common."

Needly rested for a time, watching Willum closely. His face was gray with weariness, and his eyes were bloodshot and tired. After a few moments' rest, she dug food from their packs and set it to cooking. Willum, eyes half closed, murmured, "Tell me about the angels, Needly."

It was something they told each other about, to heal the loneliness, to fight the weariness, to keep away the fear. She murmured, "I told you, *they're here, among all our busy-ness. Their shadows lie under the trees. They hang their wings in the closet of the forest, hidden among the leaves.*"

"Yes. But you've seen 'em."

"Sometimes when it's raining they come out, leaving their shadows and their wings behind. They do a dimness dance, only their naked selves glinting like wet ivory between the falling drops, silver on silver, gleam upon gleam."

"Wish I could see 'em."

"Like Grandma said*: 'Dawn discloses, but that most urgent for our sight appears in darkness and vanishes in light.'"*

"That's a riddle."

"Kind of. It means there are certain wonderful things we can see only when we're not looking for them, Willum."

Willum slept. Needly wondered about the huge hunter, about the yellow bottle she had in her sock. She had seen him drink from a bottle he had, one he carried with him. If she could get some a few drops from the yellow bottle into his food. Or drink. But how much? Grandma said a drop, a few drops. What if he took it and it didn't work, only made him sick or angry? So angry he simply killed everything he could reach? Too early to know. She had to watch, see what he did, how he did it.

It was quite dark when the hunter came back, the carcass of a large deer across his shoulders. He found Needly and Willum beside a small fire with a pot steaming over it. He dropped the deer at some distance. "Y'wanna feed 'er."

"Drag it over here," said Needly, walking toward the sleeping Griffins. "Put it here, where she can reach it."

"Take a leg for us'n."

"We have food. Take some for you, if you like."

He took a bloody slab from the hindquarter, then dragged the carcass over to where Needly stood, beneath the Griffin's beak. She pointed. He dropped it and retreated toward the fire. Needly whispered, "Dawn-song, if you're hungry, the man has cut the hide. You can eat what's exposed."

"Leave it for Mama . . ." A breathless whisper.

"There'll be plenty for Mama. It's getting dark, and I won't be able to do anything more until light, so eat. Then curl up beside her and go back to sleep. Do you need water?"

The little one limped across the harsh grasses and lay down next to the carcass. While she tore pieces of meat from it, Needly examined her feet one by one, rubbing salve into the abraded pads. She reflected that

Griffins really were not designed to walk, though their front legs were very catlike. The back legs were catlike, but the feet were stranger, with fowl-like attributes including huge curved talons that did not retract fully. That too made walking difficult. Or it was perhaps possible that they merely chose not to walk and thus never strengthened their legs or developed calluses on their feet. When and if she got a chance, she would make two pairs of Griffin shoes!

"Don't need water," said Dawn-song, chewing sleepily. "The meat is nice and juicy and warm."

And fresh, thought Needly, feeling momentary sorrow for the deer. It, too, had deserved to run and live and be. Humans should have evolved as herbivores. They would have been very different. Not so quarrelsome. Not at all violent . . . except during breeding season.

"Mama," whispered Dawn-song. "Will Mama be all right?"

"She's better," said Needly. "Are you listening to me, little one?"

"I'm listening."

"That bad man must not know you can talk. Understand. Do not say a word where he can hear you."

"I heard you tell Mama."

"Good. Just be very patient. You see, food has come. Water has come. And somehow, from somewhere, I hope help will come, too."

INEVITABLY, MORNING CAME. SURPRISINGLY, BOTH the children had slept well, though that was due more to exhaustion than tranquillity. Needly, resting against Sun-wings' side, had felt her move painfully in the early hours and had fetched a pan of water for her, water with a few drops of the stuff that stopped pain. Needly herself had needed no help to fall back into sleep the moment she lay down.

As soon as it was light in the morning, Needly woke. She took a long look across the clearing at the sleeping form of the hunter, a hummock beneath the trees, snoring with great, irregular eruptions, like a volcano with an upset stomach. The meat he had taken last night was partly eaten. She didn't see any kind of drinking vessel, cup, bottle that she could sneak anything into. If he carried one, it was in a pocket. As soon as she was sure he was not going to wake at the least sound, she took Grandma's long red scarf from her pack, the one that had served as a Namer's headdress. It was lined in white silk, and she snipped the threads holding the white lining to the other side, then began unraveling the silk threads that made it up, each thread the length of the entire, long scarf, winding each one around a smooth stick. Needles she had, thread she had, but not the lengths and lengths of it needed to sew a Griffin's wing together. The warp threads would be long enough, and both lining and bright outer layer were heavy fabrics, not fragile ones. The lining threads were preferable, as they had no dye in them. Dye might not be good in a wound. Once the threads were wound carefully on the stick, she would soak the assemblage in water with some cleansing stuff in it so it would surely not infect the wound. Then she would double the thread and use her darning needle. It would be strong enough and long enough to go through the Griffin's hide. During the morning, she took several more pans of water to Sun-wings, the last one dosed again with Grandma's recipe for healing and another few drops for pain. The substances that controlled pain had a tendency to cause sleep as well, and Sun-wings went back to sleep shortly after drinking it.

"What you gonna do?" asked Willum from among his blankets.

"I will endeavor to sew up her wing," said Needly very seriously. "The big lump over there is still asleep. Be sure to let me know if he stirs or wakes."

"N' if he asks me something?"

"You've been to furrier college, Willum. Just answer the man."

Willum chewed on that for a moment or two and then grinned at her. He looked better this morning—or at least less tired.

Sun-wings was a mountain of flesh to be climbed, and Needly climbed it as carefully as possible, foot on left front foot, walk up left front leg to joint, climb onto upper leg, walk up that to shoulder. Climb onto shoulder, which she managed by hanging on to clumps of hair. She stood there examining the injured wing. She wanted access to the injured part of the wing, but it lay against the great creature's side and back, and Needly was burdened with the pan, a water bottle, her bottles, and a great many lengths of thread carefully aligned and wound. She tried it several ways, eventually returning to Willum to say, "You'll have to help, Willum. I can't get the wing into position, not alone."

"I was watchin' you, thinkin' about it. You wanta start at the upside end, by the bone?"

"Where the tear is nearest the bone, yes. I didn't realize until now that it's built more like a bat's wing than a bird's wing. It has feathers, but it also has long, fingerlike bones in it, to spread the wing out, and it's torn from the big bone down along one of those fingers, as though Despos caught a claw in it, near the wing shoulder—she has two sets of shoulders! The claw caught the membrane and ripped it all the way to the outside edge. So I'll start at the top. If we're very careful not to stretch either side, we should come out even at the bottom. And if we don't, it'll be better if the extra tissue is at the bottom, where I can kind of trim it off or just leave it. It's mostly very strong muscle tissue with nerves and blood vessels running through it, but there are two layers of skin to sew.

"I figure I'll do a bit of the bottom skin, then if there's flesh I can just pull together with a stitch here and there, I'll do that and put some healing stuff on it, then sew the same length of the top skin. Eventually, the stitches will have to come out, so I don't want many inside. Maybe the skin will hold it close enough it can heal inside without stitching. Then we'll move down along the wing and do another stretch. The big muscles in her wing shoulders aren't hurt . . . well, they're not cut, at least. They may be badly bruised from the fall, but with the feathers and fur, I can't see whether they are or not. You'll have to hold the skin for me. Oh, and we have to wash it first and trim away any dead tissue and put some of the medicine on it as we go, and be sure our hands are really clean."

Willum stood, hands on hips, cheeks puffed out, looking at that long length of wing. There was a word, one of Needly's words, in-ter-min-able. That's what that was.

"Yes," said Needly, as though he had spoken. "It will be virtually in-terminable, so we'd better get started."

She was reflecting that Willum was not what someone well schooled would have called thoughtful. He was not at all stupid, but he had been born and grown in a village where most things, actions, reactions, and distinguishing characteristics had been defined for centuries. The people rarely had to explain anything to anyone except children, and even with them, most instruction was of the "Watch and you'll find out" kind. Wordless, or at the best terse, and always by example. The result was that Willum was not incapable of thought, but he lacked the tools of thought. He lacked the words he would need to describe or define unfamiliar situations, unfamiliar things.

She knew that just now, he knew he felt very shivery inside, but he had no word for insecure. *Lust* he knew by recognition. That was what the bull felt for the cow, the boar for the sow. Maybe he had recognized it in some of the villagers. *Fear* he knew because there were natural things to fear: lightning, forest fire, flood. Certain people, perhaps. *Impudence* he knew, though not by that name. It was what he couldn't get away with where Ma and Pa were concerned. *Hunger* he knew, and *desire* he knew, for it was almost like hunger.

What she did not perceive was the depth of his feelings about her, feelings so complicated that he had no language for them at all. He had no word for *cherishing* or being in love. There was sadness at the possibility of loss; wonder at the possibility of continuance; sick terror at any threat. His body went into brief fits of shivering and wanting to cower or shout, but he had no label for it, so he struggled with his weakness. The familiar thing closest to it was *sickness,* so he feared he was sickening for something, and he could not allow himself to sicken, could not allow himself to weaken. Strength, he understood, and weakness. Ma had, once in a while, been weakened when the labor of harvest had worn her down to, as she said, a nubbin. When that happened, her children had helped her to bed and made her mint tea with a great deal of sugar in it! Sometimes even with a bit of the stuff in the emergency bottle!

In the village, men avoided weakness. They did not push themselves to that point. They walked as farmers always have done, seldom if ever without destination, each step taking them somewhere needful. If the fence needed fixing, their feet went there. If the cow needed milking, their steps led there. Each step was timeless and necessary, and there was no strength wasted on wayward wandering, wondering, or discovering. *What the villagers called growing up consisted of giving up any urge to wander or wonder. As for discovery? What was there to discover? The family had been here forever.*

The order and simplicity of village life had required no more than a sparse vocabulary. Now, into this limited but familiar word-world, Xulai's teaching had come, and Abasio's, and then Needly's—each of them full of words that had led Willum onto branching paths where he had no landmarks. Paths with fear alongside of them, wonder at the end of them. Sometimes, as now, sitting atop a Griffin and holding her wounded flesh between his hands, he felt he could do better if he did not try to think at all. Abasio had said something like that. When thinking got hard, some people just stopped trying . . . Chipmunk brains.

So, as both the huge hunter and Sun-wings went on sleeping, he tried to turn off his brain and concentrate on each simple step, helping Needly lay the tissue of the wing back on either side of the wound, gently, carefully, cleaning it as they went. The stuff she used softened it as well, so she could see what was alive and what was not. Then, lying carefully on the uninjured part of the wing, Needly sponged each length of the bottom skin clean, sponged it again with the healing medication, trimmed off any dried tatters with her tiny pair of scissors, then stitched the skin together, very carefully, locking each stitch. On top of the stitched skin, she pushed the torn tissue together, soaked it in the infection-fighting stuff, put stitches into that as well, not as closely as in the skin, then repeated the sewing with the top skin. Then they moved a few handspans farther toward the edge of the wing and repeated the process.

"You gonna have enough thread?" Willum whispered.

"I only unraveled half my scarf lining," Needly replied. "Hand me another end. This length is used up."

Dawn-song awoke, tore meat from the carcass near her mother's head, went to the spring to drink, went into the trees briefly, and returned to lie next to her mother. Sun-wings slept on. The children were halfway down the long slash in Sun-wings' flesh when Yung For'ster stopped snoring with a loud explosive honk, sat up, and shook himself awake. He, too, went off into the woods, then returned to build up his own fire and cook—that is, half char the outside of—another chunk of the deer flesh.

" 'Longs it gonna take?" he grumbled.

"Several days," Needly replied, her needle slipping through the layer of flesh, which was growing thinner as they neared the edge of the wing. She and Willum had been cleaning the feathers as they went. Only a few had been lost, and the chances were good that they would regrow. The tiny sockets that had held them appeared unbroken . . . or uninjured. It was difficult to tell which word applied.

"You hungry, Needly?" asked Willum.

"Yes. But I don't want to quit. Can you make me a sandwich?"

He slipped from his place and went to their packs, where he assembled some rather dry cheese and some equally dry bread. Regarding this with disgust, he took his own knife to the venison, cutting several very thin slices that took only moments to brown above the coals, the slices tilted so the juices would run down to a rock at the side where he had laid the bread to catch the dripping. He put the cheese on top, watched it melt, then assembled the sandwiches. They smelled savory, at least, and he carried them back onto the Griffin's back or side—yes, side, he decided. He and Needly were actually stretched along the huge ribs that ran from the backbone down toward the grass. He wondered, very briefly, if Sun-wings had ever counted her ribs. Probably not. She was lying just a little on her right side, not to injure further the wounded left wing. When they had eaten their sandwiches, they wiped their hands with stuff from one of Needly's bottles, then Willum took up his flesh-holding job once more. Interminable though it had seemed, they were nearing the end of the task. For'ster, having eaten, was bored with it all. He took his bow and arrows and departed once more.

"When you finish sewing, is that it?" asked Willum.

"Sponge it one more time with the healing stuff. I can only do the top. I can't get at the underside of the wing."

"I'll lift it," murmured Sun-wings drowsily. "Unless you don't want me to move."

"You can lift it when I'm ready," said Needly. "Just don't flap it. This stuff of Grandma's has been known to heal a bad cut within two days, but no sense ripping out what's taken so long to do."

"Grandma. She would be a Silverhair, ah?" Sun-wings's tone underlined the word as important.

"I guess. Her hair's white, but I always thought that was because she's old."

"You know who the Silverhairs are?"

"I think some kind of . . . special people who know things most people don't."

"They're people left over from a long time ago," said Sun-wings in a dreaming voice, as though she heard a voice from some other place. "People who know how things fit together. Stars. Mountains. Trees, Peoples." There was a long pause. "Worlds, too, I think. Suns, planets, something called a . . . galaxy."

"When you say a long time ago . . . ?"

"Before men came. Became. What's the word they use? Evolved.

Before the world was. Silverhairs are among the beginners, the starters, the world seeders. So I was told."

"Who tole you that?" demanded Willum.

The Griffin spoke softly, as in a dream. "A very old man who lived at the top of a very tall mountain in that continent south of this one. The whole west side of that continent looms like a wall, and he lived like a cricket in that wall. He sucked dew and rain from the stones for drink and birds brought him food, and still he was thin as a reed. He told me the whales told him about the Silverhairs. When the whales were land-living creatures, they met the Silverhairs. They were shaped like whales then. Later, they shaped themselves like people. Now the whales remember the Silverhairs in their songs."

"How could he talk to whales from the top of a mountain?" asked Willum scornfully.

"He had not always been at the top of that mountain," the Griffin said drowsily. "When he was young, that mountain had been deep in the sea . . ."

Needly objected, "But Grandma looked like people; like me, I mean."

"He told me Silverhairs can look like anything they want to." The Griffin chuckled, as though in that moment pain were forgotten. "I thought, when he said that, that he might well be one of them, a Silverhair in the shape of an old man. He told me Silverhairs have no shape of their own."

Needly sat on Sun-wings' vast side, mouth slightly open, forgetting to chew the last bite of her sandwich. She was thinking of her mother. "And . . . I suppose they can interbreed with other creatures, if they want to."

"I suppose," whispered Sun-wings, already half asleep. "If they want to."

Needly looked at the work she and Willum had done. She had only to sponge this last little sewn bit, and then, when Sun-wings awoke enough to stretch the wing out, sponge the other side of the wing, and she'd be finished. Her whole body was stiff from the position she'd had to work from and the way she'd had to reach, stretching almost past endurance. Now it was done. She gathered her tools and supplies and slid down across the ribs, dropping off the edge of the belly with an unintentional "oof."

"Um," murmured Sun-wings, her eyes shut. Needly wasn't surprised. She had given the great beast a large dose of the pain stuff in order to keep her quiet while her wing was being stitched together. The deer carcass was nearby, and Needly took a good look at it as she passed. Sun-wings had eaten a good bit of that, too. Good. One had to balance keeping wounded creatures comfortable with keeping them awake enough to eat and drink. Serious pain made it difficult. Grandma had doctored sheep and cows and horses as well as people.

At their fireside, Willum was waiting for her.

"You're tired," he said. "I'm making us some stew for later. It smells almost as good as yours."

"It smells better than mine. What did you put in it?"

"Summa this. Ma always does." He held out his hand, full of small, fragrant bulbs.

"Wild onilic! I never have any luck finding onilic!"

"Y'have to look for bright-beetles! Those little bright red ones with the spots on their wings?"

"Spotty ladies? They lead you to onilic?"

"They nest in the onilic-sign. Early springtime, Pa used to pull the bushes out of the field, and they'd be red as blood at the bottom, from thousands of bright-beetles."

"Show me!" Needly demanded.

He led her to the far side of the clearing, a stretch of dry, sandy soil where stiff, swordlike leaves thrust upward, a narrow, thick clump of them, tight together at the bottom, spreading at the top around a dried spear of flower stalk, thick through as Needly's arm and as tall as a man. Willum pulled two of the leaves apart and stared down between them. Their bottoms appeared to be resting in a puddle of red paint, paint that squirmed and shifted. Bright-beetles. Spotty ladies. Hundreds . . . thousands of them.

"Only one problem," said Needly. "This isn't an onilic plant. It's something else."

"It's what I said, it's the onilic-*sign*. It's got an old-time name. Yucka. That's the name. The onilic is nearby, underground, you know that."

"You mean this plant, this yucka, grows next to where onilic is?"

"Yeah. 'Zackly. Ma calls 'em 'companion plants.' Look there, that's onilic," and he pointed at the bunches of fleshy, tubular leaves scattered nearby.

She stared at him, frankly at a loss. Until this moment she had not thought it possible that there was anything her grandma had not known. For sure, she had not known this. A sign, a sentinel plant.

"Are there others?" she whispered. "Companions."

"Oh, sure," said Willum, yawning. "Dozens of 'em. That's mostly how Ma finds stuff to flavor things, roots and bulbs and leaves, and stuff. It's like Ma says, country people don't get half the credit they should for the stuff they know. There's tasty little things like mushrooms that grow on a certain kind of tree roots. Pa never liked 'em, but like Ma said, that left more for her n' me! There's a kind of moss that grows on certain other trees that smells like . . . smells good. Country people stuff pillows and mattresses with it and it keeps fleas away. And I know another plant that stops pain, too. It's a kind of flower. It has a big seedpod in the middle, shaped sort of like a cup with a lid, and when the petals drop, that pod is full of sleep juice. The women in Gravysuck make little slits in the pod and the juice oozes out and hardens. Scrape that off and you can keep it in little jars for when people are hurt or real sick."

"Do you have any of it with you?" His description sounded rather like Grandma's description of her pain stuff.

He shook his head. "Ma said I couldn't handle any of her remedies—that's what she calls them—unless I learned all about finding them and making the juice or powder or whatever, and I haven't had time yet to learn about those things because Pa said the farm came first. But I know some stuff about it, just from hearing her talk. She said it had to be taught, parent to child. Ordinary, it'd be Ma to the girls, but she was planning to teach me instead, because I'm int'rested an' neither of them's int'rested one bit. She'd teach you. No question to that!"

Across the clearing from them, the Griffin stirred into momentary half consciousness. She lifted her wing, slowly stretching it, and it opened. The Griffin was staring at Needly, or through her. "When will I fly?"

"Not for a while, Sun-wings. It's all right to move the wing, but don't let the man see you can move it. And you can't heal unless you go on eating . . ." She had the pan ready with the stuff and moved toward the Griffin. "Hold your wing where it is so I can sponge the underside of it."

Willum, however, had already clambered onto the creature's side to hold the wing bone aloft so the Griffin did not have to strain to hold it. Needly was quick, and administration of the medicine took a very short time. They slid to the ground once more, the great wing folding behind them.

Sun-wings made a sound of discomfort, sighed. "The bear should have found help by now."

"What bear?" the children said in unison. They were standing by her head by now, looking up into the huge eyes.

"One who talked. He knew . . . the man you were traveling with . . ."

"Abasio?"

"He knew Abasio. So did his friend Coyote, also a talking creature. We were all at the great battle near here, a few years ago. The two creatures found me here, they brought me what food they could. Rabbits and fish. They had no way to bring water. They were already on their way to find Abasio and tell him what happened."

"When?"

The Griffin's eyes closed and she breathed heavily. "I took you children on one night. That next day we moved to the new cave. The next day Golden-throat came. The third day they brought the eggs, and we all flew to our nests. That afternoon Despos wounded me. Bear and Coyote saw me fall, I think. The animals were frightened of me, but when I called to them in words, they understood and replied! I begged them to find Abasio." Her eyes fell shut, as though with embarrassment. Griffins did not beg. They ordered. "They left two . . . no, three days ago. They thought it would take them two days to get to the foot of the mountains, by the road."

"Then he could be back here by tomorrow!" Willum turned a face that glowed with happy surprise onto Needly. "By tomorrow, Needly!"

She reached for his hand. "Perhaps. If Abasio was at the foot of the mountain himself. If the animals did not have to hunt for him. But it's wonderful to know that someone is on the way."

The Griffin breathed deeply, the huge bellows of her lungs stirring the lower branches of the nearest trees. "Abasio may be coming, yes. And you have already helped my wing. Can you tell me what is wrong with my leg?"

The children went to look at the Griffin head-on, peering along her right side. "If you can pull the injured wing close to your backbone and roll a little bit onto your belly and left side, I can get a look at your right leg. If it's just bruised, some of the same healing stuff as I put on the wing will work for the leg, too. If it's broken, we have a problem."

"Impossible?"

Needly reached out a hand and actually stroked the Griffin's great shoulder. "Nothing is impossible, Sun-wings. Nothing is impossible."

The children went to stand on her other side while the great beast strained, thrust, managed to roll slightly toward them.

"Can you move it?" called Needly.

Sun-wings shifted, crying out in sudden pain. Willum saw at once what the trouble was. "Her leg is jammed up against a rock!"

"I should have checked this yesterday!" Needly cried.

"Do not fret, child. I don't think I could have moved yesterday," whispered Sun-wings.

Needly and Willum labored at the stone, digging around it until they could get Willum's walking stick far enough into the hole to lever it loose—though they broke the stick in the process. When they managed to roll the stone out of the hollow it had been half buried in, Sun-wings strained to lift the leg that had been cramped beneath her. She grunted deeply as she managed to straighten it out to the side, and again as she bent it under her in its natural crouched position. They children looked it over, looking for blood. "We don't see any injury," Needly called. "Of course, we can't see the bones. My guess is that when you fell, you jammed your leg against the half-buried stone. You were too weak and stunned to lift yourself out. It's probably bruised, but now that you have it in a better position, it should become less painful."

They circled Sun-wings once more, stopping at her head so that Needly could whisper words of encouragement. From behind her, Willum, who had been holding himself quiet and being helpful and trying desperately not to think of what that For'ster could do to Needly, what he might do to both of them. Might do to Dawn-song and her mother if they couldn't figure a way out of this, only he couldn't . . . hadn't, not yet, maybe couldn't at all . . . Surreptitiously wiping away a few tears, he put his lips together stubbornly. "Nothin'," he said to himself firmly, quoting Needly. "Nothin's impossible."

CHAPTER 10

Cultural Confrontations

THE DARKNESS IN THE CLEARING WHERE XULAI AND Precious Wind were waiting was full of murmurings, rustling, fluttering, a myriad of moth and bat sounds.

"The fork in the road is several miles east," Precious Wind said, her own voice a mere whisper. "They should be getting close about now."

Xulai murmured, "Ever since his adventure with the men who were going to rob Saltgosh, Willum has been defining travelers on the road as 'Friend or foe: we just don' know.'"

"Willum sounds like a terror," Precious Wind murmured in return. There was no need for their extreme caution. No one could hear them from the vicinity of the Artemisian camp. The atmosphere of the almost silent mountain seemed to require it, but surely the actual situation didn't . . . Of course, she had just arrived. Did she know what the actual situation really was?

Xulai mused, "I'm sure he likes to think he's a terror, but there's something gallant about him. The care he takes of Needly is surprising!"

"Nothing prevents small boys from having large ideals, once they know such things are possible. It's alerting them to the possibility that's sometimes difficult. Tell me about this place he was reared. What did you call it? Gravy . . . ?"

"Gravysuck." Xulai went on to describe the town, Willum's ma, the uncle called Lorp.

"A Lorpist!" Precious Wind exclaimed loudly, immediately clapping a hand over her mouth. "That almost made me forget we're supposed to be hiding out. *Lorpists!* Ooh, yes. We've met Lorpists along the coast and in several places on our way cross-country toward Artemisia. The last group of them we met—five of them, men, I suppose, though they looked rather more like pictures I have seen of prehistoric apes—saw the rings in my ears and decided they needed to examine the whole group of us for what they were pleased to call 'wholeness.' We would, of course, strip in order to allow them access."

"I trust you escaped them?"

Precious Wind had a very mobile, expressive face. Xulai could often interpret whole orations without hearing them. Or, at least, know what was coming, as now, when her friend's lips curved into her recently-very-well-fed-tiger smile: "Well, since I had *ul xaolat* it wasn't a fair fight, I admit. I told the group that my god insisted that all men are complete only when they have no hair and nothing resembling a testicle. They cried heresy. I declared a battle of the gods, Lorp and his deity against me and *ul xaolat,* which had already painlessly removed all the features mentioned from each of them. Cries of dismay degenerated into violent argument. Some thought ritual suicide was the answer. We left them still arguing."

"The Lorp we knew was destined for the 'cata-pull-it.'" Xulai went on to repeat Willum's description of the process, concluding: "He had died before being launched, but it was all more than a little strange. Many of the small villages we've traveled through have been strange . . ."

Precious Wind went to the wagon door, peered out into the darkness, where nothing seemed to be happening, then returned, shrugging her shoulders and twisting her head from side to side. She dealt with emergency situations very well, but waiting for things to happen invariably gave her a stiff neck and a headache, probably from clenching her jaw. "I don't have answers to all the riddles of what went on in this area. Those who do know the answers say they are still too busy to discuss the matter."

Though Xulai had grown more accepting over the past few years, occasionally she still reverted to fury at whole generations of "fiddlers" who had been involved in her own genetic heritage. Abasio, though he had been interfered with at least as much as she, did not fret over it. He said one's ancestors had always influenced who and what one was. The addition of a little purpose to the process did not seem to him worth fussing about when there were so many more immediate concerns needing attention. Abasio, however, was not there at the moment to calm Xulai down.

"I wish someone would discuss the matter," Xulai said in a venomous tone. "I know the why well enough, but I'd very much like to be told the when and who and where of it. There had to be some reason for all this local genetic interference beyond our becoming capable of producing sea-children!"

Precious Wind summoned patience. "Well, of course there was something beyond that, Xulai! Yes, someone had to create the first sea-egg. That was your mother. Yes, someone had to swallow that one to enable more to be produced, and then produce them! That person was her daughter, the Princess Xulai: you! That was a tricky part, because we were fighting random forces left over from the Big Kill that wanted to stop it happening! To say nothing of that killing machine's sorceress daughter who killed your mother.

"*But that was less than half the battle. Then the sea-eggs that you produced had to be passed on to others, and they had to be hatched in environments that were prepared to accept them! Didn't they?* You've been disappointed in the people who refuse, but what you should have felt was amazement at how many young people have accepted! Would you have guessed so many would be willing and capable of the change? And when they proved to be both willing and capable, did you believe that fortunate result was entirely due to the warm personalities and eloquent salesmanship shown by Abasio and Xulai?"

Xulai was stunned at the question. "We have thought we were doing it rather well."

"Did you think the planners *left it totally to chance* that you would do well? Most of the people who are accepting now have been moved in the direction of acceptance for at least four generations."

Xulai stopped breathing. After a moment she gasped. "I thought there were other teams doing what Abasio and I are doing, teams spreading out from Tingawa."

"They aren't doing quite as well as you are, mostly because none of them have sea-babies yet. The fact they are having any success at all, however, may be attributed to an extensive genetic predisposition! You and Abasio were the . . . the tip of the iceberg. A lot of people were fiddled with, not just you. And I really don't understand your irritation, Xulai. People have always selected their mates on the basis of their characteristics. All that was done, here, was to see that those with useful characteristics met one another. You and Abasio were merely introduced. You weren't forcibly locked in the bedroom together!"

"Presh!"

"Well, you weren't!" Precious Wind rubbed the back of her neck, moving her hands down onto her shoulders. She ached. The journey had been tiring. She too was in a "Why me?" sort of mood, and surprised at that fact. Serenity was a much-valued virtue among Tingawans, but she was finding it increasingly difficult to maintain even a semblance of it. As Xulai herself put it, "Things keep happening!" Sybbis and her gangers. Lorpists. Griffins getting demanding. Children being abducted. *Probably very important children.*

She repeated a discipline jingle to herself, one her own grandmother had taught her, managing to achieve a mild, almost indifferent tone: "One of the men who has been working on this project for most of his life told me that 'this part of this continent' was among those selected because it had accumulated an extremely broad spectrum of genotypes from all over the world. It had been settled and resettled in prehistoric and primitive times, from various directions."

Xulai made an angry face. Precious Wind murmured, "This area west of the mountains was geologically stable and there were no wars happening in it; that made it a magnet for people seeking to improve their lives. They came from everywhere; when they got here, they interbred, mixing themselves thoroughly. Our people saw it as a place ready for intensive recruitment. We, our people, were interested in the inevitable genetic drift in the area. We wanted to encourage some genetic clusters that mightn't have turned up accidentally. Or not until it was too late."

"Inevitable genetic drift?" Xulai raised a beautifully formed and very irritated eyebrow. "Who says, inevitable?"

Precious Wind allowed herself to feel angry. "You are determined to believe you have been ill treated. Well, *we should have taken your discomfort more seriously, but it is not too late.* It should be possible for us to set things right for you. I can arrange for that to happen."

"Not likely!"

"Oh, yes. I can. Tingawan medics can erase memory. I will tell your grandfather how deeply you resent the fiddling; we'll take you to Tingawa, where they will erase your memory. Then I will personally settle you in another life in a place where no one has done any recruitment or selection at all. No man wants to think of himself as unwanted, and Abasio is an extremely attractive man. We can relieve him of memories of you, which—inasmuch as you resent his part in it—I'm sure he'll agree to. Among the various Sea Ducks, I'm sure we can find another attractive woman who's been given a sea-egg, and I'll make sure the children are taken care of while he gets one lined up."

Xulai looked at her blankly, as thought she had been struck by something very large and heavy. "That's not . . . I wasn't . . ."

"Yes, you are, you were, you have been, constantly carping about it, and it's going to become an impediment to the entire project. It's as though everything we've achieved, your mother's life, her death, must take second place to your irritation at being part of it. Xulai, if we hadn't hidden you, you wouldn't have survived. You know that as well as I do. But if you really don't like your present role, we can take you out of it!

"Do you know how much you hurt Abasio when you complain about the planning that went into your meeting each other? It's as though you're saying you'd have chosen someone else if you had free choice. How do you think that makes him feel? Perhaps he's wondering if he couldn't have made a better choice as well. Perhaps we can find someone else who's delighted with him and the children, and you can exercise totally free choice to go wherever you wish and do whatever you wish."

"I didn't mean that." Now she was on the verge of tears. "I didn't. It's just . . . I'm not sure anymore who I am! No. There's no *anymore* to it. I've *never* been sure who I am!" She shook her head.

Precious Wind, weary of the entire discussion, asked, "Make up your mind. If you want out, we can take you out. We can minimize Abasio's pain in the doing of it. Where did you intend to go with this discussion, Xulai?"

"You said the people we've been recruiting have been . . ."

"Predisposed . . ."

"Predisposed to accept our story. How?"

"Well, let's suppose people in Area One were found to have a high level of adaptability. Let's suppose in Area Two the people had a high level of practicality. Our first move might be to send a job recruiter from Area One to Area Two, and from Area Two to Area One. They would all be recruiting people of reproductive age to take jobs in the other area. Anything that gets people moving between the two areas will result in a certain amount of intermarriage. In three or four generations, many of the people in these areas turn out to have a high level of practical adaptability. That's an oversimplification, but it's essentially what happened.

"Then, since it was *absolutely necessary* that the sea-children project have a *high initial acceptance rate* in order to succeed, where would you send the first people who had swallowed sea-eggs? Hmm? You'd send them to areas known to have a larger-than-average number of adaptable, practical people, Areas One and Two."

"So that's why we're here!"

"The project has a limited time span, so it has to focus on getting an initial high rate of acceptance. Once we reach a certain critical level, momentum will take over, but we can't afford to waste any time or effort on people who are headed toward atrophy, like those few murderous villages you've told me about. We've already developed a system of prescreening, so our recruitment won't even visit such places. And you have to admit, they have been in the minority."

"There couldn't have been many places like Burned Hat," Xulai growled. "They rejected all possibilities of survival. Their beliefs were more important than their lives. I really struggle to understand that!"

"It shouldn't surprise you in the least. Way back before the Big Kill, people were told they were overpopulating the world; killing the oceans; using up prehistoric aquifers. Even in the early twenty-first century, when people knew they were adding billions of humans that the world couldn't feed, they disbelieved the world was getting hotter, less friendly to life. Even after the famines started, after all the aquifers ran dry, certain religious groups still disbelieved it."

"Oh, come on, Presh!"

"I'm not joking. While millions of children were starving at various places on the earth, some religions were still insisting that it was sinful to prevent excess births. I'm fascinated by the religions of that time. Without exception they simply denied reality. They were completely myth-driven. Self-inflicted pain was a common religious practice . . ."

"How did they arrive at that?"

"Pleasure wasn't justifiable for any reason, Xulai. In those days people were encouraged to offer up *pain* as a sacrifice to God. If a man crawled ten miles over thorny ground to a certain shrine; if he arrived bloody, infected, perhaps crippled, and offered this bloody, dirty mess as a sacrifice to the Creator, it was considered praiseworthy. Now, let me ask you: if it was offered to you, would you want it?

"In the real Creator's universe, almost all creatures are born with good, strong bodies and with organs that allow them to see, to hear, to feel, and to learn; in the Creator's universe, pain is there to warn us when something is wrong and needs help or protection. Now, why would the Creator of the universe be pleased when someone throws a bloody, suffering broken person back in the Creator's face and says, 'Here, whoop-dee-do, I'm giving you a lot of bloody pain as a sacrifice.'"

Diverted from her original plaint, Xulai thought it over. "I guess it'd work only if their god is a sadist."

"Well, Xulai, they already *know* their god is a sadist because they'd been told it had invented hell. Only a sadist could have invented hell! Of course, *before* that particular God invented hell, men had to invent that particular God. That tells you something about mankind!"

Precious Wind sighed. "Sybbis is a perfect example of what I'm talking about. She's requiring people to ignore reality and worship her, and she uses pain as the tool. She doesn't understand that people—all creatures—have evolved to seek satisfactions out of life. If they get none, they either die or rebel."

"What's she doing here?"

"Right now I believe she is explaining her authority over Artemisia."

Xulai stifled laughter. "Sybbis? Her authority?"

"I'm judging from what I know about her. The Artemisians have been attempting . . . diplomacy with her. They have to stop ganger raiding parties killing the farmers, stealing their stock, burning their barns and haystacks. The Artemisian delegation tried to convince her that farmers must be exempt from being raided, because they create the food we all eat, and once she kills them and takes the food, there will be no more food." Precious Wind frowned, shaking her head. "Perhaps she imagined food would appear at royal command. The Artemisians are waiting for her to get the point. We don't believe she's stupid, just misinformed or . . . perhaps uninformed."

Xulai, brow furrowed, shook her head. "No, Presh, sorry, I think you're wrong. I think she is stupid. She has a kind of ignorance that goes very deep. It's a . . . *depth of habit* that's even more difficult to modify than stupidity is."

"Girl, the ganger women had to have seen farmers bringing food into the city. They had to have seen them selling it!"

"If that's what you and the Artemisians have been basing your argument on, you're wrong! Abasio has told me all about that ganger life! The women reserved for the ganger top men certainly did *not* see farmers bring food into the city, and they never saw them selling it!" She settled herself more comfortably, obviously ready to lecture.

"The gang houses were typically buildings with four or more stories. The top floors and the roof were occupied by the gang leaders' women and daughters, with a locked and guarded door between them and rest of the house. Female servants—older women, unattractive women—went back and forth, but the top-caste women never left their quarters except for trips to the nearest bathhouse with an armed escort every few days. They did not move about the lower floors. They did not go to their men. The men who owned them went to them.

"It was the men, the gangers themselves, who observed things brought to market, and it was usually the men who went to the market and bought food. And they did *buy* it, because the farmers stopped bringing food to town if they didn't get paid. From the roof, however, all the women could have seen was the men going out and returning: returning with captives, returning with loot, returning with weapons—all of them stolen. How would the women know that food was in another category?

"If the Artemisians are trying to show Sybbis how farming works, they're wasting their effort. She'll continue the pattern she's familiar with: men go out and steal stuff. That's what that bunch headed for Salt-gosh was doing, and it's a pattern that will stand up under more pressure than Artemisia can bring to bear. What made them think she'd learned anything?"

Precious Wind shook her head in dismay. "I said the Artemisians are waiting for her to get the point, but the point was based on an assumption Sybbis would know something about where food comes from. If what you've said is accurate . . ."

She was silenced by the sound of shouting out near the road. Almost simultaneously Kim flew through the door of the wagon to sprawl breathlessly on the floor.

"Gangers," he gasped. "And that queen of theirs. A whole flock of 'em."

Precious Wind took *ul xaolat* from her pocket and poked at it.

They felt nothing happening. Xulai had had enough *ul xaolat* experience to know one could *feel* nothing happening. There was a sense of cessation: a momentary stoppage of all sound, sight, smell, a feeling she called "the whoosh." It was a creepy feeling that did not become less so with repeated experience.

Precious Wind said, "Now you can open the door and we'll see what's going on."

They left the wagon and stood outside on the road. They were, at most, only a quarter of the way up the mountain, looking down onto darkness broken by the campfires around Arakny's camp. The ganger group, lit by torches, had stopped east of the camp, leaving a gulf of darkness between themselves and the Artemisians. Torches grouped and shuttled across this darkness: a dozen from the gangers to the Artemisians, that dozen plus a few more back to the gangers.

Kim went up the ladder onto the wagon roof and settled himself to watch. The two women climbed onto the wagon seat.

"Arakny has been challenged and has gone to talk with whomever," said Precious Wind in a voice that betrayed deep concern. Xulai had thrown a new light onto the relationship between the ganger queen and the Artemisians, and Precious Wind felt an abrupt sense of insecurity. She'd allowed herself to feel amused about Sybbis.

"What reason will the Artemisians give for being out here?" asked Xulai.

"Every year they come this way two or three times late in the fall to collect pine nuts. I'm sure Sybbis's spies have reported that to her. Also, they bring groups of the younger people from Artemisia out here several times a year to let them get to know one another away from their separate lives, men doing this, women doing that. You, of course, will call that fiddling with them."

Xulai stuck out her tongue. "Abasio mentioned some separation by gender roles in Artemisia."

"Well, they have different songs, or I guess 'chants' would be a better word. They do not have a tradition of what I would call music, certainly nothing like the music you told me the Saltgoshians have."

"Being able to sing was the single greatest worry the Saltgosh people had about becoming sea-people. They wanted to know if they'd still be able to sing. Their music is remarkable."

"The Artemisians howl more than they sing," Kim objected. "That's what the people up in those valleys say about them. They howl."

Precious Wind thought about this. "From what you've told me about Saltgosh music, I can understand why they'd think so. That's why I used the word 'chant,' and I think that's more accurate than 'howl.' Though, come to think of it, I've heard the children sing melodies . . ."

"Maybe what the adults do is a ritual."

"Could be. Or it could just as well be some traditional style created by some prior storyteller."

She leaned forward, as though to get a closer look at the distant camp below. "Now what's happening down there?"

A group bearing torches had left the Artemisian encampment and moved westward, the loose cluster gradually stringing out into a line. Xulai counted a dozen torchbearing riders, each streaming sparks into the darkness. The torches came almost to the canyon entrance, clustered and milled about briefly, then headed back the way they had come.

Precious Wind murmured, "One rider left the group."

"I saw it," said Xulai. "But only because we're above them. I doubt anyone could have seen it from down there. One of the returning ones is now carrying a torch in each hand, arms extended! Now what is that about?"

Precious Wind managed a derisory chuckle. "If Arakny wanted to send a message up to us, she wouldn't want anyone to know she'd done it. So she'd send a dozen riders out on an errand to . . . find something she lost, perhaps. If she's used that excuse, one of the riders who'll be returning to camp already has the 'lost' item in his pocket. He'll return it with loud rejoicing."

"Arakny is that clever?"

"Arakny is more than merely clever. She's her mother's heiress apparent."

They watched the returning riders split up into twos and threes going off in several directions. Precious Wind nodded. "No one will realize that one of them is missing." She stood up, stretched, moved restlessly about. "How long did your horses and wagon take to get from this point down to where you camped below?"

It was Kim who answered. "Two and a half days from the morning when we learned the children were taken. The mountain is very steep along this side. As you see, the vertical distance isn't great, but each switchback is extremely long."

"Is it as bad as the road up the cliffs east of Woldsgard?" Precious Wind asked.

"Worse, so far as being tiresome," Xulai replied. "In daylight, the gangers will be able to see this wagon!"

Precious Wind muttered, "We won't let the rider come all that way. It'll waste too much time, even if he uses the 'scrambles' you mentioned earlier, Kim. I think Arakny needs to tell us something we can't observe from here. Very early in the morning, I'll create a space at the nearest switchback, move the wagon out of sight, then hop down to meet the messenger. He won't cover any great distance in the dark, and I've become very good at line-of-sight jumps. From what Kim says, I should be able to pick a suitable place near the bottom of the road." She took the device from her pocket and poked at it. "Telling it to wake us at first light tomorrow."

Kim mumbled something about sleep, and they soon heard him pulling out his bedding. Xulai gaped a yawn. She hadn't realized how tired she was. She turned to Precious Wind. "Do you want the inside or the outside of the bed?"

"I'll take the inside," said Precious Wind. "If you have to get up with the babies . . ."

"Not *if*! When," said Xulai. "They've been sleeping through the night, but everything's been strange the last few days." Her own words caught her by the throat and she gasped.

"What is it?" said Precious Wind."

"It's just . . . I hope Willum and Needly are sleeping through the night. Safely."

"Tell me about Needly," asked Precious Wind, hoping to turn Xulai's mind from the children's peril.

Accordingly, while they readied themselves for sleep, Xulai told her about Needly, what she saw in the girl, what she had heard from her and thought about her and supposed might be true, interrupting herself with yawn after yawn. After a time she fell quiet, breathing softly, while Precious Wind stayed thoughtfully awake. Silverhairs. Odd. In Tingawan, Veli, short for *velipelot,* "wise-heads," a common term for respected elders, could be translated as "silver hairs." Sages. Old people. The same word was used for the invisible powers that Tingawans believed protected life on Earth. The Old Ones. Miracle workers . . . ?

The thought did not keep her from falling asleep, as Kim did beneath the wagon, as Xulai did next to her in the bed and the babies in their baskets beneath it. None of them saw the huge wings at the top of the sky as they slashed again and again, their curved blades cutting slices from the dwindling moon. The wings were larger; much, much larger than those of the female Griffins.

A GOOD DISTANCE SOUTH, IN a hollow beneath a fallen tree, Abasio, blanket-covered, lay curled against Bear's furry belly, Coyote curled against his own. Bear carried his own blanket in his thick, dark hide. Between the two creatures, Abasio was warm but still not able to sleep. He estimated they would find Sun-wings's clearing the following day, midafternoon, perhaps, if they weren't delayed by any one of the fearful possibilities Bear and Coyote had listed, with amusement, earlier in the day.

He had seen the campfires, the smokes. The idea of meeting one or more of the forest men worried Abasio more than any of the other putative dangers. Only once in his life had he felt more in peril than during that strange journey to Woldsgard, for no reason except that he had been told to go. Inspired to go. Bred to go. In total, he had met or seen—sometimes at a comfortable distance—perhaps twenty of the men he had called hermits or hunters. He had not felt safe within sight of any of them, whether they were alone or in pairs. All of them had moved in an aura of fury, a barely concealed enmity toward the world.

At the time he had not been able to understand his reaction. The traders he had encountered dealt with these forest men from time to time seemingly without risk. They had recommended he follow certain nonconfrontational protocols that would keep him away from them and protect him if he came too near. Still, he had felt threatened, and some way into the trip he had finally realized why: each sighting or encounter with the forest men had given him the same feeling he had had when he and Olly had been discovered and tracked by Ogres.

Back then, they had unhitched Blue, left their wagon, and run, as far and as fast as they could, knowing they could not move without leaving their scent behind them. One of the Ogres had smelled them! Abasio shriveled inwardly at the memory of that vast, wet snuffling, closer each time they heard it. Neither the forest men nor the Ogres moved faster than a walk. They did not run. They didn't even seem to hurry, but each step was very long and they did not tire. Pursuit was inexorable. Abasio and Olly had no defense, no weapon. Terrified, they had clung together, thinking themselves lost.

And they would have been lost, except for Coyote and his tribe, howling, dancing, luring the creature into a confrontation with a monster as terrible in its own way as the Ogre had been in his . . . or hers. Or its.

He had considered the possibility that the northern men had been fathered by one kind and mothered by another, fathered by a man on an Ogress, for example . . . Or fathered by an Ogre on a human woman? Though it might be remotely possible that they were genetic discards, creatures intended as Ogres who had not grown to the desired size?

All of which was the stuff of nightmares. Even before they left, he had urged Bear and Coyote to avoid meeting any forest men at all. The two of them had talked—that is, had communicated—with certain forest dwellers who were moving along ahead and to either side of them. Small things that lived in trees. Small things that flew. Meantime they stayed alert for the smell of campfire smoke. So far, they'd had to deviate from their original heading only once, to avoid the territorial claim being made by a belligerently bugling bull elk. Toward evening, the horses, smelling water, had sniffed out this pleasant glade protected from the wind by a wall of stone, diagonally cracked and emitting a slow, shining seep of moisture that sleeked the stone on its way to the tiny pool at the bottom.

"One-frog pool," remarked Coyote.

"Is that how pools are measured?" Abasio asked.

"Um," agreed Coyote. "Even hungry, y'never eat the frog in a one-frog pool."

Abasio had tried to decipher the meaning of that, realizing in a moment that it was the same statement he had made about the male Griffin. Even if threatened, never kill the male Griffin in a one-male-Griffin world. Even if it meant tolerating terror.

Which people did, all the time: tolerated terror in fear of something worse!

And how often had terror come upon them because men wanted to be godlike? Because men wanted to create something in a dozen years that would have taken millennia to evolve, or never would have evolved at all?

The fiber that made Griffin bodies light enough to fly was not organic, yet it grew somehow. Little likelihood it would ever have evolved. Only man-created creatures had such materials. Man had created creatures who felt all the pain that natural creatures felt, but who did not have ten thousand years of history sustaining and guiding them in crisis. They did not have instincts developed over millennia. Their kind had no history. They could not say as the birds did: *"When we were hatchlings, our parents taught us to fly to a better foraging ground when autumn came. It was not far away. Each century our people flew a little farther, for the continents were moving apart, slowly, slowly, making our winter foraging ground farther away. When it was a hundred miles farther, we flew it still, and when it was a thousand, we flew it still, and so we have flown north in summer and south in winter for thousands and thousands of miles over hundreds of thousands of years. Because we always have done it, we still do it!"*

Only recently—in terms of Griffin years—had the Griffins been rearing young. They had no history to tell them how young should be reared. Griffins existed only because men had wanted to make legends come true. How could man teach a legendary animal to do something the legends had never described? Did the Phoenix fly south in the winter? Did the Griffin hibernate? And why did men have to have legends at all? Wasn't there enough wrong in this small, real world to keep them . . . us . . . busy?

Abasio yawned wearily. His head hurt. The task he and Xulai had been given was straightforward. Go, find the people who are willing to live in the seas, help them do it. Oh, but the complications: one small, stupidly courageous boy; one small girl with a strangeness about her; the two of them making an accidental pair who did not feel at all accidental, who felt, in fact, like a fated, perhaps doom-laden pair. Abasio was unutterably weary of the fated and doom-laden, and if anyone knew about fated lives, he did. Olly's fated life. His own. Xulai's. The babies'. And now Willum and Needly. A fated life always seemed to carry a fated threat with it. As if no being could be created without the accompaniment of a shadow. It was that, really, that bothered Xulai, though she refused to believe it and covered it up with pickiness. Precious Wind usually talked her out of it. Or he could, when he had the time and the energy.

The worst of it was that the pursuing shadow did not seem impersonal. The following things weren't merely hunting meat. Their appetite was for a particular scent named . . . who? Was it him, Abasio? If so, why? Why would the appetite seek Needly? Surely Willum was not significant enough to warrant such pursuit. And if none of them, then perhaps Xulai? As she sometimes seemed to think.

If one only knew what form the shadow would take! Was it Ogre if on legs? Griffin if on wings? And if beneath the sea, some monster yet unseen? Or from beneath the earth, what? Or was it one thing, one terror that included them all, one horror that changed shape to fit the circumstance?

Whatever it was, it brought the *Ogre feeling,* a dark veil that had pursued him in fits and starts since they had faced those giants below Saltgosh, followed him up the valley, across the mountain, growing stronger whenever they had spied those campfires burning among the forests, those wraiths of ghost smoke dancing above the trees.

It shouldn't be happening! After the war at the Place of Power, the Edges had agreed with surface-dwelling peoples that they, the Edges, would eradicate Ogres. Man and Ogre could not coexist when one was the preferred food of the other. People had come from Tingawa to meet with people from each Edge, "just to check," as Precious Wind had said. They had gone back to Tingawa reporting the Ogre situation would be taken care of. Had the Edges really intended eradication? Or had they merely smiled, nodded, let others suppose they had agreed without meaning to do anything about Ogres? Why should they take the trouble? Ogres could not get into any of the Edges. If they were eating other humans, let the other humans worry!

Sun-wings had threatened the lives of the new sea-people, threatened them with death inflicted by the Griffins' *kindred of the sea.* Had the Edgers made sea monsters? The Edgers made things for amusement, things they could watch. Could they have watched any such creatures? Not in those Edges on this side of the Stonies, for there was no ocean near enough. Had there been Edges near the ocean? And had anyone ever made an inventory of Edge-made monsters? The Edges had been in competition with one another, so they had not shared their secrets. How many mythical or semimythical creatures had been created? How many of their manufactured monsters still lived, lurking hidden, unidentified, utterly unexpected?

Nonetheless. Nonetheless. He breathed deeply and tried to empty his mind so that he could sleep. He would think about the babies . . . sea-babies laughing in the pool, darting through glittering shallows; shimmering sunlight falling through aspen leaves, wafers of golden light glinting across gleaming little faces . . .

That worked. Bailai and Gailai's little faces, gurgling at the sky. Rosy mouths open, shrieking: "Mama, Dada, Illum." "Wish-fish," Willum's mother had called them. Dark little eyes peeking here and there. Quick little hands grabbing at the world. The children, happily at play. Yes. That worked.

Sometimes.

VERY EARLY IN THE MORNING, when the sky was just light enough to let her see what was around her, Precious Wind slipped out the window above the bed without waking Xulai, hopped to the nearest switchback, made her way among a few sizable boulders to a fairly flat, lightly forested pocket invisible from anywhere around them except the sky. There she cleared a place for the wagon. The *ul xaolat* had to move a volume of stone and a few trees somewhere else. There were certain strictures built into the device. It would not kill any sensate thing unless told to do so: local beetles, lizards, birds, ground squirrels, were moved before the stone was displaced harmlessly but by no means silently. Precious Wind did not doubt the people down on the flat could have heard the noise, but it had sounded only like the rockfall it actually was. Though the resultant dust cloud was obvious, a fortuitous breeze moved it silently southward to hang among the treetops a goodly distance away.

She went back to peer under the wagon, making sure Kim was in what the device would recognize as a definable contiguity, then stood upon the step and moved the wagon with ancillary humans into the newly created space. Though the transition was instantaneous, the move woke Xulai. "Is it light already?" she mumbled, reaching for her clothes.

"We're already out of sight," Precious Wind informed her, cheerfully, as she came in the door. "We're off the road at the nearest switchback south to where we were last night. I'm about to hop down the road and meet the messenger. I'll be back by the time you have the breakfast fire started. The less smoke the better, I should imagine."

From the outer edge of the road she focused on the farthest clear space she could see clearly along the roads below her. In those places where the trees on the downhill side of the road were tall enough to tower above the road itself, the rising sun threw black shadows upon the roadway. She would jump down into these shadows, hidden from the downhill side, and no one in the camp below would see a person materialize out of nothing. She *went* to the chosen place, peered through branches down to the next, and repeated the process. It took five jumps before she saw the rider a short distance ahead of her. She sat on a stone at the side of the road and waited for him.

"Ma'am," he said as he dismounted. "I can't see the wagon, so I guess you moved it."

"I did," she replied. "You're Deer Runner, aren't you? What's happened, Runner?"

"Well, ma'am, Arakny's been meeting with the queen." He shook his head at some remembered idiocy. "She has a great pree-ten-shus throne in her wagon, did you know that? And another little one beside it . . . for the little boy!"

"I don't imagine the little one enjoys sitting on it much."

"Well, it's no potty chair, but still, I 'magine not. The queen, she thinks she needs to be queen of the whole area down at the foot of the mountains, and she wants the Artemisians to de-clare them-selves her vassals." He kept a perfectly straight face during this announcement.

"Vassals?" The word blurted. He licked it in and swallowed it. "Vassals!"

"Oh, indeed, yes, ma'am. Arakny's some puzzled where Sybbis got the word. Says it sounds like to her somebody else, maybe, put the idea of vassals in her mouth." Deer Runner rubbed the back of his neck in mute incomprehension. "So Arakny has told her that when their ceremonies down there are over, she'll take up the matter with Wide Mountain Mother, but that'll have to be when the tribes all hold their annual winter meeting. After first snowfall."

"Odd. I'd never heard of such a meeting."

"No, ma'am, none of us had. Heretofore." He grinned at her. "Useful word, an't it. I 'heretofore' ha'n't heard the word 'heretofore,' I don't think. But Arakny says it's useful, and what Arakny says usually goes, so as far as the outside world is concerned." He smiled sweetly and chanted, word by word: "So, though we had not heardtofore—of such a meeting heretofore—we must've had one every year—for as long as we remember."

"Which is clear back to yesterday."

"Yes, ma'am, at least that far, though if asked, I'd be inclined to stretch it back to the time of our foremothers."

"How did Sybbis react to all that?"

"Oh, very . . . royally, ma'am. Waved her what you call it . . . kind of a stick with a onion shape on the end of it, looks like gold, maybe. Wasn't, though. Not heavy enough. She dropped it and it just sort of rattled. Like tin."

"I think it's called a scepter," said Precious Wind. "A symbol of royalty."

"Well, the queen she waved her royal-ness very symbolically, and the queen she announced she would grant us poor Artemisians time to make the only possible decision. And then the queen royally announced she would leave a guard to see that we returned to Artemisia without interfering with the 'pervision wagons' she was expecting to come over the mountain from 'that salt place,' while her royal self would return to Catland to await our formal announcement of vassalage, which we must make as otherwise we will be wiped out, to the last man." He frowned, his voice grating.

"And last woman, presumably?"

"She didn't mention that. Maybe she got a good look at Arakny's face and decided it wasn't the time to push it." His expression changed to one of rejection, as though he wanted to spit, and his voice had deepened into formality. "The real reason I think Arakny sent me is that she thinks you need to know what the ganger queen brought with her. From somewhere the queen has obtained . . . an advisor. Great big fellow. Strange kind of man. Smells . . . bad. Unpleasant, say. NO! Truth is, he stinks worse than anything I've ever smelled before."

"Dirt? Sweat?"

"No, ma'am, compared to his smell, dirt and sweat are the sweet flowers of spring. He stinks something more like . . . like something rotten. Bad rotten. He seems to breathe it out. A heavy smell. Makes you want to get away and take deep breaths, as though the smell keeps you from using air."

"Where did he come from?"

Runner shrugged. "He was walking alongside. Didn't notice him in the dark. Not until they lit the fires and he showed up. He's too big for any horse to carry."

Precious Wind started to say something but stopped herself. Better the Artemisians not start speculating. One could not fight panic after it had started. She murmured, "Big. How big?"

"Half again as tall as me. Four—five times as heavy. His bones are more like the bones in horses or cattle. And there's the smell."

"Like something rotten?"

Deer Runner stiffened, adopting an enunciatory pose, one hand beating out the tempo: "This HORrible CREAture the QUEEN has GOT is LIKE something ROTten that LIVES in ROT n' ALso was PROB'ly beGOT in ROT." Alternate emphases varied in pitch, up down, up down.

Precious Wind smiled. The tribal lore masters were already creating chants. "Would you say he smells like a dead body? That smell?"

"Come to think of it. Yes. You don't forget that smell . . ."

"Better you don't talk about it, Runner. Tell Arakny that Sybbis may have brought it hoping we would show fear or throw up from the stench or something equally aversive. I know it's impossible not to see the thing or smell it, but the less we seem to pay attention to it, the better off we'll be. Runner! *Be sure she lets people know we don't need to display fear because we have weapons that can dispose of the creatures.*"

"We do? We being who?"

"I do, and we'll be back with you soon. We don't want to use the weapons if we don't have to, so ask Arakny to do what she can to quench any talk about the creature, any notice, any obvious sniffing or gagging or whatever, until I've had a chance to learn more about it and make some decisions regarding it. Will you carry that message, please?"

"Yes'm. Hold down the talk about the . . . big man. Arakny said to tell you the queen will probably leave ganger spies behind. Or guards."

"I'll manage them; don't worry about it. Here, let's save you some time and effort." She urged him to remount, asked him to lean forward and cover the horse's eyes, then took hold of the horse's bridle and moved them the next place down the road. Two more hops and they were on the flat. Another hop, and they could see the Artemisian encampment just beginning to stir. The rider, whose mouth had opened at the first jump and had not closed during the process, said something that sounded like "Ouishuc."

Precious Wind removed his hands from the horse's eye, and the mare blinked at her in some confusion. She said, "Let her rest for a few moments. Let her have a little drink from the stream over there. Animals and children have a more accurate sense of place than grown men do; they rely less on their eyes and more on that inner sense, so she's a bit confused. Don't let her move until she finds herself and settles, then ride slowly back and tell Arakny I will return to our site behind the camp as soon as the queen and her entourage have taken themselves out of sight. Tell her I'll take care of any guards that Her Royal and Most Rigorous Majesty leaves behind."

"Just . . . take care of them?" he panted out, one quick breath, still staring around him.

"Yes. It's part of my weaponry, Runner, not a personal skill. Tell her I'll do it quietly and without a fuss. I think poor Sybbis needs to get out into the air more. Do more gardening." Sybbis definitely needed to learn where food came from. She thought a moment more. "Are there other women in the ganger group?"

"Yes," he said, putting his arm around the horse's neck and patting her. "She has some men she calls commanders. They have women with them. They call them wives like the northerners do, but the women looked more like slaves to me. We know there are quite a few women in their big camp, the main one they call Catland."

"Why did they bring women with them, do you think?"

"Oh, ma'am, my thought is they're captured women that've come with this bunch to do the cooking. Ganger men can't cook, they've never done it. For sure, Sybbis has never done it. Since everyone in Artemisia goes camping and hunting and fishing, men and women both know how to do decent camp cooking at least, and wherever there's a clan house, there's sure to be a baker with a big oven and people who dry or preserve fruit and vegetables for winter, and at least one family that makes corn and flour flats for those who don't want to bother doing it at home. In Catland there seem to be about half as many women as there are men, but we don't know whether they're volunteers or captives or some of both."

"Spoils of battle?"

"More likely just taken, grabbed off while picking mushrooms or fishing or what have you. Some families have lost a mother like that, and we've had to scramble to find somebody to nurse some new babies."

"Odd, she can be queen of it all, but other women can have no authority."

"Some of us thought it was what you might call peculiar."

"Well, it will keep until I return. A question, Runner."

"Yes, ma'am?"

"How do you think the gangers would react to losing their queen. Say she just up and disappeared. Along with her child."

"They've got one or two ganger men might try to hold their camp together," he said thoughtfully. "Don't think they could do it, though. Only reason she can is the story. None of the others are much connected to the story."

"The Abasio the Cat story, you mean? Her connection with the hero of the war at the Place of Power?"

"That's the one," he said thoughtfully. "The story gives her a little . . . a little reputation. Now, the big man, if he's as big a talker as he is in body, he could maybe hold on to most of the men. If he's not a talker, probably not. Not if they could get away without his seeing. Or maybe not if they could kill him."

"You mean he might hold them through fear! Yes, possibly he could. But you haven't heard him talk?"

"No, ma'am. Far's I know, nobody has."

"In future, Runner, why don't you call me 'Presh.' That's what my friends do."

She placed her hand on his shoulder, and he bowed—only very briefly—but when he raised his head she was gone. "Ouishuc," he said once more. The horse snorted, agreeing with him.

Ul xaolat now contained the new wagon location, close enough for Precious Wind to reach it in one jump. She returned just as Xulai was setting the kettle above a very small and virtually smokeless fire. Before tucking the device away, Precious Wind used it to cut a narrow cylindrical hole through the forest, an aerial tunnel through treetops, invisible from any direction except directly through it to the camp below. While the three adults fed themselves and the little ones, they kept an intermittent watch. By midmorning, most of the ganger troop was moving back to the east along the road, the queen's towering "advisor" shambling beside the queen's wagon. A score or so of the gangers remained behind, all of them armed with various edged weapons.

Xulai had watched the departure with a strange expression on her face. Catching Precious Wind's glance, she flushed. "Ogre-human crossbreeds. Assuming there are such things, that's one of them, down there."

"Ah," said Precious Wind. "Of course. It raises some interesting questions, doesn't it? Was the creature told to offer its services to Sybbis? Or was it simply left where she could see it and acquire it? Or did she buy it from someone? And do you think Sybbis knows who or what it is? And how can she ignore the smell?"

Xulai considered the matter. "As to the smell, it may be no worse than the stench that was common in the city of Fantis. According to Abasio, they had no systems for disposing of dead animals or human waste or any kind of filth. All of it was simply dumped in the alleys, on the streets, in piles—including any bodies, animal or human, that had accumulated. According to Abasio, the city reeked, but after a while people didn't notice it anymore. So Sybbis and her gangers may not notice it as much as someone would who has always breathed the clean air of the desert. As we mentioned, she doesn't think about things very much."

Precious Wind accepted a cup of tea and breathed in the fragrant steam. The thought of breathing stink all day, every day and night, made her feel ill. "If someone could get to her with a different set of . . . I can't say 'ethics.' Gangers have no ethics. Priorities, perhaps? With different priorities, she might be quite useful, but the ganger priority is the only one she has."

"That being *'Take what you want.'* And *'Me first.'*"

"That sums it up very nicely, yes." Precious Wind glanced around them at the campsite. "If we clean this place up quickly I can probably move most of those guards by afternoon."

They drowned the little fire and buried the ashes, carefully erasing all evidence of their presence including footprints. Precious Wind jumped them back into the woods behind the Artemisian camp. Leaving Kim and Xulai with the wagon, she "cleared the area" by strolling along the south edge of the camp until she encountered the first ganger guard. "Pardon me," she called, "can you help me?" She approached to lay a hand on his arm, and they vanished. In a very short time she returned, quite alone. She repeated this six more times, then retired into the woods, where she joined Kim and Xulai for a cup of tea.

"Are you going to move them all?" Xulai asked, who had been watching the process with something halfway between amusement and stirrings of what she thought might be conscience.

"I've moved all of them that were on this side of the camp, but I'm running out of locations to put them. I want each of them to be alone, so they won't threaten anyone in their new location . . ."

"But they're not . . . wounded or anything?"

"Of course not," Precious Wind replied haughtily. "Any kind of wounding would be both unnecessary and incompetent. There are a dozen more of them, and I'll have to spend some time creating new destinations. You wouldn't know of a landmark that's unmistakable, would you?"

Kim offered, "The thing Abasio called the Listener, Xulai. Nothing else like that anywhere."

"He's right," Xulai agreed without enthusiasm. "It's not in what I'd call a convenient location, but it's huge. A kind of curling red stone— that is, it's said to be red at sunrise. It's green most of the time, and it coils up from the ground and circles up to the north, then back toward the south, like a huge skinny ocean wave, only frozen in time."

"Where did you see it from?"

Xulai shrugged. "We were just below the pass, weren't we, Kim? No! I remember the sign we saw right after we passed the thing. It said 'One day to Findem Pass.' We were looking northeast. How many switchbacks from that sign, Kim?"

He turned away, counting on his fingers as she went on: "It was only visible from that one curve on the road. That near the top, the roads between switchbacks were a lot shorter."

Xulai nodded, remembering the weird effect the thing had had on Abasio. "The thing really didn't show up very much, but it had a very odd effect on Abasio. I think we were on the third switchback from the top when we saw it."

Precious Wind ate her breakfast while she consulted her folder of maps. Various landmarks were noted, as were the roads used by the king's tax-hogs. She counted three down from the top, examined that stretch of road, then took *ul xaolat* and vanished once more, intending to start from the place their wagon had been this morning.

Several Artemisian men from Arakny's camp filtered into the wagon clearing shortly thereafter.

"My name's Deer Runner, ma'am," announced their spokesman. "Your friend spoke to Arakny, and she sent us just in case any of Sybbis's guards wander anywhere near your wagon. If you don't mind, ma'am, I'll just stay here with you."

Xulai didn't mind. "What're Sybbis's men doing?"

"Oh, they're standing around the northern two-thirds of our camp, looking bored and hungry."

"They don't seem to know that a third of them are gone," said Kim. "No one has ever told them how to organize themselves, and they don't know. Their queen didn't leave any one person in command of them. How do they respond to problems?"

"They probably don't respond to problems, ma'am. I would imagine they often encounter a bad problem they didn't see coming . . ."

" . . . or live long enough to see it depart . . ." suggested Precious Wind.

Xulai poured a cup of tea and handed it to Deer Runner. "Tell us about Catland. Everything you know . . . or suspect."

Deer Runner accepted the cup of tea and relaxed, leaning against the wagon. "Well, when the Catlanders got here, it was Midsummer and they started out with a camp. Most of 'em had tents. When they noticed that most of our buildings are 'dobe, some of 'em learned how to make 'dobe. Sybbis told 'em to build a wall around the camp. They built the wall and spent some time putting pictures on it. That was very bad problem number one because by the time they had enough bricks made and dried to build that wall, fall had come and it was turning cold. About then, maybe, they realized they should have built houses instead of a wall." He sipped at his tea, shaking his head.

"So, they had a very chilly winter. Soon as it got warm enough for 'em to make brick again, they built some shelters. They needed clay and they needed straw to make more bricks; they had to bring the clay and straw to them or go to where it was, so they tried to steal some wagons. They ended up with arrows through them, so they decided to set up their brickwork place where the clay was and buy wagonloads of straw.

"First thing they built was a house for Sybbis, and they had a look at the men's houses at Wide Mountain and built some bad copies of those for the men t'sleep in. We suggested they should build a cookhouse. We even offered to show them how, but they said they could see how. Since they couldn't see the foundations, they really didn't see how they were built. Their houses had no foundations under 'em. That was another bad problem. Once it came to snow, the bottoms of the walls got soggy. 'Dobe'll do that, and the walls started caving in. You need to put rocks where the walls are going to go, and you need to slope the ground on the outside away from the wall and ditch it—'landscape it' is what Arakny calls it—so the water drains away. And you need to slope your roofs so the water runs off of them on the downhill side so water drains away.

"By that time, some of the men had built houses of their own, an' they've gone on like that for several years now." He grinned to himself. "'Course, like I said, they didn't put any foundations under the buildings, so they're startin' to crack pretty bad."

"No overall plan?" asked Xulai.

"Not s'much as a line in the dirt even. No streets between things. Inside that wall everything's crowded together. Next bad problem they didn't see coming was that nobody figured out where to put the shit. It got pretty deep before they finally thought maybe they'd better have a special place to put it instead of just droppin' pants wherever."

"Who cleaned it up?"

Deer Runner shook his head. "Nobody. Finally Sybbis sent one guy to Wide Mountain Mother to ask her what to do. Seems wherever they came from, that's the way things had been, just shit, dead bodies, filth, trash everywhere. One of Wide Mountain Mother's family showed them how to dig earth closets. Most a' the buildings are outside that wall now, so they got room. Houses inside the wall hafta empty pots into earth closets outside the wall."

Kim said, "You said there were pictures on the wall?"

"Yup. There's one of the guy, CummyNup. He's sorta the main one over there. Then there's one of Baso the Cat."

"What does he look like?" whispered Xulai.

Deer Runner considered the matter. "Ooh, well, it's got real bright red hair, standy-up ears, round eyes, muzzle sticks out like a cat, with great long whiskers on either side of its mouth—long fangy teeth in that mouth. Looks like a cat." He grinned. "When Sybbis told the painter to put him on the wall, that's what CummyNup told the painter he looked like, a real cat."

Xulai grinned at this, thinking of Abasio's possible reaction. She anticipated telling him he did not in the least resemble his eidolon. Arakny had said there was a definite resemblance between the picture of CummyNup and Sybbis's son. CummyNup wasn't with this group. He had possibly been left in charge of the main encampment.

"How did they ever end up down here?" Kim demanded.

Xulai thought back to what Abasio had told her. "When the few remaining gangers left the city, most of them came south. Sybbis was the daughter of one of the gang chiefs. She was bought by the chief of the 'Purples'—that's the gang Abasio got recruited into. The Purples made up the largest group left when everything in Fantis fell apart, and on their way south they gathered up the remnants of other groups."

"But she rules? How?"

She shrugged again. "She was the daughter of a gang chief. She was bought by old Chief Purple to be the wife of his only son, a boy who never matured physically—in his twenties he had a body like a little boy of seven or eight. Abasio said old Chief Purple wouldn't admit it, not even to himself, that the boy was not a normal man. Sybbis knew that her father had ruled his gang. When the whole city fell apart, she gathered up the remnants and took her father-in-law's place."

Deer Runner nodded. "Well, that could explain it: she believes she's inherited his power, and she has a few powerful enforcers around her who pretend to believe that. They're the ones who actually run the place."

Xulai offered, "Precious Wind says it's good to have a putative but nonessential leader for enemies to focus on. Someone the group can lose to assassination or accident without feeling the loss or endangering the structure."

"Pute-a-tive but non-essential. That pretty well fits," murmured Deer Runner, with a sideways grin. "So it's someone among the men who's the real power, probably this CummyNup!" He scanned a circle around them. The number of guards had dwindled. "When you figure Precious Wind is coming back?"

"Whenever she loses the other thirteen or fourteen guards."

Deer Runner straightened up, abruptly losing his folksy manner and homegrown speech. "Tell her I congratulate her on her activities. Nicest job of dispersal I've seen in a very long time. As for Sybbis, she thinks she's 'building an empire,' but she has no idea what an empire is. She brought her gang south because someone told her it was warmer in the south. If old Chief Purple was still alive, I'd say he'd be the one giving the real orders. Either that or the guys who pretend to take her orders but really give their own. It doesn't matter. She's already set the place up to fail . . ."

"Like how?"

"Lady, you haven't been here, but Abasio has, and he'll verify what I say. This geographic area can't support a heavy population. Wide Mountain Mother rules a very widely spread population of people whose numbers are limited and who live almost entirely off the land. For efficiency and defense, each population cluster is assembled around a small local plaza which is located in or near the special resources a village needs. These places are always near water and near forests; can't bake bread without firewood, can't build houses without rafters."

Xulai had taken a notebook from her pocket and was taking notes as Deer Runner went on. "Each place will have a baker—less wood needed for one big oven than for fifty little ones—but there's only one wheelwright in the whole area. Only one tile maker and one kiln. One healer in each place, but only one or two surgeons in places specially equipped for him or her and the students. A surgeon has to teach as well. Originally we hired a man from way east of here, and he taught others. There's a medical school way east of us. Wide Mountain Mother picks two or three people out of each generation to send there. Seven years, it takes, to graduate from there.

"Each plaza doesn't necessarily have the whole variety of special things in it, but Wide Mountain Mother keeps a rider, at least, in every population center—that'd be a little house and stable with three or four good horses and some local family providing him with food and doing up his laundry and some local boy caring for the horses. That's so the word can get out and people's needs can be met quickly if there's a problem somewhere.

"From Wide Mountain Mother, three riders go to in three directions, to stations one, two, and three. From each of them, three horses go out, that's nine. And three from each of those, that's twenty-seven, thirty-nine locations in total. Fourth riders are the last one to catch the tiny places. There's about fifty little communities. All of 'em get the word within two days. Same thing works in reverse if some small place wants to alert the people to something—a group of marauders, a pack of wolves bothering the sheep, something like that.

"Outside each settlement there'll be some farms. If the land provides the right kind of ground, there'll be an orchard. Most essentials are found locally, grown locally, or obtainable by a crew spending a few days at a time to go get or make whatever's needed. Things not locally available that we need to trade for are carefully planned by Wide Mountain Clan. There'll be a farrier somewhere, and a blacksmith, and so on . . .

"If someone needs a house, someone pays the wagon man and the lumber man to go to the mountains and come back with a load of tree trunks for rafters. The bricks will be made at the nearest 'dobe brick works, which is the most convenient place to find clay, sand, straw, and water. If you have a tank wagon, water can be transported to wherever the clay and sand are found. If you don't have a tank wagon, everything has to go where there's water. That place becomes the center for brick production.

"There are several potteries that make cups, pitchers, big jars with tight covers to store things bugs or mice might get into. Pottery has to be fired, that means firewood or dried cattle dung. The dung is actually easier to gather and lighter to transport. The women spin and weave—the sheep are theirs. There are tanners here and there to take the hides from the animals hunted for meat. There are carpenters and wood craftsmen here and there. Each of these efforts may involve several people who do it as their primary productive activity. I believe you understand what I'm saying."

Xulai nodded. "I hear you say there's a lot of planning and adjusting necessary to keep everyone fed and healthy and happy and employed in providing everything the people need."

Deer Runner nodded agreement. "When Sybbis left Fantis, she stayed awhile on a farm—that's according to CummyNup—but nobody mentioned what time of year it was. Certainly it wasn't long enough to see the whole cycle from seed to harvest. She could have helped weed rows of carrots without connecting the growth to anything she ate at Purple House. So, the first winter her people were down here, they managed to accumulate enough food by raiding farms north of here, killing milk cows for meat and taking the grain and vegetable harvest. The people they raided weren't our people and they'd refused our offer of help, and when spring rolled around, the farmers packed up their remaining stock, loaded everything into wagons, and went east, toward the forest lands. There were enough of them to build a stockade, share the labor, and get settled in by winter. They're still there; we send riders back and forth, we keep in touch. The second year, there were no farms within raiding distance and people in Catland went hungry."

"They didn't raid Artemisia?"

"We had our defenses in order. Raiders ended up with arrows through them. We made a point of leaving the bodies where they'd be found. Catland got the message. After that, Sybbis—or whoever issues orders in her name—quit raiding the farms, *but that's not the issue.* It doesn't matter whether she tries to *steal* food or *buy* food or *trade for* food. *The local area cannot produce enough food to feed hundreds of totally nonproductive people.* The gangers have no skills. If they'd stayed up near where Fantis was, they'd have had year-round snowmelt streams off the mountains and they'd have had deeper, better soil. If they'd learned to farm and stayed there, they might have managed to live fairly well."

Xulai said, "I get the point. The population has to fit the environment, not the other way round."

"Exactly. This year Sybbis heard about Saltgosh, so she's sent a troop of men to raid Saltgosh for winter provisions."

Kim had been listening quietly, but he snorted at the mention of Saltgosh. "The men she sent are dead or captured."

Xulai murmured, "If they can sing, they might stay captured. Sing or not, they won't come back. We took their horses, Saltgosh will have taken the men. I don't understand what keeps any of them here. If she doesn't get the Saltgosh food, her men will go looking for farms to raid, despite what they've been told."

Deer Runner massaged his forehead, as though even thinking about the gangers was painful. "She's already lost over a third of her men to death or departure. We have the advantage. It's our home ground. Gangers are alley fighters, they have no weapons effective at a distance. Our people are hunters—excellent bowmen . . . and women. Just as Saltgosh does, we keep watch day and night. Any raiders Sybbis sends out don't return. If Sybbis were to take them east, a long way east, she'd find big rivers, deep soil, places where there's enough water to grow their own food, places where they could survive. Even back near Fantis, she'd find that. But she has none of the skills she needs to rule a sizable group of people."

"Who could she learn them from?" Kim asked.

Deer Runner gave him a brotherly pat on the shoulder. "A good question, Kim. Who indeed? How has she managed to get through these last years? They haven't succeeded in raiding for food. Where did they get it? We have the feeling someone is running her, keeping her here: probably somebody left over from Fantis that tells her what to do but stays out of sight."

Xulai looked up at this. Someone running her? The real manager or gang leader. She would have to tell Abasio that, the moment he returned . . .

Deer Runner yawned, stretched, and headed from the clearing, saying, "I've done enough frittering. Chances are Precious Wind has distributed the rest of the Catland guards. Think I'll go see if I can find her."

Evidently he did not find her. Shortly after his departure, and from the opposite direction, Precious Wind returned to the wagon to make a sandwich and talk around bites of it. "That thing is called the Listener by the local people, who say it's always been called that. It gave me an anchor point for dozens of forest places not too far from villages of some sort. Probably it's the area Needly came from. Is everything quiet here?"

Xulai replied, "Except for Deer Runner. He went off to look for you. He's really quite interesting."

Precious Wind flushed. "Artemisians can fool you that way. Except for the few like Wide Mountain Mother and Arakny, by and large they give you the expressionless face and the monosyllabic talk, and you'd swear they're ignorant as a gopher. Then they drop the mask and become quite . . . fascinating." She chewed, ruminatively. "I'll go looking for him when I'm finished."

She finished her sandwich and went off through the trees, leaving Xulai to stare speculatively after her. Was it possible that Precious Wind was . . . attracted to an Artemisian? Precious Wind? Icily logical Precious Wind? Precious Wind who usually eschewed emotion as though it were contagious? Hmm.

Precious Wind returned shortly after noon—not to the wagon, but to a place near the junction half a day's wagon journey southeast of Arakny's camp. There she seated herself on a conveniently placed fallen trunk, shut her eyes, and recalled the map of the area she had examined when she had joined the Artemisian group to come north. The map had shown a long finger of fractured stone pointing from the roots of the mountain out into the desert. Several miles wide at the mountain end, the finger dwindled gradually in both width and height as it came southeastward. On each side of this finger was a road, the northern one coming down from Catland and turning southeast along the ridge, the southern one down from Findem Pass to run more nearly due east on the finger's other side. Where the finger pointed, at its eastern end, was the Gap—pinched between the end of the finger on one side and by the Devil's Whatsit, or Devil's Ah, on the other. Here the two roads joined to continue generally southeast, across one of the few wagon fords of the Big River—a ford built by, maintained by, and whose tolls were collected by Artemisia—and thence on to Wide Mountain Plaza. The wide, low mountain for which the community was named was farther east, stretching itself along the horizon.

The Gap, barely wide enough for the road, was almost a day's wagon trip from Catland itself and two or three hours from Arakny's camp, which meant Sybbis's group should soon be approaching.

Northeast of the junction were two rounded and heavily forested hills separated by an almost cylindrical stone formation. The hills were densely covered with a dark juniper forest and watered by subterranean springs that had formed a pool near the road. Among polite Artemisians, the hill was called the Devil's Whatsit; among the more vulgar it had a dozen jocular titles, all of which were amply substantiated by any topographical map. The formation was in all particulars shaped and furred like a gigantic whatsit.

Precious Wind had entered the Whatsit's location into *ul xaolat* on her way from Artemisia and had chosen it as the place from which she could get a closer look at Sybbis's large and stinking companion without being observed. Her jump had brought her to a hidden spot at the tip of the finger, and from there she made a quick line-of-sight jump across the Gap onto the rock formation that extended eastward into the low forest covering the hills on either side. Though the east end of it disappeared into forest, this western end was bare stone, too exposed for her purpose, so she sight-jumped farther back to a higher point where she could see the passing wagons without being seen. From this lookout she used the waiting time to chart the surrounding area with *ul xaolat*'s map functions—something she'd been doing regularly during her journey. Many areas of this continent had not been surveyed in recent centuries, and as the lands of the earth were gradually being covered with water, at some point in succeeding centuries it would no doubt be useful to know the configuration of the sea bottom. All travelers with the necessary equipment were urged to record the topography of any area they happened to travel through.

She heard the ganger wagons before she saw them approaching. Almost immediately upon hearing the crunch and jingle of the wagons, she heard other sounds from the forests on both hills, one at either side of her ledge: branches breaking, heavy crunching of lower growths. She stiffened. Something very big was moving from behind her toward the road. She glanced around quickly, almost in panic. Though much of the forest was low, there were occasional oaks and a few invading groves of tall pines, a nearby one of which had a stout branch protruding three-quarters of the way up. There was no time to consider whether it would work or not; she simply concentrated on the angle made by branch and trunk and made a line-of-sight jump, throwing her arms around the trunk of the tree to keep her from falling thirty or forty feet to the ground below. Her feet were not secure; the branch was not flat. Slowly, carefully, she found a branch to grip on either side and was able to put her back to the trunk of the tree and lean against it. The wind was in her face. Both leafed and needled branches surrounded her, half from the pine she was in, the rest from an intrusively friendly oak. On either side of her, still invisible, the very loud noises were approaching.

She whispered to *ul xaolat*. It obeyed her command to level the branch she was standing on—without cutting her feet—and to cut a sight channel through the foliage, like the one she had cut from atop the mountain road. This one ended at the fork in the road below. Trees nearby trembled and creaked, their branches whipping as though in a high wind. Vast shadows obscured the speckled sunlight, then moved past with a grinding sound as if . . . trodden by monstrous feet. She found herself holding her breath. Sound and motion passed near her, below her, and went on toward the road. A tiny breeze lifted from the soil beneath the trees and rose to where Precious Wind clung. She gagged, spit, spit again as those who had come out of the forest went down the hill. She'd smelled them. Now she could see them!

She clung to her tree like a tick to a dog, forcing herself to breathe slowly, to make no sound. The stench made her saliva run thickly; she leaned forward and held her mouth open so it could drip onto the soil. Still gagging, she saw the drivers of the wagons at the end of her sight tunnel. Since leaving the area near the Artemisian camp, all the gangers had donned masks that covered their noses. The creatures from the forest loomed above the wagons, twelve feet tall, their stench now visible as an ocherous haze that roiled around them as they joined their fellows to make a double file on each side of Sybbis's wagon, two files of six, a dozen on the left, a dozen on the right. The whole caravan marched away to the northwest. Precious Wind waited until she could no longer see them, not even the tops of their heads. It took that long for her to be able to breathe normally, think normally, act . . . relatively normally.

She had no wish to go down to the soil where those creatures had walked. She entered the series that had brought her from the camp and returned there directly from the tree, successive locations blurring around her. Once there, she took the time to wash out her mouth, several times, then went looking for Arakny. She found her with Xulai and Kim, at the wagon, and told her that all the guards left behind by Sybbis had been taken elsewhere.

Arakny was accustomed to leadership, as was Precious Wind. There was a moderate though polite tension between the two of them, which Precious Wind tried both to grant and accept gracefully. She was the stranger, and several things she had done recently were enough to upset the Artemisian territorial sense. She was not surprised to be greeted with slight approbation.

"The poor guards you've abandoned out there may starve," said Arakny.

Precious Wind shook her head very slightly, replying mildly, "Every one of them is carrying enough food for several days. Before I left them, I told each one they would find settlements inevitably if they followed the streams I showed them. I told them if they did not act belligerent, likely they would be accepted. They need not starve." She paused, grim-faced. "Arakny, Xulai . . . there was . . . how can I say it? When I moved them, they were not angry. They were not upset. At the time I thought there was something odd about their *appreciative acceptance* of their situation. Their gratitude."

"Gratitude?"

Precious Wind's legs were trembling. She sat down abruptly, holding out her trembling hand.

"Presh! What is it?" cried Xulai.

"I see the kettle steaming. Tea. First. Please."

Tea was forthcoming. Precious Wind took the cup to the edge of the trees, rinsed her mouth with it, spat, did it again. Taste came back gradually. She sipped. The other two were regarding her with pale, strained faces. She breathed deeply, drank, waited until her head had stopped pounding.

"Arakny, I decided to watch Sybbis's group on its way back to her encampment or village or whatever we call it. There's a hill at the fork in the road . . ."

"I know the place. We call it the Devil's Whatsit. I'm told there used to be a pair of devil cats up there."

"It's still an insightful name!" Precious Wind gasped. She took a deep breath and went on: "There was a wind from the west at the time. I went up onto the stone promontory to watch the wagons go by, but as they approached, I heard something moving in the woods east of me. I spotted what looked like a good perch in a tree and hopped up to it, ending on a branch quite a good distance from the ground. What I'd heard was a massive, heavy sound, so I . . . I stayed very quiet and remained where I was, luckily high enough to be unnoticed. Did I mention there was a light wind from the west?" She paused, willing her voice to stop trembling before she went on. "We all thought Sybbis had one . . . very large attendant, counselor, whatever. There were two dozen more of them. The others were hidden on that hill, in the woods, and they lined up on each side of her wagon and marched off toward Catland. All the people in the wagons were wearing masks. The stench and the taste were unbelievable."

Arakny paled. Kim clenched his hands and drew a deep breath. Xulai stared. "More of them? In the name of everything holy, Precious Wind. More of them?"

"Many, many more." Precious Wind rose and went into the trees to rinse out her mouth once more. She glared at her misbehaving hands, making them stop shaking. It took a moment before she could say the rest. "It certainly explained why the guards she left here were glad to be removed from the area. Well removed. I'm fairly sure some of the stinking creatures are female. Sybbis seems to have a breeding population."

IN THE GLADE FAR UP the slope of the mountains, Needly and Willum were resting. During the morning they had taken turns massaging Sunwings' right rear leg. When the pain showed no signs of diminishing, Needly had treated the leg with the healing medicine and also with another one of Grandma's potions, only a tiny bit, a few places on the leg touched with a moistened twig. Less than a drop overall. Needly cautioned Willum not to touch the twig, and she laid it carefully on a flat stone, covering it with another. "Grandma told me it was stone juice," she whispered. "It's in her notebook, and I saw her make it."

"What's it do?"

"Preserves. If there's someone badly wounded, you know, and you have to get help for them, and you don't think they'll last until you can get there, you put a drop of that on them, on their tongue, if you can, or over their heart. And it stops them, preserves them, holds them unharmed until you can do for them. So, I figured, the teensiest bit on that leg, maybe it'll keep her from hurting it worse if she has to move."

"How do you bring them out of it?"

"The antidote is in Grandma's notebook, and I have a little bit of that. Or Grandma said it wears off. I should've asked her more about it . . ." She turned aside, hiding her face. "I thought I had more time with her . . ."

"You think Abasio will come?"

"I know he will."

"I wish he'd hurry," Willum muttered. "Be nice if he could get here before that giant gets back." They were both in agreement. Yung For'ster was growing increasingly impatient.

They had no luck with their wishes; the hunter returned soon thereafter, in no very good mood. He stood not far from them, bow in his hand, staring at Sun-wings. "She ready fer me t'skin 'er?"

"No," said Needly. "Not yet. Just a day or two, now that we have her properly tended to."

"Got to thinkin'," said the man, strangely. Even the word "thinkin'" came slowly to his mouth, as though someone or something else had put it there from a considerable distance. "Got to thinkin' better practice the skinnin'."

Needly stood up from her place by the fire. "When she is ready, we will guide you. No practice is necessary; you already have the skill."

Willum, moved by a strange urgency, went to Sun-wings' side. Obviously frightened, Dawn-song lay trembling against her mother's body as she had done almost constantly since their arrival.

"Nah. Gonna practice onna li'l one." He moved strangely, tottering. Needly was completely familiar with that movement. How many times had she seen Gralf move like that. Or Slap or Grudge. The giant was drunk! Where had he found drink? When men were like that, one could not talk them out of things. They did not listen. Or understand.

"It's better not to practice when you've been drinking," she said very calmly. "You could ruin both hides, lose all that gold . . ."

"Nah. Li'l one's no good anyhow." He wiped his mouth with the back of his hand, mumbling, "Ahgar said nobody wans li'l ones. Practice on her. Gotta killer firs', though, so she don' bite . . ."

He raised the bow to his shoulder.

Willum saw where it was pointed. Without thinking, he leapt.

Needly saw all four of them: the giant, Willum, Dawn-song, Sun-wings. She threw up her hands, words ready in her mouth . . .

Too late: the giant loosed the bow. The arrow flew. Willum had thrown himself in front of the little Griffin, and the arrow pinned him there.

That was what Bear and Coyote and Abasio first saw as they topped the rise: the boy shot through, pinned, eyes wide, Needly running toward him, the giant's face grinning as he turned, reaching for another arrow . . .

Bear did not hesitate. Downhill he could move very fast, and before the monster could raise the bow, Bear was behind him, powerful front legs reaching around the hunter, great, raking claws—sharpened each time he tore a great stump apart, each time he raked roots from the earth—digging deeply into the hunter's fleshy neck. His hind feet raised, climbed the creature before him as though he were a tree. Bear's great jaws gaped at the creature's neck, and his canine teeth, long as Abasio's fingers, buried themselves deep into either side of the hunter's neck, ripping it loose from the skull, rocking first to one side, then the other, tearing the flesh, ripping the throat. Blood jetted into the air like a fountain and a stench rose around them like smoke . . .

And there everyone froze, unable to move or think or do anything at all during that long, long moment in which the light left Willum's eyes . . .

XULAI HAD BEEN SITTING ON the wagon step, peeling the last of the potatoes they had brought from Gravysuck. She shot upright, crying out, a long, piercing scream. Precious Wind heard her and came running. Xulai was standing erect, head back, back curved as though some intimate agony had struck her and she had tried to move away from the pain.

"Xulai? Are you hurt?"

"The children," she moaned. "The children, Precious Wind. The children. Oh, no, no, no . . ."

"Xulai!" Her name was shouted. She came to herself.

Precious Wind said, "Who do you hear in your mind?"

"Abasio. Abasio."

"Is he there, with them?"

"He must be. I saw it. Yes. It was Abasio seeing it . . ."

"Then he will return at once. He will need help. Let's get up to the site he will return to."

Arakny was summoned, the herbalist healer with them was summoned, a number of the men followed them, and they climbed to the site Abasio had recorded before he left them, just a few days before.

Abasio had not waited an instant. By the time the contingent from the Artemisian camp reached the clearing, Sun-wings and Dawn-song were there; so was Bear, slavering, coughing, covered in stinking substances, red and ocher, his eyes wild with fury; Coyote, nose twitching, lips snarling; the horses, shivering all over, Abasio with his arms across the horses' backs. And Needly, busy at Dawn-song's side, stanching the blood that ran from a wound. And at Sun-wings' side, quite still, Willum lay, still and white as death, the arrow through him, hard as stone.

A TEMPORARY SPACE WAS MADE ready in the Artemisian camp, and the Griffins were moved into it along with Willum and Needly. The healers from Artemisia were summoned. All said that Dawn-song was not seriously hurt. Needly submitted to them samples of the potion she had already put upon Sun-wings' torn wing, on Dawn-song's wound, as well as the other potion she had administered to Willum and put on Sun-Wings' leg. She explained what her grandmother had said about the stone medicine, explained that she herself had observed it being made and that the instructions were in her grandmother's notebook. She found the notebook, held it open while the Artemisians copied the information about stone medicine and the antidote. She retrieved the book and shook her head when they suggested they take it with them.

"Copy anything you can use, but the book is all I have left of her. I'd rather keep it with me." She went on to explain that she'd put the stone medicine on Sun-wings's leg, to prevent any permanent damage from happening while they were getting away from the hunter, and on Willum as quickly as she could reach him.

Everyone with some experience of herbal remedies or healing went to examine Sun-wings's leg. It was not as warm as the rest of her. She could not move it, but it caused her no pain. It did not smell of rot. It was as though she had acquired a stone leg that blood no longer bothered to go into or out of. As for Willum, Willum was stone.

"And how long will this preserve the person?" one of the healers asked.

"If it's a whole body, long enough for that body to fix itself before the heart starts beating again. I know Sun-wings's heart hasn't stopped. I put only a few drops on her leg, just enough to hold her leg as it was. Grandma once told me about a man who had a spear through him. They used stone medicine, then they took him somewhere and removed the spear, and after quite a long while his body healed inside and his heart started beating again."

"You're speaking of surgery. We have no surgeons. The Edges have surgeons, but they don't let outsiders in. Tingawa, of course, has surgeons."

"No," said Needly, out of a terrible calm she had found inside herself and that she did not dare depart from. "They didn't cut, they just pulled out the spear. The man lay there for a long time, perhaps a year, and then he woke up and the hole through him was healed. The stone holds the person safe while the body fixes itself. It's like it stops time. Or slows it way, way down. Like a stone experiences time. Different for a stone than for a tree, or for you or me. That's why it takes so long to heal itself."

They examined Sun-wings's wounded wing, finding it to be healing with extraordinary rapidity. Needly explained the ingredients that went into the healing lotion. "Ah," said an Artemisian herbalist to another. "Ah, yes, I've heard of that," moving from one little discussion circle to another.

By the end of the morning, most of the Artemisians who lived in other areas were on the road back to their homes; Precious Wind and Xulai were using the far-talker to seek advice from Tingawa; Needly was brought in to describe the stone medicine plant to the Tingawan at the other end. Willum was laid in the bed of the wagon, the arrow gently cut off even with his skin in back, only enough protruding in front that it could be pulled from the wound when and if that seemed appropriate. Needly sat cross-legged beside him, her face ashen, her hand laid lightly upon his chest.

"Willum," she whispered into the hovering void she could sense around him. It was a place of stillness. She doubted it had a location or reference to any known point upon the world she knew. Just now it was where Willum was and it was held around him. "I didn't know what else to do, Willum. Don't die, Willum. Just wait. Just wait. You don't need to wake up and you don't need to die. Time isn't moving where you are, Willum. We're going to figure something out. We really are . . ." and meanwhile the tears fell from her jaw onto her skirt, cupped between her knees, until it was as sodden and chilled as her spirit.

SUBSEQUENTLY THERE WAS A GOOD deal of talk: discussion among the Artemisians, loving words between the Griffins and Needly, mild argument between Abasio and Xulai, a subdued, sorrowful, and yet relieved exchange between Sun-wings and Dawn-song, even a few puzzled words from Kim. The discussions of possibilities ended with the decision to move the Griffins, mother and daughter, to a currently empty storage building that stood at one side of the plaza of the Wide Mountain Clan. Once they were there, Wide Mountain Mother's closest associates could help the feeding and treating of the wounded mother; there the Griffin child would also be safe and well tended to. Those who had traveled from Saltgosh could park their wagons nearby, the horses would have pasture. Everyone would be a safer distance from Sybbis and her tame horrors, if they were tame. Once that move was made, everyone could take a deep breath and try to decide what should be done next.

Abasio, meantime, was busy explaining to representatives of the men's groups what he had heard the huge hunter say. He had repeated it to himself, over and over; now he repeated it to them. "He said, *'Nah. Li'l one's no good anyhow. Ahgar said nobody wans li'l ones. Practice on her. Gotta kill 'er firs', though, so she don' bite . . .'* We were behind him, we heard him clearly. That's exactly what he said."

"The girl child had heard no previous reference to this person or thing the hunter called Ahgar?"

"She's so upset about the boy that she can't think straight. She says give her a little time, and she'll think back at what they heard. When he said he would practice on the little one, she told him it was better not to practice when he'd been drinking. He'd ruin the hide. You do understand this was a pretense she and Willum had set up? To delay things, hoping somehow to either get away or be rescued . . ."

"And your own feelings about this hunter?"

Abasio said, "My feelings are irrelevant. I can take you there to see for yourselves! Wide Mountain Mother wants to jump to the plaza to check out the building before the Griffins are moved. Xulai will go with her. Before they do that, we can jump to the clearing where we found the children. Unless something has found the body edible, it's probably still up there where we left it. Bear grappled with the creatures and ripped out his jaw and throat. He's been trying to get rid of the taste of the thing ever since! I can take several of you there and back this afternoon. We can even bring the body back here with us, if that makes sense."

There was agreement. Bear and Coyote would go with Abasio and a group of a dozen hunters. Precious Wind would go along to be sure all the right buttons were pushed. Several of the Artemisian women would also go, Arakny among them. Precious Wind hooked the *ul xaolats* together so that the same journey lists could be shared; then those making the journey assembled around Bear, Coyote, Precious Wind, and Abasio, all linked by touch of hand.

They went.

The Artemisians who had not before known of or experienced travel via *ul xaolat* stood in shocked silence for a moment, trying to orient themselves. They had been moved to the center of the open space, and Abasio pointed them up the hill where the great carcass lay as Bear had left it. Some men moved out to the edges of the clearing, fingering weapons, keeping watch. Bear and Coyote went to examine the carcass. Their previous journey had been precipitous; there had been no time for inspection. They were immediately joined by Precious Wind, Abasio, and Dark Wolf, one of the hunters.

"By all the gods of earth and water, wind and sky, he stinks!" the Artemisian hunter exclaimed. "And he's almost as big as that one with the ganger queen. I have never encountered such a stink."

"Ungh," agreed Bear. "He tasted rotten, awful, too. Left a coat of something on my teeth. Been chewin' leaves ever since; haven't got 'em clean yet. Wasn't like human."

"When have you tasted humans?" asked Abasio.

"I've tasted you," said Bear. "When we found you, I licked your leg and you jumped like a frog."

The Artemisian took another analytical breath and made a face. "The body stinks like that one with the queen."

"'S not just dirt," said Bear. "Abasio says he smells like Ogre. It's a different smell. Nothing else smells like that. You ever smell Ogre?"

Dark Wolf shook his head. "Never have. Hope I never will."

Abasio said, "It's definitely like Ogre smell; worse, maybe. The thing may be a human-Ogre half-breed. Maybe some Troll genetics in there."

Coyote said, "A hybrid. That's what the old man called me, the one who taught me words after I could speak."

Dark Wolf turned to find Abasio behind him, pacing off the length of the carcass, which he and two others had pulled straight on the ground.

Abasio muttered, "I was talking about the created creatures not long ago with Xulai. We thought giants might be pure human genetics, with all the size controls turned off. I have a dreadful feeling that they don't stop growing. They keep right on getting bigger as long as they can get food. Trolls were an animal-human genetic mix. My guess is human and either wild boar or some kind of big cat or bear or a thing from far away called a hyena. Bear says from the smell, he's sure it's wild boar. I'm almost positive that Ogres were the result of a breeding between giants and Troll females. This man isn't as big as an Ogre, at least, not the Ogres I saw some years ago. They were maybe a third again as tall. But he's a lot bigger than any man I've ever seen. I'm generally thought of as tall, and he's half to two-thirds again my height."

One of the hunters asked, "Is there any advantage to taking the body back with us?"

Abasio nodded. "Yes. The very great advantage of getting him away from here so the ones who made him or use him won't know he's dead. He knew someone or something. He came back drunk. He got the drink from someone. He talked to someone about a Griffin hide, someone named 'Ah'g'r,' or 'a Gar.'" He made a face. "That's as close as Needly can come to the sound. I think it's a corruption of 'Ogre.'"

Coyote said, "It could have been that, Abasio, but maybe it was more like 'A Gar.' Like you'd say 'A hunter' or 'A trapper.'"

"More like a label than a name?" Abasio rubbed his head, which ached.

Precious Wind said, "Possibly! It is also perfectly possible it meant 'Ogre.' Xulai and I believe the creatures are at least partly Ogre. Which reminds me that I have unpleasant news for you, Abasio. We thought Sybbis had one of these creatures as a kind of guard or who knows what. She actually has at least twenty-four of them, some bigger than this one. Precious Wind thinks she has a breeding population of them. And Coyote is probably right. 'Ogre' or 'a Gar' might be the collective label for what they are."

Arakny offered, "It makes sense, as much as anything does in this mess. That's what Sybbis calls her new . . . consort. She speaks of him as 'uh Gar.' " She glanced at Precious Wind. "*A* Gar, of whom there are . . . obviously others."

Precious Wind turned toward Abasio. "Xulai says you connect this creature to the men you met in the northern forests, when you were on your way to Woldsgard, some years ago."

"There are similarities, yes, but the northern men didn't stink like this. They smelled bad, but it was a sweat, smoke, dirt smell that men accumulate in the forest, in and out of campfire smoke, skinning animals, getting blood on them, bathing seldom, if ever. Their smell was similar, but nowhere near this strong. I think the northerners were all, or almost all, human, maybe a little bit of something else in an ancestress back several generations."

Arakny mused, "So if Ogres are the result of Giant-Troll female breeding, could these be the result of Troll females bred by those northern men? And could they, looking into the past, be the result of some experimentation—of which there seems to have been entirely too much!"

Precious Wind said, "Remembering what the child—Needly—said, can we assume this one went somewhere to meet with another one? During the time before he came back, drunk, and shot Willum? Could he have spoken with someone from Sybbis's camp?"

There was a moment of half-whispered babble. Abasio bowed his head in thought. "Sybbis was at your encampment. Right? Last night. Was the person she called a Gar there with her?"

There were murmurs, heads shaken. None of them had gone near the ganger camp.

Precious Wind murmured, "My map shows just one unpleasantly

rocky ridge that extends between the Catland road and the Findem Pass road from their junction all the way up into the mountains. We're facing the south side of it here, and it's not far across. It's difficult terrain, but it's no real distance to speak of. I think it's possible this one could have crossed the ridge and met with someone from Catland." She shook her head in frustration. "I left my genetic analysis equipment in Artemisia, Abasio. I need to take samples from this body . . ."

"Let's simply move the whole carcass," Abasio countered. "Someone may come looking for it. I'd as soon nothing was found here. Its kinfolk may be vengeful." Though heaven only knew what its kinfolk might be!

Bear hruffed for their attention. "Coyote n' me can go up the hill a ways and hang around for a few days to see if something comes lookin' for that one."

Coyote murmured, "You'll be going back to Artemisia, though, so it'd be a good idea for a person to come get us so we don't have to walk to Artemisia."

Abasio asked, "In case something does come looking for this one, can you scratch some dirt over the blood, maybe a few branches. Here and down there where the Griffin was?"

"Can't do anything t'hide that smell," said Bear. "It'll still stink!"

Precious Wind spoke decisively: "Let's do this: Bear and Coyote will stay here as they've offered to do. I'll jump the group and the body back to the camp, but I'll return here immediately with some stuff that will hide the smell. Then if you, Bear, and you, Coyote, are willing to keep watch while we get everyone moved back to Artemisia, I'll come back around sundown—how long do you want to keep watch? How about I come at sundown three days from now, and every night after that if you two are investigating or following someone?"

"Y'gonna take that stinker to the plaza?" asked Bear.

"I don't know what we'll end up doing with the body, but I'll definitely be back very shortly to kill the smell, and I'll be back again in three days to get you."

"Countin' today?" asked Bear.

"Today is one, tomorrow is two, day after that is three."

Bear nodded. "Well then, do it, before something else comes outta the trees at us. You might bring some food when you come back. There's water here already."

It was done in one dizzying journey, the intermediate stops blurring past their eyes as they went.

Precious Wind went to her own wagon; her own stock of potions and scents; even peeked in on her own dear friend in the nearby wagon—Xulai lying on the bed with the babies asleep beside her, face still streaked with tears.

Precious Wind shook her gently. "I think Abasio went to clean up a bit. I left the body outside the camp if you want to see it. I have an errand, but I'll be back very shortly."

She was gone. Xulai barely opened her eyes; she'd been grieving over Willum. Still half asleep, she went outside to have a look at the body of the hunter. Swallowing her disgust, she knelt beside it, half rolled, half pushed one filthy sleeve up away from the wrist, gagging at the smell as she did so. Under the cloth, the skin of the creature was greenish, whitish, grayish with writhing, branching veins beneath, almost like tendrils of moss. She leaned close. The veins of color moved! She picked up a twig from the ground and thrust it at the skin. It penetrated. The white layer tore, rolled, showing what might be a more "human" skin under it.

The shirtsleeve she had rolled away was coated on the inside, beginning about the elbow, with a layer of something black that looked much like . . . tar? Some kind of waterproof coating that was dry? Why was it there? To keep the white layer from seeping through the clothes? And how thick was the white stuff? She pushed the stick in, measured it against her index finger. From the tip of the finger to the top of the first joint. An inch. The stuff seemed to end at the bottom of the neck, and on the arms halfway to the elbow. She thrust her stick at the bottom of the trouser legs. On the legs it ended a bit above the ankle. She touched it. It felt like . . . clay. Wet clay. No! More like tallow. She pushed a fingertip into it, then watched as the indentation slowly returned to its original shape. Able to hold its shape but soft. Flexible. Permeable?

She stood up, putting her arms around herself, gritting her teeth, demanding the trembling, frightened inner part of her to stop shaking. She moved to the head of the creature and used the twig to separate locks of hair. The scalp was the same, a thinner layer there, only the thickness of a piece of sheepskin lying against the creature's scalp, the texture of a soft soap, all of it emitting the same oily, rotten, deadbody smell.

Carefully she put it into words. Visually, except for the veins of darker color, it most resembled a greenish-grayish tallow. She cut slits in the clothing to determine that the coating covered the entire body except where it was exposed to the sun and air: the lower arms and hand; the face and neck. It probably did not extend to the soles of the feet. Someone else would have to remove one of those huge boots. She had no intention of trying. And Precious Wind could very well examine the creature's sexual organs for herself!

Arakny approached. Xulai thrust her twig at wrists and ankles, muttering a cursory description of what she had seen and thought. She suggested that the body be covered with something so it couldn't be seen from the air—who knew what other creatures may have been devised to keep watch upon these! Then she returned to her bed and did not open her eyes again until Precious Wind wakened her several hours later.

"I've jumped the Griffins to the building in Artemisia. Wide Mountain Mother was getting the Griffins set and arranging for food and water. There's a plot just outside they can use for sanitary purposes. Sun-wings seems to be comfortable, and the little one is fine. Really, a very appealing little creature! I've jumped the body of the hunter into Wide Mountain Plaza temporarily. I just came back here to be sure everyone was moved. Those who don't want to be jumped are on their way back there by road. So, if you're agreeable, I'll finish up by moving you and Abasio and the babies: wagon, horses, and all."

"Is everyone ready, Blue and Rags, Kim?"

"Just waiting for you to say 'go.' They're all outside, touching the wagon, including Blue and Rags."

Xulai nodded and Precious Wind moved them, hop, and hop, and hop, and then a pause while she entered a new destination. "I'm putting us into a space they've cleared, near the stables at Wide Mountain Plaza." She went outside and stood next to Abasio, her hand on his arm.

They hopped once again. There was the sound of voices, the sharp crack of an ax splitting firewood, the smell of smoke. While the others moved away Abasio slowly turned, staring around him at the Wide Mountain Plaza. He had been here before, with Olly. Looking out through the gateway to the low hill across the river, he saw the long men's houses, their tiled walls still riotous with color, all of them facing onto the dance ground with its long benches for the elders and the open-sided but well-roofed Drum House where the drummers and drumheads could make their thunders while they were protected from the rain. That's near where the gangers had grabbed him, that other time, in that other world.

On either side of Wide Mountain Plaza were other houses and plazas, and others beyond them, all the female heads of families of Artemisia: Wide Mountain Mother had been elected for life: Mother-Most, head of the clans. Others were here: High Cliff Mother; Black River Mother, Stone Valley Mother—some dozen of them, formally considering themselves of different matrilineal families, but all of them with a shared history, tribal language, and dedication to stewardship of the earth. He and Olly had come here, to this house, carrying the clan neckerchiefs Olly had designed and dyed, the sign of the thistle. Prickly. Rather like Wide Mountain Mother herself. He turned. The wagon was gone.

Coming up beside him, Precious Wind laid her hand on his arm.

"Where are we supposed to be?" he asked.

"Your wagon's around behind that house with the red door, Abasio. There's a little grove and a well and outhouse there. It's near a stables and pasture. I brought us all in a bunch and then put our mixed animal–people group where they'd be . . . suitable. There's a shed there with bedding straw for Coyote and Bear, when they arrive. I checked with Wide Mountain Mother first. Are you all right?"

"Kinda drowning in memories," he said. "That time was all . . . well, it seems a lot longer ago than it really was. The Place of Power, up on the mesa, it was . . . something out of a nightmare. In one sense. And something straight from heaven in another." He simply stood, staring into the distance, finally saying, "I'll go over to the wagon in a bit."

Precious Wind left him to struggle with the past and went to see if she could do anything for Xulai and the children. Sometimes children did not react well to being hopped. They, like animals, seemed to have an inner sense of place. So far, however, the twins had taken it in stride. Stroke, that is. No, they didn't swim like that. They wriggled, like fish. They had taken the move in sinuously.

Xulai met her in the doorway. Kim, followed by Blue and Rags, passed her on his way to the stables. Xulai asked, "Where's the rest of the herd?"

"Jumped them into a pasture outside the town just before I came here. Offered any of them to Wide Mountain Mother that she'd care to keep."

"Abasio?"

Kim shook his head as if in sympathy. "He's out there remembering the last time he was here. I think that's when he met Coyote and Bear and a bunch of survivor gangers tried to haul him back to Fantis."

Precious Wind remarked, "At the moment I think he's a bit lost in memories."

Xulai nodded. "He would be, yes. Did your de-stinker work? Up on the mountain?"

"Dear love, once I have poured some of that stuff about, no one can smell anything else for days. It isn't unpleasant, just very strong. The mountain clearing where our animal friends are does smell very strongly, but it does not smell of the creature."

"May I suggest—"

"I've already poured my de-stinker on the places the body had been . . ."

"What's it for? Why do you have any such thing?"

Precious Wind shook her head. "It's used to track animals in doing area studies. You put some on the feet of an animal and turn it loose, then you can learn how far it goes and how it familiarizes itself with a new area. It's actually diluted before it's used, and followed by a little smell-meter. After talking to Wide Mountain Mother, I also had a look at the body and took various samples. I thought the thing ought to be buried, and she agreed, so I hopped it and a few men out into the desert. *Ul xaolat* is good at digging holes, and we dug a very deep one. It took all the men to roll the body into it. We filled the hole and the men stamped it down, then we poured de-stink on the soil and piled sagebrush over it. I think something might come looking for it, and it's remotely possible something might detect the stench of it even through my de-stinker. Buried deep, it's less likely to be found."

Xulai turned from the door, yawning. "You might want to go *dig it up,* Presh. As I was about to remind you: you know those devices the laboratory in Tingawa came up with, the ones they were using on the shape-changed animals so they were sure not to lose them?"

"Locator buttons?"

"It might be a good idea to look at the body to be sure it doesn't have something similar inside it. If it does, and somebody comes looking for it . . . they'll come straight here. The fact it's buried won't matter."

Precious Wind stared, glared, and disappeared. It was several hours before she returned, wet hair streaming down her back, deeply layered in towels and carrying an armload of dry clothing. "It did indeed have a locator," she snarled. "I cannot forgive myself for not thinking of that! Stupid not to have realized something would want to keep track of the things! The device wasn't exactly like ours, but it obviously fills the same function. It was quite an exercise in . . . arm's-length dissection."

"Where had they put it in his body?"

"You don't want to know."

"You've had a bath," Xulai commented, unnecessarily.

"By the Great Litany, yes I've had a bath! Maybe a dozen baths! The bath woman put me through so many changes of water in the bathhouse I thought I was going to dissolve. Have you seen the bathhouse? They have a hot spring feeding it! I couldn't take the additional samples without touching the thing and I stank to high heaven. She wouldn't let me out until she couldn't detect the smell. She said she values her position with the tribes and would not want anyone to complain of an indecent smell."

"But you got samples?"

"There are several full sealed cans of the stuff in that storage compartment under my wagon. They can stay there until I can get them to Tingawa. The body is now reburied, and I took the locator button way, way, way out in the desert and dropped it into a very deep crack in a rock formation alongside a chasm. I left invisibly small devices to record anyone who came looking. If someone or something can trace it and comes looking for it, I should be able to see who or what it is."

"Did you look at the button, see what it does?"

"Well, it locates, obviously. It broadcasts its location continuously, so it can be tracked. They will know where it's been. I'm hoping they'll think it was a malfunction or that it was picked up by some animal or bird: all that flying across the countryside. The device seemed to accumulate some information about the body itself. Measurements of something. There were registers for various categories, but I don't know what they referred to. I had *ul xaolat* record the device in detail, so we'll figure it out later."

"I didn't know it could do that."

"The complete list of what *ul xaolat* can do would make a sizable book. It takes a very long time to master the use of the devices, that is, if one wishes to take advantage of every possible usage. I can't imagine why any one person would, but then it wasn't created to be used by just one person." She picked up the *ul xaolat* that was lying near Xulai and began to poke at it.

"Are Bear and Coyote staying on the mountain?"

"Yes. By the time I got back there, they'd found a comfortable overlook where they can see the clearing without being seen. Behind the clearing where the Griffins and the children were, there's a rock wall topped with a ledge. Behind the ledge is . . . not what I'd call a deep cave, but it's certainly a sheltering hollow, small entrance, sizable hollow, far enough out of the weather that Bear and Coyote can stay warm and dry. Something nonsmelly has used it for the purpose. Needly and Willum had carried blankets down there, and Bear had gathered them up, so he and Coyote have something to sleep on. I gathered up the children's other supplies and provisions and brought them back with me. They had to leave most of them behind, in the cave where Sun-wings had kept them before they set out to rescue her. Needly says she can find it from the place we found them, if we want to recover the supplies. I thought she and I might go up there and do that in a day or so.

"The same spring that fed the pool the children used comes down through the place Bear and Coyote found, and though I was prepared to go get provisions for them, there was most of a deer carcass in the clearing. I hopped it up where Bear and Coyote can get at it easily. It had been partly butchered, but it's fresh enough that Coyote and Bear tell me they won't need to hunt for the two more days they'll be there.

"I set up their overlook as a new arrival point on *ul xaolat* and erased the clearing as a destination." She held it up for Xulai to see what she was doing. "I'm taking it out of yours right now, so none of us can blunder into it by accident. We wouldn't want to arrive there coincidentally with more of the hunter types, whatever they are. We'll relieve Bear and Coyote in a couple of days. If they haven't seen anyone, we can replace them with pairs of hunters who are used to the woods. They won't mind spending one or two days at a time, and I think we'll want to keep a watch on that hunters' camp for a while, just to see what or who turns up."

Xulai whispered, "I'm so utterly thankful Bear was with them. That body was enormous. He's another like the ones Sybbis has, isn't he? Have you any idea what that coating is on the outside of its body? Were the veins in it still moving when . . ."

"They were, for a while." Precious Wind shuddered. "Even though the thing was dead." She sat down to put on the stockings she was carrying, following them with trousers, a shirt, and shoes. Finally, she opened her personals kit on the chair beside her, threw the towel around her shoulders, and took a comb from the kit.

Xulai said, "I don't think the wormy things are part of the stinker, Presh. The wormy things take a while to die after their host is dead. They obviously live off the host . . . bloodstream, maybe. Lungs, too, maybe. I believe that smell is the smell Abasio has always called the Ogre stink."

Precious Wind separated the left side of her hair into strands and began braiding it. Xulai took another comb and began working on the right side. "According to what we've put together, the hunter came back to the camp drunk and said 'Ahgar' or 'a Gar' or an 'Ogre' told him nobody wanted a Griffin hide from a young one, so he should just kill the young one." Precious Wind burrowed into her personals kit and brought out two beaded cylinders, thrusting one of them onto the end of her braid and twisting it tight. "We've now seen twenty-five of the monsters. How many of them are there?"

Xulai put the other cylinder on the braid she had finished and left Precious Wind to pin the braids into a crown. "'Yung For'ster' could have talked with one of the Gars from Sybbis's camp without much trouble. Or it could have talked with someone who makes or directs his kind of creatures. I feel that makes more sense than another one of his own kind telling him nobody wants a small Griffin skin. That kind of instruction sounds like it came from a human, to me."

"How could that one get back and forth from the Griffin clearing to Sybbis's camp? It would be a two-to-three-day journey from here without *ul xaolat*."

"No, it wouldn't. That's what I'm saying. Something that size moves faster than an ordinary human. Longer legs, longer steps. It took

Abasio two days to get to that clearing from the foot of the mountain, but if someone from Catland went up the mountain, west of the ridge, it could have met the hunter halfway, at some prearranged spot."

"And all we know about them is that there are more than a few of them?"

Precious Wind nodded. "We'll know more when we can get some of the samples analyzed. It's of some importance to find out how many there really are, and where they are, as well as whether they are a re-producing population or individually created. I'm thinking in terms of logistics. Things that size must eat enormously, and I'll wager they're carnivorous only. We need to be sure—"

"Could Sybbis be feeding them . . . people?"

Precious Wind shuddered uncontrollably. "Captives? It's probably within the ganger frame of reference, yes. It would explain the attitude of the guards Sybbis left here. The ones I moved to other places. They were very glad to go!" She stared into the distance for a moment or so. "All the people here think the hunter Bear killed is at least part Ogre, don't they? There's no excuse for these creatures," she snarled. "None at all."

Xulai made a strange, strangled noise, half laugh, half sob. "No excuse at all! Nor for Griffins. Nor for Trolls. Nor perhaps for children like Needly, and perhaps not for people like me. Meddled-with crea-tures. Living things created purposefully. Nothing natural about us!"

Precious Wind paled, seeing that Xulai was trembling. "Shhh. Don't upset yourself. We've had this discussion before, and you know it's non-sense!"

"I'm not *upset*. I'm *terrified* for us, Presh. Terrified. I love the babies but . . . sometimes I look at them and wonder what they are. How are they mine? Are they mine at all? What is my responsibility for them? Griffin says *we must guarantee her children's future as we are guaranteeing our own. Because we made them.* I didn't. You didn't. What is our responsibility for Griffins? What about our responsibility for these ghastly, stinking monsters! The accusation would be the same in both cases. *Mankind made them!*"

"You just said it, Xulie, dear. You didn't. I didn't."

"Humans did! Is there such a thing as collective guilt?"

Precious Wind sighed, rubbing at her forehead. "Religious people taught so, a long time ago. They called it 'original sin' because some early ancestor committed some supposed indecency—I've forgotten what it was."

"Committed! And went on committing!" Suddenly Xulai was weeping, and nothing Precious Wind could do would comfort her. The older woman sat beside her, holding her, wondering how she herself would have responded to being created as the new Ave, the birth mother of *Homo aquaticus*. Raising children totally—well, no. Not *totally*, but *greatly* different from oneself. Children who would not share one's own childhood experiences. No gathering at the dinner table in the evening. No playing ball in the meadow. No bedtime stories as one tucked them into bed. Children whose own childhood experiences one could not fully share. To love children who might never return that love . . . not as had been traditionally expected. When one really thought about it, weeping did not seem at all . . . irrational.

"What's wrong?" asked Abasio from the door. He too looked bathed. His hair hung in wet curls around his forehead.

"Nothing," Precious Wind replied, trying to smile. "She just gets overwhelmed about being Ave, every now and then."

He grinned, a wry grin. "Avam doesn't always have it so easy either."

Precious Wind made a half bow in his direction. "Has either of you read the daily reports on *ul xaolat*? The one you and Xulai were using?"

"What daily reports?"

"I needed to remove the location of that clearing up the mountain from your device, and I accidentally hit the daily-report combination. Your *ul xaolat* has a very low opinion of you." She showed Abasio the combination and left him reading the reports that popped up in sequence on the tiny screen. As she left to return to her own quarters, she heard Abasio's explosive "Idiots, are we! Xulai wondered what happened to those burned trees. Well, if it wants work to do, I'm sure I can find just loads!"

Precious Wind stuck her head back through the door. "Abasio, remember, you *cannot* retaliate against a device. It's like kicking the wagon when the axle breaks! And if you've got it stacking a winter's worth of firewood somewhere, some other poor soul may be drowning in a swamp for lack of power to transport out. The revised models are really snippy, and there's no way to get even with a device. They don't get bored, they don't get tired, they can't be punished. I wish they could. I've tried.

"You can do what I do with mine: *ignore it.* OR you can retaliate against the man in Tingawa who did most of the revisions while imprinting them with his personality. His name's Bung Quai. Just tell it, 'Yes, Bung Quai.' 'No, Bung Quai.' Every time you do that, he gets a resonance itch. At least we can feel like we're getting even."

FROM THEIR HIDING PLACE ABOVE the clearing, Bear and Coyote stood alternate watches. Coyote said he couldn't stand one, but he'd lie down one. Bear admitted it was the easier thing to do. "Problem is, when I do it that way, I keep goin' to sleep," he said.

Coyote thought about this. "Well then, that's why humans say they *stand* watches. So they don't go to sleep. Though I've seen Abasio so tired he was asleep standing up."

"If we could figure out when the critter, if there's a critter, was comin', it'd be easier. I mean, if we knew it was comin' at night, we'd sleep through the daytime."

"Men mostly move around in the light."

"Right. But if this thing's half Ogre, which is what I think he is, then he moved around at night just as well as in the sunshine. Better, maybe. They're sort of like Trolls, you know. Trolls don't like the sunlight one little bit."

"Because they've got weak eyes. They can't take the sunlight. They go blind."

Bear said, "Shhh. I hear something . . ." They rose from their mossy couch beside the tiny pool and crept to the ledge of rock overhanging the clearing below. The trees between allowed a partial view of the clearing. Bear expelled a breath audibly, suddenly catching himself as one of the creatures below raised its head and sniffed the air. There were three of them: one smaller than the hunter Bear had killed; two about the same size. Two male, one female—that is, both Bear and Coyote believed it was female, though there was nothing specifically female-shaped about it. It shared the general shapelessness of the dead one, huge stumpy legs and arms, a thick torso, a neck as thick through as the head. The two watchers shared a look of confusion. The appearance didn't equate with the smell. Part of the smell was one they associated with females in general, and one of the figures looked . . . bulbous.

"Nah heeer," drawled one of the creatures. "Ah'gar nah heeer. Nah mell Ah'gar."

"Whurs?"

A giant shrug from another. "Nah heeer."

"Whuh mell?" asked the third.

Another giant shrug.

Bear whispered, "The little girl said the one I killed talked clearly, didn't she?"

Coyote nodded. "Maybe it had like . . . a quarter Ogre in it, 'stead of half."

"N' you think these're half?"

Coyote nodded, watching the creatures below. "When these go, I'll follow. I'll come back here for you. If Precious Wind comes for you before I get back, have her come back each evening until she finds me. If I don't . . . get one of my kin to track me and get me out, or kill whoever killed me."

Bear nodded ponderously. He could move as silently as Coyote, but not as quickly. Not that the creatures below seemed capable of much speed. Still. He was willing to wait. There was water, food, even a sheltered place to sleep. He rested one paw briefly on Coyote's back before the canine slithered off one end of the ledge and down the slope among the trees. When the creatures left, he did not see Coyote follow, but then, he hadn't expected to. That smell . . . either of them could track that without fail, even though this end of the stink trail had been softened by the stuff Precious Wind had spread on the ground where the hunter had bled and died. Maybe tomorrow he'd backtrack that trail and see where the thing had gone.

CHAPTER 11

What Are Stinkers Made Of?

COYOTE SLIPPED AMONG THE TREES ON A TRACK along the south-facing slope that was more or less parallel to the monstrosities' path, forested slopes below him, snow-crowned blue peaks appearing between treetops to the north. He had tried following the creatures at first. Impossible! They . . . emanated—a good word Abasio had taught him—they emanated a stink fog that attached itself to anything that came along behind them!

"Off to one side," Coyote snarled to himself, "offside and uphill," making a breathy chant of it, *up-hill, up-hill, up-hill,* while trying to determine exactly how far uphill he needed to be. So far, he'd found no outer limit of the smell. The word "smell" didn't even say what it was! There was no human word he knew that was bad enough for what it was, and if humans had no word for a thing, animals who spoke human didn't either.

Coyotes had their own language, of course. There were howls: curse howls; mourning howls; celebration howls; the "Gather now" howl for a hunting pack. Then there were yaps: insult yaps, "Hurry up" yaps, "Do it outside or I bite" yaps for cubs who fouled the den or strayed from the pack. That one was actually more of a snarl. And of course there were other snarls for a variety of unpleasant occasions. When the pack did a sing, they used all of them, plus what Xulai called "yodels." Even using the whole vocabulary, nothing any coyote or pack could possibly howl, snarl, yap, or yodel would describe this stench. Even running water picked it up! When the creatures waded through a stream, the water immediately darkened with a roiling cloud that spread in all directions, even backward, against the flow! Filthy clouds of it that seemed to stay right there in one place, getting stronger the longer it got smelled! It was the same color Coyote had glimpsed when the largest of the creatures had pulled at the neck of its shirt. It should have been flesh, but it didn't look like flesh. Of course it might have color. Abasio said most things did, but Coyotes didn't see color—not that they needed it; their noses more than made up for that.

It had been obvious from the first that the stinkers had a destination even though what they were following was more of a suggestion than a trail. Nobody'd been on it lately. The only good thing about the stinkers was that they kept moving and they changed direction only to go around things. Or the path did. Also, they were too big to move quietly. Coyote could hear them at quite a distance, and he'd taken advantage of that by following from the far edge of their noise! Anywhere near and even the sunlight stank!

Stinking sunlight would make a good start of a curse howl! For a while he amused himself thinking of all the good words the stink would ruin. Lots of the words Abasio's Olly had taught him back when she was . . . alive. Some nights when she couldn't sleep she had come out of the wagon and taught him words. Good words. "Grace" was a willow in a soft wind. "Sparkle" was sun on ripples. "Solemn" was sun sinking beyond the hills with long, darkening clouds reaching into the distance and no sound anywhere . . . That was before she'd gone up in the ship to save the world, and from the middle of this stink Coyote wondered if it was worth saving! Her words were good words to think, but if the stink was in his nose, he couldn't think words at all!

He put his head down and ran, ran hard, until he was so far ahead of them he couldn't catch a whiff of them. He was gulping for air, his front paws tearing at the ground before he even halfway caught his breath. By that time he had his nose in the hole he'd dug, sniffing the moist earth. Pine needles and mold. The soft smell of damp soil. The melting scent of something mushroomy. A tang of bugs, maybe ants. It didn't matter what it was so long as it was something other than the . . . things, they weren't even creatures, just . . . things.

Next time Bear could do this following. The stinkers moved slow; that was Bear's usual speed. Better yet, Bear did not have a doggish, coyote-ish, wolfish nose and he could probably tolerate this quite well, but for Coyote, never again! After breathing deeply for some little time, he sighed, shook himself, sat up, and listened. Nothing. He backtracked. They had decided to spend the night in a clearing. He glanced at the sky. It was almost night. So much had happened, so fast . . .

He retreated to the place he'd been, where he couldn't smell them. A fallen tree offered shelter, a hollow that had been dug by something else, something he couldn't smell, so it hadn't been here for a long time. He crawled into it thankfully. He'd hear them when they woke and moved in the morning.

He slept deeply, waking to light and to the sound of branches cracking and crunching among the trees behind him. The stinkers were catching up to him . . . no! They had turned. Why? They'd been headed west. Now they were headed north, into the mountain instead of along it!

He went back quietly—though they didn't react quickly, the monsters had very good hearing. He found them lurching awkwardly uphill, this time on a real trail, one that looked very well used. He'd been in such a hurry to breathe, he'd crossed it yesterday without even seeing it! It seemed to be leading them out of the trees, and when that happened there'd be no way for him to keep out of sight! He sat down, momentarily baffled as the stinkers straggled into the sunlight, a little way up the slope of the clearing beyond. Then they stopped.

Now what? Coyote expelled his breath in a long, silent sigh and lay down to evaluate the situation. Abasio said *evaluate* meant not to do anything really stupid without thinking about it first. He also said sometimes there wasn't any smart thing left to do, so one ended up doing a stupid anyhow. Sometimes Coyote knew Abasio was joking with himself; other times he knew Abasio was joking with himself to keep from feeling something else. But still, thinking about the situation wouldn't do any harm—starting with the trail . . .

The trail the stinkers had followed until now had been just barely. (Xulai said that a lot. "Are these pans clean enough, Xulai?" "Just barely.") The trail they had just reached was wide with a surface lower than the surrounding soil. Now that he was thinking about trails, he could make out other trails of the "just barely" kind coming through the trees from different directions. That meant some stinkers came from here, some from there, and somewhere else, and when they got here . . . there were lots of them. If that was true, there might be more stinkers coming right now. If this was where they were headed, why did they sleep out in the trees last night?

Prudently, he squirmed his way into a thicket, burying himself where he could still see the big new trail and all of the clearing beyond. From the forest's edge the ground sloped up toward a cliff so tall that the trees at its top were only a fuzzy line, a kind of fringe, like the edge of Xulai's shawl. The wall was highest at its center, gradually lowering as it curved outward on either side, as though someone—someone with a round jaw, like humans, not a narrow one like coyotes—had taken a big bite out of the side of a hill. The sidewalls closed off the area at both sides; the new trail led out of the forest and straight into a gaping darkness at the bottom of the cliff. A hole. A big hole. Big enough for two or three of the stinkers to go in side by side without bending over.

That was it. There was nothing else, no possible cover except a man-high ridge of stone that came out of the cliff just to the right of the hole, ran straight toward him, and extended a little way downhill, into the forest. From this side of the ridge, no one could approach the entrance without being seen, and there were shadowy hints of movement inside that opening, as though something was waiting there. Coyote didn't want to meet whatever it was!

Under cover of the tees, he left the thicket and clawed his way over the ridge, sliding down the other side. It was a tilted double layer of stone, darker on top of lighter. Coyote couldn't see colors but he could see darker and lighter. The really black layers were lava from deep inside the earth. The light-colored ones were ashes—sometimes almost white—or all sorts of medium-colored sand. And the river that ate down through them had been doing it for millions of years. Coyote had had no thought that included *million,* so Abasio had told him to think "All the pieces of sand in the bed of a river." That was *millions.*

Coyotes had only four numbers. There was one, a few, many, and more many. Many was the same as the pack number. Generally. A many had its own smell. Each coyote had its own smell; with a few, each one smelled separately (a mama and her cubs was a few); pack smell was all the coyotes added together. If anyone was missing, it was pack smell missing something. If anyone was new, it was pack smell with something added. Xulai had told him the most difficult things about giving animals speech had been to fit words with how their brains worked rather than changing their brains so much that they would lose their coyote-ity, or their bear-ity, or their horse-ity.

She gave him a word howl: *"Coyote-ities, bear-ities, both have necessities! And I confess to be utterly sure that it is plain to see, incontrovertibly, creatures must keep their identities pure!"*

Coyote had remembered that! He could actually howl it! Except for all the *T*s and *P*s. *T*s just wouldn't howl. He had to make *L*s out of them. Xulai said when one creature's words didn't fit another creature's brain, they had "incompatible vocabularies." On their way to find Sun-wings, Abasio had told Bear and Coyote about the people from Earth who had gone to another world a long time ago, and they had met creatures who had "incompatible vocabularies" with humans. All well and good, as Abasio would say, but what about tongues that just didn't bend that way!

This mountain with the hole in it might be a volcano that hadn't completely cooled down. The hole might be a lava tube. Lava tubes usually came in bunches; sometimes they had water and warm places inside. Coyote was very thirsty and tired—and now that he'd quit running, he was cold. The idea of someplace warm, with water—that idea was very . . . appealing. "Appealing" was being warm with fresh meat.

Over in the clearing, the creatures were shifting uneasily and mumbling to one another. Coyote lay quiet, still searching for cover nearer that hole. The only possibility seemed to be a pile of rocks next to the ridge, about a third of the way to the cliff. If he stayed close to the side of the ridge, the pile would hide him from the entrance. Of course, if something was looking down on the area from above, they would see him or they wouldn't. That was one of those no-smart-things-left-to-try situations. "Sit-u-ation" was the right word. He'd heard Xulai say, "Abasio, we have a situation." In a situation, you just went ahead because there was nothing else to do.

He skulked along the bottom of the ridge to nose the rock pile. Lichen. Lichen took a long while. Not as long as a million, but long. He tested a stone with a paw, pushing hard at it. It didn't move. Lichen on all the surfaces, cracks filled with dirt that things had taken root in. The dried old roots were still twisted among the stones, so the pile was cemented together by soil, root, rain, and time. Solid. He climbed it slowly from the side away from the stinkers. At the very top, three sizable stones had an even larger one resting atop them, like a three-legged stool with very fat legs and a nice, dark hollow in the middle and a slot between two of the leg rocks that was just big enough for him to squeeze through. The next slot over let him see the dark hole. Perfect! Abasio said that a lot, usually when he fixed something. Until it broke again, then he said other things.

The stinkers still weren't going anywhere. No one was noticing him. But. Something was biting at him! What? A smell? Actually another smell getting through the stink? Danger mixed into the stench, trying to tell him something. He had a flash of memory, Mama with one paw firmly placed on his small, wriggling back, holding him down and quiet until she identified some new smell. Mama hadn't had human words. Words had come later, much later, long after he'd left Mama and the den. He didn't remember much about its happening to him: except that he'd been very, very scared when the first words had exploded in his head! *You are Coyote!* Up until then, he'd just been self-smell.

The new smell was *oil*. The word "oil" yattered at him like an angry crow! *Oil* went with machines. His insides were giving him all kinds of reasons why a tunnel smelling of machines was not a good place for a coyote. Machines always had humans attached, and the first thing most humans did when they saw something with fur on it was kill it. Brain strongly suggested that if running away was not possible, being very quiet might be the best alternative. There was a word for that, too! "In-con-spic-u-ous," and he already was: under cover and lying down. He was hungry, thirsty, but he was inconspicuous. He let his body sag into the gentle cup of soil time had blown across the stones. He was used to daylong walking and running, but the stink of the creatures was like being sick. Every part of him ached. The thought came dimly. He would have to ask Abasio. Could smells do that?

Movement beyond the ridge caught his eyes. More stinkers! He had to count! He could, when he had to. His three and a new three! Six of them, now! A flick of excitement! So. Something was going to happen! This was why the creatures spent the night in the clearing. They weren't supposed to be here until now! He laid his jaw gently onto his crossed paws, considering the dark opening across from him. It might be a lava tube. Places like that provided winter cover and warmth for whole tribes of forest creatures. Stone tunnels weren't as comfortable as earthen ones, but they sometimes led to chambers warmed by hot water. Bear and Coyote, between them, knew the location of a dozen such places: always warm and generally safe, though too hard to be comfortable in, in their natural state. The water often tasted strange, but it was usually all right to drink . . .

The mumbling became momentarily louder. He raised his head. Two new stinkers. That made eight . . .

He went back to thinking about burrows. Coyote remembered being with a man—long before he knew Abasio—a man who had been sent to find the coyote cubs who had grown up able to talk. They had spent the night in a rock cavern. In the middle of the night, Coyote had wakened to find his own front paws working at the stone, trying to make it comfortable. The man was watching him and writing something down. That night he had given Coyote a blanket, and the next day he had taught him to do recipes. Recipes were chains of words you stuck in your head about doing things that weren't instinctive. "Instinctive" was like howling, hunting, or mating, but creatures—even humans—needed recipes to remember complicated stuff. "Complicated" was a bunch of main things with a lot of branches going off in all directions. The thicket he'd hidden in was complicated.

Coyote's first recipe had been "making a bed." "Making" meant putting things together. Birds and mice and rabbits were born with instinct for "making a bed." They used twigs and straw and fur. Coyotes had to learn the recipe, then do it: bite off bunches of grass and low-growing twigs of pine; carry them into a cave or hole among rocks, or into a hole in the ground after you had dug a long tunnel to it. Grass made a softness on the rock, and fleas didn't like the smell of the pine sap. Once he had the "making" idea, he could do other things with it.

Coyote had taught "making a bed" to Bear, even though Bear didn't really need it. Bear had his own bed, a nice fat layer under his fur that didn't get sore no matter how long he slept on it. Coyotes ran with their noses to the ground a lot of the time, smelling the way, so coyote heads weren't high above the ground, and it was hard to carry things very far in their mouths. Carrying a rabbit home to the pups was about it. With Coyote, it was more dragging than making. Bear hibernated in winter, which Coyote did not, but warmth was a good thing no matter where the warm came from. In winter it was good to be curled up against Bear's furry, warm hide, listening to the weird dream sounds Bear made while his belly rumbled.

Lost as he was in such musings, more than half asleep, his head and ears came up at the sound of a shout from up the hill. He counted. There were now eleven stinkers, and the shout had come from a thing standing outside the tunnel—a thing completely covered, arms, hands, face, body. The face had eyeholes with . . . something in them. Glass, maybe. Under all that, it was the right height and bulk to be a human. The stinkers shifted and muttered. They didn't want to do whatever the human wanted them to. Finally one of the ones Coyote had followed shambled up the hill with the others following, one at a time. Another human had come out of the tunnel; he held a small, probably black thing in front of him. Abasio had told him: "Just say dark-colored. Or medium, or light. That's enough to give us the idea." As the stinkers approached, the second man pointed the small dark thing at the stinker and the second man fiddled with something he was holding. When somebody did twitchiness, that's what Abasio said: "he fiddled with it." That was how Coyote got language. Someone had fiddled with him.

"Where's babble babble babble?" one of the humans said, nasty-voiced.

The front stinker mumbled something. *"Godair nodair ghohn."*

What was it saying? *Go dare node air gun?* This was one of the ones that had come to the place where the Griffin was, where Bear had killed a stinker. Coyote mouthed the sounds. "Go dare . . . there, no there, gone"? Yes! "I go there, it was not there, gone." The killed stinker was gone, all right! Precious Wind had jumped it all the way back to Artemisia.

The human did a quick fiddly thing, like . . . writing something. Abasio and Xulai did things like that, put recipes down so they could remember them. Recipes and lists. Recipe words went across; list words went down, one under the other. This one was probably a list of the stinkers because this man knew one was missing. If it knew one was missing, then it could tell the stinkers apart. The other man kept on talking as the other stinkers went past, one at a time. Coyote could barely hear him, but it was definitely a human male voice. When all of them had gone inside, the two humans followed them.

Coyote heard no door or gate closing. No sound of anything shutting. The opening was just that. Open. Open or not, he wasn't going in there. Nothing the stinkers had done had told him anything worth reporting on, not yet. Even though he needed to find out more, he still wasn't going to do a stupid and use a human hole into that mountain. If the mountain was a dead volcano, there was probably another way in.

He got to his feet, stretched his legs carefully, one at a time, and descended the rock pile to take a closer look at the cliff. On this side of the ridge, it actually made a little . . . dip, a kind of curve away from him. Also, this side had holes in it that couldn't be seen from the other side of the ridge: holes not big enough to be human entrances but big enough for coyotes. He sniffed at one or two, no human smell. Good. No stinker smell either, which was even better. Now, if he just weren't so tired and thirsty. Very tired; very, very thirsty. He lay panting for a time, considering what else he might try. Around him the trees spoke with soft-wind voices. As his panting slowed, the voices grew louder, not wind sounds but real voices—much muffled by echoes. Definitely human.

He arose resentfully and tried to locate the sound source. It had no direction. It was as loud if he faced one way as the other. He closed his eyes and looked at the cliff again. This time a shadow on the cliff wall before him looked different. Part of it was behind the other part. There was an opening behind it. A man would have to stoop over to get in there. Then he'd have to keep going, because he wouldn't be able to turn around!

It was wide enough for Coyote, and he could turn around anytime he needed to. After the second turn, it was completely dark but the voices were clearer: no words, just the murmur of saying, asking, answering. Like chickens did. *Cluckety-cluck-cluck? Clu-awcketty-clawk!* When chickens did it, Xulai said it was conversation. "Nice grasshopper, warm sun, ooh, beetle. Yum."

He pushed his left side against the wall and moved along it. The tube got larger the farther he went. A sudden pain in his foot stopped him, and without meaning to, he whined. The whine went off into the darkness, echoing.

He didn't have time for a curse howl. And this wasn't the right place! Instead he muttered one of Abasio's short curse words and lay down to investigate his left rear foot. A sharp stone. Something like a sharp stone. It hadn't cut him, yet. No blood.

"Thanks be to God," he said solemnly. *That was a man-saying, one that Abasio, Bear, and Coyote had talked about. And Blue Horse, too. Not Rags. She said god-talk bored her. Recently some of the talking animals had decided that if men had a god, then animals should have them, too. The humans' god was something like humans, only invisible, bigger, stronger, wiser, everything-er than humans were. So now some of the talking creatures had created their own gods. Blue said some of the horses at the farms north of Wellsport had a horse-god, a wind-swift Stallion Lord that led his mares and foals across the sky, their hooves making thunder and striking lightning sparks from the sky. Abasio said hooves made sparks only if horses were shod, so the sky horses had to have a blacksmith up there somewhere—a sky farrier. Humans, some of them, prayed to their god. Some people did it constantly. Praying was telling the god stuff. The animals had decided a long time ago that since gods were supposed to know everything, telling them stuff was a waste of time, so it must be that the people were just lonely. Xulai said that was the real reason most gods existed. People got lonely and scared and needed someone to talk to.*

Coyote muttered; digging his teeth into the crevice between his toes, getting his teeth on whatever it was he'd stepped on. There. Not a stone, something metal-tasting, small, sharp; no blood on it or on his foot, which was a good thing. The thing was mostly smooth, but his tongue felt rough places on it. He spat the silvery thing against the wall of the tunnel, picked up a few small stones to cover it, peed on them well enough to find it easily, and lay back down, still thinking of deities.

Horse-gods. Blue said he'd never heard of an animal deity who actually helped any animal. Abasio said human gods didn't really help people either. When something nice happened, though, men said their god did it, and when something bad happened, men said they were being punished. But some men did bad things all the time and never got punished, so evidently the god got distracted a lot. No matter how useless gods were, men still made up lots of them, even evil ones. Animals had enough trouble without inventing a trouble god. Coyote had tried to create a picture in his head of a coyote-god. He couldn't do it. He had thought up a good god howl that would sound like wind, a great wind with a . . . million coyote voices in it. Suppose he got a really big pack together and taught them the howl, would the coyote-god appear? If it did, what would Coyote pray for? In-visibility, in-smellability, in-hearability. Now, these would come in very useful! Think of the chicken coops he could raid!

Not that he would. Of course. Not if anyone was watching. However, if there happened to be a coyote-god listening, he, Coyote, would be grateful for water. And something edible!

He yawned, and the yawn woke him slightly and encouraged him to get his legs under him. This was not the time to go to sleep. He needed to see what was to be seen—assuming there was light in here somewhere. At least he could find the voices and find out what they were all about. Then he could sleep. The tunnel was smooth-floored. He could trot along it at a fairly good rate—definitely one of those routes Abasio had called a lava tube. Though it curved, it did not seem to branch, not on the side he was staying on. His breathing had its own echo. If the way branched on the other side, the echo would be different. The way wasn't steep either, which was another blessing. It simply went on into the mountain, sloping very gently upward—all lava tubes did, because the melted stuff had run downhill. The air was flowing in the same direction he was going, coming in from behind him, carrying only a tiny odor of the stinkers. Air was good, footing was good, but the darkness was absolute, so he went slowly, keeping his fur against the side of the tunnel as he walked steadily onward. That was another Abasio trick. If you were in the dark, keep to one side of whatever place you were in. If you had to get out, turn around and keep your other side in touch with the wall. And of course keep smelling and listening . . .

And listening! Had he heard a plink? And a trickle! Maybe there was a god of coyotes! The sound came from up ahead, in the direction he was going. Yes! His eager nose encountered a film of moisture sliding down the side of the tunnel, accumulating in a long, narrow hollow at the bottom of the wall before seeping out through a crack about a paw and a half above the bottom. He lapped it up, waited until it filled again, and drank it all, and three more times. That was better. Hunger would wait, but thirst didn't wait for anything. The water had a volcano taste.

Sharp. It wasn't his favorite water taste—that would be either *fish* or *frog*, preferably with green stuff—but it wouldn't hurt him, he knew that.

His widely opened eyes caught a flicker, like a darkness gulping a lighter shadow. It came again. Firelight. He slowed, crept forward around a corner. What might be firelight and daylight, both, and then a suddenly glaring white light from something else, and a windy, rushing sound! Like a storm coming! The tunnel ended a short distance ahead at a coyote-sized, egg-shaped gap, little end upward, bottom nicely scooped for a coyote to lie in. He crawled the last little way, turning his head sideways to poke one eye over the edge without his nose showing.

He was looking down and across at a sizable cavern! On the floor was the thing he'd seen first: a flicker of firelight. People, fire, and . . . some kind of machines! Coyote shuddered, remembering machines from the war at the Place of Power! Some of them were wheel things that ran by themselves. Even after the Place of Power had died, there were some wheels-by-themselves-runners going back and forth among the Edges.

The cavern was round, roundish. Not smooth round but like a huge, lumpy half bubble. If the floor was a circle, he couldn't see the part that was under him and behind him. So, his recipe would say it was like a very big bubble and he was looking down from more than halfway to the top of it. He could see the sky through a stone-toothed, star-centered hole to one side of the top. He could tell it was the west top because of the star. It was called the morning star, or the evening star, either one. Abasio had taught him why this crazy star stayed so close to the sun: it wanted to mate with the sun because it was in heat. That was a human joke that didn't make sense even when people explained it. It was the first star you could see at night and the last one to blink out in the morning. The strange white glare came from lamps on the lower walls—that is, the ones he could see. The part he couldn't see might be empty. The men didn't even look in that direction.

A line of pens stood along the cavern wall, each pen holding stinkers, assorted sizes, none really small. Male or female? Some had hair on their faces; some didn't. Two of them were different, more like the one Bear had killed. They even had bows, like the hunter. Did that mean anything? He counted. Two paws equaled ten stinkers in each pen.

The three he had followed were just now entering the cavern. Coyote counted ten pens; that was one foot, twice on each toe, another foot of pens, and two more feet. Four double feet of pens, each pen with ten. He whispered it to himself, remembering it. A man came in holding a long rod connected to something he had strapped on his back. Abasio had a thing like it, made out of stiff cloth. A kind of bag to put things in, when he didn't have the wagon. To pack things in. He called it a pack. "Packing" was like "making," only push instead of drag. Maybe push harder, too.

The voices from below got louder. The men were looking at what they were doing, they didn't look up. Coyote eased himself forward so he could put his long nose over the edge and use both eyes. The stone was as dark as his fur. If he didn't move, if he kept perfectly still, chances were they could look right at him and not see him.

They were working around a . . . built thing. How would he tell Abasio about it? He had to find words in his "compatible vocabulary." First, it was lying flat on the floor. It looked like a . . . kind of gate made out of metal. Bars very close together going one way, another set going the other way like . . . like Xulai's grill over the fire! *Grill!* The grill thing was lying flat, and under it was a curved shininess. It looked like a bowl, like Xulai's big bowl she made green food in. He yawned and closed his eyes. Just for a minute.

Coyote had never figured out why men ate green food all the time. Coyotes ate green food only when they had pain in the middle. Abasio said dogs did, too. Horses, sheep, and goats and other creatures like them ate green food all the time, but why did men eat green food? The thing down below looked like Xulai's bowl for green food, only this one was metal. Xulai's bowl was made of clay baked in an oven, and he, Coyote, was not to stick his nose into it. Said Xulai.

He was dozing off again! Hunger could do that. Make you sleepy. His head jerked up. The two stinkers with the bows were being let out of the pen, and they came over to the inside edge of the bubble, the part Coyote couldn't see. After a little while there was a splash! There was water back there! Then he saw others with bows, more like the first ones. He counted them on his feet, one double front foot, two double front feet, that was two eyes, then one double back foot, two double back . . . no. Almost two double back feet but one was missing. That was one face of double feet. Abasio would help him figure it out. All his feet one face around except one missing, and THAT was the dead one, for sure. All of the hunters got to go wherever the splash was.

At one of the pens, the man with the pack was pushing at the stinkers with the long rod thing that had something like two fingers on the end of it. No. Finger and thumb. Like pinching. The human said something loud. The creature in the pen took its clothes off. Each one had a shirt-jacket top that wrapped around and fastened, trousers that tied in front, and boots. That was all. The man took each thing and laid it next to the pen. The clothes were black inside. Like the cloth Abasio used to cover the chicken coops to keep them from getting wet.

Coyote felt his nose wrinkling again, felt his ears flatten, the way they always did when he saw something nasty or dangerous. Without their clothes the stinkers were . . . were just . . . nasty! The naked one howled: a foot-in-the-mouth-complain-roar. Not pain. Like he had his head in a hole. The human pushed at him with the long rod, making him move out onto the grill. The thing's feet didn't go through! So there had to be something else on top of the grill, something he couldn't see from up here. The grill thing was holding up something else. Maybe mesh. "Mesh" was the word for the stuff on the chicken coops. With its clothes off, the stinker looked like a ball of white fat with darker worms in it. Dirty white with squirmies. Nasty!

Some things were nasty for Coyotes, even though Xulai said she'd never seen anything nasty enough that a Coyote wouldn't eat it. Abasio had told her that was an insult, so she apologized. It was not a proper apology. She didn't lie down, belly up, and whine while he sniffed her, so it was NOT a proper apology. It was only a human apology, just saying "sorry." Coyote would rather Xulai had lain down belly up so he could give her a good sniff, but female humans were funny about being sniffed.

His head jerked. He'd been dozing again! Sniff dreaming. He wondered if other creatures dreamed in smells. He did not want to sniff that thing on the grill. Water came out of the end of the rod the man was holding. Steam billowed out, so it could be hot water. That was why they wore those long coats! The human was washing the white stuff off the stinker. The white stuff was falling on the grill in thick chunks; then it got soft and dripped down into the bowl while the stinker turned around and around, making a kind of wolf-owl-eagle noise, like two pieces of metal rubbed together howl-screech-scream on and on while the stuff on it came off and dripped down. Off its head, too. It didn't have any of the stuff on its face or feet or hands. Everywhere else, though.

With the white stuff off, he looked like a human man, more or less. If the flabby, dangly part in front worked the way it did in humans, this stinker was a male. That part was not tidy. Coyote liked that word. "Tidy." Neat. Coyotes had neat ones. Dogs did, too. Horses, sometimes, except when they got all excited and then they were just disgusting. Like puppy poop dangling all the way to the ground! Humans' parts were no better, at least men's parts weren't. That's why they had to wear clothes. It would be very painful crawling over rocks or through thorn-bushes with that dangly thing hanging there. And women's baby-milk parts! Why didn't they shrink back neatly when the puppies . . . babies were weaned? No, they stayed dangly, just like men's parts, and they had to wear clothes. They didn't have fur. Naked skin with no fur made no sense at all. Except for frogs. And fish.

Coyote stayed where he was while the next one was washed off. This one had no dangly part. Maybe it had breasts, he couldn't tell with the general flabbiness. And it was round! Like it had pups inside! Coyote gagged. More of them? The whole world needed none of them, not more of them! And here came the stink! Coyote saw it rising up toward him. A kind of gray cloud in the air. All the people down there had masks over their faces, masks with tubes and things over their noses. Coyote had only his paws to put over his. It wasn't bearable! He turned and trotted back down the tunnel. The air was flowing up the tunnel toward the cavern! Abasio said hot air went up, so the air in the cavern was warmer, right, and the hot water made it warm, too, and it went up and out that hole at the top. That's why they had the fire! To make the air go up! And the air from the tunnel would flow up behind it! It was going past him, now, on its way out. It would be unbearable only if he put his nose over the edge. He sometimes wished he had a face like Abasio's. Abasio would be able to put his eyes over without putting his nose over!

On the other hand, Abasio couldn't smell anything. Coyote didn't know why human people even bothered with noses. They weren't de-signed very well. The man said men were made in the image of their deity. Whoever made the deity ought to be ashamed! "Ashamed" was what pups felt when they soiled the den and got nipped for it. Humans ought to be ashamed with noses like that.

He lay quietly, head on paws, facing away from the opening as he dozed, the sounds from below telling him the washing was going on, variations in howls telling him different ones were being . . . washed. Some voices were more howl-y—female maybe? If the round one was having . . . young ones, it meant the things mated. Coyote gagged. The idea make him feel like he'd eaten grass.

Eventually, the howling stopped. A very loud metal clang brought him back to the hole. The stink cloud had gone out through the top, and something was sliding out under the grill. It went out until it covered the bowl and dropped with a *whoosh-clang* sound. The wagon door went *whoosh*. The kettle lid went *clang*. So this was a big lid! With the bowl covered, the smell was . . . not so bad, and after a bit it was almost gone, but there was a noise . . . Howling? Screaming? Very high and shrill, like the tiniest birds, only lots of them: maybe like a bunch of bugs yelling, many, many little tiny voices. Yes, like a . . . a huge swarm of those sting-y ones: gnats! The pens were full of naked, washed stinkers covered with dark worms that sounded like gnats. Well, maybe not worms. Squirmy things. Skinnier than worms. Not as thin as hair, though. All over their bodies, these things that squirmed and wriggled and lashed about, screaming. Worm fur. That's what they were, worm fur! The men pushed the clothes through the bars. The stinkers smelled the clothes! They could identify their own clothes by smell! Coyote didn't believe anything that smelled that bad could smell anything else. He would ask Abasio for a word for that! When they all had clothes on, the noise stopped. The worms didn't like the light! That was why they screamed!

It was getting to be more than Coyote could remember. Everything he had seen had to go into words, and he had to remember the words. When animals like Bear and Coyote were given speech, their brains had to be changed to hold words, too, and learning words was sometimes hard. He took a deep breath and looked hard at the naked shapes. They were probably males and females. All of them were covered with that wormy stuff. It wasn't fur. It wasn't hair. It was something else. He didn't know what. He didn't want to know what!

The two hunters came back from the part of the bubble he couldn't see. They had their boots and trousers on and were putting on their jackets. They had worms, too, but not very many. One of them had a patch of the white goo on his back, and the man yelled at him to go back and wash it off. It wasn't very thick. Not nearly as thick as on the other stinkers. It might even be a different kind, since they hadn't collected it in the bowl with the other stuff.

Finally, all of them had their clothes back on and were being herded out of the cavern. Back out into the world. To do what?

Maybe they were going to feed them. Maybe that's why they came here. To be fed. Coyote blinked, yawned, put his paws over the edge of the hole, and forced himself to stay awake because the bowl was being lifted up from underneath, some kind of metal legs pushing it up. One side of it had a nose on it, sticking out; there was a word for that nose. A spout! *Spout pours out!* A hole opened up in the floor. The opposite side of the bowl pushed higher, and higher. The lid slid back a little, and whatever was inside it poured out of the spout into the hole. It was pale-colored. That's all he could tell. Pale-colored and runny. Had it been cooked, maybe? It didn't smell as bad as it had smelled before. It hardly smelled at all. As he moved, his foot touched a pebble he hadn't noticed. It rolled off the edge.

Then noise. A screaming noise, not voice, not human, machine noise. All the men turned around, started looking up at the walls, up through the top hole. Other men came in, yelling. Coyote pulled away from the hole and went back around the first corner of the tunnel, turning to put only his head around the corner, flat on the floor, tight against the corner, watching. A fluttering noise. *Bametty whacketa, whacketa, whacketa,* on and on. Something came toward the tunnel hole, something spinning. A light came into the tunnel. Coyote pulled back. The light went to the corner, played around over the rock, over the floor, didn't come around the corner. Abasio said light couldn't turn corners unless people put mirrors up to bounce the light on. The *whacketa, whacketa* noise went away. Coyote waited a bit before going back toward the hole. The flying thing was outside another hole, shooting the light inside. The big noise had stopped.

Someone down below yelled. "Fahs awarm . . . ak a wrrrk."

"Fahs awarm," Coyote repeated to himself. Oh, yes. Abasio said that sometimes. "False alarm." "Alarm" was when you saw a forest fire coming. "Alarm" was when you heard a wolf pack in your territory or the nearest spring got fouled by something. Humans made really loud noises when there was an *alarm,* to let everyone know. A pack of coyotes did, too. Coyote breathed deeply, wondering if the falling pebble had created the *alarm*. The spinning machine flew around a bit longer before it settled onto the floor of the cavern, against the wall in the space he couldn't see. They must keep it down there, next to the water the hunters had washed in, out of the way.

Below him, in the cavern, the white lights went out, one by one. The rushing sound got softer each time a light went out. The lights had been making the noise. A kind of loud hissing. Like . . . when Xulai cooked things in a pot over the fire and put rocks on the lid. She said the rocks held the steam in. They made the water hotter, and it hissed and whistled. Finally all of the lights went out. The creatures were gone. All the men were gone. Nothing there but the grill thing and the pens, and the lanterns, and fading light coming in from the sky. It was almost night. He needed food. He needed to sleep. But first, he needed to get out of this place.

Following his own smell, noting that nothing had come in behind him to change the scent trail, he went back the way he had come, stopping only to drink again and to pick up the piece of metal he'd found, carrying it in his mouth. As he stuck his head out into the clearing, a gopher stuck his head out of a hole, not a coyote length away. It started moving away . . . not fast enough! He ate it skin and all, cracking the bones up small and being careful not to nick the bitter round piece in the middle of it. He pushed that piece away, next to his metal thing he'd dropped when he saw the gopher. When he'd licked the blood from his face, he picked the metal thing up and went farther along the edge of the cliff, sniffing other holes until he found one he liked. It smelled of fox-a-long-while-ago, but it still had a warm bed of dead leaves and grasses. He had never met a talking fox, and he wondered vaguely for a few moments if there were any. If the bed's owner came home, he'd find out. Foxes and coyotes weren't friends, but they weren't food either. Tomorrow he'd go back to Bear; someone would come to take them to Artemisia and they'd give him real food . . .

IN ARTEMISIA, PRECIOUS WIND was suffering from fulminating frustration. "Oh, I wish we could jump the ocean," she said for the hundredth time. "We just don't have the equipment here!"

"I know," Xulai replied, trying not to sound impatient. "Presh, that's what you've been saying. You've said it over and over for hours! Saying it doesn't help. You can't jump the ocean. You'll be able to when they build the floating way stations, but they haven't built them yet. Or until somebody builds a factory to make flying machines like they used to have. So either leave me here and get yourself to Wellsport and take a ship . . . or send somebody else. Or for heaven's sake, talk about something else. Tell me why you're in such an uproar."

"I told you! I told you it was the compounds in that fatty stuff that came off the body."

"You've said that, yes. You haven't said what's disturbing about them. Are they dangerous, poisonous? Do you find them so intriguing you can't wait to analyze them? What?"

Precious Wind collapsed on the wagon bed. Xulai was feeding the babies, both of whom were sleepy and fractious and, in Precious Wind's opinion, should be let alone to have a nap instead of having that relentless spoon shoved into their resentful little mouths. New mothers were sometimes too terribly conscientious. If the Tingawan-granny rule is five meals a day, five it is, even though babies are like dogs, can't count but know when they're full! She bit her tongue and decided not to mention it again. What had Xulai asked? Oh, yes. The stuff on the body.

"I'll give you my reasoning so far. We know these creatures have been manufactured, and we know they have some human genetics. Right?"

Xulai nodded, frowned, received a face full of spat-out mashed carrot, and threw the spoon against the wall in frustration. She bundled up the babies and laid them in their baskets, where they decided to fuss. Xulai shoved their baskets under the bed and pulled a blanket down to make it dark. In half a minute the fussing stopped.

Xulai rotated her head, stretching her neck to loosen the muscles, sighed deeply, and said, with a fairly good pretense at calm, "If you make a human genetic assumption to start with, I'll go along with it." *Anything to make you happy, Presh!*

"So they've been manufactured. Some parts of them may have been purposeful and other attributes may have happened as a kind of side effect. We don't know which. We know there are various . . . types of them. Some are fairly articulate—the one Bear killed: that one talked to Willum and Needly . . ."

Xulai commented, "To be clear: we're putting stinkers who speak understandably and engage in complex activity in a class we're calling the 'hunter type.' Right? We're thinking that sort might possibly include or be related to the ones Abasio met during his trip through the northlands. Right?"

"Yes. That group—which we believe are referred to as 'the Gars'—is at one extreme. The one Bear killed had a name, wore clothing, and could talk. He spoke of a father who had died, so he knew something about families. He could use a bow, build a campfire, and evidently knew how to find his way around. He knew where to go to get liquor or something similar. Abasio did not say the northern men smelled like the body does, so they may be related only in matter of size."

Xulai said, "If the one you've been examining is at one end of a class of beings, a . . . genus? Then at the other end of the class you'd find something with similar genetics but without speech or clothing. A monster, like Ogres or Trolls . . ."

Precious Wind looked up, suddenly attentive. "Say that again. A monster like . . . ?"

"Like Ogres or Trolls."

"Ogre. Agra. A gar. That word the creatures used that we haven't been able to translate. Could it be 'Ogre'?"

"I suppose it could. That doesn't mean the creatures attribute the same meaning to the word that I do."

"I wish we knew if all of them have worm things growing on them." Precious Wind noticed Xulai's shudder and frowned. " 'Worm things' isn't a scientific term. I don't know what else to call them, not yet. The hunter does have them. A very sparse coating of them."

"How about the stinkers Sybbis has?"

"We don't know. Presumably they're in the same class as the hunter. That type is between man size and giant size, and it is human-shaped. Since the hunter killed game for himself, we know they eat flesh. From my examination of the body, we assume they are bisexual—though we can't be sure until we find a female one. Only male ones may have been created, as with the first giants. I'm almost certain that it's the worm organisms that create the fat layer on the outside of the bodies. I'm definitely sure the fat layer is where the smell comes from. We may suspect that layer was purposefully designed—it includes some very interesting compounds—but we have no proof of that."

Xulai murmured, "And you want all those questions answered."

"I do, and some of them might be answered rather quickly if I could get samples to the labs in Tingawa. *Ul xaolat* can do quite a bit of analysis, given properly preserved samples, but I don't even have the facilities here to prepare samples properly. The wormy things from the dead stinker disintegrated almost immediately. Even the ones I'd put into preservatives didn't last very long. I had less than an hour or so to look at them. They're almost . . . well, if I had picked one up not attached to its host, I would have said it was a separate organism, something like a tapeworm. They have a tiny air bladder. They're tubular with three openings, one buried in the body, one that excretes the fat, and another one connected to the air bladder. The few still alive made barely audible sounds when exposed to light."

"If you get another chance to collect samples, ask Needly if she'll give you some of her rock medicine. That would preserve them."

Precious Wind slapped her forehead with her fingers, snarling at herself. "Yes. Of course! I'll ask Needly to put a drop of the rock medicine in a vial for me, and I'll carry it just in case we come up against a live stinker."

She took a deep breath, as though preparing to begin saying it all again. For what would be the sixth or seventh time . . .

Very deliberately, and concentrating intensely upon sounding calm and rational and not screaming, Xulai said, "Oh, Precious, in case you hadn't noticed, it is late afternoon. I'm about to find Abasio and start fixing our supper." She slowed her voice, speaking very clearly: *"You did promise to pick up Coyote and Bear tonight. If you left right now, you could bring them back by the time our meal is ready. They're probably hungry and they may have information you'd find helpful."*

Precious Wind looked out the wagon door at the sky, mouth dropping open. "You're right! It is late afternoon. I'd lost track. And you're also right that they may well have some useful information. Where's the . . . ? Ah, there it is." She took *ul xaolat* from its resting place on a shelf and went out, calling, "Be back in a bit. Better have Kim roust out something for Coyote and Bear. There wasn't a lot of that carcass left, and they may be quite hungry by this time . . ."

Abasio passed Precious Wind on his way into the wagon. "She going after Bear and Coyote?"

"I fervently hope so," snarled Xulai.

"You sound . . . a little, uh . . ."

"Irritated, annoyed, upset, stressed. Yes."

"At Precious Wind?" He could not keep the astonishment out of his voice. He tried again, more soberly: "At your good friend and longtime virtual sister, your dearest companion in the world?"

Xulai laughed, stopping abruptly with her hand over her mouth. It had been a rather—well, lunatic sort of laugh. She swallowed. "'Basio, motherhood is turning me into a witch, and Precious Wind is helping do it. She's been in here for hours, talking. She's angry that she can't jump all the way to Tingawa. She tried analyzing some of that stuff from the body, the fatty stuff, and the wormy things that produce it. She can't tell what it is or they are, but she *won't stop talking about it, every detail, lamenting that she can't go there, that she can't do it here, over and over and over.*"

"You say lamenting . . . ?"

"Over and over."

"That's very Tingawan of her. I've noticed—"

"Abasio! Don't."

"What?"

"Don't start about the incredible tenacity of Tingawans. Their tenacity, their ethical behavior, their sensitivity, their elegance, their whatever . . . Sometimes I get very tired of the Tingawan pedestal. I didn't grow up in Tingawa. I'm not accustomed to sainthood. I never aspired to it . . ."

"Sainthood?" Abasio looked puzzled. "What's that?"

"People talk about Tingawans as though they're perfect. Sainthood . . . it's a long-ago thing about people who were so perfect while they were alive that they were believed to have gone to heaven to help God by doing miracles."

He frowned. "A miracle is just an incidental good thing, the opposite of an incidental bad thing, which is an accident. Incidents occur naturally through interaction of matter, living or inert, and if someone is watching who makes judgments, that person might identify some as good, some as bad, and some indifferent."

"Well, some religions told people that all the good ones are miracles, rewards given you by some saint or other. And once people got used to that idea that all good things are rewards, then it followed that all bad things are punishment. After that there weren't any accidents anymore, just people getting shoved around by the saints. Or gods. Which doesn't matter! Except sometimes people talk about Tingawans as though they were saints. Or gods. Which they aren't. You should know that. I'm tired of trying to be perfect. Sometimes I hate the whole . . ."

He started to say something deliberately amusing, but her expression stopped him. Maybe it was not the best time for that. Instead he put his arms around her, holding her very gently. "I can understand that the Tingawan mystique might be very wearing, yes." *Pat, pat, pat.* "Precious Wind does get very intent upon things. Remember her wolves?" He smiled into Xulai's burning, furious eyes. "I will never forget the feeling I had"—*pat, pat, pat*—"when I was suddenly surrounded by that ring of intent yellow eyes! Hungry yellow eyes. And there sat Precious Wind, completely at ease." *Pat, pat, pat.* "She is strange, my love, but we are very lucky to have her with us, strangeness and all. At least the creature she's intent upon now is dead! She's not collecting a pack of them. And the thing is buried. It's not following us, looking hungrily at us as the wolves did. Constantly." *Pat, pat, pat.*

"She'll get one to follow us if she has the chance," snarled Xulai. "And she'll expect us to make it welcome."

Abasio ignored both tone and content. "Now, what may I do to help with our supper? Shall I see what's available for the animals if they come back with her?"

She shook herself and took a deep breath. "No. No. I don't need food kind of help. Come sit beside me with your arm around me. I need you to tell me we're doing fine, doing well, we aren't stymied by anything, we're accomplishing our mission, we're . . ."

He sat, embraced, and said in his most authoritative voice, "We are two dedicated and wonderful people who are contributing to the survival of the human and other races. The world will remember our names in perpetuity." He sat and hugged as directed, very gently, rocking her slightly to and fro. Neither of them said anything else for some little time as Xulai gradually relaxed. He could feel the tension leaving her. He decided the situation called for something more demonstrative . . .

Just outside the wagon, women screamed in terror!

"She's back," Xulai said petulantly, leaping to her feet. "She must have brought Bear."

"You stay here," he said. "Just sit. I'll take care of whatever . . ."

Precious Wind had brought Coyote and Bear. Several women who had been shucking corn had seen Bear solidify within a few feet of them. Abasio calmed the Artemisians, soothed Bear, and then introduced soothed-Bear to calmed-Artemisians and calmed-Artemisians to soothed-Bear. Then, since he had noticed several of the men fingering their knives, he stood and made a short conciliatory speech concerning the inadvisability of hunting and killing speaking animals. One of the hunters expressed rude disbelief as to the animal, the speaker, and the subject. Abasio said it again, more loudly.

Wide Mountain Mother, eyes only half open, stalked from her house, drawing her disarranged clothing around her. With uniform malevolence she scowled at Precious Wind, Bear, Abasio, and hunters, raising her voice to remind them of the war that had taken place some five or six years ago in which they had been aided by talking animals.

Precious Wind apologized for having returned so thoughtlessly.

Wide Mountain Mother closed her eyes and shook her head, and spoke again, loudly, emphasizing her scorn and disbelief that anyone sensible would materialize large animals of a type known for ferocity in the middle of a working camp.

Precious Wind began to apologize again.

Wide Mountain Mother left in the middle of the apology, closing her door behind her, loudly.

The hunters, muttering discontentedly, went off to the men's camp to discuss the ethics of not killing previously acceptable prey animals who have, for some unknown and probably unholy reason, acquired language.

Xulai, who had been well on her way to becoming relaxed, contented, and loving, reverted at once to the mood of snarling irritation in which Abasio had found her.

Abasio sighed. At least the babies were still asleep.

SEVERAL HOURS LATER, WIDE MOUNTAIN Mother had finished her much-needed nap. Humans and creatures had been given mildly spirituous liquids and considerable amounts of food. The world had settled into evening. Seven people sat around a small, comfortable fire near which Coyote had just used Xulai's salad bowl and cooking grill to recount his adventure with the stinkers, ending the tale by licking his jowls and recalling his fortunate encounter with a gopher. Precious Wind, Xulai, Abasio, Needly, Arakny, Wide Mountain Mother, and Bear had heard it from beginning to end, without interruption. Around them at a little distance, other Artemisians, men, women, and children, had gathered to listen.

"Nice rendition," Abasio commented.

"Rendition? What's that?" Coyote said, trying not to snarl. He was tired!

Xulai knew exactly how he felt. She reached out to run her hand along his fur. "Boiling fat off meat or hides is called rendering, Coyote. Abasio has made a bad pun about your telling being a rendition. It's not really very funny." She giggled helplessly to herself, trying to ignore Wide Mountain Mother, her face as rigidly solemn as though cast in metal.

Arakny, believing Mother was still somewhat irritated at the day's confusions, shook her head warningly, including everyone present in the gesture.

In fact, Mother was more grieved than annoyed. Everything that was happening weighed upon her. Her own people were used to her and she to them. Both understood their parts in life; hers to make sure everyone knew what they were to do; theirs to do it. New people, new things, were troublesome. Always. She sighed audibly, at which the others became even quieter as she looked up and spoke, so softly that the silence had to continue if they were to hear her. "I'm not really angry *at* anything, Arakny, certainly not at anyone here. I don't really know who or what to be angry at!

"The word I want is . . . 'distressed.' I *am* distressed and I imagine everyone else here is also distressed. We didn't create these stinker things, but there's very little doubt some humans did. With Coyote's very generous and dedicated help in finding their purpose, with Precious Wind's assistance in taking one of them apart, we now know quite a lot more about them. Unfortunately, at this point everything we have learned contributes to our confusion. However, I try to remind myself that problems are like that. For a while *everything new you learn just makes it worse.* Eventually, it falls into some kind of shape, but in this case there's been nothing yet to help us solve the attendant problems—the ones that really concern us.

"If I say something incorrect, please stop me. When Precious Wind brought the body back here and had a good look at it, we already knew the stinkers excrete a substance all over their bodies. We now know it gets washed off of them, by human beings, presumably at intervals. Coyote saw four hundred of the stinkers gathered for that purpose—do I understand that correctly, Abasio, Coyote? Each pen had ten in it, and there were forty pens?"

Abasio and Coyote conferred. Yes. That was correct. Ten in each pen, nine stinkers and one of the hunter type, who presumably killed meat for his group. Human meat.

Mother nodded. "Also, when Precious Wind did some very elementary tests on the stuff the creature excretes from its skin, she saw that the material—what was it, Precious Wind?"

"When dissolved in water, it attempts to gather itself, to make a shape, but the shape doesn't hold."

Mother said, "I was distressed at the idea of a few dozen of these creatures! Multiply that by tens! There's so much we don't know! We don't know who the humans are at the processing site. We don't know whether that processing site is the only site. We don't know whether the group Coyote saw is the only group. We don't know if there are more than four hundred of the creatures plus a few extra, such as the ones with Sybbis. We don't know if the creatures seen with Sybbis were part of this gathering or are of some other type. I see Xulai is making notes, so note these items, please; we may return to them.

"It was centuries ago that the waters began rising. Scientists found an upwelling of water in the South Pacific that seems to be chemically different from the rest of the world's ocean waters. They found or postulated or theorized a cavern in the earth's crust that was leaking water into the surface oceans. They measured the possibility with their devices and told us that it contained only enough water to raise the level all over the earth by a few feet. People moved uphill and away from the shores and life went on. The scientists told the population when the water, at its then-current rate of flow, would stop. That time came, but it didn't stop. It just continued to flow. There was a flurry of recalculation, but the people who did it came up with the same answers and the same enigma. The water was still coming, into the bottom of the ocean. And we didn't know where it was coming from. We still don't know where it's coming from.

"However, as soon as it was known that the water wouldn't stop, another great project began, a genetic project that extended, generation after generation, culminating in the birth of Xulai and Abasio's twin children. This was, in part, spurred by the Visitation, the title assigned to an event in Tingawa when a prophet or scientist or madman appeared to provide a translation, so he said, of some research done on genetics prior to or during the Big Kill. This information proved invaluable in the work that followed and culminated in the birth of the sea-children."

She turned to face Xulai and Abasio where they sat beside each other, the children on their laps. "Those of us who worked on the survival project—some of the people of Artemisia, many of the people of Tingawa, some from other places and peoples in the world . . . Xulai, Abasio, all the people we knew, everywhere, were *totally satisfied that the human part of the problem was solved when your children were born.*" She turned toward Precious Wind, suddenly demanding, in a voice ragged with emotion, "Isn't that true?"

Precious Wind bowed to her.

Mother went on "When those babies came . . . many of us . . . we simply wanted to shout with joy. It had taken lifetimes, many lifetimes of struggle, and when your family returned to us, here, Abasio, and we saw your children's faces looking up at us from . . ." She gulped, then laughed. "Looking up at us from a pool of water, and those little eyes looking right into our own . . . we rejoiced. Little fingers grabbing our hands, little mouths tasting the world. I can't remember ever being happier. Here they are, a new people who can create lives that will be more than mere survival, lives that will have an elegance of their own." Mother turned away, wiping at her eyes.

Several of the older women gathered around her. Everyone else sat, at a loss. Wide Mountain Mother had not, ever, lost her calm, determined manner. Not ever. Until now. The circle was quite silent, even the onlookers were still except for one shrill voice: "Mama, why is Granmama cryin', Mama?"

Wide Mountain Mother turned back toward the group. "Forgive me. They were not tears of unhappiness. I still weep with delight whenever I see the children, but now I am feeling fear for them as well. Someone or something may be threatening us. These stinkers are being created by someone, somewhere. It has to be the Edges, there are no other possibilities on this side of the world, and Precious Wind has used her far-talker to reach Tingawa. The Tingawans have not seen anything similar. From what Coyote has told us, it is apparent the creatures are being . . . farmed. They are turned loose to graze, each group of nine with a hunter to furnish them with game. Then they are summoned to return to a place where they are stripped of the stuff that exudes from their skins. That stuff is the crop. We know it is organic. We know it is alive. We don't know if there are many more of them—"

"Nuh!" said a voice from the outer ring of watchers and listeners.

Mother looked up. "You think not, Deer Runner?"

"Forgive me interrupting, Mother, but there can't be many more if they eat meat. We know what eats big meat: us n' the big cats. Bears, sometimes, but they don't really hunt meat and they'd rather have fish and eat a lot of other stuff besides." He turned toward Bear. "I'm right, aren't I?"

Bear nodded ponderously. "There's bears that hunt meat, but they're big white ones that live up north, not the ones around here. And those stinker things aren't quick enough to eat little, fast stuff, like rabbits."

Deer Runner went on: "And we know there's not many big cats. I been lookin' for a skin for three years, haven't seen one I could kill with a clear mind. Mothers with little ones, a few. I saw only two young ones, last year's kittens still staying close to known territory. One big male. Not enough to hunt any. If you got hundreds, maybe thousands of those . . . things up there, they have to eat something. If there was that much game, there'd be more cats."

Wide Mountain Mother nodded. "He speaks truth, Abasio. If they eat meat, they have to get it somewhere. There isn't enough game to feed thousands of them. Possibly not even hundreds. Coyote told us he wondered if the creatures were being fed by the humans, after they were washed. It doesn't matter, the meat would still have to come from somewhere."

Bear interrupted. " 'Scuse me, Mother Lady. Guess you don't think like a meat eater'd think, but you forgot about the most meat there is. People meat."

There was a moment of utter silence. "Wouldn't we have heard?" said Arakny at last. "If there'd been predation, wouldn't it be known?"

Precious Wind muttered, "Even if there hasn't been, yet, predation on humans may be *planned*. We wondered what Sybbis was doing with the creatures. One possible answer is that she may be feeding them."

"But why would Sybbis have some of them?" cried Needly. "What does *she* want them for?"

Abasio put Bailai on the ground. "There's a definite connection between her and old Chief Purple. Old Chief Purple bought into one of the Edges outside Fantis." Bailai had crawled over to Xulai, who was still holding Gailai, and reached for his sister's foot, tugging it toward him and putting her big toe in his mouth. There was a ripple of laughter from the watchers. Abasio looked down, shook his head, and took Bailai back on his lap.

Wide Mountain Mother beckoned, whispered into a woman's ear, and the woman and a companion went to relieve Abasio and Xulai of the children.

Relinquishing his son, Abasio said, "Sybbis is not bright enough to instigate a plot, but since old Chief Purple is involved with the Edgers, he may be paying her or simply ordering her to keep some of the creatures. I don't know what he'd pay her with, but I know she's afraid of him . . ."

"Could be payin' food," offered Deer Runner. "She's havin' trouble feedin' her people."

Precious Wind interrupted, returning to her description of the body. "I should have mentioned that the hunter Bear killed had a locator device inside it. Such things are coded and can be used to track the creature . . ."

Both Abasio and Wide Mountain Mother exclaimed at this.

Precious Wind said hastily, "I didn't think of it, but Xulai did. The device has been been cleaned of any trace of us—and it's been put in a place that can't be associated with us. Also, I've left a spy-eye device nearby to record anyone who comes looking for it. I don't think it's likely, but there's a chance we'll get some idea of who's using it."

Abasio frowned. "Is there a possibility its movements have been constantly recorded? Would the record show that body swooping back and forth when you used *ul xaolat* to move it and dispose of it?"

Precious Wind shook her head. "Coyote said the men expected that one to show up. If they'd had a record of it being swooped about, they'd have known it wasn't going to appear. Besides, I recently learned that *ul xaolat* doesn't actually *move* things through space. It reassembles them in a new location, so no swoop actually occurs. I doubt if they bother to record the creatures' daily movements. They aren't studying the creatures; they already know the creatures. They probably made the creatures, and we have to find out what the stuff on their bodies is and what they're doing with it."

Wide Mountain Mother looked around their circle, shaking her head slowly, hands raised in question. "So, is that everything we know?"

"No," said Xulai. "Arakny said we hadn't heard of predation. On our way here we came through an area which should have had several villages in it. The last one, Odd Duck, was shown on the tax map, which means it's fairly recent. We found . . . evidence that the inhabitants had been eaten."

"Eaten?" asked Wide Mountain Mother. "Evidence?"

Precious Wind gritted her teeth and spoke through them angrily. She got to her feet. Her face seemed suddenly almost too narrow, as though it had pinched itself inward, focusing on something too unpleasant to allow comfort. "I did not finish describing my study of the body of the hunter. Earlier we questioned whether the creatures might be feeding on human prey. I think it is beyond question. I have proof they eat people."

"Them, too? As well as the giants? Human people?" cried Arakny.

Wide Mountain Mother asked, "What evidence do you have?"

Precious Wind's face showed her disgust. "When Xulai reminded me that the corpse might be carrying a locator, I went back and had *ul xaolat* dig it up and move it out into the desert. I took samples of the fatty stuff. It seemed to dissolve in water, to make a uniform solution, but then it coalesced, drew together, moved and changed, trying to form a shape, extruding what I took to be organs of some kind, then . . . sucking them in again and trying with something else. It didn't last. The whole substance broke apart into liquid layers . . ." She made a gesture of frustration. "I need to send some of the stuff to Tingawa. I don't have what I need here—I'm not even knowledgeable enough myself to find out what it is . . ."

"So you *don't* know what the creatures feed on?" Arakny asked.

Precious Wind flushed. "Sorry, I went off on a tangent! Yes, we *do know* what they feed on! *Ul xaolat* examined the digestive tract of the stinker. It found a skull, not whole, as Xulai described in Odd Duck. Just pieces of a child's skull, and pieces of pelvis, a half-grown child perhaps eight or nine years old."

Wide Mountain Mother's face convulsed in disgust. Abasio said, "If we're right about the heritage of the thing, genetically it's part Troll or Ogre or both. Those and Ghouls—which I've been told of but have never seen—are the only Edge-created monsters that were built to feed on humans."

Xulai's lips were drawn back in distaste. Abasio put his hand on hers. "On our way here, in the valley northwest of Saltgosh, we found droppings, Mother. Human-looking but huge. There were three little skulls in them, human babies. There was a skeleton hanging on a fence, a person evidently caught as it fled. Skull was bitten in two. However, the thing that did it was *not* one of the stinkers we've been talking about. *It was much, much larger than any of them.* The population of giants includes at least one breeding couple, and they've been feasting on humans. The people of Saltgosh have already started an eradication program, they've killed several of them, and personally, I think they'll manage to kill them all."

Mother said, "Deer Runner has said there is not sufficient game, but he was not thinking of humans as game. Now we must. Could the hunters among the stinkers have been providing them with humans as food?"

No one answered. Mother said, "What do you think, Abasio?"

"I suppose it's possible. The four hundred that came to be stripped of their product may have assembled from a very wide range, and that number may well be the maximum that can be sustained. They aren't free-ranging; they're under supervision of some kind, probably each ten assigned to a different hunting area. I believe they've calculated that four hundred of them will provide enough of whatever product is being harvested. The purpose of which we don't know. However, we can put a watch on the place, and the next time they come there, we can follow them back to their home."

"They were born and grew up somewhere," said Needly. "The one that shot Willum, he spoke of his father, who died, and was buried. That is, *some parts* were buried. He said the parts they didn't *keep to use again.* I wondered whether maybe the stuff they ooze is made by a separate organ. Something they put into a little one to make it grow up and become a stinker."

Precious Wind cried, "You didn't tell us that!"

"I didn't remember it until just now."

Wide Mountain Mother stared thoughtfully into the distance for a moment, then turned to look directly at Coyote. "Coyote, you went along the edge of the mountains to get there? Mostly flat ground? Low trees?" She looked around at the group questioningly. "Doesn't that sound like the route to the Oracles?"

"You mean the not-people? They're farther along in that same direction, not much farther, though," said Coyote.

"You call them 'not-people'?"

"They don't smell like people. They don't smell like anything alive I've ever smelled. And I don't think they're people, they're all one thing so far as my nose knows."

Wide Mountain Mother took a deep breath as she looked around the circle, from face to face. Despite the fine wrinkles that circled her eyes and mouth, her eyes were large and clear, the deep brown of a forest pool. Her thick gray braids fell to her waist, framing a face of enormous dignity. She smiled a strange, humorless smile, as though in wonder at the subject under discussion, then exhaled audibly.

"One would have thought that when the Big Kill was over, the Edgers would come out of their holes and join the human race. They preferred not. Not only have they stayed in their holes, they have been a constant annoyance to the rest of the human race. Even now, when the Edges are confronted with the same disaster as all the rest of the world." She paused, took a deep breath, and said slowly, word by word: "Here, I think, we come to the center of the matter, do we not, Arakny?"

"We do, Mother. Nothing we know explains the source of the water or the slowness of the process, almost as though something has given us just enough time to adapt. *Just enough* to accomplish our transition into sea creatures. *Just enough* for us to reach all the people now on Earth with the opportunity to take part in that transition. That particular timing seems so fortuitous one has to consider the possibility it is no accident."

Wide Mountain Mother nodded. "Also the water keeps coming in a volume that *is larger than the planet itself!* As one of our women said,

'Then it's coming from somewhere else.' Think on that when you wish to lie awake at night!" She paused, noticed Abasio's expression. "What is it, Abasio?"

"Do Artemisians believe in dreams, Mother? Repeated dreams, so completely repeated and so memorable that the dreamer thinks he is receiving a message?"

"I would not necessarily disbelieve. Have you been having such a dream?"

"I'm not saying any of it is clear or sensible or true. This is the message I'm getting, that's all. In a repeated dream, I hear conversations about us, conversations about Earth. The problem of Earth. They all say our problem is that we have no 'bow,' or not enough bow or not enough of us have it. They say we don't listen to our world. Or we can't hear it. In its briefest form, the message is always the same. *We were killing our world, and our world asked a world called Lom for help. Lom passed the request to another world. And the other world was huge and had too much water and was glad to help, through a wormhole.*"

"How Long has this been going on, Abasio?" Arakny's voice was very calm, very kind. Precious Wind gave her a quick, rather suspicious look. Arakny was speaking as she might to someone she was being very careful not to startle because he was out of his mind. Seeking information without upsetting the informant! Really presumptuous! Whatever Abasio was, he was not crazy.

Xulai saw the same implication and scowled, raising her eyebrows at Precious Wind.

Abasio gave Arakny an "I know what you're up to" grin and shook his head. "Arakny, my mental health is excellent. My recent dream life, however, has been a little bit like reading a book without a bookmark. Each time I go there, the book opens at a different place and it's difficult to know what comes in between or how it connects. One character turns up in different dreams, and it greets me by name. It knows I'm there. For all I know, it engineers the dreams. If I believe the dream, I believe the water is being sent purposefully."

"Why?" asked Mother.

"To get rid of us," Abasio said. "All of us humans, because we were destroying the planet. The world called Lom didn't have the wherewithal to provide help, so it reached out to another world—a huge ocean planet. You don't know where the water's coming from, Precious Wind. Nobody on Earth does. That's because it's coming through a wormhole that empties into a cavern inside our world and gets pushed up into the bottom of the sea. The planet that's sending the water wanted more dry land for its crop."

"For its crop? Which is what?" Xulai demanded.

"Fligbine. I think it's a euphoric drug of some kind."

Arakny and Xulai shared a pitying glance.

"You asked!" he said angrily.

Wide Mountain Mother said, "Lom is the world, or world part, to which two ships were dispatched a thousand years ago. They went from the Place of Power."

"So Xulai told me. I hadn't known of it until she told me, in Salt-gosh. And yes, Arakny, I'd been having the dreams *before* we reached Saltgosh."

Wide Mountain Mother smiled, a real smile. "I don't discount your dream, Abasio. It fits too nicely with my suppositions to be ignored. Unfortunately, we have an immediate threat which must be given pre-cedence: a threat from the Edges. We have accepted the fact that our world will be drowned. Despite their initial skepticism, even the Edges had to accept it as fact. All of us who cooperated with the Tingawan researchers and workers are devoted to the task Abasio and Xulai have helped accomplish." She shook her head fretfully, grimaced. "But, from the beginning, the Edges have refused to help with it or to take part in it."

"Refused?" Abasio looked up in amazement. "You mean, they were invited?"

It was Precious Wind who answered. "Oh, yes, they were invited. I've read the records. There were a lot more of them when they were first invited. Then, as recently as a few decades ago, when we knew we were getting close to the project goal—your babies—Tingawa sent ambassa-dors, not to one Edge only, but to each of them. There were, I believe, forty-seven of them left in our area at that time; fewer than half of those are left now. The Edges told us to run along and play. What they actu-ally said, in almost the same words in every Edge, was 'No thank you, what you're doing is useless, we have our own plans.'"

"And that's exactly what worries us," Wide Mountain Mother snarled.

"The Edges have always been insular. Each Edge must consistently prove itself superior to every other Edge. The point Arakny and I have been talking around, what we've been almost afraid to say, is—if the Edgers really have their own plans, then we should be scared to death. *What the Edges have planned in the past has usually been harmful to the rest of us.*"

"I thought they just stayed to themselves," said Xulai.

Arakny laughed. "If only they would. We can thank the Edges for the disease that ravaged Fantis. We can thank the Edges for turning their giants loose on us. On one former occasion, we found it necessary to get rid of a giant. We went to the Edge responsible and put it to them. We knew they had placed devices in all their creations they could use to turn them off. They refused to act—"

Xulai interrupted. "Arakny, forgive me, but what was the manner of refusal? Angry. Bored? What?"

"Their manner was quite jocular. They laughed. As if they had forgotten they needed anything from the outside world."

"Thank you," Xulai murmured, making quick notes. "I'm charged with the responsibility of reporting and I'm trying to document as we go."

Arakny went on: "Since they felt they didn't need the outside world, we decided to teach them otherwise. They had observer devices out at some distance that could see who was moving about, passing through, and so forth. We found and blinded all their devices. We kept watch on the sites and captured any repairmen. We intercepted their usual shipments of food and detoured the food wagons to our territory, paid for the food they had brought, put it in our warehouses, and told the drovers the Edge had died off of a plague, they wouldn't need food in the future.

"The Edge responded by turning some warrior devices loose on us, but prior to beginning this conflict, we had obtained some devices of our own from Tingawa. After some months without food, they turned off their giant. At a great distance. We didn't remove our people and let food get through to them until we checked to see that it was truly dead. We didn't know about the insect problem then, but it had wandered out into the desert to die, which I think may have made a difference. Bodies dry out instead of rot. Larvae die. We acted as harshly as we did because the Edges talk to one another, and we wanted to be sure that no other Edges got the idea it would be fun to push us around. Historically, the Edges have been amused by things like that." She clasped her hands in her lap and fell silent. The entire group seemed to be holding its breath.

Wide Mountain Mother, shaking her head, beckoned to one of the women and was given a cup of something steaming that was evidently soothing. When she had drunk it, she managed a smile.

"We clan mothers have discussed this—interminably, I'm afraid! We had to convince ourselves over and over that this inundation is true. We had to ask ourselves over and over why it has come upon us and who has brought it upon us. Until today, that question had no answer. I will not accept Abasio's dream as absolute truth in all details, but I'm sure there is truth in it! There is, however, one thing we have never doubted. The Edges are planning something inimical to us. Why else would they refuse to cooperate with the rest of us?"

Silence.

Precious Wind broke it. "The answer you received from the Edges sounds almost like a threat. 'What you're doing is useless,' weren't those the words? They seem to indicate that our efforts would meet with disaster."

Abasio growled, "Have the Edges said *nothing* about their own plans?"

Wide Mountain Mother shook her head. "Precious Wind quoted them exactly, Abasio. Their entire response consisted of the words 'No thank you, what you're doing is useless, we have our own plans.' Some of them varied that by omitting the 'thank you.' Recently I have paid more attention to their exact words, however. By calling our efforts 'useless,' they could mean 'wasted,' or they could mean 'Whatever you try, we will prevent you.' This makes more sense if you put it in the context of the traditional Edger attitude toward non-Edgers, accepted as a religious belief. They really believe all humans who were in any way *important* were created and survived in the Edges during the Big Kill. They really believe that any humans who survived the Big Kill outside the Edges are insignificant trash people who survived accidentally, no credit to themselves. When Edgers eliminate outsiders, they really believe they're taking out the trash."

Precious Wind gritted her teeth and spoke through them angrily. *"We have to find out what they're doing with the stinker stuff."* She got to her feet. Her face seemed suddenly almost too narrow, as though it had pinched itself inward, as if she was concentrating on something too unpleasant to allow comfort. "I'm almost sure they're making something alive,"

Xulai, however, was mentally chewing at something, her face very tense. She suddenly leapt to her feet, crying, "Oh, oh, they couldn't. Abasio. Remember what . . ." Her voice ran off in panic-stricken silence.

Abasio had risen and gone to her immediately. He turned her to face him. "Xulai, what?"

"I was thinking . . . remember what Sun-wings said. She said our sea-children could be destroyed by the Griffins' 'brethren in the seas.' As though she knew there was something waiting in this great ocean, something that would make anything we did useless! If the Griffins were created by the Edgers, they may also have created other creatures we've never even seen. The Edgers could know what else is out there. And maybe that's the reason they won't cooperate with us. They know it's useless! They've already put something in this ocean . . . something that won't let us live! Or maybe let anything live."

"Xulai, she said IF!" cried Needly. "Sun-wings said '*If* we didn't help them'! So she didn't mean something already there that she . . . that the Griffins couldn't . . . couldn't control."

Xulai sat down again, still white-faced. Abasio put his arm around her. Wide Mountain Mother nodded, surveyed their small circle. "How nice. A new terror to join the rest. Can we tell that particular panic to go play with the dozen or so other terrors, horrors, and impossibilities for the moment? Perhaps tomorrow we will have time to give it its due?"

She looked around the circle, noting their expressions. "No, you all want to DO something." She shook her head, mouth clenched. For a moment there was complete silence. She raised her head. "VERY WELL . . .

"We will all meet here tomorrow, midmorning. Each of you remember to bring several handkerchiefs and a complete list of any deities you've heard of, eliminating redundant deities under different names. One Earth goddess will be sufficient, for example. And then we will join in violent motion, screaming, sobbing, calling out in unison for help and sympathy. It will do no good, but everybody rushing about will amuse the children and I am told it releases tension."

The group watching had grown larger. There were grinning nods from the clan mothers in the group; others stared, mouths open, or exchanged bewildered glances. The shrill voice rose from the fringes once more. "Mama, I wanna watch evabody rushin' 'bout an' be amuse!"

Into the quiet that followed, Arakny cried, "Then what is that ganger queen doing with dozens of such creatures? What is our so-called Queen Sybbis intending to use them for?"

Precious Wind answered, "I've used our far-talker to discuss Sybbis's visit. The people in Tingawa think she was making—or was directed to make—a reconnaissance to find out how strong you are, and how determined. Something or someone had to have told her the Artemisians were on the road that goes up to Findem Pass. The one stinker who was with her may have been a spy."

Xulai asked, "Does Tingawa think the things are smart enough to—"

Precious Wind threw up her hands. "They don't *need* to be smart. Any one of them could be planted with electronic devices to tell the Edgers what's being said in the camp, what's being done in the camp, and very probably what Sybbis herself says and does. It, or Sybbis, may have attempted to plant devices in your wagons. If people haven't checked, they should.

"Further, Tingawa thinks if she's being induced to feed the creatures, she will soon send her gangers to take captives. If she's been induced to house them or to let them hunt, we need to find in what area, where. We need to know if people are disappearing. Are families in remote areas still there, safe, or are they gone? Arc there signs that remote areas have been occupied?"

From among the listeners, voices rose in confusion, a babble through which Wide Mountain Mother's voice cut like a knife. "Hush. Confusions of words don't help. Let us pick a direction in which we can move. We have one that may be useful.

"First: the Edges tell us they have their own plans.

"Second: the Edges have the technology necessary to make creatures; they have done it for generations in the archetypal villages.

"Third: they are now making creatures that eat human flesh and create a strange, fatty substance on their bodies that behaves, Precious Wind tells us, like a living organism.

"Fourth: they are harvesting that substance from a breeding population. And all this indicates what?"

Xulai spoke. "We need to find out what they're doing with it, and where they're doing it."

Mother nodded. "Exactly. We need spies." She looked around the circle. "Is Deer Runner here?"

"I'm here, Mother."

"Will you find those of the scouts who may be near? We need to set up a Find, Follow, and Observe network."

Runner sped off toward the stream that separated the men's houses from the plaza.

"Would she keep the creatures in her own camp?" asked Arakny of no one in particular. "Could she?"

Abasio shook his head, stood up, and squirmed, stretching his shoulders and back, knotted from sitting too long on the ground. "Let's consider what little evidence we have. Sybbis's people wore masks. The people Coyote saw at the rendering works wore masks. The men Precious Wind relocated away from Sybbis and Catland were *grateful* for being moved. This indicates fairly clearly that people can't live in close association with them without masks, that they aren't accustomed to them, and they hate having them around. They certainly can't live all the time wearing masks, so the stinkers aren't with them ordinarily. However, the gangers claim to control a big territory. Coyote and Bear have told me they've talked with other creatures, and a couple of valleys that used to have human settlers in them are now empty of human life.

"There's a connection here we should keep in mind. Old Chief Purple and Sybbis have a connection, possibly a fairly close connection. Old Chief Purple bought his way into one of the Edges.

"The gangers can evidently tolerate the stinker Sybbis had with her, or perhaps tolerate it for only a short time. At the moment she may see that one as an added symbol of power, like her throne. The other dozens of them . . . perhaps they're a display of power by the Edge that left them there in the woods for Sybbis to pick up on her return journey. We weren't supposed to know about them, so who was? My guess would be they are being used against Sybbis's people, to keep them cowed. I have very little doubt Sybbis's people know they eat humans. They've been told, or they've seen it happen. That's why the guards didn't mind Precious Wind getting the stinkers away from Sybbis.

"And all that leads me to believe that the Edge where old Chief Purple was, or still is, is central to this whole thing."

Quiet came, a long, apprehensive quiet, broken at last by Bear. "Lady, you took that thing apart? Would you say it'd be killed easy? Could a arrow kill it?"

Precious Wind nodded. "Arrow through the heart. Yes. The anatomy is approximately human."

"I tore one a' 'um's neck apart. It was real nasty. Arrows, they're good. Better if y'didn hafta touch it."

Wide Mountain Mother said firmly, "Bear, most of our scouts are excellent bowmen. When Deer Runner returns, we will begin set up a F, F, and O net to monitor traffic between and among the Edges north of us and the area Coyote has identified. There must be some kind of headquarters there, something or someone who has information, would you agree?"

Abasio took a moment before answering. "If they eat people, there have to be people in the area. If all the prey is gone, we can expect the Edgers to move. If they're developing something for use after the waters have risen, they need to have access to deep water."

Mother agreed. "We will use our best bowmen, but for the time being we'll avoid guns. We can kill and bury the hunters quietly. Without them, we assume, the other creatures cannot live. Abasio, Precious Wind, we have to find out what it is the Edgers are doing. We have to figure out how to do that without their knowing it, at least for a time."

Silence fell again to be broken by Needly's small, piercing voice, ringing with the clarity of a bell. "Mother, I know this discussion has been very important, and urgent though it is, Xulai and Abasio and I must interrupt our part in it to fulfill a more personal responsibility.

"Who is going to tell us how to get Willum to the House of the Oracles?"

Xulai turned toward Needly in sudden horror. *She had forgotten. For a time she had completely forgotten Willum.*

CHAPTER 12

House of the Oracles

ABASIO WAS, AS USUAL IN THESE DREAMS, IN the middle of the pool . . . or, more accurately, above the middle of the pool. He was invisible to the two women and seemingly to the creatures coming and going on their constant errands. The tower structure with its shimmering pool and lofty lines had been designed to convey a feeling of tranquillity and peace. He could feel it, feel that others felt it, including the statue of a woman that lay on a block of stone not far away, lips tightly compressed, her eyes half shut, almost slitted, as in anger, arms open as though reaching for something.

It began as it always began: *The little girl, who looked to be about six years old, said, "You promised a story!"*

Her mother said, "I know, Crumpet, but . . ."

"You always tell us no buts." This, firmly, from the boy. "An' you did promise." He was slightly older than his sister. A year or two, perhaps.

"Oh, tell Crumpet and Crash a story, Jinian," said Silkhands. "I enjoy them, too."

"Once upon a time," Jinian began, her voice fading into a long mumble.

" . . . When mankind came, there were already creatures here who had their own ways of life, their own language, their own ideas of what was right and wrong. They were called Eesties . . . other races of people, too . . . the world kept

everything peaceful and fruitful by sending messages to every thinking creature in the world . . . they took crystals from the pool to pass on to other living things . . . actually chemical messages that went right to the brain . . . man paid no attention to the messages or the way things were . . . man destroyed it.

"So, the children of Lom hated us . . . we began to multiply . . . the more of us there were, the more destruction we did. . ."

Abasio's dream went on. Either the tower dream or the Plethrob dream. Always the same dream, as though something, someone, wanted him to remember every word of it. A little different, each time, but always the same story of repentance and loss.

Jinian continued: "And the only reason I can think of for me to go is that my talent may be restored like Grandma Mavin's is going to be, though probably only temporarily, so I can help the people there. Of course, Aunty Silk's talent was never taken away completely. Healers went right on healing people, though it was much harder . . ."

"I guess that's a really good thing," said Crash. "Mama, who's that coming in here?"

"It's the galactic officer," said Jinian, almost in a whisper. "Fixit. That's its nickname. Fixit."

"Good morning, ladies," said the person arriving.

Abasio recognized it. He had bumped into it outside Plethrob's throne room. It had six legs. He remembered that.

It came over to the pool, leaned over the edge, and took Abasio's hand. "Abasio. Remember me?"

In the dream, Abasio thought he nodded. Thought he remembered saying, "Mmph."

"I'll be seeing you soon," said the bumped creature. "Don't worry so much. Xulai worries about your worrying. It's going to be all right. Promise. Really."

"Aunty Silk, c'n I ast a question?" cried Crash.

"You always do, dear."

"Who's the glactic ossifer talking to? That man hanging out there in the middle of the pool. He keeps looking at me."

"What man?" asked the women in unison. "What man?"

"Me, I'm Abasio," shouted Abasio in his dream. "Every damned time the Dervish can see me, this Fixit creature I bumped into can see me, the children can see me, why in the hell can't you?"

LOOKING OVER HER SHOULDER, NEEDLY came into the wagon to find Xulai and Precious Wind in furious activity, neatening the wagon for its trip to the Oracles the following morning. She watched for a few moments before asking tentatively, "Xulai, did you know Abasio's sound asleep out there under a tree? He's making these really strange noises and talking to someone about a Dervish. And yelling that somebody can't see him."

Xulai had been crouched over an open drawer. She rose with a troubled expression. "Yesterday at the meeting, he told everyone about his strange dreams. They have been going on for a long time, before we even reached Saltgosh. They're haunting him. Wide Mountain Mother seemed to believe in them, at least partly. I wish Abasio could figure out why they come to him. He says it's like a book; every night it opens up at some other place, only the same people are involved all the time. Dreams shouldn't do that. Should they?"

"Have you ever asked what he's dreaming about?"

"Not really, no. Do you think I should? I thought talking about it might only make it worse."

Xulai took a tiny garment from the pile at the back, shook it out, and shrieked—in surprise, not revulsion. The shirt had been mouse-occupied. Mouse landed on the bed and leapt to the floor, five baby mice landed on the bed along with everything else that had been in the drawer. Needly was first there, removing her shoe, laying it on its side with the heel against the wall, the opening toward mama mouse. Mouse saw the shoe as a nice, dark cave and ran for it, down to the toe. Needly wrapped a handkerchief around the shoe and rescued the mouse-lets.

"You have a mouse in your shoe!" Xulai expostulated.

"It's the easiest way to catch them, Xulai. Mice like to run along walls because that's where they find holes, and most people wear shoes, or boots, so they usually have one handy. If you put your shoe down like that—on its side, heel against the wall, toe out, open top toward the mouse—it'll run into your shoe, down into the nice dark toe. Then you just wrap something around the top, to keep it from jumping out while you relocate it." She grabbed a piece of bread from the food cabinet and limped purposefully toward the trees, shoe in one hand, bread and mouse-lets in the other.

When she returned, reshod, she found Xulai, Abasio, and Precious Wind emptying the wagon. Xulai, rather red-faced, announced, "Having mice in drawers simply verified that the wagon needs a good cleaning! We're making the trip to the Oracles in the morning, and the wagon should be mouse-free before we go! What did you do with them?"

"I found a nice hollow log back there. I put the mouse family in it, along with enough food for today. It's near water and there's lots of dried grasses with large seeds. Mama mouse will be fine. How can I help?"

"Fold down the outside table, be sure it's clean, empty one drawer at a time onto the table, wipe out the drawer, and shake things out. Fold and put them back if they're clean. If anything is dirty or mousy or chewed, leave it outside and I'll look at it there."

Precious Wind went to fetch wash water, and Xulai stopped in mid-fold, staring at the wall. "Needly. Abasio's funny about telling me things that he thinks might be upsetting. Upsetting to me, I mean. What he thinks might upset me, he wouldn't necessarily think would upset you. Could you . . . sort of ask him about the dreams? Yesterday he said he'd had the dream again and he wondered what normal felt like. He said he wondered if fated persons are allowed to have a normal day. If he's really having some kind of . . ."

"Puzzlement," suggested Needly.

"Anxiety. Something like that. It might help him to talk to someone about it, and he won't, not ordinarily. Except to Blue. Who has limited understanding of the human . . ."

"Mind? Psyche? Personality?"

"Any of those. You could always involve Precious Wind or even Arakny. They're both very levelheaded. So am I, of course, normally, but with the babies I get—"

"—into a state of maternal confusion, which is normal to new mothers." Needly spoke in a fully mature voice.

"That was Grandma, wasn't it?" Xulai commented.

"I guess," said Needly, in some confusion. Maybe Abasio wasn't the only one being haunted. She knew Xulai was worried about Abasio, and recently Needly herself had worried about him. Every time he saw someone sit in the chair his grandfather had made—made specially to fit into this wagon, long before Abasio had even met Xulai—Abasio fussed about not making time to go visit his grandfather, who lived somewhere north of here. And yesterday he'd stomped about saying there were other teams out now; the whole future did not rest upon Xulai and him alone. He wanted Xulai and his grandfather to know each other before it was too late. He wanted his grandfather to see the children.

Poor Abasio. Needly knew he wanted . . . a lot of things, and he wasn't the only one who needed to do something else. Xulai wanted to do something else. From what both of them said, everything they'd done since birth had been fated. They wanted some un-fated time off!

When they went outside later, however, he seemed to have cheered up. "In the morning, we'll have a quick, early breakfast and make the trip to the Oracles without stopping for a meal. Since this will take us close to the country where the stinkers are or were, Wide Mountain Mother is sending a sizable number of the warriors—all of them bowmen—as guides and escort, and some of the women are going. She tells me they're provisioning a small wagon that will also carry Willum."

Xulai put the baby clothes into the washtub and Precious Wind lifted the kettle from the fire and poured the hot water over them. "How long will it take?"

Abasio shrugged. "The trip will take less than a full day, assuming no disasters. And if we get a chance, she wants us to explore the place Coyote saw. Where the stinkers got hosed off."

"Explore it?" Xulai stiffened. Exploring wasn't something she wanted to do with the children along.

Precious Wind shook her head. "Not all of us, Xulai. If it looks abandoned, a couple of the warriors and I will look it over. It didn't sound like a place where people stay permanently. I do have equipment to detect high-tech alarms and traps."

Abasio didn't argue with her. There was never any point in arguing with Tingawans. One would think one had won the argument, only to find one had reached the end of round one in a bout that could go on after one or both parties had died and passed it to succeeding generations.

Xulai took the lid off a small kettle at the side of the fire where a savory mixture of chicken, onions, green peppers, and cornmeal was warming for their lunch. "This is ready to eat. Come get your bowls, stir in some of this shredded cheese, and we'll have our lunch before we finish sweeping out."

She leaned over, dipping the big spoon into a pot that suddenly began to squirm toward her across the coals. Xulai screamed and took two tottering steps back. There was a great subterranean muttering sound, like talking mountains. Horses screamed. In the plaza men yelled, and there came a loud, crashing sound. The ground went on shaking and snarling as Xulai staggered and fell, desperately twisting to avoid the fire. Abasio tried to run toward her and was sent sprawling. Needly had been shaken off the wagon step and was ruefully fingering a skinned elbow while the world went on with its deep, terrible growling and trembling, as though trying to shake itself apart.

The noise faded slowly, though the horses went on screaming and whinnying. A great cloud of dust had formed at the far side of the plaza, from which shouts and calls were still rising, along with coughs and curses. Adobe chimneys had fallen . . . were still falling! One tottered as they watched, adding to the dust cloud. Someone shrieked for help, and they heard running feet.

"What in . . ." cried Abasio, crawling over to help Xulai, who was sitting quite still while her eyes searched for the cook pot. Miraculously, it had not overturned. "Babies!" she cried.

Needly crawled up the wagon steps and looked inside. "They're fine, Xulai. They didn't even wake up!" Needly had reached the conclusion the babies were calamitously picky but catastrophe-proof. They would take an earthquake without a quiver but could create a full-blown crisis over a morsel of potato. Baby lunch could take . . . hours! Now, if she could just find something really catastrophic to feed them, maybe a live rattlesnake, they'd probably swallow it and go to sleep!

Abasio helped Xulai up, unhurt except for a couple of sore places that would probably turn into bruises. Together they washed the abrasion on Needly's arm and put a bandage over it. Abasio went to the horses and found Blue volubly and inaccurately explaining earthquakes to Rags.

As he returned from the horses, Needly remarked, "I guess that was an earthquake?"

"Yes," Abasio agreed. "It must have happened at some distance from us. I'm trying to remember what I've heard about aftershocks. Aren't they supposed to come very soon after?"

Precious Wind muttered, "Very soon after, but not always. Abasio, look across the plaza to the southwest."

They all looked. One of the roads—that is, rutted pathways—that led away from the plaza pointed down the slope across the little stream, beside the dancing ground, past the men's houses, into the desert and away: an endless line of ruts disappearing into an expanse of nothing. Where that trail met the horizon a cloud was rising, boiling, thrusting up great billows of dust, their rounded tops caught by a wind that pushed them northwest, expanding as they went.

"Something over there either fell in or heaved up," said Abasio. The noises from the area around them had subsided. There were occasional yells, but no screaming. Abasio got up and walked toward the noise on the plaza. He returned only a few moments later to tell them a few chimneys had fallen, one old, empty house had fallen—they'd been going to tear it down soon, anyhow. People had been moved away from toppled walls for safety while they were considering what to do. No one had been killed. The worst injury was one broken arm from a fall from a ladder. The healers were dealing with the broken arm along with various abrasions and bruises. Abasio took a bit more food in his bowl, which he had managed to put down without spilling. The Griffins were fine, a little startled but fine. Sun-wings remembered other such shocks and had limped outside to see the dust cloud.

Everyone seemed to be waiting after that, for another quake, for an aftershock, for some word of catastrophe, and the only sounds were of chewing, swallowing, comments on the dust cloud off to the southwest—which continued to roil—and murmured appreciation to Xulai as the cook. Cookery was a safe subject for each of them, though for different reasons. Needly, who was trying to think of anything except shaking land, resolved to ask Xulai to teach her to cook. Precious Wind, who was tired of worrying over the stinker problem, was wondering when Xulai could possibly have learned to cook. Not at Woldsgard, certainly. The cook there would not have taken kindly to an invasion of her kitchen. Abasio was merely feeling grateful that Xulai could cook, though he didn't intend to mention it because it would set Xulai off on a rant as to whether cooking skills had been part of the breeding program.

As Needly scraped the bottom of her bowl, she remarked, "I should go see Dawn-song. She might be frightened . . ."

Abasio rose. "Sun-wings is eight hundred years old, Needly. I imagine she's soothed her child through more dangerous events. Besides, to avoid any possible misunderstandings, Wide Mountain Mother fixed up a guard post over there. There's someone reliable on duty all the time who can keep her informed about what's going on."

"Why?" asked Needly. "Surely she didn't think the Griffins would . . ."

Xulai shook her head. "Mother's not worried about Sun-wings or Dawn-song doing anything. But, according to Arakny, there's a very small group—half a dozen or so—of old lie-abouts who are griping about providing food for the Griffins. Arakny says this particular bunch haven't even provided food for themselves since reaching adolescence and taking up their lifetime careers in the fields of gripe, cavil, and complaint. All one family, brothers and cousins, and it's an inherited trait."

"They need a cata-pull-it," said Needly and Abasio, in unison. They shared a grin while Abasio explained the guard duty. "Mother put the guard over there because she thought it best the gripe group be prevented from haranguing Sun-wings and Dawn-song. When she told me about them, I told her about the cata-pull-it. She's going to tell the clan mothers about it, focusing on getting rid of certain people. They know of a swamp down along the river where they can build one. She thinks the family you're talking about may move away when they see the construction and hear about how it's used, particularly the part about being paraded about while the drum goes 'dum, dum, dum,' while the people take a vote as to whether they get cata-pull-ited or not. The useless old complainers would certainly fear the vote going against them."

Precious Wind asked for an explanation of cata-pull-its, which Abasio provided. Shaking her head, she asked, "What are we doing about Sun-wings when we go to the Oracles?"

Abasio's dissatisfaction with the entire Sun-wings problem was reflected in his face. He glanced at Needly, nodding in her direction. "I've talked with her about it, Presh. We can't carry her with us. She can limp enough to go in and out of the shelter she's in, which is helpful from a sanitation point of view, but she can't move quickly. If we can obtain more of the antidote from the Oracles, we'll bring it back with us, or have someone jump it back. The main reason we're going, of course, is to see if the Oracles can heal Willum." He stared into space, wondering what he might have forgotten that he should have remembered.

Needly said plaintively, "I feel so useless! I have Grandma's note-book, but I've never made the stone medicine or its antidote. I've seen the plants once, but I don't have any of them. They're very rare. I might look for months and not find them. I'm sure she's at the House of the Oracles . . . and I'd feel better if she told me what to do next."

Neither Abasio nor Xulai commented. They were both determined not to count on Grandma's help until they had seen whether Grandma was, indeed, alive at the House of the Oracles.

"Will Sun-wings and Dawn-song accept being left in the care of the Artemisians?" Precious Wind asked as she went to the fire to see if there was any chicken left. She looked questioningly at the others, accepted headshakes from Abasio and Xulai, then split the remainder between Needly and herself.

As she returned to her seat, she said, "I asked Wide Mountain Mother if they were having any problem feeding Sun-wings and her child. She said not, all the annoying old hunters notwithstanding. The Griffin is eating far less than normal because she's not flying. Since some of the children have discovered that Dawn-song likes to play, so they go in there and play with her. When I looked in yesterday, they were climbing all over Sun-wings, and she seemed to be enjoying it . . ."

Xulai, shocked, exclaimed, "Climbing *on* her? And she lets them?"

Precious Wind looked at Needly and shrugged. "Encourages them! Needly was with them; the children were mostly younger than she, not big enough to hurt Sun-wings. Perhaps it relieves Sun-wings' boredom."

Needly nodded in agreement. "One little boy brought her a rabbit he had snared. She ate it, told him it was very good. I think Abasio's right. It would be safest not to move Sun-wings at all if we can avoid it."

Xulai said, "Safest? She's been moved before with no trouble."

"She has," Precious Wind agreed. "And we've been very lucky that there was enough power when it was done. It could be a nasty situation to get her out in the middle of nowhere, immobile, and find there's not enough power to move her at all. However . . ." She dropped her voice almost to a whisper. "I was thinking more of the fact that she's making friends, as well as becoming a friend to a good many Arte-misians. Friendship may give us some leeway when it comes to survival questions."

"She doesn't need to go anywhere," said Needly. "If the Oracles won't come back and fix her, Grandma will! Precious Wind and I can hop Grandma back here!"

Abasio still had grave doubts about that matter, "grave" being the operative word. According to Needly, her old caretaker was dead and had been buried in Hench Valley. Of course, Willum was also dead, or petrified, though not buried. If Willum could be returned to life—which Abasio also had agonizing doubts about—then others might also. He was trying to keep his doubts well hidden and retain an open mind on these questions of survival along with questions about a good many other things. Such as Oracles! And stinkers! And these idiotic dreams he kept having!

He felt himself shaking. He was laughing! Why in hell was he laughing . . . over Fixit.

Fixit. Fixit was just plain funny. The creature felt and sounded so real. And it looked so very . . . imaginary. What were those ancient books Precious Wind had told them of? Illustrated ones, the story told in pictures. Comedic books! Well, Fixit looked very much . . . like what one saw when one had been drinking too much! BUT if they needed help with those damned Edgers, Fixit would be the person . . . creature he would turn to.

Despite Abasio's affection for Willum (tried though it had often been) and his regard for Grandma (whom he had never met), their fates faded into relative insignificance when he focused on whatever it was the Edgers were up to! The Edgers were going to be a problem, probably the worst problem they would face—and by "they" he meant any colleagues, friends, cooperative creatures who were working with them. Mother, Arakny, and the scouts and border riders had set up a network of riders, each with a spare horse, to observe and record any unusual movement in the more vacant areas of Artemisia as well as any movement from the north. Though there were very few mechanical vehicles left and very little fuel for them, the Edgers had somehow always managed to have both, supposedly from a huge buried industrial complex far east of here. It was said to have been set up originally to protect needed materials in a time of war and had gone on protecting them for centuries after the war was over. Machines wrapped in stuff that looked like spiderwebs, emerging from those wraps as though just manufactured. And, unfortunately, weapons, too.

Of all those at Wide Mountain Mother's meeting, Abasio had probably known the most about Edgers, how they acted, how they thought!
Back when old Chief Purple had bought his way into an Edge, Abasio
had run errands back and forth. He knew what Edgers were like. They
could be pleasant and affable, and turn around and stab you in the
back while still smiling. If they knew something bothered you, they'd
use it like a dagger, stick it in and then twist it! The only way to avoid
that was to maintain an appearance of uninterested calm. Of control.
NO. Not so much control as an appearance of not caring! It was wearing him down. Or the dreams were. He seemed to be the only one
struggling. No one else expressed any doubts whatsoever about Willum's future, not the Artemisians, not Precious Wind or Xulai. Making
a simple trip to visit people—creatures?—who had been visited before
without incident should not fall into the category of "things that make
one's instincts scream 'watch out!'" It made him feel foolish and inadequate, but the nerves in his back screamed danger, nonetheless. Or
maybe he was having a personal aftershock from the earthquake.

Leaving what he was beginning to think of as "the womenfolk,"
Abasio went to talk with Sun-wings herself. He had not forgotten her
threat, which she had not withdrawn, and continuing to build goodwill
between them could hurt nothing. He surprised himself by feeling an
honest affection toward her, and not because of that long-ago instance
when she'd saved his life. Affection meant . . . well, it meant another
burden. By any measure she was that! A person or creature one cared
about was the most dreadful kind. Get in trouble with any ordinary
burden: if trouble came, you dropped it and ran! If one dropped Sun-
wings, she would probably not just lie there and let you get away! And
suppose she did? Think about all that weight on one's conscience!

Burden or not, threat or not, when he arrived at the big storage barn
where Sun-wings was being cared for, she seemed more relaxed about
her situation than he was. When he went over his reasoning regarding
the Oracles, she said, "You have it right, Abasio. It is best for me to stay
here. The women in this place are kind and interesting. They feed me
and my child very well. And I am enjoying the children."

She did not mention the thing she valued most: her relief at being
in a place where she could not be seen from the air. When Despos had
attacked her, when she had fallen into that little valley, when she had

been there alone except for the hunter, it was only the second time in her life she could remember feeling . . . desperation. That was a word Needly had given her. She had said, "Do not despair, Sun-wings. Do not feel desperation!" What was the other word Needly had used? "Terror." Yes. Terror for Dawn-song. Both times she had felt that terror, humans had . . . helped. One child had rescued her hatchling, another child had sewn her wing. A day or so ago, the healers had said she had done it well. They had told her they would take the stitches out soon, perhaps tomorrow. The boy had put himself between the arrow and Dawn-song. The man, Abasio, could have rescued the human children and left her there to die. She had threatened the humans, threatened to kill their children in the seas, and they could have left her there. They had not even argued about it. They had simply brought her back without question.

So, if a Griffin needed help, where did the Griffin find it? If Despos returned, he would kill her and her child. All the other Griffins had flown to Tingawa, and she knew only two of them would have certainly helped her if they were here—the two the children said they had named Bell-sound and Golden-throat. She was grateful. She knew the word. Grateful to those she had threatened to kill. It made a . . . a confusion. It was likely the ten Griffins who had come from the land to the south were also . . . *good creatures,* but she could not be sure.

She was committed to doing her part carefully: never going out in daylight; diligently examining the night sky before she limped her way out to the place they had told her to use, the place that was always clean when she went to use it again. She spoke softly to the people who brought her food. She could sometimes smell fear on them, but nonetheless they came. The children weren't afraid. Yesterday they had brought clean, *warm* water and brushes and Needly had directed them in washing her, all seventeen of them. She had counted. Little males, little females, chattering, noisy, affectionate. That was a new word. They had been "affectionate." They had brushed her fur with wet brushes, rinsing them out, over and over. They had combed the feathers and wiped each one with cloths. She was still stiff from the fall, it was hard for her to reach, to groom . . . but, oh, it felt . . . better to be clean. And the children had done it for fun. She did not really understand fun. Dawn-song had also been groomed, had also thought it fun, but she had not been able to explain it either, except to say it felt like swallowed bubbles!

So she was depending upon humans, particularly on this one and his children and females . . . if that is how it worked. Griffins did not have . . . families. Mothers and young, yes. Sisters, maybe, if the older one had helped care for the younger. She wasn't sure how it worked with human hes and shes. She did not know if any of them were worthy of trust. But if there had been other males than Despos? Perhaps it would have been more like humans. Families. And worthy of trust to do what? What more could they do than they had done already, as though there had been no choice but to do as they did? *No choice but to do as they did.* She set this aside to think upon later. There was something there she needed to understand . . .

Now she asked, "Why are you worried? Is that the right word?"

Abasio shook his head at her and told her the truth. "I'm apprehensive. That's a little worse than worried. I don't even really know why. I've felt this way ever since Coyote told us about the Edgers and the stinkers." He rubbed his face in annoyance, trying to erase the frown lines. "I have no idea what it has to do with me or Xulai or our children . . . including Willum and Needly, but those creatures make me feel crawly."

"Crawly?"

"Like . . . something unwelcome on your body, something that itches . . ."

Sun-wings did a strange thing with her beak. While he puzzled over that, she lifted her unwounded wing, half unfolding it. "There, in my wing pit, I feel a bug. Can you see it?"

Abasio crouched to look up under the wing. He saw a bright blue thing, as long as his thumb and broad, rather beetle-ish. "You want it out?"

"I would be grateful. I can only reach there with a hind leg, the wrong hind leg. The children missed it yesterday, and it makes *me* feel crawly."

Abasio removed the bug between thumb and finger. Despite its crawliness, it was very beautiful. It had six legs, at least one pair of wings, and gemlike iridescent wing covers. "I don't recognize it."

"You would have no reason to," she said. "It's a dragon flea. Soon after Griffins were made, dragon fleas appeared. Might it be Griffins and dragons are similar species? Or perhaps we are . . . the next best thing in the flea's . . . judgment? Perhaps when some mankind made a Griffin he also made the flea, just as a . . . what would the word be? A little thing, a . . ."

"A trifle, an amusement . . ."

"Ah, I know. One of the boy children gave Needly a gift in a box. The box was . . . made fancy? It had around it . . ."

"A ribbon and a bow? To make the gift special. Is that what you're saying?"

"Yes. Something like that. So I think the one who made Griffins made the dragon flea like the bow on the box. Even though we are not dragons." She purred. "I think you are troubled by a dragon flea in your brain."

She did the peculiar thing with her beak, and Abasio realized she was smiling. She had made a joke.

He waved the beetle thing at her, saying, "I removed your dragon flea. Can you remove mine?"

She did the smile thing again, a crinkling of the tissue at the outer edges of the beak. "I can take the idea of the stink creatures out of your head, but then your head would be of no more use to you and I think Needly . . . I think both she and Xulai would be . . . cross with me?"

"Furious, I hope. That's worse than cross."

She shrugged. "Furious. That is a Despos word! Always he is furious. Perhaps there is no cure for human crawlies or Griffin crawlies. I think maybe only very . . . Needly told me the word . . . ah! Only very 'conscientious' creatures have crawlies, people so . . . 'ap-pre-hen-sive' they think of disasters ahead of time, and the thinking drives them into apprehen . . ."

"Apprehen-sion." He did not like the other words that came to mind. Terror! Horror!

Sun-wings nodded: "Apprehension. That is what I feel for our future, your little ones and mine, Abasio. Give the flea to the one called Precious Wind. She collects . . . bugs." She shifted, a little uncomfortably. "I have learned from Needly that names must have a *Namer* and a *why*. She said she and Willum were *sent* to be our Namers, and part of the *why* was our need for names and the other part was to name us suitably. Did Precious Wind have a *Namer*? And *why* is her name?"

Abasio thought the question only slightly strange. "Her parents were her Namers. As she was being born, a wind came from the sea. That wind brought rain to save crops that were dying from lack of water."

"Ah. Crops would be food? Food much needed? I see. So the wind was 'precious,' which means . . ."

"Of much value. Dawn-song is of much value to you. Xulai and the children are of much value to me, we are of value to one another. We are treasured. You and Dawn-song are treasured by us and by the children."

"Ah. Treasured. And a treasure is . . . something of value. Yes?" She sighed, a very human-sounding sigh. "Give the flea to Precious Wind. She will . . . value it! She likes new things. Especially bugs. I find that strange but interesting. With your people, Abasio, I am finding many things strange . . . but interesting. If a person does not eat bugs, then why does a person like bugs?"

"People . . . *some people* study the world around them." He stopped, suddenly remembering the Great Litany. "The *universe* around them. They seek to understand the *universe* in all its parts. Bugs are parts, Griffins are parts, humans are parts . . . all that exists is . . . part of it." He stepped back with a polite bow before wrapping the bug, which was still very lively, in his handkerchief, bidding her farewell politely, and taking the bug back to the wagon.

The wagon his grandfather had built for him several lifetimes ago— or so it seemed to him now. Though Precious Wind had a wagon of her own, she was spending most of her time with Xulai and the babies, and that is where he found her to give her the dragon flea.

"Where did you get this?" cried Precious Wind. "It's beautiful. Xulai, Needly, look at the wing covers, that gorgeous azure blue! Green and purple lights in it. It's marvelous!"

"It's a dragon flea," Abasio said. "Sun-wings sent it to you. It was itching her wing pit. She finds you strange but interesting."

"What are you grinning about?" demanded Xulai.

He realized he was actually smiling. "Both Sun-wings and I had a fit of crawlies. I rid her of hers, and she has rid me of mine." He laughed. "I didn't realize the Griffins have a sense of humor."

"*Some of them* have a sense of humor," Needly corrected without looking up from her self-imposed washup job at the dishpan. "There are sixteen adult females. Willum and I met six of them, and three of them have no humor or kindness in them: Flame-tail, Copper-beak, and Silver-shanks, as well as the male, Despos. Despos is partly scaled, and I believe those four have serpent genes in their design. Two are carrying eggs in their pockets, and the other one, Silver-shanks, has a female child, Snow-foot. However, Snow-foot was *not* sired by Despos, and she already has a sense of humor. She is a lovely little Griffin, like Dawn-song. The other three adults are friendly ones: Sun-wings and her child, Dawn-song; Golden-throat and her child, Amber-ears; Bell-sound and the baby male Griffin Willum and I hatched for her. We named him Carillon. He shouldn't have been named until he was fledged, but the name just jumped out of my throat."

All three adults were staring at her with their mouths open. "Despos?" Xulai squeaked then, clearing her throat, "Despos is who?"

"The male Griffin. He's enormous and dangerous and destructive!"

"You've seen him?" cried Xulai. "I didn't realize . . ."

"What's this about pockets?" said Abasio.

"Did you say 'baby male Griffin'?" Precious Wind muttered. "We thought there might be only one male!"

They had all spoken at once, and Needly looked up into three intent, concerned, demanding faces. She flushed before saying plaintively, "Well, Xulai . . . Everyone has been very busy since we got back. Willum and I . . . we didn't get a chance to tell you anything we did while we were . . . taken away. Not about our new cave or becoming official Namers and making up a ceremony to name the Griffins, not about our costumes or Willum's drumming or sending all the Griffins to Tingawa, or about how Griffins have pockets to keep their eggs in and how we hid the eggs and hatched one of them and fooled Despos and sent him away to the north pole . . ."

Abasio sat down with a thud. Xulai, paling visibly, sagged onto a chair and took a very deep breath. Precious Wind, reaching for her notebook, said in a firm voice betrayed by only a slight quaver, "There's no time like the present, Needly. Why don't we start with Despos and the north pole." Her eyebrows went up, very far up. "That is, of course, unless you have a more consequential point of origin from which you prefer to begin?"

"Wait just a moment," said Abasio. "No sense making her tell us twice. I think Arakny and Wide Mountain Mother need to hear this."

ARAKNY AND WIDE MOUNTAIN MOTHER joined them to hear the naming saga, everyone seated on cushions or folding chairs drinking tea, after which Wide Mountain Mother had left them. She had gone, speechless, shaking her head slowly side to side as though she feared something was loose inside it. Precious Wind, however, made an excuse to delay Arakny.

Arakny looked them over with a wry half smile. "You're looking very portent-ious. Is there some additional disaster you didn't want Mother to know about?"

Xulai took a deep breath. "Sit back down, Arakny, do. Take off your shoes, you've been twisting your feet about as though they hurt. It's nothing like that. We don't want to be thought intrusive, but we've been told Wide Mountain Mother won't visit the Oracles. Is there a reason for her avoidance that we should be aware of before we go there?"

Arakny frowned, sat down, removed her moccasins as suggested. "I don't think Mother's avoidance should influence you. They make her uncomfortable, so she chooses not to visit." She crossed one leg over the other and rubbed distractedly at the foot she had sprained during the quake. "We tell the Oracles things we think are important, and they tell us it doesn't matter. And conversely, they make remarks that to us sound incidental and even silly, but they do it in a manner that seems to indicate importance. Of course, they don't say 'this is important' or tell us why it's important, which rather destroys the value of their having said anything about it at all. We have been keeping meticulous records, however, and we've found some correlation between things they've mentioned and subsequent events, though sometimes there's a very long elapsed time between the two. That can be very annoying—especially to Wide Mountain Mother."

"Could you . . . give us an example?" Abasio asked.

Arakny stared into the distance. "Oh, there was a thing over a year ago. We had taken them a load of food supplies as a gift. They've given us to understand that such gifts are 'acceptable.' You should understand that Mother is not immune to criticism by her people, and food is considered to be a tribal resource which should not be needlessly wasted. During the unloading—they weren't helping unload, they never help do anything, but they were standing by, supervising, I suppose—anyway, two of them mentioned that it was raining in the mountains.

Two of them, a few steps apart, two statements apropos of nothing separated by a few moments of time. 'It's raining in the mountains.'

"We were not surprised that it was raining in the mountains. It often rains in the mountains. If there are any clouds over the mountains at all—Stonies or Little Stonies—chances are it's raining. They *didn't* tell us that as a consequence of this particular rain, the river was going to flood the plaza several days later during the Corn Festival."

Xulai murmured, "Corn Festival meaning lots of visitors? Dignitaries and so forth?"

"All of that, plus some. Well, we've gradually learned to . . . to *extrapolate* what the implications of any such seemingly meaningless but repeated statement might be. Distant rain might affect us how? Free association leads us to disaster words like 'drown' and 'flood' and 'washout.' Then we might ask ourselves *whose* drowning might most upset us, or *where* a flood or washout in the near future would be particularly troubling? Among other suggestions, we might possibly come up with ideas such as *While Wide Mountain Mother is crossing a bridge in the Little Stony Mountains,* or *While an important visitor is trying to reach us,* or *During Corn Festival in the plaza.*"

"Little Stonies being the small range just north of here? And difficulties which you couldn't do anything about?" asked Xulai.

"Oh, but we could! We could treat it as a mystery. We could *pretend* some enemy had set *a trap* for us, that *rain* had been given as a *clue,* and we could examine our routines to see what unpleasant event might occur as the result of rain. We could make sure Mother—or any other clan leader—didn't traverse any route until it was checked. It was time to do that anyhow, though we'd intended to delay the routine for a while; we went ahead and had the maintenance teams check trails and bridges at once. Also, since we all know this place was built near the confluence of the Wickinook and the Chawook streams, we'd have a good water source . . ."

Abasio said, "And since both these streams originate in the Little Stonies . . ."

"Exactly! And finally, since many of us are old enough to remember this plaza has been flooded in the past, we could move the festival to higher ground, just in case!"

Precious Wind murmured, "All of which, in fact, you did?"

"Indeed. Most of it required only a revision of the schedule. We found the bridge over the canyon near Black Peak had a piece of timber under it that had been chewed in half by a packrat, or a pack of rats; the maintenance team found the only trail from Shangos'k'nee had been both blocked and collapsed by a big stone dislodged from the ridge above. It's not a trail that's in constant use, but it's the only one that saves half a day's foot travel from there to here.

"Men from half a dozen places volunteered to do a quick rebuild of the trail. It's along a cliff side and dangerous if not shored up. The bridge got a new piece of timber—after we dug out the packrat nest under it—a monster nest, must have been hundreds of generations of rats. Normally the stream bed that separates the plaza from the men's houses is just that, a dry or almost dry bed. However, when an infrequent very heavy rain comes down, it is likely to pick up all manner of things, a huge dead cottonwood, for example, which will inevitably hang up on something, somewhere, with brush and deadwood piling around it. The water level rises, and the plaza is slightly lower than all the houses around it. It was indeed flooded. As we had arranged to hold the festival somewhere else, it was no great problem. It has flooded before, and we have little flood dams to put at the bottom of all the doors to keep the water from running into the houses. For that very reason, the lower parts of the walls around the plaza are laid up in stone, not adobe."

"I see," said Xulai. "Telling you without telling you could be very irritating."

"It can indeed," Arakny said, throwing up her hands. "I should point out, however, that *no one's life would have been endangered if we had not corrected these things.* The bridge was a long way from breaking; the trail block was obvious from a distance; both of these would have been routinely corrected within a short time. The flood would have been fatal to no one. It's not that we *can't* deal with the Oracles, but all this allusive *maybe/maybe-not* hinting at things seems foolish, particularly when you consider that the mention of rain was only one of about six similar mentions, and none of the others seemed to have *any relevance whatsoever.* It makes life difficult for Wide Mountain Mother. She says she has to feel . . . omniscient in order to do her job, even though she knows she isn't. I confess I don't really understand what she means."

"I do." Abasio looked up with a rueful grin. "Getting things done requires a competent person to give the orders and competent people to follow them. When I visited Ghastain it was apparent the king liked a lot of marching and flag-waving by his army. I'd never seen an army before. Anyhow, I noticed the insignia they wear. It's called a chain of command, and they told me it indicates who can get orders from above and give orders lower down. It reminded me that Xulai's father once told me he lost 'the power of command' during his wife's long illness. He said he couldn't summon it up. He was too involved with her suffering."

Arakny exclaimed, "That must be it! Mother said the Oracles made her feel *incapable*! I hadn't thought about giving life-and-death orders while feeling unsure of oneself! If there's anything the Oracles are good at, it's confusing people!"

She fell silent, unconsciously kneading the sore foot, remembering that she was possibly next in line to be Mother-Most of the clan. *Set the thought aside! Oh, please let Mother live forever or get the clans to elect someone else Mother-Most for life. Please! Even though I can't think of anyone but me who would do the job very well!*

"To answer your original question, no, I don't think Mother's refusal to go to the Oracles is anything you should worry about. You and Abasio are doing very well, supremely well. You will not do it the way the Oracles would, but that simply doesn't matter."

"What are they like?" asked Xulai. "Appearance, manner, speech . . ."

"If you see someone in bright clothes, that's one of the servants. They're young to middle-aged adults, and they're quiet. Evidently they work for a season, then go home for a season, in rotation. They say the pay is good and the work light. They aren't our people. Most of them come from farther east, where there's good farm country. Their only duties are to keep the caves clean. The House of the Oracles is actually a cave.

"The Oracles wear gray robes with names embroidered on the shoulder, which is a good thing—they look identical. It's best if you don't ask them any questions at all. Pursuing a question makes them disappear. Do not ever ask 'why?' They seemingly can't deal with *why* . . .

"Let's see, what else? The rooms they give human guests are fully equipped for human use. We started with the assumption they were male and female, no particular reason except one does label things in accordance with custom. Either the males are clean-shaven or they don't grow facial hair or they aren't sexed at all. No one of us has ever seen them unclothed. We've never seen a child among them. They may very well be identical. We have wondered if they take the shape of whatever people they are with."

"They're not like Dervishes, then," said Abasio. "I'd thought they might be."

"Dervishes?" asked Arakny.

"It's one of those dreams he mentioned," said Xulai, giving him a fond look. "He's been floating around in some other world in his dreams."

"Really?" Arakny gave Abasio a keenly interested look. "That Lom world you were talking about? Where the starships went?"

"You said you didn't know that Lom is a place-name on the world where the ships went from the Place of Power," said Precious Wind. She was staring at Abasio as though she had suddenly decided to dissect him.

"They're just dreams," he said, uncomfortable beneath that penetrating gaze. "I may have heard the name somewhere. I don't remember how it came up . . ."

Xulai reached over to take his hand. "You were explaining to Willum and me that the people in your area, where you grew up, believed that most of the people on Earth had flown to the stars in starships."

Needly came from the wagon holding a cup and a cloth and approached Arakny. "Let me put some of this on your foot." She knelt down and bathed the foot in the whatever it was and unbuckled the other shoe, saying, "Let's put some on the other foot as well. As soon as it dries, you can put the shoes on, and I'll leave the cup here. You can put it in a bottle and keep it if you'd like to use it again."

Arakny sniffed at the stuff, looking puzzled. The foot Needly had bathed felt warm, almost hot. And the pain had gone. She picked up the cloth and cup and did as Needly had suggested with the other foot. "Xulai, was it you who told Abasio about Dervishes and the other Gamesmen on Lom?"

"No!" Xulai cried. "How could I? I've never heard of Gamesmen. All I told him was what little I remembered of the messages from the ships that were received in Tingawa."

Arakny stared into nothing for a long moment, then said matter-of-factly, "There were two ships; one landed in a valley, one on a flat mountain. Valley ship you can forget. All the females left that ship when it landed, and the men stayed behind to start what they called the University, which blew itself up a few generations after landing. The mountain ship has never stopped functioning, however. They're still training cadres of technical people every generation, and they've continued to maintain the ship and provide information."

Xulai had stopped moving, eyes wide. She cried, "Information until *now*? I wasn't told that any of the receivers here on Earth were still functioning."

Arakny shrugged. "So far as I know, they aren't. The current information comes directly into the library helmets through what they call a 'wormhole alternate communications link.' The helmet people pronounce it 'whack-el': *W-H-A-C-L*."

Precious Wind stood, slowly turned. "Arakny, are you saying Earth is still receiving information from one of the two ships that went to a place named Lom at the time of the Big Kill?"

"Right. The two ships that were built on the moon over a millennium ago by the Place of Power. About a quarter of the people working on the project were your countrymen, Tingawans." Arakny slipped her feet into the moccasins, took a couple of steps away, testing for pain. None. "Needly, what was in that stuff? Never mind. Tell me later." She turned her back on them, running her fingers through her hair, pressing her head for a long moment as though to ease an unpleasant memory.

"The people from the Place of Power were never comfortable neighbors. Still, we had always tried to get along with them, and after the ships went, some of the people from the Place of Power moved down in our area and some went up toward Fantis, where, I'm told, they joined up with the Edgers."

"That's all the Edgers needed," snarled Abasio. "More highly destructive technical expertise. But I suppose everyone from there had to go somewhere else."

Arakny laughed. "Actually, not, Abasio. Most of the people are still there, in the town of Golden-trees. It's quite nice, really."

Precious Wind murmured, "From your tone, I assume it has become . . . ordinary. That's all and the end of the Place of Power? It's *ordinary*."

"Yes," Arakny agreed. "Except a few amusing footnotes. At least I find them so. There were at least two other ships sent from Earth to Lom, or Lom's planet, that were built elsewhere."

Xulai cried, "Ships no one knew about? Arakny, how in the world did they . . . ?"

Arakny smiled, shaking her head. "Since the Big Kill, people on this side of our planet forget there are people on the other side of our planet. The Place of Power wasn't the only enclave that managed to survive the Big Kill. The area called Yurope sent off at least two ships, small ones, carrying only a few hundred people each." She stopped, grinned widely, and said, "Now, you'll think I'm telling you a fairy tale, but it's a favorite thing of mine. One of the ships from Yurope carried an entire marching band to Lom. The band belonged to the royal family of a tiny principality only a few miles across: it had nothing in it, no business, no agriculture, no anything except places for people to gamble."

Abasio nodded. "The only thing I know about gambling is that when Grandpa was younger and the town had a tavern, he and his friends used to gamble for toothpicks. Everyone started with twenty or fifty or whatever, and the one who ended up with the fewest toothpicks had to buy the beer for the others."

Arakny smiled. "Well, this family gambled real money, not toothpicks. The head of the family, the prince, didn't gamble, but he took a share from those who did: enough for this family to build a ship and put it in orbit and send it to Lom . . ."

"How could they send it to the same world?" cried Precious Wind. "The Place of Power destination was a secret! It was kept secret from everyone, because of the Big Kill!"

"They no doubt bribed someone to obtain the planet location just as they bribed someone for the technology that let bodies and minds survive the thousand-year voyage. The 'mind survival' technique is very similar to the 'helmet technology.' The mind is stored; the body is preserved; the mind is fed back into the body when the trip ends. The prince and his family and his band and the families of the band members went to Lom, just as the Place of Power ships did, and they very definitely got there. Mountain-ship messages referred to them, saying things like 'The Band marched through School Town yesterday.'"

"Where are you getting this information?" cried Precious Wind. "Where's all of it coming from?"

Xulai interrupted, "Yes, Arakny, please. You're telling us things we're utterly ignorant of. I think we deserve to know . . ."

Arakny made patting, "sit down and listen" motions. "Don't get all ruffled! I'm one of Artemisia's librarians. On the surface Artemisia is a simple society. We do things in very simple ways. Our apparent simplicity gave us protective coloration that helped us survive the Big Kill. Seeing how primitive we were, no one suspected us. However, under the simple surface, Artemisia has a number of highly technical . . ." She paused, searching for a word.

"Inclusions?" suggested Precious Wind.

"Very well. Inclusions. We call the things we're given 'library helmets.' The people who give them to us call them Universal Receivers. The library helmets are the most sophisticated information-gathering-and-disseminating devices ever invented—that anyone on Earth has seen, at least. Don't ask about the power source, because I have no idea. For all I know, it might actually be sunlight, more—or less—specifically, starlight. Maybe they're fueled by the information itself."

As she had spoken, the other three had become increasingly intent.

Arakny went on: "The helmets do what you and Abasio do for the Tingawan historians, Xulai. Gather information from all sources, cross-check that information against all sources, remove obvious falsities and flaws, and retain only information that is determined to be accurate and true."

Precious Wind gasped, "That's remarkable!"

"It is. Also, the helmets can receive information through wormholes—you may recall that the messages from the ships on Lom came through a wormhole . . ."

"Just a minute," said Precious Wind. "Are you saying it's possible that all planets are connected via wormholes?"

Arakny turned to regard her questioningly. "Precious Wind, when did I say that? I said, 'Messages from the ships on Lom came through a wormhole.' That's all I said. The only thing I know for a fact is that *the planet containing a geographic area known as Lom, and this planet we are sitting on, ARE or WERE connected by a wormhole.* The helmet people told us when a ship goes from one planet to another, it leaves something like a temporary crease in space. If a wormhole subsequently touches a crease, sometimes it may turn along it, follow it. A wormhole was established at some time, between us and Lom, and since—*so far as we know*—only the flights of the ships linked the two planets, that flight *might* be when it happened."

"Are you saying the planets might have done it?" Precious Wind demanded furiously.

Arakny snarled, "Did you hear me say that? Strange, I don't remember saying that. Are you having difficulty with your ears, Miss Most-Terribly-Important-Tingawan?"

Abasio shook his head at Precious Wind. "Calm down, Presh. Get off your elephant! Listen instead of demanding. Arakny hasn't claimed any certainty about details."

"Thank you, Abasio." Arakny bowed in his direction. "Yes. I understand your frustration, Precious Wind. Frustration can beget fury, and I also get dreadfully frustrated. At one point I asked the helmet about wormholes between planets. The helmet condescended to tell me that establishing wormholes is a customary thing for a planet to do if it's a bow planet."

"How do you spell that, 'bow' . . . ?" Precious Wind demanded, still sharply.

Arakny stared her down. "It told me ver-bal-ly, as in con-ver-sa-tion. It did not write it down or spell it out. If it had, what difference would it make to be able to spell it? *B-O-W, B-O-U-G-H, B-A-O, B-H-A-O-H.* No matter how it might be spelled, it is something I can't identify, something that is probably spelled, if at all, *in some entirely different language's alphabet?* That's the way it sounded when the helmet told me, ver-bal-ly, the answer to my question. It's on my list of things to find out someday when I have unlimited free time." Her body said clearly, "When you go home to your blessed Tingawa and leave me alone!"

"Are you people here in Artemisia the only ones who know this?" Abasio asked in his politest voice.

"Firstly, not even most Artemisians know about it because Artemisians are like most other people: they're much more interested in food, sex, sleep, or the next tribal ceremony than they are in a theory of 'universal wormhole information networks.' Which spells, before you ask, Precious Wind, *U-WIN.*" She glared at Precious Wind for a long moment before resuming her account.

"Secondly, the people who gave us the helmets obviously already know about it. *Before you pounce on me, Precious Wind! No, I do not know who or what they are. They show up now and again to feed some additional information or systems into our helmets. Sometimes they give us a few new ones.* If you want more information, ask your own people in Tingawa. I understand they have analyzed the helmets and are actually manufacturing them, or a very close copy. I don't know if the Tingawan helmets have the capacity to be Universal Receivers, however, so you might want to check on that before considering them an adequate substitute. I do know that each helmet given to us contains an official description of the helmets and their capabilities and it refers to the manufacturers as Us and We, which the people of Artemisia do not find enlightening."

Precious Wind murmured, "What are they called, these people who gave you the helmets?"

Arakny said, very seriously, "We call them the People Who Gave Us the Helmets."

Precious Wind frowned. "Well, what do they call themselves?"

"We ask who they are. They say, 'We are the people giving helmets.' They don't say 'helmets,' they say something I can't pronounce. Shall we make an acronym? 'We, helmets, are to people giving'? *W-H-A-T-P-G?* Pronounced 'WHAT PIG.'" She laughed, silently but almost hysterically, shaking her head. "Or 'Helmets Us Goin' ta Give You'? That could be HUGGY. They arrive, they look human, but I believe that's protective coloration. I don't think they are human; who or whatever they are, they are an enigma. Enigma number two if we count the Oracles as enigma number one. Or vice versa.

"For heaven's sake, Precious Wind, try to accept it: *No one in Artemisia is hiding anything from you and the Grand Supreme Whatsit of Tingawa. The helmet people are enigmas. It is very difficult to get information from enigmas that is not in itself enigmatic. Which doesn't usually help and it's* NOT our fault. I cannot direct them to talk to Tingawans. And quite frankly, I wouldn't if I could. Your attitude may explain why they don't."

There was a lengthy silence while Precious Wind, her jaw clenched, stared at the still-lengthening shadows, Abasio at the grass, Xulai at Arakny, Arakny at the few golden leaves, still jittering on the trees outside.

Xulai broke it by asking plaintively, "Does the helmet know why the royal family brought their marching band with them to Lom?"

Arakny gave her a smile of gratitude. At last, something she knew! "Because the prince loved it. It was like . . . You know how some children play with toy soldiers? His band was like that. They were his toy. He was a toy prince in a toy kingdom with a toy band and he had more money than he could spend in forever! He knew of the Big Kill. He didn't want his musicians killed. And they would have been killed because they didn't care about the creeds that had been inserted in killing machines designed to kill everyone who didn't have an identical creed in his or her memory. All his lovely oom-pah, bang, tan-tara, and tweetle people would have been casually slaughtered like so many others. So this princeling, who had never in his life wanted anything he couldn't have, decided to move somewhere safe with a few of his closest friends and his band and their families. It took them a thousand years to get there, but they got there."

"How did Lom react to that?"

"The ship got there, the band woke up, got out of the ship, and gave a concert."

"Immediately?"

"As immediately as everyone could be wakened, I guess. The concert was attended by some of the natives. They gleefully accepted the presence of the band, the world accepted its presence, and the band has been marching the roads of Lom ever since, just the way they used to march the roads of the principality. There weren't that many roads when they got there. The roads have become longer and longer. Their march covers them all; that's what they do and it's all that they do.

"According to our accounts, the several races of local people love the band. The Eesties love the band. The shadow people love the band. It is in no small part due to the band that the other humans have been tolerated. If you don't have a helmet, I'll lend you one and you can sense the account. If you do have one, put it on and ask to march with the band on Lom. It's like you're right in the middle of them. It's a good idea to be on a good straight piece of road when you do it." She sighed. "Once I ended up in the middle of a river."

Abasio mused: "When I dream about that world, I'm usually in the tower, the one that was destroyed by natives and restored by humans."

"In the tower?"

"The Daylight Tower. It's a tall, round white tower. There's a huge silver bell hanging in the top of it with a circle of tall, pointy-arched windows all the way around the bell. The bottom of the tower is like the top, only the arches are taller and wider and people or creatures constantly enter and leave. Inside, in the middle, a round pool is set into the stone floor, a pool with a low, carved stone rim around it built a little bit like a seat. It's too low and the rim is too short for human people to lean against, so it was designed with other creatures in mind.

"When humans rebuilt it, they made it identical to the original tower, even using all the unbroken original stones. Almost all of the original bell metal was found and recast. Most of the stones around the pool are the original ones. There's a statue of a reclining woman on the floor, and there are other women sitting around it talking about a journey they are about to take. To come here. To help us. I think one of them is a shapeshifter . . ." His voice faded.

"Then what?" Arakny's mouth gaped breathlessly.

"Nothing except creatures coming in and going out, different ones. The reason I mentioned a Dervish is that one came in, saw me, and spoke to me. She told me her name was Bartelmy and that she was a Dervish. Usually none of them know I'm there. The other ones, that is. But the children see me and the Dervish saw me."

"What do they look like, the other ones?"

"The women? They look like human women. They say they have to go help Earth because a friend has asked them to. As a favor."

"A friend?" Xulai thrust out her hands, palms up in exaggerated wonderment. "It's so nice to know that we have a friend. Now, who might that be?"

Abasio shook his head, his unfocused eyes staring into nothing, unaware of the intensity with which Arakny and Precious Wind were watching him. "The ships went from here to Lom. That left a . . . crease? A wormhole happened, and our world used that wormhole to ask Lom for help."

"Help to do what?" asked Arakny.

"Help to get rid of us," Abasio said. "All of us humans, because we were destroying the planet. Lom didn't have the wherewithal to provide help, so it reached out to another world—a huge ocean planet. You don't know where the water's coming from, Precious Wind. Nobody on Earth does. That's because it's coming through a wormhole that empties into a deep trench at the bottom of our ocean. The planet that's sending the water wanted more dry land for its crop."

"For its crop? Which is what?" Xulai demanded.

"Fligbine. No, I don't know what it is, though I think it's a euphoric drug."

Arakny and Xulai shared a pitying glance.

"You asked!" he said angrily. He turned and glared at Arakny. "Now, don't interrupt me, just listen. I haven't really thought of the dreams as actual happenings, though I feel strongly that the *essence* of the dreams has happened. My dreaming them, experiencing them, is either a random accident or it's purposeful. If it's accidental, we can all forget it. But if I assume it is purposeful, then I am being sent a message! Not to me for any particular reason, except, perhaps, that I'm able to receive it or maybe I was nearest the Listener when the message came through!"

Xulai shivered suddenly. "*We were,* Arakny! He was . . . he had this red glow around him. Really. And we had to get him around the corner from the Listener before it stopped. He started having the dreams long before that, though."

Abasio nodded. "Yes, they started sometime before we came into Gravysuck. I don't know why I should be the only recipient. Other people here may be having the same dreams. Messages can get a bit garbled, and when it happens, it does not necessarily indicate that the receiver is broken—or *insane.*"

Arakny flushed. "Sorry."

He nodded his forgiveness. "So if I take out all the frills and the worst of the oddities and reduce the dreams to their consistent elements, we could say someone or something on Lom wants us to know they're coming. There's a creature called Fixit who's coming, and it's bringing two women from Lom. And a statue, I think. Not just coming to Earth, but coming *here.* And it definitely has something to do with Xulai or me or the babies."

"The babies?" cried Xulai, suddenly alert. "You think it knows about the babies?"

"Oh, it or they know *all* about the babies because I usually have one or both of them with me when I'm there. One of them is usually awake and sees everything that's going on. It's very strange."

"Do the women have names?" Precious Wind asked.

"One of the women is a healer, Silkhands. And the other one, the mother of the two children, is Jinian. The Dervish called Bartelmy is Jinian's mother . . ."

A murmur came from the bed, where the babies were supposedly asleep. "Ninian. Ninian?"

"That's Gailai," he said. "She baby-talks to Jinian when we go there. Bailai doesn't. He's girl-shy."

"Our children are sharing your dream?" demanded Xulai.

"Or dreaming the same dream simultaneously," said Precious Wind thoughtfully. "They're genetically linked, Xulai. If Abasio's right about his being capable of receiving, that capability could be shared with his children." She rose from her place on the grass and stood very straight, head back, forcing herself to set the matter aside and pull herself into the here and now, the current situation.

"People, I'd like nothing better than to spend a day with the helmet seeing if I can find out exactly what has brought us to this place! However! We do have something else to do first. Your dream voyages are probably outside the Oracles' purview, though we can try to open the subject with them. Our immediate problems are with Willum and Sunwings, however. And then we need to figure out the Griffin survival problem . . ."

"Wait!" cried Abasio, his face alive with sudden recognition. "That's why they're coming. Partly. To solve the Griffin problem! *That's why the shapeshifter is coming!*"

Arakny muttered, "Shapeshifter. Yes. Of course. Why didn't I think of that? All we need is a shapeshifter! And we still don't know precisely where the Griffins originated and who might have records of the genetic input . . . *I suppose you're going to tell me we don't need that now, because a shapeshifter is going to come solve it for us?*"

Abasio sighed. "Arakny, I have told you what . . . messages I've received. I do not believe I'm losing my mind. If you want to ignore dreams and visions and whatnot, then do so. We can deal only with known facts. Perhaps we can also speak to the Oracles about the Edgers. They may have some insight into what they're planning."

Arakny grimaced. "Which doesn't mean they'll answer our questions. We very rarely get any useful information from them. So rarely that's it's been suggested they should be called Obstacles rather than Oracles . . ."

And that was the conversation about that, leaving each one of them unsatisfied.

THE MOOD PERSISTED WHEN THEY started out in the morning, Arakny and Precious Wind on matched golden horses alongside Xulai, Abasio, Needly, and the babies in their wagon. The small second wagon carried their supplies and Willum's contorted, stony self, carefully cushioned, as though he could feel. Needly, for one, was not convinced he wouldn't bruise. Or feel cold. Or hurt. A dozen Artemisian men carrying bows and knives rode alongside or out in front, half a dozen of them leading spare horses. They always took spare horses. An assignment from Wide Mountain Mother cannot be allowed to founder because a horse goes lame, and these men had been assigned to take part in the Find, Follow, and Observe network Deer Runner and Mother had set up. The so-called House of the Oracles was at the far western end of the territory, and the first task of these men was to locate any sign of Edger invasion onto the northwestern quadrant of Artemisian territory. A lesser number of mounted women were going also, out of curiosity, to learn the way.

The way was already quite well known, there were no surprises. They would not need to cross the Big River. Some distance north and east of the Devil's Ah, the Big River swung widely to the west into a canyon that had opened when the Stonies had been heaved up a millennium before. South of the Devil's Ah was the last bridge over the Big River, which then made a deep cut to the southwest, a long, shallow C as it curved south and then east to run back out onto the desert, separating the southeastern corner of the Stonies from the rest of the range and carrying the river with it. It was along the southern edge of this separated region that Coyote had tracked the stinkers, and in the northern part of this same area was the cave in which Sun-wings had secreted Willum and Needly.

They met no monsters. It was almost as though the area had been swept and cleared for the two wagons and the people riding alongside. Bear sometimes walked, sometimes lay curled in one of the wagons; Coyote likewise. Coyote had not yet recovered from his journey into the rendering works. He was victim to unpleasant thoughts or memories that woke him from sleep, kicking and biting. For some reason he could not define or explain, he had brought his piece of metal with him, the one he had picked up in the lava tube. He had tucked it into a corner of the wagon, where it wouldn't get lost. He had never mentioned it to Abasio, and he couldn't explain that either, though there was some kind of memory tickling at him, a memory concerning something similar he had seen, somewhere . . .

The babies had spent most of the previous day in a small pool at the bottom of a canyon, quite near Wide Mountain Clan House. Several years previously, a hot spring had been diverted to mix with the cold water in the pool to make a play place for the children who lived in the area, and the babies had enjoyed the warm pool for hours, delightedly receiving various sets of baby minders and thoroughly tiring themselves. Today they were willing to sleep or lie on any convenient lap and watch the desert go by. No one approached the travelers. No dangers presented themselves. It was ordinary. Peaceful. Normal. It made Abasio very nervous.

The tip of a rocky ridge of the Stonies thrust up along their way on the right, growing higher as they went. To the left, ahead of them, a low hummock clad in sand and cactus appeared. When they reached it, it was backed by two taller ones. Others appeared as they drove on, growing higher the farther west they went, so that they trundled along a wide, winding way between two ranges of hills, the low, sandy dunelike ones to the south, the higher, rocky ones at the foot of the mountains to the north. Keeping his eyes on the northern horizon, Coyote told Abasio when he recognized the outline he had seen before, where the stinkers had turned north.

"Up that way," he said. "Right up at the foot of the mountain. That's where they went."

Abasio drew the attention of the troop to the place and the landmarks, but they didn't stop. A team had already been chosen to explore the area on the way back, and Precious Wind was part of it. Half an hour later, Kim and one of the Artemisian outriders came back at a gallop. "Just up ahead," the Artemisian rider cried. "The canyon's just a mile or so ahead."

Wagons were stopped. Faces were washed. Hair was combed and braided on men and women both. Various adornments were donned. The babies were undressed, washed, and reclothed. They went on.

The target canyon looked like any of a thousand others, except that it had an east-facing stone wall on which a large, square surface had been smoothed and polished to receive the carefully graven words *HOUSE OF ORACLES*.

IF YOU HAVE LEGITIMATE BUSINESS HERE, RING THE BELL. IF YOU ARE MERELY CURIOUS, GO ON BY. YOU WILL FIND A RIVER SETTLEMENT HALF A DAY'S TRAVEL WEST.

Under this, in smaller letters, the sign read:

THERE WILL BE SEVERE PENALTIES FOR THOSE RINGING THE BELL WITHOUT LEGITIMATE BUSINESS.

The wall was surmounted by a carved arch with a bell hanging in it. The bell rope hung within easy reach beside the message. Arakny rang the bell, a quick *dong-dong,* only one bell, yet it sent dissonant tones up the canyon, the echoes reinforcing one another. The wagons turned in, went just inside the canyon, and stopped within a grove of very large trees surrounding a well-used campground. Everyone, horses and people, gathered in the shade to wait. Coyote stuck his nose in the corner of the wagon and pulled out the metal bit he had found in the stinker tunnels.

"Coming," whispered Arakny. The word went through the gathering. The horses stood still. Three people were coming down the canyon toward them, gray robes as specified. Gray hair, braided, as specified. Arakny went forward to meet them. In a few moments she returned. "Needly. They'd like to see you." She held out her hand.

Needly said firmly, "I'll go alone, Arakny. I need to ask about Grandma."

Arakny's surprise was plain, but she nodded nonetheless. "Of course, child. As you will."

Needly went up the path to the place where the trio stood. She had gone only half the distance when her voice came back to the waiting group, a high, exultant scream: "Grandma!" The next moment she was in the arms of the middle figure.

"Well," said Arakny to those closest around her. "I guess that answers that question."

"When you come here," Xulai whispered, "do you usually camp out here, or do they invite you in?"

"As I've mentioned, from time to time Mother sends messages or gifts of food, and the men who deliver the items camp out here overnight before making the return trip. There's a spring of good water behind that stone pillar to your left, and the trees make a pleasant shade. When I came, they invited me in. The place is inside the mountain, built into a series of caves. It's very comfortable, but one really never knows what they'll do until they do it."

Needly came running back. "Abasio, Xulai, Arakny, and Precious Wind are invited in, and the others are invited to camp here. Oh, and Willum. Will one of the men help Abasio carry Willum?"

One of the bowmen stepped forward to carry the back end of the stretcher they had constructed for the occasion. Willum was not heavy, but his sprawled position made it difficult for any one person to carry him. The others followed them. The path was sandy. Abasio and Xulai, each carrying one of the babies, were last in line behind Arakny. Xulai happened to glance behind her at the Artemisians, who were busy setting up camp. The path behind her had no footprints on it whatsoever. She looked down at Arakny's feet. As Arakny raised her left foot, the sand filled in below it, settling itself into utter smoothness before Xulai's foot stepped down. She gulped and looked resolutely forward.

The two who had accompanied Grandma stood to one side, watching them pass. Their faces wore identical small, pleasant smiles, welcoming to precisely the same degree. One name on the shoulder was LUSS FAR-LIGHT. The other was DRON WINDLEAS. Xulai, with Gailai held against her shoulder, nodded to each, memorizing "Dron" and "Luss," receiving duplicate nods in return. She caught Needly's eye, seeing there a reflection of her own confusion. Needly kept to herself the words that had leapt to her tongue when she had turned from Grandma's arms to meet the two remaining Oracles. She had thought in that moment that they were not separate people but identical parts of one thing. One big thing. No. One larger thing, but without any . . . bigness to it. The idea was confusing and unpleasant. She squashed it, folded it, put it away until another time.

Grandma reached out a hand to Xulai, drew her close to say, "Thank you for taking care of my child."

"I'm afraid we didn't do a very good job," Xulai said, pleased that the woman before her looked precisely as Needly had described her. "We almost lost her."

"But you didn't. That's the important thing. May I carry the baby?" She reached out for Gailai, who stared into her face for a moment, then reached out and grabbed her nose. There was a sudden scurry by their feet. Coyote. He was holding something in his mouth, offering it.

Grandma stepped back, leaned over: "You want to give me this?"

He nodded. She put her hand down and he dropped the metal piece into it, a little wet. She wiped it on her skirt and then looked at it closely. Her mouth opened, made a pursed, almost whistle shape. "Where?" she asked.

"Long story," he said.

"Will you be here, with them?" She gestured at the Artemisians, busy making camp.

"Yes. With Bear."

"I'll come find you and Bear later tonight," Grandma said, pocketing Coyote's gift. "Stay close where I can find you." This time she was successful in taking Gailai in one arm and Abasio's arm with her other.

The opening was an arch, rough stone, without a door. As they came into the shade of it, Xulai saw that it was only a kind of portal. The actual door stood ajar ahead of them, three man heights tall, two man heights wide, one man height thick, one solid piece of stone, sharp-cornered, smooth as planed wood. It bore nothing resembling hinges or a knob or a knocker. When Xulai went past it, the last in line, she felt it pivot on some unseen bearing and close soundlessly behind them. When she looked back, it was invisible. Not even a hairline showed its outline.

COYOTE AND BEAR STAYED TOGETHER, near but not too near the men setting up camp and preparing their food. One corner of the wagon had been occupied by a very large stew kettle containing corn, onions, meat, Tom's toes, and a plethora of herbs. These things had been soaking all day and the kettle had been placed on a stout grid over the fire as soon as it was well alight. Someone among the Artemisian men spoke to the cook, and she ladled two large bowls full of the stew they had prepared and broke a large hunk of bread into each of them. The man set the bowls near the place where Coyote and Bear had established their own territory, at the edge of an almost impenetrable tangle. They waited for the stew to cool, then ate it with a good deal of pleasure. It wasn't fresh rabbit, but it was very good. Bear often ate vegetables, Coyote but rarely, as part of the stomach contents of something just killed or as a way to clear his own stomach if something had not agreed with him. Both found the dish filling to the stomach and pleasant to the nose, however, and when they had eaten and licked the bowls clean, they retreated into the tangle.

Some hours later, a woman came down the path from the Oracles' place. She said softly, "Coyote?"

"Over here," he yodeled, as softly. He and Bear pushed themselves to the edge of the tangle, sticking their heads out. The woman came close, looked around her, found a place to sit, a convenient log next to a tree. She said, "The log is new. You put that there?"

"I did," said Bear. Human people are so . . . what's the word, up n' down?"

"Vertical?"

"Yah. So vertical. It's hard for you to get down on our level to talk."

"Only the old ones." She laughed. "I guess that includes grandmas. Tell me about the metal piece, Coyote. Did you know what it was?"

"No. I only knew it itched me. In a bad way. I've seen something like it somewhere, but I can't remember."

"Could it be with traders? At the pass?"

It came back to him in a flash. "That's where!"

"Indeed. Well, tell me the story."

Which he did, well rehearsed, having told it several times to others. He included all the details and what various people had thought about it subsequently. "I found the little metal piece on my way in, it stuck in my foot. I picked it up on my way out. I knew Abasio wouldn't know anything about it. I didn't think the people we're staying with would know. I thought you might."

"I've seen them on things old Digger traded. I think it's a manufacturer's tag, identifying a product, Coyote. Something that was no doubt dug out of a buried city. Maybe the one under Hench Valley. It was originally probably on its way to a place near Fantis. People have told me there was a huge manufacturing plant down on the plain near Fantis. I've heard that place was and still is owned by the Edgers, and they may have made or used the stuff that had that tag on it." She turned it in her hands. "You said a man couldn't get through the tunnel you were in when you found this?"

"I said he couldn't get *in or out* the way I got in and out. It was only the entrance that was tight. But if he'd come in some other way, he could have dropped it in the tunnel I was in. Or something else could have. It's a whatsit in there, a tangle . . ."

"A maze."

"That's it. There were tunnels leading off all directions from the one where I found it."

"I'm surprised you didn't get lost."

"I was following the air. It was moving that way, up and out."

"And the men you saw were Edgers?"

"That's what everyone thinks. The Artemisians think so. Arakny thinks so. Abasio and Xulai think so. Who else could they be but Edgers?"

"You have an opinion, Bear?"

"Nope. Know nothin' about this thing. What I do know is Old Digger, up in Tuckwhip, he had miles of tunnel dug into that city. I know because lotsa us critters make themselves winter places in Digger's holes. If this came from there, chances are he dug it and sold it to a wagoner. Prob'ly the wagoner was the one they call the Gold King. He's the one buys the strange stuff, mostly. Maybe the wagoner sold it to an Edger, maybe one a' those washin' stuff off a stinker."

"I know Digger." Grandma made a face. "I'd like to ask him a few questions . . ."

"Sun-wings killed him," said Coyote. "Rotten old man."

"Sun-wings?"

"The big mare Griffin that's got people all in a . . . maze. The one that told'm to fix their little ones like they did humans so they could live when everything's water."

"Xulai told me one of the men was killed, but not who. Sun-wings killed Digger?"

"Took his head off, like a chicken. Didn't bite him. Doesn't like the taste."

"Too merciful, but appropriate. I knew his death was coming, just not how soon. Now, how do I find out what this stuff was, that had the metal tag on it?"

"It was there where the Edgers washed their stinkers. So I figure it has something to do with that. Something they use, maybe? Edgers got to go back and forth from there, you need somebody to follow them home, ask them."

"How long ago were you there?"

Coyote tried to remember: A night's sleep? A day's travel? More sleep, then Precious Wind had arrived. Maybe it was a day or two or three since? He said, "Three, four days."

"And they're not far from here."

"The place isn't. Don't know if they're still there."

"I understand that. How near here, do you think?"

"Might take us an hour, maybe."

"Well, in the morning, we may give it a try," said Grandma. "Meantime, we'll work with what we know. Precious Wind brought us a sample of the stuff that accumulates on the stinker bodies. Put that together with this tag, which we're fairly sure is a biological product, a catalyst. Well, it's simply very useful, Coyote. I'm glad it itched you. How can I repay you?"

"Chicken," said Coyote. "I'd say that's top of my preferences."

"Where'd you get that word, 'preference'? Don't remember your having that one."

"Listenin' to that Precious Wind. She has preferences, lots and lots of 'em. Mostly different from what other folks prefers."

Grandma laughed. "Indeed."

"You gonna help Willum?" Bear inquired. "That little girl of yours, she's brave as a . . . bear, but she's really grieved over that boy."

"If it weren't for the arrow through him, it'd be easy. There are medical machines in the Oracles' place. I've used them from time to time. They're very good, good diagnosticians, good providers of treatment. Problem is, the machine reports that the arrow's made out of yew. There isn't any yew anywhere around here. Where did that hunter get it, that stinker hunter?" She shook her head angrily. "Yew's poison. It's as if someone made arrows that would eventually kill anything they hit. That's wicked, pure wicked. So we're figuring out what we're going to try . . . We can't just take the rock away or he'll bleed to death."

"Thought he was like rock. Thought he couldn't bleed."

"He'd bleed if we neutralized the rock medicine all at once. We have to neutralize it as we go. Tiny, tiny bit at a time so he loses only a tiny bit of blood. He can't heal if he's stone except as slow as stone, which means he might be healed by the time the rest of us are all dead and gone. And if he isn't stone he bleeds. They have a medical machine in there. I've fed all the information into the machines, and I'm waiting for them to come up with an answer. Then we'll wake him up."

"Needly says you were stone, like him."

"I was. But I just had a place on my head where a rock hit. I wasn't bleeding. It was easy to get at and heal, didn't even break the skin very much. Even though it was lots easier than with Willum, it still took quite a while."

"You were buried there in that village. Who got you out?"

"Well, at first I thought the Oracles had. Then I thought not, but near here is where I woke up."

"Didn't they say?"

"They don't say much, ever. Especially if it's something you really want to know."

"She tell you all about the Griffin mare?"

"Yes, and her cub, Dawn-song. Now, that's a much easier thing. We can heal her very quickly. I made up a batch of the antidote after I got here. There's a little patch of that stone plant just up the hill from here, near my old home; I've kept my eyes on it for a long time. I'll take or send some of the antidote back to Wide Mountain Mother, and the Griffin's leg should be healed before her wing is. The real problem is what the Griffin said about her children surviving. Now, that's a very different matter, very difficult. Very, very difficult. Nobody's sure there's enough time left. However, there's ways and there's ways, and I'm sure there are capable people working on the problem."

"Ma'am, are you one of those . . . those Oracles?"

"No, Bear. I'm certainly not. I'm just a human who amused herself for much of her young life by making use of all that equipment and machinery they have here. I suppose that gave me a few enhancements, ah . . . improvements?"

"That'd be betterments, I guess. Blue says 'betterments.' "

"Betterments, then. I'm not quite sure what the Oracles think I am or what they regard me as being in connection to themselves. I've learned a lot of things from them—well, that is, I've learned it from the machines and devices they brought here. You know, it's very strange. They acquire these things, all kinds of things, but once they have them, they just sort of . . . let them be. They have pictures they never look at, equipment they never use. I seem to be the only one who is using the equipment, so I have no idea why they brought it."

Bear nodded wisely, looked at Coyote. "Sounds like pack rats t'me."

"Pack rats," agreed Coyote. "Can you tell us anything about them, even just a little bit?"

"Only a little bit. They're not from here. They're from another world. I know the Oracles look like humans, more or less, but I don't think they are. I think maybe they can take pretty much any shape they like. Which is another way of saying they don't have any shape. They say they're on some kind of mission. They don't say who gave them the mission. They say they have their orders. I don't know why, but I've come to doubt that." She stared into the distance; Bear and Coyote stared with her. "They've been here a very long time for us to know so little about them. I've given them credit for a lot of things . . . things they maybe had nothing to do with. Until I brought Willum . . . there's never been anything immediate that I've put to them, something that needs doing right now, and I'm a little confused by the way they act."

"Like how?"

"Well, if they were human I'd say they were embarrassed. Kind of . . . shifty. It has nothing to do with you two good creatures. Now, I promised Needly I'd be back to tell her a bedtime story. She's too big for bedtime stories, and it's way too early for bed, but she remembers how they made her feel when she was little and she wants to feel cozy. She needs a little cozy because she's had a lot of horrible lately. You two look like you could do with a bedtime story."

"We're awright," said Bear, nudging Coyote, who grumphed an assent. "Wish you good night."

"Wish you good night, good creatures, and I did bring you a bedtime something," she said, taking two sizable packets from a deep pocket and putting them before two noses. When she was a quarter of the way up the path to the portal, she heard two voices behind.

"Chicken! It's a whole roasted chicken. How'd she know I like it roasted? Whadju get?"

"Honey," said Bear, with enormous satisfaction. "Two big pieces of comb. She's a very nice old lady."

Grandma smiled ruefully. Of course she was very nice, but she didn't feel anywhere near that old.

NEEDLY HAD NOT VISITED BEAR and Coyote, for the Oracles had invited her to have supper with them. Supper had consisted of an endless series of tiny bowls, plates, vessels, kettles, each with something different in it. The food items (liquids, pastes, solids; crunchy, slimy) were a very strange assortment, by no means all delicious, though a few were. The Oracles, however, seemed to get quite as much pleasure (if, indeed, that was what they were having) out of analyzing the ingredients, the tastes, the intermixing of the tastes, the fading away of the tastes, the texture, the changing of the texture when chewed (whether unyielding or compliant), and all the other ways in which food could possibly be appreciated as they did the eating of it. Their vocabulary was limited and their comments repeated several times. The entire event took about half an hour.

Somehow it all had been very . . . like playacting? Needly had not been sure until this event, but now she was. They were not what Grandma thought they were! She wasn't afraid of them, but she didn't like them or admire them or consider them wise. They were merely . . . acting. As though they had seen . . . seen a pictured dinner party. Needly had been told of such things: Grandma's bedtime stories had been full of wonderful events and wonderful people doing wonderful things. The machines were full of such things. The Oracles had many sources they could copy. And they were simply copying, she was sure of it!

Had it not been for Grandma's having remarked that she sometimes felt the Oracles were "tasting" the Earthian environment, Needly would have been dismayed by the "dinner party." As it was, she nodded agreement when she agreed, kept silent when she disagreed, refused to eat anything her nose told her would promptly come up again, and showed proper reverence for the hosts (or hostesses) when it was over. By the time she returned to the room where Grandma lived, Grandma herself had returned.

"What did you think?" Grandma asked.

"I thought it was a lot of fuss about nothing."

"When they do things like that, it's like a game to them. I believe they don't ordinarily have bodies that need to eat. They have several of those really advanced food machines in the big reception area, did you see them?" Needly had not. "Just tell the machine what you want, and it produces it. Sometimes it asks for a recipe. I use them regularly when I'm here, but the Oracles never use them at all. Maybe their bodies soak up sunlight, though I wouldn't swear to it. The best I've been able to get them to say is first: they have to be here. Second: they have a job, a mission, a task. Third: they chose to appear as the leading life-form—that's us—and fourth: they wish to experience things the leading life-form experiences."

"Do they also pee and poop?"

Grandma looked puzzled. "How clever of you, Needly. You know, I have no idea! There's a water toilet in my quarters here, but that's meaningless. It could be for guests only. So I can only say I shouldn't be surprised either way.

"This, by the way, is probably my last visit. They were talking about something coming or their going? It's confusing, and they weren't talking to me. More like someone mumbling to themselves, really. If they go, I'm afraid they'll take all this lovely machinery with them. I'll regret that." She sat back, ready to hear about Needly's trip through the woods and whatever else the child wanted to tell her, then, startlingly, she sat up again, looking very alert.

Needly heard a humming sound. Grandma looked as though she wanted to spit. "Excuse me, my darling, but I'm wanted. I shouldn't be long."

The door thing, which faded into the wall when not needed, opened as she approached it and closed behind her. Needly decided to inspect the bookshelf along one wall, nicely filled with books, some of which she recognized. In Tuckwhip, books had been hidden except when she and Grandma were sure they were alone. Most of the people there used them to start fires. She was quite hungry, but couldn't do anything about it until Grandma came back, and a book would pass the time. She found a book of animal stories and was deeply involved in it when Grandma returned, a Grandma pale-faced and obviously unhappy.

"They can't do it," she said. "What we planned to do for Willum. It won't work. The medical machine had a report for me. It's that blasted yew wood. Who in heaven's name put that weapon into the hands of those . . . creatures?"

Needly wanted to scream or cry or both. Instead she knotted her hands together and concentrated on making them as tight as she could. And tighter. "What won't work. Grandma?"

"I told you how we planned to do it. We have the antidote that nullifies the stone, we have an excellent medicine that aids healing. The minute we nullify the stone, the yew shaft starts poisoning Willum's living tissue, and the healing aid can't fight it. The machine is running on low, I guess researching everything that's ever been recorded about yew wood or the rock medicine . . ."

"Couldn't you start working in the middle of him. Then do a tiny bit at a time, but from both sides." She turned away, visualizing what she meant. "Tell me about the healing agent. How does it work?"

"It's a liquid. You warm it to liquefy it, then pour it into a wound and it sets into quite a solid gel at body temperature—ours, that is. It has chemicals and organics in it that encourage the tissue on all sides to invade the gel and build new tissue. The growing cells actually eat it. Of course, to get the tissue to do that, you have to stop its being rock first."

"So it turns into a gel at our body temperature?"

"Oh, yes. We get it much warmer than that to melt it."

"Does the liquid set into gel immediately, or does it take a little time? I mean, does it flow at first? If there's a little opening like into a blood vessel, will it flow in before it sets?"

"Yes, if it's warm when you pour it, it stays liquid for as long as it takes to cool, longer if someone has a fever, but not terribly long."

"Oh, what would happen if we tried . . ." Needly murmured. "Suppose the shaft could be pulled out completely while he's rock, then rinse out the hole to get every splinter of yew out of him. Then maybe you could warm him while he's rock, warm enough to keep the healing stuff liquid. Plug the hole in his back, and from the front fill the hole completely with the heal-all, turn him so it will flow into any little hole, any open capillary, any gap in cells. Wait until it sets into gel. Then turn him over and be sure the heal-all is gelled even with his skin in back. When that is set, then you could try to de-rock all of him. By that time, maybe the stuff will be plugging every capillary. There will be no place for him to bleed from. That is, if the shaft isn't through his heart or something. If it isn't, he won't bleed."

Grandma sat staring at the child. "I'll go see what the medical machines advise," she said, leaving with some haste.

There were two beds in the room, one that Grandma had obviously used. Her slippers were beside it, her night water bottle was on the table. Grandma always had a night water bottle. She rarely if ever drank from it. Needly used to ask her why she had it. Grandma always said she might need it if the house caught on fire. The other bed was for Needly. Her pack was there. She undressed and put on the light sleep trousers and shirt Xulai had made for her, like Willum's. She had admired Willum's. They looked so comfortable and had turned out to be so, even though they were made from old shirts. Xulai didn't have any more old shirts. She had made the bottoms from old bed sheets. Needly lay down on her bed with the book.

She realized she hadn't told Grandma she was hungry. Of all those little dishes and kettles and vials of stuff, only half a dozen of them had been tasty. Six tiny spoonfuls. And she was thirsty. She'd have a drink out of Grandma's water bottle. She sipped . . . and stopped. That explained why Grandma had a water bottle. It wasn't water.

Grandma's room was near the reception area. She went out to find the food machine Grandma had talked about. It had a start button and a keyboard. She pushed the one and found the letters to spell "fried chicken." The machine whirred and went *thunk*. A silvery sack dropped into a bin. She took it back to their room. The chicken was hot and tasty, and she ate it with some of the trail stuff she had in her pack. Corn—some parched, some popped—and dried, fried pieces of corn flats, and piñon nuts and dried pieces of apples, apricots, cherries, and plums. Needly munched some, sipping not-water between munches. The not-water must be liquor. The stuff that was stronger than beer, which she had tasted before, in Tuckwhip. It gave one a very funny sort of floating feeling.

She dozed off for a while. The room sensed she was asleep and put a blanket over her. Only a little later, she half woke, thinking she had heard something.

The door opened and Grandma came in. She was trying to smile. "The Oracles were annoyed," she said, almost in a whisper.

"People—that is, human people—are not expected to come up with answers that the Oracles haven't thought of first. It took them some time to decide on the correct reaction. They wished to ignore your suggestion, but they decided that would be undignified. They wished to ignore the fact that your suggestion might work, but they decided it would be equally undignified not to recognize it. Therefore, they wish to congratulate you on having had a good idea. All that before I had a chance to ask the machine."

"And?" Needly cried.

"Needly, much of what I just said is . . . interpolation. Nothing was as clear or definite as I said it. When I quoted the Oracles as saying people aren't expected to come up with answers, what they actually said was 'machine job, not for person.' However, the machine didn't help much. It gave us an equivocal reading. A maybe. So we tried what you suggested. The machine is much stronger than a person, and much more delicate at the same time. It pulled the shaft out and washed out the hole to get all the bits out, if any. It warmed him until he was a tiny bit warmer than usual body temp. Not too high, it said, because there was a danger of cracking him. It blocked the hole in his back. It warmed the gel and poured it into him. When it set, it turned him over and put a little more gel in the back and evened up the gel on both sides of him and de-rocked him."

"Did he wake up? Is he moving?"

"He opened his eyes. That's all the movement he could make because he was in terrible pain. Terrible screaming pain. The machine reacted immediately. It had analyzed the rock medicine and had created some; it used the rock medicine on him again and put the arrow shaft back where it was. It's now humming furiously again, rethinking the whole thing. It doesn't want him to move, eat, do anything until everything has grown. Why are you crying? It's too early to cry. We've just started."

Needly, her eyes awash in tears, could not stop. "Grandma, he was so brave. He didn't even think, he just jumped in front of that arrow, protecting the little Griffin." She wiped her face, got out of bed, and pulled on her jacket. "I can't just lie here. Do you have the stuff to de-rock Sun-wings' leg? Where's Abasio and Xulai? I need to go tell them about Willum. They were really upset. We need to go tell them. And Coyote and

Bear; somebody needs to tell them, too." She took a deep breath, trying to remember other . . . concrete things. Definite things. "And we need to give some of the antidote to someone to take back to Sun-wings. Can I ask Precious Wind to do it? She's feeling annoyed at herself."

"I gave the antidote to Precious Wind hours ago, child."

Needly, who felt that if she had to lie still right now and not think about Willum, she would simply die, said so. Worriedly, Grandma told her in that case they would join the singsong that the Artemisians were having on the campground.

IN THE BUILDING WHERE THE Griffins were lodged, near the Wide Mountain Clan House, a clan member who had just arrived on watch looked up suddenly to see a woman walk in through the door and approach the large Griffin, who appeared to be asleep, though it was still early in the evening.

"Hey," he said. "What you doing here?"

"Is Wide Mountain Mother available? I suppose she's asleep."

"I'm not gonna wake her up, 'f that's what y're after."

"Don't need to. Can you get me a bucket of water?" She smiled.

He enjoyed her smile. "I 'spose."

"I'd really appreciate that."

He brought water. The woman spoke into the Griffin's ear, which twitched upward. A very large eye opened. The Griffin said, "I do not like hearing that about Willum!"

"I do not like telling it to you. Oh, here's the water. Whoops. Cold! Can you stand it cold, Sun-wings?"

"I'm eight or nine hundred years old. Winter on top of those mountains is not a tropical holiday."

"We're only going to do the leg so the rest of you won't get chilled. Right! Instructions are, do it once. Wait to see how much sensation comes back. If it's still dead-ish, do it again. Okay?"

The woman and the water carrier bathed the Griffin's rear right leg, every crease and dimple, then, at the water carrier's suggestion, while awaiting results, they retired to the adjacent room.

When they returned after a rather lengthy interval, they asked Sun-wings to move the leg, which she was almost able to do. It quivered, but almost was not good enough. The woman and the water carrier bathed the leg again. This time the results were satisfactory. Within moments, the leg moved freely. The Griffin stood, shakily at first, then with increasing strength. Dawn-song—wakened by the movement and the loud rejoicing—came from her bed in the corner and began chirruping in celebration.

The woman urged caution. "Sun-wings, your wing still isn't quite well enough healed for you to try flying. It doesn't need much time, maybe another day or two. Don't try it before it's fully healed or you'll rip it and we'll have to start over. As far as the leg goes, by morning you should be able to move around comfortably. Since we don't know where Despos is, you and the little one will stay undercover, yes? When Needly gets back, she's bringing some stuff that will heal the wing even more quickly and prevent scarring. Be patient."

The Griffin hummed. The woman took this for assent. "Thank you for your help," she said to the water carrier.

"Thank you, Precious Wind," he said. "That was most enjoyable. It's strange how we keep encountering each other."

"Not at all. I asked Wide Mountain Mother to put you on night guard before I left." She smiled at him again and disappeared. It would take about ten jumps to get her back to the Oracles. Such a pleasant night for traveling.

"Ouishuc," said Deer Runner fondly.

THE NEWS ABOUT WILLUM WAS circulated in the outdoor camp among the Artemisians. Most of the Artemisians had not known the boy except as a sprawled statue, but they knew the circumstances of his injury and considered him one of themselves. They built up the fire and passed around a beverage with instructions that Willum was to be the subject of concern, that all present were to send caring and concerned thoughts to him. Needly had been asked about the "naming" meeting she and Willum had had with the Griffins, and she had acted it out for them at length. They then had many questions about the big male. Everyone was conscious of their surroundings, their proximity to the Oracles, however much they were separated by thick walls of stone, and they kept it reasonably quiet. Needly and Grandma had been honored guests, given a special pillowed log to sit on and provided with full cups of whatever was being drunk. Grandma had told them honestly about the situation with Willum. If they wished to have a liquid-fueled song and prayer meeting, it was all right with her. Doubtless the religiosity part of it would dwindle as the imbibing part increased.

Needly asked, "Did you know the Artemisian people before, Grandma?"

"I knew them when I was much younger, before I was sent to Hench Valley. I grew up in a house just up the hill over there, not far. It's a very comfortable, well-equipped house, and why it's out here, all by itself, I have no idea. I suppose I'm probably part Artemisian, genetically. Maybe part Tingawan, too."

"Did the Oracles adopt you or something?"

"No. One day they were just here. The empty caves were full of equipment and stuff, all kinds of stuff. I was very young and curious—I couldn't have been more than six, Needly. Remember you at six and you'll come close to what I was like. Curious. Probably impertinent. So I hung around the place and asked questions. Sometimes the Oracles would say things for no reason, sometimes they would answer a question I had asked, sometimes they would say something that seemed to be the answer to a question I had asked the day before, or many days before. This was not as surprising to me as it might have been for other children because I lived among humans who were often dreamy and unworldly, to whom time meant little or nothing, so I already had acquired a tendency to 'fill in the blanks.' The people I lived with never corrected me, so I presumed that was the way some creatures communicated, with a lot of silences and vacancies scattered among the answers and informations. I thought I was filling in the blanks pretty well. I did it with the Oracles sometimes when they had said things or indicated things or hinted at things that I cared about a lot. As soon as I learned how to use the machines, I became quite certain that they hadn't answered because they knew the machines could answer me, and they expected me to find out by myself.

"Needly, all the grown people I had associated with were wise about something. None of them were simply stupid or ignorant. I did not realize a simple fact: *Though silence and vagueness can be a mask for profound knowledge, they can also mask total ignorance!* Sometimes silence and vagueness are *the reality.* The Oracles simply knew nothing about the things I had asked them about.

"But they had all these great machines, edubots that were . . . well, the most advanced ones that had ever been made. They were just there, up in the front of the cave, and the Oracles, they didn't seem to pay any attention to them at all. I put two and two together to get what I considered reasonable. They didn't need the machines because they had put the information into the machines to start with. So there I was, young and curious and with all kinds of time on my hands, and with machines that would answer any question I asked. That was enough. I never went farther back into their . . . territory than that. And they never invited me into those areas.

"I asked the edubots and the other equipment they have in there what I should do with my life. One of the machines I asked set off a whole series of bells and whistles and red lights and urgent messages to say that they, or someone, was looking for a particular genotype that fit me. Oh, I was smart enough to ask how they got my genotype, and the machine replied that it was well equipped to analyze spit and sweat and skin cells and . . . and . . . and. Quite honestly, I crowed over that a little. It's nice to feel special, which I did not feel at home. Every person in that house, to hear them tell it, was unique and more special than anyone else in the world, and I was merely the girl child."

"They should have thought more of you than that, Grandma!"

"Maybe they did and just didn't show it. Too late now to ask them. At that time I felt some of those machines were more . . . human than some of the humans I knew. The humans, often as not, said, 'Go away and don't bother me,' but the machines actually welcomed me. I asked if I was the one they were looking for . . . one of the ones, I should say. As I remember, their answer to that question was that I was 'the type that had been selected.' They never actually told me who did the selecting. I foolishly assumed the Oracles had.

"As for the inducements I was offered . . . when I asked what was to be my payment for being 'the type that had been selected,' I got a document printed out on one of the machines. I have no idea who actually wrote the thing. At the time I just assumed the Oracles were responsible for it all. The inducement talked about the history of Earth and the problems of people, and it offered me the opportunity to have 'children who would contribute positively to the future of the earth; the opportunity to meet men of very high attainments.' Things like that. At the bottom it said: 'If you agree, sign at the bottom and insert into slot A.' Which I did."

"Are you glad you . . . like you said, worked for them or whoever it actually was?"

"On balance, I'd say so, though I'd have preferred more disclosure and less mystery. Joshua, my first partner, didn't arrive until years later, of course, but the machines were there all the time. And when I saw the house being built near ours, of course I went over to meet the person who was building it. I was sixteen by then, and Joshua and I became very, very close, and no one at my house said 'don't' or 'no' or 'What do you think you're doing?' I didn't really think about it at all. And when we became partners, he took me to Hench Valley. No one ever explained why Hench Valley either. He built a house for me there. He left me, but he told me someone else would be coming along. The partners that arrived from time to time were really wonderful men, joyful, joyous men, capable of delight, the kind of men that . . . when you meet them, you think they have known you forever and you have known them, just that long. Our children were delightful. Though giving them up was neither delightful nor even bearable. But if I hadn't agreed to it, you probably wouldn't be here at all. You were certainly an inducement when you came along."

"So, really, you probably were working for someone else all along, not the Oracles at all." Needly gave Grandma a long, long hug. "I'm glad it was someone else, Grandma. I don't like the Oracles very much, but I still hope they can help Willum."

"You're very fond of that boy. Be very careful, child. Don't get yourself carried away if you two get older together."

"If I did, wouldn't you suppose that it was fated, just the way you were, and my real father, and Xulai, and all the rest of us?"

"Ah, doesn't it sound wonderful? Living in an age where all may be left to beneficent fate?"

"Doesn't it?"

"Sweetheart, fate isn't beneficent. Given the size and complexity of the universe, I'd guess it's pretty much random. Humans have a long history of trusting in good fortune, and it hasn't worked out very well. Every human person, tribe, community, nation, has spent millennia trusting in beneficent fortune, burning fossil fuel, sucking aquifers dry, having babies like rabbits, sucking Earth's lifeblood and raising her temperature while denying we were doing it, the whole time trusting in Luck! Good Fortune! God with a small *g*! God with a BIG *G*! Science with a BIG BIG *S*. Science with a sneer. None of which helped solve the problem because we *WERE* the problem."

"Weren't there any followers of the Great Litany then, when we were despoiling?"

"The litany hadn't been given to us then, and most of the religions were of the 'God Sits on My Shoulder' variety . . . You don't know of those? Each one of them declares he or she has a personal relationship with God. They are not thinking of the Creator of the universe when they say this. They are not thinking of innumerable galaxies, planets, and stars beyond counting. They are not thinking of an immensity, a miraculous machinery out of which life springs in a trillion forms. No. The picture they have in their minds is of a nice grandfatherly God shaped just like them who made a nice little flat garden world with a sun going around it, into which HE, always HE, inserted our first parents, whom HE challenged to be naughty, already knowing they would be because HE is omniscient. Nice and grandfatherly but tricky and sadistic, setting us up for sin so he can punish us, because, really, he likes punishing things."

"I do not understand that!"

"I'll tell you a truth, Needly. Men almost always make gods in their own image. If men make a god who likes to punish people, it's because the men like to punish people. Many men do. They beat their wives, their children. They get in fights. They like punishing things. In one country, the one that used to be here where we are . . . if they had a choice between preventing a misdeed or punishing a misdeed, their usual solution was to build more and bigger prisons."

"Preventing . . . ?"

"Oh, child. If people like to eat corn and you make eating corn illegal, what happens?"

"People eat it anyhow."

"And if people like to dance or drink liquor, or take some drug to make them feel better, and you make it a prison offense to drink, dance, or drug, what must you do?"

"Oh, I see! You'll have to build more and bigger prisons. Much bigger, I 'magine."

"It seems ridiculous, but when people are self-righteous, they really tend to prefer punishment to prevention. We talked about Mobwows a long time ago, remember?"

"*Monkey-brain* willy-waggers."

"The Mobwows have brought us to this, Needly. They're why Earth got into such terrible shape, and they're why it is being drowned. Somewhere, someone, something has finally taken notice. Maybe the REAL ONE who's REALLY in charge. A Living Planet is too important for fools go on trifling with it. The Oracles have a prediction machine in there. I've asked it. You feed in all the facts you know about a given situation, it asks questions back, you answer them to the best of your ability, and it makes a prediction. That machine is ninety percent certain that someone or something with the power to enforce it has decided to control the number of human babies born on Earth. Even when we are completely aquatic, there will never again be more than two billion of us on this planet. That's less than one-quarter of the number before the Big Kill. And no person who is not healthy and healthful will cause or have any pregnancies at all. And to keep any *willy-wagging* revolutionaries from rising up, any man or woman who tries to circumvent those prohibitions will be fixed so he can do no damage."

"If . . . if the number's set, how could anybody circumvent . . ."

"I didn't say if they *succeed,* I said if *they try.* The Oracles say . . . *And look at what I just said. I'm telling it wrong again.* The *machines,* not the Oracles, gave me the information about the number of humans that will be allowed."

"Grandma, you are not the kind of person to get confused about things. Why are you so upset about this machines-or-Oracles riddle?"

Grandma frowned, shook her head, rubbing at the two deep wrinkles between her eyes. "Oh, Needly, it's part of that filling-in-the-blanks business. I never got answers from the Oracles, and *I assumed* they didn't answer because they knew I could get the answers from the machines. And *I assumed* the answers were IN the machines because the Oracles PUT them there. I was a *child;* it seemed *logical.* In time, I learned I was wrong. I've met some people recently who have what they call 'library helmets.' Do you know about them? You do!"

"Abasio has one. And Arakny."

Grandma sighed. "The machines get their information the way the library helmets do. They don't let false information in!"

Needly put her hands to Grandma's cheeks, petting her. "So you're trying to separate the Oracles from the machines, in your mind."

"Exactly. And it's a hard habit to break." *Especially since her children, HER children, were supposedly in the custody of the Oracles. Don't think of that. Not now. Not now!* "Now, the machines—which were not made by or given information by the Oracles—the *machines* say there will be a limit on humans. Some people, those with genetic problems, won't have any children. Some will have one. Most will have two, one for the mother, one for the father. Exceptional people may have more and inadequate people maybe none, but the total number, worldwide, will never exceed two billion. Once that limit is reached, if any person or laboratory or scientist tries to exceed that limit, that person or laboratory or scientist will cease to exist."

"What about if a child dies?"

"I gathered the death rate is already built in. That third child some people will have makes up for those who die young. I doubt that a death would allow the parent to try again. Too much room for shiftiness there. Too many historic incidents of daughters being killed to make room for a possible son. The quota is per person, not per couple. No *willy-wagging* allowed! Once one's own quota is born, no more." She gazed into the fire. "How they hope to keep track of it is more than I can imagine. The only thing I can come up with is an automatic genetic response to pregnancies. After so many, a woman would simply become infertile."

Needly considered this, swinging her legs in time to the music the Artemisians were making. "Is the number they allow larger than the population of mankind now? There aren't many of us."

"I think it's a little larger, yes. The figure has to be based on balance. Not just how many humans, but also how many elephants, and how many antelope, horses, cows, sheep, goats, field mice, oak trees, coconut trees, miles of grassland. Of course, now all those things will have to be translated into their comparable aquatic equivalent: giant kelp instead of pine forests; scurrying crabs instead of mice; whales instead of elephants; dolphins instead of horses—unless they come up with an aquatic version of horses. How many of each and every single thing—all of them in balance.

"It's ironic, but when the world is covered in water, there will actually be more space than there was before, vertical space as well as horizontal space. That disturbed me a little, but the machines said that humans won't be able to live very deep down. There have always been various biomes at various depths. I suppose it'll be pretty much the same, except the bottom ones will be a lot farther down."

There was a burst of laughter from around the fire. Grandma raised her head, listening, smiled a wry smile, and pointed to the Artemisians who were singing a bawdy song, a very funny one that she had learned from the father of her fourth child. He had been a lovely man. Very . . . skilled. She repeated the words and tune so Needly could learn it. "There, you have some new naughty words to teach Willum."

Needly smiled a very small smile, then concentrated on making it feel larger. For a little while she would pretend. Willum would be all right, somehow. She would teach Willum the song. She would civilize Willum. She would grow up and love Willum! He would love her. They would each get a sea-egg and become a couple, like Abasio and Xulai. She sat singing softly in the dark, the dream wrapped around her like a blanket, holding fast to the happiness inside it.

Grandma, seeing the child's expression, did not draw her out of her joy. Let her dream while she could. At present, neither Grandma nor the Oracles nor the omniscient machines saw any help for the boy who had given his life for the Griffin's child.

CHAPTER 13

The Weigh of All Flesh

LAZILY LATE ON THE FOLLOWING MORNING, THE ARTEMISIANS were ready-
ing the wagons to return to Wide Mountain when they were startled by
a wild hallooing and the thud-shudder of many racing hooves. They
had barely time to look up before Deer Runner leapt from the lead
horse and stumbled into the arms of two friends.

"We got news," he gasped to Abasio. "Wide Mountain Mother said to
catch you before you leave. Something you prob'ly want to see; you and
the others. Can you get 'em?"

Arakny was summoned along with Precious Wind, Xulai, and
Grandma. Deer Runner, his dust-dried throat being soothed by a cup
of something hot, delivered his message. "Patrol rider came in after
dark, last night. He'd been on border rounds south of here, down the
river valley. There's been a . . . whaddya call it when the ground falls in?
Makes a pit?"

"Sinkhole," said Abasio.

"Like that, yeah. Well, accordin' to him, there's one heckuva stink
hole happened down the river valley, only it's not just a hole. It's like
the whole section of river had a seam on its bottom side and somebody
pulled the stitches out, and the whole riverbed's dropped and spread
out and then filled up with water. Like an arm a' the ocean grabbed up

at the mountains here." He took another swallow, then gargled, "Did somebody see t'the horses?"

Abasio stood aside so Runner could see the horses being watered, wiped down, petted, and praised by people from the escort camp.

"That must be what happened the other day!" cried Arakny. "That earthquake that dropped all the chimneys at Wide Mountain. You say an arm of the ocean. You mean, it's salt water flowing in?"

"Not salt water flowin' in, no, but it's sure no water flowin' out. 'Rakny, you used to ride the borders. You know the Wanderin' Lows, the place down across from Cow's Bottom Bluff? Had that big, deep pond in the middle and swampy all around it that spread all to gosh and gone when it rained? Took a long while to dry out and shrink back? An' excep' for the pond, ever' time we thought we had it mapped, it went somewhere else?"

Arakny said she did remember the deep pond and the Wandering Lows, yes, what about it?

"Well, now there's new streams—not new ones, but old ones running in different directions—comin' inta that pool, an' it's spreadin' out, and they say at the far south end there's not much high ground between it and how far the ocean's come. Like water's runnin' in from the ocean over a lot of the land south of us."

Arakny asked, "Anybody drowned, anybody's house sunk, anything like that?"

"No, that's not the trouble! Trouble is, the border riders han't been down that way in six months, so we didn't know *the blasted Edgers've put some kinda camp down there by the Lows pond*—only now the pond's a regular lake—and they're buildin' something the Mother-Most needed to know about. And she said come get you all to go with me because you'll probably be the ones best suited to see to it."

Grandma said, "I'll tell the Oracles. I imagine they'll want to know." She went slowly up the path to the hidden door, the sandy path neatening itself behind each footfall, Needly looking after her with troubled eyes. Grandma had been forced to admit that the advice she had been given over the years had emanated from machines *the Oracles had obtained or been given by someone. Someones.* The Oracles could not take credit for the information the machines produced.

They might take credit for obtaining the machines . . . if that acquisition had been an honest one. If not, the Oracles could take no credit at all, and though Grandma said she accepted that, she was having great difficulty breaking old habits of respect for the Oracles themselves. Needly felt no such ambivalence. Her certainty was growing that the Oracles were far from being the omniscient do-gooders she had come to expect. Far from being do-gooders at all.

Grandma had intended leaving Willum with the Oracles, safe from danger. Needly had insisted that Willum be returned to Wide Mountain. Even though some of them might now be making a side trip to the south, they would soon return to Wide Mountain, so Willum could as well be taken there with those who were returning. Meantime, she soothingly offered the suggestion that the Oracles undoubtedly had ways of letting Grandma know if they came up with a solution to Willum's condition.

Grandma agreed without argument. How could she not? She was spending a good part of each day regretting those decades of unquestioning trust. Had it been for a good cause? How would she know? She had started to ask the Oracles, several times, about her children, and had found her words blocked. They had not been evasive, they had been . . . deaf. As though they had not heard her. Now she felt foolish, resentful, and unanchored. Since so much of her life had been lived presumably at their direction, nothing of her plans or hopes seemed secure. No event in her life seemed as useful as she had . . . assumed.

She was beginning to obsess over details, things that had never bothered her before: the fact that she had never really penetrated into the "House" of the Oracles; the fact that she knew none of the Oracles as persons, as friends; the fact that their beneficence had been assumed on her part more than demonstrated on theirs. Oh, they had told her stories of their wanderings, planets they had visited, but they were strangely nonsequential. Scattered. Almost . . . random. She had not blamed them for the lack of clarity. She had blamed herself . . .

Abasio was asking, "How far is it down to the place this whatever-it-is happened?"

Deer Runner replied, "Cow's Bottom Bluff is where it happened. That's a *marker* for Artemisia, 'Basio. It's the southwest corner of our territory. We put a corner marker there way back, some hundreds of years. Black Buffalo's one of the border riders, and he's the one who brought word of it. He didn't ride out right when it happened; he took a day or so to ride around the area, see how far the water went, spy out where those Edgers were. He did it without bein' seen. They have weapons, according to Buffalo, and he didn't trust them not to shoot. Then he had a long ride northeast to get to Wide Mountain.

"Since it was full moon last night, we started out directly. Would have taken a lot longer if we hadn't run those poor horses half to death soon as the sun came up. From Wide Mountain to here's brought us a good way south already. So, from here, it shouldn't be more'n a day along the river, almost directly south. I brought Talking Crow and Big Beaver along. They both know the river route and it's been marked for wagons. We can make it with only a few jigger-jogs where the little canyons feed in from the east."

Grandma soon returned with Precious Wind and Xulai, all of them ready to depart. Two of the Oracles—two extremely large ones that they had not seen before—had followed the three humans without being noticed. Now one of them said, "Let us provide you with some . . . comforts. We have this . . . very nice portable camp that you can put quite near where you will be. If you will take this . . . ?"

"This" was a crystal cube about a hand's width on an edge. The Oracle put it into Grandma's hands. "When you get near, find a place that seems appropriate, speak to it saying you would like to have the camp there, and it will establish itself. It provides whatever you need if you tell it. We wish to see the thing these Edger beings are building also, so take the cube with you when you go closer to observe. It too will see and listen for us."

"You can see it from here?"

"It will send the image here. We can." They turned to Xulai and Abasio, who were holding the babies beside their wagon. "You," said one of them. "We understand you become like the creature we have asked edubot to picture for us: the octopus. You are first generation, is that correct?"

Xulai and Abasio both nodded, it was correct. The Oracles bowed very slightly and returned to their House. *Cave!* Needly said to herself. She had renamed the place. A den, maybe. A lair. So far as she was concerned, it was not a house. And what were these large ones doing? Grandma had seemed as surprised at them as everyone else, so she had not seen them before either. So far as Needly was concerned, "oracle" was merely a misleading word. Perhaps even a kind of disguise. She had not said this to Grandma. Soon she might have to.

"Supplies?" Abasio asked Deer Runner.

"You had enough for the return journey, so you should have plenty to get where we're going. Meantime, Wide Mountain Mother's sending a supply wagon directly to Cow Bluff—well, to a point far enough north of it the wagons won't run into the Edgers. It'll have enough supplies for all us people and horses to get back."

It was agreed the three weary horses would be given a full day's rest and would go back to Wide Mountain tomorrow along with Talking Crow and half the original escort. The wagon containing Willum would go with them along with Arakny's account of events so far, which she recited to Talking Crow for conveyance to Wide Mountain Mother. Talking Crow, it seemed, was named for having a memory that could hang on to lengthy, detailed accounts and recite them word for word.

The other half of the escort group, along with Deer Runner and Beaver, would accompany Arakny on the trip to Cow's Bottom Bluff today. The members of the escort decided among themselves which ones would go where, and less than an hour later the group headed south was on its way, food in hand as they went. Since they did not want a confrontation with Edgers who had invaded Artemisian territory, they rode with three outriders: one a mile ahead to the south, others the same distance southeast and southwest. The big river, which had always been named exactly that in whatever language was current . . . the "Big River" wandered deep in its canyon—one that had preceded the river rather than having been eaten out by it—as it meandered east or west as the underlying strata directed; Beaver's rock piles along the trail were arranged to indicate both direction and distance to save travel time by cutting across from bend to bend, and there were occasional well-established wagon tracks indicating that others had followed a suggested shortcut. A few very long diversions were marked with intermediate cairns indicating where changes of direction were needed to take them around the feeder arroyos constantly being shaped by rains and by spring melt from the surrounding hills.

Shortly before noon, the southwest rider came in to guide them to a shallow bend with an easy access down one of those feeder canyons: an often-used resting or overnighting point for circuit riders, messengers, and supply wagons. Horses and people went down, wagons stayed above. Fires were built and water boiled. People on private business went up two little side canyons helpfully labeled with chiseled arrows where Artemisians had built little sheds over deep cracks in the stone. Grandma was glad to find someone had provided seats without splinters, the only distraction being the pack-rat nest in the corner. This particular pack rat was only a novice, and disposing of the nest required only a few minutes' work with the shovel that Grandma asked one of the escort men to get out of a wagon for her. Grandma could remember nests that had taken a dozen men a week to dispose of. When old families of pack rats packed a nest for a hundred successive generations, they did a very solid, smelly, massive, poop-n'-pee-cemented job of it. She had, on occasion, made some remarkable finds in pack-rat nests. This one had a few items not yet cemented in—a bracelet, a ring, a strangely shaped little key. She tucked them away in her pack to be displayed on the lost-and-found wall she had noticed along one side of the plaza at Wide Mountain.

Needly observed this clearance with great interest. There were bones in the nest, and bits of glass and metal. In addition to the jewelry and the key, someone had lost a knife, several people had lost shoes, and in the last shovelful there was the very strange ring with a carved stone that Grandma put aside with the knife, asking Needly to remind her to soak it and clean it.

"Why do they do that, Grandma? Collect all that stuff?"

"Needly, I don't think anyone knows why pack rats pack. Personally, I think they have an insatiable curiosity. Anything different, they have to collect it and look at it and smell it, and decide whether it's edible or not. Especially shiny things. Or different-looking things."

"But they poop and pee all over it!"

"That's how they demonstrate ownership. They don't maintain anything or keep it safe or guard it. They don't use it *for* anything, or even intend to. Just the *getting and having* is enough for them, and they *get and have* it all cemented together. It keeps other critters from robbing them. And when you're in pack-rat country, you don't want to leave anything you value where they can get at it, especially if it's shiny."

Horses lunched on a handful of oats, a wisp of hay; people ate sandwiches made early that morning along with cups of herb tea often used by riders to prevent dehydration and relieve saddle ache. They were back on the track in less than an hour.

In midafternoon they saw Cow's Bottom Bluff. The whole mountain was called the Cow, and it lay with its back to them, its head to the east with two rock formations making the horns. At this distance, it could be a cow, though the closer they got, the less cowlike it looked. The western end was the Cow's Bottom. It was almost dusk when the south rider came in to report a forested area about half a mile ahead. "There's a low area north of the lake where the river's switched back and forth over the years. There's probably water down just a few feet through the whole area, plenty, for the trees have grown up into quite a little forest. Cottonwoods, aspens, some pines, thick enough we won't be seen from the place the Edgers have set up. The pond's a good-sized lake by now, and it's still getting bigger. We went through the woods and had a look at it. Edger men have a camp set up a bit further south and east, beyond the dunes at that end. Their usual mess! All kinds a' machines. Stinks of oil and fuel. Empty cans lyin' around." The rider, who had been schooled to leave a campsite looking as it did before anyone arrived on it, made a gesture of contempt. "The best campsite for us'll be just up ahead, hidden in the trees."

Arakny rode ahead with the outrider and walked out to meet the others as they approached. "It does look like a good place. No sign that anybody's been around here, no Edger mess. You want to check it out so we can use the *camp-creator thing*?"

The place was level and shaded. They spent a few moments walking through and around it to be sure no current four-legged resident would be displaced, Arakny and Grandma exchanged a few words, then Grandma murmured to the glassy cube she had carried in a bag at her waist. They heard a vague tinkling sound as a door opened into the forest before them. The door hummed to itself. A beam of light came through it from somewhere to stroke the horses, the wagons. The door became larger. They drove the wagons inside. Grandma murmured to the device again. Another door opened into human quarters, a large room furnished with chairs, benches, tables, a kitchen along one wall with utensils hanging above shelves. A flight of stairs led to several dormitory rooms, with beds, and two large bathrooms—multiple showers, basins, and toilet cubicles. When Abasio and Xulai came up, carrying the babies, another bedroom sprouted at the end of the hall, this one containing a large bed and two small cribs for babies.

Seeing this, Abasio said, "How in . . . well, how could they pipe water in here?"

Grandma murmured, "Wormhole, Abasio. This camp is only one of a number of gadgets the Oracles have . . . well . . ." She shook her head, determined to be truthful. " . . . gadgets the Oracles claim they've made. After they gave us the gadget, I went back inside and used the library machine." She flushed, remembering. It had seemed like a transgression to check up on them. And the result had made her angry at herself, as much as at the Oracles. "This camp gadget is listed along with its manufacturer, which is definitely not the Oracles. It seems, if I understand it correctly, the universe is full of tiny, squirmy, short-lived micro-wormholes, and if you have the right technology, you can grab one, anchor one end of it in water—a river, an ocean, or a subterranean aquifer—and the other end almost anywhere. Or you can tie the ends of a wormhole together and put a camp inside, like this one, with one door to the nearest real-space place. Clever, no? The information I read said there's a galactic requirement to replace an equal amount of whatever substances are used up each time. It seems people who travel can make arrangements beforehand with a water bank or air bank or whatever they may be using."

"Galactic requirement, Grandma?"

"That was what I read. There are evidently galactic officials that oversee certain aspects of interaction among worlds. Sometimes I get the impression the . . . the Oracles may not be . . . in compliance with some of the regulations." She frowned. She had decided to be honest with herself and others. "Sometimes I think they don't know much about the regulations!"

"They prob'ly don't and aren't in compliance," said Needly. "They give me a squirmy feeling, you know? Grandma. Like when you step on a snake, all unaware."

"Well, they do tend to be . . . evasive," mused Grandma, as yet unwilling to disillusion either herself or Needly completely. "They do, but I always just put that down to their being strange, you know. In a strange world?"

"They're not a bit in a strange world," argued Needly. "They never leave that cave they live in, and inside that cavern of theirs, wherever the part is where they actually live, I'll bet it's just like their home. Wherever their home is."

On the lower floor of the camp, the horses had been unhitched and the stable area had sprouted a water trough and two long mangers full of hay. Grandma said, "This device no doubt accessed some kind of database in order to identify horses and what horses need. Most of the species living in the galaxy are in the Oracle database. So they say. Billions of species of living things."

"*Oracle* database, Grandma?" Needly allowed herself to sound slightly chiding.

"You know, I doubt it, Needly. I'm beginning to doubt my own name. My own face in a mirror."

Needly thought the database probably existed, but thought it unlikely that the name "Oracle" was attached to it in any way. Of course, as she admitted to herself, she was unlikely to give the Oracles credit for anything at all. They hadn't helped Willum; she had been depending upon them to help Willum; so as far as she was concerned, they were useless. Being angry at them kept her from grieving, even though she knew she couldn't stay furious forever.

Someone sat down on a very comfortable chair, saying, "I wish we could see the area they're working on from in here." Immediately, to squeals of surprise, the living area produced several observation screens with code boxes below them. The screens could show any direction outside, close or at some distance. Arakny and Precious Wind began moving the view screens south, along the shore of the river-that-had-become-a-lake. It was a considerable body of water, but the only evidence of Edger use lay along the short stretch of shoreline just over the low hill south of them. That sandy stretch, between the Cow's rump and the widening lake, was messily cluttered with vehicle tracks, cans of fuel, and machines of one kind or another. Whoever had been here wasn't orderly; whoever had been here was very probably coming back.

"People," said Arakny, beckoning for them to gather around. "Listen please. The Oracles have lent us this camp device. It comes with a menu and an explanation, if any of you are interested. Ask for it, and it appears on the nearest wall in whatever language you've used. It's a self-contained wormhole that bends space around us. When we're in here we're invisible and we can't be heard. I'm setting a code word, which is my name followed by Needly's name separated by 'oops.' Arakny-oops-Needly. It's not something anyone is likely to say by accident. If you are outside fairly close to this location, you can say the code word and the door will open for you. I don't know exactly how close you need to be, so find landmarks you can rely on before you wander off. The door from outside opens into the stable, and it makes sense to leave it that way. If anyone besides us happens into this area, they will walk right through the area without noticing us. We are, so to speak, removed from the space. You will need to check the surroundings before going out; be sure to use one of those surveillance screens to be sure there's no trespassers out there before you open the door.

"Will someone please volunteer for horse maintenance? Beaver, thank you, pick someone to help you. Decide tomorrow whether you want the horses loafing in here all day or want to take them somewhere else. We passed some bits of pasture right along the river within a mile of here that might keep them happy, but we may need to leave in a hurry, so do not plan to put them very far. *Do not* unpack the wagons. Take what you need from them and put things back after use, so we're ready to leave at any time. Don't scatter your personal stuff around, keep your pack ready to go. The code for emergency departure is our usual one.

"A few of us are going out in a moment to look over the territory. We'll take a close look at that construction site while there's nobody there. We can't tell from in here whether something important may be hidden behind something else, so the screens in here can't see it. Once we get a better idea of the layout and what's going on, maybe we can rely on the screens.

"Now listen carefully: We do not want to make any contact with the Edgers, assuming that's who made the mess out there. We do not want them to be aware we know about this place. Nonetheless, we want to get all information about what they're doing here that we can, so regard this as an F and O mission . . . oh, for our guests, that's 'Follow and Observe.' If we need to leave in a hurry, we'll go straight back to Wide Mountain Plaza, so if any of you are tracking anyone or sitting up on the mountain observing their camp, wherever it is, be sure you're carrying whatever you need in the way of food and water to get home if you get stranded. The best rule is, do not leave this place without three days' food and water and a pack of sanitary leaves. If we do cut out of here in a hurry, *and if we're not being pursued,* we'll stop a mile or so east on the Wide Mountain track and find out whether we're missing anyone. If we are, we'll leave someone there with provisions and a horse for each missing person. I repeat, that'll be a mile or two along the track back to Wide Mountain. If you're finding out something important, stay with it; someone'll be waiting for you along the trail. If we *are* pursued, you'll find the usual trail sign indicating food and water caches if we've had time to leave any. If not, you'll have to live off the land. Everything will be easiest and safest for everyone if *you'll have with you what you will need.* Anyone who's tracking, please leave our usual trail signs just in case we have to come looking for you. At this stage, any information we can get will be welcome.

"I say again, if you use something out of the wagons, put it back when you're finished with it, because we may need to leave in a hurry. Don't scatter stuff about, because if we collapse the camp, our stuff will probably not be there when we open it up again. It is not an actual place! Each time we open it, it's a temporary construction! I have no idea what memory capacity it has; could be inclusive, could be none. Keep your belongings in your packs where you can grab them. If you go out, either take your pack with you or put it in a wagon. We are very unlikely to leave without the wagons.

"We assume whoever's been here making that mess along the shore will be back in the morning. In the morning, we intend to be waiting for them. Remember. If you go out, go out quiet and stay quiet. Kitchen crew for tonight will be Silver Plume, Squash Blossom, and two men. Blossom, you pick two. We'll appoint somebody else for tomorrow if we're still here tomorrow. Any questions?"

"How long will the provisions guy wait?" someone asked.

There was a brief give-and-take before they decided on three days before a rescue party would be dispatched from Wide Mountain.

And with that, they settled for the evening. Horses lay down and sighed. People ate many-eater stew and sighed. People, amazed, took hot showers and sighed pleasurably. The kitchen crew had almost nothing to do but heat the food. Empty bowls set down on tables were miraculously washed and returned to cupboards. One of the men reported that horse droppings and urine disappeared before they hit the ground. Silver Plume, experimenting, found that bringing food had been unnecessary. The camp would provide whatever food was asked for, she told them, gleefully hoisting a fancily decorated cake to illustrate the point.

Before it became completely dark, Arakny, Precious Wind, Deer Runner, Xulai, and Abasio sneaked out to look over the territory. Whatever was being done was happening down on the "beach" next to the extended water. Abasio took off his clothes and slipped into the lake, his body making the change as soon as he was completely below the surface.

After climbing out and changing back, he reported: "It fits what the rider reported. I can't see down there; I get some echoes. It's so deep that there must have been a series of caverns running more or less parallel to the river but below it. In some places the bottom of the river was evidently the roof of the cavern. There's a kind of ridge around the edge where that floor was. I imagine some water has been leaking down into the cavern for a very long time; the bottom finally weakened, collapsed, and the whole cavern system filled up with water. It's very, very deep in there, and something way, way down there is making a strange noise." It had been what Abasio would call a purposeful noise, but he'd been unable to locate the source. Considering the depth and the darkness, he had not gone far; he had been uncertain about being able to find his way out if he got lost under a stone roof.

Arakny, meantime, had sought an observation post they could use on the following morning without being observed, a place that would let them see all of the roughly rectangular space the Edgers had strewn with one mess or another, limited by the lakeshore on the west; the line of dunes on the south; and the low forest now around them on the north. East was Cow Bluff, with a long narrow trough along its bottom between mountain and a parallel ridge known as the Cow's Tail: as though a huge plowshare had been dragged along the foot of the mountain. The ridge was partly rounded, some parts of it topped with scattered outcroppings of stone; the trough between rump and tail was the only clean and uncluttered place on the site; it offered the best view and the least danger of discovery. Arakny pointed to the area and told her group to be ready to go there at first light. Everyone else was cautioned to stay out of sight and hearing.

When it was fully dark, Abasio whispered in Grandma's ear. He found Xulai, whispered in her ear, and they both went out, leaving Grandma as babysitter. They did not return until well after dark, and well after moonrise. They had taken the crystal cube with them to record the situation along the shore and the extent of the inundation, presuming there would be a way to download that information.

(Actually, the cube recorded *everything* that occurred in or near the water, and sent that information to a receiver at the House of the Oracles, including a passionate interlude on the shore. After watching this without comprehension, the Oracles decided to store what they had seen and keep it secret. Galactic inspectors had a lot of rules and were fussy about what they called "intruding on other people," and sometimes actually removed such things. With their customary efficiency, they put Abasio and Xulai's lovemaking in a secure file and pushed a certain button labeled ERASE, which their experience had taught them meant "hide." Since they had never yet remembered wanting something they had hidden, the word "erase" had never inconvenienced them in the least.)

ARAKNY WAKENED THEM WHILE IT was still dark. Abasio and Xulai checked on the babies, and told the two young women who were acting as babysitters much more than they needed to know about feeding the babies, changing them, and so forth. Since they'd been helping for some little time they were almost believably attentive.

They asked for and received toasted bread with honey but brewed their own special tea known as wake-up tea, made from desert shrubs. Arakny moved about, sending this one here and that one there. At sunrise, she led the other six observers along the foot of the mountain into the trough behind the tail. They lined up at the north end of it, close together, each behind a sheltering clump of sage or yucca.

Early as they were, they were not the first on the site. A set of rails had been laid entering the site from the south through the gap between dunes and the dark water. Along the rails two giants were propelling a flatcar that held the skeleton of a fish. A huge fish . . .

"It's a whale," murmured Arakny.

"It wasn't there last night," whispered Grandma. "The giants have probably just brought it there . . ."

The rails ran into the water. Needly whispered, "What're they doin'?"

Abasio shrugged. "My grandfather used to tell me, 'Watch and you'll find out.' I suppose that's what we'll have to do."

As the light increased, the rails were more clearly visible, coming in from the south through the gap between dunes and the widening lake. The wheeled car holding the metal monster was now about halfway to the water's edge. It did resemble a whale more than anything else. At the near end of the convoluted, cupped, skull shape of the thing, its mouth gaped wide.

"No hinge," muttered Abasio. "That jaw has no hinge. The mouth doesn't shut."

Among the observers, people made chewing movements of their jaws to determine where the hinge on the huge skeleton creature should be, but wasn't.

"Do whales have lips?" asked Needly. "Maybe it'll just shut its lips."

The framework was about six or seven man-heights long, and it included fins, hinged where they met the huge ribs curving down from a long spine, the rear half of it segmented and ending in a flat tail, like an afterthought, as though someone had said, "Whoops, it should have a tail, shouldn't it?"

"The framework . . . skeleton actually looks like bones," Xulai murmured.

"Right shape but wrong color for bones," said Grandma. "It's metal."

"I've always assumed the Edges were too constricted to hold really big equipment," Xulai said fretfully.

Arakny commented in an annoyed whisper, "Well, we at Artemisia have always assumed the Edgers would stay in their own territory. Both our assumptions have been wrong. It's obvious this group intends to go anywhere it likes and build anything it likes. The Edges had an underground manufacturing plant east of Fantis. So far as I know, it's still there. And usable."

"I'm assuming they're here without permission, Arakny?" Xulai asked.

Arakny shook her head, wondering how many days Wide Mountain Mother might take to cool down once she heard of this. "They didn't even ask! I'm virtually sure they intended to use the area without bothering to clean up after themselves. Whatever they're doing, it has to do with water, and the pond at the Wandering Lows was probably the closest calm water they could find. Mother will be very annoyed."

"They may have thought this area would be underwater before anyone else knew they'd been here," Needly murmured.

There was still nothing happening down below them but lethargic and what seemed to be pointless wanderings by the two giants. The rails were equipped with a siding, the mechanism of which was stuck, stubbornly resisting the attempts of the giants to run the flatcar out of the way. The watchers had time to become thoroughly bored before two other giants emerged from behind the dunes, pushing another car along the rails. Whatever was being delivered was shrouded in canvas, and the shape of it gave Abasio a premonitory pang. He did not have to wait long to have his suspicion confirmed. A truckload of men arrived, the switching mechanism became the center of their attention and was either repaired or unlocked, and both skeleton and the canvas-shrouded object were thrust onto the siding, where several of the men cooperated in pulling off the covering to display a long cylinder on a complicated understructure that was designed—if the various cogged wheels and levers were to be believed—to be raised or lowered as well as swung to either side.

"What's that?" demanded Deer Runner.

"I've seen pictures of them," said Abasio. "Haven't you, Xulai? Arakny?"

"Cannons," said Arakny. "They were made to throw exploding projectiles or just large chunks of metal that would kill and wreck. That's why the mouth on the fish doesn't close. The cannon is supposed to fit inside it."

"A weapon of war disguised as a whale," said Grandma, turning toward Arakny. "Do you really think the Edgers are using that factory east of Fantis? You think they've set it up to produce this . . . whale-y thing?"

Arakny murmured, "The factory east of Fantis was built mostly underground during the Big Kill. If the Edges are manufacturing anything really large, that's the only place they could be doing it. After we starved the Edges, they stopped their giant and behaved themselves, so it's been some time since we've thought it necessary to have scouts checking that far north.

"Now, however, Deer Runner has called out all the scouts, even the older ones and the young men just getting familiar with the territory. He has them covering the entire area from just north of Fantis to here. They've checked the west side of the Big River and gone as far east as Wide Mountain. They've found a lot of vehicle tracks, but there are no newly laid rails coming into Artemisia. The pieces must have been brought down separately, in wagons, and assembled here."

Several men had come to assist the giants in closing the siding switch and bringing something else along the tracks. Needly made a troubled sound and pointed. They looked farther along the beach to the south, where another skeleton was being giant-handled along the tracks toward the shore area—an infant child of the first thing. "Now, that's definitely a fish," she announced.

It certainly resembled one closely; as like to the whale framework as doghouse to castle, though the small one was much more complicated, being strung, laced, and patterned with networks and webs of various shapes and sizes. These networks ran to and through many small and very complicated-looking mechanisms at various places inside it. This framework, too, had fins and a tail, and the head end had a number of lenses curving around the front from one side to the other.

"Eyes?" murmured Xulai.

"Or windows?" Grandma suggested.

On its own smaller flatcar, the smaller fish was pushed to the end of the tracks, where four giants lifted it onto the shore before pushing the flatcar back along the tracks and around behind the dunes.

"They've got a camp or an assembly area or something behind those dunes," said Abasio. "Any known sites that come to mind?"

"Caves," said Arakny. "There's quite a large complex of caves on the south side of Cow Bluff. The border riders always kept the caves stocked with emergency rations and supplies, and they're large enough to have served as an assembly site for these things. When we get back to the camp, we'll send a team over the mountain to take a look."

Just as the huge fish was apparently supposed to have a cannon protruding from its mouth area, the smaller one had several small guns mounted atop its head, and these were now being inspected by half a dozen men who had parked a mechanized cart alongside the fish. Its shelved compartments were loaded with mechanical contrivances, spools of wire, odd-looking tools. Moving with the utmost care, two of the men took a container out of the cart, set it on a fold-down work surface, and opened what appeared to be an extremely complicated lock mechanism. One of them walked to the mouth of the fish, where he received the container from his coworker and set it down carefully while the other carefully joined him inside the fish.

The two of them alternately peered into the container and at a bracketlike device that extended across two of the ribs, meantime exchanging comments or argument, though, as Needly remarked, they seemed more puzzled than anything.

"They haven't done this before," commented Deer Runner. "It's a mystery to them!"

All conversation exhausted, Worker One finally reached into the container and removed the mystery: a carefully wrapped lump that he and Worker Two attempted to affix to the bracket. This required one or both of them to go back and forth, inside and outside, as they decided different tools were required. After the third upheaval, the taller of the two simply stayed outside and passed whatever items were requested by the inside man through a gap in the skeleton.

"Deer Runner's right. They haven't done this before," said Needly, craning to see. "If they had, they'd have known what to take in there."

"Use these," said Arakny, handing a thing forward. "Put it to your eyes . . . no, the other end. Now turn the wheel until you can see . . ."

"What is it?" whispered Needly.

"It's like the long-looker they had in the tower at Saltgosh," said Xulai. "It magnifies things that are far away. The one in Saltgosh was very big. These are tiny in comparison, and two linked together, one for each eye. I think they're called 'duoscopes.'"

Arakny said, "They make them in the east somewhere. That is, I assume they do, because the traders from there sell them. We bought a few dozen of them for use by our border riders and scouts. I put this pair in my pack, thinking they might be useful, but I'd forgotten about them until this morning."

Needly passed the glasses back. "Xulai, Precious Wind, look at that thing they've put in. Up above the bracket. They've unwrapped it."

Xulai looked, gasped, passed the instrument to Precious Wind, who made a face and passed it on to Grandma.

"As I feared," said Grandma. "I see a transparent spherical container of a . . . I believe it's a brain. It could be a human brain, though some other creatures have brains of similar size."

Far to the left, at the other end of the work area, the workers had given up on moving their cannon. They were moving toward the smaller construction, stopping at a respectful distance to watch. Grandma passed the duoscopes to Needly. "Your eyes are best, child. Tell us what you're seeing."

"The . . . the brain's in a transparent kind of globe, with liquid in it. The globe is mounted on a complicated metal base. The man inside keeps turning it over and looking at the bottom of the metal part, then looking at the place it's supposed to go. When he turns it over I get glimpses of the bottom. It's not flat or smooth, it's octagonal. There's a place on the bracket thing that could also be octagonal—we're just high enough above them for me to guess at that, it's hard to tell because the bracket's almost edge-on. I think that must be what the brain globe is supposed to connect to. He keeps turning it over and looking back and forth and talking to the other one. Something's in the way or it isn't made right. The part on the bracket has wires . . . lots of them, all different-ent colors, running from it all over the inside of the . . . framework, the skeleton. Wait. Ah! He wiggled something and made it fit. Now there's bubbles in the liquid around the brain. Can you hear the hum?"

She took the glasses from her eyes to listen, cocking her head. The others nodded. Yes, there was a hum. All of them heard it but Grandma, who shrugged. "I can't hear it, but I'm making note for the Oracles that there's a hum."

"Won't their recorder thing notice the hum?" asked Abasio.

"Of course it will."

"Then why do you—"

"I have told them I may not be available in the future, that is, after this particular problem with the Edgers is solved. Wide Mountain Mother and I have agreed to discuss our . . . relationship with the Oracles. Until Wide Mountain Mother and I decide what our particular arrangement, if any, is going to be with them in the future—for instance, providing them with food is certainly unnecessary and unwarranted given their access to food machines and the fact they have paid for nothing Artemisia has given—I thought I'd keep things as usual, no matter how silly it seems." Particularly inasmuch as they might still have her children. She put the thought away resolutely. She could not afford to dwell on that, not now!

Needly interrupted. "The man inside is coming out—no, he's stopping just inside the mouth. There's a . . . well, it's like a bunch of switches . . ."

"Control panel," said Abasio, who, while he and Xulai were in Tingawa, had spent a good deal of time in the workshops.

"Well, he's pushing things on the control panel. I can't tell what. There are about twenty switch things and button things, and he's only pushing a few of them. Okay, now—no, the other man is bringing him some stuff." She took the glasses away from her eyes. "You can see him. He's got a hose that goes to . . . a tank of something on the cart. I didn't see that before."

"He just uncovered it," said Abasio. "It was behind the wagon."

They were silent, watching. The tank was obviously under pressure. The worker was attaching something to the end of the hose. "Nozzle," said Abasio matter-of-factly. The hose was directed through the wire mesh at the far side of the interior. The man at the control panel looked at the other, received a nod, then pressed one of the bars on the panel. The hum changed, became piercing. The man left the control panel and went some distance away from the thing; the other pressed on the nozzle, which began to project . . . stuff, some kind of coating that stayed on some surfaces, but merely dropped off of others. Gradually one network was coated with something white and waxy- looking.

"It's just staying on parts of it," murmured Needly. "How does it know which parts?"

"That's just what it looked like," said a voice from behind them. Coyote.

"What are you doing here?" asked Abasio in surprise.

"Same as you. Findin' out. Bear n' me got here last night."

Grandma said, "Coyote, what do you mean? *'That's just what it looked like.'*"

"When the big kettle they cooked the stinker stuff in got poured out, that's what the stuff looked like. Only not so white."

"Processed to take out impurities, perhaps?" Precious Wind suggested. "I have to get some of the stuff to Tingawa so they can analyze it . . ."

"Shhh," said Needly. "Watch. He left a hole on the far side, and now he's going over there. He's spraying the inside toward us."

The hose man came to the front of the construction and pointed his hose into it with a continuous circling motion. He finished, shut off the hose, walked over to his partner, and stood watching the fish.

"It only stuck to some of the things inside," said Needly. "Kind of a network. See. It goes to different places inside and it goes to a web that's stretched all over the outside. It's changing color."

The sprayed material was solidifying as a shiny, dark red coating, stretching smooth over certain wires and controls, falling off others to collect in a liquid puddle. A second hose was brought into play to suck the liquid out.

"What does that red network look like to you?" Precious Wind asked.

"A diagram," said Arakny. "It's like a . . ."

"A diagram of a nervous system," said Xulai. "My grandfather has a wonderful pre–Big Kill book on physiology. It's full of pictures like that, as if creatures were cut in half and all their nerves and muscles and organs were different colors so you could see how they all fitted together. I don't understand how the stuff stuck to just certain wires, though. That thing is full of wires and shapes . . ."

"That hum we heard. I imagine they were running power through just one set," said Grandma. "The stuff sticks only where there's power. See the man at that control thing, he's checking the network and writing things down. He wants to be sure there aren't any . . . bare spots or anything."

Precious Wind said eagerly, "That would explain . . . remember, Xulai, when I mentioned making a solution of the fatty stuff off the hunter. I said it coalesced. I was using *ul xaolat* at the time, so I would have been in an . . . area of power. That's why the stuff was trying to make a shape!"

"Watch," said Needly. "They've . . . put power into a new set of wires, I think."

The first things to solidify had been in a network of strings, knots, and threads. The second one was similar, slightly different in color when it had solidified, as were the third and the fourth, leaving the inside of the shape latticed and surrounded with networks. The fifth set of things to be sprayed was more bulky, made up of sheets, ropes, and cylinders. The procedure was the same, and they heard the hum. The color this time was blue.

"Those look like muscles," said Abasio. "Now, how in the world can they get the same stuff to form different kinds of tissues?"

"We don't know it's the same stuff, Abasio." Needly peered at the man with the hose. "He could be connected to a whole bunch of different tanks of the stuff. We can't see where the hose goes. Maybe the leftover stuff is being sucked back, then they connect the hose to something else. They're not wasting it. Each time they spray, they suck up all the stuff that drops down."

The fifth round had taken much longer. The men doing the spraying had had to move to various vantage points, get behind, over, under. The blue stuff also took longer to settle and acquire a slightly shiny surface.

"What's next?" muttered Precious Wind.

"Organs. Glands. The thing is probably intended to eat and excrete, and I don't see any template for anything like that." Arakny reached for the glasses in Needly's hand and focused them on another group just arriving. "Now I do."

A new cart had arrived, this one carrying not only a mass of flexible balloons, hoses, and strange-shaped mesh objects but also a crew of half a dozen tiny men who plunged into the fish and guided the newly arrived material into place, fastening here, fastening there.

"Guts," said Deer Runner. "They're givin' it guts. What are those little people? Somethin' they've made?"

"Midgets, perhaps," said Precious Wind. "They aren't artificial, Runner. Midgets have always been with us. Every genetics lab would have saved the genotype. At one time, way back, some of our people thought if things got really rough here, not enough food to go around, we could impose that genotype to shrink the human race and use less food. As for what they're doing now, it's close quarters in there, so they needed very small workmen. The Edgers may have been collecting them for ages."

Grandma said, "Coloring the various types of parts helps identify them, I suppose. Can we consider the wires and shapes and inflated things inside it to be templates? Patterns? Do they dissolve after they're covered, or do they stay? Each set of patterns is a different color, and each set has power run through it separately?"

Arakny said, "Or, it could be that each set is coated with materials that will react in certain ways with the stinker material. Maybe the stuff can take any shape it has a pattern for or whatever shape it's stimulated to take. I too wonder if the templates dissolve after the substance dries. Amazing."

"Perhaps it all dissolves except for the brain," said Arakny. "That's real."

The construction went on. Each layer of material was allowed to dry. Liquids were brought out and pumped into certain ports. Something bulgy began to expand and contract, then others began to move. Heart. Lungs. The little people left the creature's innards, proceeded south, past the dunes, and disappeared. Coyote, who could see farther south than the others, noted that as soon as they were past the dunes, they began to run. Now, wasn't that interesting? The various parts of the "fish" had begun to pulse, pulling in fluid or gas from somewhere, inflating to fill the space behind them.

"The thing's filling up. The whole thing!" Needly managed to whisper and scream at the same time.

"It still needs a skin," whispered Xulai in return.

"I do not have a good feeling about this," Grandma growled.

"There's the skin," remarked Abasio. The hoses were deployed once again, this time on the outside, all of the outside. The skin was gray when it dried.

Grandma spoke again, now demandingly. "How far are we from them, Abasio? Never mind. However far we are, I don't feel we have enough protection here."

Abasio looked around them. They were lying just below the crest of the ridge, here covered with sand and with only the clumps of yucca or sage at the top, no barriers or protected places around them. Grandma's uneasiness was connected with what was going on below them, so any danger would come from that direction, and he had learned to trust her instincts. Not far to their left, along another stretch of ridge, the underlying stone protruded at the top of the ridge, making an effective barrier. He nodded toward it, and Grandma immediately scrambled in that direction. The others had heard the slight panic in her voice and followed at once. Each of them found a place at the top of the ridge that had an exposed chunk of solid rock next to it. Though all of them might have been momentarily exposed to view, all eyes among those down on the shore had been totally concentrated on what was being done with the fish. The entire process had taken some hours. The sun was above them, center sky.

Abasio had picked up on the old woman's caution. The nice thing about excess caution was that it almost never killed anyone. He passed instructions back along the line of them: "If *anything* looks the least bit worrisome down there, don't keep watching! Get your entire body and head behind a rock."

From the end of the line, Coyote looked them over: at the far end Arakny, Needly, Grandma, Deer Runner, and Precious Wind; then Abasio and Xulai, then himself . . . and up the hill somewhere, he heard Bear snort. Now, when had Bear showed up? Coyote squirmed a hollow in the sand, behind his own rock, his nose between his paws and his eyes fixed on the thing on the shore. By shifting himself sideways, he could see a bit farther, right and left.

Now the men had put all the hoses away and were busy removing whatever it was that had covered the various lenses and antennae on the fish, sheets of something that came away without tearing, though they were now heavy with the sprayed material. The men were careful not to touch it. They used long pincers, pulling away each section of film and dropping it into a waiting canister with a swiveling lid. The others, including the giants, watched and muttered. One of the human watchers had brought a bottle, which he passed around.

The sprayers completed their work, closed up their carts, and joined the larger group. Another bottle materialized, and the two sprayers were toasted, everyone miming a raised glass. The giants looked at the men and grumbled, miming drinking. They wanted some, too. One of the men spoke reprovingly to them. The watchers heard his shouted words. "Later, at the cave, just wait." The giants went farther down the shore and sat on the sand, legs crossed before them.

Another vehicle approached from the south, one equipped with yet another tank—this one a vivid red and labeled hugely down the sides

ACTIVATOR. DANGER. This vehicle had a nozzle mounted on top; it turned and backed toward the fish. The driver, wearing an all-over covering with face mask, got out to stand beside a tall mechanism at the side of the truck, the top a blank screen, below it a square array of buttons.

"What's that?" Needly asked. "The thing on the side?"

From beside her, Grandma answered. "The bottom part is a keyboard where a person can spell out instructions to the machine. The top part is a screen where the machine's responses will show up. I think."

"How did you know that, Grandma?" asked Needly.

"It looks like the food machines at the Oracles. You used it, didn't you?"

"Food machine?" said Abasio.

Grandma murmured, "I have no idea where they got it. If I get hungry at night, I can go to one of them and ask it for whatever I like, and the machine either creates it or obtains it, and puts it in a drawer for me. I pull open the drawer, and there it is, hot or cold, whichever. Sometimes I have to put in the recipe first, but never more than once. It always remembers. When we were there last I had something called 'turkey enchiladas with green peppers and sour cream.'"

"What's that?"

"Something I found in the Oracles' collection of books. One of them has recipes in it, for all kinds of things So I fed the recipes into the machines, and when I'm hungry, the machines make the food. The enchiladas were very tasty."

Xulai resolved to acquire, by any means possible, such a device. The thought of sour cream and peppers made her mouth water. She told her mouth to behave. They would have breakfast when they got back to the camp. Maybe she'd ask the camp for . . . enchiladas.

The man beside the truck was now busy pushing buttons, using all his fingers, doing it quickly. Lights came on, spelling out TARGET ACQUIRED.

The man pulled a visor down over his face. His entire body, including his hands, was covered. He pressed a button. The gun on top of the tank shot out a widening cone of red mist that settled over the smaller fish; the nozzle on the truck dropped, hummed, a fine, direct line of fluid shot into the mouth of the thing, the nozzle spun, then it stopped. The entire fish was now a rather bright pink. The sign lit up: TARGET ACTIVATED.

The man leapt into the vehicle and drove it away, quickly. All of them but Needly and Grandma watched it go. It was Needly who cried, "Look. Look."

The fish was shaking, trembling. The fins moved, moved again, lashed as if in fury. A high-pitched scream came from the thing, part mechanical, part . . . organic. The thing turned itself toward the water, the fins came forward, tried to drag it again and again, gaining only a few inches at a time. The scream increased in pitch, became words . . . "NO . . . NO . . . TURN IT OFF NO TURN IT OFF, HURTS, HURTS, BURNING, BURNING. WATER GOT TO GET TO WATER AAAAAAAA . . ."

The scream went up the scale into a shrill howling as the fish erupted into-thousands of screaming shards that blasted away in all directions from a wide, scooped hole in the sand.

Grandma had yelled "get down" at the first scream. Every member of the group watching from behind the rocks had ducked! Metallic bits shrieked over them and into the trees and along the bottom of the mountain behind them. Uncountable bits landed between them and the shore, many of them moving, trembling, trying to crawl. Down on the beach the situation was pure horror! The men and the giants had been showered with debris, including the waxy stuff that had been sprayed on the fish, the waxy stuff that was now activated . . . alive. The men screamed and tore at it, flung themselves into the water, trying to wash it off.

Xulai, responding as she would in any emergency, jumped up, ready to help.

"No," Precious Wind cried. "Abasio, don't let her go. None of you. Don't go near a scrap of that stuff. Every tiniest piece of it will have to be burned. Coyote, your nose is going to be our guide out of here, so don't go anywhere. Just stay with us."

Below them, on the shore, the men had fallen. Some still made noises. Others were silent. Even from where the observers were, they could see limbs half severed, faces eaten away. The giants had been hit, too, in the eyes. Their deaths had been quick, eaten through the eyes to the brains, in an instant. Their bodies were still being eaten.

"What in hell did they think they were doing!" cried Abasio.

"Growing new bodies for themselves," said Arakny and Precious

Wind, as though with one voice. "Seagoing bodies," continued Precious Wind. "They planned to put their brains in bodies made out of the stinker goo, goo their bodies created from humans the stinkers had eaten. They probably planned to swim and kill and eat what they killed and go on living."

The truck down on the shore had started its siren. The sign on its side blinked on and off, repeatedly: TRIAL 9: FAILURE . . . TRIAL 9: FAILURE . . . TRIAL 9: FAILURE. . .

"That siren's going to bring someone else," said Abasio heavily. "Where's our closest cover, Arakny? The place the Oracles gave us? Right." He raised his voice. "Please, everyone pay attention. As you can see, that stuff is deadly. We must not touch that material. We're going out in single file following me, and I will follow Coyote if he'll start us out . . ."

Coyote looked at Xulai, who pointed in the direction of the stable-cum-camp: "That way is our closest safe territory."

There was a consensus as they went, pointing, murmuring, everyone's eyes raking the ground before them. They set out in single file. Arakny beckoned Grandma and Needly past her so she could keep an eye on them. Coyote leading, they went to the north. The crawling bits of stuff were everywhere. Coyote went a few steps at a time, sniffing, double-sniffing, using his eyes as well. Abasio, behind him, checked each step. It seemed much farther than they'd remembered, in time if not in distance. Abasio found a clean piece of metal, turned it over with a stone, found the other side clean, and used it to flip the closest stuff farther away. Deer Runner followed his example. By the time they reached an area where Coyote could smell no more, where none of them could see any more bits of the red-tinted fattiness, writhing, twisting, trying to crawl, each person in the line felt as though miles had been walked.

Looking behind them, they saw that it wasn't as far as it had felt. They still had a good view of the area. The large whale shape was in clear view, along with the cart from which the brain had been taken. The ACTIVATOR: DANGER truck had evidently gone back where it came from. The big whale was still there. The giants had been eaten, almost to their waists. Their bottom halves still sat, slowly disintegrating.

Grandma said, "We can summon help from the observation post. The Oracles could probably supply us with what would be needed . . ."

The group cast glances at one another, doubtfully. Arakny said firmly, "NO. Before we make plans to do any cleanup, and definitely before we attempt to involve the *Oracles,* let's see what the Edgers do. That truck said 'Trial Nine.' I think we can assume they've had at least eight failures before, so they may have devised a way to clean up that will be quicker and safer than anything we can do. Let's get inside and watch. It's this way!" Arakny moved into a grove of stunted trees, saying loudly, "Arakny-oops-Needly."

The door opened and they all went through it . . . hurriedly. There was a sudden demand upon the bathrooms.

Grandma, just inside the stable entry, turned to Coyote and Bear, putting one hand on Coyote's head, the other on Bear's shoulder. "This place is something the Oracles loaned to us," she said. "We can't be seen, felt, or detected from outside. Don't ask me how it works, I don't know. Kitchen is over there," pointing. "Let me know if you're hungry or thirsty. Beds and bathroom up those stairs. You can stay here, with the horses, or inside." She stopped, noticing some nervousness on the part of the two horses who had stayed in the stable. "Better go either upstairs or outdoors, but don't go anywhere near where that mess happened. This is an observation room, observation windows along that wall, the code we set for the shore area is S A."

"Whats a Es Ai?" Bear asked Coyote.

"Writin'," said Coyote. "I can't do it."

"I'll show you," said Needly, who was already glued to one of the screens, moving it back and forth, finding nothing alive but the crawling bits of flesh. "It just shows you a little piece of the place at a time, but it's a lot safer than being out there."

Abasio came to stand next to her. "What would happen if we put some of that stuff in a bottle?" she asked. "Suppose we fed it, kept it alive, then used it against a giant. Just throw it at him."

Xulai shuddered. "That stuff came off a stinker. And you know what the stinkers ate. They eat humans. And giants eat humans. And that's what the stuff they were making the fish out of eats also. It eats humans or things that eat humans."

Needly slowly shook her head. "Xulai, it lives only when the activator stuff is sprayed on it. They sprayed the white stuff all over the small fish with the brain in it, and no one was even wearing special clothes. It wasn't until the activator was added that everyone was scared."

Xulai nodded, rubbing her forehead. "Yes, of course you're right, Needly. I knew the white stuff was harmless. Precious Wind took samples of it from the stinker that Bear killed. She and I both touched it with our bare hands . . ."

"We did," agreed Precious Wind. "It smelled terrible, but it was harmless. Flies lit on it and flew away again. However, the trial they conducted out there this morning verifies why they are experimenting with it. It does attempt to take a shape. I told you about making a solution of the stuff and watching it try to coalesce. The problem, of course, is that we don't know what shape it was trying for, and evidently the Edgers don't know either! If I had to guess, I'd say 'embryonic stinker.'"

Abasio said, "I wish we knew exactly what they're trying to do. If it tries to take a shape in the flask, then it does have at least one shape it can take. All those wires and nets were their attempt to force it into other shapes, force it to make tissues that do other things, and it won't go!"

Arakny had found her own window and focused it on the shore. "Abasio, part of what they're doing is trying to fix the shape and make it permanent. That's what the activator stuff was meant to do. However, Edger expertise was almost entirely electronic and mechanical, not genetic. Oh, I know, they produced giants and various living characters for the archetypal villages, but they didn't design anything new. A giant is just a human being with increased bone structure and the genes that govern growth turned off. *IF* they made the Griffins, they used known sequences. Eagle and bat wings combined, lion body, feathered, and eagle beak. They'd have made little ones first. Then, when they had the pattern, they'd make the bigger ones. *If they did it at all. Somehow, I think the Griffins are too beautiful to have been made by Edgers.*"

Needly remarked, "Add in the fact that Griffins talk. I think that would puzzle Edgers."

Precious Wind smiled. "Needly, Coyote has a voice, and Bear, and Blue and Rags. The speech center can be copied. It takes different genetic signals to build in different creatures, but the device built is pretty much the same in each case. But it works only if the creature's brain is . . . speech discerning. It isn't accidental that the creatures first domesticated by man are those who discern meaning in speech. I don't mean they understand the words, but they know different sounds have different meanings.

"The thing about all this that baffles me is why would Edgers think the shaping can be guided by a brain? Growth and development aren't brain-directed! They're purely genetic. Cell A next to Cell B always makes Cell C. When enough Cell C's get into a bunch, that signals the next one will be Cell D . . ." She shook her head furiously. "We have learned one thing, Abasio. *We do know what they're trying for.* They are trying to grow an aquatic body for a human brain."

Arakny added, "And don't ignore the fact that *the thing did move,* the fins did move, it tried to get into the water. That brain was thinking before it died: thinking and talking and hurting."

"You think they've succeeded?" Xulai was appalled.

Arakny frowned at her feet, thinking. "No, but I know what Precious Wind is thinking. They wouldn't have expended all that time and effort unless they had had positive results in earlier experiments. Probably with something smaller. What we saw out there involved an enormous expenditure of time and effort, and treasure—that is, whatever they use to buy things with. Without some positive results, would they go so far as to acquire a human brain?"

Abasio put his hand on her shoulder. "The Edgers wouldn't consider it was going far to grab a human brain. Believe me, if they wanted one, they'd grab one at any distance, with no compunction whatsoever!"

"You people," yelped Coyote, who had his eyes fixed on the window showing the shore. "If you want to see who came to clean up, they're down there."

They turned. Indeed, they were down there, trucks carrying humans, dressed in all-over protective gear, working in pairs, one of each pair carrying a device that spat flame, the other helping him locate moving bits.

"They've done this more than a few times before," Abasio remarked, heaving a deep breath. He remained at the window, watching the men work. One couple was in trouble. Moving bits were climbing their clothing. Someone else picked up a torn shred of metal and scraped them off."

"I think you're wrong, Abasio," said Precious Wind. "They haven't done this before. If they'd had anything like this happen before, all of those workers wouldn't have been sitting around down there without protective clothing, just watching. This trial was based on some previous success . . . Look down there now!" She pointed to one side of the screen.

There were several men who seemed to be onlookers: no hazard clothing, no moving about. Abasio fiddled with his window, bringing the picture closer. "Oh, for the . . . !" he exploded. "Well, this removes all doubt!"

Xulai said, "What is it, Abasio? Someone you know?"

"I didn't really know the bastard, but I definitely recognize him. The man on top of the blue truck, the gray-haired fat one to the right, that's old Chief Purple." He turned to the group, raising his voice. "When I was a boy, I ran off to the city and joined a gang, the Purples. Gang chiefs accumulated treasure by digging into the buried city for things the Edgers wanted. Story was, old Chief Purple found something one of the Edges wanted a lot. He got hold of enough of whatever it was to buy himself into one of the Edges just outside Fantis. He spent most of his time there. He left his son behind to take over as chief of the Purples. Poor little rodent couldn't have been chief of an empty mousehole. He had never matured. Old Chief Purple couldn't accept that he was sexually and mentally just a little boy. He bought Sybbis as a wife for the kid. That's the same Sybbis who is now the leader of the Catland people and owner, supposedly, of a couple of dozen huge stinkers. I'll bet at any odds she's keeping them for papa-in-law, old Chief Purple. His private supply! To provide the substance for his own whale when the time comes!"

Arakny bared her teeth. "All of this establishes the definite link between the Edges and the stinkers. And they still seem to be creating giants, though the ones that were here today didn't seem inclined to eat babies."

Abasio shook his head at her, saying, "Arakny, please keep in mind that if these giants are the same as most of them now—a different sort from the ones who took part in the Place of Power war—then they'll eat people unless they're prevented from doing so. These were probably created to be workmen, so they were made with a block against eating humans."

"Ah," she said. "Well, if the four they had here were the only ones, they're gone now. Enough. We have the link. Are we agreed that we need some of that stuff they called the activator? We should probably get a sample to Tingawa, if we can. The Edges have the better part of two centuries yet before they drown. They can do a lot of damage in that time. How many men died down there? Including the observers? Thirty, fifty? They weren't all Edgers, by any means."

Abasio pointed to the screen. "They're leaving. They're headed back the way they came. I guess they just came to see the extent of the disaster."

The others turned to the screen, watching the truck turn around and move away, no one looking back.

Xulai turned toward Coyote. "Coyote, could you follow the ones who're cleaning up? When they finish down there by the water, they'll go back to wherever they're camped or based. They were here not long after sunrise this morning, and the cleanup crew showed up very promptly after the explosion, so it can't be far from here. Some of us will wait here for you to come back." She looked up at Arakny. "You want to know where they are, don't you?"

"We do," she said.

Coyote drew himself up, as high as his legs could push him, and said to Grandma. "I think that would be worth . . . several chickens, don't you?"

"Oh, I should think so," she said. "Perhaps as many as ten, delivered at intervals."

"Roasted!" said Coyote, saliva dripping from his tongue.

"Oh, very definitely roasted."

"That truck is leaving," said Needly. "If you're going to follow it . . ."

Coyote was out the door, circling east and then south up the hill behind the ridges they had lain on earlier. Wherever the truck went, it would come out south of that hill. He yapped as he went, and several of the group saw Bear come out of the trees and amble after him, not hurrying.

"If the Oracles ever look at what their food-supply machines are doling out, they are going to be wondering what I'm doing with all those roasted chickens and combs of honey," Grandma murmured to herself, watching the two creatures scuttle over the hill and disappear in the south. "Such good, helpful creatures." She put her hand in her pocket and pulled out the metal tag Coyote had given her, murmuring to herself, "This might be enough by itself. Depending on records, of course. Old records . . ." She thought for a moment. "I *will not* ask the Oracles."

"What's Tingawa doing for bears?" Abasio murmured to Precious Wind.

"Cross-breeding with polar bears," she said. "The ice caps are still going to be there and the ice will be more extensive than it has been in hundreds of thousands of years. There'll be plenty of room for bears." She headed for the door.

"Where are you going?" called Xulai.

"They may have missed one chunk of that stuff," she said. "I want a sample."

"Take this," said Grandma, handing her the crystal cube that had furnished their quarters. "Tell it what you want. If there is any of the stuff unburned out there, it'll tell you. And by the way, did you intend to pick it up in your bare hands. What were you going to carry it in?"

No reply. Precious Wind flushed.

Grandma shook her head. "You do have a habit of getting too narrowly focused, young woman. Stop and think before you do anything. Tell it what you need." She indicated the device. "It'll probably think of something."

The group left turned to food, more as a diversion than because they were hungry. Xulai checked on the babies, who had already been fed to repletion. As Xulai and the others chewed their food, they chewed at the subject without coming up with any new revelations and finally decided they had no reason to stay where they were. Once they were sure the cleanup crew had gone somewhere else, they moved around the charred site, picturing everything they saw, taking notes, taking samples. The crystal cube, which Precious Wind was now calling the Provider, came up with sample holders, tongs for grabbing things, even gummed labels. It did not come up with any samples, and Precious Wind found only two, eating her shoe. She managed to get them into a vial before the leather was quite penetrated.

"We can be back at the Oracles by tonight," Precious Wind announced. "If Grandma and Needly want to go there to return the Provider they lent us."

"Willum will be partway back to Wide Mountain by now," said Grandma, who had decided she really didn't want to go back to the Oracles. "There's no reason we shouldn't head in that same direction. We can always send a messenger to drop the cube off at the Oracles' place. If we take something in our packs to eat on the way, we'll save some time."

"Leave a riding horse here," said Abasio. "A horse and a couple of blankets. I'll go up there in the woods where Bear was and wait for him and Coyote. I won't be far behind you." He whispered to Xulai, and she nodded, reaching into the bag she was carrying. She handed him *ul xaolat*.

"Read what it said in the daily reports," she murmured. "It's a nasty, sarcastic device. Don't forget to tell it 'Yes, Bung Quai!'"

"Just what I need," murmured Abasio, putting his arms around her. "A sarcastic assassin. We'll all be there soon."

"I'll stay with 'im," Big Beaver offered. "Us n' the animals'll be back tomorrow or the next morning. 'Less'n that Coyote gets into trouble or somethin'."

Precious Wind and Deer Runner also volunteered to stay with Abasio. Before collapsing the "comforts" provided by the Oracles, they asked the camp to provide various food items they could pack for the journey. The rest of the group packed up and headed north, where an hour later they met the supply wagon Wide Mountain Mother had sent. The arriving wagoners expressed themselves in terms that Mother would never be allowed to hear, turned the wagon around, and headed back the way it had come. At least now they had company.

BEAR AND COYOTE TROTTED UP and over the Cow's rump, through a stunted forest of evergreens, along the Cow's backbone, and far enough down the south side that they could see the desert below. Some distance to their left they spotted a large cluster of vehicles and the end of the railway that had extended from this place to the site of the destruction behind them. They moved along the side of the mountain until they could see several men moving in and out of a cave, almost below them. The two animals moved carefully forward until they were almost directly above the cave opening, hidden in a growth of low juniper. The truck that had sprayed the activator was parked in front and the driver was just sitting in it, not doing anything except maybe talking to himself, as his mouth was moving and he kept making violent gestures.

The men working below did not seem interested in what they were doing. When the truck with Abasio's old ganger chief on it showed up, winding its way among the rocks, most of the men disappeared inside the cave. On arrival, all the occupants of the truck but one followed them into the cave. The one who stayed outside was a rather fat man, half bald, with bulgy eyes, a very long nose, a large, ugly scar across his forehead, and a dark face—Abasio had told Coyote he would see Chief Purple's red face as dark.

The fat man yelled into the cave—if that was what it was. Bear and Coyote were above it, and couldn't really tell. It was deep enough, at any rate, to hold a wagon and team of eight horses, one of the lead horses saddled, which two of the other men drove out and left standing, one man holding the lead team while the other one loaded things into the wagon.

Bear said, "That wagon's shiny. Shines like water."

It did shine like water. Like the little metal thing Coyote had given to Grandma.

The driver of the alarm truck got out. His face was dark, too. If both of them had red faces, it probably meant they were both angry. The driver was yelling something, waving his arms, kicking at things, finally turning on Chief Purple and hitting him with a clenched fist. The blow was returned, the fight continued until Chief Purple kicked the man low on his body and then hit him on the neck when he bent over. The driver lay there, perfectly still.

"He fights pretty good for a fat ol' man," said Coyote. "What's he doin' now?"

"Gettin' something outta that alarm truck. Looks like . . . what're those? Looks like balls kids play with, but shiny. Metal. See, he's turnin' the part on the side. Like it was a honey jar. They're like cans with a top that turns around to make it tight. He's takin' the rope off the side of the truck . . ."

"'Basio called it a hose. Looks like a rope but it's hollow in the middle."

Bear nodded. "Hose. He's fillin' those cans. You 'spose that's the stuff that blew up?"

"Probly." They watched while Chief Purple filled his containers and screwed on the tops. One of his men took the containers and put them in the shiny wagon while Chief Purple climbed onto the driver's seat. One of the other men mounted the saddled lead horse. Men boiled out of the cave, a dozen mounting onto horses, the others getting into the other vehicles by twos and threes. Coyote had seen guns before; the people at the Place of Power had had guns; most of these men were carrying long guns. Chief Purple stood up on the wagon seat to talk at them. A speech, Coyote decided. He was making a speech. His voice was loud, and it carried well.

"Had enough of these blasted fish people tryin' to change humans t'suit theirselves. 'Nuf a' these female boss Artemisians. 'Nuf a' all of 'em. We're goin' to the heart of 'em, the place they do the changin'! We gotta poison that'll spread! Goin' to the heart of 'em and kill 'em all. Poison the water where those fish children live, t'ones south a' here, t'ones west a' here. Then we'll get a ship, cross over t'that Tinkywa place, an' kill t'ones there. No more a' this turnin' humin bein's inta fish. Alla Edgers 'r comin'. Meetin' us at Big Mountain!"

There was a ragged assent from the men. Many of those on horseback were leading saddled but riderless horses.

Bear said, "Somma them horses prob'ly belonged to somma those dead people the fish blew up."

Coyote grunted an agreement, then asked, "Where's Big Mountain?"

Bear snorted. "Alla mountains 're big. Wouldn't call 'em mountains if they wasn't big."

Chief Purple jerked his head at the man on the lead horse, who kicked the horse and its companion into movement. The wagon moved off, headed eastward. The cars and trucks fell in behind it, the dust of their going drifting eastward, as though following them.

Coyote mused, "Why's there a rider on that front horse?" Receiving no answer, he mused a moment more and nodded to himself. " 'Cause it's too far out in front for the driver to see what's there, I guess."

"T'other one, he's finished playin' dead," said Bear, indicating the driver that Chief Purple had left on the ground. The man crawled over to a rock and pulled himself up, shaking his head, then started walking around, kicking at nothing, talking, his voice getting louder and louder. A light breeze brought his words: "Rather die than be put in one a' those fish things. What kinda person'd wanta be put in there? Nobody! Nosir, damn it, nobody! Crazy idjits, how many they gonna kill afore they stop it? Think they're gonna live f'rever? Two hunnert years! Who's had any chil'ren anytime recent? Who's gonna be left in two hunnert years? Nobody much lef' *now* but that idjit n' people he's bought. Oh, Gold King, he's one for buyin' he is. Thinks he c'n buy livin' f'rever. T'hell'th it! I say, t'hell'th it!"

Eventually wearying of this, he went into the cave, emerged holding a burning stick that he threw at the activator wagon as he dived down behind a rock. "Duck," said Bear. The truck blew up like the almost-fish had. None of the debris reached as far as Bear and Coyote. Satisfied, at least for the moment, the man went back into the cave. They continued to watch. After some time he reemerged, leading a saddle horse and followed by a dog. He stood looking around himself for a long moment before mounting and riding off southward, out of Artemisia, away from the direction the Gold King had gone.

Coyote stood up and shook himself. "Let's look around inside n' then go back to Abasio."

Below him, there was a tremor and a roar, fire spouted from the cave entrance. Bear watched the flames die, then nodded to himself. "Let's not look around inside," he said. "No tellin' what else he's got goin' off down there. Let's just go back to Abasio."

CHAPTER 14

The Official Arrival of Balytaniwassinot

THE SHORE OF THE NEW LAKE BECAME NOTICEABLY longer over the next few hours. The mess left by the cleanup crew was not cleaned up. After a time spent idly deploring the mess, Abasio took the *ul xaolat* from his pocket, pushed what he assumed was the proper button, and asked, "Can you clean up that mess down there? Remove all devices, material, everything, and return it to its pristine state? Without using power that any other person may be in desperate need of?"

The tiny screen went blank for a moment before words appeared: *At last, someone sensible. Yes.* Things on the beach began to disappear. Rails vanished a bit at a time. Equipment vanished, also a bit at a time. Scars made by burning something or other vanished. Tracked sand erupted in tiny volcanoes and subsided, smooth. By the time the sun dropped toward the mountains in the west, everything looked just as nature plus an earthquake would have left it.

Precious Wind grinned and pointed at the device. "Xulai told you about it, did she?"

Abasio made a face at the thing while saying, "Thank you, Bung

Quai." They resumed sitting in reasonable patience halfway up the mountain, waiting for Coyote and Bear.

Abasio heard a sound. "What is that?" he asked no one in particular. The others listened. The sound was a variable hum with an occasional *plunk-plunk* noise. They could not tell what direction it was coming from. The hum went on, rising and falling in pitch as though something mechanical might be trying to remember a tune. The plunks grew more frequent. Another hour passed and Precious Wind pointed out toward the lake, where bubbles were boiling up from the waters below. As though air were being pumped into the water. Or a cavern had been uncovered.

"Something hollow there and the water just reached it?" Abasio offered.

"Somehow I think not," said Deer Runner, pointing.

Out in the center of the new lake something very large emerged. The bubbles that had accompanied it stopped. Hum was replaced with whir. The thing came toward the shore, came farther toward, reached, rolled up on, an almost spherical thing, four men high and wide, dark-blue-blackish-greenish: flattened on the bottom. It had four wheels, two close together at one edge of the flat side, and two across from them, farther apart. It appeared to have no openings or features whatsoever. Intragalactic modules were not known for their looks.

While the watchers on the hillside stared in total incomprehension, ruminations continued inside the emergent thing. The *arrival* had been *planned* and had *happened,* but *the arrival* had not *happened as planned.* That fact had preoccupied the occupant of the intragalactic module, IGM, for most of the last three days.

The occupant, Balytaniwassinot, also known as "Fixit," operator of the IGM, was a galactic sector agent, GSA, who had not intended to cause an earthquake when it had *officially* arrived some days ago. There had been several prearrivals of both agent and module that had occurred covertly, unassumingly, some centuries ago. So long as they never learned about those previous visits, a great many persons in higher-up galactic supervisory positions (HUGSUPs) could continue filling their working time with harmless self-admiration. They also knew nothing about the dream interventions Balytaniwassinot had created, which

was also a good thing. What they did not know of, they could not investigate. What they did not investigate, they could not recriminate.
Dream interventions were Balytaniwassinot's own invention, and the
agent intended to keep them strictly to itself. Putting a thing or idea or
person in someone's dreams was an excellent way of planting familiarity with that thing or idea or person in someone's unconscious mind. By
this time, Abasio should know all about Lom and Plethrob and the sea
planet Squamutch, which would greatly reduce the time he would need
to become assured of their reality.

The intragalactic module was equipped with an automatic log. The
agent also carried a log that it wore at all times except when sleeping. If
it removed the log at any other time, it screamed at him. Both logs were
"required." Either or both of them constantly recorded every breath,
blink, twitch, fart, belch, action, and uttered word of the module occupant. If an agent did anything at all, the log would record it. Later,
an inspector would look at this log, perhaps to barely glance, perhaps
to intensely scrutinize. Therefore, in the current situation, it was absolutely necessary that the log report *only* items confirming that the IGM
had just arrived on Earth for the very first time! Actually, a short time earlier,
agent and module had—as on numerous previous occasions—landed
unseen and unheralded, done what was needed, then departed, meanwhile expunging all log entries concerning the matter. Like the dream
interventions, the expunging methods were of the agent's own invention. No one but Balytaniwassinot would have been capable of figuring
out the single, albeit extremely complicated way in which official logs
could be expunged without leaving any sign at all of the expungement.

Shortly after leaving-in-order-to-rearrive, the logs were allowed to
record the new approach. The sensors said there were people gathered
nearby who would see the module as it landed or shortly after descent,
therefore a *witnessed initial arrival* should occur without problems.
The protocol absolutely required that all initial arrivals be witnessed
by local inhabitants; that the arrival be *recorded* (including statements
made by the arriving official in the local language, offering friendship,
brotherhood, trade contracts, voting rights, or whatever other inclusive
word seemed appropriate), and that copies of that recorded arrival be
provided simultaneously to all planetary population groups. In cases
where modules had made contact without a *properly witnessed initial ar-*

rival, whole planetary populations had fallen prey to rumors of invasion from space.

This arrival would have been properly witnessed IF the module's automatic landing sequence had not considered the surface to be landed upon as a *solid* part, when in fact the *solid* part was actually *below* a *liquid* part. Either the charts were wrong or something out there had been modified. OR, which Balytaniwassinot gravely suspected, it was piloting an *improperly programmed module*! Balytaniwassinot's usual module was being refitted, and this one had been offered as a temporary replacement.

When arriving on any NEW planet, any properly programmed IGM automatically engaged the "analysis of landing site" series before setting down. This planet, Earth, was considered to be NEW—that is, new to sector scrutiny, though it was far from new to Balytaniwassinot. IF the "analysis of landing site" had been engaged, it would have detected water where no water had previously been, and there would have been no crash. Instead, the module had plunged loudly through the water and into the fabric of the world, occasioning a considerable quake. The module seemed to be undamaged, but there had been damage to the local fabric, which had to be repaired to prevent further subsidence. IGMs were not routinely equipped for repair while submerged; it had taken a good deal of both time and originality, during which the module had been invisible underwater. The people, persons, local inhabitants who were *needed* to make this a *witnessed initial arrival* had meantime dispersed. Dispersed completely! Leaving no sign they had been here where there had been a considerable clutter of persons and equipment before!

When Balytaniwassinot had first arrived on Earth a long, long time ago, the planet had indeed been NEW to galactic visits. At that time ten or twelve hundred years ago, Earth had not been listed. Since it had been unlisted, it had also been unscheduled for inspection, evaluation, or analysis. When Balytaniwassinot/Fixit had happened upon the solar system, Self was merely taking a little side trip, an unscheduled dawdle, an unauthorized wander. It was notable that even on that occasion, very shortly after being hired, Fixit had already figured out how to fiddle the logs. Indeed, if it had not figured out how to fiddle the logs, Self would not have accepted the job. Some creatures, Self told itself, were simply not designed to accept supervision.

So, on that long-ago first visit, without authorization or any previous information, Fixit had landed to do a preliminary analysis only to have the analysis forced upon it. Fixit was new to the job, a neophyte, but it had taken only a glance to learn that the planet was all wrong and getting wronger by the hour. The dominant race had largely wiped out all other creatures. The world had overheated. Something called a Big Kill had been or still was going on, and it was eliminating most of the dominant species. Since members of this dominant species (beings that were mostly myth-driven and incapable of analytical thought) were the source of the world's wrongness, their reduction in numbers was probably not a bad thing.

But, the longer Fixit stayed, the more of the dominant species it met, the more troubled it became. If the remainder of the dominant species had been *uniformly wrong*, any galactic officer making an evaluation would have done its duty and would have immediately eliminated the species, notifying the Supreme Council it had done so. That officer would in all probability also have received a bonus or upgrade in pay or position.

But the species, what was left of it, was *not* uniformly wrong, and Balytaniwassinot was *not* just any galactic officer. Balytaniwassinot felt the members of the species who were *not wrong* did not deserve elimination. Though in the minority, they had bao and were therefore worth considerable effort. Besides, Self's pride got in the way. At that time Self was still young. No one in authority had ordered Fixit to save those of Earth who had bao, a task that would require great amounts of time and ingenuity. Given the cost, it was unlikely anyone in authority would have done so. However . . . one might attempt it on the sly.

The problem as Balytaniwassinot saw it was: *Separate the part of the population who are myth-driven from that part who are bao-driven. Myth-driven persons believe they are immortal, god-governed, god-shaped, that the universe was constructed just for their use. They also perceive that their directive deity drives them not through reason, but through reward and punishment, like livestock.*

Bao-driven people do not believe they are immortal or that they are shaped like god or that the universe or any world in it was made for their use. Therefore, those who are bao-driven should be willing to change shape, disvow ownership of the planet, and refuse to be motivated by threat or reward that is contrary to reason.

That was it. Problem and solution. Mankind could be given the choice of turning into something else. Balytaniwassinot spent considerable time thinking about what that something else should be and was influenced, to some extent, by recent visits to aqueous planets in the Yugrit sytem. That would take care of the actuality. Balytaniwassinot would have to take care of the paperwork! And the paperwork would have to go back to a time before Balytaniwassinot had been born!

Starting from that point, the best solution Balytaniwassinot could devise required a few very brief time trips back a thousand Earth years or so from that time. Modules were equipped for time travel. Time travel was seldom if ever approved in areas that were interdependent as a time-line change on one world might have an adverse effect upon a linked world, setting up a chain reaction. However, Earth had had only *one* extra-system contact with a world part called *Lom,* on Ocalcalcalip, and though there had been some information shared subsequently, there had been no further physical involvement. Changing the past on *this* planet *after* that contact would not affect the other planet. Once the initial shove was given, the plan would require interim adjustments to keep it moving in the right direction, but if successful, the bao-driven population would be saved.

The first thing to be done was to create an Order to Exterminate Species and get it into the files a very long time ago. The dominant species had already given grounds for extermination and, indeed, was already exterminating itself, so the file would merely establish that galactic officers may have put a finger in the pie. So to speak. All those killing machines and wars and so forth, in fact anything the dominant species had done, would be presumed to have happened in accordance with the extermination order. All such orders were required to "seem" natural to the planet's history, so that part would be easy.

Then to save the members of the dominant race that *did not* deserve extermination, there would have to be some kind of exception made. Balytaniwassinot studied the species. It watched them. It looked at the things they had done and not done. Eventually, it drafted an Amendment Resolution.

Amendment Resolution below, voted unanimously by Galactic Supreme Council preliminary to carrying out the order:

Re: Mankinds. Order Exterminate Species (WmQr988856082).
Remarkable talents shown by a minority of this species indicate the possible presence of bao: individuals possessing bao
are invariably exempt from Orders to Exterminate Species. To
identify those individuals with bao, present individual mankinds with an extermination problem solvable only through
bao, allowing those with bao to survive.

Getting the papers into the files was no problem. All agents spend
an apprentice century. Balytaniwassinot had spent its apprentice century as a file clerk. The files were foolproof. Everything was entered
five times in five different ways, but Balytaniwassinot knew them all.
First some documentation to establish that this planet had been listed
before. Then the OES defining it as a plague species, and dated long
enough ago that no one remained in office who might have known
about it. And finally, the Amendment Resolution allowing interference
to protect those with bao. All of it long enough ago that no one would
be surprised to have forgotten about it. To Galactic Officer Balytaniwassinot, the planet was NEW. Self imagined its surprise when it dug into
the files and found the planet wasn't new at all. What a shock it would
be! Tsk-tsk. And again, tsk.

However, the intervention had to have happened way back when. It
expunged all reference to the planet from the logs, then *(as he told himself later, to get it moving before Self lost its nerve)* Self returned to Earth and
made a millennial jump back, at which time several preliminary tasks
were accomplished.

First: The pathetic, half-dead little world spirit of Earth was encouraged (covertly) to send a plea for help to the world part Lom on
Ocalcalcalip. Actually, Self had had to bribe the Earth World Spirit.
Self had promised to send her somewhere else that did not have mankinds or anything resembling mankinds on it. Poor thing had done
nothing but grieve over her poor world for centuries, and she had
earned a long vacation.

Second: Self had gone off to Ocalcalcalip (O'kl-KAL-k'lip), where
the world spirit of the planet part called Lom (a creature known as
Ganver) passed the request on to the ocean planet Squamutch, where
Balytaniwassinot, under a (false) diplomatic identity, had already con-

vinced the ruler the planet needed more dry land to grow more of its cash crop, fligbine. Squamutch was a very large ocean planet with only a few islands suitable for growing things. Fligbine was a euphoric drug much in demand. Fixit assisted in acquiring and diverting a wormhole to carry away the excess water, one end on Squamutch, the other deep in the oceans of Earth.

Third: The scientists of Tingawa were provided with some advanced research on various genetic applications along with the information that in ten to twelve hundred years, the earth would be underwater. Balytaniwassinot had enjoyed this visit. It had gone in disguise as "Wazeer Noht" and had spoken through a voice synthesizer. It had later learned that the visit was now known as "the Visitation."

When Self returned to present time, water had been flowing into Earth for a thousand years. Tingawans had argued for centuries about the flooding forecast. All the figures checked out. The earth would indeed be underwater. Wasn't it lucky Tingawan scientists had received this information about certain genetic discoveries as long ago as they did. No one was upset or disrupted enough to start a national or international panic, and there was plenty of time for world-drowning changes to creep up on them gradually.

Luckily, Balytaniwassinot's people were extremely long-lived. Short-lived agents would be no use at all, so galactic agents were chosen only from among the long-lived peoples. Thus Balytaniwassinot could look forward to the next couple of dozen or so human generations, and now (though Balytaniwassinot was actually making a follow-up visit to his last half-dozen follow-up visits), as far as the omnipresent log was concerned, THIS VISIT HERE AND NOW WOULD APPEAR TO BE THE INITIAL ARRIVAL. Accomplished, of course, in accordance with the "FIRST ARRIVAL PROTOCOL."

The next item on *that* protocol was to sense the surroundings with the *full* array. Those watching from the hillside, having witnessed the emrgence of the spherical thing, saw a tall, spiky prong emerge from the sphere. The prong went up and up and up, extruded several spines; then it twirled and twirled and went *ploonk* back where it came from.

Something gleeped.

"What in the devil . . ." snarled Abasio *(the witness).*

"What's it?" demanded Coyote *(the other witness), who had just arrived.*

The gleep indicated the presence of *Oracle*. This current trip, in current time, had been authorized on the basis of two items: *Oracle* being item number one. Though it was a perfect cover for its operation, Balytaniwassinot had really rather hoped this was a mistake and there *would not be* any *Oracle*. It would have preferred a worldwide plague! It had hoped in vain. Tsk, and again, tsk, and a sigh. All false hopes abandoned, Self would take a deep breath and then do the next step in the protocol. Self accordingly breathed heavily, not once but three times, and uttered a brief curse. The log would record its annoyance at the very idea of Oracle. This was not only allowable but expected!

Item number two in authorizing this trip had been a rumored conspiracy to kill off an entire species of naturally evolved creatures on the world Earth by drowning: a novel method when applied interplanetarily. The creatures destined for termination were known as mankinds or humans, and oddly enough, the Galactic Congress had long ago voted eradication of this same race on the grounds that it was a plague race because it had left its home planet and infected another planet. Yet another case of the left wallub not knowing what the right finglesnitter was up to. This one was easy. Balytaniwassinot knew exactly where the paperwork was, having put it there!

There had been one minor annoyance. Representatives of an antidrug organization who were visiting the court of Plethrob on Gobanjur were appalled to find the people of that planet uniformly addicted to fligbine. The delegation had been even more appalled to learn that the large ocean planet Squamutch was diverting much of its oceans to a planet called Earth in order to dry out more of its own surface. This was being done to allow even larger crops of fligbine to sell to Gobanjur. The organization appealed to the Intelligent Creatures Rights Organization.

It had therefore been necessary for Fixit to arrange that the entire diplomatic corps attend a banquet also attended by several Gobanjurians who had just returned from worlds where no fligbine had been available. The normal, unhampered behavior of undrugged Gobanjurians was both witnessed and experienced. The diplomats who survived had subsequently presented their point of view forcibly to the antidrug organization, which had promptly withdrawn its complaint.

In the face of this diplomatic brouhaha, the order for eradication of mankind had been temporarily suspended—and some interfering creature had pointed out that *innocent* threatened species had a right to wipe out the threatener. Planet-wide drowning, however, despite the level of provocation by the threatening species, was not *species specific,* and the Galactic Congress had *NOT voted to wipe out snakes, butterflies, elephants, earthworms, eels, mongooses, okapis, ostriches, owls, oysters, or a list of other creatures that seemed endless.* The rumored conspiracy did, however, enable Balytaniwassinot to get oh-so-very-casually involved. "Oh, while I'm down that way, why don't I add this silly flooding brouhaha to my agenda." Having involved Lom, Ocalcalcalip, and Squamutch initially, Self now needed to extract them, painlessly he hoped.

So to work! After all, Balytaniwassinot's nickname was "FIXIT." FIXING was what it did. Now Self's *official* task was to investigate this whole three-planet-involved world drowning without committing an "Arbitrarily Imposed Solution," the dread AIS that had cost so many galactic officers their rankings. Once intelligence emerged upon a planet, Fixers were forbidden to use "Arbitrarily Imposed Solutions." One had to accept freedom of choice in order to work for the Galactic Affairs Office. *Intelligent beings who had developed language were supposed to be able to solve their own problems regardless of how many times certain ones of them had proved they couldn't solve getting out of bed (or equivalent) in the morning (or equivalent).*

Balytaniwassinot knew the supposed "conspirators" quite well: Ocalcalcalip, which contained the separable geographic part (a peninsula) named Lom. That one was easy. *"Yes, Lom had some reason to help the Earth spirit wipe out mankind, but Lom's world-part spirit had no information concerning other living, speaking creatures that would be at risk. Lom's involvement was therefore innocent."* This had the advantage of being true. Besides, Lom had made an offer of remediation, and Balytaniwassinot had accepted the agents of this reparation: three travelers (female mankinds, one of them made out of rock) who had volunteered to assist in adapting to sea life such creatures as Griffins along with any others who wished to be adapted.

The other world involved was Squamutch, *which—provably—had donated the water in order to solve an agricultural and cash-flow problem, also quite innocently.* Any planet was allowed to change its life balance to make it more productive.

And, as for Gobanjur, one would simply not mention Gobanjur! Galacti-
cally, Gobanjur was considered an embarrassment. Not every planet had a ruler
whose . . . sexual parts had been increased to the point they had exploded during
a banquet for the diplomatic corps. Ambassadress Malanako had brought suit for
sexual assault after being hit in the face by fragments of said parts. Note: Under
great pressure from galactic officers, the Gobanjur congress subsequently replaced
the Bigger-Bigger male rulers with female persons chosen on the basis of ability.
(Bigger-Bigger sexual parts had been achieved by force feeding of certain foods
and drugs, and elections had been replaced by committees with measuring tapes.
These organs had been useful only for display, as their size and weight eliminated
any possibility of being used in any other way.)

The observers were not troubled by eliminating mankind, but they
were troubled by the ancillary effects. Foremost among them was the
imminent threat of extinction to other, innocent Earthian species: Griffins, yes, but also thousands of species of running, flying, squirming
creatures, all still extant and needing perching places or solidity beneath them.

However, there *was* no real threat of extinction! Foreseeing several
hundred years ago that mankind would be lethal to any world it lived
upon, Balytaniwassinot had begun to prevent its happening! Breeding
populations of every single Earthian creature either already had been
or soon would be moved to a wonderful world without a single mankind
on it. Balytaniwassinot had found the unoccupied world a long time
ago: mountain and plain, jungle and desert, river and lake and sea, all
well populated by vegetation only, none of it sensate. Balytaniwassinot
added nourishing Earthian vegetation to this untouched world after
determining that this would not injure any native vegetation. When one
took up a square mile of jungle to a depth of fifty feet, and a square mile
of ocean reef with a similar underlayment, and transplanted them onto
another world a few thousand years ago, all kinds of things crawl out
and multiply.

Then, subsequent to this discovery, every time Self went out on a
trip, Self took along a mover full of Earth creatures, transporting them
several millennia back in time once on the planet, so they'd have a long
time to multiply before the next load arrived. Balytaniwassinot stopped
by to check on progress at some point during every trip. Every living
thing had been moved in order of the food chain, most edible and

smallest first. Lots and lots of little fish before any bigger fish. Lots and lots of mice before things that lived on mice. Self was now at the point of moving the big fellows: the big herbivores and predators: elephants, rhinos, hippos, crocodiles, whales . . . maybe not whales. Whales and dolphins would continue to be very happy on the new earth. Some of them were at the top of the food chain except for mankinds, and they might enjoy humans on a more fluid earth so long as the humans were unarmed.

(Fixit had had a junior colleague who had majored in sea-world linguistics work up a whale lexicon, figuring Earth's sea people were going to need it. The whales had told him they weren't going to stand for any nonsense, so dropping off the lexicon at the Sea Duck installations was one of the things he intended to do this trip. Since human lungs couldn't manage the sounds, they'd have to invent a whale horn that would. Helpfully, Balytaniwassinot had arranged for the construction of a prototype.)

All this activity (except for the time travel) was buried in a report Fixit had made a very long time ago, making quite sure that the report was buried in the files where it could be found if someone looked for it—as Fixit had repeatedly done, whenever he wished to append an updated detail. Of course, someone would have to look for it very hard. "Yes, I knew I had reported it! See there, I reported the whole thing, and when I didn't hear to the contrary, I figured I could go on with it." By the time anyone went hunting, the stamped approvals supposedly provided by "higher-ups" would have outlasted the stampers. He had picked the really ancient higher-ups, the ones with the shortest life (and attention) spans. The last one, old Fliggerybat Nognose, had died just last trip, but that was unquestionably his stamp! No one else would think of using the Nognose nostrils in their coat of arms!

So, reason number one for this trip to Earth had been dealt with. No one had acted maliciously. The two planets that started the flood did so for innocent reasons—well, reasonably innocent—and all was working out well.

Reason number two for being on this planet was still to be dealt with. Balytaniwassinot had dealt with Oracles before and had not liked it—them—then. His opinion was not likely to change now.

Well, he would deal with the Oracles. And finally, as addenda, there would be all the little Listener requests for help that had been accumulating for quite some little time. Pleas. Screams. Childish, but nonetheless pitiable tales of injustice and evil referring to the basic issues and adding dozens of others. Oh, yes, dozens of them. Self had them on Self's memo leaf together with identities of the requesters. Persons known as Grandma and Willum and Needly and Xulai, and even Abasio, who did not even know he had submitted a request. Oh, Balytaniwassinot felt it knew them so well.

Time to move on! Self was muttering, occasionally yelling. Yes, the landing had gone badly but the damage had been rectified. Let headquarters determine who, what, or which was responsible for issuance of an IGM that had not been properly programmed. THEN it would be of consequence and Balytaniwassinot looked forward to testifying against whatever *thrumdraggit gatiplogs* had been responsible.

Irritation overcame prudence and the words "thrumdraggit gatiplogs" rang out across the shoreline and stirred echoes from the far hills.

"What's a thrumdraggit gatiplog?" asked Beaver thoughtfully.

"Shhh," said Precious Wind, pressing the buttons on her ul xaolat *for linguistic search and retrieval, universal. After some time, "gatiplog": term of derogation, literally dirt eater. "Thrum": small, ugly animal. "Draggit": misshapen.*

The IGM sensed people present. Good. It would be a "well-witnessed arrival" after all. Announcing one's presence was always an interesting interlude. Sometimes even amusing, as when one had to round up native creatures fleeing in terror and paralyze them temporarily. Or when one happened upon a world that conducted conversations in smells. Or a world on which the first word of introduction required four days, galactic time, to say in color emanations. Still, in general, introductions were creators of jollification. Self pushed a few levers, turned a small wheel, and the surface module cast about itself, rather in the manner of a large dog smelling out a trail before trundling away to the northeast, following the horses and wagons of the travelers. Inside it, Fixit leaned back and sighed. *How many Earth years ago was it—not counting the time trips—that Self had begun its plan? Several hundred years spent arranging for A to be born and when grown up mate with B and give birth to C, who when grown fathered D and then E, who gave birth to F, G, H, and finally I, who when grown fathered J, marvelous J, a really fun companion who—just a few decades ago—began playing role after role after role with a seductress named Lillis, as J had been repeatedly reequipped to do so.*

Now that the last act was about to be played out, Self had actually become quite fond of some of the characters. Lillis/Grandma (wouldn't she be surprised if she knew!). And little Needly. Amazing. And the other young one, this Willum. Self had had *nothing whatsoever* to do with the planning of Willum, and what a strange young creature it was! Balytaniwassinot's people were quite differently reared, but sometimes Fixit actually envied the mankinds some aspects of their fathering and mothering.

Last act coming up. Climax. Finale. And the opening to the last act would be at the end of the trail the horse and wagon had made, the trail Balytaniwassinot was following with no apprehensions whatsoever. Because . . .

If it didn't work? If total failure resulted?

No one would even blink and it would not be held against Fixit.

Since "mankind" was included in the mix, total failure had been the forecast.

From Cow Bluff's rear end, Abasio watched something resembling an extremely large spherical turtle move out of the water and roll purposefully away in the direction of Wide Mountain Plaza. He said to Precious Wind, "Would you mind telling me what in the hilarious halls of the utterly ridiculous that is? And where's it going?"

Precious Wind said nothing, but Coyote, who had just arrived, replied, "We dunno. But we can track it, 'Basio."

"A blind man with two left feet could track it! It's got wheels. It makes four separate great, round ditches in the sand."

"Thas true. Just thought we'd offer," said Bear. "You got anything for breakfast?"

It was the unanimous decision of the group consisting of four humans, four horses, one coyote, and one bear that they would have breakfast before following whatever the thing was—that was following the wagons and horses—that were undoubtedly going to be following the supply wagon—that was following its own trail back to Wide Mountain Plaza.

The IGM had decided to improve the landscape. (Balytaniwassinot was napping and had neglected to turn off the optimize switch governing travel conditions. During most of the trip the horses et al. found themselves on a paved road.)

THAT NIGHT THE PLAZA WAS lit with several fires. Lathered horses had brought slightly-in-advance warning of the approach of the Thing. The Thing had approached without deviating from its course. What was possibly the straightest road and probably the only paved road on the planet now joined Cow Bluff and Wide Mountain Plaza. When it woke, Balytaniwassinot knew it would have to remove the paving if the man-kinds didn't want it. Arbitrarily Imposed Pavement was no doubt con-trary to policy. The module rolled to a stop in the plaza.

From the surrounding buildings people emerged, some looking rather fearful, others merely interested. Abasio and his group rode up to surround the Thing. Some of them, including Abasio himself, dis-mounted. Others teetered nervously atop weary steeds.

There was a loud clang, and a wedge-shaped piece of the Thing came loose at the top and the sides. Falling to the ground, the piece formed a ramp, wider at the bottom, down which came . . . something.

It was willowy, said Abasio to himself. Willowy and yet probably very strong. As a young willow tree might be if made out of steel cables. Roughly an erect cylinder or trunk, it walked on angled limblike limbs arranged around the bottom, six of them, each ending in a sorta-foot, lead foot different from side foot different from hind foot. It had several, six, arms that were also limblike. The arms ended in various numbers of fingers that were obviously designed for various purposes. Several seemed to be intended as screwdrivers; one was unmistakably a spoon. Abasio found himself searching for a finger ending in a cork-screw. None. Pity; he'd had hopes.

The being had a nodule at the top that might be regarded as a head. After a moment or two it really appeared to be a head, as it had suddenly acquired a nose, mouth, two eyes, two ears, and . . . what was supposed, Abasio thought, to pass for hair. With each ensuing moment that passed, these features grew more . . . familiar. It was adopting local . . . color.

"I greet you," said the creature. "I am titled Balytaniwassinot. I come from far away and bring greetings from the galactic overlords, whose humble servant I am."

No one said anything, so what the hell? Abasio filled in. "We greet you in return. We are . . . amazed that you speak a language we can understand. Did you fall, drop . . . plunge into that lake back there?"

"Unfortunate but true. It was not . . . supposed to be there. Planetary charts are no longer accurate. There have been great . . . changes in recent . . . periods of time. Is this not true?'

Abasio nodded. He supposed so. The creature he confronted was not half as scary as the three he'd confronted under the Gaddir House, and they hadn't eaten him. Chances were, this one wouldn't either. He cleared his throat. "Are you here for some . . . ah, purpose?"

Good, good! thought Balytaniwassinot. At least purpose was recognized. Could not get on with job until purpose was noted. "I am . . ." It paused, adjusted its resonator for clarity. "I am titled Balytaniwassinot, also short-named Fixit! I will explain name. 'Baly' means first-chosen one, eldest in family. 'Tani' means gender, I am a tan second gender of my five-gendered people. 'Wassinot' is earned name, last part of name given when creature manifests skill, talent, propensity. In my case, 'wassinot' was given because of propensity to mend, repair, put in order, reestablish purposeful use of things. In your language 'wassinot' would be . . . 'fixit.' I am therefore Eldest Tan Who Fixes Things. You may call me 'Fixit.' I am . . . an official of the galactic . . . ah, supervisory group. I have been sent."

"Sent by whom?" said someone else.

Balytaniwassinot turned. A person wrapped in a colorful shawl-blanket approached. A person who by its own manner defined itself as "important." Balytaniwassinot bowed. "Personage," he said.

"Why are you here?" asked the personage.

"One was sent. One was told to find certain loci." Balytaniwassinot unfurled its memory leaf from under its fourth arm and referred to it. "One may find oneself anywhere in a galaxy by depending upon a concatenation of loci. There is present near here one female . . . Griffin. Griffin being a human-constructed, self-aware, basically mammalian, formerly mythical being with wings and the features of eagle, lion, and so forth. Is this so?"

"This is so," said one of the creatures.

Balytaniwassinot said, "Check mark." Self made a check mark, noting the local time and the galactic date. "Also is present, one female young of this Griffin?"

"This is also true." This answer came from someone else.

Balytaniwassinot directed its face to smile. "You see, check mark, another check mark. Is also here one very large female mountain? Ah, maternal mountain?"

The creatures looked at one another. The personage before Self spoke: "I am Wide Mountain Mother."

Balytaniwassinot allowed personage to see Self suffered confusion. Being confused always pleased newly approached races. It diluted one's impressive superiority, allowing one to seem more . . . local. "One is not mountain," it said with intentional bafflement and a slight hint of charming confusion.

The speaker turned and pointed imperiously at the eastern horizon. "Do you see the end of the desert there?"

"It is apprehended."

"Do you see that far to the north, that way, it rises and goes a long, long way south before it lowers itself again?"

"I do so perceive!"

"Most mountains stand among other mountains and most of them are tall. That one is alone and very, very wide. It is called Wide Mountain. Our people here are the Wide Mountain people. I am Mother-Most of those people, and I am Wide Mountain Mother. Do you understand?"

"One apprehends. Another check mark! Now. Does one have here a Griffin demanding for its child, children, future in the seas?"

"We do."

"Check mark. Does female offspring of same concur in demand?"

"It does."

"Check mark." Balytaniwassinot let the scroll extend farther. "Does world suffer incursion of creature calling self 'Oracles'?"

For a moment no one spoke, then Grandma said, "I'm afraid it does. Yes."

"Label pertaining to self?" Fixit directed a digit at her pointedly, as though it had no idea who or what she was. Fixit had been present at her birth, though unnoticeably.

"I am called . . . Lillis, or, more often, Grandma."

"You are knowing said Oracles?"

"Yes," she said disconsolately. Her whole world was going to hell in a handbasket. She just knew it.

"Check mark. We do proceed, do we not? Now, also, is one here recognizing name 'Crash'?"

"I do," said Abasio, as though in a dream. "He's a boy. Son of Jinian. He's somewhere else."

"Somewhere else being Lom section of Ocalcalcalip. Where is Crash-son-of-Jinian being seen by you?"

"I have repeating dreams. In my dream he's in the tower, damn it. Always in the tower."

"Describing tower, please. Also does one here have recognition of statue of woman? Very unhappy woman?"

"The tower's white. It has a bell and a pool and the statue of the woman was in the tower," said Abasio. "Every damned time."

"Very good!" crowed Fixit, smiling broadly to remove the residuary apprehension that was still detectable in the surrounding . . . throng, group, assembly. "Broad Geological-Protrusion Maternal Creature, can you provide help to move a heaviness out of intragalactic wormhole module? Men? Strong, yes? Something to use for rollers. Yes?"

They all watched, as though in a trance, while several logs were fetched as rollers for a dozen of the Wide Mountain men to use in rolling a stone statue of a contorted woman out of the . . . wormhole ship, down the ramp, and onto the plaza.

"Oh, poor thing," cried Xulai and Precious Wind, almost as one voice.

"Not long poor thing, not long," said Balytaniwassinot. "Very soon thousand-year time is up. Woman received thousand-year stone curse on Lom. Self not understanding curse methodology, but is evidently powerful on Lom. Curse is stone-for-one-thousand-years. However, curse is not intelligent. Curse cannot compute slow time or fast time; years there not so long as years here; added centuries due to crossing very many galactic time zones. Add fact also: wormhole time is compressed! One cannot go home again. Too soon ago. Now. Only few more points to check off list. Do persons here know spirit of planet. Urth, not?"

"We call it Earth, yes," said Xulai. "I . . . we aren't aware of a spirit . . ."

"Being unaware not surprising. Too many mankinds always sucking makes very weak, sick spirit. Trees fall, spirit weakens. Oceans stink. Spirit weakens. Never very strong. All those ice ages, extinctions. Then plague of mankinds. Weakening, very weakening."

It turned and called, its voice suddenly becoming a piercing sound that fled from where they were to the farthest mountains and retuned as echo: "Gaea! Gaea!"

They were silent, and it was not until several moments had passed that they saw the tiny, virtually transparent being standing next to Balytaniwassinot. The galactic officer patted it on its . . . upper protrusion. "T'cha. Poor thing, poor thing, why didn't you ask for help? Umm?"

"Din't know how," it whimpered. "Hiding. 'Most no place left to hide . . ."

"She'll need remedial care," said Balytaniwassinot, fixing them all with an unmistakable glare. "This is despicable what mankinds have done to her. I'll be taking over for her while she's in rehab and you will not try any of your nonsense with me. Oh, she's in bad shape. Oh, shame on you. Shameshameshame! All of you."

"I resent that 'all of you' bit," said Grandma. "Some of us have been doing our very best to stop the misuse—"

"And much good has your best done! Fiddling with Oracles. You don't have time for . . . Ah. I think my companions on this journey are stirring." It went into the ship and returned after a time with two women. One older, but not aged. One quite young but with an air of strain and loss in her face. Immediately, two women from one of the surrounding houses moved forward. Wide Mountain Mother nodded at them, and they escorted the two passengers toward the nearest house, Mother's house. Placing and replacing the rolling logs, the men pushed the statue along behind them.

Mother said to Fixit, "We presume hospitality may be offered, hot tea. A comfortable place to sit and talk?"

Balytaniwassinot nodded. Then it made a noise, rather like a trumpet fanfare. When all eyes were fixed on it, Self began to orate, hands raised. "Much time ago from this place two ships went to Ocalcalcalip. Unfortunate choice in one respect. Silly world spirit there played dolly house with planet. Each room separate little piece. No doors. No stairs. Nothing connected, nothing allowed to connect. Ocean tides messy, washes up things from ocean bottom. Spirit moves moon away, stops tides. Now no ocean currents to speak of, reefs cutting them off. Spirit doesn't like wind, makes things dusty. Fixes planet so it is without winds. Mountains cutting them off. Everything local, small, cute.

"One part of planet, off by itself, peninsula name of Lom. In spiritual vacuum Lom develops its own spirit, arising out of need. Lom spirit is calling itself Ganver! Original world spirit doesn't mind, has enough trouble keeping everything clean, pretty elsewhere. Lucky, your ships go to that place: Lom. Otherwise all people on ships die of being bored, wearing dolly dresses. Oh, shame! Ocalcalcalip world should have been fixed long time ago! Am fixing now! Spirit has been moved to nice little asteroid with lots of meteor holes needing curtains with ruffles, no atmosphere to hold dust, no water to make mud, everything very neat. Former sectional spirit, Ganver, will be taking over planet Ocalcalcalip."

"Do you mean that really happened?" gasped Grandma. "Curtains? On meteor holes?"

"I speak . . . meteor-phorically but truly. Spirit was more interested in orderly than in fertile, more interested in pretty than in useful. World was god-awful mess. But neat. Happens sometimes. Galactic large projectile has nifertug with second-sex child—*wait, words ambigmeous . . .* Need REFERENCE." The last two words were uttered as a command. Behind it, in the ship, a light went on. A sparkling device appeared above the creature's head.

It nodded and went on. "Ah, *Bigshot* has *friend* with *daughter.* Daughter aspiring to be planetary spirit. Bigshot pulls ropes, ah . . . *strings* . . . arranges for girl getting job. Spirit has no big image, sees only small things. Cannot see forest for tall wooden growths. Cannot see mountain range for big rocks. Cannot see pasture for grass. Thinks wind unnecessary because is blowing dust or because wind is not pretty. Tsk. Mistake.

"So, in absence of sensible planetary governance, several local places of Ocalcalcalip grew their own spirits. One of them, Ganver, is now taking over planet. Installing weather there now! Creature had good sense, good feedback systems by way of chemical signals. Good local place. Your ships landed there. Ganver, good, kind creature, didn't know mankinds are plague. Didn't know poor design meant creatures breed like small four-legged grain thieves! *Lookee me, lookee me, I got big whacky-doodle. I like play with big whacky-doodle, make many baby.* Right?"

Grandma spoke in a distant voice. "Sounds like you've met Mobwows before."

"Mobwow?" Fixit uttered the command again. "REFERENCE." The

device reappeared. "Reference says *you* make word! *Monkey-brain*. Willy-wagger. With Oh Oh?"

"How did you know that? Needly and I were the only ones there!"

"Reference is everywhere. Simultaneously absorbing words, sound words, smell words, touch words, all communication methods. Reference is very good spy. Has ears everywhere. And eyes, noses, oh, yes. Mobwow! Very perfect word! Will remember word!

"Fixit is experienced agent. One thousand years in training. Now on nine thousand nine hundred ninety-ninth job. Next one, I get new hat, with gold on." Balytaniwassinot smiled brilliantly, rainbows reflected from its teeth, splashing off in all directions. "You are not only plague in universe! I have seen others. Some worse. Some turned over new record page and became reasonable creatures. I will talk to you, Grandma, about Mobwows and Oracles. I think you already know about them, it. Amateurs. Never answer questions, no? Afraid they may say wrong thing. Cannot allow self to say wrong thing. Pretend to be mysterious. All creature needs to do to seem wise is to keep communication system inactive. Others think silence sign of wisdom. Not unfounded. In many, silence would be sign of wisdom. Not Oracles. Oracles have no wisdom, only able to act mysterious. It/they don't answer? Because it/they don't know. Good mechanics, though. Something wrong with your filth flusher. Oracles very good at thinking up Arbitrarily Imposed Solutions. Oracles say, 'Remove filth flusher, tell creature to excrete on tree root.'

"You had creature on this world much like Oracles. I forget name. Will remember . . . ah, yes, was called Poly-ti-shun. Famous for Arbitrarily Imposed Solutions: AIS: *'Have problem? Person doing something we disapprove of? Pass law against, build more prisons.'* Was made extinct during Big Kill. What is saying? *Even black cloud has silver lining.* Yes?"

Balytaniwassinot seemed to take a deep breath. It shook its head, then smiled again. "This Earth is not bad place. Seems worth saving, no! We will see what can be done short of AIS, and I know you will help me willingly, with energy and dedication. So I will stay awhile. Eventually, my passengers will want to return home. Ah . . . even the third one, see. No more rock. They stay now for a while before I take them home."

They all turned, following its gaze. Outside Wide Mountain Mother's house the men had been unable to roll the statue through the door, and during the process the statue had softened and was trying to get up. Wide Mountain women were already beside her, helping her up. Her clothes were falling into dust. Wide Mountain Mother snatched off her shawl and wrapped it around the former statue. They moved into the house.

The visitor suddenly snapped its fingers, or what might have been fingers. "Saying 'rock' reminds me. Another loci. You have boy who is rock, wounded? Here?"

"Yes," cried Needly. "Yes we do. Willum."

"My passengers. Those women in the house? Aha! I will tell story. Be listening carefully.

"I am on Lom, recruiting Ganver to be world spirit for whole planet, we are near Listener, which is crying plea for help, help, help. Cry for help is coming from planet you call Earth. Here. Person called Needly is asking help from Listener here on Earth. Person called Abasio is asking help. Person called Grandma—that one is you, right? Asking help. Also Xulai pleading help. This Listener on Lom and the one on Earth are very closely tied. All the time messages, back and forth, back and forth. I am telling Ganver what is trouble, Earth is being drowned. Ganver says it knows all about it. It happens because long ago, before so much weakened, Earth spirit has asked for mankinds to be exterminated because mankinds are killing planet.

"Plea for help has long ago been answered by Ganver, who has asked Squamutch to send extra water to Earth to exterminate mankinds. Mankinds refuse extermination, change themselves into fish. Or something similar. In meantime, boy is rock, boy is wounded, very fine exemplary boy much needed by certain creatures destined to be *pivorot* . . . Reference! . . . that is . . . nexus, pivotal, ah . . . *necessary good persons*. So Ganver is saying it knows solutions to problems. How Griffins can go to sea. How boy can be healed. How everything can be done with consent of persons involved. No AIS. NO Arbitrarily Imposed Solution! Ganver is sending three women to fix situation. That is why they are here, partly. I have brought one shape-changer. I have brought one healer. I have brought one witch who is also linguist. Ganver has restored some talents just for this purpose. Since they are here, fortuitously, they will no doubt, along with other things, help take the rock from the boy."

Balytaniwassinot did something that sounded like a sigh. "Now, for today that is enough. Abasio, will you visit with me for a time? I like simple two-person conversation to become more familiar. We will wander about, learn . . . environment? Yes? I have small mover that flies. I will leave the big one here. We will return soon." And with that, it gestured for Abasio to go into the turtle, then went in and shut the door.

Needly, Grandma, Xulai, Precious Wind, Deer Runner, Coyote, and Bear . . . were left standing in the plaza alone.

Xulai said hesitantly, "We could go over to the wagon and have some tea. I left a kettle keeping warm on the fire before our . . . can't call it a guest, can I?"

Precious Wind growled, "More like the guy who works for the guy who really owns the property we thought we owned, only it turns out we don't even have a lease. And how did it know about Willum? And all those other . . . 'loci.'"

A door opened across the way. Arakny. She stepped outside and beckoned. "All of you, come on in over here. It's chilly out there, coming on for snow, I think. Bear, you and Coyote, too. I have honey. And chicken."

It was the house the three women had been taken into, the three women who were now sitting quietly, drinking tea. Arakny went to one of them. "Everyone, this is Silkhands. She is a healer. The woman next to her is Mavin. She is a shapeshifter, and she is called Mavin Manyshaped . . ."

"I don't believe that," growled Bear—in Bear—to Coyote.

The third woman spoke—in Bear—to Bear: "Just watch her."

And the shape-changer woman turned into a bear. A very nice-looking bear, though small, in order not to rip the clothing she had just been given. Bear felt an unseasonal urge. Bear in dress changed back, whispering, between beautiful bear teeth, "Zorry."

The second woman, Jinian, spoke to Bear again—in Bear. "Don't get any ideas, furry socks. She can make her claws as long as your foot."

Xulai cried, "I thought they'd taken your talents away! I thought you couldn't do those things anymore."

Silkhands answered. "Fixit told you. Jinian and I have had our talents returned, just for this trip. Mavin never lost hers. She fell prey to a curse that was to last a thousand years. The way time gets twisted in wormholes, that's how long it took us to get here. I know Fixit kept taking little side trips through loops that added fifty years there, a hundred somewhere else. Then it'd reverse it on the way back, so we wouldn't have been gone that long. So, Mavin can change shape, and I can heal people, and Jinian can talk to any creature that will talk back and do some witchery, and together, we think maybe we can do something for . . . a boy, and a Griffin, or maybe many Griffins and maybe some other creatures . . ."

"Or maybe," said Needly wearily, half dreaming, "all the creatures on our world."

FIXIT OFFERED ABASIO A DRINK. "You drink happy-making, sensory-negating liquids?" the creature asked. "I have checked database that says you do, including some harmful. This one will not harm you. If you don't like, say so, I have it mix something else."

Abasio inclined his head in what he hoped looked like gracious acceptance. The liquid provided was extremely pleasant, smooth, flavorful, tangy. He sat in one of the several seats around the perimeter of the circular room, noting the picture stuck up above the control panel.

"Is that your child?" he asked.

"Child?"

"Your family . . . offspring. A young one of you created by you?"

"Oh, you mean Blamfos. NO no no. Not the way we do things. No. That one in the picture is twigpit. That is, special-occasion g'forz, food! No, Thanksgiving turkey? No, that is archaic. Christmas pudding? Database says even more archaic. What do you have for special-occasions food?"

"Pumpkin pastry and smashed apple drink for harvesttime. You say that's a picture of food! It looks exactly like you. You mean you eat your own . . ."

"Oh, no, no, no. Would you appreciate explanation?"

Abasio wondered if he could get away with saying no. Decided not. "I would appreciate explanation, yes."

"You have two type persons, right. Male female, right. Fertilizer and accepter, right?"

Abasio considered this an oversimplification, but he said, "Right."

"Our people have five type persons: isk, tan, blag, wurf, and dibble. Are more formal terms, but that is what we usually say. Is bad courtesy, sometimes insult, to call by wrong name. I am tan, so-called First Fertilizer. On your world you are first and only fertilizer and your woman is first and only accepter. On our world Isk is first accepter.

"My world has long, long year. Oh, my, yes, so very long. Winter on my world becomes . . . eternity. It is cold. Ziprogs invade the house, build nests, carry diseases. Everyone catches diseases. Everyone going 'phoo, phoo, phoo' from the lung all the time. Understand?"

"It's cold and uncomfortable, mice invade your houses, you all catch what we call colds, you sneeze on each other, and you're just generally miserable."

"Yes, *is misery*! Good substitutive word! So when world turns more toward sun, comes what you call spring, it is like heaven. 'Heaven' is suitable word for nicest possible imaginary place? Good. We have warm little wind. Happy little frillies on trees. All the isks and tans begin to feel . . . oh so warm and happy and . . . like exploding. You know feeling?"

Abasio flushed. What he was drinking gave him a hint. "Yes, I understand."

Fixit put its hands to its neck, just above the multishoulders, and pointed at . . . well, Abasio might have called them eyelids, a circle of them, a dozen or more, all the way around the neck. "Here, this area called k'fum, it begins to feel very warm and it begins to swell, what is inside grows big." It smiled. "They get VERY BIG and they *protrude* and on the ends they have things like . . . whiskers. Do you know whiskers?"

"Hair," said Abasio, pointing to his own.

"No, thicker than that. But at the end lots of things like hairs . . ."

"F . . . fl . . . filmens. Filaments!" said Abasio.

"Good, yes, two kinds filaments, red ones and brown ones. And all along sides of filaments little . . . nodules, tiny, hundreds and hundreds of them. Those are being willimoxies, red ones, brown ones."

"I shee," Abasio murmured. He didn't, but it might get clearer. His mug was almost empty. Balytaniwassinot refilled Abasio's and its own.

"Meantime," it said, "isks is having similar thing happening. K'fum might be called, in your language . . . *REFERENCE needed!* . . . 'fringe.' That is good word. All around necks of isks and tans are being fringes. Time goes warmer and warmer until one morning all isks and tans wake up feeling OH, MY! All isks and tans run out into fields, people running from everywhere, laughing, and once in fields, isks and tans, they dance. Wind comes up and they dance, they dance, the willimoxies on brown filaments, they begin to swell up, bigger and bigger, brown willimoxies get like balloon, and then they burst! Isk ones burst, tan ones burst, air is full of dusty, smoky . . ."

"Sper . . ."Abasio tried to say.

"Spores!" cried Balytaniwassinot. "Yes, that is right word. Breeze is mixing them, mixing them, meantimes, red filaments of fringe has become all sticky, red fringe is swirling, catching dusty smoky spores. Soon all tans, isks fall down, exhausted from dancing. They sleep there all day. No one bothers. Is bad to bother.

"While they sleep, fringe dries out. Later, isks wake up, tans wake up, go about business. Fringe is now drying out! Hanging around . . . neck like . . . collar. No one very sensible, you know? Silly. Like when drinking k'pir, what is in your cup. Like that. Then is coming rattle time!"

"Rattle time?"

"All along each filament of fringe all red willimoxies are becoming golms. Not *quite* what *seed* is, but something like that. Hard, with shell, and makes happy little rattle when the isks move, the tans move, happy little sound. Everyone hears the sound and laughs, even blags, wurfs, and dibbles. Days and days go by, everyone smiling. Time for fixing soil in fields. Turning over, making smooth, making soft, putting good things in soil. Everyone does that, young ones, old ones, every person helps, even pet quizzinogs out in fields digging, digging. You have quiz-zinogs? To catch ziprogs?"

"Cats," murmured Abasio. No, cats didn't dig. "Terriers dig and catch mice. Yes, many people have them."

"Good. Is always good, finding similarities. Now comes golm-swat time. Need coolish day, must be little breeze, no big wind. Isks and tans dance in the fields, jump up and down, hit own fringe with fingers, hit other people's fringe with fingers while singing swat song. Have special fingers for swat. Other peoples gather around edges of fields also singing. When we swat fringe, shells break and ripe golms fall to the ground. Dance must be very active to make golms fall evenly, all over ground. Golms have tiny, tiny legs. If one falls too close to other one, on ground, it will move over. When isks and tans are finished dancing, all the dried pods have fallen off, the parts have shrunken and pulled back into neck, lids shut.

"When isks and tans finish dancing, blags go dance in field. If is no breeze, may wait a while, a day or so. All along back and side arms of blags are sacs that hold what is like mist. Four arms, four sacs each arm. Top one has genetic part for isks, next one is for tans, then blags, then wurfs. Blags dance in pairs, using front arms to press on partner's sacs, now this one, now that one, round and round making little puffs of mist. Little breeze spreads mist. Mist is different colors, it swirls and moves. Blags wave arms, whirl around, sing, dance, wave, until growing part is spread evenly, everywhere. People watching also sing blagging song. Each separate part has its own song.

"Dancing has packed the soil down. Now is time for wurfs. Sun is going down, getting cooler. Must be just cool enough. Wurfs line up at edge of field. You understand are many fields, many places, local people use local fields, different days different places? Maybe not all on same days but when weather is right? Wurf has hands out at sides touching hand of next wurf, looking straight down field, just so far apart, very even, the wurfs march across field, singing plibble song, funny song, plibbing as they go . . ."

"Plibbing?"

"Excreting liquid. *No, no, not waste-produce liquid!* Not dirtiness, no. Fertility liquid. Not covering whole field, no, just spraying here, there, wherever. Like you would take tiny mouthful of water and sploosh it out. Human childrens play so, sometimes? Have play things to sploosh water at one another? Wurfs have gland behind knee. In the marching, wurf bends so"—Fixit did a deep knee bend—"and so, and so, and each time, little puff of liquid spurts out. Where the plibble falls on golms, those golms *at once become maybe-people.* As soon as golm is touched with tiny drop of plibble-mist, it buries self. Is very funny to see. Just-grown persons, you would say 'childs,' they take magnifying glass to edge of field, laughing at funniness of golms burying selves."

Abasio tried to visualize this. "Why ish it funny, Fishit?"

"Just is. Tiny golm, covered all over with legs, all legs going like . . . windmill—you know windmill? Round and round? Very . . . industri-ous. Funny, so little, so . . . vigorous.

"Then, when the wurfs are finished, everyone goes home and the maflipluks—maflipluk is family, you see—sit at supper table in family house and pray for rain. This is done as a courtesy. We have a very rcliable world spirit who always assures rain at the proper time but is courteous to say 'please send rain' and 'thank you for sending rain,' respecting world spirit."

"You did say 'maybe-people'?"

"Yes. Very soon all golms sprout and grow. Those not plibbed are not-people, not-people is food; those having been plibbed are maybe-people. Isk, tan, blag, and wurf have contributed to maybe-people, but they have no nerves, no brain. No feelings. No senses. No emotions. Just good vegetable/animal, very delicious, very nutritious.

"I see you are confused. I am told our planet has very strange genetic systems, but we are accustomed to it." Fixit patted Abasio on one shoulder. "You will understand . . .

"So, time goes by, all the ones in fields, including the not-people and the maybe-people, grow up, put roots down. Machine goes through field cutting narrow paths, leaving rows of not-people and maybe-people in between to grow, to get half tall." Balytaniwassinot stood and put two of its hands at about its midpoint. "So tall as this, half tall. Now inspectors go into fields, look at maybe-people, see how developing, decide whether developed enough to ring bells for choosing time. All of us, isks and tans and blags and wurfs, go into field—walk up and down paths, look carefully at maybe-people, see best ones we can find. Tallest ones, best-shaped, best color. Count arms and legs, feel to see if muscle growing well. Look in mouth to see chew plate forming. Look at shape of node at top to be sure is room for face and hair. Mark all good ones with color spray. Color spray says, *'This one is maybe-person suitable for final choosing.'*

"Then some time later, long enough for maybe-people to get almost full height, inspectors set choosing day. This is separate for each field. Not all fields grow alike. Isks and tans and blags and wurfs go down the rows again, and each person looks only at those approved with color spray, looks and looks, and each chooses two maybe-people that are close together, best two they can find, close together. Only best ones; out of thousands only two. Those two are now *chosen ones* and chosen labels are put on those chosen two. Those two are chosen to become people!"

Abasio found that getting his tongue to make words was becoming difficult. He set the liquid down and resolved not to finish what was in the glass. "You shay labels?"

"Labels are made special by selection department. Selection department knows how many people world is comfortable with. At beginning of year, part of new year celebration, each worthy person receives two labels. Unworthy persons, those who have done evil, no labels. World does not risk unworthy person raising another to be unworthy. Self, Balytaniwassinot, gets two labels with my name on, with my registered number on. Two labels only for any person: never more! When person receives labels, person puts them away safely. No replacements! No mistakes! Only last year a blag was cooked for stealing label. This is a very bad thing to do! Shameful for that blag's maflipluk!

"When labels are all on, everyone finished, all the pairs chosen, fertility officers check off everyone against list. You understand each field has its own people? Mostly people living nearby—all are on list. If someone did not choose, if someone's label is missing, they check! Maybe during year that one wilted or is wilting now; maybe that one is afar on duty for galactic office; maybe that one left labels with family member with certificate allowing family member to choose for the one who is far away. Fertility officers check all such things, remind people who did not show up to come to field and choose, correct records, and not until all checking is finished do they make announcement. 'Choosing is finished.'

"Only then, finally, come the dibbles. Some dibbles are already standing in field next to pair chosen by friend or member of maflipluk. Others go into field and pick pair without knowing who chose. However chosen, each dibble picks one pair. When pair is located, dibble will very carefully dibble both of them: one of pair for chooser, other one of pair for dibble's self. Dibble also has two labels, different colors; and has flag with name and number. Dibble puts one color label on one dibbled for self, puts other color label for person who chose that pair, puts flag in ground to show this pair now *chosen,* and *dibbled,* and *labeled*! Person calls out to fertility officer to check, fertility officer calls out name on pair, names are written down, and flag is recorded. If are not enough dibbles to come out even, fertility officer asks dibblers who have already dibbled one pair to dibble one of a chosen pair for someone else—only one, since there is no dibble for that pair. When all is finished, every already-person has one *dibbled one,* also called *chosen one,* or *becoming-person.* All these names mean the same thing, all are used with dignity.

Only after being dibbled do the chosen ones acquire nerves and brain and consciousness of self."

"They're the ones who are becoming . . . whats?"

"Camrath-selipedes-nosti-famikines. Which I am. Which my people are. Once the *maybe-person* has been dibbled, it is a *becoming-person*. It grows brain, nerves, face, develops gender. This is when we learn what gender chosen one is. Until then, no one knows or cares. We have saying, 'Food has no gender. Families welcome all.' This is happy season, fields full of green, here and there maflipluks of already-people—that is, 'grown-up family' spending time with their becoming-people who are still growing, talking to them about becoming wurf or tan or whatever it is. If one's chosen is a wurf, and one's maflipluk—family—has no wurf, one may be inviting friend who is wurf to come talk to one's chosen. This is time for teaching what is breeding role, how to behave, vocabulary. Sometimes songs. Some even teach reading, though Self thinks it better to wait until one's chosen is ready to go home. In field, sometimes, when learning words, there is a certain regrettable . . . naughtiness. Using impolite words. Self always says: 'They had to learn it from an already-person, and that already-person ought to be ashamed!' "

Abasio was amazed to realize he was visualizing this whole thing. Seeing it. "When are they ready to . . . go home?"

"When big growth roots on bottom of feet dry up. You understand our year is very long; more than fifteen of your years. All this growing has taken a long, long time, and in time you would call autumn, when one's chosen is fully grown and ripe, growth roots have become dry. When almost completely dry, maflipluk comes to help new person get loose from roots. That is when whole maflipluk comes together to name the new person. Maflipluk has decided on name together. Maflipluk helps new person walk first steps on way home. Many new-persons' legs being tangled as it learns to walk, much laughing, much singing, much introducing of new ones and old ones."

Abasio took a deep breath, wishing he had taken notes. "If you need a dibble for every one of them, then there are more dibbles than there are any of the other genders." Abasio wasn't sure of this, but it had seemed so, going by . . .

"Oh! Forgot important thing. You are right, must be more of them, but they have already been something else by then. All dibbles begin as something else, then when it is getting older, parts used in reproduction become . . . inactive, other parts ripen. Then person becomes dibble. All of us become dibbles in time. Dibbling is final, very serious step of being-person. Dibble can even reject a chosen one, force a person to choose again. We have no such things as inexperienced, novice people being dibbles! No!"

"And the picture up there *is not* a picture of one of your . . . ones you've . . . chosen?"

"No. That is only maybe-person, or as we say after choosing, 'a wasn't-person.'"

Abasio struggled with it. "You mean, once all the dibbling is done, then the ones not dibbled are not maybe-people anymore. Because all the chances to be people are gone? So now they're just *wasn't . . . weren't-persons?*"

"True That is picture of maybe-person that was never dibbled. Instead was potted and put in special greenhouse at our home to become twigpit, food for special occasion. Is being fed special goodness at its roots. Homecoming feast requires twigpit. Summer festival requires twigpit. Welcoming new family member requires twigpit. That is the twigpit picked out for homecoming dinner when Self returns. Roasted and stuffed and served with k'pir sauce, like the stuff you are drinking. K'pir is fermented g'forz."

Abasio was still struggling with cannibalistic images. "And after all the new-people are taken home from their roots, what happens to the rest of the field of . . ."

"Were-not-people," it said helpfully. "Inspectors go through field to be sure all new-people are gone, taken home. Usually by then a left-behind-person would be known; someone would have seen lonely becoming-person with no visitors; someone would have called inspector to come see what needs doing. Only if very recent disaster happened and whole maflipluk was killed, new-person might be left behind. Inspectors take them and arrange . . . adoption. Only when all new-people are taken then reaping machines process all not-people for food over winter. Many good recipes. In winter only special-occasion twigpits in greenhouse are fresh g'forz, rest is all packaged. Of course, we eat also many other things; the world has many gardens, orchards, fisheries.

We have very nice kitchen; we have member of maflipluk, family, who is dibble: Fantarisa-vitonka. Fanty is excellent cook! Dib even took *classes* in cookery! Many dibbles are good at cookery. They give such attention to detail. We joke at dib, such a fussy one cooking!" Balytaniwassinot smiled, shook tan's head at the memory, saying, 'Do not touch that minced glabthrot, take from mouth this instant! I am needing for recipe!'"

Abasio found himself wondering just how this arrangement could have evolved. He visualized ancient fields full of omnivorous creatures struggling away from their drying roots, stumbling out into the world, stopping to take a bite out of a wasn't-person every now and then. He shook his head. "And so . . . who do you live with, and what is your home like?"

"Oh, Self's maflipluk has very nice house at edge of dancing fields. Big family room and kitchen. Each family member has own study-bedroom-sanitation-grooming-room. Bedrooms have very good soil beds. When house was built, maflipluk sent to planet known for quality of self-sifting bedding soil, all little clods breaking down by themselves in daytime. While one is asleep, little night roots come out all over, take goodness from bedding soil. In morning when one wakes, night roots reabsorb into body. Every so many sleeping times, new sprinkle of goodness is sifted onto bed. If one is wakened, for emergency, roots all sticking out, one gets up looking like quizzinog! All furry. Most dis . . . repu . . . table."

"But you also eat food?"

"Oh, yes. Food is for taste, for amusement, for fun, for sitting around table together. Now that Self is eldest except for one dibble, most of family are ones Self has chosen or chosen ones of my chosen ones: danced, recepted, planted, fertilized, chosen. One for every year. Of course, years on our planet are very long. One may choose only . . . *at most* four of its own in a lifetime. Two or three is more usual. Wurf who made me first chosen, that wurf and Self were partners for many trips, but wurf wilted last year. Two of Self's chosen have chosen ones of theirs, even the eldest one of theirs has one of its. It is a good . . . family."

It reached onto a shelf, took down a little box, and rifled through it, handing Abasio a picture. It showed eight creatures, of five very different varieties though all shared a similar body shape. One had very odd knee joints, another a noticeable swelling of the arms. He recognized Fixit at once. And there was another like it. Two tans. And, according to Fixit, who pointed out the easily distinguishable types: two isks, two blags, a dibble, and a wurf. "One of our dibbles, the good cook Fantarisa-vitonka, chosen one of that isk at end of row, was taking picture," said Balytaniwassinot, wiping a furtive tear from his breathing duct. "I was chosen one of wurf in picture who is wilted now. Oh, I will be glad to be home."

Abasio could not help himself, he reached out and patted Fixit on the nearest approximation of a shoulder. Fixit smiled, saying suddenly, "Abasio, do you have bao?"

"I've heard the word," said Abasio carefully, without emphasis, something inside him at full alert. "I can't remember ever having heard it defined, though. Something to do with respect, I think."

"This world, is it belonging to some kind of collective? Council? Ruler?"

Abasio considered this, his eyes fixed on the cup of whatever it had been. *Happy-making, sensory-negating liquid* . . . that just might tend to make a person silly enough to say something . . . dangerous. Well, he and Xulai had discussed precisely this question. At some length! Wasn't that propitious. Convenient. Appropriate. Foresightful! Damn right!

"No," he said with apparent unconcern. "Certainly not that I know of. If it's conscious, I suppose it belongs to itself. You spoke of its spirit, but I have no idea whether spirits think in terms of . . . ownership. I suppose a spirit might say 'my world' just as I might say 'my job' is to do this and that. It doesn't mean the job belongs to me forever, it just means I'm currently responsible for it. I suppose a world would belong to itself, that is, collectively to all consciousness on it or in it. Or to whatever collective it might have decided to belong to or have been admitted to for its benefit. Or if none of those apply, then I really don't know. I doubt anyone except the Creator could claim complete ownership of it, if even the Creator cared to do so." *And if that didn't cover all possible bases, nothing would. Thank heaven he'd rehearsed it over and over. And don't forget to warn Xulai! Needly wouldn't need warning. Or Grandma.* "I imagine you, Fixit, for example, might say of this planet, 'It's one of my worlds,' meaning you're responsible for it but not asserting ownership. Why do you ask?"

"Oh, just curious," said Fixit, smiling sincerely. It had been fairly sure, but it was nice to have it confirmed. Fixit liked Abasio. Fixit had counted on Abasio. Fixit was glad he would not have to end up drowning Abasio.

CHAPTER 15

The Matter of Bao

WHILE ABASIO WAS BEING ENTERTAINED BY FIXIT, THE three women who had arrived on Fixit's ship, plus two weary animals who had walked all the way from Cow Bluff, were being cared for by Wide Mountain Mother. First, she and Arakny had set about meeting the needs of the women, particularly Mavin, the one who had been stone. On emerging into flexibility, her clothes had fallen into dust around her.

Jinian had cried, "We never thought of it. Silkhands and I brought clothing, but we never thought of clothing for Mavin."

Arakny wrapped her in a robe. They all had a cup of calming tea. Bear and Coyote had a drink of cold water, then happily accepted Mother's offer of a warm room with a large bed that Mother had first covered with an old blanket. Silkhands saw them limping and insisted on looking at and treating their feet with a salve that stopped the pain. They were asleep before she closed the door on them. Meantime, Arakny had suggested that the women who had come with Fixit might enjoy the bathhouse and a change of clothes in her spacious wing of the house before meeting to discuss the reason for their journey.

There were tubs for everyone; Jinian washed Mavin's hair and brought her up-to-date on affairs back in Lom. The most difficult information to give her had been about the talents, the loss of talents, so

Jinian concentrated on the compensations. Jinian's husband, Mavin's son, Peter, was well. Mavin now had grandchildren. No, a thousand years hadn't passed in the way Mavin would have supposed if she had heard the curse before fossilizing. When they returned to Lom, only a decade or so would have passed since Mavin was petrified.

Mavin dealt with all this by returning to outrage—in a furious mutter—at the fact no one had had the sense to put new clothing around her so she wouldn't be displayed naked in the plaza. Jinian reminded herself that Mavin, at the time of her petrification, had been in a fighting frenzy, and nothing in the stony time between would have served to calm her. She whispered this supposition to Wide Mountain Mother, and everyone concentrated on being soothing. By the time Mavin had been dressed in the clothing Arakny had provided and emerged from the room, clean and warm, her hair neatly braided, she had calmed down and was beginning to grasp a general outline of what was going on.

"All those clothes!" Mavin remarked to Arakny as they passed the large side room with shelves on all the walls, the room from which she had been outfitted. "It's like a shop! You have children's things, too."

"Well, I guess it *is* a kind of shop," Arakny confessed. "I think we can clothe you decently while you are with us. This is what we call our emergency store. It's where our people bring clean, wearable used clothing that children have outgrown or women have grown tired of. Some women who love to sew or knit make new things especially for the emergency store. We have wedding gowns of various types, just in case an eloping couple happens by. Any of it can be provided to people who need it: if someone is trapped away from home by weather, or has had an accident on the road, or has been attacked by some unprincipled wanderer—or"—she gave Mavin an encouraging smile—"someone who has been petrified for a long time. You are the first we have had in that category."

"Not one I recommend," said Mavin, looking around. "Nothing for men?"

"We have little-boy things here. Clothing for men and boys old enough to prefer being dressed by father than by mother are stored in similar fashion in the men's house, across the stream and the dance ground. We keep a supply of other necessities, too, sanitary and grooming supplies; the men's house has razors. Basically, we try to keep on hand what someone would need who had been flooded out or burned out or robbed on the road. Though that very seldom happens anymore."

Mavin said innocently, "I will bet you that all donated shoes and boots are the same size."

Mother frowned at her and murmured, "I don't know why that would be."

"Don't you have women who come in here and claim they're all the wrong size?"

Arakny laughed. "Oh, yes. You're right, Mavin. Mother, remember the wheelwright's wife whose wagon got hit by lightning?"

They laughed together remembering the number of pairs of shoes the woman had tried on, and, indeed, they had all been the wrong size. "Three pair fit her perfectly well," said Mother. "But she was determined to be upset. I'm glad it was at the shoes and not at the supper."

Mavin was sufficiently soothed and recovered that she actually smiled at that. Meantime she was thinking what a sensible situation this was. The men and women didn't try to live together. They obviously met, to suit themselves, when it suited themselves, but they didn't try to live together. That would have solved her problem with her . . . her son's father, back on Lom . . .

When they rejoined the others in the large, firelit living room of Wide Mountain Mother's house, the group had grown in size. Half a dozen local women who had seen the turtle arrive had decided since Mother was having visitors, Mother would definitely need several dozen small fruit-stuffed pastries, some fresh cookies, perhaps some spice bread. Wide Mountain Mother introduced the visitors from Lom, at first being surprised that they all understood one another so well, though on reflection, she realized the ships that had taken Earthian people to Lom all those centuries ago had been built here and had departed from here; the machines in the ships spoke the language spoken on this part of Earth; the books that had been saved on this continent were in that same language. Here and there small print shops still printed books, not many and not often, but those that were printed were in that same language, and Volumetarians had for centuries distributed them discreetly: a dictionary here, a children's book there, a book of fables, a book of basic science, a book of history so the Big Kill would not be forgotten. Village schools still taught children to read the languages the Volumetarians had persisted in keeping alive and uncorrupted. Thus the three women returning from the stars were both understanding the others and being understood by them.

By the time Mavin joined them, the group had already become engaged in the motherly or grandmotherly activity of bragging about offspring and circulating pictures of children and grandchildren or, in two cases, great-grandchildren. Cameras were virtually unknown in Artemisia, where the women treasured little portraits drawn or painted by traveling artists who made the circuit every few years memorializing youth or weddings or anniversaries. Jinian had brought some high-tech pictures of Crumpet and Crash from Lom, where the Mountain ship was still turning out people trained to design things, build things, and take pictures of things, and she immediately sat down next to Mavin, putting the pictures of Crash and Crumpet into her hands. She identified them as Crash and Crumpet. "They have much longer family names for proper occasions."

"Peter's children?" Mavin murmured. "And yours . . . Are they good children, healthy and bright?" She accepted Jinian's nod. There were tears in her eyes. If it weren't for this trip, she would never have seen them! The last shreds of resentment faded. Whatever they wanted her to do . . . she'd do it.

The traditional words about the children were said, with varying degrees of sincerity, while Needly listened in amazement. Nothing done in Hench Valley had prepared her for womanly gatherings with heaping platters of sweet things on the table, endless cups of tea, and a seemingly unlimited number of pictured offspring, each and every one of whom—despite their quite ordinary appearance—were said to be cleverer, prettier, and nicer than any other children anywhere. Jinian, who had two of her own, doubted this and actually winked at Needly on one occasion when the bragging threatened to go into orbit.

Much to Silkhands's confusion, the gathering paid only brief attention to the most urgent situation involving the visitors. Jinian and she had traveled some light-years in very short elapsed time—wormhole travel was faster than light, though since there was no light in wormholes they had had no impression of great speed—and they had arrived ready to do whatever needed to be done about something called a Griffin, only to be caught up in this offspring contest where Mavin was being shown pictures of her son's children, whom she had never met, by her son's wife, Jinian, who had had no trouble admiring other people's children.

Silkhands herself, however, was having trouble breathing. *Somewhere near her was another child, a child whose spirit was trapped and suffocating, crushed and in pain. No one was paying attention.*

The mutual admiration still showed little sign of tapering off some-time later when Abasio and Fixit joined the group. Two chairs were moved in from another room and the newcomers sat down. Abasio had some difficulty in lining up chair with body as he sat between Silkhands and Needly. From across the room, Xulai looked at him with raised eyebrows. He shrugged, then nodded, then smiled. Yes, he was squiffy. Yes, his smile said, he was definitely squiffy. However, his face said that the person, thing, creature responsible for his squiffiness, whatever he, she, it, or they was, was a very pleasant . . . creature.

Xulai, awash in tea, sighed. Men had all the fun. Bailai and Gailai were asleep in an adjacent room, and despite all the child talk around her, she had not mentioned them once. One did not want to remind people that all their bragged-on children could not, in their current much-admired forms, produce descendants who would survive the coming inundation. Under the circumstances, it would not be fitting for the mother of the future to do her own bragging about children who would. Wide Mountain Mother, who had met Bailai and Gailai, gave her a look that carried both sympathy and understanding.

Needly was very conscious of the confusion and disturbance in sev-eral minds in the room, including that of Grandma, who was sitting next to her. Needly had always thought of Grandma as she thought of the mountains—solid, eternal, and immovable—and she had main-tained this judgment despite Grandma's probable misjudgment of the Oracles. Even mountains had an occasional crevasse. Needly had doubted the Oracles from her first contact with them. She had felt Grandma's need to believe in them without knowing the basis of that need. To go on believing in them, however, Grandma had had to ignore their having been no help with Willum, which Needly could not ignore and would not forgive. As though to echo her pain, she heard Abasio ask Silkhands, who was sitting between him and Jinian, whether she had as yet seen Willum.

Needly heard her mutter, "Is that his name? I have come all this way to do something important. I am sitting in a room where I can feel a spirit suffocating, trapped, in agony, a boy. His pain is my pain—no, I have not seen him—and why are we sitting, talking, talking, talking?"

Abasio took her hand in his own and pressed it, whispering, "Give it a few moments."

"Tell me about the stone medicine again, what's it made of?" Precious Wind queried Grandma.

Needly produced the bottle, which Precious Wind smelled.

Grandma then repeated what she had said before, producing her little notebook, which had a drawing of the plant. Fixit whispered into its note taker. Silkhands fumed.

"Then what is the antidote made of?" Precious Wind asked.

Grandma told her. The notebook was perused. Finally Precious Wind turned to Arakny and said, "It's nothing I ever learned about. It's not among the herbal remedies I know."

Jinian remarked, "If I hadn't seen this notebook, I'd have said it isn't herbal at all, it's magic—a curse in a bottle and an anticurse in another bottle. Exactly the same curse that kept Mavin as a stone."

"But it required that plant to make it," Grandma objected, rather sharply. "And there was no invocation, as would be required with either curse or blessing!"

Silkhands bit her lip and snarled silently into her teacup. She had not come all this way to discuss herbs! She caught Abasio's eyes on her. He winked. How could he! He patted the air, saying without saying "be patient." Needly gave her a sympathetic look. Silkhands attempted to be patient. The others obviously didn't know what it was like for her, though she thought the child had an inkling of it. She could feel the discomfort, the struggle going on, a spirit trying desperately to get loose, screaming that it was being compressed and suffocated. No one else could detect it. They went on talking.

"Sometimes plants are elements of spells," said Jinian. "But when we—I mean the circle of women I work with—when we speak of herbal remedies, we mean things that are made of plants only, no so-called enchantments added. No prayers to or invocations of any outside force except the acknowledgments that all practitioners of the art make to other powers."

"I remember the curse words well enough," snarled Mavin. "They were the last ones I heard before I became rock."

"They have the same effect," Jinian said. "But they are not interconnected. *They imprison the mind and the spirit as well as the body.*"

"I'm so glad that's been cleared up. Now, *if someone will just pay attention!*" muttered Silkhands.

Needly's patience cracked. She cried angrily, "Can we please quit talking about the rock solution? It doesn't matter how it is made, or how the antidote is made, or who knew how to make it. *All that has nothing to do with Willum's problem!* It's not the rock solution or the herbs or the recipe that's the problem, it's that Willum will bleed to death if we unrock him!"

Everyone gave her sympathetic looks. Precious Wind asked, "When they used the antidote on Willum, did they pour it into the wound after the shaft was drawn out?"

"No. They sprayed it on his body." Grandma began to describe in great detail what had been done, what had been tried and failed . . . Needly made a gesture of complete frustration.

"Is it warm where you have the boy now? Is he close by?" Silkhands asked very loudly, staring at Arakny.

Arakny looked up, startled. "He's in a room here; no, it's not very warm in there."

Abasio said, also loudly, and with a sidelong glance at Silkhands. "Then, since our visitors have come, at least in part, to help him, why don't we bring him in here?"

Released from pointless politeness by Abasio's voice, Silkhands said, also loudly, but in her sweetest, most patient voice: "Oh, that's such a good idea! Now that we know *every aspect* of what *the problem* is and *every detail* of *what's been tried, why don't we have a look at the boy who is suffering, though I know no one in this room but me hears his spirit screaming for release!*"

"I hear him," cried Needly in an agonized howl. *"I've been hearing him ever since that arrow hit him!"*

Silence fell like a stage curtain. Wide Mountain Mother put her hand over her mouth in embarrassed awareness. There was a healer here who knew more than any of them, and they'd gone on talking around her, ignoring the boy, thinking of him as though he really were only stone. She was momentarily ashamed, then resolute. She would make up for it. She would . . . find a way to make up for it. Until now she had rarely needed to consider whether someone else might know more about things than she herself did. Especially . . . extraterrestrials. She realized suddenly that she had been pushing them into the same class into which she had put the Oracles, who, from her experience, knew little or nothing.

Xulai, Abasio, and Needly, however, had risen and gone immediately into the neighboring room to fetch Willum. He had been put on the bed just as he was, clothed as he had been when the arrow struck him. Rock or not, Needly insisted they cut off his bloody clothing and put pajama trousers on him before they wrapped him in a blanket and brought him to the place Mother had cleared for him, on the floor in the center of the room, in front of the fire. He was resting on one shoulder, one hip, and one elbow. His rock-hard body was cold.

Silkhands asked for pillows to push under his elevated portions so that he didn't look so uncomfortable, explaining as she did so that even though she knew his *body* was feeling nothing at all, if he looked uncomfortable, she felt uncomfortable, and that was no way to feel when you were fiddling about with people's insides! "The agony is there!" she remarked with a certain deliberate brutality. "It is not physical. It's like being crushed in a cage." She looked around her at a circle of horrified faces. "He won't remember that part," she said. "I can promise he will not remember, even though he was left like this for a very long time." *And maybe next time they'd concentrate on what was important instead of on how nicely little Cecily draws pictures of kittens and how cute Booboo is in his bunny suit.*

She folded the blanket with ostentatious care and put it to one side. Needly held out a bottle and whispered, "Put some of the antidote on your hands, Silkhands. Whether there is magic involved or not, the intention is still part of the mixture, is it not?"

Jinian overheard her. "It is indeed, but who told you?"

"It just seems logical. So much of magic and herbal lore seems to be in what is meant."

It could do no harm, Silkhands thought, putting a few drops on her palm and rubbing it into her hands, then laying her hands on the boy. If he were closer to the fire he would be warmer. She let the feeling penetrate, sending ghost fingers to carry the antidote into his flesh.

Into his rock. She could get in there, but oh, it was difficult. *Like drilling into stone.* Yes, *they had been right about that* . . . she *would* need the antidote. Make a mental note. *Chatter is not* always *irrelevant.* Ouch! Finger pricked on that one! Something in there not fleshlike.

"Ah." She looked up to locate her fellow traveler. "Jinian, I know it's difficult if you're working alone, particularly in a strange environment, but if you can summon a little witchery, we could really use a pulling spell. This wound was supposedly washed out, but there are splinters and sharp little shreds that were embedded. That's probably why nothing that's been tried has worked. The debris is all along the wound, and while I might be able to pull on the bits and splinters, I want them to come out of the hole, not through flesh. That would only make things worse . . ."

Jinian thought for a long moment, feeling herself at the center of everyone's attention. Well, that would help. She could use that focused attention. Perhaps "like to like" would work under these circumstances. "I need a clean cloth, a small one, maybe a handkerchief. It must be very clean, white, if possible, no dye or perfume. And it would be very helpful to have the shaft that was pulled out. Was it kept?"

Yes, the pieces of shaft were in the room where Willum had been. Someone went to get them while Wide Mountain Mother offered a folded, very clean, and neatly ironed handkerchief from her pocket.

Jinian looked around the room, stopped at Needly, nodded to her, saying, "Spread the handkerchief out on Willum's belly. Abasio, this was what? An arrow shaft? I need a little piece of it, please?" Abasio went to the fireplace and used his knife on a piece of the yew shaft, letting the dust fall into the fire. He brought Jinian a fragment. She laid it on Willum's chest, near the wound. "Silkhands, you're right-handed? Put a little of the antidote on your right hand, put that little piece of wood between two fingers of that hand, then hold that hand cupped, palm down, over the top of the wound. Visualize bits of sawdust rising into your hand. Try to hold that thought. We're going to summon like to like. Now, please, don't talk, anyone." She cupped her own hands before her face and began murmuring into them, her voice rising and falling, sometimes pleading, sometimes commanding. Then she turned slightly toward Silkhands. "Raise your hand, just a little. Now move it over the cloth."

Jinian murmured again, and a tiny shower of sawdust fell from Silk-hand's fingers onto the handkerchief.

"Don't anyone touch it," said Jinian. "I bind it where it is, using it to summon the rest. Now, to loosen the rest of it, a couple more drops of the antidote on your hand, Silkhands, and when your spirit fingers go in, think of them pushing the antidote ahead of them and then around and behind the wood, to loosen it. Ready? Now, we'll try that again."

They did it again, producing another, slightly larger shower of saw-dust that included several actual splinters, then repeated the process thrice more. The last time there was nothing.

"Feel any more at all?" Jinian asked Silkhands.

Silkhand placed her hand over the wound and after a moment shook her head. "Just rock. I can tell you what I've found so far. My talent won't touch the stone, so the antidote is necessary; you may make note of that fact for future healers if this stone medicine becomes well known. I can't unlock the flesh without it. But, as we all know, if we unlock the flesh, he will bleed. So far I have unlocked only tiny places behind splinters and dust; now we need to think of some way to put just a few drops of the antidote halfway down that wound. Help me think of a way to keep him stone except for that one little place."

Wide Mountain Mother said, "I have some straws, hollow ones. You could suck some of the stuff into the straw, put your finger over it, and let the stuff out inside him."

"It'll just run out," said Needly.

"Not if we turn him so the line of the shaft is level," murmured Jinian.

"Chairs," said Arakny. "If we put his top on one chair and his bottom and legs on another, we can turn him and brace him with pillows until the channel's level."

"We could test it with colored water first," said Needly. "To be sure it's level before you use the real stuff."

"Why don't we make something smooth the same size as the shaft and just insert it from the back?" said Abasio. "That'll hold the antidote where you want it."

"A moment," said a new voice. "I think I can solve your problem." Fixit thrust an arm between two of them. "Look at finger, please. Finger is extensible. Finger is softer than something we might carve."

A finger, the middle one of three on the hand, visibly grew in length. It really looked more like a tentacle than a jointed finger, being very smooth, the tip completely flat, like the cross section of a cylinder. "Can this be inserted? Is swat finger. Never mind, Abasio will tell you what it is for. Assuming antidote will not dissolve finger, I can maintain length for some time."

"You didn't show me that trick," said Abasio.

"Did not seem necessary to go on at length about swatting willimoxies . . ."

"No, I think we've pretty well covered that subject . . ." Abasio muttered. There was absolutely no reason why thoughts of swatting willimoxies should make one feel as if one had been caught by one's mother reading . . . what was it called? Pro . . . Por . . . He couldn't remember, except that it was supposed to be naughty. On Balytaniwassinot's world, being naughty was evidently holiday fun! NO. WRONG. On Balytaniwassinot's world, there was no naughty, only good, healthful, very public, multisexual exercise. With difficulty he brought his mind—recently almost totally occupied by images of hundreds of wildly, ecstatically gyrating Fixits—back to the present problem.

"Put it there," ordered Silkhands, who waited while the galactic officer positioned himself behind the boy and helped her shift Willum's body until the fingertip surface was level, allowing the antidote to touch the stone evenly all the way around. She placed her hands on the boy's chest, murmured "Now, Fixit, push just a tiny bit farther toward me, that's it. Hold it just like that. Now, nobody move, please." She tipped one drop of the antidote into the hole in the boy's chest, then laid her hands over the hole and closed her eyes. "Oh, very good! That made a nice soft place there, right there, and the softness almost circles the hole. Needly, can you put in one drop more? Good. I've found a vein needing repair. I'm doing that."

Needly watched her closely. She didn't move. Her eyes were closed. But Needly could feel something . . . as though Silkhands was panting from extreme effort. Needly's own muscles tensed in sympathy. Silkhands was reaching for something. Jinian moved to stand between the fire and Silkhands and laid one hand on Silkhand's shoulder, barely touching. Needly felt Silkhands drawing something . . . power from somewhere, from Jinian. Jinian was getting it . . . from the fire. How did they do that?

Silkhands murmured, ". . . another one. Poor little guy did get messed up in there, but he was lucky. His heart is only the thickness of a fingernail away from this hole, but that tiny bit makes all the difference. All right, I've done that one. Now we're going to convince some lazy cells that they need to multiply very quickly and fill in across the gap to make a little plug. Hold your finger there just a little longer, Fixit. It takes a little time, everyone think nice thoughts."

Someone said, "We could sing something?"

"Do not sing!" said Jinian hastily. "Just be very calm. Very, very calm. Think of things that join, people holding hands, glue sticking two pieces of paper together, two clouds melting into one, a stream flowing into a river . . . Yes, yes, there. Very good, it's joining." She leaned back for a few moments, her hands still. "Now he has two holes in him, one from front, one from back, but the middle has a very thin little partition across it. Thank you very much, Balytaniwassinot. You may remove your finger now. Wash it, please, just in case there's any of that stone stuff on it. I detect you are part, perhaps the largest part, vegetable, so you should be immune, but that's only an impression. When we have finished with this, I would like to touch your interesting flesh again.

"Now, Abasio and Jinian, turn the boy to the left—no, the other left. I need access to the hole in his back. Thank you. More antidote please, just a drop or two on my fingers. Thank you, Mother." Silence, and more silence broken by Silkhands's murmuring, "Ah, we have encountered a nasty. Tsk. Not really broken, just pushed very brutally to one side, bruised. I can fix that. And again, more antidote." She held out her hand and Mother put several drops on the palm. Silkhands laid it on Willum's chest. "Nothing really bad there, just . . . Someone mentioned healing stuff that did a very good healing on the Griffin's wings? Does anyone have it? Needly? Will you fetch it, please? No, no, Arakny, I'm fine. I'll just hold it until she gets back."

Silence. People breathing very softly until Needly returned. "That's wonderful," said Silkhands, sniffing the open bottle. "If you'll put some in a very clean spoon, just a tiny bit. Yes, now drip it in. One drop at a time. Right. Now I've fixed all the bleeding places, starting at the skin on his back, working between the ribs in back, fixed the wounded places in the lungs, alongside his heart, still forward, and now we're at the ribs in front. Turn him over, please. The arrow went right between them, both front and back, which was good. Very good! That means no bone splinters!"

Needly thought laughter. Willum had told her the rib story. She would tell Willum they *had* counted his ribs. From the inside.

Silkhands turned her head, stretching neck and shoulders without moving her hands, as though she were in pain. "We're closing off those little places that would bleed, moving toward his skin, getting close." Abasio leaned forward with a clean cloth and wiped her forehead, which was beaded with sweat. She thanked him with a smile as she turned toward Grandma. "Grandma, I don't want him to wake up for quite a little while after I'm finished. Every cell of his body that touched that shaft is going to need a little time to knit together, and there are nerves there that will scream. Though the stone medicine affects the whole body, I find that flesh becomes a different kind of stone than bone does. It's like the difference between sandstone and basalt. When the shaft was pulled out from between the ribs, the *rib-stone*— which is more abrasive than *flesh-stone*—rasped splinters and dust into the wound. We've disposed of those, but the stone that preserved his life complicates things now. If we use much more of the antidote, he's going to . . . lose the rock that's keeping him steady. We need to keep him perfectly quiet until all those frantic little cells along the wound manage to extend into the gap.

"Does anyone know of something I can get into his blood that will make him sleep? I can put it in from where I'm working right now. I can put him to sleep myself, but he'll struggle against it, so I'd have to sit right beside him for hours and it's very tiring and there's only one of me, so something material rather than mental would be more reliable . . ."

The clinking of bottles drew her attention to Needly, who had not left the room this time but was shuffling beneath her skirts. *Which was evidently where she carried them? What an assortment!* No matter. "Oh, Needly, thank you. Now, what's in this? Poppy, right? I know about that. We have that on Lom, from seeds brought from Earth originally. And there's no other ingredient? And no liquid but clean water?"

"Distilled water," muttered Grandma.

"Perfect, Grandma. You made this? Well then, you know the efficacy of your materials. This is going to go directly from the wound into his bloodstream a tiny, tiny bit at a time. Will you decide how much would be needed to keep someone his size asleep for several hours if given as an injection rather than by mouth? Better yet, if possible, is there a dose we can give him safely that will keep him asleep for up to a day or so? If that would be too much all at once, we can do a series of doses, whatever we can do most safely. Measure the largest safe dose, then put a little bit of it in a very clean little spoon. We'll need to dilute that, will we not?"

There was a scurry as Mother went to fetch a spoon and, from a neighboring room, a slender glass cylinder obviously made to be used for measurement. There was a quick discussion of using boiled water to dilute the poppy juice. Jinian volunteered to purify the water and did so by murmuring at the cylinder. The water moved into two distinguishable layers, and the bottom bit pretended to be a solid while Jinian poured off the purified top. Arakny handed Grandma a clean towel on which to polish various items. Grandma received this with a nod of thanks, and she, Silkhands, and Needly muttered together. The antidote would be needed to de-rock the veins while Silkhands moved the blood. Needly poured some of the solution into the glass; Grandma regarded it thoughtfully, gave Willum a calculating look, added a few drops more before transferring some of the liquid into the small spoon.

Silkhands murmured, "Needly, you have a steady hand, will you drip it in slowly, just drop by drop as I ask for it? It will take a while. I won't ask for another drop until I've got the last one moved, and I have to wait for each drop to undo the rock ahead of it before I can move on . . ."

Needly, at Silkhand's nod, dripped one drop at a time into the wound, with long, breathless pauses between.

After what seemed an eternity during which not one of the women in the room spoke or even seemed to breathe (later, Needly was inclined to think this had been a miracle), Silkhands murmured, "Good, let me move some blood in the nearest veins to pull it in through the capillaries and spread that around. Now I want antidote on him, right here where my hand is, so I can get the stone out of the heart. I don't dare try to get it pumping yet; it would be pushing against stone. Better I just move it a tiny bit at a time. It is interesting that once in the vein, the antidote continues to work, removing the stone in front of it. This is going to take a while. I wonder. Considering how the stuff works, let's put quite a bit of the antidote right here, under my hand, and let me see how far I can get it into him. Hmm. That works, it seeps down by gravity,

unlocking the flesh as it goes. *Still a little stiff.* I need to push it down farther, just a drop or two more of antidote. Thank you, Needly. Can you
and Grandma start at his arms and legs, working down from shoulders
and hips, putting the antidote on your hands? His pajama legs are full,
just push them up to the hip joint and work down from there. Let's do it
as quickly as we can. Think of invisible fingers pushing each dose down
into him and then spreading outward. Good. Now that the first dose
in the wound is fully dispersed, we need to do the same thing with the
next dose, still from the wound directly into the blood."

The room was utterly silent; people seemed to have forgotten how
to breathe. After what seemed a silent eternity, Silkhands took a deep,
aching breath. "Good. Now he is not going to bleed into the wound. I
should have asked before: were there other injuries? I didn't feel any,
but there might have been something minor? Good. Now we need not
use any more of the antidote. There's enough antidote in the blood that
as the blood liquefies, it moves the antidote with it, changing what little
stone is left. Right now I'm pushing it. Can't start the heart until it can
pump freely. We can let more of it penetrate from outside. Let us turn
him over and push a bit more of the antidote into and onto him and get
all of him back to flesh."

In a few moments the contorted arm relaxed. A collective sigh
came from the whole room, long-held breath expelled. Then the legs
straightened, and finally the twisted body relaxed. By that time, Willum
was in what appeared to be a sound sleep on a blanket in front of the
fire, still warming up. A bandage had been wound around his chest,
covering the two wounds. He was lying on his back, a pillow under his
head, another under his knees. Needly was sitting next to him, wiping
tears from her eyes and hoping. From across the room, Abasio could
see a pulse beating in the boy's neck. Silkhands had his heart beating.

She said, "If there's any little area of stone left, the antidote in the
blood will dissolve it. I'm amazed that the stuff seems to be totally
benign. The body accepts it as though it were natural to it."

Grandma said, "Wouldn't be much good if it couldn't bring life back,
would it? Wouldn't deserve the title? The two work together, stone and
un-stone. Like they hold a person's body between two healing hands."

Silkhands smiled. Yes, they did indeed do that. She very much
wanted to learn the constituents of both the stone medicine and its

antidote. And *she very much wanted seeds to plant when she got back to Lom. People too wounded to treat could be held in stone until one had the right people to work on them!* She went to sit next to Fixit, her hands on one of its arms, her senses deep inside it (which tan did not feel), explaining how those with the healing talent had worked on Lom. Perhaps it could assure that the healing talent, at least, would continue.

"It may have been given by Ganver, but there at the end you weren't using anything but yourself," Fixit said quietly. "Ganver told me about the talents he had given originally. They bear his finger, his . . . signature, one might say. His . . . flavor. They are recognizable. Yours was only you."

"I know," she whispered. "I think all the talent did was just show me how. Perhaps the ability exists in a good many people, and proper training might well let them use it. And I'm wondering if other talents—Mavin's, for instance—might not be the same."

"I wish I could duplicate the Ganver person," the galactic officer lamented, almost in a whisper. "Such an original thinker. That geographical chemical feedback system it had, making the area where people live behave like a body with various organs. Unfortunately it kept everything a bit too placid; the world body wasn't prepared for trauma. It hadn't developed any defenses. Tell me, was fixing this boy your reason for coming?" *Fixit knew very well what the reason had been for the three women's coming. Now the log had to be informed as well. Verisimilitude. "See, see, the galactic officer had no prior knowledge at all. None."*

Silkhands yawned, shaking her head slowly, her neck reluctant to move from its concentrated rigidity. "No. We weren't told of the boy originally; his injury was something that happened more recently, and we only heard about it when we were almost here. Our reason for coming had to do more with the flooding situation and some unforeseen problems it had caused with other creatures. Particularly the threat it posed to the Griffins. Jinian can tell you if you'd like to hear more about it."

It gave her a puzzled look, then bowed in Jinian's direction, saying, "Perhaps I need more of the background, yes." *As though he did not know the background from one end to the other!*

Jinian held out her cup. It was refilled. "Do you know how reproduction takes place on Lom?"

Fixit's mouth dropped open. Of all the . . . Well, no. Self honestly didn't. And what had that to do with . . . ? Self shook tan's head at her, a very recently acquired human gesture.

"Well then, you do need more of the background, Fixit." She settled herself to speak.

"You've described Ganver as a world spirit, for that part of the world it controlled. I knew Ganver. Ganver took an interest in me, tried to educate me, tried to help me understand what was going on, and it talked to me of bao.

"At that time I had no idea what 'having a child' meant to the Eesty race. It takes five individual Eesties to create a new life, one of each of the five genders. The act itself is called 'a gathering of perfection.' During that act, or one might better say 'ceremony'—it's as much spiritual as physical—one of the five participants dies . . . or rather, gives up its life. One life is given to create one or two new ones: there's usually only one new life, but sometimes the new life splits into two during the ceremony, resulting in nonidentical twins . Almost always, the Eesty that dies has already lived a long, complete life and is willing to take part in a 'gathering' because its own life is no longer rewarding. The ceremony is performed only among deeply sincere friends—their meaning of 'sincere' includes a whole lexicon of positive emotions. Love, respect, honor. It is noteworthy that Eesties incapable of these feelings can never achieve a 'gathering.' A *bad* Eesty cannot reproduce itself.

"Given this sacrifice on the part of one participant, each new life is deeply freighted with all kinds of generous, loving associations. To have the new life betray everything the 'gathering' stood for, to denigrate the life that was given, is almost unknown and would be deeply traumatic, particularly for the four surviving gatherers. This betrayal is what Ganver's child did, and Ganver blamed mankind for it to such an extent that he approved—that is, Lom approved the wiping out of mankind."

"So, Ganver is assisting to open wormhole to bottom of Earth's ocean," Fixit mused. "But Lom didn't know there were creatures here that live for a thousand years or more as well as speaking animals who are also self-aware."

Abasio nodded. "But the Griffins soon let it be known."

"That is true. And Ganver heard it," Fixit replied. "Ganver realized if the Griffins were going to adapt, they'd have to do it in a way that could happen all at once."

"Didn't I say so!" Abasio reached out to Xulai. "That's exactly what I said!"

Xulai laid her hand on his. "Yes, you did, dear. Is that what's going to happen?"

Fixit went on: "Ganver had, itself, created a life-form that could change, all at once. It was known as a shapeshifter."

"Ganver consulted some of us hated mankinds about the problem," said Silkhands. She smiled wearily. "It held no animosity against healers or against Jinian. After hearing all about the problem, we two suggested that the Griffins—and perhaps some other creatures—could be given shifter organs and taught to use them. Shapeshifter talent requires an individual organ, located in the brain. When all the other talents were lost, however, the shapeshifter organs vanished as well."

"I suggested to Ganver that it create such an organ for us," said Fixit, making a four-handed gesture of frustration. During its career it had very seldom felt frustrated, but this *Griffin-drowning* problem had been confounding from the beginning. "Ganver said it couldn't remember how it had done it in the first place . . ." Fixit's voice trailed away dolefully.

Jinian cried, "Ganver really couldn't, Fixit! Ganver was so depressed it was in no condition to do anything, and we couldn't wait for it to recover. Silkhands and I talked about it endlessly, and then she mentioned something about Mavin having been turned to stone for a thousand years. It had happened during an all-out war with some very unpleasant witches, but her shifter organ was presumably still intact, inside her. AND Fixit said he could make sure we traveled a thousand years on the way here." She turned to smile at Mavin, who was sitting next to her. "We spun over and over through a great many of what Fixit called 'time loops,' but Fixit did it perfectly and Mavin woke up when we arrived. Silkhands and I told her about the plan."

"Which is?" asked Abasio.

"Which is to use Mavin's shifter organ as a pattern from which to assemble a copy inside each of the Griffins, using their own tissue."

Mavin was skeptical. "Even if you're born with the organ, it takes a lot of time to learn how to use it."

Xulai shrugged. "We have two hundred years. How much time, really?"

"Well, not that long! I was typical, I suppose. I remember hiding and spending hour after hour making my toes longer and shorter. It's scary. You wonder what will happen to your heart if you change something close to it. Or your brain!" She shook her head, and shrugged again. "I worry that we may get everyone's hopes up when we don't really know whether it can be done."

Jinian said, "Well, each of us is here to attempt it, and I'm here to assist. Since all this creating and installing and teaching may involve communicating with various kinds of creatures, it helps greatly if someone can reassure each creature in its own language that one is really helping, not threatening."

There was a long silence. Xulai moved uncomfortably, frowning. "Forgive me but . . . if you create an organ inside a creature, it would not be genetically transmitted to its young, would it?"

"People keep saying that given talents aren't hereditary, but that *can't* be accurate." Silkhands made an irritated gesture. "Ganver didn't create an organ in me. One of my parents or grandparents was given the healing talent—*given* it—but I inherited it. It became part of the family genetics. So I know that when the talent was given, it was given in a form that transmitted to offspring. Two healers invariably had healer children."

Mavin, who had almost slipped into a doze, said firmly, "She's right. My son inherited shape-changing from me. Some, but not all, other families inherited their talents. And when two parents had different talents from each other, the child inherited a mix. Remember the *Index*?"

"Index?" Fixit looked up with sudden interest. "What is index?"

"*The Index of Talents Together with a Compendium on Proper Costume and Behavior in Game,*" Silkhands announced, biting off each word as though hating the taste of it. "That was the title of it. A book all properly educated gamesmen were supposed to learn!"

Jinian added, her voice holding a mixture of laughter and frustration, "There were eleven 'normal' talents, plus the few special ones like mine. There were gradations of the strength of each talent. In the *Index*, it was supposed that there were eight strength variations. If one inherited the same talent from both parents, that was strength eight. If one inherited two different talents, each one was strength four. Four different talents from four different grandparents would be strength two for each one, and eight differently talented great-grandparents might end up giving a person strength one in each one. It was more complex than that, of course, because one's parents may have inherited half a dozen different talents in different strengths. At any rate, the *Index* listed over a thousand types, some of them completely theoretical, each with its own dress and title. In school we were supposed to learn them all! I suppose some of the teachers actually did."

Abasio still looked puzzled. Jinian thought a moment before saying, "Let's suppose you inherited one-quarter seer—that's seeing the future—and one-quarter herald—that's really just enunciatory yelling except one can be heard miles away—those two talents would give you the ability to tell when someone was going to die, for instance, and a very loud voice to tell them about it. Then suppose you inherited strength one or two in some combination of dead raising, transporting, and flying. What were you?"

"Wasn't that a Banshee!" Silkhands laughed. "I only saw one, ever, this floating, screaming, skull-faced creature. We had to learn the costumes, too. Banshees wore floating black-and-gray draperies with long black-and-gray hair, and a skull mask with their own eyes showing through. And they screamed, of course. Whatever it was that Ganver gave us in the beginning, it definitely included the genetic coding to pass it on."

Abasio muttered, "If Mavin passed it to her son, that means it's still got that potency. If hers is identically copied, it should become potent in the Griffins. Precious Wind has done a great deal of genetic work in recent years, and she's gone out to use our far-talker to consult with the laboratories in Tingawa. I imagine she will also consult the library helmets?" He looked questioningly at Arakny, who reached for the notebook she always carried in her pocket.

"Whatever they try to do for the Griffins should be done through the male line," said Needly. "Please remind Precious Wind of that while she's talking to them, Abasio. There are supposedly sixteen females, but we know of only one new male from a nonlethal sire, Carillon, the baby Bell-sound has. If you can make the change descend through the male line, in his half of the equation—and he's still a baby—then it will go on to all of the next generations."

Xulai said, "But the baby Griffin won't even be grown in two hundred years, Needly."

"I know," she replied. "Your son, Bailai, won't be grown for years, but his genetics won't change. They're the same in newborns and mature people."

Abasio said, "Needly, Precious Wind is using the far-talker just outside. Would you make sure she remembers about the little male?"

As she left, Needly decided on another suggestion she would make to Precious Wind. It would be better if the three hostile Griffins could be taken somewhere else to live. Undoubtedly Mr. Fixit could arrange that. She already had a very good idea what he would do about all the other animals . . . or might have already done. He was going to do a Noa Zarc, one of the old antibao stories that Grandma had told her. Fixit would take breeding stock of every type of living creature to some other world with no mankinds on it, then sterilize the ones on Earth well prior to the final flood so they could live out their lives and not drown.

As Needly left them, Silkhands murmured to Wide Mountain Mother, "The plan was for me to create a shape-changer organ in each of the Griffins, out of their own cells. I understand there are ONLY sixteen of them. At the moment even ONE sounds terribly complicated, and I'm getting too tired to think . . ."

"You've worked your heart out, dear. Of course you're tired. You need a soft bed! All of you do. Arakny can tell me later whatever decisions you reach."

She murmured to Silkhands as she led her away, with Mavin and Jinian following. Arakny began collecting teacups and plates from all over the room and stacking them on the table. Others of the neighbors bid her good-bye and left, one or two at a time. Only Fixit, Abasio, Xulai, Arakny, and Grandma were left, to be rejoined a few moments later by Needly.

Grandma tried to speak, choked, cleared her throat, and tried again. She was struggling with the disappearance of her own children. Little Sally and Serena. Golden-haired Jules. Lilt-voiced Sarah; Jan and Jacky. "Mr. Fixit. Please, before you all get involved in this Griffin business, can you find out if these Oracles have my children or know where they are. My sons and daughters. I was told the Oracles had devised a genetic program that would be of benefit to the world, and my children were supposedly the result. I was told they would be sent to some destination arranged by the Oracles. I want to know where they are. I want to know

if they are happily, productively occupied . . . and I want them back!"
She paused, gulped, and went on: "Someone dug me out of that grave
in Tuckwhip! Someone brought me to the Oracles. Someone found the
antidote and used it. At one time I'd have believed the Oracles did it.
Now I don't believe that. I want to know who did it!"

Needly looked at her in horror! Was that it? *Of course it was.* Oh,
Grandma. She gritted her teeth and desperately tried to think of some
way she could help. She looked up to meet Xulai's eyes, full of understanding. Xulai nodded, shrugged, held her hands open, the meaning
clear. There was too much going on, all at once, to deal with this now,
but she would help.

Xulai muttered something, and Fixit looked intently at her. "Xulai?"

"It was hearing Grandma use the word 'children,' Fixit. Since the
Edges are responsible for a lot of the trouble going on, and we're considering retaliation, we need to remember it's not just men in there;
there are probably women and children, too, perhaps women and children who had nothing to do with giants and mechanical whales and
possibly should be removed and given a chance at something else?"

"No reason not to."

The door opened again as Precious Wind came in from outside to
announce triumphantly, "They think it's perfectly possible to copy the
organ once we have one to copy from." She turned toward Fixit. "It
seems they can analyze and study it while it's in place, no need for any
kind of surgery. Their machines can scan and duplicate. The Griffins
aren't identical to one another, but the ones like Sun-wings are very
similar, genetically, and they don't think rejection would be an insur-
mountable problem once the first one is adapted. We have to take our
three visitors to Tingawa, of course."

Fixit remarked, "We? Our? Including you?"

Precious Wind flushed. "If you don't mind. I'd like to go, too. And,
just by the way, we still aren't sure where the Griffins originated, though
everyone seems sure it was the Edgers."

"The nice ones simply seem too nice to have been created by Edgers,"
Needly said. "If they did create any, they did the bad ones. Please don't
forget what I told you about the bad ones?"

Fixit spoke. "Bad ones? Some are . . . evil?"

Needly explained while Fixit made notes on his memo leaf.

"I will add this to list," said Fixit. "Where are creatures now?"

"The sixteen females we know about are in Tingawa," said Precious Wind. "They admit there may be others somewhere in the world, but all those they know of are there." She turned toward Needly. "Tingawa advised me that all ten of the unnamed Griffins are awaiting the arrival of the Namers. I gave them the news that Willum is recovering."

Needly shivered at the memory. "I thought . . . maybe the emperor or somebody would do it?"

"Oh, the emperor is quite willing to do so, Needly. After you and Willum come and conduct a ceremony so he will know how to do it in the future."

Needly cried, "Oh no, but . . ."

Precious Wind crowed, "I can't wait to witness the ceremony!"

Xulai and Abasio, both of whom remembered Needly's vivid description of soot-striped faces and bonging and *eeeai, eeeai, ohwa* being chanted, could not hide their grins as they thought of Xulai's very dignified grandfather, emperor of Tingawa, naming Griffins. Oh, they wanted to be there to watch!

Precious Wind went on: "Also, they have a solution for reproduction during the period between now and the little ones' maturity. The variation among all the Griffins is minuscule, except for the sequence that identifies the Despos lineage. Tingawa thinks it possible to use a few cells from the baby male to sequence and build fertile sperm. Interesting?"

"Artificial inseminating?" cried Fixit. "How good if so!" *And of course there's the very nice male Griffin that Self has stashed in the mountains, far to the south. He's been sleeping there about five hundred years, but he can be awakened and introduced to the ladies at any time.* "When Willum is recovered I will take you both to Tingawa so you can teach the emperor how to name Griffins."

Precious Wind said, "And yes, Needly. They will use cells only from the list of approved donors. And yes, before you ask, the baby male can provide what we would call the Y chromosome in humans, so they won't all hatch girls."

Needly refused to consider another naming ceremony. Not today. "Precious Wind, how can we find out where the Griffins were made and who made them? We're pretty sure it was done in the Edges, but there must have been at least two locations to have ended up with these two, very different populations."

"Is it important? Right now?"

"Sun-wings threatened us with creatures beneath the sea. If inimical Griffins were created in a particular place, is it not likely the sea creatures would have been made in that same place? We haven't put that on our list of problems, but it is a problem for us, isn't it?"

Fixit beamed at her. "So clever, this child. What is parentage of this child?" *As though itself had not been intimately involved in the parenting of the child . . . well, intimate at one remove.*

Silence.

Needly was used to hearing silence on that question. She said, "Grandma doesn't know who fathered me; and she is surprised her daughter mothered me because her daughter is . . . not a competent person. At all."

While it was unlikely that anyone in the universe was more familiar with Trudis's genetics than Fixit, he managed to keep his face in a properly listen-and-learn expression as Needly went on.

"Nobody seems to know who fathered me or my siblings. There were at least two other girls and three boys born at the same time, and they all disappeared. People talked about a Silverhair being the father, but nobody knows who or where they are! Someone must know! Grandma really is my genetic grandmother, though, and my mother is really her daughter. I know Grandma thought for a while my father might be somebody from the Oracles."

"Male reproductive human not produced by Oracles," said the galactic officer. Its face was twisted in a strange expression that conveyed revulsion, annoyance, and fury in about equal proportions. "Oracles not capable of reproducing hair follicle—not even if given supplies, equipment, set of instructions, and trained assemblers!"

Arakny cried, "Oh, but Fixit, they make wonderful things. When we went to see what the Edgers were doing, trying to make new bodies, the Oracles made us a portable camp, and it even provided for the horses—"

"DID . . . NOT . . . MAKE," said the galactic officer with a scowl, or what they interpreted was intended as a scowl. "*Please do not make Self say again!* Oracles incapable of making anything more complicated than dung pile. Oracles are . . . plausible liars, actual idiots. Do you still have item?"

"I do," confessed Grandma in a choked voice. "We were going to return it to them."

She offered the crystal cube and Fixit took it from her, turning it about among several arms and hands. It pointed. "See, there, look close at corner, stamped in crystal: it says 'Manufactured 243/58417/0999epj117/.' That is galactic date. Always galactic date is in numbers used on planet of purchase. It says 'fct. Oxel 235.' That means produced by Oxel factory 235. Oxel is very large manufacturing concern making very good equipment for interworld travelers, portable housing facilities, any size: factories 202 through 465 are set up on meteor belt of third planet of Ariaxne in the Frad system in this galaxy. One through 201 are in neighboring system."

Xulai cried, "Oh, I'd love to have one of those camps. Think how much easier it would make our job, Abasio. Hot water! And the children could stay clean! And so could I."

Abasio said, "And we could really sleep at night without keeping one ear open for assassins. Unfortunately, I don't know what we've got that we don't need that we could pay with, sweetheart."

Fixit murmured, "Leave that question for now. We will think of something. At moment I am interested in tying up loose ends. Are you familiar with resolution adopted by Galactic Supreme Council concerning extermination of mankind?"

"You mean the reason why we're being flooded," said Abasio.

"No, no. Flooding was informal decision made by World Spirit of Earth, and assisted by two other world spirits. Resolution of Galactic Supreme Council was as follows: 'Present mankind with problem they cannot evade; see if they will respond adequately, properly, and with bao. If not, then mankind will be mercifully expunged. If they respond sensibly, the council will work with them to improve their species.' World Spirit pulled . . . REFERENCE needed! . . . carpet from beneath pedal extremities of council, but we have already discussed this. I am interested in knowing about this bao. Are you knowing what is bao?"

As though I have not known about bao since I was a becoming-person. First lesson ever taught to Balytaniwassinot, long before it became Fixit, first lesson taught any of our people is always about bao.

"There's that word again," cried Arakny. "What is bao?"

"Grandma knows," said Needly. "She told me."

"So you can tell them," said Grandma. "I've done enough telling."

For a moment Needly stared into the distance, arranging her thoughts. Abasio and Fixit took advantage of the pause to raid the cookie plates on the table. When quiet came and everyone seemed settled, Needly folded her hands in her lap and began.

"Early mankind evolved sufficiently to create language, and this set them apart from other living creatures, so far as they knew, for while they were not the only creature with language, they were the only ones whose language they understood. They knew the earth was flat. They saw the sun rise in the east and sink in the west, so they knew it went around them each day. They saw the moon and stars do the same thing. It was obvious to them that they, humans, were at the center of everything, and since they were at the center, they assumed themselves to be the purpose for which sun and moon were made." She stopped, taking a sip from her almost empty cup. Arakny, who had left the pot warmer on the table, refilled it for her.

"Everything they saw reinforced their idea that man was at the center of everything. Stone was there for him to use as axes and pounders and spearheads. Animals and fish were there for him to eat. Shells found along the shore were good for making needles and beads. Fire was there to keep man warm and scare predators away. Women were there for pleasure and to make babies.

"At night, around the fire, they listened to the old men, those who had lived many summers, tell the stories they had learned from their old ones. Those first old ones knew the list of names. First name was his father—or perhaps the chief's name. Next name was the father or chief before him. Next name was the one before that, and the one before that. They memorized the list of names and recited it around the fire, all the way back to the first man. The first man was the one who had started the list. Maybe there were eight names, or fifteen, or twenty, but the first name was the first man who ever was, the one the Creator had made. They recited this list of names and taught it to their sons, and when they learned to count, they even assigned these old ones a certain number of years of life. And because man was a maker of things, they knew everything had to have been made by something, the Great Maker.

"Those who lived in the northern hemisphere watched the sun rise and saw that it came up in places that moved along the horizon from north to south. They learned the farther north the sun went, the warmer and longer the days were; the farther south it went, the colder and shorter the days were. They made a mark on the cave wall, one mark for each day as the sun moved back and forth, learning how many days it was from the longest day until the longest day came again. It was always the same number of days. The Great Maker had made it that way for man. Sometimes, however, the cold time went on past the proper line on the wall. The old men talked it over and decided the Maker might have gone to sleep and forgotten to put more fuel on the sun to make it hotter, so they built a big fire and danced around it, yelling, to wake up the Maker and get him to heat up the sun. It seemed like a good idea to do it every year when the temperature change was supposed to happen, just to remind the Maker they were there.

"The old men were the ones who remembered all this. They were too old to go hunting, too old to fight off the lions, but they were the ones who remembered: they remembered the list of names, back to the first man, the way to mark off the year, the way to build the fire, and the right words to use when they reminded the Maker to send the sun back, the way they had fixed the wounds that healed well, the way the fever came and how it went away when they chewed willow bark, the way to the northern valleys where they went in summer to hunt deer. And gradually, over the centuries, the old men became a separate kind of being. They became a separate caste with knowledge of law and healing and dealing with the Maker. They were not all old. Perhaps a young man had been crippled in the hunting, he could join them to learn. There was so much to learn. They learned revelation, invocation, and nomination—the laws by revelation, healing by invocation, and leaders by nomination. They became the shamans, the witch doctors, the priests . . ." She paused for a sip of water.

Arakny asked, "Were there no women among them? No wise women?"

"There were," said Grandma, "but they were individuals, almost always. Loners. The men formed clubs, societies, often *secret* societies, passing the *secret knowledge* on to their sons. The women mostly stayed close to the earth, herbs, planting, animals. The men grew away from it. They forgot the actuality of creation and began to populate their visions with gods and spirits and demons. They became the first professionals by owning the three great professions. Law. Medicine. Religion. Interestingly enough, these fields at one time were held to be the only three in which highborn men—that is, gentlemen—could engage without polluting themselves with physical labor." She turned toward her granddaughter. "Go on, Needly."

"When men invented writing, they finally had a way to preserve the knowledge of the old men by writing it down. They wrote the stories of their ancestors, of their histories, of their lineage. They wrote down the proper way to summon the Maker and remind him of his duty toward his people. They wrote down how man was at the center of everything, a particular favorite of the Maker. When they had finished, if anyone questioned the writings, they said the Maker himself had dictated what they had written down."

Grandma interrupted. "We must remember that all during these thousands of years before writing was invented, the stories were retold thousands of times, and the tribes separated and the stories were not remembered precisely the same by all of them, so the northern man might tell the story differently from the southern man, and so on. Even after writing came, there were differences."

Needly took a deep breath. "All the generations of life before that first-remembered father were forgotten. All the generations of living without language, all the generations while language slowly emerged, all those generations before they learned to make fire, all the generations while they learned to make spears and clothing. All those forgotten generations were as if they had never been, but some things remained constant, the guiding beliefs of mankind: historic man had speech and writing; the universe had been created for historic man; everything had been created for him." She paused, reaching for her cup, for her throat was dry.

"May I help tell the story?" asked Arakny. Both Needly and Grandma nodded. "Once the old men had decided on something, it was hard for them to let go of it. When people learned the world was round, not flat, when people learned the earth went around the sun, not the sun around the earth, the old men owed their allegiance to the story rather than to the truth. Wise people, good people, tried to change the old men, but by that time the old men were powerful. They were kings with armies. They were religious leaders with their own kinds of armies, and they taught that the false was true and the truth was false. The world was flat. Their book said so. The sun went around the earth. The book said so. The world was four thousand years old. Look, count up the generations of men listed in the book, the book says so. The first man's name was so and so. Their book said so. Women were the cause of sin and imperfection. The book said so. Truth was unimportant. Believe what's in the book. Most people could not read in those times, and the important men didn't want them to learn to read. They might not understand it. They might get the story wrong. They would read it themselves and tell men what to believe."

"Aha," said Fixit, who had listened to all this with great attention. "But why was this believed? Did not all men have eyes, ears, senses? Could not all men think and measure?"

Grandma said, "Of course they could. But the old men were in power. They had authority. They determined that everyone had to believe what they said, and if you didn't believe it, they would torture you until you did, and if you still didn't believe, they burned you to death. And if someone wrote a book that contradicted THE book, then they burned the book. They said no one should read any books but the ones they approved. Better yet, men shouldn't bother learning to read, or shouldn't bother reading if they already knew how: the old men would tell them what to think."

Arakny said grimly, "The old men had to build fences and gates around what people could think and read and believe so they wouldn't stray. One gate was called 'hell,' for people who disobeyed them, and another gate was called 'heaven,' a reward for people who behaved properly and didn't ask questions."

Grandma said grimly, "And the old men fought every new thing that was learned. If new discoveries were made, people must not be allowed to listen. They must not listen to the age of the earth, they must not listen to how man evolved, they must not listen to equality of women, they must not listen to restricting population. They must not listen to the truth, because the old men who ran things liked things just the way they were. *With them in power.* With riches and power coming from a steadily growing population, for the old men urged that man procreate without cease to build their armies."

The door had opened across the room. Wide Mountain Mother stood there. Both Needly and Arakny nodded to her, and Mother said very loudly: "And finally they did the very worst thing. They said, 'Don't pay attention to the evidence, don't look at the numbers, don't believe the science. *The Maker put all that evidence there just to fool you and test your faith, and if you fall for it, you'll go to hell.'*"

"Aha," cried Fixit. "So they say, in other words, that their Creator is a liar and a trickster and a . . . what is word for 'pain lover' . . . REFERENCE needed! . . . ah, yes, *sadist.*"

"Yes." Grandma nodded. "Only a sadist would create hell. Only a sadist would create a god who would create hell, and that is one of the keys to bao. Those without bao accept the existence of a god who is a liar, a trickster, and a sadist. The god of selfish humanity, the god of me-first humanity, the 'Crawl on bloody knees and offer your pain to me' god. The god of 'Build more prisons.' The wee, tiny 'Sit on my shoulder' God of use-it-up-and-worry-about-it-later. Monkey-brain willy-wagger humanity. The God of Mobwows."

"But those who have bao," Needly went on, leaping up from her chair, "they know the Creator never lies or tricks or tortures anyone. Pain was given to all living things by the Creator, not as punishment but so they can be warned of danger: it warns us that the fire burns, the sharp edge cuts, the sickness must be treated quickly to be cured. The Creator who gave us that warning is no sadist."

Fixit gave her a smiling glance. "Your grandma is teaching you this?"

"Yes," Needly said. "And I believe it."

There was a long silence, broken at last when Wide Mountain Mother said, "The rule of the old men was the way most of mankind lost bao. Or perhaps was never allowed to find it."

Fixit cocked its head and asked, "And what does 'bao' mean?"

Grandma and Mother shared a long look. It was Mother who answered. *"Bao is the acceptance that mankind is part of the fabric of the universe, not the purpose of it. Humanity is meant to live as part of creation, not as the owner of it or to make war against it."*

Grandma said, "To accuse the Creator of planting lies in the universe in order to trick mankind into hell is the worst obscenity man can commit, for intelligence cannot evolve in a universe that lies. The universe changes and evolves over aeons, but it does not lie. It may be misinterpreted, and often is, but *it does not lie.* Men may lie, doctrines may lie, books may lie, kings and princes and priests may lie . . . the universe does not."

There was a thoughtful silence. Balytaniwassinot was busily adding to its notes as it muttered to its personal log. *("See, see galactic dates on note leaf. Oh, why am just now learning how mankinds were misled? New information! Why have I never heard it before! Both lateral hearts are pounding at how surprised and amazed I am! Be sure to note, log, how hearts are pounding!")*

Precious Wind remarked, "I have mentioned my fascination with pre–Big Kill history. There is a historic parallel with today. Those without bao do not see a universal fabric of which they are a part; each of those without bao has his face at the center, his family and friends, radiating from him like the spokes of a wheel, and no one else has importance. There was a cult of this self-importance on Earth in the twenty-first century. It was called something like My Face First or See My Face. Those who took part in it were without bao."

Fixit nodded, remarking, "This is also what Needly was distinguishing among Griffins, those with bao and those without. Is this bao being genetic?"

Silkhands shook her head. "It's a mystery, Fixit. I don't think anyone has been able to determine exactly how it is transmitted. I know children who have it, but I have also seen toddlers whose eyes glow with hunger to consume and use up, and defile. The first word they learn, the last one they utter at the end of a lifetime of greed, is 'mine'! Yet others get so deep into being the fabric of the universe that they are almost indistinguishable as individual people. It is as though they become absorbed into all that is and it shines from them like light."

There was a long silence that Fixit broke. "You tell it very well." And it sighed vastly. "Even now?" it said. "Knowing size of universe, age of universe, vastness, number of planets . . . even now some mankinds think they are purpose of universe?"

Grandma stood up and shook herself. "All men don't, no, but it's still being taught, Fixit. It is taught in churches! Oh, not the Kindlies, they wouldn't, but there are others. You can tell the ones who are corrupted by it. Unless a thing serves them in some way, they don't see it at all. And if they see it, it's theirs to destroy." She sounded as though she wanted to cry, for she had come to feel that the Oracles she had trusted were probably among those who had no bao.

Someone sighed deeply and was echoed by someone else again.

Into the silence came a drowsy, wondering voice from the next room: *"Where's this place?*

"Oh, oh, is she hurt?

"Where's Dawn-song?"

And then, demanding: *"Where's Needly?"*

Needly cried out in a mixture of surprise, concern, and joy! Their sleeping medicine hadn't kept him asleep. Willum was awake.

Grandma ran to get Silkhands, who came stumbling with sleep to lay her hands upon the boy immediately, exclaiming that he should not be excited, so the group split up and went off in various directions. Balytaniwassinot took Silkhands aside and spoke with her for a few moments, after which Abasio gently carried the boy into the turtle, where Balytaniwassinot put a piece of equipment over his body, left it there for a few moments, and then invited Silkhands to look at the results.

"The scar's gone?" she cried.

"Could not have done it while foreign substance prevented care. Would not have helped him. But once you and witchery woman had accomplished the impossible, this healer could do things very fast. Keep him quiet for one day. One day is all that is needed." Of course, with rather extensive reprogramming, the machine could possibly have removed the sawdust and splinters of the yew shaft, but Balytaniwassinot hesitated to think how long that would have taken. If he could have obtained permission to do it at all! Still, it would provide an interesting footnote in his trip report.

Willum could not be convinced Dawn-song was all right until he was carried, again gently, out to the building where Dawn-song and Sun-wings were housed. He wanted to stay there with Dawn-song and Needly, but was talked into spending a couple of days as Wide Mountain Mother's guest, until he was thoroughly healed and would not run the risk of destroying some of what Silkhands still considered to be fragile membranes that were holding parts of his body together. Certainly it would do no harm for him to rest, even though Fixit knew the healing was happening with great rapidity.

It was evening. People were weary, even those who had slept during part of the day, Willum, among others, was ensconced in a large, soft bed in Wide Mountain Mother's best guest bedroom, and outside his door were shifts of guards charged with keeping him *placid, unexcited, and quiet for at least one full day.*

Before Abasio fell asleep in the wagon, surrounded by his own family, warm in Xulai's arms, his ears full of baby babble of "Illum, Illum, Illum," he learned of the guards' assignment. His comment, made only to himself, was "Fat chance!"

CHAPTER 16

Fixit's To-Do List

THE TALK ABOUT BAO WAS NOW ON THE log, and it had sorted people very neatly, and even though Fixit had already assigned most of the people and creatures it had met into bao and nonbao categories, having it on the logs would give him official sanction. Everything falling into place so neatly had allowed Fixit to sleep very well during the night, and thus refreshed, he was in the proper mood to deal with the Oracles. Abasio had mentioned Grandma's need to know what had happened to her children, which Fixit had foreseen. Indeed, it was the one episode in this entire plan that Fixit felt ashamed of. He simply had not been able to think of any other way to do it! Nor had his partner in the endeavor, one well known to Grandma, who had been in on it almost from the beginning!

Fixit asked both Abasio and Grandma to make the trip, using the Listener as an excuse. They should learn the way things could be ordered through the Listener. Fixit had spent large pieces of the previous century planning this particular visit, and it hoped to wind up all the unfinished business before it left. After the centuries it had spent (*which it never would admit to, no, not even under torture*), Fixit was not leaving with things half solved, merely hoping they would work out. Right now it would focus on Abasio and Grandma and the other one—Fixit's silent partner, Jay, Grandma's changeable friend—for it believed that trio could probably carry the project forward . . . even though two of the three knew nothing about it at all.

Besides, Fixit felt a kind of sympathy for both of them. Fixit had been involved in their lives for a very long time. The problem of Earth: the lack of bao; the total idiocy of its environmental destruction; the fact that its inhabitants had come within a knife's edge of killing themselves off (which a majority of the council had approved their doing and had encouraged their getting on with); the fact that that they were, indeed, a plague now spreading into the galaxy. The vote of the Galactic Supreme Council had been so close. Finally it had come down to a simple challenge found in the Order to Exterminate Species.

" . . . To identify those individuals with bao, present individual mankinds with an extermination problem solvable only through bao, allowing those with bao to survive."

Naturally, the council was still arguing about what the problem should be, and what the response should be. Left to the council, mankind would have gone extinct before its members made up their minds. Fixit had decided upon an AIS, an Arbitrarily Imposed Solution. Which, of course, had to happen all by itself because Fixit did not intend to lose his rank. Or his sense of self-approval.

The plea from pathetic little Gaea, the world spirit, had been arranged. Fixit had taken care of that. Then the response of Lom—Fixit had spent endless days with Ganver, encouraging it to pick up the duties of world spirit, continue the weeding out of the humans, saving the bao ones: the presence of the three women who had come from Lom was indicative that some of them were capable, useful, and appropriate and should be allowed to live and reproduce. Then the request to Squamutch had been arranged. And the subsequent flooding, timed very carefully to allow adjustment. (During the same elapsed time it had taken Fixit to accomplish this, the council had called to order seven hundred and eighty-seven committee and subcommittee sessions to decide what should happen on Earth.)

All that, climaxing in the last, final, most important thing: the response of mankind—at least of the better ones of the race. To meet the challenge, they had to choose to *change themselves to fit the environment* rather than yet again trying to force the environment to accommodate them. AND delightfully enough, *they had to do it individually!*

None of the humans involved realized what a memorable decision this had been. The betting among galactic workers had been nine to two against. No Earthlings knew that decision was the only thing that had allowed mankind's existence to continue. The real threat had been "change or be eradicated," and the decision had to be made now, not two hundred years from now. *Only the ones with bao would swallow sea-eggs and make the change, only the ones who would make the change now would survive to reproduce sea-children.* Those who would not change would die. *And, of course, there was still the final problem. That final threat was still there. The final question hadn't been asked yet.*

Some of them would be told, of course. It was up to Fixit to decide who and when. It had previously thought it would be Abasio and Grandma; it had added a few names to those two. All of them had dedicated their lives and had suffered extreme losses. They had proved capable of self-sacrifice. It did not seem to Fixit that their labor had been appropriately recognized! Well, it couldn't be, really. The true story might never be allowed to surface. Still, Balytaniwassinot was determined to "Fixit." Let, as it were, the quizzinogs out of the carrying sack for a few persons to deal with. Not just yet. A few were not quite ready yet. But it would make friends and see how things developed.

"I have received award," Fixit announced to Abasio and Grandma. "My name, Fixit, is name Self was given for thinking up method Self calls MIF, which stands for Massive Immediate Fix."

The two humans exchanged puzzled glances but seemed interested.

"I will explain," said Fixit. "I am agent, you know? Agents have come to Earth for a very long time. Always before, agent received what you might call niggles? You know niggles?"

Grandma said thoughtfully, "You mean, people complaining about something, not screaming emergency or anything, just sort of whining about it. Griping, we call it."

Fixit nodded. Tan had perfected the nod and other human bodily signs in front of a large mirror. Also frowns, sneers, "shrugs"—a raised shoulder movement indicating puzzlement. Humans still used a great variety of prespeech signals. "Griping, yes, good word. And what is usually done about niggles?"

"Usually nothing. People are busy, they have more urgent things to do . . ."

"Exactly. This is way things were done in my environment, also. Niggles came, no one did anything. Niggles accumulated. No one did anything. Finally niggles became, as you say, emergency. Or some disaster happened but no one connected disaster to niggles. You understand?"

"You're saying a lot of time was lost, a lot of effort expended, sometimes even lives were lost or, maybe, planets ruined because no one took action," said Grandma.

"Exactly! So, in my program each niggle is examined to see if it is what you call 'balloon' or 'seed'! Balloon is much air inside nothing much, seed is something that may grow like weed and put roots halfway to center of planet! And if is seed, no matter how tiny a seed, have machine to examine for what might happen. If machine says 'whoops,' this means look at seed very carefully. Sometimes 'whoops' is whole millennium away. Century is quite common. More usual is like large part lifetime. When do you think is time to handle 'whoops'?"

"While you can still sweep it into the dustpan," said Grandma.

"Right. And burn it right now, before it blows away," said Abasio.

"Even if whoops is many, many years away?"

Both its guests nodded, glancing at each other, smiling, as though both remembered things that should have been handled a long time ago.

Fixit said, "So, is of my mind entirely so. Niggles become item one of my system. Check every niggle and do it as far in advance of trouble as possible. Even if trouble is lifetimes away. Then Massive Immediate Fix may never be needed." He heaved something very much like a sigh.

"Used to be galactic officers went to problem area. Might be three problems, three different planets, not far apart, but Agent Arp might be assigned to planet one, Agent Berp went to planet two, Agent Carp went to planet three. All close together, wormhole close, you understand? So Agent Arp found out what was problem, he needed item Arp-item-one for little job and worker Arp-worker-one, who knows how to install item. Went on with problem, found needed another item for another little job, sent for Arp-item-two, worked way down list.

"Meantime, Agent Berp, nearby, requisitions Berp-item-one and Berp-item-two. Items get mixed up. Item Arp-item-one arrives in Berp system, agent there did not requisition, returns item. Meantime, nearby,

Agent Carp has also ordered same item, which at that moment is quite close but in process of being returned far away.

"Now both Arp and Carp waiting for same item. Worker Arp-worker-one, arriving at Arp site, is knowing how to use Arp-item-one, but that item not present. Arp-worker-one gets disgusted, leaves to do emergency job elsewhere. First agent still waiting for item. Eventually worker and item arrive in same system, by that time agent has moved on, no one remembers what problem was. And so on."

"Sounds likely to me," said Abasio. Grandma nodded.

Fixit continued: "Was not unusual! Unfortunate, but not unusual. Self did study. Counted time spent, time wasted, time other jobs delayed because of equipment not on hand, workers coming and going, different workers doing exact same jobs in close-by areas, wormhole traffic heavy back and forth, back and forth. Superiors granted permission for Self to try MIF. Massive Immediate Fix.

"Next job: Self requisitions one Massive Fabricator, six analysis experts, one skill gathering—this is group of people, usually of very different races of creature, whose skills reinforce and supplement one another. A skill gathering is very powerful, very time-consuming to bring together (such creatures have many commitments), but once together, immensely able to quickly make statement: *These things should be done.* No hang-ups problems with a skill gathering—do not confuse this with ordinary committee, which requires no expertise from members, talks forever without getting anything done. In skill gathering, no one wastes words: what one does not know, another does. Each one speaks *only to own field of expertise.* Says it one time only: 'Do this!' Gets up and leaves when it has said. Then scheduling manager fits what each one said into plan.

"Also, Self brings much other equipment. Self gets all problem areas located, fifty, sixty areas. Self divides them into clusters by contiguity, anywhere from three to five is good so long as they are close together. We go to one cluster of three locations. Self takes one GDE, that is 'galactic day equivalent,' for using skill gathering. Using same, we determine base cause of niggle in each place, see likelihood of disaster projection, and analyze corrective measures on three separate planets, each member says what must be done, then skill gathering sent on to next cluster. Meantime orders are sent to Massive Fabricator same day, workers briefed late that same day. Second day, all material and workers delivered, self-generating process begins and will continue; third day inspector looks at fix process, tweaks if necessary, and we are on way to next cluster. Fixed processes are checked at intervals thereafter, to be sure proceeding as planned.

"Estimate to do each cluster the normal way, half year, galactic time. My way, three GDEs. Normal expense, each single one, ten times what my way cost for all three. Self presents report to high panel. High panel says wait until we see if it works. I go on with other projects; eventually high panel says, yes, it works, you are given name FIXIT. Teach others how to use. Now everyone but old gnafflesnorts does it Fixit way.

"Gnafflesnorts claim there was no problem to fix in two of three places. Self points out that niggle on first world indicates an irreversible planet-wide famine within one hundred years. Niggle on other world indicates all life will be wiped out before end of century due to war between and among three races fighting over living space; trees used by one race being cut down to make room for burrows used by another race, both being killed by water-living race seeking to flood both areas."

"Let me guess," said Grandma. "Gnafflesnorts were not comfortable dealing with likelihood or probability."

Fixit whooped. "Gnafflesnorts unable to act on anything short of world being covered with rotting bodies. At that time they are happy to meet, shake heads or other body parts, saying equivalent of tsk-tsk, then issue report saying what might have been done earlier, along with interdiction of planet until life reemerges, when and if!

"Gnafflesnorts are immutable, unchanging, rather die than change, soon will die, so those identified as gnafflesnorts are now given only twiddly little problems that are not really problems and everyone lets them alone, happily talking forever how to solve nothing much."

"Why do you use them at all?" Abasio asked.

Fixit drew itself up and adopted a strongly judgmental expression. "Why, good-ness gra-cious, gnafflesnorts very im-por-tant crea-tures. Related to other very im-por-tant crea-tures, like head of council or vice president. Cannot do without gnafflesnorts. Gnafflesnorts must be allowed to die in office. You know syndrome?"

This oration had taken up most of the time needed to reach the House of the Oracles. The ship took up most of the clearing next to the sign and bell, and Fixit dropped the ramp onto the path. Fixit pointed a device at the bell, which rang and went on ringing. When an Oracle appeared, the Fixit told it to get its whole group, person, singularity out here where he could look at it. Grandma was watching from inside the flier. If the news was . . . really bad, she wanted to be able to cry without anyone looking at her. She stood at the top of the ramp, grasped Abasio's hand, and held on to it as though she were drowning. He put his arm around her shoulders and pulled her close.

The Oracles came out, a few at a time, forming a small group that got larger and larger. Abasio stopped counting at fifty, for he noticed a strange thing happening. The ones at the center of the group began to lose shape, to amalgamate, drawing others in at the edges, the process continuing, until by the time the last ones had joined the group, the Oracle was one large lump of gray something, perhaps six or eight man heights wide and one very short man height tall, covered with silvery hair. During this process he felt Grandma shaking beside him, her face expressing pain, disappointment, dislike . . . fear!

Abasio had been instructed to say and do nothing. To disguise the fact that he too was shaking, he leaned casually against the doorframe, pulling Grandma with him, his arm around her. The flier was called "expansible" by Fixit, which evidently meant it would become whatever size was necessary to move who or whatever needed to be moved. Abasio felt very strange and tried to analyze how he felt. He was interested, a little horrified; he felt a weird desire to giggle; and there was a very a slight shudder of nausea. Grandma was trembling, and he held her even tighter. She was afraid, though weirdly enough, he felt it was going to be all right. For no earthly good reason, it was going to be all right. Fixit's presence was . . . inexplicably reassuring.

Fixit spoke to the thing. It spoke about Grandma. It said she had had seven children. It said those children had been taken from her. It demanded to know, at once, where they were and what they were doing.

The Oracle thing shuffled. Abasio bent over and looked at the bottom edge of it. Feet. The thing had scores and scores of feet. A mouth opened somewhere and the thing said, "They're well."

"That does not answer the question."

Pause. "What was question?"

"Where are they now, and what are they doing?"

"Gaaaa . . . haven't decided yet . . ."

"Where are they now?"

"In workshop."

"Doing what?"

Four voices spoke. "Nothing." "In storage." "Since put there." "Long time ago."

"You will immediately split off a small portion, send it to the workshop, and take Grandma's children out of storage and bring them here."

Half the aggregation began to move.

"No, no. I said small portion. Maybe one-tenth of that!"

A triangular piece of the Oracle slid out of the whole pie, split into the more familiar gray-clad Oracle shape, and hastened into the House of the Oracles.

From his position by the flier, Abasio heard Grandma muttering, "I'll kill it. I'll kill the whole damned thing. Oh, I'm so angry . . ."

They waited for what seemed to be quite a long time. The Oracle grew restless, shifting from side to side, like water sloshing in a bowl. Fixit lifted a hand and something shot out of a nozzle on the flier, falling on it like mist. The Oracle became very, very quiet.

Inside the House, someone shouted. Someone else. Several people, young girls and boys, came out of the portal, skirted the Oracle, and gathered around the galactic officer. They appeared to be in early adolescence, oddly clad, as though dressed by someone who was not accustomed to clothing.

"I know them!" cried Grandma, escaping Abasio's grip and fleeing down the ramp from the flier at a run. "They've grown, but I'd know them anywhere. Oh, Jacky and Jules, how tall you've grown. Sally, still chewing your nails I see. Sarah, Jan, where did you get those haircuts? Serena! Oh, look at you. You're turning beautiful. Who'd have thought . . ."

The six young people stared at her. Jacky said tentatively, "Moms?" The one addressed as Serena asked, "What'd you do, Moms?" Sarah complained, "They said you'd come get us real soon," and three of them said, almost in unison, "You got older!"

The part of Oracle that had gone into the House returned to its brethren. Fixit did the thing with the nozzle again, and the Oracle flattened against the ground, ending up the thickness of a doormat. It did not move. Fixit remarked in a conversational tone, "I cannot decide whether to simply destroy the whole mass of it. Or split it up into little tiny pieces and scatter them across the universe. Or confine the whole ridiculous pudding in a very small ice cavern on an asteroid with an extremely long orbit for the next several thousand years."

It turned toward Grandma. "Data bank on this planet includes a creature called a . . . luggage mouse. No, no. Packing mouse? No, rat! . . . REFERENCE needed! . . . Packing rat?"

She nodded, suddenly very alert. "Pack rat, yes."

"Grandma, this creature, Oracle, is also packing rat. Everywhere it goes, picks up everything. People. Creatures. Artifacts. This thing here, that thing there. This person here, that person there. Does not use. Does not care for. Does not dust or clean or keep in order. Simply aggregates! Buys time-stop storage equipment to keep live things interminably. Buys workmen, puts them in storage thinking will need someday. T'chah! Finds empty place. Calls this place 'warehouse' or 'storeroom' or 'temple' or 'House of Oracles.' Calls it something, anything, no matter what. It is only holding place for acquisitions. Not place of caring for, just place to put and forget. No sense to acquisitions. No taste. No beauty. Sometimes, accidentally, individually, items are beautiful or marvelous. Sometimes are ugly, unpleasant but expensive. Creature thinks if a thing expensive, must be good, even better if one gets for very little. Creature likes 'bargains.'" He stamped back and forth several times, working off his annoyance. (*Fixit thought he did annoyance rather well. He had practiced it, over and over.*)

Abasio said, "How old were the children when they left you, Grandma?"

"Around three or four years."

"How old are you now?" he asked the one called Sarah.

"I think about twelve, maybe a year or two more," she said. "Our Pas left us here and told us not to worry, make music and be happy. We went to school for a while. Then we worked for the Oracles a while. Then we . . . then I don't know what happened."

"When you went to school, were you all the same age?"

All six nodded.

Fixit turned toward Grandma and said sympathetically, "They stored each one until they had them all, then schooled them for a while, probably with edubots. I know they have edubots because they use them themselves—with them, the knowledge does not stick, but if they use the edubot just before an encounter with outsiders, they retain enough to give them a fleeting aura of reliability. Often they use an edubot just before such encounter, so they will seem . . . intelligent. Then they worked them for a while, we must learn at what! They look to be in good health. Are you . . . capable of taking on a family of six adolescents?"

"Well, I was one once," raged Grandma. "Had my first child when I was only five or six years older than these. I think those Oracles owe me!"

The doormat of Oracles quivered at the sound of her voice, and Fixit used the spray again. *(This time furiously, pretending to rage! See. See how angry with this creature I have become! Actually, as scapegoats go, Oracles made very good ones!)*

Grandma was raging on: "I think they owe me a great deal, including enough resources to have a place to live, maybe over in Artemisia, among people I can respect, and I'll need a couple of people to help with the housekeeping and cooking. And it's got to be a big house for all eight of us, there's Needly, too. Nine, if Willum stays with us. Which he'll probably do, at least sometimes."

Fixit had his memory leaf out. "Let's do an inventory."

They went through the House of the Oracles. Fixit methodically, Grandma snarling, Abasio incredulously. The natural cave had been partitioned off into room after room after room, some furnished for people, some simply full of things they had collected. Furniture. Art. Rocks. Gold. Clothing, closet after closet after closet of it. Different colors. Shoes, boots, sandals, slippers, things Abasio didn't recognize that seemed to be used for walking on snow. Several more-than-life-sized wood carvings of female human nudes of a racial type Abasio did not recognize. Huge tables. Everything was pictured and listed by the memory leaf.

They went through what Grandma identified as guest quarters. Furnished in accordance with some pictured hotel or guesthouse, without personality or color, adequate and no more.

"I stayed here," said Grandma. "Needly and I brought Willum here. I've stayed here many times, out at the front here, and around the food machines and another room or two equipped for human occupancy. I never saw any other human here, though I know some Artemisians have made brief visits. I never saw the rest of it, all those storage areas, all those machines. I used only the information machines and edubots that are up front."

They investigated servants' quarters. Almost identical to guest quarters. Empty. Evidently the servants had . . . recently decided it might be a good idea to be elsewhere? Abasio wondered at this. Grandma had lived nearby in her youth. She had visited here many times. She had been told that her task in Tuckwhip was arranged by the Oracles. She had assumed her children had been returned here or at least through here on their way somewhere else. She had recently returned here with Needly and others . . . Possibly she had spoken to one or more of the servants about her missing children. More than possibly Needly had spoken of them! Of course she had! Perhaps one or more of the servants knew there were children "in storage" here and had put two and two together. Having done so, they had felt it wise to depart. Now where were they? Fixit resolved to find a few and ask questions. The Oracles were still an enigma, and it was curious as to what they did with themselves all day.

Fixit and its helpers returned to the outside world, which felt cleaner.

One of the children came hesitantly toward them. "Sir, are you going to . . . empty out the place?"

Fixit nodded. "You are Jan, yes? I plan to empty it, yes."

"Please, our work is in there. Please do not empty out our work."

"What is your work, child?"

"Music, sir, or ma'am, or—"

"'Sir' will do as well as anything. You say music?"

"Yessir, our instruments, and the music we've written, and the music we have made records of . . . all our work."

"Can you gather it all up and bring it outside. Abasio and I will go away for a while . . . What is trouble? You made a shaking . . ."

"If you go away, the Oracles will . . . will put us back . . ."

"There will be no putting back. No nothing. The Oracle will lie there like rug. Like unattractive, dirty rug full of crumbs and spills and house-pet mess. You may walk all over it. Wipe feet on it. Let pet animal soil it. Spill paint on it. Suggest ugliest paint possible.

"Now, you collect your work, all of it, everything you value, clothes, whatever. Edubots, too, if you like. Bring it out here and Abasio and

I will be back soon. If something is too big for you to move, put it on list. No, no, to save time, I will bring out fetcher." Fixit came back to the flier and pushed buttons. Something came across the sky, stopped. Something came down from the thing in the sky. The thing in the sky went away.

The children were gathered around the thing. A featureless sphere with knobs on top. "This is Fetcher model XQ99," said Fixit. "Press button on top to wake up. Say the word 'follow,' it will follow you. Take it to the thing you want. Point, say, 'Fetch this and follow.' It will take thing and bring it. Bring it out here, say, 'Put down.' If many things in same place, say 'follow,' then point at each one and say, 'Fetch all these things to put-down place.'"

"Sir, I am Jules, sir. It isn't very big."

"Doesn't need to be big, Jules. Uses force fields. Can lift whole house if required. Try it, you will appreciate. I will see to further transport when we return. Is that satisfactory, Jules?"

Jules spoke to the machine, which followed him around in a circle. He grinned and set off, followed by a very intent little machine. Fixit turned to Abasio and snarled, "Was there any room in there that you found attractive? No. Of course not. Oracles have no taste. They are like sticky tissue for bugs."

"Flypaper," said Grandma. "I'd almost forgotten flypaper. Yes, that's exactly what they're like. No sense. A few moments, perhaps an hour's excitement in acquisition, then decades of inattention while acquisition rots. No sense. And no cherishing! Just stickiness."

"What're you going to do with it?" Abasio asked Fixit, indicating the pancake-shaped Oracle.

"Nothing for moment. Self does not think anything will eat it, though Self is willing to risk possibility. Self intends selling contents of the House, as is, less anything Grandma or the children might like to keep. There are some good educational machines in there that are generally useful for anyone seeking information . . . cooking, animal training, nuclear physics, philosophy, lovemaking for bisexual, trisexual, group sexuals, how to build houses for birds, how to build your own space fleet in owned-grassy-property-behind-house . . . REFERENCE needed! . . . *Backyard!* . . . or in building-made-for-storage-of-vehicle . . . REFERENCE needed! . . . *Garage!* The rest of it will be sold to provide exactly what Grandma has asked for. House in Artemisia, enough funding to provide for help. At least thirty—forty Earth years' worth of whatever one needs, expendables, things for house, foods, drinks, clothing for growing young ones. These young ones may not be much help for a while. Self wonders what they were taught in the Oracles 'school.'" *(Self knew very well what they had been taught in school and it was more than adequate for their very well-planned futures. They had received everything they needed, or Balytaniwassinot's name was not Fixit!)*

Fixit turned and called to Grandma. "The food machines are working, there's plenty of space. Can you and children wait here, get reacquainted, while Abasio and Self do some business?" Then he went close to her and murmured, "We will solve this situation. Please, find out what your children have been taught, what they have done. We must provide for interests, for future development, for all kinds learning that may interest them . . ."

Grandma—though appearing to be in an eccentric orbit among and around joy, fury, and confusion—agreed to all or some part of this by nodding, shrugging, weeping, and laughing simultaneously.

"Feel free to kick Oracle when you go by, jump up and down on it," said Fixit. "Perhaps the children would join you in the activity." As Fixit moved away, Abasio heard it mumbling to itself: "All emitting a distinct aura of fortunate accident. Suitable. No harm done. Coming out as planned. No aura of unsuitable purpose. Suspicious one might say someone, something messing about!"

"What are you going to do with the Oracl . . . Oracles?" Abasio asked, when they were in flight once more.

"It—it is an *it*, not a *them*. Galactic office has been uncertain how to classify Oracles. They/it are very strange arrangement, all one thing genetically identical. One puts out bud, eventually bud can detach, reattach. Each bud part has only tiny piece of brain. Brain does not grow very much, but body grows and grows, parts split off, parts pretend to be separate people, put different label on each one, label generated by computer. All very nice, BUT when real person says, 'Good morning, Mard,' or 'Go commit an indecency on yourself, Mard,' part labeled 'Mard' does not answer or react."

"You mean the part cannot remember the name of the part?"

"Is so, yes. There is one brain for whole aggregation. Brain splits, each thing not very smart. Keeps on splitting, still only one same-sized brain as in beginning. Makes whole thing ridiculous. Eventually gets very large, becomes whole crowd of very stupid things making silly remarks. *But it thinks it's smart. Acts as though very smart.*" It stopped, rubbed its head with two sets of arms, all four hands busily massaging. "*NO. Said that wrong!*

"*I am falling into Grandma trap. Oracle acts so strange that* other creatures think it must be smart! *From somewhere creature got word 'Oracle.' Word 'Oracle' is miraculous. Creature says usual stupid things, but is now getting great respect for people believe it is being* oracular! Self must examine history to determine where title 'oracle' was adopted, or given. Title 'oracle' allows stupidity to pass for wisdom. I think this happens often with humans. Person calls self oracle, seer, prophet, leader. People think the name means powerful, of large intelligence. Means nothing except that creature has adopted label. Ha! Does silly things like with Grandma's children, then forgets all about it."

Abasio thought of Arakny and shook his head. "Arakny is going to be furious! She was telling me how the Oracles casually mention something without explaining it, and how the Artemisians have to extrapolate from that to know what's meant."

"If Self forgets to tell her, you tell her: *nothing* is meant. Entirely fortuitous if something it says ends up connecting even slightly to any reality at all. Is actually only very small stupid brain making imitative noises. Could do same opening book at random, pointing at word—how you say 'covering seeing organs'?"

"Blindfolded."

"Ah, word not sensible. Do not understand 'folded' part. Eyelids, perhaps, folding? To say again, might as well look at book blindfolded, get same as from Oracle."

"How did the Oracle travel? Surely it/they can't have invented space travel on their/its own?"

"Original Oracle planet is being on main travel routes. Convenient location, so Galactic Traffic Office is putting galactic sector repair post there. At that time not familiar with Oracles. Transport ship needing repair, landing there. One or more Oracle dividing up, either . . . beg ride . . . REFERENCE needed! . . . *hitchhike* . . . or paying for transport."

"If they pay for transport, what do they pay with?"

"Is strangeness that. Pay with yribium. Not known where Oracle gets yribium, but it is found where Oracles are. Is used to make many things. I have only seen it in shapes . . . is word . . . REFERENCE needed! . . . *ingots?* Cylinders so long as my shortest arm, so big around."

It made a circle with thumb and one finger of two hands, a diameter about twice that of a broomstick. Fixit's shortest arm was as long as Abasio's from elbow to wrist and seemed to be used mostly for rubbing Fixit's scalp in frustration. Abasio started to say something but Fixit was in full cry on the yribium subject.

"Until now, always, people wanting yribium have gone to Oracle planet, scraped up luggub after luggub of soil, refined substance from soil, put soil back. So to travel Oracle maybe paid yribium, maybe hitch-hiked itself. Someone is picking it up on one planet and letting it off on another planet, still on main travel route. Oracles ending up on six, seven planets. Still dividing up, still pretending to be something. That is how it is getting here to Earth. This piece of it has been living here . . . for a long time, Abasio.

"The Artemisians have been giving it food for a generation or more. They are thinking space-traveling people must be intelligent, so they . . . are consulting it. Paying for *consultations* with some of what we found inside. Got oracular answers. Meaningless! Self feels surprise! Self would be thinking Wide Mountain Mother is smarter than that. And Grandma, too. Even smart people are believing something mysterious must have . . . wonderful-ness.

"Ah. We are here."

They had landed on the ledge next to the Listener. The sight of the Listener still made Abasio queasy, but if he turned his back on it, or stayed in the flier, it was merely an itchiness. The galactic officer took up a position next to the strange growth-device-implement and engaged in an unintelligible and interminable conversation. Part of the negotiations seemed to involve transmitting pictures of the inventory and provisions of a great many location numbers and galactic time codes, during which Abasio dozed off.

They went back to the House of the Oracles, where the Oracle(s) were still doormatting the entrance, their (its) top surface now criss-crossed in all directions with footprints. Fixit considered the sizable pile of things outside, did one of tan's message-sending routines, which resulted in a brief wait, just long enough for Fixit to move restlessly about the pile, poking at it while the children looked on rather worriedly. To Abasio, the pile seemed to contain every instrument known to any musician plus some things that seemed as likely to be instruments of torture as they were of sound, and the pile seemed of a volume impossible to move. The whole area was abruptly shadowed by the turtle's soundless arrival above the pile. It emitted voluminous amounts of papery sheets that dropped onto the pile, where they hissed at one another as they slithered and folded to wrap the entire pile—pausing once to squeal peremptorily for another few sheets—binding all into one bumpy bundle the size of a small house, which was then lifted and carried away eastward. The flier made some expansion noises as Grandma and her children came aboard; then they all returned to Wide Mountain Plaza. The house-sized bundle sat at one side and a large silver disc hovered over it—an immense silver disc that had managed to shadow the entire plaza and some of the surrounding countryside. Suspended beneath it was what could be the bottom—that is, the basement floor—of a very large house. At the center of the plaza stood Wide Mountain Mother, lips compressed, steadily tapping her foot.

Abasio was first off the flier. When the children emerged, Mother's foot stopped and her mouth opened. Abasio was at her side, lips near her ear, before she had a chance to speak. "Those are Grandma's children. Born one at a time except for the twins, over a period of some eight or ten years. Each one was taken by the Oracles when he or she was a toddler. They were put 'in storage,' which is a way of saying their lives were stopped until the Oracles had collected all six of them. Then they woke them up and played school with them for a while, then played employer with them for a while, then put them back in storage. Which is where we found them. The galactic officer has negotiated to have a house built for them."

He looked deeply into Mother's eyes and purposely smiled the smile Xulai called "seductive," doing the sidelong look that invited the listener into his private thoughts, lowering his voice as though disclosing his hidden heart with all its secrets. "Grandma has expressed a wish to live in Artemisia, where she would be able to visit with you and Arakny. She has formed a great respect for you both, and it would be a good environment for children who are going to be very puzzled about life for a time. Though her philosophy is very like yours, she hesitates to suggest it, as she's not one of your people. If you prefer her to go somewhere else, of course, that's perfectly understandable.

"That thing hovering up there will put the house down wherever is decided. The big bundle over there is the contents that will go into the house. If you would rather Grandma and the children not be here, Fixit and I will find someplace near a town or community where they'll be welcome. I imagine Saltgosh would welcome them with their usual beneficence . . ."

Wide Mountain Mother flushed. She had been prepared to feel outrage at Fixit, at Abasio, at persons innumerable. She was still outraged, but her target seemed to have moved. She was remembering how many times the Artemisians had provided the "Oracles" with food; how many times they had paid for "consultations," she only wished she could tell the . . . things what she thought of them.

She said, "Well, of course they may settle here. I'll let her pick . . . there are three or four close places . . . However . . . I was somewhat upset by the arrival of . . . what is that *thing* up there?"

"That's what Fixit calls a Massive Fabricator. It's just delivering the house, wherever you and Grandma decide to put it—and don't hesitate to tell her if it would be more suitable elsewhere! Fixit takes a Massive Fabricator and a dozen other things I know absolutely nothing about on jobs with him, her, it, or them. Its work method is to bring a great squad of backup people and equipment along and keep them within easy reach. The people, persons, organisms who come along with the Fabricator probably lie around playing gambling games up there while waiting to be called, which, considering the efficiency with which Fixit operates, I don't imagine is ever very long. Otherwise, it says, everything takes forever and costs escalate and mistakes are made.

"Then Fixit comes in with some kind of special committee of experts that makes a list of things that must be done and how they must be done, then that list is handed over to a scheduling expert who puts each thing in order of doing, then Fixit presses the do button, and it all happens more or less at once. Anyhow, that's what I, as a rather amazed observer, believe has happened. The pile of things to the side includes the musical instruments the children have used, plus some other equipment. The house is all finished except for your telling Grandma to put it somewhere else or somewhere in Artemisia and whatever systems you feel it should be connected to, if any. It doesn't have to be connected to anything: it can be fully self-contained." He turned and waved to Fixit. "I'll go fetch Grandma, and the two of you can tell him yes . . . or no, and we'll take it elsewhere."

He turned to see Needly gaping. She ran toward him. "Are they her children, Abasio? Really? What did those Oracle things DO?"

"They put her children in storage and then curled up and went to sleep for several years. How's Willum doing?"

"Silkhands says he's healed. The thing Fixit used on him speeds up the healing. He could probably climb a mountain right now, if he needed to, but everyone's trying to keep him quiet for at least a day, and it's driving him crazy. They finally gave up and carried him over to see Dawn-song so he'd calm down and sleep. Mother Griffin keeps petting him, but he just keeps saying he's been sleeping for days and days and wants to get up. So she's got him pinned down under her talons, telling him Griffin stories."

"Where's Xulai? I want to tell her we have the portable camp."

"You do? Didn't you have to give it back?"

"As it happened, I don't think the Oracles are going to ask for it. The position they're in right now, they probably won't be asking for anything, except perhaps, 'Please wipe your feet before entering.' "

Needly set off to find Xulai for him, and he sat on the bench beneath the shade trees. Across the plaza Grandma and Wide Mountain Mother were nodding and gesturing. Suddenly past them, there was a flurry of upturned soil, as though invisible shovels were digging a ditch. He watched, bemused. A minute went by, two. Five small fliers appeared and zoomed around the edges of the place he was watching, the place the two women were watching. The sky darkened. The house was descending! Soundlessly, its basement sank into the hole. Large holes appeared around it into which a dozen full-grown trees descended, several around the house and one on either side of the steps leading to the porch, which was long and wide and shady and already well equipped with rocking chairs.

Xulai came around the corner with Needly, both of them stopping in astonishment. It was a very large house and it had not been there when Needly left to look for Xulai, perhaps five minutes ago. Needly went toward it, touched the porch rail, stood staring at it in disbelief. Xulai saw Abasio waiting and came toward him, shaking her head.

"I don't believe it," she said to him. "I mean, I do believe it, but gracious. Do you suppose it's furnished inside? Beds? Sheets? Pillowcases? Pots and pans?"

"Knowing Fixit, I would say definitely yes. And some gadget that will let Grandma or any of the children return any items they don't like and receive others they do. Only I'm betting they won't because Fixit has probably used some personality analysis machine to determine what each one of them prefers. I mean, that's just being efficient, isn't it?"

She giggled. "He's—I mean, *it's* quite a wonderful . . . being."

He/it was indeed. Abasio had the germ of an idea, but there was one thing still left undone. "Wait for me. I want to speak to Fixit for just a moment."

Fixit was standing next to its flier, helping Mavin, Silkhands, and Jinian get on board along with a seemingly endless clutter of small gifts they had been given by the Artemisian women. When he saw Abasio coming, it came to meet him.

"Is trouble?" Fixit asked.

"Just a niggle. A promise I made to a man. I get the itch that it may fit into something else, maybe." He explained what it was.

"How very strange a request! In a few moments we will depart, but I will arrange to obtain what you need. I have small, very fast messenger that will return it to you here."

Raised voices drew their attention to the far side of the plaza, where Grandma and children were gathered around the new house, evidently arguing as to who ought to be first inside. The children won and lined up behind Grandma, who led the way as they all disappeared inside. Meantime, the three women from Lom had managed to get themselves and their paraphernalia aboard; Fixit waved good-bye and headed for his ship, leaving Abasio to murmur "pollen, pollen, pollen" over and over to himself. He had almost forgotten the pollen.

Needly and Grandma and her other children were inside their new house. Willum was being told Griffin stories while he was held firmly under Sun-wings's foot. Wide Mountain Mother was in her house, possibly having a nap. Fixit was, at least momentarily, gone.

"Where are the babies?" Abasio whispered, afraid to break the quiet.

"Precious Wind is babysitting in her wagon."

"Ahhh," he said, allowing himself to leer. "Then we have our wagon all to ourselves?"

CHAPTER 17

Willum Gets His Ride

WITH THE DEPARTURE OF FIXIT AND ITS SHIP, everything had fallen into an almost miraculous calm. Early evening came. Light muted. Sound softened. Footsteps slowed. Abasio sat with Xulai, Needly, and Wide Mountain Mother on a long, comfortable bench beneath a shade tree in the plaza, all four of them enjoying the fact that absolutely nothing was happening.

Needly murmured, "Grandma and her children are getting acquainted. The house is really nice. We each have our own room. It's just about perfect."

"Yes," said Abasio. "It looks very . . . residential. I saw the Fabricator had already provided shade trees. Very large ones."

Needly nodded her unequivocal approval. "The thing in the sky looked around and saw how things were done, then it did one to match. It got the trees from the mountains, and it planted small ones in their place."

"How many rooms does it have?" asked Xulai, with a touch of envy.

"Grandma has a bedroom and bathroom all to herself. And there's a girls' wing, with three bedrooms, one for each one of us, and a boy's wing, too, and each bedroom has its own toilet and basin! Then there's one big huge shower room for girls and one for the boys. It's wormhole plumbing! They run the water near a star to heat it! It has huge kitchen with everything to cook with, but the best thing is the music room. They do make wonderful music, Abasio. They're going to teach me. Serena says I have a nice voice. I can sing, sort of sing, but I didn't know I could do it at all because that's the last thing any female would want to do in Hench Valley. Evidently my mother couldn't sing, but Grandma can, and she says it skipped a generation. And the house has a separate living room and the hugest dining room. The table has chairs enough for twice as many of us."

"Has it indeed?" said Abasio thoughtfully. "Has it indeed! Well, sharing a shower room is quite acceptable." He nodded gravely. "After all, sometimes Xulai, you, and Willum, the babies, the horses, Kim, and I all have had to share the same tree."

Needly giggled. "We did, didn't we." She looked up. "Oh, there's Bear and Coyote!"

"They went to sleep at my house," said Wide Mountain Mother. "Poor things were worn out."

The two animals ambled over. Stretching out on the ground, Bear said, "We was so tired we didn't wake up until just a little while ago. Didn't nobody care 'bout where those Edgers went? Them as was buildin' fish bodies?"

Abasio started, flushing. "Oh, Coyote, Bear, there's been so much going on we're losing track of what we're trying to do! We do need to know about that."

Coyote lay down at Abasio's feet and recited what he and Bear had seen, describing the containers that had been filled from the truck, and concluding, "He took some stuff out of the truck the spray came from, you know, the one we saw? N' then him and the driver got in a fight. Or t'other way round. Driver was yellin' at him how long was it gonna go on, all this killing people t'make fish, and who's gonna wanta be in the fish two hunnert years from now. Anyhow, Old Purple, he knocked the driver down and he took off in that wagon, Abasio. Eight horses. Maybe twelve riders and a whole bunch of other trucks and things." He turned to Bear. "Isn't that what happened?"

"Near as I could tell. He didn't make much sense, and he was so mad his face was all swole up."

Abasio grimaced and rubbed his forehead, wishing greatly that

Fixit had not chosen just this time to go off to Tingawa. "If he headed north, he's headed for Edger country or west, one or the other. He wouldn't go east or south. If he's headed west, he'll have to cross the Big River, and on our way from the pass, we used the only bridge that'll take wagons and trucks; it's the one northwest of here. He can't take vehicles across the river anywhere else unless he goes north almost to Fantis."

"He'll be going through Artemisia," said Wide Mountain Mother. "He has to, to get to the bridge."

Coyote laid a paw on Abasio's knee. "Listen, 'Basio. There's somethin' worse. That Chief Purple, he was yellin' about the sea-children. He was sayin' he's got poison t'put at all the Sea Duck places t'kill the sea-children. He was yellin' about the only one to go on livin' was the Edges, nobody else."

Xulai drew in her breath, paling. Abasio got to his feet to pace a three-step square, back and forth, muttering, "Sea Duck. He wouldn't know where to find Sea Duck Three, and he has no way to get to Tingawa, so he's headed for Sea Duck One. He'll have to go through the mountains. When he left, where were you? Up on the Cow? Which direction did he go from there?"

Bear moved his left front paw. "We were on the sun side of that Cow Mountain, up above his cave. He was headed around that Cow Mountain, n' he had to go the long way. No way he could get that wagon through where that whale blew up. Couldn't get through that little forest n' all the sand piles inna way."

"You mean where we had the camp?"

"Yeah. He couldn' go that way. So he went aroun' the mountain t'other way."

Abasio cursed himself for not waking Bear and Coyote earlier to find out what was going on. If old Chief Purple had headed around the east end of Cow Bluff and angled west to come up the east side of the Big River, he could already have crossed the bridge. It had been less than a full day's trip south to Cow Bluff from the Oracles, slowly, with loaded wagons. It had been a full day ago that Coyote and Bear had seen the men depart.

Bear mumbled, "That wagon a' his. It's real bright. Sun shines off it like off water—"

"Just a minute," cried Abasio. "A wagon painted . . . could it be gold, Coyote? Painted to look like gold?"

"What's gold look like?" Coyote asked.

Wide Mountain Mother took a chain from around her neck and held it out, twisting it so that the small pendant on it sparkled. "Like this, Coyote."

"Yeah, painted to look like that. Why?"

"Then Grandma was right!" cried Needly. "Grandma knows about him. She says he's the same man as that one you called Chief Purple."

"How does she know him, Needly?"

"In wintertime, the Hench Valley men spent most of their time digging in the buried city. Then, come springtime, they'd haul everything they'd found up to Findem Pass to sell to the traders. Grandma used to go up there, see what was sold and bought, and she saw the Gold King and his wagon when he bought stuff from Old Digger. She even talked about the kind of cans Coyote described. That tag Coyote found? She thought it was like the ones on those cans, and that's what made her think it was some kind of chemical. She thought the little tag Coyote found would confirm it, but Precious Wind said Tingawa can't identify it."

Abasio growled, "That stuff might have been what Chief Purple used to buy himself a place in the Edge."

Xulai stared down at her knotted hands, frowning. "Tingawa doesn't know what the tag identifies? If the Gold King only bought a few cans of it, up there at the pass, he either had to have some of it already, or it had to be mixed with other things in that 'activator' truck."

Abasio mused, "The truck had several tanks on it, the mixture probably wasn't explosive until it was mixed, and the various substances were probably mixed as they were sprayed. Otherwise, the activator could have been too dangerous to have around. They must have thought they'd solved the explosive problem . . ."

Xulai offered, "Maybe they had solved it. It didn't blow up until something went wrong with the . . . what, the wiring?"

Abasio grunted. "Possibly. Well, if Tingawa can't identify the substance, we've got to get hold of some of it! The quickest way might to go back to Cow Bluff and find the red truck that sprayed it . . ."

Coyote yelped, "Nah, 'Basio, that's what we're tellin' you. Him and the driver had a fight. Purple knocked him down, and he didn't move. But then, when Purple and all his men left, the driver got up off the ground and he went in the cave and came out with this burning stick, and he threw the stick at that truck and blew it up!" said Coyote. "He was yellin' about nobody wantin' t'be in a fish—"

Bear interrupted. "Sayin' wasn't gonna be anybody lef' in two hunnert years to go inna fish."

Abasio shook his head, his hands curling into fists. "Sounds like he used dynamite to blow up the truck; they still use it in mining, even at Saltgosh. And, if he destroyed the truck to get rid of whatever went into the 'activator' substances, he's probably also destroyed any supply of them they had in their cave." He rose, stalked about, muttered, "Hell of a time for Fixit to take himself off to Tingawa." He came back to Coyote. "You didn't have time to count the men, did you?"

Coyote swung his jaw from side to side, meaning no. "Happened too fast. Lots, though. Really lots. Two paws, five or six times, maybe."

Abasio kept up his pacing. "If Tingawa can't identify the tag, then the only way it can be identified is to get some of the stuff and have Tingawa . . . or Fixit . . . tell us what it is. If the Gold King's wagon is past the bridge, it'll be headed up toward the pass."

He was thinking furiously. It was late afternoon. The sun would go down soon, and the cavalcade of horses and trucks would have to stop. Unless some of the trucks and cars still had headlights. Very few did. Batteries were almost an extinct creation, but if anybody had any, it would be old Chief Purple's bunch. Who knew what might be found in the buried factory east of Fantis? Someone had to see to that. He'd talk to Fixit when he came back . . . which could be far too late.

Xulai murmured, "Bear, can you tell us again what sort of container he put the stuff in?"

"They was 'bout as big as your head. Real shiny, like sun on water. With a round place where a lid screws onto like a honey jar, and a kina . . ." He reached out to touch her belt.

"Belt? Strap?"

"Like that, yeah. A strap across the lid to hold it so it wuddn' get open by mistake. And there was a hose at the side of the truck he got 'em from, that's how he filled 'em. And he put 'em in his shiny wagon, an' all those other men came runnin' out and got inta their cars n' trucks, n' they drove off. They had . . . what's those . . . ?" He looked questioningly at Coyote. "T'kill things with?"

"Long guns, Xulai. Long guns," said Coyote. "The kind that shoot really far."

"Did you hear him, Abasio?" she cried.

Abasio was glaring at nothing. "Yes, I heard him. Rifles. Chief Purple was always and is now as bad a stinker as his . . . creatures are. The problem I'm struggling with is that once he gets past Saltgosh Valley, he'll be in the forest. Maybe Fixit can locate him, even there, but I don't know that he can; we don't know when Fixit's's coming back, and if Old Purple gets to Wellsport . . ."

"That Old Purple, he's got a two-paw hitch . . ." said Bear. "And he 'uz out front. Didn't nobody go past him."

Abasio stopped pacing and turned toward Needly. "Do you happen to know, has Sun-wings been flying?"

Needly cried, "Oh, yes, Abasio. Before the healer lady from Lom left with Fixit, she looked at Sun-wings' wounded wing, and she put some new stuff on her, and then Mr. Fixit took a portable machine over there, and between the two of them, they healed her wing beautifully, not even a scar, and—"

Wide Mountain Mother interrupted: "Meanwhile, they were giving most of the credit to you, my dear, for the wonderful job of field surgery you did."

"I need to go talk to Sun-wings," Abasio muttered.

"What about the glactic guy?" asked Coyote.

"The galactic guy had to run some sort of galactic errand." Abasio turned away, fuming. Yet another Edger plan. What kind of mind would come up with a plan to kill everyone else and leave the planet for the Edgers? Even the driver of the truck seemed to have figured that out. Edgers were a dying breed. Couldn't the old fat man see that? No. The old fat man couldn't see past his nose. The old fat man not only did not have bao, he was off the scale the other way. He thought the whole universe was centered on him personally. Well, he wasn't going to get away with it. Not damned likely. Abasio turned back toward the rider. "I think I know how to handle this." He turned and ran across the plaza, headed for the building the Griffins were still occupying.

Sun-wings was dozing when he came in. She lifted one eyelid, yawned, and greeted him with a sound rather like a purr. Then, "Yes, Abasio?"

"I understand you've been flying."

"I have," she said with great satisfaction. "There's a little pull in the membrane of the wing, but the healers assure me it will lessen and finally go away."

"Are you flying well enough to go to Saltgosh, carrying a passenger?"

"Why would I want to do that?"

"Because our hope of letting men survive, and our hope of giving you what you've asked for, are rapidly escaping from us. One of the Edgers—you know who I mean?"

"The ones we call the 'gophers.' Yes."

"Long and long ago, an artist among them created you, Sun-wings. You and the others like you. He was a great artist because he made you beautiful and sane and marvelous. We are being visited by a shape-shifter who can help you and your children take a form that will swim and float and fly when the world is covered in water. However, doing it requires a substance . . . a material. One of the Edgers, the one called the Gold King, has taken the substance and he's headed for Wellsport, across the mountains. There are a great many other Edgers in vehicles following him. They have weapons. He is going, we think, to sell the material to someone else. We can stop him, but I need to get word to Saltgosh now, in a hurry, and the only way I know to do it is to send someone."

"I can convey a message."

"Sun-wings, even for such a purpose, I, *we* are unwilling to risk your life. The people in Saltgosh are very nervous. They've added some heavy weaponry which could hurt you badly. My idea was, if you'd take Willum—"

"The boy?" She laughed. "I dangled him when I took him from place to place in the mountains. He was . . ." She sought for the new word Needly had taught her. "Indignant."

"Couldn't you let him sit on your shoulders, in front of your wings. See, they have a watchtower over there. If you fly into the valley low, past the watchtower, land down in the center of it, not threatening at all, and Willum gets off and runs toward the watchtower, they'll know you're not dangerous. He can deliver the message, and then you can bring him back."

"The message being?"

"That they need to chop down one huge tree to block the road that runs west."

She closed her eyes for a moment, then nodded. "You need to force the wagon to take the north road into the long valley where the giants are."

"You know about them?"

"They're very visible. Whenever I flew over that valley, I screamed a few times, just to bring them out. They keep on growing, you know."

"You mean, they're still getting bigger?"

"They were. The strange visitor, I am told, has sprayed them with something to shrink them, but it will take a long time. Perhaps it will only stop them growing. We were wondering when they would stop growing. I was told once, long ago, by someone, that there is a limit to what bone will support. I was also told that in prehistoric times there were huge creatures, as large as the giants. Perhaps they had bone like ours, not the same as other creatures, but not . . . unnatural. Do you expect the giants to stop this . . . Gold King?"

"We think they will, yes. If we make enough noise to attract them. When I came through there, Willum's hollering was all it took. The stuff we need is in two metal canisters. About as big around as my head. Very strong canisters. The giants attack because they're hungry. Probably the canisters will survive any attack the giants make. Probably they will leave them alone."

"Then, probably, my sisters and I can fly in later and pick them up?"

"I had thought someone could pick them up. We actually need only one of them. Or they're small enough that you could carry a bit of netting, roll them into it, and carry both of them. Both of them together may not be as heavy as some prey animals I know you've carried. Needly has told us about her stay with you, of course. She's very fond of you and Dawn-song."

"Fond," murmured Sun-wings. "This is like what? Loving?

"Like that, yes."

"And Willum?"

Abasio laughed. "He'd still rather ride you than a horse, and it isn't that you are more intelligent or better spoken, because Blue, the horse, is an extremely intelligent and well-spoken creature. I think Willum is in love with the idea of flight."

"I can take the boy," she said. This was the boy who had given his life for her child. Oh, yes, she could take this boy.

"You'll be landing in the pasture below the town. It would be nice if you could avoid eating any of their livestock while you wait for Willum to deliver the message."

"When is this to be done?"

"It's too late to go today. Dawn, in the morning."

"Then, if I'm not to eat one of their goats or sheep, you'd better ask someone to bring me some early breakfast."

Wakened before dawn, Willum was in a state of disbelief. He kept saying, "Oh, wow."

"Willum. You! Are! Not! Listening!"

"Oh, wow. C'n I go all the way to Gravysuck and show Mom?"

"I've changed my mind, you can't go."

" 'Basio, no, no."

"Then shut up and listen."

Willum clamped his hand over his mouth and appeared to give Abasio his full attention.

"This will not do unless you can follow directions. You'll fly over Saltgosh, down into the meadow, about halfway, so the Saltgoshians will see that Sun-wings is not attacking. She'll land down in the meadow. You get off. You'll carry a flag, and you'll wave the flag like crazy at the watchtower while you walk up the meadow toward the town. They've moved down to Snow Town, so the people who'll see you are in the watchtower. You tell them the Griffin is waiting to take you back. You tell them I sent you. You find somebody, anybody, and ask them to find Melkin. You give Melkin the letter I'll be writing while you are getting dressed to go flying. Once Melkin has read the letter, ask him for an answer.

"Now, repeat back to me what I just said."

"Y'mean now?"

"I mean now."

"I . . . I . . . guess I didn't . . . hear what you just said."

Abasio just looked at him. Willum began to turn red. Abasio shook his head. "Then you can't go. I'll find some local child who wants to do the job and can listen to instructions. Perhaps Needly would go. She's lighter. It would be easier on Sun-wings. I'm sorry to have bothered you with it. I guess you're just . . . too . . . stupid . . . to learn."

Willum turned a color very close to purple. "'Basio, say it again. Please. Just say it one time again."

Abasio said it again slowly. When he had finished, Willum repeated it back to him, getting it mostly right. They did it again, and this time Willum got all of it right.

"This is your one and only last chance, Willum. You foul this up by yelling or yodeling or any other kind of nonsense, and you are going home to Gravysuck. Up in the air, you keep your mouth shut. I do not want anyone looking up to see what's up there, getting the idea Sun-wings has captured a child, then trying to shoot her, do you understand me? What did I just say?"

Willum repeated what he had just said. Abasio could hardly believe it. He went on:

"You are to be silent. You are to find Melkin and give him the message which will ask him to give you an answer. If the answer is yes, you may stay there long enough to see what happens. If you can get the stuff from the wagon, that would be marvelous. The cans are melon-shaped, pumpkin-shaped, round, like your head . . . and there's two of them. If the answer is no, you have to get back here fast and let me know. And if Sun-wings tells me you've made a single sound out of line, you're going home with the next wagon headed west. I'm telling her the same thing, so if you forget, be sure, she'll remember. If you do anything to endanger her life, she has our permission to drop you and leave you wherever you fall."

"When do we go?" asked Willum.

Abasio snarled, "What do you do if the answer is no?"

Willum turned a deeper red, his face contorted in concentration. "Come back and tell you as fast as I can. We can, that is."

"You're going to go now," said Abasio, who had noticed that the large washtub in which Sun-wings's meals were served was being re-trieved from her building. "As soon as you eat something, put on a double sweater and your jacket."

He stood in the sun, head down, trying to not-think. So many things could go wrong.

Someone tugged on his arm. One of Grandma's children. "Abasio, Mr. Fixit said give this to you." He held out a small packet. "He said it took some getting. He said time travel. Can anybody really do that?"

Abasio shook his head. "Thank you, Jules. This is a miracle. The one thing needed to guarantee success, and here it is! I don't know about time travel, but if anyone could, it'd probably be Fixit."

Sun-wings came out of the building and extended her wings, repeatedly, first one, then the other, then both, stretching them to their limits, moving them high, meeting over her back, then down, so far as the earth would allow.

When Abasio approached, she said, "I think a rope loop, in front of the wings, just behind my front leg shoulders and held down, tight, by one of my front feet. In that way, the boy can put his upper legs under the rope, his lower legs back, and his feet tucked under it. Then I can tighten it gently—is that right word?—with my foot, but it does not choke me. He will hang on to the rope with hands, too."

They tried a couple of lengths before finding one that was comfortable for her. Abasio said, "Don't fret over Dawn-song, you know we'll take care of her until you get back." Willum came out of the wagon warmly dressed and muttering about blankets on fish—Xulai had obviously seen to dressing him. Abasio unbuttoned the boy's jacket, lifted the sweaters, and placed the message beneath the shirt, next to Willum's skin. "There may be some other stuff in that wagon, Willum. I don't know what it looks like. It's called yribium. If it's in ingots, it'll be short, thick, very heavy sticks. If you see anything like that, grab some of it."

He took hold of the boy's chin, looked beyond him to speak to both him and Sun-wings. "Now, this is important. The woodsman over there in Saltgosh is not going to want to cut that tree! You give this to Melkin. It's pollen from a male tree like the one you have to cut. It's something their woodsman has wanted for years. He'll cut the tree if you give him this. You've got an inside pocket in your jacket. I'm putting it in that pocket, and I'm buttoning it so you can't lose it." *And pray to heaven that it contains what Fixit said it does.* He turned to meet Sun-wings's eyes. She seemed to be smiling.

"I'm going to climb the stone place they call 'Two Old Men Pretend- ing to Be Buffalo,'" Sun-wings announced, turning toward the asp grove at the foot of a tall formation of stones that did indeed resemble two hunched old men humped over like buffalo. When they arrived at the formation, she said, "Willum, climb onto my back by holding on to little bunches of feathers, not just one, it may pull out."

He did so, his face tight with concentration. Abasio handed him the flag they had prepared, bright red, like the Saltgosh singers' caps. Sun-wings climbed the rock, talons and claws gripping and shifting, Willum lying flat against her back. Once he was on top, she told him to get his legs under the rope; then she put a front foot into the rope loop, tightened it over Willum's legs and her shoulders, and told him to bend his knees and tuck his toes under the rope and hold on tight. The next thing Abasio knew, she had launched herself downward, wings opening just before she hit the ground, then lifting, lifting. He saw her circle to gain height, then turn toward the west.

On her back, Willum was caught halfway between ecstasy and terror. They were circling higher and higher, and he was suddenly glad of the extra sweaters. It was cold up here. Maybe Xulai had been right about that. She sometimes was right about things. Most times. They were headed west, over the road. There was a hill on the horizon, and they were headed for that, reached it, went over it, and began climbing again. The mountains ahead of them were higher, much higher.

She circled up and up on the rising air from the sun-warmed slope below, moving farther west with each turn until at last she tilted to one side and Willum saw the top of the pass beneath them, the pale scribble of road descending on both sides. The sun had risen far enough that there was good light to see by, though none shone directly on this western face of the mountain. The Gold King's wagon was already one-third of the way down the side, cars and trucks strung out behind it, weapons protruding from every window. Since the Gold King had an eight-horse hitch and seemingly a light load, the wagon was moving very fast. Willum had never seen a wagon move that fast; one horse of the lead team carried a rider, and the accompanying riders were also at full gallop. He had extra horses, too, following along behind.

Sun-wings slipped over the first range of peaks, tilted, and sailed down the valley on the far side, past the Listener, turning from valley into valley, not flapping, just gliding through the rising air, slowly descending as they went. There ahead of them was the watchtower.

Willum sat up straight, held on with one hand, and waved the flag with the other. As they went by, he looked to his right and saw two incredulous faces staring at him through the watcher's gap in the stone. Sun-wings dropped as they went down the meadow, then began to circle, losing altitude and frightening a herd of cows into a frantic stampede. Lower and lower yet.

He leaned forward and called, "That pasture right underneath us. That's for people to camp and there's no stock in it. That'd be a good place." It was also out of sight of the wagon coming down from the pass place.

Sun-wings swerved, looked down, then her wings came high behind him and they were down. He loosened his hold on the rope and slid from the Griffin's shoulder.

"I'm going to walk up toward them," he told her. "I'll be back."

"Take your time," she said. "I need a drink of water."

She walked toward the river, starting yet another stampede two pastures away, this one of horses.

Willum went straight across toward the salt works, still waving his flag.

Several men emerged from the salt works and came toward him. One of them was Melkin. Willum remembered having to . . . well, to apologize to him. He felt his face turning red.

"Willum," Melkin said, his voice a little tight. "You seem to have acquired quite a mount there."

"Don't think I 'quired her," said Willum. "Think I was just the lightest one they had to send." He struggled with his buttons. "Sir, gotta letter in here from Abasio. He said important. Real important."

Seeing Willum's struggle with several layers of sweater and jacket, Melkin helped with the buttons. He read the letter, muttering to the men at his sides. "Weapons," he said. "Do you know what weapons they have, Willum?"

Willum concentrated very hard on what Abasio had said to the others just before they took off. "I heard him talking while I was gettin' dressed. They got long guns and lots of 'em. 'Basio says you've got bigger weapons'n that, but 'Basio thought it'd be better if you just weren't 'vailable or visible when they came by, just sorta not there so no matter what they got, if there's nobody there, then nobody starts shootin' anything. Since ever'body knows you're all moved down to Snow Town, those gangers, they won't think anything 'bout your not bein' there. But they gotta take that road where the giants is."

"That's a helluva big tree," muttered one of the men. "Take a while."

Another commented, "It'd have to be, to make them go the other way. Otherwise they'd just haul it off the road."

"Can't take long," said Willum. "That wagon is one-third a' the way down on this side and he's comin' downhill with a light load an' a eight-horse hitch and the riders at full gallop an' I don't know how many cars and trucks behint him with those guns stickin' out the sides."

"Go ring for Gister. He's the best woodsman. We can use one of the big salt saws."

"He's not going to let you cut that tree!" several of the men cried in virtual unison.

Sun-wings called, "Willum! The package Abasio gave you. Before we took off."

Willum got red in the face. He really *had* listened. He dug into the inside pocket of his jacket. "This is stuff from a male tree like that'n we hafta cut. It's called . . ." He frowned again.

"Pollen," said Sun-wings. "The trees grow near Tingawa. That's where Fixit got it."

Willum grinned. "Abasio said this will make seeds, to grow new ones."

"Gister's been looking for a male tree for over thirty years!" cried Melkin.

"Well, he wouldn'ta found it around here. They grow where Sun-wings said."

The men went off in different directions. A bell began to ring, a strange *b'bing* sound. Melkin, noting Willum's puzzled look, explained. "There's four message bells. Small, middle, big, and huge. Different tones to each one. We hit it with different kinds of strikers; metal makes one sound, wood makes another, wood with a leather wrapped around it still another. Each man who lives or works away from Saltgosh has his own signal. That signal you heard was Gister's, the middle bell hit with a wooden mallet. If we did *b'bingy*, on that same bell, that'd be his boy. Anyhow, Gister's the one'll tell us where to cut and how deep, so it'll come down right over the road."

Willum was furiously thinking of all the talk he'd overheard while they'd been getting him dressed. "So you'll keep all your folks safe and away from that wagon when it comes by you? And not leave any tools out where they could maybe get'm and clear the road? An', I jus' thought, there's that buncha Edgers with 'em and their guns. So, after the wagon goes through, if we go in there past the notch t'collect the stuff, if the giants don't . . . get ridduv 'em, THEN 'f you had some men with weapons ready, that might be a pretty good idea."

Melkin grinned at him. "Thank you for the suggestions, and yes, I agree it'd be a pretty good idea. I'm glad we're down in Snow Town, though. We'd be vulnerable if we were still living up in the town. Oh, we'd get all the people down, but they'd have to leave all their possessions behind. Do you know why this guy took the stuff?"

" 'Cause he's got somebody wants to buy it for, oh, a lot of gold. A great lot. But what these men want is only the Edgers should be left alive when the waters come. They wanta kill ever'body else an' specially the sea-babies. An 'Basio and Mr. Fixit, they need that stuff to figure out what them Edgers're up to so they don't . . . kill a lot more people."

"They want to be the only ones left alive? The Edgers?"

"Yessir. And they're the ones that're messin' things up, makin' things like those giants. Did you know they were still growing?"

"Still? Who says?"

"Sun-wings, the Griffin! She says. Her folk have been watchin' them. She says they were still growin', but they've been stopped now by Mr. Fixit. Now they're getting littler."

"You need anything before you go back? Or does she?" Melkin stared at the Griffin, shaking his head. He'd seen Griffins, now and then, at some distance, but never this close. "If you're going to park somewhere and watch what happens, you'll have to be high, and it's cold up there, so you should have a blanket. I'll bring you one. And could I . . . be introduced to her?"

"Sure. But be nice. She's very polite." Willum remembered Digger. " 'Cept when she's killing somebody, I guess. But she doesn't like the taste of people. So you're safe."

Melkin was introduced to Sun-wings and got into a conversation with her about the giants while Willum went hastily across the pasture to the privy the group had used when they had camped here previousl̵ He had really, really not wanted to wet on Sun-wings. Somehow, tł just wasn't the relationship he wanted to have, but it was really cold up there and sort of swoopy and he really, really had to go.

When he came out, a woman was coming down from the town with a sandwich and a blanket for him. It was Liny, the tailor's sister, the one who'd made all the cookies. (*They'd met her before but he hadn't swiped anything from her, so he could just say thank you without being ashamed or having to apologize. He'd really never had that feeling until Abasio had taught it to him. Probably because there wasn't anything in Gravysuck worth stealing.*) Liny asked if the Griffin would like anything.

"Any raw meat," Sun-wings replied. "A piece about the size of that boy." And then she laughed, and after a moment the woman laughed with her. Still, she returned in a little while with two men carrying a leg of something that kept Sun-wings busy for some little time. Flying had given her an appetite. Recently she hadn't really been eating much.

Gister showed up. The men began to move machinery. Sun-wings suggested Willum get on her shoulders while she climbed a sidewall. Waving farewell, Willum did so. The men not busy moving machinery stood staring as the Griffin climbed to the top of the south wall. Looking at the drop, Willum put the folded blanket under his bottom, his legs under the rope, bent his knees to clamp down on it, tucked his toes under, and gripped it tight, closing his eyes and concentrating on not throwing up as she launched herself down, then WHAP and they were headed up. She circled, higher and higher. He heard machinery below them; a huge-wheeled block-cutting machine was slicing into the south side of the tree.

High and higher, they went. The machine shrieked. Higher yet. Willum looked over his shoulder as they crossed the watchtower. The tree trembled. Sun-wings heard it and turned so they could watch the huge bulk of it tremble and tremble while the men ran to get away from the trunk. The tree shook and leaned and came down across the road to the west with a crash that buffeted them, high as they were. Now the men came back and were trimming away the growth around the other road, making the way to the notch more visible, more . . . Willum thought about it. More usable-looking.

Willum looked back once more when they were above the pass. The watchtower wall blocked his view of the Saltgosh Valley. It did not block his view of the switchbacks on the western side, and the Gold King's wagon was maybe six or eight roads lower than it had been, the followers strung out in a long line behind it. He still had the twelve riders, but there were slightly fewer of the trucks. He spotted two of them higher on the mountain, gushing steam into the cold morning air. Willum turned his attention back to the wagon and visualized it going through the notch . . . not. If the wagon stayed in front, they'd have to stop every truck, then unhitch the horses and shorten the harness to make it just a two-horse hitch—no way more than a two-horse hitch could get through there, then go through, take the other horses through, then rehitch. The sun was lower. It was midafternoon. Sun-wings sculled, catching an updraft, using it to lift, then to slide.

Willum leaned forward. " 'Basio wants to know if they go through, and what happens."

"I can land somewhere if you're cold."

"Just if you're tired, Sun-wings. Otherwise I'm fine."

Willum grinned. Oh, it really might be worth learning to listen. He finally figured it out. If you wanted to do anything NEW, you had to *listen* for what was *new*. Everything back in Gravysuck was OLD. He had *listened* to things Xulai told him on the trip, because they were NEW things, but *bein' told what to do* was just OLD stuff. Anyhow, it had felt like . . . seemed like . . . no, it just used some of the same words like it was an OLD thing, but what he hadn't figured out was it *couldn't be* OLD when Abasio or Xulai did it, because *everything* they were doing was a NEW thing. That's why they were so tired all the time, because doing NEW stuff all the time meant you hadn't got used to it or figured out the easiest way to do it yet, or figured out how to get out of doing it yet, and that was why they got so . . . peeved at him.

He finally figured it out. He was going to try really, really hard, to learn to listen.

Sun-wings found a place on a southwest-facing side of a peak, almost at the corner of the north and east valley walls but cupped and sheltered from the northeast wind and warmed by the afternoon sun. She lay upon a ledge, fluffed out both feathers and fur to hold the heat from the sun-warmed stone while the boy cleared some of the sand and gravel that had accumulated at the bottom of the wall to make room for her legs. Then he snuggled into the warm notch between her left front leg and rib cage, covering his legs and her front feet with the blanket.

"Don't your feet get cold, Sun-wings?"

"They have a venturi tube in each one of them."

"What's that?"

"A place where the blood is forced through a tighter place that makes it move faster. Birds have them in their legs. Otherwise their feet would freeze in the winter."

"Who told you that?"

She paused, suddenly thoughtful. "I don't . . . I don't remember. Someone did. Before I was grown. Long, long ago. *Venturi tubes and dual musculature in the upper back, and unequal weight distribution of internal organs,* many things like that. I shouldn't be able to fly, you know." She sighed. "But I do."

They looked down on both sides of the wall, Saltgosh to the south, the Valley of the Giants to the north. It was truly a valley of the giants, for the huge creatures were readily visible, two or three of them moving about at any one time, one or two of them tall enough that their heads were almost even with the tops of some trees. They must have been a long way west when he and Abasio and Xulai had come through here before. Two of them were what Abasio had seen when he went back in the notch that time. Willum tried to identify different ones and count them, but they all looked alike. No clothes, of course. How did they keep warm in the winter? There seemed to be at least five, maybe one or two more. In the Saltgosh Valley, people were busy moving livestock: all the cows and horses were disappearing among the trees. Though the people had been moved down some time ago, the animals were let out on pasture daytimes until it actually snowed. Sun-wings nudged his leg and pointed with her beak, and he saw the water was building up behind the huge dropped tree trunk. Some still ran under the trunk in the old riverbed, but more was diverted into the northwestward flow, through the notch. He nodded sleepily.

It seemed a very short time before they spotted the Gold King's wagon approaching the watchtower, and Willum realized both he and the Griffin had fallen asleep for a while. Sun-wings's beak was resting on his shoulder. He rubbed his eyes, letting his elbow casually shove the beak a little to wake her up. The horses were still running and the Gold King's entourage was alert, weapons at the ready, looking all about themselves for any hostile action and finding none at all.

Willum could look almost directly down into the town. It seemed completely dead, no sign of life at all. The place might as well have been deserted. The wagon and horsemen thundered on—the sound clearly audible even at their height—covering a distance about halfway to the split in the road before any of the riders seemed to notice that they would have to take the right-hand fork. From the back side of the east wall, unseen, Sun-wings and Willum dropped into flight and circled high above to look directly down on the notch, then returned to their former resting place.

"Notch is bigger'n it was," Willum remarked when they were back on their high terrace. "Looks like those giants been pullin' stones outta the way."

"Do the men in the city know?"

"Dunno," said Willum. "They'll know if they help us, down there, because they'll see it. Otherwise, we sh'd stop and tell 'um."

"We'll see," said Sun-wings. The Gold King's wagon was approaching the barrier. It stopped. The men and horses milled about, the driver got off the wagon and looked at the other route. Finally he gestured and the mounted men went toward the notch, entering it one at a time. They emerged on the giant-valley side, milled about, returned to the south side. There were no giants in sight. All the horses were unhitched, then the front two were rehitched.

"I'd a sent summa those cars through first," murmured Willum.

"I imagine anyone who calls himself a king is more interested in being first than in being smart," murmured Sun-wings. The wagon started through with just two horses pulling it, several men staying behind with the unhitched ones. There was some confusion, some coming and going, someone carrying a rope.

"It's slippery in there," Willum explained to his huge friend . . . well, he guessed she was his friend. "I think the wagon may've slipped off the road. When we went through, Abasio had a rope on the outside a' the wagon so it wouldn't slide."

Eventually, the men got the wagon on the road and edged out on the giant-valley side. Two other horses followed, and the men got busy hitching them to the wagon once more. Sun-wings nudged Willum with her shoulder and pointed with her beak—beyond the men. There, approaching them one behind the other, were two giants. The men prob ably didn't hear the footsteps over the noise of the water. Willum leapt up, put the blanket by the gravel and scooped a quantity of it onto the blanket, grabbed the blanket by the four corners, and turned to watch.

What happened was almost too fast to follow, men turning, seeing, screaming, running back through the notch, the way blocked by the next group of horses coming through, the first giant arriving, lifting his foot to step on the wagon and crush it like a nutshell, the men using their weapons like little cannons. They made little puffs of smoke with what was probably a *bang-bang* noise. The sound barely reached Willum and Sun-wings, *whup, whup*. The other giant arrived; there were two more approaching from another direction, then suddenly, horses were grabbed from above and jerked off their feet, their frantic struggles stopping when their heads were bitten off, another foot came down where the wagon had been, a huge mouth expelled a knot of harness that evidently resisted chewing. Blood ran across the giants' chests. Abasio had given Willum some little distance glasses. Needly told him she'd used them to watch the fish being constructed, and now he used them to watch the wagon, very carefully, noticing where the wagon was, how broken it was. The right side of it had ripped off. A giant tipped it toward that side, and everything dumped out—cans and cans, yellow, all alike, rolling away along the road, a couple among them different, shiny like metal. A foot came down on them, moved on. The metal things were still there, pressed into the ground among the yellow cans. Too small, too round to have been crushed. He heaved a deep breath. There was also a clutter of other things, like little sticks, those were probably the other things Abasio had wanted.

Willum tried to count the number of men eaten. There had been twelve riders and at least two in the wagon plus all the drivers of cars and trucks. All the horses were dead, being carried away. One of the men was hiding, keeping perfectly still behind a tree. That must be the purple one, fat, older than the others. With all the yelling the giants were doing, he didn't see what was coming at him from behind. None of the giants wore clothes, and this one was definitely female. She had the man dangling by one leg before he had a chance to yell. He was the last one. Now the giants were picking up bits and pieces of things from the wagon. Putting things in their mouths, sacks of something. One of them wandered away toward the west, toward where Odd Duck had been. He was making a noise, a kind of moaning. Others followed him. The female one turned toward the north. She had half a horse dangling from her hand and was going to take it home, wherever home was. A pair of human legs protruded from the corner of her mouth.

The moaning turned into a screech, then a howl.

"Was there something bad in that wagon?" Willum whispered to Sun-wings.

"I heard someone say the Gold King was going to poison Sea Duck, if he could get there." She nodded toward the notch. "The men in those vehicles aren't going to go through, Willum. I thought they'd turn around and head back, but they aren't."

The men were not. They had gathered around someone who was waving his arms, apparently yelling to them. Heads nodded, the men who weren't already carrying guns took them from the vehicles, and the whole group, some fifty of them, started marching up the road toward Saltgosh. A couple of men aimed their weapons at the town on the ledge and shot at it.

Sun-wings murmured, "They intend to use the town for something. I wonder. Those cars and trucks take something to make them run, don't they? *Fuel,* Abasio says. Fuel is what makes things run. He says food is people fuel. Maybe they're running out of it."

"When the wagon went over, there were lotsa those yellow cans inside. Can you see colors, Sun-wings? Coyote can't, I know. Maybe that was what it was."

"I can see color, yes. All my sisters can, so far as I know. Could the yellow cans be fuel?"

The Edgers were approaching the edge of the salt works. Suddenly every window in the town sprouted weapons, and a deadly barrage was aimed down at the massed Edgers. Half of them fell, the rest ran toward the path that led upward to the town.

"That is a very stupid move," remarked Sun-wings. "They aren't really very . . . intelligent, are they."

" 'Basio said something wunst 'bout Edgers breedin' in so much they lost their brains. I told Needly wunst about that, y'gotta breed out some. Otherwise . . . whoops. Looka that!"

The first half-dozen climbers had gained the top of the path and had promptly fallen backward onto half a dozen others, the whole group plummeting off the stairs—Willum noted for the first time that the protective rail had been removed. There were now only about a dozen of the Edgers who were alive and seemingly unwounded. A shout reached them, evidently from within the houses. Someone among the Edgers huddled on the stairs threw his weapon down. In the salt works, men appeared, aiming upward, and others came out of the town, aiming down. The rest of the Edgers threw down their weapons.

Sun-wings glanced at the sky. "There's a moon tonight, but I think we'll ask your friends for some help in getting in there and picking up the two things you want before dark. I don't want to get caught on the ground, and I don't want you to get caught halfway up to a place I can drop from. AND, I don't want to stress this wing by taking off from the ground or chill it by flying at night. That watchtower of theirs can tell us when the way is clear."

"I'm gonna be a little heavier," said Willum. "Just for a little bit. Just in case." He climbed back on her shoulders, the gravel-laden blanket held in his arms. Sun-wings dropped into flight and returned to the meadow below the town, carefully flying by the watchtower so they could be seen.

Melkin met them almost as soon as they landed. There was a great howling from over the northern wall. More than one giant voice.

"We saw some of it," he said. "What was in that wagon?"

"Abasio said the Gold King was going to poison the water around Sea Duck," said the Griffin.

Willum agreed. "That was parta that ganger leader thinkin' the Edgers was 'spose to be the only people left alive when the world's all water. I think the giants're so hungry by this time they'll put most anything inta their mouths. I think at least one of 'em ate the poison. If there's any of it left, you might want to get rid of it some way before it kills somebody."

"The things you needed?"

"I think I saw the metal things, and they look all right," said Willum. "They were in real shiny kinda cans, metal, shaped like a melon. Sun-wings n' me saw 'em fall outta the wagon, right beyond the notch, and one of the giants stepped on 'em, so they're a little buried, but not broke, I don't think. Right there just inside. But that one giant, he's just stampin' around in there. I think maybe Sun-wings n' me can get ridda him."

He went back to Sun-wings and talked to her. "Yes," she said. "I can do that. Now?"

They took off once more, this time circling to get only a little higher than the northern wall. Sun-wings asked, "You want to come at it from the front?"

"The front and a little higher, so it'll hit him in the eyes!"

"Then let it go when I say so." She circled to gain a bit more height, turned, and flew directly at the giant's head. He was howling, kicking at the wagon, waving his arms aimlessly.

"The minute he looks up," said Sun-wings. She screamed. The giant, mouth open, turned directly toward her, arms coming up. In that same instant Willum dumped the blanket load of gravel and sand, which continued forward and down as Sun-wings drove her wings down to carry them over the creature's head. The gravel caught the giant full in the face, mostly around the eyes, and he howled even louder, stumbling back from the wagon, turning to run in the opposite direction.

They turned back and were down within moments. Sun-wings was panting. She lay flat, her wings widespread. Melkin ran up to them. "Is she all right?"

"Have somebody bring her some water," mumbled Willum. "She's scared. So'm I." He knew exactly how she felt. His heart was pounding as though it wanted to break out from behind his ribs.

Melkin gave instructions while he and Willum were walking across the pastures toward the notch. When Willum could spare the breath, he mumbled, "There's something else in there I should take a sample back to Abasio. We thought if you'd keep watch for us, I'd sneak in there and grab them and bring them out by the road. That is, if all the men who were with the Gold King are dead."

"There were twenty horses."

"I counted fifteen they bit the heads off of."

"If the giants that're poisoned die," said Melkin, "the others'll eat them."

"Then they'll die, too. But that'll take a while. I'll tell Fixit when we get back. Fixit'll think a' somethin to get ridda the bodies."

"You want to try it now?"

Willum looked up at the sky, then back at Sun-wings. "While the light's still good enough."

Half a dozen of the men went with him. Five horses had escaped back through the notch and were tangled in harness near the entry. One of the men went to cut them free while the rest went through the notch, carefully, using the hand rope Abasio had strung there. Four of them kept watch in all directions while Willum went on with the other two. The giant he had blinded was blundering around a little north of them, not far. They could see another one farther back, to the left. Neither of them seemed to be paying any attention to the notch. Willum found the cans pressed deeply into the soil, but Melkin had brought a shovel with him, and they were out in minutes, scratched, slightly dented, but whole. Willum reached into the wreckage of the wagon. There were many yellow cans of something or other and several dozen bars of metal. Had to be metal, they were so heavy. Not long, but very heavy. He passed these and some of the yellow cans to the others and they handed them back through the notch to the far side. They themselves were back through the notch before the giants noticed they were there.

"Something we came back to tell you, but I 'spect you noticed," said Willum. "D'jou notice they'd been pullin' away at that notch. D'you know about Mr. Fixit?"

"You mentioned him a couple of times earlier today, Willum. I don't know the man, no."

"Well, firs' thing, he's notta man. Not ezackly, but somethin' like," said Willum. "Came in a spaceship, looked kinda like a turtle. I mean the ship looked like a turtle, Mr. Fixit looks like a tree, sort of. Fixit says he can shrink those giants—only Abasio says he's not a *he*. He's an *it*, I guess. Anyhow, Fixit can shrink the giants. Or Abasio says there's a weapon that'll kill them if Fixit's here to get the dead bodies away. Fixit's gone for a while, but it's comin' back. If they don't all die from that poison, Fixit'll come fix 'em for you."

Melkin nodded. "These cans are vehicle fuel, and there's more in that wagon. We'll take those if Abasio doesn't mind, and we can always use the horses, too." Laden with the rods of metal and the two spherical containers, they emerged to lay the salvage on the stump of the huge tree. Liny found a piece of net they could use to hold the cans. Willum weighed the cans carefully in his hands, weighed the other thing, decided on one can and one bar, and asked Melkin to put the others away until he retrieved them later.

"Why're you leaving some?" asked Melkin.

"She's been hurt," said Willum, running a fond hand down Sun-wings's shoulder. "An' her wing's just healed, and those things're heavy an' so was that gravel we hit the giant with. We'll come get the rest of them when she's rested some. Or maybe Abasio'll send a wagon. Or maybe the guy in the turtle ship will come pick them up. Fixit looks really . . . strange, but nice, an' he'll 'preciate your holdin' on to 'em for it. I keep wantin' to call it a him." He tied the net securely and set it beside Sun-wings' foot so she could carry it rather than add any weight on her shoulders. Then it was just one more climb, one more swoop, one more WHAP, and they were on the way home.

"You tired, Sun-wings?" asked Willum.

"Just a little," said Sun-wings, who ached deeply.

"Take it easy goin' back, then. Just slip through where it's easiest."

And she did. They came down through the dusk in one long, virtually motionless glide, low over the pass, over Artemisia, the outskirts, the farms, the edge houses, and at last, as darkness fell, a circle of fires that marked the plaza. Half the population of the area seemed to be tending the fires and waiting for the Griffin and the boy. Sun-wings dropped, braked against the air, dropped again, and was down in the center, crouched, panting.

Willum didn't realize he was tired and cold until he stumbled and reached his hands toward the nearest fire. Abasio caught him and carried him to the fireside. Precious Wind, Xulai, and half a dozen Artemisians helped Sun-wings into her house and brought her a large container of something warm and savory-smelling. Needly arrived with a crew—including all six of Grandma's children—who sang continuously as, armed with brushes and warm water, they climbed carefully and gently all over the Griffin's body once again, grooming her until she shone. The brushes, Sun-wings thought to herself, seemed to work well in relieving the ache. As did what they called music. She had not heard music before. She drank deeply of the tub of thick something . . . soup, Needly said. Chicken soup, with bits of things in it. Grain. Vegetables. Meat. Not a Griffin's usual diet, but it tasted . . . marvelous. Like eating and drinking both at once. She relaxed, ran her bill along the furry back of Dawn-song—who had also enjoyed some soup—and the two Griffins purred, not noticing that they were, separately, in harmony with the song.

The can and bar lay on the plaza, still tied in their netting. Abasio heard about the abortive battle the Edgers had tried to start in Salt-gosh, also about the additional can and rods of metal and the other contents of the wagon that were in Saltgosh, whenever they wanted to go after them, but that Willum had thought Sun-wings might be "kinda too tired" to carry back just them. Concealing his interest in Willum's sincere concern for Sun-wings's welfare, Abasio put the salvaged items away carefully in his wagon. Tomorrow, when Fixit came back, it could pick up the rest. Fixit would take the accumulated bits and pieces of whatever it was Fixit needed to make shape-changer organs for the Griffins. And, perhaps, for other things, too. Certainly for creatures like a bear. And a coyote.

And maybe an Abasio. Though he already had a shape that would do for aquatic living, it would be more gratifying to look like his son than like an octopus. Not right now, for those feet would not help him do his current job, but perhaps later. And perhaps some of this could be sorted out when Fixit got back, tomorrow.

FIXIT RETURNED BEFORE DAWN. WHEN Abasio rose, he left Xulai and the babies still asleep, and took care not to wake them. The IGM was sitting in the plaza. Fixit saw Abasio crossing the plaza and came out to invite him to breakfast. "I have human food in the flier. Come have morning meal with me."

Abasio fetched the materials Willum and Sun-wings had picked up and took them with him, just as they were, wrapped in the netting. Fixit stowed the whole bundle in something he called an "analysis locker," then they sat at a small table that first extruded itself from the floor and then extruded plates with food on them. Abasio was offered and accepted ham and eggs and fruit juice, while Fixit was putting what appeared to be sugar and cream on something that looked like porridge and was probably—Abasio thought— dried, then minced, then stewed not-people.

Fixit referred to its memo leaf.

"On way back, Self told survey ship to find all places identifiable as Edges." It shook its head at Abasio, wearing an expression Abasio might have called "troubled." "Have inventory of each one, Abasio, very accu-rate, though very sad making. How many men, how many women, chil-

dren? Xulai much concerned about children, spoke to me of children."
It shook its head. Abasio was learning to read its facial expressions, and
it was wearing one of distaste. "Abasio, *not* many children. Very few, very
fat children. Not very many women either. Only men were very old ones.
Women, too, mostly old. Those few peoples, not speaking much. Not
interested in anything much. Sleeping most of time. Seeming strange,
somehow."

"I don't imagine they get much exercise," said Abasio.

"Making metal fish for people brains not exercise?"

"Willum and Sun-wings think there were around a total of fifty
Edger men involved in that fish-building business. The Edges I knew
of, outside Fantis, would have had that many men in any one Edge. It
sounds to me like they're dying off."

"You think when city died . . . ?"

"I do think it, yes. Whether the Edgers realized it or not, they depended on the city. They depended on the farms. When the sickness
hit the city, wiping it out, I think that spelled the end for the Edgers as
well. Wide Mountain Mother speaks of disputes her people had with
Edgers. Once farms stopped providing food, once communities like
Wide Mountain stopped tolerating them, they began to die. This fish
business was sort of a last gasp. If I had to decide what to do with them,
I'd just sterilize any that are still fertile and let them alone. Any able-
bodied Edgers who still existed were probably in that bunch that got
wiped out in Saltgosh. Old Purple was eaten by a giant. Inasmuch as the
Edges made the giants, this is perhaps poetic justice."

"Some few were taken prisoner, not? We can go talk to such?"

"Not a bad idea. We want to pick up the rest of the stuff from that
wagon anyhow."

Fixit looked up and rose as a bell on the front of the analysis locker
made a chirping sound. After examining the gauges on the locker, it
announced, "Aha. Now, that is interesting, is it not? The metal bars the
boy brought. They are yribium."

"I know. There's more of it in Saltgosh. The stuff is heavy and Willum
didn't want Sun-wings to try and carry it. It was her first long flight since
she was wounded."

Fixit wasn't listening. It had its teeth in a bar of yribium and was
shaking it into submission as it went on exultantly, "Was meaning to

tell you. I went back to Oracle cave to roll up Oracle mat and take it up to turtle for disposal. When I roll mat up a little, I see all beneath it layer of white! Very heavy little crystals, white. Always, everyone thought yribium was *in soil* of Oracle planet, thought Oracle picked only planets that *had* yribium. Is now evident this is not so. Yribium is being somehow . . . excreted by Oracle. This Old Purple person, this is source of his wealth. Not Gold King at all. No."

Abasio said, "You mean the Gold King was trading stuff to the Oracles? And getting paid in yribium!"

It gave itself a shake, quivering in annoyance. "No one is ever studying Oracle. Someone should study Oracle!"

"Are you allowed to do that? Allowed to take one apart? See how it works?"

"No. Am not allowed. Should be allowed, however."

"What do they look like, under their clothes?"

"Clothing is not clothing. Is part of creature. Looks like robe? It is like little thing of stone or wood or pottery . . . REFERENCE needed! . . . *Figurine!* Solid at bottom with feet carved on. Should be study of knowing how Oracles secrete and excrete. It is almost only reason they are being allowed to continue living. I am probably sending whole assembly of them, it, to one huge planet, heavy gravity, far-off travel route, with clear signs saying no landings. No more travel for Oracles."

"Why heavy gravity?"

"Hard to look like upstanding person in heavy gravity. Hard to pretend to be separate thing. On heavy planet could only be separate puddle. On heavy planet might even evolve intelligence!"

Abasio had resolved last night that he would find out what was really going on. He said in his most tactful, soothing voice, "Look, Balytani-wassinot, I believe everything you tell me, really . . ."

Fixit tried very hard to look appropriately flattered. "Yes, Abasio. Is there a problem?"

"It's this whole story about what's going on here. There's something wrong with it. For instance, somebody or something was . . . is running Grandma's life. I know how that feels. That somebody or something sent men to live with her, to father her children. I've been through that business of being selected and sent somewhere, too. Now, she's an intelligent woman. She's able to tell a good man from a bad one. She told me about the men they sent to live with her. She said in all important ways they were alike, and she liked them. Well, Xulai and I—we know about that. We like each other, too, and our lives were arranged for us. We know why. But why was Grandma's life and the lives of all those men? She says they were all *good* men, capable men, kind men. The children were—are all bright, good kids. *Immensely talented.* They are not traumatized by this whole . . . stupid Oracle business. They seem to be . . . thriving. This does not seem accidental to me. And it's certainly not something these so-called Oracles could have managed."

"Fixit agrees. Oracle didn't manage," said Fixit. "Something using Oracle as . . . how you say, finger of feline? . . . REFERENCE needed! . . . *Cat's-paw!*"

Abasio shuddered. "Wouldn't *you* know? Wouldn't *your head office* know?" He stopped. There was music coming from somewhere. Music. Orchestral music. He had first heard orchestral music in Tingawa, not before, not since. This was coming from Grandma's new house. "The children have moved their music, all those instruments . . ."

Fixit remarked, "I helped them move in. Used small moving devices you saw. Piano was why we had to send for big ship. Little flier does not stretch to piano. Or harp. Or thing called Suzie-phone. Self is assured this is what it is called. Makes strange *oompah* sound like mating call of Flobstummel, marsh-water denizens on second planet of Glom. Interesting place. I think maybe when this world is all water, I bring pair of Flobstummel to visit you."

"Your people must really have long lives, Fixit. Afraid I won't last that long."

Fixit made a face. Sometimes even his own life seemed too short to get everything done that needed doing. "That is true, Abasio. Sometimes I am forgetting. Now Oracle matter settled. Grandma matter settled. She has children, house, Needly, also. Needly wants to go with Willum, Willum wants to go with you. Self thinks that is good. They will be help for you, when you have finished recruitment job—no, truly. *Do not be shaking head with sad expression on face. Job is NOT forever.* I am knowledgeable. You *will* finish job—then children can come live with Grandma. Or maybe you will not want to give them up. Self think they will grow wanting sea-eggs together.

"All things progress: little World Spirit of Earth has gone to rehab.

New Earth World Spirit arriving very soon. Giants have been sprayed with *Shrink-eze, patented product of Shrinkables Corporation, motto of corporation, 'Makes big problems into no problems.'*"

"Oh," cried Abasio. "I forgot to tell you." He explained the *ul xaolat*'s forecast regarding dead giants. "If the giants over near Saltgosh died from that poison, can you get rid of the corpses?"

"Oh, yes. If shrinking too slow and you wish to hurry matter, you may kill giants and I will dispose of corpses. Will send message to mover in orbit. Mover can locate any dead giant bodies, transport said bodies above planetary orbit plane, then propel said bodies toward the sun. Cremation in sun no problem. Any we do not find dead will be shrunken. They shed only a little bit each day, but it goes on and on. In half your year, they end up size of small creature lives under mushroom."

"Gnome? Pixie? Imp?"

"Some such kind word, yes. First shrinks to eating rabbit, then is eating mouse, then cricket, then ant, then mite, then no more giant. You know, Self has taken Lom women to Tingawa. Precious Wind also in Tingawa. Interesting. Precious Wind had samples, jars of what Edgers were washing off stinkers. Yes, Coyote told me stinker story while you were busy. Stuff of stinker is like . . . human primal material. Silkhands can make anything with it. Shape it, it becomes living! She has already shaped it into shapeshifter organ like Mavin's. Only problem, shape is ephemeral. Does not hold."

"Did anyone tell you what the Edgers were trying to do with it?"

"Oh, yes. Self saw. All was recorded on device in portable camp. Self saw."

"Did you see that other substance they used, at the end. Before everything blew up?"

"Self did see. Activator."

"That's what you have in your locker with the yribium. We didn't have any of the activator stuff until Willum brought it back. There's another container of it in Saltgosh. The people in Tingawa believe that's what makes the thing keep a shape permanently. Tingawa thinks it's a necessary ingredient in making organs for the Griffins."

"There should be more in the truck it came from."

"It isn't anymore. The man who was left had . . . a temper tantrum, blew it up with an explosive."

"So I need to take this to Tingawa! You will come with me?"

"You know, Fixit, Xulai and I do have a job to do."

"Very soon you will getting back to it. You are not losing time. Think! You will have portable camp. This will make you safer. Make camp at night, put horses, wagon, selves inside. Push button, hay comes for horses. Push button, water for horses. Nobody can find you. It weighs almost nothing. This will make travel easier. Better for horses, too. Self has looked at wagon. Self thought maybe a flier, but Xulai says no, it would . . . frighten people. She says these villages are very low tech. Very con-ser-va-tive, which means every brain cell filled with old ideas, sometimes ideas three, four, twenty generations past. Living ideas change, like all living things. Ideas that do not change begin to rot at bottom. Must be turned over, like garden soil, or begin to stink.

"So you must keep wagon, but wagon can be modified to look the same but weigh about one-tenth. Portable camp accesses things like food, hot water, from other places via miniworms. Cuts down weight. Also, Self has ordered attachment that bakes cookies, has own access to ingredients. You get low on cookies, tell wagon to make just how many you need for then. Also, it will be better for Needly and Willum, who want to go on with you. Xulai says she will school. I think you take basic edubot with you for Willum! Edubot a bit heavy, so we pack it in wormhole and hitch it like trailer. Do not think Needly needs much school, but she will enjoy."

Abasio sighed. "One thing I've wondered."

"What's that?"

"It looks like you can do almost anything, you and your Massive Fabricators and your wormholes, and so forth. How come no one has suggested stopping the waters rising?"

Fixit made a small shuffling dance, all six legs in simultaneous movement. Abasio interpreted the movement as one of embarrassment.

"Well," it said. "Best reason is we can't stop."

"Can't? You can go zipping around the galaxy, interdicting planets right and left, and you can't stop the water coming from Squamutch?"

"It IS stopped coming—from Squamutch. Squamutch is sending no more. That we did first thing, stop it from Squamutch." Which was quite true, *once enough water was already on the way.* "But wormhole is already full of it. All downhill from where it is. Enough to drown planet. Cannot be detached and allowed to run out into space, become danger to interstellar commerce. Cannot be moved. Wormholes, once anchored, become intransigent. Dislike being pushed. Push one, it tangles two others, then four. Before you know it, massive galactic mess taking endless time to untangle."

"You said best reason. Is there another one?"

"Of course. Reason water was started in first place. Galactic Order to Eradicate mankind is still in effect. Mankind is biped walking around on land. That mankind is ruining planet. *Do not tell me new leaf has been turned over by mankind. Will not believe you.*" Fixit sighed, stared longingly at the picture of the homecoming dinner: twigpit.

"What about the stinkers? Silkhands says the stuff they exude is needed for making shifter organs."

"Galactic Head Office says stinker material interesting, but not unique, can be produced and provided if needed, says Arbitrarily Imposed Solution to eradicate stinkers is permitted in this case since stinkers truly incapable of making any decision. I will take care of eliminating stinkers, cleaning out mountain where washing of stinkers took place. I have given information to Tingawa how material may be made without necessity of eating humans to make it. Humans or whatever else one may be trying to create."

"You mean, they excreted . . . that is, exuded the essence of whatever they ate."

"The essential basis. That is correct. One other ingredient needed to make organ hold shape. Great surprise."

"What ingredient?"

"Yribium." Fixit stared at Abasio with all eyes, unblinking. A small quiver at the corner of its mouth reminded Abasio of something. Sunwings: her laughter betrayed only by the quiver of tissue at the sides of her beak.

"You are making jest with me," Abasio suggested.

"Never would Self do such a thing," Balytaniwassinot murmured, putting three of its hands over its face.

"You would and you are! Really? Yribium! Well. Isn't it a good thing we didn't throw the Oracles away. Can we keep it/them and make it/them yield yribium?"

"It would be slavery."

"I don't think you can enslave something that has no brain."

"Is interesting question. We will submit question to the galactic court. We will need to keep creatures only a few thousand years awaiting decision. A mere . . . cosmic blink of the eye. Meantime, I will go to Saltgosh to pick up rest of stuff. Every few years I will go flatten Oracles and make good use of yribium. If you can find truck driver, maybe he could tell you what activator is, that would save time. Otherwise . . ." It shrugged all six shoulders. "Let it alone. Tingawa capable of determining what stuff is."

Abasio, remembering Xulai's birth, let it alone. He simply could not imagine that Tingawa was still creating people . . . breeding people born to do certain tasks, jobs, fill certain positions, crossbreed certain people. No, that really wasn't it. He could imagine Tingawa doing the genetics. He couldn't imagine the . . . moral dimension. What had gone on in that Tuckwhip village and elsewhere in Hench Valley had not been genetics. It hadn't been something someone could take apart and figure out in advance. It had been almost a miracle. It simply could not be Tingawa. Meddling. Again. He smiled, thanked Fixit for his help, and shaking his head, watched the ship's virtually instantaneous departure.

Blue stuck his head over Abasio's shoulder and said, "Alone again, Abasio? Do I understand that Rags and I and the other team are to have accommodations? Hay on command?"

"Well, it seems so. If we can find that truck driver, it'll give us a piece of the puzzle."

"Tell that Jinian lady. She'll talk to some birds, they'll talk to some gophers and foxes, they'll talk to an eagle or two. In no time, they'll find him."

"Blue, that is an exceptionally good idea."

CHAPTER 18

A Road Ends: A Road Begins

WHILE PEOPLE FLEW AND SEIZED AND STRUGGLED ELSEWHERE, while Oracles excreted yribium and Saltgoshers cut salt, while Wide Mountain Mother administered and Arakny dreaded her future, Grandma sat on the front porch of her house in Artemisia, lost in daydream. The big trees around it screened it from other houses, so she wasn't out in public view, not that she was hiding, just enjoying being pleasantly quiet and, for the moment, alone. The house was half full of children. Earlier, she had been watching a wagon that was approaching from the west. She had watched it, or watched the dust trail it had kicked up, almost all the way down the mountain. As it neared the bottom, it disappeared. The dust cloud still showed above the trees, now and then.

Wide Mountain Mother had a spyglass in her dining room that allowed her to see that road that came from the pass to the west, or went off to Cow Bluff to the south-southwest, or vaguely north by west to Catland. The only direction Mother could be surprised from was the east, and there were riders out in that direction to prevent surprises from happening. Mother thought there had been quite enough surprises. A year ago, would she have thought of grooming a Griffin? Making Griffin-style soup? Adding a nonhuman star traveler to her usual guests?

Precious Wind, Mavin, Silkhands, and Jinian were in Tingawa. Abasio should be returning soon with Willum and Xulai. Grandma yawned. Needly and Serena came out with a tray. They put it on the little table beside her.

"You don't even need to move," said Needly. "There's stewed chicken with cornmeal dumplings."

"And apple pie," said Serena. "I learned to cook at the Oracles. The edubot that taught cooking was really great.

Grandma murmured, "I enjoyed the music earlier."

"Oh, that music room is splendid. It actually has acoustics. I thought everywhere had acoustics, but Jules says echoes and reverberations are *not* acoustics. He and Jan argue about it all the time. Enjoy your supper."

And they were gone. Perfectly self-contained, capable, good children. She took a bite of chicken and dumpling. Children who could cook! HER children. She wiped a tear from the corner of each eye. It was certainly nothing to cry about! Well, it *was*. In a sense. In that she had had absolutely nothing . . . almost nothing to do with it.

When she had eaten, she dozed off a little. Recent events had been rather trying, exciting, fearsome. She still couldn't believe most of what had happened. When she woke, she realized several hours had passed. The sun was low on the horizon. The dust trail she had been following down the mountain was now approaching on the western road. A large wagon, another one some distance behind.

Needly and Serena came out to sit beside her.

"Can you see who's in that wagon?" Grandma asked.

"I think it's a Saltgosh wagon," Needly replied. "It's blue, and Willum says theirs are all painted the same: blue with 'Saltgosh Mines' painted in yellow on the side."

Willum appeared, racing toward them from Wide Mountain Mother's place, Abasio and Xulai strolling behind. Abasio called, "I think we're going to have company."

The three of them settled on the porch steps. The wagons kept coming, slowed, turned into the plaza, paused, then came across the plaza toward them. Xulai said, "That's Burn Atterbury driving the front wagon, Abasio. The music director from Saltgosh."

Needly stood up very straight and walked to the front of the porch, staring. Two men were on the seat of the second wagon, an older man was driving the front one. In the wagon were five youngsters, about her own age. Two girls. Three boys. Five . . . "Grandma," she whispered.

"Yes, Needly. I see."

"Silverhairs?" said Xulai. "Abasio, they're . . ."

"I see," he said. "How . . . very interesting. Xulai, aren't those the five young singers we both enjoyed so much. I thought they had black hair?"

"They probably did," said Grandma, crisply. "I'd have made sure I kept them dyed if I'd been he. Atterbury's no fool."

Mr. Atterbury climbed from the front wagon, coming toward Xulai and Abasio, bowing in Grandma's direction. "Mr. Abasio," he called. "Ma'am. I've . . . well, I've come to make a confession, is what I have."

"You've had them since they were babies, haven't you?" Abasio asked, his voice perfectly calm and friendly.

The man flushed red and rubbed his jaw. "Yes. Sure have. Was told they were in some danger and needed to be kept hid. And then, of course, you saw how they turned out. They were quite an asset. I hate to give 'em up, I surely do. Had no idea when you were there at Saltgosh that you were the ones I was supposed to give them up to!"

"Who brought them to you?"

"Man with hair the same color as the little ones. One or two at a time. Brought them, like I said, to the Home. With money, like I said, to pay for them. Story I told you was more or less what he told me, just not the all-at-one-time family tragedy I made it out to be. I have no idea who or what the real family is."

Needly stepped down from the porch and offered her hand. "Their real family is mine, sir. They are my two half sisters and my three half brothers. Wouldn't you agree, Grandma?"

"Oh, yes," she said, sighing. "I've wondered and wondered where they'd got to."

Atterbury nodded ponderously. "Well, I got a message from the man who brought them originally. Back when he brought 'em, he said he'd let me know when it was safe. And he said it was safe now, and you'd be here in Artemisia, and you'd have room for . . . the family."

"But he didn't tell you who the family was?" Grandma lifted her eyes, noted the man's weariness for the first time. "Oh, for heaven's sake. Needly, get the boys to bring out some chairs; it's cooler out here than inside. Let those children down from the wagon and get them something to drink. Are you hungry?" she called, and was answered by shy nods, then more energetic ones. "Can you feed them all, Serena? They look famished."

"I'll get a meal ready," said Serena, going first to the wagon to invite the silver-haired boys and girls inside. They climbed down from wagons, boys and girls, and trailed off into the house. Serena figured that even if the food wasn't ready yet, she was pretty sure they could use a bathroom.

Grandma relaxed, knowing she needn't worry about there being enough food in the house, not even if a few dozen people happened to drop in. Among the things salvaged from the Oracles' pack-ratting had been several of their "shopping carts," a wheeled device with a large basket and a control panel. One could buy any of hundreds of items in the cart catalog once a credit account for the cart had been established. One named the item, picked from the array offered, pointed out the item one wanted, and the item appeared in the cart. According to Fixit, Grandma had several decades' worth of credit because of past-due payment for services rendered. Grandma was so surprised at the idea of having credit that she had not asked services to whom. She should have asked that. Meantime, it made the shopping for small food and sundry items very convenient. Wide Mountain Mother even came over from time to time to borrow a cart, carefully deducting the amount of her purchase from the "land rent" Grandma had insisted she be charged for the house site. (*Needly and I are not of your people, Mother, and Artemisia does not owe us free use of your land. We will not be contented unless you let us pay an appropriate fee for your truly invaluable help.*") Of course that declaration had had to be repeated a few times!

"It's a long, long way from Saltgosh," Grandma said to the four weary drivers. "What? Three or four days?"

"With loaded wagons, about that," said Atterbury, taking the chair Abasio offered him.

The others followed suit, one remarking, "Yes, ma'am, about that. Saw that young one there," pointing at Willum. "Flying in on a Griffin. Now, that's something one does not see every day. The young'uns"—he waved at them inclusively—"they started right up working on a symphony, *The Flight of the Griffin*. Lots of violin, cello, swooping. Strings do good swooping sounds. Second movement has to do with giants, a lot of bass horns in that one, and barrel-drum giant steps. Got a good start on it, too."

Sally came out with glasses and a pitcher. Not long thereafter, others appeared with trays for the grown-ups, then trays for themselves. For a time there was only a contented munching, the rattle of ice in glasses, the clink of forks on plates.

"You've got a full wagon load," murmured Grandma at last, putting her plate down and nodding at the second wagon.

"Musical instruments mostly, ma'am," said the driver.

Boys boiled out of the house, surrounding the wagon. Boys brought out instruments from inside. Boys outside got theirs out of the wagon. Girls carried their trays inside and returned with instruments of their own. One of the silver-haired boys took up a horn and played a brief phrase. Others echoed. He went on, was echoed; within moments they were all either singing or playing, the theme repeated, extended, harmonized upon, a second theme introduced by a bassoon, the two interwoven . . .

"They're kinfolk, aren't they?" Atterbury whispered, shaking his head in amazement. "The ones I brought and the others. Those others, are they yours, ma'am? All six of 'em."

Grandma could only nod. Her throat was too full for her to speak.

"I would say they are a specially selected strain," Abasio offered. He wondered how Fixit had managed it. Of course, he couldn't *be* sure it had been Fixit . . . but he *was* sure. How far back had that . . . creature gone? Back before Grandma, that was sure. Probably back before her parents, whoever they had been . . . or further. How long ago had all this started? Could it have been over a thousand years . . . ?

Wide Mountain Mother came toward them from her house. Abasio went in and fetched a chair for her. They were running out of chairs.

"I came to offer as many bedrooms as needed," she said quietly to Serena. "The older gentlemen look about ready to drop."

Serena smiled her thanks. "Two or three bedrooms would be welcome, I'm sure. Our younger visitors . . . family members will do fine here with us. Each of our bedrooms has two beds in it, almost as though the house knew they were coming. Do you suppose it really did? Grandma hasn't said how we're related, but we're definitely related. Musically, if no other way. We've invited our new relations . . . to stay with us. We've fed Mr. Atterbury and the men driving the other wagon, but they would probably like a warm bath and a quiet place to sleep. And, Mother, could someone take care of the horses? Mr. Fixit didn't think of a stable first time around. None of us did and that's something I guess we need to learn about . . . horses."

Mother looked at Serena weighingly. *My, what a sensible girl.* One would have to keep an eye on that one. "You don't need to unload wagons tonight, Serena. I've sent a messenger to the men's houses to ask if they will stable and care for your horses and arrange for protecting whatever's in the wagons." She turned to the men. "Mr. Atterbury, would you and the other gentlemen like to come across with me? It's the house right over there." Though male guests who were Artemisian were usually sent to the men's guesthouse, if they came from a society which usually cohabited, as Saltgosh did, Mother often invited them to stay with her.

One of the boys darted to the wagon to get the men's belongings, was followed by another, and they trailed away to Wide Mountain Mother's house. A few moments later, several men came down the hill from the men's houses and drove the wagons back to the barns and stables that were near where Sun-wings and Dawn-song were still domiciled and where Blue and Rags formed a welcoming committee.

On the side of the porch, Willum whispered, "Y'won't need me anymore, Needly. Look at all this family you got."

"Don't be silly," she said. "Young women do not marry family members."

"M . . . m . . . marry?"

"I definitely intend to marry a Griffin flier. And since you're the only one I know of, I'm afraid it will have to be you. Not any time soon, of course. Eight years, maybe. Or ten. Not until I know you've learned to listen."

"Oh, 'course," he said, both relieved and . . . well, mostly relieved. "Is Mr. Fixit coming back? I think Grandma needs some more rooms in this house. Lookin' at all those girls, definite she needs some more bathrooms."

NIGHT CAME. MORNING CAME: a large houseful of young people who had talked themselves to sleep, finally, in the very late night . . . or early morning. Now Grandma was once more alone on the porch, quietly darning a sock. Or she had been before she fell asleep. She dreamed she saw someone approaching. He sat down next to her on the porch, leaned back, and crossed his legs. Was it Fixit? It could be, she could dream of Fixit. Such a strange creature. It was the first time she had really looked at it sitting quietly, not moving about like a hurricane. No, like a cyclone. Self-contained but very dust raising!

"Is it the truth, what you told Abasio about your . . . reproductive habits?" she asked, waking up just a little.

She dreamed that Fixit abruptly changed shape. Now it had only two legs, and it looked terribly familiar. Like someone she had once known. Known very well. Whoever it was nodded thoughtfully at her and said, "If you're speaking of the reproductive habits of the Camrathsexipedes, they are fully documented in archives in the galactic center nearest them. They are of great interest, being probably the most complicated form of reproduction achieved by any race."

She awoke, eyes fixed on the sock she had been darning, voicing her vague thoughts. "You sound sort of uninvolved."

"Well, practically speaking," the person sitting next to her said in a very familiar voice, "a moment's consideration would establish that should be the case. I don't know what human involvement in Camrath-sexipedian reproduction would amount to. I rather think it would not be tolerated."

She opened her eyes wider, gave up on the dream, and finally came wide-awake, saying in amazement. "Joshua!?"

The man in the neighboring chair smiled, a much-loved, well-known smile. "Greetings, my love. I am told by those who have managed our lives that management has now . . . retired, gone, given up. No more manage-ment. We may . . . draw away the veil, as it were. Stop keeping secrets."

His face shifted, only slightly. She was now looking at a . . . silver-haired man of enormous charm. She simply stared, forgetting to breathe.

"Take a breath," he/it/they said. "I am *not* shapeshifting. I do have a gadget in my pocket that creates a kind of visual overlay, an image. Actual variations from reality are minor."

She gasped. "You're . . . you're Needly's papa. I mean, you're all six of their papas. I mean, the six ones born in Hench Valley." The darn-ing egg slipped from her lax finger and rolled. He picked it up from between his feet. "You're all six of thems . . . their . . . sires. The silver-haired ones, I mean, maybe I think . . ."

And maybe I don't, and I'm dreaming and maybe . . . She pinched herself. *Nope. Awake.*

"And Calepta's," he said. "And Brian's."

"And the other three? Father to them all?"

"Father to all, yes, in a manner of speaking. Though not in any intimate sense. You, for example, evolved, just as Balytaniwassinot's people did. As Feblia's people did."

"Feblia?"

"A character Abasio sometimes dreams of. It annoys him greatly, poor man. He really, really has done a magnificent job of work, hasn't he? Kept his temper, mostly. Hasn't abused anyone. Loves his fishy children. Loves his foreordained and eight-armed wife."

"Are you going to tell me you fathered . . . ?"

"Abasio? Xulai? No, no. Not at all. Abasio and Xulai are precisely as represented, the work of a thousand years of Tingawan genetic ingenuity." His face had shifted again, and his body. He was now someone she had known very well. Galan's father. "And except for the children borne by you, my love, the others were all conceived without any attendant intimacy. I approached the women individually, suggested a drink, provided a drink, they drifted off into dreamland. A small but complicated device was employed—without the necessity of either party removing clothing—and the women were left with very nice dreams of how they were impregnated. Even Trudis, though what may constitute a nice dream with her would probably not bear close examination."

"You were also Trudis's father! It would have been incestuous."

"Horse breeders would have called it line breeding. In any case, it didn't happen, it wasn't necessary."

"All of them, the whole dozen of them, mine and the Silverhairs." She found herself growing angry. "Why?"

"For the sake of bao, love. No, don't argue and *do not* get angry. You have no grounds for anger. NO. Just take one minute to consider *one* question. Will you do that?"

She glared at him angrily. "One and only one!"

"The question has a preface: *Monkey-brain willy-wagging man has dominated and ruined his planet. His world asks for help in eliminating monkey-*

brain man. Several other worlds cooperate in doing this by helping to drown monkey-brain man. Monkey-brain man refuses to be drowned and turns himself into creature who can live in the oceans.

"Now, this is the question. *Given a thousand years or so of mankind living in the sea, what do you think will happen to those seas when they are dominated by monkey-brained man, who has changed his body so he could live in the water but has done absolutely nothing to change his brain?*"

The idea lay there, like a . . . pile of manure in the road. Suddenly there. Stinking. She saw undersea factories spewing toxic fumes that bubbled darkly upward, breaking at the surface into a thin film of sticky, unpleasant iridescence. She saw slicks of this oily, foul-smelling substance—sprawling islands of it. She saw sea creatures lying on the surface, their gills clogged, dying; babies like Gailai wearing breathing masks and goggles. Realization came in a single, overwhelming wave!

"Oh, Joshua," she sobbed. "Oh, we'll do it again! All over again, and our lives will have been all wasted. All of our lives, our work wasted . . ."

He put his arms around her, shaking his head, wondering what vision of the future she had seen among the terrible total he had imagined. "No. We refuse to let it be wasted. We have two centuries and—"

She cut him off, finding herself badly off balance. "Who is *we*, Joshua? *Who?*"

"Let's say a few children of Earth who came back home to help."

"I have no idea what you're talking about."

"Do you trust me?"

"Do I trust you to what? To be charming, yes . Amusing, yes. To show up in a new shape every few years . . . I suppose I have to take it on faith that's what happened. I'll assume for the moment what you've just said is all true—"

Now he cut her off. "Yes, and who or what do you know of who could 'show up in a new shape every few years'? Hint. You had tea with one of them recently . . ."

"A shapeshifter? You don't mean Mavin . . . ?"

"Not Mavin herself, but definitely her countrymen. Recruited. On Lom. By Fixit. A LONG time ago. Long before Ganver had his temper tantrum and took all the talents away. Long before the earth began to drown. Fixit's people are a remarkably long-lived race."

"Recruited?"

"Recruited on Lom, and put, so to speak, in cold storage. Just as your children were."

"Why, that sneaky . . . that sneak!"

"That sneak is an official interferer who believes it easier to fix problems if he gets a head start on them and whose ancestors have believed the same. That official interferer's ancestors had been asking similar questions since the first humans left Earth and were sent to Lom. A race might be allowed to destroy its own planet, but the moment it leaves that planet it becomes an infection. The current official interferer— one known as Fixit—asked that terrible question the moment the earth spirit called for help, and it called for help for centuries and centuries and centuries! That interferer then went to Lom, looked about, found a few male shapeshifters who had bao. It then put said shapeshifters into . . . storage; storage interrupted from time to time by educational trips and attendance at meetings and having said shapeshifters' genetics fiddled with. It then built its own mini Massive Fabricator by recruiting several people with varying talents and, as I said, putting them in cold storage also. Thereafter, Fixit called upon them as needed."

"And your talent is . . ."

"Why, charm, of course. Charm and humor and being a generally delightful character. Not a bad carpenter either."

She stared at him, lost in a weird delight mixed with a terrible confusion. "But that's an intervention, Joshua! It's not bao. It's not fabricky at all, and bao says we're just part of the fabric, you know. We are not the purpose of creation. We are not a creature that has been specially created and anyone would intervene for specially. I do believe that!"

"You're saying 'anyone.' No, the Creator would not intervene for 'anyone' of its creatures. But another 'anyone' might. 'Anyones' have been interfering with one another since the dawn of time. You are one of the anyones. Xulai is. Abasio is. For example, did you make that sock?" He pointed to the one she had been darning.

She hadn't really looked at the sock before. It didn't look as though it had been hand-knitted. "No. It's one of Willum's. Needly told me his socks were all holes. Someone back in his village probably made it. Or it was bought from some peddler going through. Someone in my family told me about knitting machines. Maybe there are still places where people use machines to make ordinary things like socks and mittens and winter hats . . ."

"Yes, you didn't make it, but you're darning it?"

She looked at the sock in her hands. Not a pretty thing but . . . "There's wear in it yet."

"It suffers from an absence of part of its substance. And even if one didn't make it, one could still be interested in mending it?"

"Well, of course one mends things. Otherwise one would be spending a fortune on underwear and socks and winter mittens . . ."

"Yes, one would." He sat back in his chair and stared into the west, where the sunset was beginning to color the horizon over the mountains. "So if one had a race of people who were useful in various ways but certainly not the center and purpose of the universe, and if that race of people by and large, unfortunately, had an unfortunate absence in part of their substance, anyone might be allowed to darn it. To fix the hole in their nature. One might use various implements to mend it. Perhaps a Lillis-shaped darning egg, and a Needly, and someone skilled at the job of being a well-intentioned male hank of yarn."

"One being who?"

"One being a human person selected by Balytaniwassinot to fulfill a certain role and prepared for that role by being given an intensive education on the future of mankind." He frowned. "Oh, and one who found a certain person named Lillis to be irresistible. The other candidates were enthusiastic, but not nearly as enthusiastic as was *this* candidate. We were allowed to choose; that was part of the deal. The Camrathsexipedes are a remarkably ethical race. Except for occasional jesting, they tell the truth as they breathe, being unable to live without either air or veracity. Fixit would not have allowed me to attempt pretending an enthusiasm I did not feel."

His face moved as though it were liquid, expression and shape wavering. She put out her hand to touch it, the touch turning into a caress. "An egg and a needle and yarn and a dozen young ones. All of them brothers and sisters?" His face settled into familiarity. "Now you look like Joshua again."

"Is he your favorite one of me?"

She struggled to remember. "He was . . . the Joshua you was just the only one who . . . who wasn't in Hench Valley. I did hate Hench Valley so. Anything done there was done under a shadow. Not being there made life sunlit. But he wasn't a separate he, was he. What you are saying is that all of you were one you."

"All were one and one was all. You are correct. Fixit had several candidates, me among them, and I won the job by being several good candidates for it."

"You mean, by being several people I could be very happy with. Each one of you? Who weren't really that different! Which makes a good deal of sense. So much easier to have one all-purpose man than doing them by dozens." She tried the thought. It had awkward corners, but . . . but it could be made to fit. It actually could explain . . . rather a lot. "So all of them were you. I'm glad. That way I don't have to mourn for any of them, and I don't have to feel a fool for being foolish over all of them. Did you make up all that business that Abasio was telling us about Fixit's people. All that dancing and pibbling and fringe swatting?"

He shook his head slowly and emphatically. "Fixit itself told Abasio all about it. I had no part in the telling, but I will say the Camrathsexipedes breed in exactly that way. I was not in cold storage the whole time. I have had guided tours of some quite remarkable worlds, during one of which I witnessed *from beginning to end* the procreation procedure of Fixit's people. Fixit also had to tell Abasio about it so it would be in his log. Nobody knew about all the tours I'd already had . . ."

"You told me his people were totally ethical."

"I did. And Fixit knows that sometimes it is much more ethical to ignore a regulation than to obey it. Especially regulations made by people who are in high office because they have used low tactics to get there and are often regulating things for their own profit. Fixit's people derive great pleasure from what amounts to a good deal of healthful community exercise. Admittedly, it is strange, and if you knew how it evolved, you would think it even stranger. Each step in it evolved over many millennia in response to a particular environmental danger. When one learns how each step developed, one can only admire and revere the Creator, for relying on evolution makes everything perfectly reasonable. As is everything in the universe, perfectly reasonable— once you know everything there is to know about it."

"You're not . . . HIM, are you? Or HER, IT, or THEM?"

"You mean the Creator? Don't let your bao slip, Lillis! Reason should tell you the Creator would not bother with such a matter, truly. Earth is not even a blip in the fabric of the universe. This is simply too small a matter to be of interest. No, I am a human minion, a descendant of people who were on the ships that went to Lom, a descendant who inherited shapeshifting as my talent and who was recruited by Fixit to do covert work part-time for one particular minor branch of the Galactic Affairs Office. Their overview is large, but not universal. There are no records of my recruitment or my equipment."

"I imagine you're really busy," she said, the sadness in the words not her intention at all. Nor the tear that dropped onto the sock she had been mending.

"Ah, Lillis. You're lonely."

Now the tears were a flood, choking her, so the words were drowned. "Well, of course I am! It does somehow make it a great deal easier to know you were all the same you, you know, so I'm not a . . . what did they used to call them in the old books? A loose woman."

"A passionate, loving woman who thought being faithful to an ideal was more important than being faithful to any particular male creature who came and went as the mood took him."

"Him, it, or them! But I'm still glad they, you were all the same . . ."

" . . . the same . . . minion. And, Lillis my love, *I'd so much rather you didn't say 'were.'* I didn't *stop* being, you know. I still *am*. I've worked part-time until now, but it's full-time from here on out."

"You still are what?" she cried. "I'm very well read, but I don't know what a 'minion' is! And if you were always the same one, then why didn't you just stay in Hench Valley the whole time? Why all that back-and-forth-ing?"

He frowned, very slightly. "Because the children could not be identical. They are not copies of one another. One does not make an orchestra of all oboes. Or violins. Or cymbals and kettledrums. Each is an individual. And in order to assure that, one had to be . . . what is it that Xulai is always fussing about?"

"Being fiddled with!"

"One had to be fiddled with. Rebuilt. No, not really rebuilt at all, as a shapeshifter, that came automatically, but I did have to be reequipped."

She choked on her tears again, trying to laugh. "You had . . . have very nice equipment."

"Thank you. I particularly like the shapely nose and this manly jaw."

"That's not what I—"

"No? What else *could* you have been thinking of?" He sat there, quietly staring at her, a slight smile coming and going. "How old are you, Lillis? You were seventeen when we met. Our firstborn was . . . were the girls Sarah and Sally. How old are they now?"

"They are apparently postpubertal. How 'post,' who knows. Did they age at all while those creatures had them?"

"Unfortunate creature, the Oracle . . ."

"While those idiots kept them in storage. Did you know about that?"

"I did. They were not suffering. They were not conscious. They were merely arrested. As you were."

"As I were what?"

"Arrested. Everyone calls you 'Grandma.' Yet . . . your hair is not gray. I see no lines in your face. If I had to judge, I would say you are probably in your early to midthirties. One reason for Hench Valley would be its everlasting sameness. You could (and did) miss great chunks of Hench Valley time without noticing it at all because *Hench Valley did not change.* A three-year chunk there, a five-year chunk here, it would still be the same. You wondered, 'Why Hench Valley?' That's why. Though you only had six of the babies, it took a sizable chunk of time to accumulate a dozen children . . . thirteen, if we count Trudis.

"Besides, we *should* count Trudis. As it turned out, you were right to fight for her. When we got to that stage, the Silverhair stage, she turned out to be the only one to have the genetic mix that was needed. Which was a good thing."

She gave him a look of frank disbelief. "Don't tell me you planners and conspirators didn't have such a person located in advance."

"I wasn't one of the planners and conspirators. They did have such a person in mind, but they had neglected to recruit a real seer when they recruited me. A seer would have told them the person they were depending on would die before her contribution could be made. Which she did. Died."

"Chastised to death in Hench Valley, no doubt."

"No. *That* they could and would have prevented, but she was not kept under constant surveillance. One cannot prevent a woman deciding to go visit her mother in the middle of the night by way of a mountain trail which she had no doubt traveled hundreds of times, and, as she rounded a corner, being confronted by—way, way below his natural range—a pugnacious mountain goat going the opposite way. It is probably unnecessary to speculate whether, when on a narrow trail, a pair of horns and four feet firmly planted will always outperform two feet totally surprised."

"Do you mean Ma Beans! *That was why she fell?*"

"She woke in the night with a premonition of death, thought it was her mother, and went to prevent it."

"You're inventing that."

"As a matter of fact, I'm not. She told her sister she was going and why. You knew her?"

"I helped her in childbirth. Several times. The babies were always early and died within a few days. I'm sure it was a genetic thing. I told her how to prevent the pregnancies. She said no, she was going to keep on doing what she wanted to do. I had her help me, I thought it might show her where things were going wrong . . ."

"Her mother probably told her not to walk the trail after dark. But she kept on doing what she wanted to do."

"She had a good reason for staying pregnant, Joshua. Her man of the house didn't chastise her when she was pregnant. Oh, Joshua or whoever . . . What am I supposed to call you? I don't want to talk about Hench Valley. I want Hench Valley to . . . go away."

He leaned close and put his arm around her, whispering urgently, "Listen to me, Lillis. I am your fairy godfather and can grant your wish! Hench Valley has only about half a year to go. At which point it will be gone." He hugged her. "The two little girls who are still there will disappear. The Home at Saltgosh has agreed to take the two little girls. They are mentally very slow but they willingly do easy tasks like dusting and washing things: dishes, pots, pans, floors. They love music. They enjoy food and any bit of new clothing puts them into ecstasies. Their lives are not without pleasure. In the Home, they will be well treated, probably even loved, much as a pet is loved, and they will be protected.

"In Hench Valley the last fertile woman has recently gone through the 'change' and this is known throughout the valley. Very shortly, now, the men remaining in Hench Valley will know females have to be found if they're to continue pointing at some hungry little boy and bragging that 'he's one a' mine.' They will decide to go over the pass, down toward Catland and Artemisia, where they plan to steal a 'whole buncha wimmin.' There are far fewer men left in Hench Valley than you might guess. They've been leaking away for the last decade. They will, of course, follow tradition by first dancing around the fire and getting thoroughly drunk.

"While still in that frivolous state, as they approach Catland, they will encounter Sybbis escorted by a large group of her gangers, all well armed and not drunk. Sybbis will be on a mission to find out what has happened to *her* stinkers, left in her charge by old Chief Purple. This meeting of the two groups will result in carnage. None of the Hench Valley men will return to Hench Valley."

"And?"

"And nothing. By then, all the stinkers will have been . . . disbanded by Fixit. They are not a race of people; they do not have the abilities necessary to survive, even if taken to some hospitable and untenanted planet; they are without mentality and have no emotions but a recurrent mating urge and consistent hunger. There are no female hunters, the male hunters will be relocated to live out their lives.

"In Hench Valley, after a quiet and really rather enjoyable winter, when spring comes the few older women and the scatter of little boys remaining will be looking for a leader. Someone to guide them and their remaining livestock out into the world. Perhaps a small committee of female Artemisians could be persuaded to undertake a rescue mission?"

"And you know this how?"

"The likelihood of each event is well over the ninetieth percentile. As is the probability that Sybbis, while hunting for her stinkers and getting involved in the fray between her gangers and the Hench Valley men, will be very slightly scratched and will subsequently die of an easily preventable infection. This will result in the population of Catland being dispersed into the surrounding countryside. I have not described the interventions which will help this whole plot along, but they are simple and nonviolent."

"If the infection is easily preventable . . ."

"Sybbis will refuse to use an antiseptic solution because 'it stings.' "

"And you know this how?"

"You and I played games, love. Remember? We played cubies, some-times: one asks a question, then one rolls the cubies and writes down the letters on top, and if it's a long question maybe they are thrown twice. Then you make up the answer out of the ten or twenty letters you have."

"You played cubies to determine the future of Earth?"

"It's only a similarity. For questions pertaining to something the size of a planet, one needs something a bit larger and more reliable, so one has this enormously complicated machine that figures out likelihoods. One tells the machine everything one knows about a situation. Then one asks it to research the situation and give the likelihood of X hap-pening. Or X and Y and Z. Or the whole alphabet. And the machine asks for certain other information, which one provides—after taking some time and effort to find it out—then one goes around and around with the machine, refining the information, changing it here, goosing it there, and eventually it says the likelihood is even both ways. And then one asks this and that and the other thing, and when one has spent enough time changing the variables, one learns that there are a couple of little interventions, as follows.

"If someone goes to Grief's Barn in Hench Valley in the afternoon of a certain day this coming spring, and asks a certain Pa what the men are going to do now that there are no childbearing females at all left in Hench Valley, everything I mentioned will happen."

"With a couple of little interventions?"

"First intervention was having someone go in and get the little girls out of there before we ask the question. Second intervention is some-body getting there and asking the question. Fixit and I will do that."

"Why do you have to get the little girls out?"

"They are not bright, but they are willing and seemingly tireless, and will do almost anything to please others. Which can be a deathtrap we wish to avoid. Because we don't want them trying to please the men of Hench Valley, do we?"

She shuddered. "No. I wasn't thinking."

"The machine forecast death by gang rape if we didn't get them out first, so we're getting them out first."

"And everything we did, you and I and the Home that kept the Sil-verhairs and the stupid Oracles and Needly and . . . everything was because that sort of machine said DO?"

"That machine doesn't have a DO button. A human person has to decide to do. Fixit's machine, now, oh yes, it has a DO button, but he's in another line of business."

"Which is what, really?"

"He's in our business, our DO thing, yours and mine. Our business is about increasing the share of the population who have bao."

"From what to what, increased?"

"Well, various extraterrestrial populations were polled. Virtually everyone asked thought it was perfectly all right to drown a population that had fewer than one in ten with bao, and that held true right up until we hit fifty percent and then decreased the higher we went. At sixty percent, they voted do not destroy, but do intervene. HOWEVER, while drowning mankind met with general approval, those who were questioned pointed out that there were a great many other self-aware creatures on Earth who had not been involved in despoiling the planet, and these creatures would also perish. This was a definite NO-NO. Which is the opposite of DO. This includes the Griffins and all the other creatures that want to go on living."

"Is Fixit really here?"

"Oh, yes. He's here. Somewhere. He's actually been doing what he says he's been doing. Both here and on the other side of the planet. It seems there is still a side besides our side to the planet, and there are as many or more people left over there. Different languages, same concerns. Fixit is fixated on fixing things.

"His to-do list today includes a visit to Tingawa to double-check that people haven't been fibbing to him about the Griffins having a few bad eggs. That's a Fixit joke. He lets me borrow his ship sometimes. If I decide to stay . . . he'll leave the little flier for me—us—to use. He'll appoint me—us—an ambassador or something."

"If you decide to stay? I thought you were a native here, that you lived here."

"I do live here, I *have* lived here. But I could move on. Depends on what kind of offer I get. From this woman. See, that's why I'm here, *stealin' wimmin.*"

She stared at him with something very much like hope in her eyes. "Is it possibly a woman with thirteen children? If one counted Willum."

"Yup. That's the one."

"And who, exactly, is the one doing this woman stealing? Joshua? Or one of the others."

"I thought I'd sort of let it be whoever it was on any given day. Unless this woman takes a dislike to one of them. See, that way, if she gets mad at one, he can just get lost for an indeterminate length of time . . ."

"Until she cools off?"

"Or warms up, whichever."

"You took the Silverhairs to Saltgosh."

"Whichever me was available, yes. You heard them there. Singing. Did you know that Needly sings just the way they do. As you and I do. I remember our singing while we were building that house. I imagine our singing these days would be sadly out of practice, but it was a pretty good house and very good singing."

"I've got a pretty good house now. It has room in it for . . . at least one other person if he didn't mind sharing a bedroom. You'd never be more than one at a time, would you?"

"It is my understanding that it's impossible to do that. Did you just offer an invitation?"

"Well . . . it's just that someone has to solve that problem you've presented."

"Which problem?"

"The one where the *monkey-brain* inherits the oceans."

"Oh," said Joshua. "That problem. Yes. We have to get to work on that one. Isn't it a good thing, my love, that you and I have still a good many years to live?"

BALYTANIWASSINOT HAD BID THEM FAREWELL. He did leave Joshua his flier together with a document identifying him as a deputy something in the bureau of something else with the authority to do a great many decisive things if he found it necessary. Remarkably, this document had actually been approved and stamped by persons in the bureau who were currently alive.

Abasio had said, "I'll sort of miss him, it, them, you know. He was . . ."

"Different?" suggested Joshua, who had been introduced by Grandma as "my first husband."

"Oh, my yes. He was different. I hope he enjoys his homecoming twigpit. With sauce."

Joshua smiled. "And you're you moving on, northward, I understand."

"Not for a while. Xulai and I are both feeling . . . overstimulated. There's been a great deal happening. Both Xulai and I feel that we'd like to have some time just to relax. No huge problems, no threats, no hiding in the forest to escape assassins. Just quiet, being among friends, listening to the children's music. And when we do move on, I want to stop and visit my grandfather and let him meet the sea-babies. There are half a dozen villages and small towns up this side of the mountain, so we won't be deviating too far from our assigned work. We'll go north, on beyond Fantis, there are several towns not far north of there, then east, then we can work our way back southward again."

Joshua smiled and nodded. "Lillis and I would like to go with you. As a matter of fact, Fixit assigned me to join you on this next trip to familiarize myself with the surroundings. We have our own wagons and our own portable camp. Balytaniwassinot ordered them for us to 'make up in some small way for the unpleasantness caused by the Oracles, who should have been removed from the galaxy long since.'"

"Did they get removed?"

"It's an interesting story. You knew how Fixit squashed them and misted them into absolute . . . flatness?"

"I do. I found it gratifying."

"Well, he was going to roll that mat up and transport it in that form to whatever place it was that had been chosen to put the thing, and when he started to roll, guess what he found on the ground under it?"

Abasio shook his head, then remembered. "Oh yes! It was yribium?"

"Yribium. Yes. Squashing them evidently pushes it out. After he garnered all the yribium, he un-flattened them. Evidently occasional flattening does them, it, no damage. Fixit intends to put them in a kind of zoo place somewhere and flatten them at intervals. He thinks his headquarters will probably gather all of them up, wherever they are, and put them in one place or several places near one another where they can be profitably flattened on a strict schedule. I think—though I'd rather you don't speak of it—that he intends to keep at least one colony for himself, one he can use to finance some of his . . . covert operations."

"Covert . . . ?"

"Like saving mankind from extinction. If it hadn't been for Fixit . . . well, just say we came very close."

"So . . . this yribium is valuable? Isn't that part of what Willum retrieved? He's longing for a reason to go flying again."

Joshua grinned. "Oh, yes. It's valuable. The Oracle, so-called, had been pack-ratting items from the Gold King for decades, giving yribium in exchange. It was the necessary ingredient to stabilize the stinker fat, which can, by the way, be manufactured perfectly well without involving stinkers who eat people. Or eat Griffins. Or eat any other life-form that we may want to make special organs for. It can all be done perfectly well in the laboratory."

"And the stinkers are gone?"

"Gone. Yes. Euthanized. They are almost unable to feel pain, but still, Fixit did away with them, the few who were left, very mercifully. That and everything else seems to be falling into place. There has even been some talk of giving shifter organs to the new people, like your children."

"Why?"

"Oh, in their current form they won't be able to dive as deep as . . . whales, say. If they could shift, they could occupy the ocean all the way down."

"And overpopulate it!" Abasio snarled.

"Not necessarily. I'm told the new world spirit will definitely put an end to that, should it ever begin."

SEVERAL THINGS OCCURRED BEFORE ABASIO and Xulai decided to move on. Hench Valley lost two little girls who were not very bright but were very industrious. The Home at Saltgosh gained them. Both girls and Home benefited from the relocation. Then, seemingly, there was a strange confrontation on the mountain road above Hench Valley between the Hench Valley men and Sybbis's gangers. Sybbis was said to be seriously ill. CummyNup, who was evidently Sybbis's partner and the father of her son, had taken the boy and gone east, where his mother was said to be living. CummyNup's mother had never approved of Sybbis.

Several women from Artemisia planned a trip to Hench Valley in the spring, just to see if there was anyone there needing help.

And finally, when Abasio and Xulai did set out to visit Abasio's grandfather, it was as a considerable entourage. The leading six-horse hitch wagon held Grandma, Joshua, and all six of Grandma and Joshua's children. Blue and Rags' wagon, now with a second two-horse hitch, carried Abasio, Xulai, Willum and the babies, plus Bear and Coyote when they got footsore. These two were followed by another six-horse hitch bringing Needly and Needly's five half sisters and brothers: a total of twenty-one people (and roughly as many horses), counting Bear and Coyote but not counting the three outriders. Such loads in normal wagons also laden with food supplies, clothing, hay, oats, tools, rope, tea, cookies, and so forth would have been heavy for even a six-horse hitch, but the three wagons carried only the people. In each wagon, however, one of the people carried a portable camp that contained its own supplies of water, food, bed linens, and the like, plus everything else that people, creatures, or horses might want, these things all stowed in miraculous little wormholes that came trailing weightlessly along after the wagons like invisible puppies bumbling along after the jingling, clanging, chattering, occasionally harmoniously singing mother dogs.

Kim was still doing his outrider duty along with two of Wide Mountain Mother's scouts who had volunteered to provide additional protective services. Abasio had insisted these services were to be confined to riding back at top speed to inform the wagon train if anything looked even remotely dangerous, strange, or in any way remarkable.

"Are you sure you want to do this?" Abasio asked Grandma. "Some of these villages are really . . . well, they're foul. Dangerous. Hateful."

"Well, the children will just have to practice their singing, I guess," said Grandma. "They tell me they're very good at it, and it usually calms people right down."

"That would be nice," said Xulai. "To be calmed down."

"What's the first village called? And where is it?"

"It's north, along the mountains, just beyond where Catland was. Before its tragic end. Did they ever get Sybbis's tomb built?"

"I think they sort of gave up on it," said Joshua. "They never did learn to build with adobe, so it was suggested they just bury her. So I heard. And then Abasio and Xulai want to stop and visit with Abasio's grandfather, and his place is two or three villages beyond the one we come to first."

"But that's lovely," said Grandma. "We'll enjoy that, too. What did you say the name of the first village was?"

"It's called Vexing," said Abasio. "The man who founded it had no memory. People would ask him where he lived and he'd say, 'Now, that's vexing, I can't think why . . .' And everyone ended up calling it 'Vexing.' It's a bit larger than the villages we've been going through. Several hundred people. According to the reports we have, the people have taken their attitudes from the name of the town, so there's almost no likelihood of anyone wanting to make the trip to Sea Duck, but it's on the way, so we'll see what we can do."

It was a two-day journey north of Artemisia. They passed two Edges. The walls around each of them were still there, but the gate was open and no one answered when they called. Though there were stairs leading down, the place had the smell of rot, and no one wanted to explore. Late in the afternoon they came upon the outskirts of the town, a line of half a dozen small farms arranged along the road like beads on a string. Abasio was surprised when the children leapt out of their wagons and lined up in front of them.

"Heads up," whinnied Blue. "You there, second hitch, Grandma's wagon! I said heads up!"

"What in the . . ." Abasio cried. "Xulai, stop them. They might be hurt."

"I think not," Grandma said. "Relax. Just watch."

The horses began to prance. Ordinary wagon horses do not prance, but the eight pair pulling the first two wagons were doing a creditable job of pretending to. All they needed, thought Xulai, were some plumes and a virtually naked rider decked in sequins . . . it was sequins, she thought . . . little shiny things. Now, that might be fun!

The children were marching in front of the horses, singing. Several were also playing stringed instruments, tapping little drums.

"I stand with the chipmunk and elephant, I stand with the whale and flea," they sang. "In the midst of a wonderful universe that was not made for me." People came out of their houses, down from their porches, leaned on their fences as the children sang, "I'm only a part of the Creator's art; it was not made for me."

The children reached out their hands, still singing. "I stand with the planets, the stars, and the sun as part of a perfect design. Because it was made for everyone, I may not call it mine."

Xulai came onto the wagon seat, the babies on her lap. The people of the village ran alongside. "Oh, look at the babies, look at the babies. Stop, stop, let us see the babies."

The Silverhairs took the melody. "The planets whirl, the stars are aglow, life moves from the sea to the land. There come ages of sun and ages of snow, everything as it was planned. All of it a part of the Creator's art, and it was not made for man . . ."

And the children sang, "We're only a part of the Creator's art, we're not the reason why, so lift up your voice, rejoice, rejoice, as every day goes by, that you're simply a part of the Creator's art, and not a reason why . . ."

They stopped singing as people came out with gifts. A basket of fruit. A cake. "We heard you were coming. Can you stay a day or two? Oh, tell us about it all. Isn't it wonderful!"

Abasio gave Xulai a look that said better than words, "What is going on here! What has happened?"

Grandma got down from her own wagon and walked back to Abasio's. "Is it wide enough for three up there?" She climbed up, seating herself next to Xulai and taking Bailai onto her lap. "Good afternoon, young sea-gentleman," she said, giving him a blubby kiss on his tummy, at which he screamed laughter.

The singing went on. The laughter went on. Horses were unhitched and led to water, given oats, given a polishing. Willum whispered to Needly, "We shoulda brought Sun-wings. Coulda sold rides, I bet."

"Oh, Willum," said Needly. "Sun-wings and Dawn-song are in Tingawa getting their shifter organs and learning how to use them. You'd better watch your tongue around them when they come back. They may turn into something dreadful and eat you."

Someone built a fire in the village center. Someone brought things to cook over the fire. Abasio answered questions. Xulai answered questions. People watched the babies' trousers being washed out. Food was passed from one to another. Babies were passed from one to another. Drink was passed the other way. Late in the evening, they had listed twelve young couples who would be going south, to Sea Duck 3.

"What fun!" they cried. "How exciting!"

When the fires burned down, Abasio sat down on the very comfortable bed provided by the portable camp. When Xulai sat down beside him, he murmured, "What just happened?"

"I don't know," she said. "I really don't. I'm just going to sit here and think about it."

Abasio said, "I'm going to take a short walk. Be back soon."

He soon found Grandma, sitting outside her own portable camp with Joshua, who looked up with a grin and said, "That was nicely done. Looks like things are working out."

"I'd like an explanation," said Abasio. "Is it hypnosis?"

"No, no!" said Grandma. "Not at all, Abasio. Hypnosis is replacing one's one judgment with that of someone else. What you saw today is the releasing of one's own judgment from impairment. As Fixit recently explained to me, *monkey-brain* is a kind of pattern in the mind. Most humans are born without any pattern in that part of the brain, but they get imprinted very soon. Certainly by the time they begin to talk. Words are part of the imprint. There's the word 'mine.' Little ones learn 'mine' very quickly. Often it's the first word they learn. Certain things belong to certain people, and other things don't. By the time they're half grown, they've learned that the whole world is chopped up into pieces that belong to different people. Those people own it, different ones different parts of it, but all of it is owned by people. If people want lumber, they go cut down a forest. The fact that other creatures live in the forest doesn't matter, because the forest is a *mine*, somebody took it or bought it. The word 'mine' starts the idea, and it makes a pattern in the brain, and that pattern is the start of *monkey-brain*. The pattern is contagious. Parents who have it pass it on to their children, and before children are grown they know humans own everything. They've acquired *monkey-brain*. And once someone has *monkey-brain*, they're immune to bao."

Abasio frowned. "It sounds hopeless. I didn't realize . . ."

"Well, we've thought it was hopeless. The people who were working on it got onto the right track when someone realized the response in the brain was actually an electrical trail, reinforced by time and custom to make a quirk in the way the brain was wired, and that if one found the right disrupter, the pattern could be disrupted. One-by-one reprogramming was too time-consuming. What was wanted was a cure as contagious as the disease. It was pointed out and we learned that certain kinds of music have always been contagious. You know what I mean? The tune that you can't get out of your head? It just keeps popping back in? The music the children sing is like that. You can't get rid of it. You start humming it. Whistling it. It's a . . . disruptor. It disrupts the *monkey-brain* pattern, breaks it, splits it up into nothing."

Needly took up the telling. "And once that *mine* pattern is broken, people can think past it. They see the stars are stars. They see the sun that's setting over the mountains is a star which is part of the fabric. They see their Earth is a planet, which is part of the fabric, and they see themselves as a thread in the fabric of the world, a world which does not die when one of its threads reaches its end and is followed by another thread. They can know that happens, and let it be all right without *willy-wagging* or having to promise themselves some kind of afterlife. Their thread is picked up by another thread that will continue the fabric, and their part in it will always be there, because in reality time does not pass. It always is in the mind of the Creator. The new pattern allows them to be contented with that."

Joshua mused, "The young people in this village will very soon head off in all directions, singing. Every one of those who volunteered to go has a good voice and some talent with some kind of instrument. They will find other villages that will shortly thereafter go off in all directions, singing. I have Fixit's flier. It will expand to hold all of us if we fly across the eastern ocean and visit the towns that are over there. Who will then head in all directions, singing. Fixit has predicted that as few as fifty initial locations will blanket the globe inside ten years."

Abasio shook his head slowly, still finding it hard to believe. Knowing it was true, but finding it hard nonetheless. He waved at them, turned, and went back to the wagon that was actually a camp disguised as a wagon, leaving Joshua and Grandma sitting with their arms around each other, watching the sun that was a star, that did not belong to mankind, be hidden as the world (which did not belong to mankind) whirled slowly away . . .

Watching as the edges of the galaxy blinked into view. (No, we do not say "our galaxy." We say "the Milky Way" or "the galaxy in which the planet we have named Earth is found," but not "*our* galaxy.")

Watching as the earth turned away into a darkness that was full of stars that were suns that had planets going around them that had life on them that did not belong to mankind.

Watching a universe that seemed far less dark tonight than it had been at any time in the last several thousand monkey-brained *willy-wagging* years.

THE GRIFFINS? AH, YES.

Sun-wings admitted she had threatened mankind with monsters that did not exist, though she had been certain they would exist, for she had watched the Edgers building their mechanical whales.

And did everyone know about the wonderful male Griffin Fixit had found in the continent to the south? He'd been there all the time, carefully staying to himself, never seen by Despos, never having to fight him. He was a little foggy about just where he had been or who had taken care of him there. It was almost as though he had had a fairy godfather who kept him hidden. But he was fine. And so good-natured! All the females thought so.

Poor Despos. Fixit's ship had found his body up there the north pole. It really got cold up there. Despos had never been cold before, so he didn't realize lying down to have a nap wasn't a good idea. Especially for one with serpent genetics.

The shifter organs created for Sun-wings and her sisters worked very well. The Griffins amazed themselves, and one another, however, by refusing to agree upon a new shape and deciding individually what shape they would adopt when. When they felt like swimming, they would swim. And when they felt like flying, they'd do that! All babies came from the egg, however, as Griffins, and wasn't it nice that Fixit had taken three of the Griffins to a whole world of their own, via wormhole. Two of them had eggs, one of which was male. If they didn't kill each other—for they were extremely quarrelsome—they could have a whole planet almost to themselves except for large, prolific fish that made excellent eating.

Because, as Fixit explained to her mother, Silver-shanks, wormhole travel wasn't good for children, little Snow-foot had been left behind and had been adopted as Dawn-song's sister. And Needly's. And Willum's. And everyone else's in Artemisia. The Artemisians had become very fond of Griffins. Snow-foot didn't seem to be missing her mother or her aunts at all.

The water from Squamutch? Ah, yes.

Through Fixit, the World Spirit of Squamutch sent a gift to the new World Spirit of Earth: several plants of the celebrated Squamutch water lily. Rooted in the seafloor, the miles-long stems would reach the tops of the tallest mountains and the full-grown pads were larger than the playing field of one of those ancient outdoor games humans had played. Kick-sphere? Put-down-ball? Whatever it had been called, the pad was big enough to hold a small village. One large panel of leaf, curved into a half cylinder, with two semicircular endpieces, made a house. Peel the outer green layer away, one was left with a translucent membrane: a window. The cut edges of the leaf grew into the leaf below, and the house went on being alive. And the lilies reproduced readily, very readily. Each seed pod made two boats, each flower petal a blanket. One of the first things done by the educational department of the confederated tribes of watery Earth was to offer classes in aquatic architecture.

The new world spirit? Ah, yes.

And at last the new world spirit arrived. He emerged from the sea off the coast near Tingawa, and emerged, and emerged, and emerged. He towered into the sky, and his trident pierced the clouds. He had a curly beard and an enormous laugh and a trumpet made out of a huge, curly shell. His name, he said, was Neptune, and he was on lengthy, perhaps interminable vacation from a large solar planet previously given that same name under the mistaken apprehension that it had water on it. Which it did not. Nor, unfortunately, did it have any appreciable life on it, and really, unless one was for some *inexplicable* reason *fond* of *gases,* there was very little amusement to be had out of them. This world, however . . . this one was going to be fun!

The new spirit was particularly grateful to Fixit, for Fixit had taken giraffes away. And elephants. Warthogs. Hippos. Also lions, tigers, leopards, wolves, weasels, foxes. About fifty kinds of antelopes. Had Earth really needed fifty kinds of antelope? Well, luckily, Fixit had taken all of them to a distant planet named Terra Firma, so the new world spirit would not have to struggle with them! Lovely forests, prairies, mountains, lakes, small seas there, but no mankinds on Terra Firma, and no creature that might evolve into mankinds. Any creatures that might evolve into a mankind sort of thing had been taken elsewhere, to a world where survival meant strenuous, continuing effort. No forests to chop down. No mines full of metal. Destruction would be, in every case, counterproductive. Mobwows very probably wouldn't survive it.

Still, all the creatures that Fixit had not taken away had to be adapted to living in the seas. The new Earth spirit couldn't wait until the oceans were full! So much to do! Gracious, but there was still so much to do! Whales now. Leviathans. He had to learn whale and he was finding it difficult. Could one of the small beings who were turning into octopods help him out by introducing him to the Sea King, the Kraken, who no doubt spoke whale? No, no, it *was quite all right for Kraken to retain the title of Sea King.* He, Neptune, was the Sea GOD, not to be confused with the Creator, merely a member of a subrace, and HE, Neptune, had titles enough already.

This was really going to be so much fun! Now, did everyone here understand about bao? Because if they didn't, Neptune was going to start giving classes. Required classes.

The End. Ah, yes. And bao . . . to us all.

Author's Note

Author's note, following, include a note on the chronology of the books whose characters are mentioned in *Fish Tails,* as well as the story of the Kindly Teacher.

Chronology

The books that precede *Fish Tails* are not listed in the chronological order of their publication. This listing follows the chronology of the story, though the publication date of each book is given.

The story begins with *The Song of Mavin Manyshaped* (Ace Original, March 1985) in the world of Lom, to which humans from Earth came some time before. The first character met is Mavin Manyshaped, a young woman who helps her sister escape a life of pain and abuse, and then escapes a similar fate by taking her younger brother, Mertyn, and absconding—in the guise of a horse. She meets the wizard Himaggery, a man of many and vast enthusiasms, and kindly Windlow the Seer. She will not stay with the wizard, but she promises to meet him twenty years later. Leaving her brother in Windlow's care, she begins her search for her sister.

In *The Flight of Mavin Manyshaped* (Ace fantasy edition, June 1985), she goes far across the seas to look for her long-lost sister and finds her in one of the strange cities of the chasm, cities that hang forever in structures built upon vines that hang between the great beasts of the land above and the weirdly wonderful creatures of the chasm bottom. Mavin's sister dies in giving birth to twins. Mavin brings her infant nephews back to the lands of the True Game so they may be raised among kin in a shifter demesne. The time for the twenty-year reunion she promised Himaggery is coming closer.

In *The Search of Mavin Manyshaped* (Ace edition, September 1985), no one knows where Himaggery is, except that he is sought by the deadly shadow. The Daylight tower and bell have been destroyed and the shadow is free to eat all living creatures. Mavin finds Himaggery in a form the shadow cannot recognize; she brings him through a long, dangerous journey to safety, stays with him for a time, and becomes pregnant—a fact that everyone in the place recognizes—except Himaggery. His many and vast enthusiasms, Mavin realizes, don't leave room for him to really look at anyone, certainly not a woman or child; besides, if her child should be a shifter, it will need special rearing. She leaves Himaggery to have the child elsewhere. He says he will find her. When he finishes this latest project . . . or the next one . . . or certainly the one after that.

The story of Mavin and Himaggery's son, Peter, begins with *King's Blood Four* (Ace edition, April 1983). It is the story of Peter, a boy of unknown parentage, fostered in School Town and there taught the rudiments of the True Game. The people on Lom came from Earth, long ago. The talents that make them gamesmen and gameswomen were given to them by Lom. Those who received no talent are mere pawns, a separate class of beings, all too often sacrificed "in play." In this book, Peter is betrayed, taken hostage, held for a ransom he has no way of paying. It is here he first meets his cousins, and sees his mother for the first time since she left him in School Town, shortly after his birth. It is while he is captive that his talent comes to him, out of nowhere, and he learns he too can shift . . . into almost anything. He escapes, taking with him his fellow captive, the healer Silkhands.

In *Necromancer Nine* (Ace edition, September 1983), the boy must find his mother, Mavin Manyshaped, who has left a set of enigmatic directions. In finding her, he at least partially finds himself. There is a puzzle in the lands of the True Games, and Peter, Windlow, Himaggery . . . all are seeking to solve it

In *Wizard's Eleven* (Ace Original, February 1984), the boy becomes a man, knowing who and what he is and regretting what he is, for he is a gamesman, which means that his best friend, a pawn, is unworthy of friendship. To gamesmen, the untalented are mere pawns, now awaiting death in the game. By this time he has met the girl named Jinian, and together with her and the eidolons of the first, great gamesmen, they fight a great battle of the dead with the dead for the soul of their world.

We meet the girl first in *Jinian Footseer* (a Tor book, September 1985), a child who for no discernible reason is treated with scorn by her family, who is despised by her supposed mother, abused by her supposed brothers, taught witchcraft by several old women in and about the place, has a marriage arranged, seemingly to her advantage, but is fortuitously kidnapped, escapes, and finds her own way to School Town, where in time she is joined by the six other women who make up her "Seven" in witchcraft.

In *Dervish Daughter* (a Tor book, March 1986), we learn of Jinian's true parentage, and she finds herself fighting a lonely battle for the soul of Lom, against a mysterious creature that calls itself an Oracle and seems to be a devil.

And in *Jinian Star-Eye* (a Tor book, August 1986), she prevails, learning she has a talent that she alone possesses. She joins with Peter to unite the present with the past. In their claiming of the world for their own, the talents given by that world are taken from them.

Then in *Plague of Angels* (Doubleday, 1993), we meet Abasio, the farm boy turned ganger turned mystic who flees from a dying city and on the way meets a girl named Olly. They go toward the city from which the ships flew to Lom, all those centuries ago. Olly is captured and taken into the city, fulfilling a long-promised destiny, and leaves there in the last spaceship, taking with her the threat that would have meant death to the world. Abasio is left alone except for Blue, the horse who somehow, along the way, has learned to talk. Abasio believes the ability to converse is a gift from the great beings he can think of only as angels, a gift so that he will not be left totally alone.

And, in *Waters Rising* (Harper Voyager, 2010), we meet Abasio and Blue again, now seeking a child named Xulai, whom he has been told he will find in Woldsgard far to the west. One last monster left over from the Big Kill tracks them relentlessly as their travels lead them to far distant Tingawa, and to the birth of their children, the first sea-children, the twins Bailai and Gailai.

And finally, in *Fish Tails*, Abasio and Xulai and their children travel though the sparsely populated land, stopping in villages to recruit those who are interested in becoming sea dwellers. While on this journey, they welcome strange visitors from far-off Lom, Mavin Manyshaped, Jinian Star-Eye, and Silkhands the healer, returned to the land of their origin. These three have been called by the spirit of the planet to come and assure that the other creatures of Earth—particularly self-aware creatures like the Griffins Sun-wings and Dawn-song—made by man and for whom man must be responsible—are also made ready to live in a world that is forever to be an ocean without a shore.

(Balytaniwassinot learned, by the way, that the Edgers were responsible for making the Griffins, not the Edgers around the old city of Fantis, but those that lived on the west side of the Stonies, in the land that is lost. From what we can learn, there were two places from which Griffins came: an Edge, not far west of where Wellsport is now, which was drowned when the seas came in; the other an Edge far to the south-west on the southern continent. That one may still be in existence, and if there is time, we may send an expedition to find it. I am told it would be helpful to know what genetics went into the making of the Griffins, even though Precious Wind tells me that the Tingawans are very close to figuring it out on their own.)

The Story of the Kindly Teacher

Once upon a time there was a very kindly man, a good teacher, who wished to help people. Each day he put on his robe, took up his staff, and went among the people of the earth telling them his teaching. Each time, when he met a group of people, he said, "I have a gift for you, this is a good teaching, which can lead to happier lives. My teaching is this: be kind."

(If there are children listening, this is where we put our fingers to our lips and nod at them, as though saying "listen.")

People heeded the good teaching and many lived happier lives. There was only one instruction in the teaching: be kind. There were no sacrifices demanded, no offerings required. There were no rites that were obligatory. It was all very simple. "Be kind," the teacher would say. Then he would give some examples of kindness—to people, to chickens, to bees, to horses. There is a song he wrote . . .

Be kind to all creatures, wherever they be;
Be kind to the robins who live in your tree;
Be kind to the sparrow, be kind to the finch,
Be kind to the inchworm and give him his inch.
Don't hurry, don't worry, don't grab, and don't clutch;
Don't drive yourself crazy by doing too much.
(These two lines are sung by women)

Be kind to the husband who gives you a pain,
you know he can't stop, there's a flaw in his brain . . .
(These two by men)
Be kind to your wife when she fusses and nags,
Wives who are hugged do not turn into hags.
(Everyone)
Be kind to the gopher, be kind to the mole,
Be kind to all creatures who live in a hole.
Be kind to the cricket who lives on your shelf.
Be kind to your critics. Be kind to yourself!

Many people disregarded the Teacher, but they were no worse off than before, so the teaching did not hurt them. Those who listened did have happier lives. The Teacher was old and a little lame, so some of his followers offered to help him, three of them in particular. One was a Drover, one a Lawyer, one a Soldier. These men admired the Teacher and told him they respected his teaching, and always as the Teacher went from one place to another they would hear him say, "I have a gift for you, this is a good teaching."

One day the Teacher had a sore throat and could not give his teaching, so his friend the Drover said, "I know your teaching, word for word. I can tell it, Teacher." And he went out among the people, saying, "I have something good for you: this is the only true teaching."

When the Teacher heard what the Drover had said, he told him, "I don't say the *only true* teaching, my friend. I simply tell people that it is a good teaching."

"Oh, but, Teacher," said the Drover, "that is because you are modest. Everyone knows your teaching is the best one. Besides, people will only really pay attention if they think they are getting the very best of anything. Some of them ask me questions. Just today a man asked me, 'How can I be sure being kind is right?' I told him how I do. So long as the oxen don't wander, I'm kind to 'em. If the oxen wander, I touch them with the whip, to bring them back on the road. I keep a close eye on them. I don't let them wander off to eat grass or drink water when they have hauling to do."

The Teacher sighed, for that is not the way he taught; he would have been kinder to the oxen, but he was kind to the Drover, and thanked him for his help. And those who listened to the Drover thought the teaching was the only good one, and when they saw the whip he carried, they knew it was for using on people who didn't stay on the right path, and they bought whips to show other people what teaching they believed in.

It's all right to be kind, but not when there's hauling to do.

Time went by, and one day the Teacher was ill and could not give his teaching. The Lawyer asked if he could be the substitute, and he went out among the people saying, "Before I tell you the teaching, I have new rules for you, so before we talk about the teaching, you must learn all these rules about how you must live, for only those who live in this way can really take advantage of the teaching." And he made the people sit down and write copies of the rules as to what they could eat and when they could eat it and how they should dress and who they could associate with and how much money they must contribute to the Lawyer for his time. When the Teacher learned of this, he said, "I always tell people my teaching is a gift, not a rule they must follow. And I never talk about money."

But the Lawyer said, "Oh, Teacher, that is because you think everyone is as kind as you are. If you want to be able to tell your true followers from other people, you must make rules that set them apart from other people, and you must make them memorize and recite the rules, and you must also make them pay for your words." And he said, "People really value only what they pay for, and you will grow rich in the process."

The Teacher was upset, but he was kind to the Lawyer. Those who listened to the Lawyer saw he carried books and a bag full of gold, so they learned his rules, and the subrules that went with his rules, and the exceptions to the rules and the details that went with the exceptions, and they bought copies of them all and studied them every day. The Lawyer had taught them it was all right to be kind, but one had to follow the rules first, and *they were so busy learning and following the rules, that's as far as they ever got. They never found time to be kind.*

The Teacher grew older. He sometimes found it hard to stand up to give his teaching. The Soldier told him he knew the teaching word for word, so he went out among the people. The Soldier told them, "Before I tell you the teaching, line up there and give me your names so I can enroll you among our followers. If you have babies or children, they must be enrolled as soon after birth as possible so God will know who they are. God recognizes only the ones WE enroll. God pays no attention to people under any other label. Your children must come to class and learn the teaching. They will listen carefully, repeat every word after me, and they will be tested on how well they remember. You will join your brethren in marching and you will stay in line! Once you have joined, you may not leave us. Anyone trying to leave our rank and file will be hunted down and burned for being a heretic. You may in time do some kindness, but you have to conquer first and get rid of all the ones who don't believe." Then he marched up and down, he marched up and down, with the sword at his side going *clang . . . clang . . . clang . . .*

When the Teacher heard of this, he was very upset, but he was kind to the Soldier, even when the Soldier said, "You are too easy with the people, Teacher. You need to have a great army of right-thinking troops, for they will give you the power to put your teachings into law, and that way you can take over the government and enforce your teachings among everyone. The ones who are most rigorous, you will make officers, and they will discipline the people. You need more power! I will take these people and drill them over and over until they obey without thinking. Then we will conquer everyone else and teach them in their turn!"

And those who followed the Soldier bought swords of their own and became very militant and warlike. They enrolled their children as soon as they were born and told them they must not associate with other people who might not know the Soldier's way. They sent their sons to become officers of the troops and their daughters to be teachers in the schools, and they learned to sacrifice and feel pain and offer it to God, and they waged war on those who did not believe what the Soldier believed. It was all right to be kind, but . . . *But you had to conquer first and get rid of the people who didn't believe.*

The Kindly Teacher was saddened. He knew he had failed his own teachings when he let his friends teach in his name. He did not want to force his teaching on people. He did not want to gain power over others. He did not want to make his teaching into law. He did not want to grow rich. He wanted only to offer a good teaching that would make life happier for many. Now he was too tired and old to go among the people and give them his teaching. In sorrow, he died. He was buried by the Drover, the Lawyer, and the Soldier, all of them weeping over his grave. Then each of them went his own way.

And in time the Drover died. The Drover had three friends who knew the teachings, word for word, and they carried on by creating the *Church of the Teacher's Drover.*

And the *True Church of the Teacher's Drover.*

And the *Reformed True Church of the Teacher's Drover.*

And they each taught something different, but they all had a whip.

And in time the Lawyer died. The Lawyer had many followers who knew the teachings, word for word, and they carried on by creating the *Church of the Teacher's Lawyer.*

And the *True Church of the Teacher's Lawyer.*

And the *Reformed True Church of the Teacher's Lawyer.*

And each of them taught something different, but they all had many, many rules; and very—large—bags—of—gold.

In time the Soldier died, and he was remembered by the *Church of the Teacher's Soldier.*

And the *Militant Church of the Teacher's Soldier.*

And the *True Militant Church of the Teacher's Soldier.*

And the *Reformed True Militant Church of the Teacher's Soldier.*

And by the *Absolutely Reformed and Truly Most Militant Church of the Teacher's Soldier.* And they all taught something different, but they all had swords. *Clang, clang, clang . . . Clang, clang, clang . . . Clang, clang, clang.*

Every few hundred years, a new person would arise with yet another idea of what the Teacher had probably meant. One time many killed at his direction, and that was called the Teacher's Crusade; another time many tortured in his name, and that was called the Teacher's Inquisition; another time many hated in his name, and that was called the Teacher's Reformation; but no one ever heard what it was the Teacher had taught. Then, of course, men slaughtered men until there were no more men to fight.

There are still those who follow the Teacher in dealing with others—not his Drover, his Lawyer, or his Soldier. They carry no whip to punish, accumulate no gold to bribe, carry no sword to kill. They do not buy influence to make their belief a law, they do not threaten the pain of hell or prison, they do not deal death. They study no book, memorize no creed. If attacked, they defend themselves, but the way of kindness keeps peace among them. For the Kindly Teacher told them this:

If a man seeks to make his faith a law, this action alone disproves his faith, for the law cannot define kindness.

If a man seeks to buy his faith into prominence, this action alone disproves his faith, for money cannot buy kindness.

If a man seeks to kill others who believe otherwise, this action alone disproves his faith, for those who kill are not kind.